شاهنامه
فردوسی

Shahnameh

THE EPIC OF THE PERSIAN KINGS

FERDOWSI

Translated by AHMAD SADRI

Edited by Melissa Hibbard and Hamid Rahmanian

Liveright Publishing Corporation

A Division of W. W. Norton & Company
Independent Publishers Since 1923

Printed in the United States of America

For information about special discounts for bulk purchases, please contact W. W. Norton Special Sales at specialsales@wwnorton.com or 800-233-4830

Book design by Hamid Rahmanian
Manufacturing by Lakeside Book Company

ISBN 978-1-324-09380-0

Liveright Publishing Corporation
500 Fifth Avenue, New York, N.Y. 10110
www.wwnorton.com

W. W. Norton & Company Ltd.
15 Carlisle Street, London W1D 3BS

10 9 8 7 6 5 4 3 2 1

The Kufi-style Persian calligraphy *Shahnameh Ferdowsi* in the opening and closing of the book was developed in Khorausan, Iran, the birthplace of Ferdowsi, during the time of his versification of *Shahnameh* in the tenth century. Calligraphy by Mohsen Ebadi.

This book is dedicated to first-generation Iranians who seek their roots within the garden of humanity.

This edition of *Shahnameh: The Epic of the Persian Kings* was made possible with the generous support of the

Mowafaghian Foundation

CONTENTS

PART I
MYTHOLOGY AND EPIC TRADITIONS

PART II
HISTORICAL TRADITIONS

PREFACE

OVER A MILLENNIUM AGO, the Persian poet Ferdowsi of Tous meticulously compiled and transformed age-old mythological and epic tradition into a fifty-thousand-verse tome, *Shahnameh*—a literary masterpiece that remains a cornerstone of Iranian cultural heritage. Not only does this text preserve the Persian language but it also serves as a mighty bridge connecting modern Iran, navigating through the historical mist, to its illustrious pre-Islamic era. Even in the twenty-first century, the mythological figures and heroes of *Shahnameh* continue to converse with their own people. This resonance is palpable in the streets of various Iranian cities, where people rally for their freedom and self-dignity against oppressive rulers. The legends and customs of *Shahnameh* inspire unity and provide new generations with a playbook for resistance. It serves as a poignant reminder of the flourishing ancient traditions of the Iranian people.

Navigating the vast landscape of any mythology can be daunting for the average reader, and *Shahnameh* is no exception. I recall trying to avoid it entirely in my teenage years, perceiving it as an imposing tome filled with intimidating poems. Although poetry is infused in our culture, and the young and old alike can recite poetry by heart, I feared that I needed special knowledge to decipher the verses of Ferdowsi. This led to many disagreements with my father, who ardently wished for me to explore its depths—unbeknownst to us both that one day my whole life would be engulfed by this epic poem.

My journey into the world of *Shahnameh* started in 2009, with an abridged, six-hundred-page illustrated edition. I created the illustrations and tasked the responsibility of translating the work to Dr. Ahmad Sadri, a brilliant collaborator and immensely knowledgeable writer. For me, it was important that the work be translated by a native speaker who was not only familiar with the subtleties of the language but also steeped in the culture that embodies *Shahnameh*. In fact, this edition of *Shahnameh* is the first English translation by an Iranian, providing a layer of authenticity and cultural nuance that is unique to this edition. In terms of the stylistic method, I drew from my filmmaking background and approached this project with the guiding principle that I have employed in all of my work as an artist: prioritizing character-based narratives over events and minimizing side stories. This would surely present *Shahnameh* as both compelling and accessible.

Since publishing the illustrated *Shahnameh* in 2013, I have continued to mine Ferdowsi's magnus opus, creating new works based on its various stories, including an audiobook edition; two pop-up books, *Zahhak: The Legend of the Serpent King* and *The Seven Trials of Rostam*; and two comic books, narrating the love stories of Zaul and Rudabeh and Bijan and Manijeh. I've also written and directed four theater productions for the stage: "Zahhak," "Feathers of Fire," "Prince of Sorrows," and "Song of the North." Each of these projects serves as a narrative conduit for the tales of the heroes and heroines of *Shahnameh*, tailored for the modern world.

Amid these projects, it felt important to embark on an expanded reader's edition that comprehensively encapsulates the entirety of *Shahnameh*'s narratives. With this vision in mind, I returned to Dr. Sadri and posed the Herculean task of completing the translation in full. He and my partner, Melissa Hibbard, who worked as the story editor, collaborated to ensure that this translation maintains accessibility and coherence, allowing readers to effortlessly follow the narrative without losing track of the many new characters that come on the scene in the second half of *Shahnameh*—a true testament to their dedication and skill.

As an Iranian immigrant in the United States, I've observed a misrepresentation or lack of representation of Iranian culture free of political association in the Western world. Since the 1979 Islamic Revolution and the subsequent mass migration of Iranians to the West, our narratives are often passed through a political prism and confined to current affairs, imparting them with an expiration date. But to me, Iran has always been a timeless symphony, an opulent composition of intricacy and grandeur. The complex tapestry that makes up Iran—its diverse lands, peoples, and customs—as well as its turbulent yet fascinating history, merits the attention of the world. And so, I've dedicated my life to creating work that hopefully captivates the imagination of the public with Iranian culture. It is my fervent hope and optimism that, through this carefully crafted edition, English readers will encounter *Shahnameh* in a way that transcends mere accessibility: this book is an invitation to a timeless saga that is both enlightening and invigorating, offering a rich and immersive experience of Persian storytelling.

Hamid Rahmanian
2023, Fictionville Studio
Brooklyn, New York

INTRODUCTION

The Book of Kings—the King of Books

THE PERSIAN LITERARY MASTERPIECE *Shahnameh* or "Book of Kings" was composed around 1010 CE by Abu al-Qasem Ferdowsi, a man born in the village of Pauzh, in the Iranian province of Khorausan. It is thus the first cousin to the English epic poem *Beowulf*, the French *Song of Roland*, and of the Chinese magnum opus, *The Great Tang Records*. One thousand CE was clearly an age of magisterial composition. Indeed, despite its uncontested Persian providence, *Shahnameh* has been read as a multicultural text, incorporating many of the literary traits found in other great examples of world literature. Reuben Levy, the late Cambridge professor of Persian, described it as something of "an amalgamation . . . [of] chapters in the book of Genesis, the *Odyssey*, *Paradise Lost*, Chaucer's *Canterbury Tales* and Shakespeare."

Shahnameh is all those things and more. It can hold its head high in the company of other great epics like *Gilgamesh*, the *Mahabharata*, the *Ramayana*, the *Aeneid*, the *Nibelungenlied*, and of course the *Iliad* and *Odyssey* of Homer. At one and the same time, *Shahnameh* is a global masterpiece and Iran's very own "nationalepos" (a fabulous term coined by the illustrious Iranologist Theodor Nöldeke in the 1930s). It is kept alive today, in no small part, thanks to the illustrated or calligraphic manuscripts of the epic that the princes and kings of successive Iranian dynasties continued to commission. Artist Hamid Rahmanian's illustrated edition of *Shahnameh*, published in 2014, continued the tradition, providing a fresh and rich synthetic visual approach to this foundational work of literature. *Shahnameh* presents the "essence" of Iran, and delves into the Iranian soul. In flowering language it tells the sweeping saga of the fifty or so kings who governed it, from the creation of the world until the fall of the last indigenous royal house.

Shahnameh is, in itself, a milestone in the history of Iran. Its composition marks the end of a glorious era that had unfolded over the centuries, with first the Medes, then Cyrus and the immense empire of the Achaemenids, which had made Greece and the rest of the known world tremble. Iran's rich history continued with the intrepid ride of the Parthian horsemen, whose Arsacid (Ashkani) dynasty had in turn harassed and vexed the Roman Empire. Finally, the Sassanians, stubborn rivals of the Byzantines, had closed this long chapter of ancient Iranian history when Arab Islamic invaders entered Iran and conquered the land. The Arab conquest of Iran in 651 CE brought about the eventual decline and collapse of the old Zoroastrian religion, while the rise of Muslim Arabs coincided with an unprecedented political, social, economic, and military weakness in Persia. For Ferdowsi, at that point, history stops.

And still, it is the longest literary composition ever written in the Persian language, running over fifty thousand couplets. It is structured chronologically, one king's reign following the other, and explores the motivation and personality of each ruler who, without exception, always faces some kind of personal or political crisis. The kings are not necessarily the most memorable figures, however, for woven into the tapestry of Iran's monarchical past is a strong, colorful, and distinct heroic thread that exposes stories of the exploits, successes, trials, and tribulations of the heroes who seem to define what it means to be a good ruler. Best known of these hero tales is the epic cycle about Rostam, the ultimate Persian *Pahlevan*, a "strong man," firm of body and resolute of mind (although not at all averse to playing the trickster). In Ferdowsi's hands, Rostam, despite coming from an Iranian border area, becomes *the* symbol of heroic Iran: when he is at war, he identifies himself as an Iranian and when he fights, he does so as a vassal and a champion of the shah; in fact, Ferdowsi makes it clear that Iran's shahs need Rostam far more than he needs them.

Ferdowsi molds Rostam into the national champion par excellence—a position he retains today, unchallenged. It is right that his stories dominate *Shahnameh* in its popular perception, if not in page count.

Scattered throughout the docudrama that is *Shahnameh* is a heady mixture of love stories, Iranian folklore motifs, and the remnants of multiple oral traditions drawn from many places; there is a fixation on power, ethics, and fate; family discord, treason, loyalty, heroism, treachery, faith in God, patriotism, pride, and shame permeate the story of Iran and its people—from rulers, nobles, and champions to slaves and peasants.

In Persian, *Shahnameh* means both "the Book of Kings" and "the King of Books." No wonder. Few peoples can be proud of having such a great poet as emblematic as Ferdowsi to represent them, for his masterwork is Persian to its core. Through its composition, he revitalized—and thereby saved—the Persian language at a time when it was in danger of being supplanted by Arabic. Yet in spite of his eternal fame, the details of Ferdowsi's life are obscure; even his name is not well established. According to various sources, he is sometimes called Mansour, sometimes Ahmad, or even Hassan, son of Hassan, or son of Ahmad or Ali. But Fath bin Ali al-Bundari, who translated *Shahnameh* into Arabic, two centuries after the poet's death, is undoubtedly to be trusted when he calls him al-Amîr al-Hakîm Abou-l-Qâssem Mansour bin al-Hassan al-Ferdowsi al-Toûsi. "Ferdowsi" is obviously a pen name (*takhallos*), although it is unclear why it was chosen. It could be that his powerful patron, Mahmoud of Ghazna, gave it to him as a mark of esteem, for the name has the same source as the English word *paradise*. Derived from the Median *pari-daiza*, via Old Persian, it designates a surrounding wall delimiting a hunting reserve or game park, and then the park itself. Among the Greeks, the word *paradeisos* was borrowed from Old Persian to designate a royal residence with an extensive garden where it was good to hunt, to rest, and to feast. It also passed into Hebrew in the form *pardes* and it persisted in the Persian *päliz*. Finally, the word entered into Arabic as *ferdow*, "paradise"; it is from this that the poet's penname derives.

He is said to have died at the age of seventy-one, after thirty-five years of work, but the revision of *Shahnameh* continued until 1019 or 1020. The date of his death remains controversial: 1020 or 1025 are both proposed. Posterity remembers especially his shady relations with Mahmoud of Ghazna, who was supposed to remunerate him generously in coin as soon as the masterpiece was finished. But the great medieval poet Nezami Aruzi reports that after the poem was completed, a copy in seven volumes, Ferdowsi, accompanied by his professional reciter, went to Ghazna to present his masterpiece where—because of the slanderous gossip circulated by Ferdowsi's enemies or perhaps because of the Shi'ite leanings of the poet—Mahmoud handed over twenty thousand dinars instead of the sixty thousand dinars Ferdowsi was promised. Exasperated and distressed, Ferdowsi took himself off to a hammam, where he drank beer and divided his payment between the bath-servants. Fearing Mahmoud's anger, he left Ghazna and took refuge in Herat, then in Tus, where he is said to have composed a violent satire against Mahmud. Filled with remorse, and on the advice of his vizier, Mahmoud sent to Ferdowsi camels loaded with indigo, worth twenty thousand dinars. Legend has it that at the moment the camels entered Tus, the body of the deceased poet left the city through another gate. Scholars debate the veracity of any or all of these "biographic" details, but they make a fitting tale for a poet who was a master storyteller.

The social class to which Ferdowsi belonged, the *dihqans*, who were chiefly landowners, had quickly converted to Islam with the coming of the Arabs, but they had certainly not forgotten the history and cultural world of pre-Islamic Iran. On the contrary, the *dihqans* were keen to keep the memory of the ancient kings alive. Ferdowsi only continues this tradition, but with the talent that real genius confers. The ninth century witnessed a renaissance of Zoroastrianism among the Iranians who used the reactivation of the old faith to push back against the Islamic regime of the Arabs. Most of the Pahlavi (Middle Persian) texts that we now possess date from this period. National fervor and religious revival helped to stimulate Ferdowsi's creative spirit. Besides, he was guaranteed a huge audience of sympathetic Persian-born readers and listeners.

The Iranian epic tradition can be traced back to antiquity. The old Avesta, for instance, preserved early Iron Age stories of ancient kings, some of which were inherited, albeit indirectly, by Ferdowsi. After Alexander of Macedon's conquest of the Persian Empire, the Seleucid era saw a process of Hellenization that would eliminate a whole section of the Iranian past until the prestigious adventure of the Achaemenid dynasty would be completely erased from the collective memory of Iran. Even the name of Cyrus the Great eventually disappeared and remained unknown to most Iranians until the nineteenth century. Only the name of Darius would survive the centuries; Darius III, the last Achaemenid great king, appears in *Shahnameh* as Dara, the valiant but ill-starred opponent of Skander (Alexander).

The epic genre flourished again with the arrival of the Parthian dynasty and, little by little, the national spirit was reborn and chased away most of the Hellenizing influences that had dominated Persian culture. Under the following dynasty, that of the Sassanian, whose cradle in Fars was the same as that of the Achaemenids, epic and historical literature seems to have flourished. We know that at this time "Books of Kings" were composed in Pahlavi or Middle Persian: the *Kār-Nāmag ī Ardašīr ī Pābagān*, "Book of the Deeds of Ardeshir, Son of Papak," for instance, was a popular prose-tale about the birth and accession to power of Ardashir I, the first of the Sassanian kings, while another text, the now-lost *Khwaday-nāmag* or the "Book of Lords," seems to have been a history of the kings of Iran's last pre-Islamic dynasty. Tragically, the great literary products of the Sassanian period were destroyed during the Arab invasion, an even more devastating fate for the culture of ancient Persia than that brought about by the Greeks.

Ferdowsi was able to draw all his documentation from manuscripts that still existed at his time. These were probably texts translated from Pahlavi into Persian. Consequently, there has been much discussion about whether the poet knew the Pahlavi language. This is not impossible. Despite the difference in the writing of the Middle Persian script, the Pahlavi language was still comprehensible to Persian speakers; it was merely a very archaic form of Persian. Many texts had already been translated into Persian, such as the long-lost *Shahnameh* of Abu Almansuri (composed c. 947 CE), and from the beginning of his own great work

Ferdowsi alludes to it and reports that he had an illustrious predecessor in the person of Daqiqi, too, an already famous poet of his time. Daqiqi had undertaken to compose a "Book of Kings" and he had written a thousand verses of it by the time he died. Paying homage to Daqiqi, Ferdowsi took them up in his own work:

> There was a book from long ago,
> which contained many tales,
> but it was scattered around the hands of the *mobads* (Zoroastrian priests),
> a part of it was owned by every scholar-priest.
>
> A hero appeared, a descendant of the *dihqans*,
> brave and strong, wise, and gifted,
> who quested for old, old stories
> And hunted for lost tales.
>
> One by one the *mobads* narrated to him
> the sayings of the kings and the revolving of the world.
> When the hero had absorbed their words
> he wrote a celebrated book
> And it was a wonder of the world
> So that princes and peasants praised it.
>
> Along came an articulate youth (Daqiqi),
> skilled with words and of nimble mind.
> He said, "I will put this book into verse."
> But he died and the poetry remained unwritten.
>
> Should I try to get a hold of that book
> and start putting it into verse myself?
> I consulted loads of people . . .
> I had a good pal in town:
> we were two peas in a pod!

He said to me, "This is a brilliant idea!
Just go for it!! Get it done!
I will get you a copy of the old stories
in written form! But get on with it!
You are smart and still young,
and you have the gift of bringing heroes to life.
Go and rework this royal book,
and get fame and fortune from men of worth."
(*Shahnameh* 1:12–14, 115–31; trans. Lloyd Llewellyn-Jones)

Ferdowsi must have thrown himself into a formidable research challenge as he attempted to track down these old texts, and even find people who still spoke the Pahlavi form of his language. Oral tradition was still very much alive at the time and in his text the poet often mentions his informants. Still, despite the relentless research, the reigns of certain ancient kings had already fallen into oblivion, and Ferdowsi was obliged to fill in the gaps with general observations or moralizing maxims.

History thickens throughout the narrative of *Shahnameh*. A long mythological section begins the poem, which is followed by a segment full of legendary characters (many having a historical basis); finally, the poem moves into its proper historical phase with the dawn of the Sassanian dynasty. The mythical narrative opens at the court of the first king of Iran, a land which is, of course, located at the center of the world. The king, who is the product of God's love for Iran, undertakes cosmic combat against the minions of Ahriman, God's evil adversary in traditional Zoroastrian cosmology. Fire is discovered, the demons are tamed, and Persia's culture and civilization swiftly develop. Jamshid, the fourth king of this primeval dynasty (Pishdadians), establishes a rigid social hierarchy composed of four classes: priests, warriors, farmers, and artisans. Jamshid is a Solomon-like figure, dispensing justice and charity all around him. He rules from a palace called *Takht-e Jamshid*, the "Throne of Jamshid," a magnificent construction of stone that had been brought down from heaven. From there he governed the world for four hundred fifty years. In Ferdowsi's day, the ancient ruins of Persepolis, which projected up and out from the desert sands that had swallowed them, were interpreted at that great heavenly monument, and today Iranians still know the archaeological site of Persepolis as *Takht-e Jamshid.*

Jamshid, and all rightful kings, are said to possess a divine essence or charisma (*farr*), which can be visibly manifest surrounding their person as a divine halo of light (as is seen in this edition), an aura, or a totemic animal such as a wild boar, ram, or falcon, but should a king misbehave, act unjustly, or anger God, then the *farr* may abandon him. When Jamshid succumbs to hubris, he loses his *farr* and his throne falls to Zahhak, a power-hungry but naïve Arab prince who is corrupted by the kiss (and culinary arts) of Iblis (Satan) and turns into an oppressive and bloodthirsty tyrant. Feraydun, a descendant of Jamshid, with the aid of Kaveh the brave blacksmith, manages to pry the throne away from Zahhak and restore his own family to establish the Kayanid dynasty. Freedom and justice return to Iran. Just before he dies, however, Feraydun divides his kingdom between his three ambitious sons, and in no time at all, their jealousies lead to fratricide and embroil Iran and its northeastern neighbor, Touran, in a long and bloody feud.

Rostam, a trickster warrior of enormous size and strength from nearby Zabolestan (Sistan), steadfastly defends the Iranian Kayanid dynasty in all of its wars with Touran. Rostam, son of Zaul, son of Saum, son of Narimon, is from the Garshasb family, and his mother, Rudabeh, is the daughter of Mehraub Shah Kaboli. The Garshasb family was one of the most important Iranian families, and its men were known for both physical strength and wisdom. After Ferdowsi finishes with the extended, but compelling, story of Rostam, the mythical era begins to blend into a quasi-legendary historical period, with the story of the last Achaemenid kings, Darab and Dara (Darius II and III). In what is essentially a book within a book, the *Skandarnameh* ("Book of Alexander") section of *Shahnameh* gives its focus to the exploits of Alexander the Great (Eskandar).

The *Skandarnameh* comes at the point in Ferdowsi's narrative where myth morphs into legend and legend turns into history, the intersection where Ferdowsi overwrites the "what happened" with the "what is better." According to Ferdowsi, Darab (Darius II) was married to Nahid, a daughter of Philqus (Philip II), King of Rom (Rome, or the west), but shortly after their wedding he rejected her (the poor girl had the most dreadful halitosis), and sent her home to her father. Unknown to Darab, she was pregnant with his child, and when she gave birth, Philqus raised him as his own son and named him Eskandar. Meanwhile Darab took a Persian wife and she gave him a son, Dara. After Philqus's death, when Eskandar came of age, Dara, who had become king of Persia, demanded tribute from Rom, but Eskandar decided to withhold it. Now, war erupts between the two kingdoms, and Eskandar defeats Dara in three battles and captures Istakhr (the area around Persepolis). In a fourth battle, Dara is killed by two of his own men, whom Ferdowsi names as Mahyar and Janusayar. Eskandar finds the king as he lies dying, and weeps with him for his misfortune. Dara gives Eskandar his daughter Rhoshanak (Roxane) in marriage, bestows the Persian Empire into Eskandar's hands, and then dies. This is a key moment in the epic's narrative and in the conceptualization of Iran's history: Eskandar is rewarded the Persian Empire thanks to his military prowess and his charismatic leadership; but, as Ferdowsi has made his readers aware, the empire was his by birthright and through blood. As the firstborn son of Darab, Eskandar was always destined to sit on the Persian throne, and through his death, Dara, Eskandar's half-brother, rights the dynastic wrong and allows destiny to triumph. Eskandar, the Persian prince, takes his rightful place among the great kings of the past.

Why did Ferdowsi feel the need to rewrite the history of the Macedonian invasion, a truly bloody and catastrophic moment in Iran's long history? And why did he need to rehabilitate Alexander III by turning him into an Achaemenid prince, heir, and king? The answer must lie with the Arab invasion of Iran because, for Ferdowsi, the Arab conquest was an apocalyptic event, the nadir of Persia's long, celebrated past. To utterly villainize the Arabs and their total occupation of Persia, he needed to write out the bloody invasion of Iran by the Macedonians and turn it into a positive. *Shahnameh* has room for only one true villain.

Following on from the *Skandarnameh*, the poem fast-forwards through the Greek Seleucids and the east-Iranian Parthians, who are given very short shrift by Ferdowsi, and picks up again with the revolt of Ardashir, who, in the post-Alexander era of fractured petty kingdoms, overthrows the regional ruler Ardavan with the assistance of Golnar, Ardavan's counselor-cum-concubine. This leads to the establishment of the Sassanian dynasty, foreordained because Ardashir is a blood heir to the throne of the king of kings. The poem then focuses successively on the historical Sassanian kings, some of whom (Ardashir, Bahraum-e Gur, Nushin-ravaun, and Khosrow-Parviz) feature more prominently than others.

Throughout the epic poem, the ruler's success as both a reveler and hunter-warrior distinguishes him as a worthy and legitimate sovereign. The pairing of *bazm* (battle) and *razm* (banquet) as the ultimate royal activities is an ancient concept with roots in pre-Islamic Iran and is a recurring theme in *Shahnameh*. Ferdowsi insists that the ideal royal virtues include bravery, prowess, skill in hunting, wisdom, honor, humility, and levelheadedness, but nowhere does Ferdowsi beatify kings or attempt to hide their character flaws, which often are the cause of calamity or tragedy for themselves or those around them (as is the case in the story of the impetuous Kay-Kavous). Oddly, the very best princes (Iraj, Seyavash, and Esfandiar) die before taking the throne, while the ideal shah (Kay-Khosrow) abdicates his throne for fear of falling into hubris and the abuse of power. Ferdowsi also probes the question of fate and questions whether humans have any kind of free will, and he laments the tragic forces that so often compel kings to make enemies, to quarrel with their sons, and to humiliate the champion warriors to whom they owe their thrones. Father-son conflicts are a particularly tragic hallmark of the work, and by and large end badly for the son (Rostam and Sohrab, Kay-Kavous and Seyavash, Goshtausp and Esfandiar), but all the way through *Shahnameh* we can sense Ferdowsi trying to replay patterns of dynamic conflict in hopes that better outcomes can be had. Sadly, that rarely happens; in Ferdowsi's world, virtue is not rewarded, and Fate and Time overpower human works and wisdom.

Ferdowsi's magisterial poem offers its readers instruction by exploring how the kings of old governed the world and why the world has been handed down to us in such sad state of disarray. This is why Ferdowsi, after writing fifty thousand couplets, ends *Shahnameh* with the Arab conquest of Persia, which he, even while writing as a Muslim, depicts as Iran's greatest tragedy.

Lloyd Llewellyn-Jones

FURTHER READING

Davidson, O. M. *Poet and Hero in the Persian Book of Kings*. Cambridge, MA, 2013.

Davidson, O. M., and M. S. Simpson (eds.). *Ferdowsi's Shahnama: Millennial Perspectives*. Cambridge, MA, 2013.

Davis, D. *Epic and Sedition: The Case of Ferdowsi's Shahnameh*. Washington, 1992.

Friedl, E. *Folktales and Storytellers of Iran*. London, 2014.

Gazerani, S. *The Sistani Cycle of Iran's National History*. Leiden, 2016.

Ghazanfari, K. *Perceptions of Zoroastrian Realities in the Shahnameh*. Berlin, 2011.

Hämeen-Anttila, J. *Khwadaynamag: The Middle Persian Book of Kings*. Leiden, 2017.

Hoyland, R. G. *The History of the Kings of the Persians in Three Arabic Chronicles*. Liverpool, 2018.

Kassock, Z. J. V. *Karnamag i Ardeshir i Papagan: A Pahlavi Student's Guide*. Fredericksberg, 2013.

Levy, R. *The Epic of the Kings: Shah-Nama, the National Epic of Persia*. London, 1967.

Llewellyn-Jones, L. *Persians. The Age of the Great Kings*. London and New York, 2022.

Llewellyn-Jones, L., and J. Robson. *Ctesias' History of Persia: Tales of the Orient*. London, 2010.

Nöldeke, T. *The Iranian National Epic, or, the "Shahnamah."* London, 1930.

Rubanovich, J. *Orality and Textuality in the Iranian World: Patterns of Interaction across the Centuries*. Leiden, 2015.

Shayegan, M. R. *Aspects of History and Epic in Ancient Iran*. Washington, DC, 2012.

Yamamoto, K. *The Oral Background of Persian Epics*. Leiden, 2003.

TRANSLATOR'S NOTE

THE TRIPLE TEXTURES

Shahnameh begins with a brief mythological introduction comprising 9 percent of the extant poem. These are not creation myths. The four kings of this period (Gayumart, Hushang, Tahmuret, and Jamshid) were civilizers: they discovered, invented, and taught their followers such skills as hunting, irrigation, farming, smelting, sailing, and warfare. They tamed the beasts of their enchanted world and dragooned its demons to carve palaces out of stone and unravel the secrets of the arcane art of writing.

Over half (53 percent) of the poem is dedicated to the epic period. This is the age of heroes. Demons and angels are rare in this dispensation, and they are treated with a measure of skeptical distance when they appear. Epic kings live by the moral codes of civilization rather than inventing them. The most salient survival of the mythic past in epic times is that the kings continue to rule by their "divine sanction" (*farr*) that emanates from their faces as a charismatic halo. But, unlike the "divine right of kings" in medieval Europe, *farr* is an evanescent gift. A king risks losing his halo if he neglects the royal arts (*honar*) of fighting, feasting, and generosity or acts with selfish impetuosity, spurning the council of practical reason (*kherad*).

Kings Jamshid and Nowzar forfeited their divine sanction due to their hubris and indolence. The *farr* of the irascible King Kay-Kavous steadily waned until he was obliged to retire in favor of his grandson,

Kay-Khosrow. This prince, whose mother and grandmother were of Touranian stock, was known for his courage, wisdom, and dedication to Iran, which is how he won the crown in a contest with his full-blooded Iranian uncle, Fariborz. The epic period is the most dazzling part of the poem. This explains why professional reciters of the poem, over the centuries, have focused their attention on these stories.

The poem ends with a historical account of the last pre-Islamic dynasty of Iran, comprising the remaining 38 percent of the poem. If we liken the mythic and epic parts of *Shahnameh* to Hesiod's Theogony and Homer's *Iliad* and *Odyssey*, the historical segment of it resembles Herodotus's Histories. Pivoting from epic to history in *Shahnameh* is smooth. Rather than starting with the historical sketch of the Macedonian invasion of Iran, the poem begins with the "Alexander Romance" that had been circulating in the area for over a millennium.

Recapitulating the Arsacid or (Ashkanian) dynasty (247 BCE–224 CE) in a few lines, Ferdowsi turns his attention to the Sassanian period (224–651 CE). The interminable Persian-Roman wars were waged or fought by a score of Roman emperors, from Crassus and Alexander Severus to Heraclius. About half of these appear in *Shahnameh* with the generic title of Caesar. As might be expected of a work commissioned by the royal courts, Iran's victories against the Romans are augmented while such setbacks as Nersi's crushing defeat in the battle of Satala (298 CE) are edited out or given short shrift. The eastern neighbors of the Sassanian Iran consisted of the Kushanians, the Hephthalites, the Kidarite and Nezak Huns, and various Turkic confederations. *Shahnameh* lumps all these as Touranians or Turks whose leaders are identified by the title of khagan.

Despite these shortcomings, the historic *Shahnameh* remains a valuable resource for social and cultural disciplines. To begin with, the poem's sequence of events after King Piruz (459–84 CE) corresponds with the Sassanian record. More important, the historic part of the poem is a portal into Iran's late antique zeitgeist reflecting the political philosophy, social ethos, theological controversies, state administration, and libido economy of the period. This is why we have included such material as the pithy comments of philosophers at the funeral of Alexander and the edifying discourses of Buzarjmehr, although they do not advance the story. One can find similar value in Ferdowsi's own comments that frame the stories. These lines have all been translated in verse to set them apart from the body of the stories.

DIVERSITY, PATRIOTISM, AND MORALITY

Shahnameh is not a Persian exercise in self-adulation. In the poem, one finds ample evidence of chivalrous conduct by the enemy as well as unbecoming conduct by the Iranian side. Undoubtedly, Piran, the Touranian field marshal, and Khosh-nauvaz, the Hephthalite khagan, are treated with sympathy by the omniscient narrator of *Shahnameh*, who enters their private chambers and records their solitary prayers for peace and justice.

One could make a case for the claim that *Shahnameh* is a thousand years ahead of its time in certain theological and moral respects. However, it would be surprising for a twenty-first-century reader not to find something to quibble with in a thousand-year-old text. For instance, a combination of abuse and misogyny is evident in the shocking treatment of the slave girl Azaudeh by the arrogant King Bahraum V. Occasional ethnic and religious stereotypes about Kurds, Baluchis, Turks, Arabs, gypsies, Jews, and Christians—not to mention such heretical sects as the Manichaeans and the Mazdakites—can be found in the poem. And yet we must warn against the modern nativist readings of *Shahnameh* and the equally absurd critique of the poem as a racist screed. Most of the evidence for such anachronistic caricatures comes from inauthentic additions or out-of-context quotations.

THE ESSENCE OF THE IRANIAN IDENTITY

Shahnameh ended with the Arab conquest of 630 CE. This was a disaster for Iran. But the Iranians preserved their identity by holding on to their language and calendar after converting to Islam. Ferdowsi, who finished his *Shahnameh* in the year 400 of the Islamic calendar, was at the pinnacle of the renascence of the Persian language.

Today, men, women, and children in Persianate societies from Asia Minor to the borders of Hun China recite lines of *Shahnameh* by heart. The book continues to be read at family gatherings and performed by professional reciters in the teahouses of Tajikistan, Iran, and Afghanistan. Such practices have been intensified in post-Islamic-Republic Iran.

It was my awareness of the role of ordinary speakers of Persian in upholding their poetic birthright that gave me the courage to embark on the path of translating this work. I remember the first public performance of *Shahnameh* that I witnessed at age seven, somewhere near the city of Karaj. The professional reciter (Naqaul) wore a leather vest studded with shiny spikes and wielded a short cane that turned into a sword, a mace, and even the neck of a neighing horse. He paced rapidly back and forth, producing sound effects for galloping horses, clanging swords, and lacerating javelins. Sonorously intoning the lines of *Shahnameh* in the middle of his prose narration, the performer brought to life the last scenes of the battle of Rostam and Sohrab. I still remember the pictures I made in my head as he went on. The session ended with a cliffhanger as the hero, Rostam, climbed a pile of rocks and put his neck in a self-made noose to take his own life. Then he kicked the stones and they crumbled under his feet with a terrible sound: Khorrr!

Later, I learned that this scene belonged to the scripts of the Naqauls and was not in any of the authoritative copies of *Shahnameh*. But the knowledge did not diminish the impact of that performance. I, too, have used such additional stories (e.g., Rostam's taking of the White Fortress and his slaying of a musth elephant) to flesh out the account of his coming of age.

ABOUT THIS EDITION

We are fortunate to live in the age of great discoveries and masterfully prepared critical editions of *Shahnameh*. The nine-volume Moscow version was superseded by the canonic, eight-volume Khaleghi-Motlagh edition, based on the 1217 Florence manuscript. The latter was discovered by Angelo Piemontese in 1978. Another serendipitous discovery occurred in 1932 when the Egyptian scholar Abd al-Wahhab al-Ezam collated the fragments of an Arabic translation by Fath b. Ali al-Bundari al-Isfahani. This work, named *Al-Shahnameh,* was commissioned by the Ayyubid ruler al-Mu'azzam Isa (1198–1227). I have closely followed the Khaleghi-Motlagh text with occasional references to *Al-Shahnameh.* Although on a few occasions, the sequences of events are slightly modulated for a smoother narration, no stories are skipped or relegated to summarized margins.

The 2013 illustrated edition of this *Shahnameh* contained the mythological and epic dispensations that comprise a bit under the first two-thirds of *Shahnameh.* The current version includes the entire work. The story is told with a relentless economy. Only persons with speaking lines have been named, and once a character is introduced, we follow them, adding as much psychological depth and human interest as could be squeezed from the text.

To keep the text user-friendly, we have eschewed diacritical marks. To distinguish the long Ā vowel ("tall" as opposed to "apple"), I have used "au" as in "Paul." So Zāl and Sām are spelled Zaul and Saum.

Also, I have preserved the prominent authorial voice of Ferdowsi, the poet who versified one of the prose compendiums of the ancient legends commissioned by the Samanid commander of Tus, Abu Mansur b. Abd-al-Razzauq (d. 961 CE).

Unlike Homer, Ferdowsi does not claim to be possessed by a muse. The poet's somber voice brackets every story with philosophical commentary, and it occasionally breaks through the narrative like a Greek chorus to regale the audience with the story's moral. Nor is Ferdowsi above using such occasions to complain of his poverty and old age, mourn the death of his young son, or express his fear of death before finishing the poem—which he completed after thirty-three years (from 977 to 1010 CE). It is as if the poet was deliberately humanizing himself to counter the larger-than-life image we all have made for him.

The translator of an ancient text can claim to be only somewhat objective about the task. Changes in intellectual and historical horizons over the past millennium have been enormous. Our understanding of masculinity, patriotism, gender, and nationality has undergone a great transformation. Our lifeworld and cultural sensitivities have changed, and not always in predictable ways. Rudabeh, Tahmineh, the young Soudabeh, and Manizheh, the heroines of the epic *Shahnameh*'s four love stories, initiate romance and succeed in their sexual conquest of their enemies. The word "enemy" is chosen advisedly as all these stories occur across national boundaries. The iconic "other" of *Shahnameh* is often the object of romantic interest. The Arab might be seen as the ultimate enemy that crushed the Iranian empire and ended the epic of the Persian kings. But the quintessential hero of the poem, Rostam, is born to a mother descended from an Arab "Serpent King."

The national epic of Iran never dehumanizes the enemy. To be sure, there are some evil Touranians who deserve their vilification. King Afrasiab and his scheming brother Garsivaz top that list. But, his other brother, Aghrirat, shields a group of Iranian captives from execution and pays for it with his life. To complicate the question of identities, this dreadful enemy king also happens to be the maternal grandfather of the Iranian king Kay-Khosrow, who defends him as a worthy opponent in the presence of his incredulous knights.

My collaborators Melissa Hibbard and Hamid Rahmanian (who read, reread, listened to, and critiqued several permutations of this translation) and I have toiled on this volume with the hope of someday encountering someone who has become familiar with *Shahnameh*'s intrepid heroines and heroes. This arduous labor of love will have been worthwhile should we hear one day that the four sweeping and increasingly human-centered tragedies of Sohrab, Siavosh, Forud, and Esfandiar have become as familiar to our English-speaking audiences as those of Oedipus, Hector, Hamlet, and Lear.

Ahmad Sadri

Shahnameh

The Epic of the Persian Kings

In the name of the Lord of life and reason, the sublime,
God who conceived us but can't be conceived,
For He is beyond our ken, and above our space and time.

The maker of the moon, the venus and the sun
Who gave us reason and enjoined us
To acquire wisdom and pass it on.

Ponder these tales but don't call them fables and lies.
Some of them conform to reason. The rest are
Esoteric truths that have come to us in disguise.

Part I

Mythology and Epic Traditions

CHAPTER 1

The Kings of Yore: Gayumart to Zahhak

THE FIRST KING: GAYUMART*

No one knows for sure how the first kingships began
Or who was the very first to wear the crown of sovereignty
But the forefathers have related the tales of one such man.

As the sun entered the constellation of Aries and the world rejoiced in the glory of spring, a man named Gayumart ascended the throne of the world and began his rule. Wearing a tiger pelt, he took residence in the mountains with his companions, and inaugurated the customs of preparing food. He was tall as a cypress tree and his face shone with the halo of divine sanction like a full moon. Animals of the world, carnivores and herbivores alike, humbled themselves at his threshold and pledged their obedience. He reigned for thirty years.

The king had no enemies in the world but for the archdemon Ahriman, who was the source of all darkness in the universe. Rankled by envy, Ahriman conspired with his son Khazarvaun, who resembled a fearsome wolf, to crush the new king. Crowds of demons flocked to Khazarvaun's evil cause.

But the king had a wise and handsome son named Siamak, whom he adored. He beamed whenever he saw him, and dreaded the thought of being separated.

One day, the angel Sorush appeared to the handsome prince and warned him that the devil's forces were on the move. Outraged, Siamak gathered an army to stand against the prince of darkness. He wore only the hide of a tiger, as armor did not exist yet, when he went to wrestle with Ahriman's son. Khazarvaun threw him to the ground and mauled him to death.

When Gayumart heard what had happened, he fell off his throne,

* All personal names in the present edition are transliterated from our critical edition of *Shahnameh* by Khaleghi-Motlagh et al. Foreign personal names and locations have been recorded in accordance with current English usage.

clawing his face and crying tears of blood. All inhabitants of the land, both man and beast, came to share in their king's sorrows. After a year of grief, the angel Sorush appeared to the king and advised him to stop mourning and prepare to avenge his son's death.

Gayumart was getting old, and the world needed a new leader. So, he decided to entrust the command of the war of revenge to Siamak's son, a lad by the name of Hushang. King Gayumart would always be at the heart of the army, but now his grandson would lead the charge. His forces consisted of men, fairies, tame beasts, leopards, and wolves. The scion of Ahriman fearlessly led his army, raising a great cloud of dust. The two sides fought hard, and in the end, the demons were defeated. Hushang took Khazarvaun by the neck, ripped his hide, cut off his head, and threw his lifeless body to the ground. Having exacted revenge for his father, the young man went back to his grandfather and gave a report of his victory. Gayumart was content that Siamak's death had been avenged before death carried him away from this world.

Gayumart's reign ended but his legacy remained
Sorrows and pleasures of this life vanish in time
What endures is the good name one has made.

THE SECOND KING: HUSHANG

Young Hushang ascended the throne after his grandfather and declared himself the ruler of the seven realms. During the forty years of his reign, the second king spread justice and enriched the world as he was commanded to do so by God. He smelted iron and inaugurated the use of new instruments such as hatchets, axes, saws, and maces. All these inventions were only made possible after he accidentally discovered the secret of fire.

During a hunting expedition, Hushang saw a snake slithering in a cleavage of rocks and threw a piece of flint, aiming for its head. The missile missed its target, hitting the rock face, but a spark flew. Thus, the astute king learned how to make a spark into a fire. That night he made a bonfire and drank with his companions in celebration of his discovery. He was the first to celebrate the Persian festival of Sadeh, which occurs on the fortieth day of winter.

Having mastered one element, the king soon embarked on conquering water by teaching his followers how to irrigate their crops. He then pioneered the art of making bread out of harvested seeds, and trained his people to hunt wild beasts for meat and pelts and even how to domesticate animals.

Hushang was a great king who avenged his father and improved the world with his innovation, but he, too, succumbed to death, that common fate of all humans.

THE THIRD KING: TAHMURET

After Hushang, his son Tahmuret ascended the throne and ruled for forty years. At the outset of his reign, the young sovereign declared that he would disclose what was beneficial but hidden and that he would cleanse the world of evil. He taught people the secrets of breeding new and stronger animals and the arts of shearing, spinning, and weaving wool. He tamed cheetahs and falcons to help man hunt.

Above all, Tahmuret subdued the demons that lurked around, killing two-thirds of their population and imprisoning the rest. This is how he earned the title of Demon Binder. Some of the demons pleaded for their lives, saying they would teach him an art with many benefits if he let them live. Tahmuret set them free to reveal their secrets, and, lo, they taught him the art of writing in thirty languages, including Roman, Chinese, Arabic, and Persian.

For thirty years, he ruled and spread the knowledge of various arts until it was time for him to die. Then the Demon Binder was succeeded by his son, who would become a truly magnificent sovereign.

THE FOURTH KING: JAMSHID

The young King Jamshid wore his father's crown and declared himself both priest and king. The world took refuge in his protection, and all submitted to him, including birds of the sky, demons, and fairies. Jamshid charmed the iron and fashioned armor both for men and warhorses. He established a tradition whereby champions were encouraged to taunt their enemies and seek glory on the battlefield.

Among the crucial inventions of King Jamshid was his creation of the social classes. He divided the people into four castes: the clerics, the warriors, the farmers, and the artisans. Each profession was given its exclusive purpose. For fifty years the king allowed the four vocations to take root.

Jamshid allotted the next fifty years of his reign to build his empire. He coerced the demons to fashion mud into bricks and mix water with plaster to build palaces and bathhouses. They also carved blocks from granite boulders in accordance with the rules of geometric design to erect magnificent buildings. Then the king mined gold, silver, and precious stones such as rubies and amber. He extracted and refined perfumes, including camphor, musk, ambergris, and rosewater.

It was this king who founded the field of medicine. He built ships and crossed watery passages that separate the landmasses of the world. These and his other contributions to human civilization consumed another fifty years of the king's long reign.

Having accomplished all of this, the exalted Jamshid built a jewel-encrusted throne with the aid of his divine sanction. The throne would be held aloft by demons whenever the king wished. When his throne was lifted to the heavens, the king looked as radiant as the shining sun. The inhabitants of the world gathered to behold the king in wonderment and rained a shower of gems on him. One such day coincided with the first day of spring. Iranians called that day Nowruz and solemnized it as the eve of the Persian New Year.

The ancient kings gave us the gift of a peaceful holiday
Calling for wine and musicians at the onset of spring
They forgave their foes and drank their worries away.

For the next three hundred years, Jamshid ruled in justice and triumph. His subjects, both human and demon, obeyed the glorious king who was aglow with the halo of divine kingship.

But the king lost his way, allowing himself to be seduced by the temptations of vanity. After all, insofar as he could see, he was the omnipotent sovereign of the world. Confident of his supremacy, the great king called together the elder noblemen and the clerics and declared: "I am the one who made the world good. I am the one who initiated the arts and transformed the earth. Everyone must recognize my ascendancy. Your satiety and safety, your garments and comforts, are all my gifts. I have banished sickness and death from the world. You are beholden to me for everything. I am the one with the crown of kingship, and none can challenge my preeminence."

The noblemen and the clerics lowered their heads in silence and dared not oppose the royal declaration. But the die was cast. Once Jamshid uttered these words, the divine halo of kingship scattered from around his head and his fortunes swiftly declined.

Here is an excellent piece of advice that a wise man gave
To an unskilled ruler seduced by temptations of pride:
"When you are made a king, adopt the humility of a slave."

Chaos filled the kingdom for twenty-three years. Steadily the noblemen, the knights, and all worthy followers left the royal throne, appalled as they were with the king's hubris and conceit. As his authority eroded, he was further inclined to arrogance and iniquity. Finally, the king was forced to abandon his palace and go into hiding.

In the meantime, in a nearby land, another king was rising.

THE RISE OF THE SERPENT KING

There was once a noble and God-fearing Arab king named Mardaus. He had stables of well-groomed Arabian horses and was rich with many flocks of milk-giving lambs, sheep, and goats. He was generous to people in need.

Mardaus had a son by the name of Zahhak, who was sometimes known as Bivarasp, which meant "owner of ten thousand horses." Impetuous, petty, and ruthless, he was unlike his father in every respect. The wicked prince loved only his horses and spent most of his day in the saddle.

One day at dawn, the devil Iblis came to the prince disguised as a kindly adviser. Zahhak was mesmerized by his guest and asked for his guidance. The mysterious visitor agreed to offer his advice, but on one condition: the prince had to agree to follow Iblis's directives and to keep their conversation a secret. Zahhak pledged his obedience, and Iblis spoke: "Why should an old and decrepit father reign when he has a worthy son like you? The time has come for you to wrest power from him and rule the world."

Zahhak was tempted but did not wish to shed his father's blood. He said, "Give me a different piece of advice, for this cannot be done."

Iblis said, "If you refuse my advice, you have broken your promise to me. And then your father will continue to rule and you shall be nothing but an inferior subject."

At this, the ambitious prince finally allowed himself to be seduced by the devil, becoming complicit in the plot to murder his own father. Iblis dug a pit on the way to a garden where Mardaus went for his devotions. When the pious and noble king rose at dawn to perform his prayers, he fell into the pit and broke his back, and Iblis filled the pit with dirt.

Soon after Zahhak took his father's throne, Iblis returned in another disguise. This time he appeared as a young man adept in culinary arts and took over as the king's chef. Iblis was a sorcerer in the royal kitchen. He fed the new king a delectable diet of animal flesh to make him as fearless as a lion. This did wonders for the new cook's reputation; people at that time were not used to exotic foods. Iblis flavored his meals with spices and zests and brought such dishes as partridge, pheasant, and the roasted sirloin of a calf to the royal table. Delighted by the talents of his capable and creative cook, Zahhak offered to grant him a wish: "What is your pleasure? Ask and you shall be given."

The disguised Iblis said, "My heart is full of your love, my king. My only wish is to place kisses upon His Majesty's shoulders."

The favor was granted, and when he kissed the shoulders of the king, Iblis magically dissolved into the ground. Suddenly, two black serpents sprouted from the king's shoulders, and he screamed with horror. He tried everything to rid himself of the blight. He even ordered the serpents to be severed at the root, but they grew back like the branches of a tree.

The king called on the physicians of the world to devise a cure, but none could rid him of his affliction.

Then Iblis appeared to Zahhak for a third time, in the guise of a skilled healer. He recommended that the serpents be fed the brains of young men so that they would not harm the king and might eventually die of their own accord. Thereafter, as his henchmen beheaded young men daily to feed their king's voracious serpents, the Arab king inclined himself to evil, and soon mastered the black arts of witchcraft.

THE TYRANT ZAHHAK RULED FOR A THOUSAND YEARS

Meanwhile, Jamshid's loss of divine charisma had plunged Iran into confusion. Since he had given up his sovereignty, pretenders to the throne had risen and fought each other for dominance. Iran needed a new mighty king to settle disputes and restore order to the land. Searching for their new sovereign, the Iranian noblemen and knights came to settle on the fearsome Serpent King of the Arabs. They went to Zahhak, swore their allegiance, and ushered him and his army to the palace known as the Throne of Jamshid.

Thus, the Serpent King began his long, brutal rule over Iran. He immediately commanded his minions to search for the fugitive king. This search lasted one hundred years until Jamshid was found hiding somewhere around the sea of China. Zahhak had the doomed king sawed in half, an order that filled the world with terror.

After seven centuries it was time for Jamshid's demise
In the blink of an eye, he was swallowed by fate
As a speck of straw onto rubbed amber flies.

Zahhak then commanded his henchmen to drag Jamshid's horrified sisters, Shahrnauz and Arnavauz, out of their palace and forced them to join him in wedlock. He corrupted them, as one can only teach what one knows. Zahhak was unjust and knew nothing but the evil trade of witchery. He was also in the habit of killing any soldier with a beautiful daughter to possess the helpless maiden himself.

Time passed, and the snakes on his shoulders continued to demand the lives of young men for their daily sustenance. Only a handful of the victims escaped due to the mercy of a few good men in the tyrant's employ. But most of them perished appeasing the appetite of his serpents, or as victims of his other dark whims. In this manner, the terrible ruler tyrannized Iran for nearly a thousand years.

One night, sleeping with the fair Arnavauz in his chambers, Zahhak woke up screaming from a nightmare. In the vision, a young warrior attacked him with an ox-headed mace and tied him up with leather cords. Then he put a packsaddle on his back and dragged him to Mount Damavand for imprisonment.

Arnavauz said: "Nothing should frighten you. You are the king of the seven realms and the sovereign to man and beast alike. Gather the soothsayers and prognosticators of the land and charge them to uncover the name of the man who is destined to kill you. Then you can easily eliminate him."

Zahhak followed this advice. When the wise men had gathered, he said: "Tell me about my end. When is it written for me to leave this world? Who will inherit my throne? Reveal this to me or suffer great pain."

As the assembled wise men investigated the matter, their lips dried, and their faces paled. They stood to suffer whether they told the truth or withheld it. Finally, a brave and wise man rose and spoke: "Stop the vain illusion that you will live forever. We are all destined to die. The name of the man who is fated to kill you is Feraydun. He has not yet been born. But one day he will pummel your head with his ox-headed mace. Then he shall bind and drag you down from your throne."

"But people don't act without reason. Why would this man assault and bind me?"

"Because you will kill his father and butcher his beloved cow."

Zahhak collapsed upon hearing this. Upon recovery, he sent his deputies to track down impending signs of his future nemesis throughout the realm.

THE RISE OF THE RIGHTEOUS KING

Born to a woman named Faranak, Feraydun was luminous with the same divine halo of kingship that had once adorned Jamshid.

He was still an infant when his father, Abtin, fell victim to Zahhak's minions, who had been on the prowl for young men to feed the serpents of the tyrant. When Faranak heard that her husband had been murdered, she was grief-stricken and worried for her son's life. In desperation, she took her newborn to a righteous cowherd for protection. As the baby Feraydun was hungry, the cowherd gave him to a cow named Barmauyeh for nursing. The gentle Barmauyeh was famous for her dazzling colors.

Three years after entrusting his son to the cowherd, Faranak had a premonition that Zahhak was closing in on him. In distress, she went to the cowherd and said: "A divine fear has entered my heart. My life depends on this child. I am afraid for his safety. I shall take him away from this land of witchcraft. I will go to the slopes of the Alborz Range."

Soon after their escape, the tyrant tracked down the farm where she had sought refuge, but Faranak and her son were nowhere to be found. Discovering that Barmauyeh had nursed Feraydun, he slew the cow, killed the cowherd, and burned the farm.

Having narrowly escaped the tyrant's clutches, Faranak ascended to the heights of the Alborz Mountains and entrusted her child to a hermit who lived there, saying: "Oh, holy man of God, I am a bereaved widow from the land of Iran. This child of mine is destined to end the reign of Zahhak. A cowherd brought him up to this age on the milk of the noble cow Barmauyeh. Now it falls upon you to accept his charge and lavish on him your fatherly care."

The kind hermit took pity on Faranak and accepted the task of rearing the tender child. When Feraydun reached the age of sixteen, he bid farewell to the hermit and came down from the mountain to ask his mother about his lineage. She said: "Your father was Abtin, a man of noble birth who was descended from King Tahmuret. The terrible king Zahhak had him killed to feed his serpents. Then Zahhak heard that you would overthrow him. We had to escape, and for your safety it was necessary for us to separate several times. Before I brought you to the hermit, the noble and magnificent cow, Barmauyeh, nursed you. After our departure the Serpent King came to capture you, and, in his rage, killed the innocent and gentle cow."

Feraydun was incensed: "The lion gains his courage in action. It is time I wielded my blade and avenged my father. I shall raze the palace of that sorcerer."

Faranak scolded her son: "This is not the way you will seek revenge. How can you fight Zahhak, who is able to rally a hundred thousand men from every realm under his control? You are drunk on the wine of youth. Don't endanger your life on such a reckless adventure. The people will rise to your cause when the time comes."

THE STORY OF KAVEH, THE BLACKSMITH

Zahhak became increasingly obsessed with finding Feraydun and Faranak. Their names alone stirred a great fear in his heart. One day he gathered the notables and clerics of his kingdom. "I have a fierce enemy, but he is in hiding," he declared. "I do not underestimate my enemies, puny as they might be. I intend to gather a great army of men and demons to confront this foe when he rises. But first, we must prepare a proclamation testifying that I am a just king, and it must stress that I have eschewed falsehoods and iniquity."

Fearing the wrath of the king, the dignitaries endorsed the proclamation declaring the tyrant to be the most just king in the world. At this time a man appeared at the gates, loudly protesting his wrongful treatment. Zahhak called on him to come forward and speak.

"I am Kaveh, a harmless blacksmith," he said. "But you keep pouring a torrent of fire on my head. You are the king of the seven realms, but it seems that our share of your great wealth and power is nothing but misery. Tell me, by what accounting is it my duty to sacrifice my son to feed your serpents?"

The king ordered his men to release Kaveh's son, and in exchange for this favor, he asked the blacksmith to sign his proclamation of justice.

Kaveh grew angry as he read the deed proclaiming Zahhak's righteousness. He roared at the dignitaries who had endorsed it. "Hell is your abode, you minions of the devil. You are sycophants surrounding an unjust king. Let it be known that Kaveh does not bear witness to this false document. Nor am I afraid of this king!"

With this, he tore the proclamation to shreds and strode out, firmly asserting his defiance. Astonished at the boldness of Kaveh, the dignitaries turned to their king and asked why he had suffered a mere blacksmith to tear up the royal proclamation they had signed. Zahhak was puzzled himself. "I don't know. As soon as I heard his voice it was as if I was paralyzed. I don't know what came over me. Nor do I know what will come of this."

Upon leaving the palace, Kaveh called upon the people of the capital to overthrow their tyrannical Serpent King, and great masses flocked to him. Hoisting his leather apron on a lance, Kaveh walked ahead of the crowd, chanting:

Let those who long for Feraydun
Lift the yoke of the accursed Zahhak
Before walking with us in communion.

Kaveh knew where Feraydun lived and directed his rally toward his town. His followers grew as he marched, and soon he was leading a veritable army behind his makeshift standard. When the multitudes reached the dwelling of their providential leader, a cry of astonishment went up from the household. The young man Feraydun took Kaveh's banner as a good omen. He treated it with respect and added three silken strands of crimson, yellow, and purple to it. From then on, the blacksmith's apron became the symbol of the Iranian throne. Although each king would adorn it with their own precious gems, the name of the leathern banner remained the *Standard of Kaveh*.

The arrival of the rebellious blacksmith was the sign that Feraydun had been waiting for. The time was ripe for his uprising. He confronted his mother with these words: "The moment has arrived for me to stand up and lead this revolt. But I need your fervent prayers. Don't worry for me, just put your trust in God, the Creator of the world."

Faranak wept with joy as her valiant son took charge of the men who had come seeking his leadership. Before leaving town, however, Feraydun stopped at the blacksmith's sector of the bazaar and ordered the fabrication of an ox-headed mace. The ironworkers forged the splendid mace in tempered steel. Only then did he lead his rebellious army toward the palace of the Serpent King in the city of Jerusalem.

The army stopped at an Arab oasis to rest along the way. That night the divine messenger Sorush came to Feraydun and taught him the secrets of undoing magical spells, a skill that he would need in his fight against the witchcraft of Zahhak.

To reach their destination from Iran, the army of rebellion had to cross the Arvand River where the Tigris and the Euphrates merge. But the boatmen refused to help them pass, as Zahhak had forbidden unauthorized passage. Furious at hearing this, Feraydun waded into the angry waves of the river. His companions followed suit, and in one magnificent movement, all the troops crossed the mighty Arvand. The march continued until the city of Jerusalem was in sight.

The ominous outline of Zahhak's palace was visible from a great distance. Feraydun knew those soaring vaults could not have been constructed by ordinary means. The castle had to be enchanted. He swiftly stormed the gates, slew all of its sentries, and galloped into the courtyard. Wielding his ox-headed mace and using the instructions of the angel Sorush, Feraydun disenchanted the edifice and brought down the high canopy that crowned the castle.

Feraydun looked around for Zahhak but did not find him anywhere. He then reclined on Zahhak's throne and called for Shahrnauz and Arnavauz, the lovely sisters of King Jamshid, who in their ageless beauty rivaled rosebuds and narcissus petals. But first they had to be cleansed from the evil influence of Zahhak. Having been bathed and purified, the princesses emerged from the inner quarters, staggering as if they had been awakened from a trance. After regaining their composure, they greeted this intriguing stranger.

Arnavauz said: "Who are you, and what is your name? What is your noble origin? It took great courage and prodigious fortune to challenge the witchery of the mighty sorcerer Zahhak. We cannot begin to tell you of the suffering we have endured in this palace."

He replied: "I am Feraydun, the son of Abtin, who was killed by the Serpent King. I spent my childhood on the flight from the tyrant Zahhak. A noble cow was my nursemaid and a mountain hermitage my home. I have come here to terminate Zahhak's reign of cruelty and bloodshed."

Arnavauz recognized Feraydun as the man prophesied to end the reign of their captor. "The Serpent King is not in his palace," she said. "He has gone to India searching for potent spells to prolong his rule. As if it weren't enough for him to shed blood to feed his serpents. Now he has taken to more ghoulish practices, including bathing in young blood to enhance his powers."

IN THE SERPENT KING'S PALACE

Zahhak had a caretaker who looked after the affairs of the court in his absence. His name was Kondrow, and he lived some distance away from the palace. When the caretaker heard that the castle had been conquered, he rushed to the audience hall and found a young stranger lounging on the royal throne, flanked by Zahhak's favorite wives. He kept his calm as he approached, pretending nothing unusual had transpired.

At the foot of the throne, Kondrow complimented the intruder's royal halo and wished him long dominion over the world. Feraydun asked him a few questions about the daily operations of the castle and then charged him to prepare a feast, complete with musicians and good wine. Kondrow obeyed his new master's command and prepared the banquet. While festivities were in progress he sneaked away and rode off to inform Zahhak of the catastrophic events in his palace.

"Exalted king," he exclaimed upon reaching him. "A young lad has scorned you, riding into your castle on horseback and breaking your spells. He is reclining on your throne as we speak."

"No matter," said Zahhak, not wanting to lose face by appearing surprised. "He is a guest in our palace."

"But, Your Majesty, what kind of guest wields a deadly mace? He's killing your demons and wearing your crown and royal sash!"

"Don't whine about this man. It is said that an insolent guest is a good omen!"

"Well, in that case I am sure the great king can explain what this insolent guest wants with His Majesty's queens," Kondrow elaborated. "He sits on your throne, caressing the lovely face of Shahrnauz while allowing Arnavauz's ruby lips to nibble his other hand. And he does all this in broad daylight. When the night casts its darkness upon the world, this guest is sure to take even more liberties with the raven-haired queens of His Majesty."

Zahhak finally lost his temper. Cursing Kondrow, he declared: "You will never work in my court again!"

"Frankly," he replied. "I doubt you will ever see your court again. Nor are you in a position to offer or deny me a job. You will do well to take care of your own affairs, since it appears you have been plucked out of your palace like a strand of hair from a piece of dough."

Zahhak quickly gathered an army of demons to storm the city and waylay the intruder. But the troops of Feraydun got wind of the invading army and engaged them at the approaches to the city and then in the narrow alleyways around the castle. As a fierce battle raged, the people of the city rose in a rebellion against their tyrant. Some of them fought in the streets and others rose to their rooftops to rain a shower of bricks and tiles on the hordes of the Serpent King, chanting:

We detest Zahhak, who clings to his throne,
And Feraydun, whomever he might be,
Makes a better king than this vile carrion.

As the battle raged around the palace, Zahhak donned his full body armor and climbed to the palace roof using his lasso. From this vantage point, he espied Shahrnauz holding an intimate discourse with Feraydun, no doubt speaking of the evil character of the tyrant who had once ruled the palace. Blinded by jealousy and rage, he lowered himself into the courtyard and drew his dagger to kill Shahrnauz. But Feraydun dropped him to the ground with one mighty blow of his mace. His helmet had cracked by the pounding. All it would take was one more knock to finish him off.

At that moment, the angel Sorush reappeared and warned Feraydun that it was not decreed that the Serpent King be killed at his hand. Instead, he was to be taken to Mount Damavand and imprisoned there. Feraydun tied Zahhak's hands to the saddle of a camel and dragged him to a deep cave under Mount Damavand's dome, where he chained him to the ground.

One millennium after the evil one's usurpation, a legitimate king was about to ascend the throne of Iran. Feraydun issued orders that people who had fought for him should surrender their arms and go back to their occupations. Fighting was a task restricted to the warrior caste.

And thus began the five hundred years of a glorious reign.

Feraydun avenged his father and put Zahhak in chains,
Banishing the unjust and appointing noble men to office,
He settled his affairs and staked his claims.

Feraydun was not made of ambergris and musk
Nor was he an angel. He was but a righteous man
Who practiced virtue from dawn to dusk.

Through good deeds, he gained his legendary fame.
If you are just and generous, you, too, can be
A latter-day Feraydun by a different name.

CHAPTER 2

A World Divided: Sons of Feraydun

Feraydun ascended the throne when the autumn arrived,
Naming that day Mehregan, a holiday of bonfires
And many joyous celebrations, he contrived

To burn ambergris and saffron and imbibe the ruby wine,
And thus began the five-centuries' tenure of an exemplary king
Whose just reign none can, in fairness, malign.

A RIGHTEOUS KING WEARS THE CROWN

Faranak rejoiced that her son had won the Persian throne. She bathed and purified herself, gave a bounty to the poor, and enriched her friends. Then she loaded precious jewels, garments, and weapons on a convoy of golden bridled Arabian horses and sent them to her royal son. Feraydun kissed the ground in thanks and accepted his mother's gifts.

The nobility also seemed joyous, showering their new king with gold and gems at the various crowning ceremonies.

When the festivities ended, Feraydun voyaged around the world, building up all that had fallen into disrepair. As the royal expedition neared its end, the world resembled a garden of paradise. The king established the Persian capital at Tammisheh, east of the city of Amol, and officially began his reign.

At fifty, the king had three sons, all tall, handsome, and deserving of the crown. The first two had been born to Shahrnauz and a third to Arnavauz, the sisters of Jamshid. Feraydun had not named his sons as he wanted them to first prove their mettle.

As the time came for the princes to marry, the king charged a wise nobleman named Jandal with finding three brides born to the same parents. Jandal searched the world for brides who would be worthy of the royal house of Iran and discovered that Sarv, the king of Yemen, had three lovely daughters. He traveled to the court of Yemen, kissed the ground, and said: "I am a humble messenger from the mighty King Feraydun. He sends his greetings and confirms your tenure on the Arab throne. My king desires that your daughters be betrothed to his royal sons. There is no doubt that the princesses of Yemen would be suitable matches for the princes of Iran."

The king of Yemen wilted like a jasmine flower plucked from the branch, for he was devoted to his daughters and did not wish to part with them. But he knew it was impossible to refuse the king of Iran as the fate of Zahhak was fresh in his mind. Sarv consulted his allies in the land of the lance-bearing Arab tribesmen. They pledged their allegiance in war should Sarv defy the new Iranian king. But he chose the wiser path. He was ready to follow the directives of the great Feraydun. But he also loved his daughters and was loath to send them to faraway kingdoms. Thus, he told Jandal. "It is my right to meet the princes who propose to marry my daughters. I must be sure that I am entrusting my beloved ones to men who have justice in their hearts."

Jandal kissed the throne and departed. When Feraydun heard what Sarv had required, he summoned his sons and advised them to travel to Yemen and prove their worth, for Sarv was a wise and discerning king.

The three princes of Iran each took a band of loyal warriors with them to Yemen. King Sarv plied his future sons-in-law with riddles and trials of prowess. They proved to be equal to all of the posed challenges. Sarv reluctantly consented to the marriages and called for a celebration. He blamed providence for depriving him of the chance to bequeath his kingdom to a male successor. Now he would have to endure a painful separation as well. Why should he have had daughters instead of sons? But, when the festivities began, the king found himself in better spirits: "One must honor a child who is refined and respectful," he declared. "It is virtue, not the gender of a child, that matters."

When the lavish ceremonies ended, Sarv bid his daughters farewell and sent them off with a caravan of camels loaded with their rich dowries, toward the capital city of Iran.

When Feraydun heard the news of the departure of his sons from Yemen, he determined to try their mettle before giving them names befitting their characters. To this end, he transformed himself into a fire-breathing dragon and waited by the road. As the caravan of the princess brides and their husbands approached, the dragon roared and blocked their way.

The king's eldest son was stricken with fear. "A man of good sense never picks a battle with a dragon," he said before running away.

The second son notched an arrow in his bow, declaring, "I always fight when I am challenged. Neither lions nor dragons scare me."

The third son, however, spoke directly to the dragon: "Remove yourself from this road if you know the name of King Feraydun. We are the sons of that exalted king, and you block our way at your peril."

Feraydun, who had heard enough, stopped the trial, and vanished. The caravan continued its journey and finally reached the capital city of Tamisheh, where the king welcomed his sons back.

"I was the dragon that attacked you," he told them, seated regally on his war elephant, ox-headed mace in hand. "And what you went through was a trial. My elder son, who sought the way of prudence, will be called Salm, meaning peace. He will not be blamed for escaping the dragon because recklessness in battle is closer to madness than courage. My middle son, who was ferocious in confronting the dragon, will be known by the name of Tur. And my youngest, who combined courage and prudence, will be named Iraj."

At the eve of the three royal weddings the king had his astrologers cast the horoscopes of his sons. They all had been born under the signs of fire. The cunning Salm's planet was Saturn, in the constellation of Sagittarius. The headstrong Tur's planet was the bloody Mars, in the constellation of Leo. And the brave and trusting Iraj's planet was the moon in the constellation of Aries. The stars had portended that conflict was brewing.

DIVIDING THE WORLD

Feraydun had spent a long time in consultation with astrologers and seers to determine the proper division of his kingdom. Having named his sons, he was now prepared to divide his vast dominion among them. Salm was given Rome and the lands on the western horizon, and Tur was allotted the kingdom of the eastern provinces, where the Turks and the Chinese resided. After this declaration, Salm and Tur left for their domains to rule as sovereigns. Then it was time for Iraj to receive his share of the empire: the middle kingdom of Iran, along with its Arabian provinces.

And thus, the prosperous and peaceful reign of Feraydun continued until the pallor of old age painted over the flush of his youth. His sons, by contrast, continued to look evermore handsome with the vigor of youth.

But things had soured between the brothers. Salm had long begrudged his younger brother, Iraj, for inheriting the best part of Feraydun's kingdom. One day, he sent a message to Tur:

> We are sons of a great king, all deserving of the crown. I was the eldest and the most deserving of us. After me, you were the one set to get the lion's share of our father's kingdom. But the unjust king gave the middle kingdom and its Arab provinces to Iraj, banishing us to the outer reaches of the world. No one can blame us if we resent this unfair division.

The impetuous Tur felt a wave of rage rising in him as he listened to his brother's message. He sent back this response:

> What you said is true. Remember how our father deceived us in the guise of a dragon when we were young? He's the one who planted this blood-soaked tree that has borne bitter fruit. Let's speak in person. This matter has festered long enough.

When the two brothers met, they agreed to send a wily priest to their father to communicate their bitter feelings. But even a clever envoy could not hide the impudent tone of their message:

> Greetings from your two sons. You are old, and it is time for you to depart this world. Only a misguided man clings to life after his time has come. God gave you the world, but you have been derelict in your duties toward the Creator. You did not divide your

> kingdom in justice. You gave your youngest the heartland of Iran and relegated your elder sons to the desolate ends of the earth.
>
> Now take the crown off the worthless head of the boy and banish him to some obscure corner. If you refuse, we will bring upon you the armies of Rome, China, and Turkistan. Beware, our mace-wielding horde is on the move and it will slay Iraj if he stands in our way.

The messenger arrived at the glorious palace of Feraydun, whose tall ramparts scraped the clouds. He passed through a wondrous avenue where lions and leopards were tied on one side, and war elephants stood on the other. Magnificent warriors who wore delicate garments and carried glittering weapons crowded the halls of the palace. Mesmerized by the splendor of the court, the envoy offered his abject apologies for the severe message he was about to deliver to the king.

"Don't worry," Feraydun said. "I don't fault the messenger."

When the recitation of the letter was complete, the king said, "These impure men have sold their souls to the devil. Relay this message for me:

> You have spurned my teachings and become vicious creatures without shame before God and man. I, too, was once young. My hair was pitch-black, and my back was straight as a tall cypress. The world that bent my back is still at work. It will bend your back, and it will not stop at that. Know that I did not divide my land on a whim. Nor did I play favorites. I consulted the wise men who know the ways of the stars on this crucial matter.
>
> My time has indeed arrived to leave this world but heed these words of advice: the demon of greed has overcome your reason. Why else would you choose worthless soil over your brother?
>
> The world has seen the likes of you. It has not kept faith with them and will not be kind to you, either. Remember that you will one day face divine judgment.

When the envoy left with the king's message, Feraydun turned to Iraj, who had been by his side. "Your brothers were wicked, and they have become even more so since they were sent to rule over fierce peoples," he said. "They will bring great armies against us. A brother is a brother only as long as he acts the part. Be wise, and do not open your arms to embrace a drawn sword. Eat their breakfast before they devour your dinner. And seek no confederates in the world, for righteousness is your only true ally."

"I will not fight my brothers," Iraj responded. "Let them have my crown, for I have no abiding love for this office. Nor will I fight my brothers over worldly possession. I will tell them that this world is an unfaithful lover, which was false even to the great King Jamshid. If you permit me, I will go unarmed to Salm and Tur and mollify them."

Feraydun was taken aback by Iraj's disposition. "Your brothers are declaring war against you, but you propose to win their hearts. You are like the full moon whose nature is to shine and make the world beautiful. They seek to shed your blood, and you speak of making peace. And yet, it is unwise to place one's head between a dragon's jaws. Take some soldiers along and carry my letter to your haughty brothers:

> In the name of the Creator. This is a letter to my sons from their father, who once wielded the heavy mace and the long blade. You are each a rising sun in your own right, brilliant and fierce kings. I was the emissary of light to the world of darkness and the herald of hope. At my age, all I want is the happiness of my sons. The brother you despise out of greed has given up his crown and comes to you without an army. Treat him as the younger brother he is to you and look after his welfare and safety.

Iraj took the king's sealed letter and set off to meet his brothers at the head of a small contingent of soldiers. Salm and Tur brought their armies forth to receive their younger sibling. The three met but there was no meeting of the minds. Two hearts brimmed with hatred while one throbbed with brotherly love. Salm and Tur glared at their brother and seemed to resent his serene countenance and the fact that their troops were obviously charmed by his nobility. Warriors gathered in small groups, telling each other that Iraj deserved to be the king of the world.

Salm heard these rumors and went to Tur in great agitation, saying: "Did you see how our soldiers did not take their admiring eyes off him? They want him to be their king. We begrudged him the rule of Iran, but now he is laying claim to our kingdoms."

The wicked brothers spent the entire night conspiring. In the morning, they descended on Iraj's tent and declared; "You are younger than both of us. How did you get to inherit our father's realm while we were banished to the barren hinterlands of the world? We will not stand for this."

"Calm down, my elder brothers," Iraj replied, "and you will get what you want. I don't want to rule over the east or the west. Nor do I want the kingship of Iran. You take it all. The power that is gained in hatred will bear only bitterness. On the day of our death, we will have only a brick for our pillow. I have given up the throne of Iran. I will not fight you over it."

Enraged by Iraj's composed manner, Tur jumped to his feet and hurled a golden dais at his head. Severely injured, Iraj pleaded for his life: "Do you have no shame before God and our father? How can you so wantonly take a life? One shouldn't even kill an ant. You don't need to make a murderer of yourself. I assure you I will disappear into obscurity, and you will never see me again."

Tur did not respond to this plea. Instead, he pulled a dagger from his boot and beheaded his young brother.

There was a noble prince who excelled over his peers
He had everything but was betrayed by the cruel fate
Verily, there is no justice in this vale of tears.

Tur sent the severed head of Iraj to Feraydun with this message: "Here is the head that you raised above us. Put the crown of our ancestors on it if you wish."

Their grim work complete, Salm and Tur returned to their own western and eastern realms.

AVENGING THE PRINCE

To welcome Iraj back from his mission of peace, Feraydun had arranged a lavish reception. The throne was adorned with turquoise, and the crown glittered with added jewels. War elephants marched under the city's decorated gates, driven by drummers in festive garments. In the palace, an elaborate feast was arranged, with wine and gifted musicians.

But to the expectant crowds' dismay, a camel appeared on the horizon, shrouded in a cloud of dust. At the gates of the city, a rider dismounted, tears streaming down his sallow face. Holding a strange golden chest, he approached Feraydun. Attendants rushed forth and lifted the lid. Under a sheet of perfumed silk lay the severed head of Iraj.

Feraydun lost consciousness and fell off his horse. The throngs that had gathered at the palace gates to welcome Iraj quickly transformed into a mourning procession. Devastated at the demise of his beloved son, the king set fire to the young prince's palace and prayed that he would live to avenge his death.

Feraydun's dark night of despair persisted for months until he learned that one of the young prince's consorts, Mauh-aufarid, had given birth to a beautiful daughter. Feraydun embraced the infant, who resembled her father, and reared her in the royal court until she came of age and married the king's nephew, Pashang. In due time a son was born to the young couple, and a nurse rushed the baby to her royal master, ecstatically announcing, "Behold, a second Iraj!"

The king rejoiced. He had a strong sense that his dear son had been reborn. He named the boy Manuchehr and saw to his proper education. Iraj's son was a prodigious student of the royal arts who quickly earned the king's admiration and the army's respect. Feraydun gave Manuchehr the keys to his treasure houses and called upon his army commanders to pay their respects to his crown prince. In the ensuing celebrations, great heroes such as Shiruy, Saum, and Qauran, the son of Kaveh the blacksmith, rained a shower of emeralds on the young man who would avenge his father.

The new, hopeful spirit at the court of Feraydun was no secret to Salm and Tur. They had heard about the rise of Manuchehr and feared that the day of their reckoning was nigh. To mollify their father and prevent the coming war of revenge, the malevolent brothers sent a rich caravan loaded with precious gifts to Feraydun's court along with a letter carried by a glib envoy:

> May the divine halo of King Feraydun shine forever. This is a letter from two unjust men whose eyes are full of tears and whose hearts are branded with the indelible guilt of their wickedness. Their shame is so great that they dare not look upon the countenance of their father. Hence these lowly slaves have sent an envoy rather than coming to beg for mercy themselves. The wisdom of the learned sages is now confirmed: evil deeds are surely punished.
>
> But what could we do when our destiny was written in this way? Even ferocious lions and formidable dragons cannot escape the cunning of fate. We blame the abominable devil for deceiving us. We were possessed, and our judgment was corrupted.
>
> Now we hope that our crowned father will forgive us. Our guilt is indeed great, but we believe that the king's forgiveness is greater. Thus, we request that Manuchehr honor us with his presence. Send him to us with a great army so we can wash the old hatred with the tears from our repentant eyes and soothe his aching heart with our rich treasures.

Joined on his right side by Manuchehr in his regalia of the crown prince, Feraydun reclined on his royal throne. The heroes of the army stood at attention, displaying their golden shields and maces. The envoy of Salm and Tur was ushered in and seated on a golden dais. The emissary gave a moving performance in submitting their apologies and extending their offer to host Manuchehr. The king patiently listened to the message before speaking: "The evil heart of those men is on display like the sun upon the sky. I have heard all that you have spoken. Now take your blood money and your empty words back to those shameless rogues and tell them: 'You sent me Iraj's head in a golden chest and left his body to the beasts of prey. Now you profess to love Manuchehr and express a wish to see him? You will soon see him in full battle gear at the head of an avenging army. You will answer to him and his commanders, Qauran, Sarv, Shiruy, and Saum.'

I wanted to avenge Iraj myself, but the rules of filial piety forbid a war between a father and his sons. Now Manuchehr has grown, a branch from that mighty tree. He will wage war, refusing your insincere pleas and bribes."

The envoy trembled as he took his leave to deliver Feraydun's message. After hearing their father's rebuke, the guilty brothers knew war was inescapable. "We must kill that lion cub before he sprouts teeth," said Salm. And with this, they gathered a great army on the plain of Haumun and prepared for war.

Feraydun charged Manuchehr to take the battle to the enemy: "Salm and Tur have arrayed their forces. It signifies a hunter's good fortune when the antelope wanders into his range."

"I shall gird my loins to avenge Iraj," Manuchehr said. "I don't have much respect for these armies, since I don't see a worthy opponent among them."

The armed forces of Iran left Tammisheh, marching behind the Standard of Kaveh until they rested at the elm forest that bordered the plain of Haumun. Manuchehr and his lieutenant, Qauran, came out of the woods to review the flanks. King Sarv of Yemen stayed back, at the heart of the army.

Tur came forth and addressed the Iranian scouts sent by Manuchehr to report on the strength of the enemy: "Remind your upstart king that Iraj had only a daughter. He had no son to avenge him. This man who is your leader has no claim to the throne of Iran."

"I will take your message to Manuchehr," one of the scouts replied. "But it would behoove you to think of your own predicament before sending such messages. This army is massive, and your men will surely lose their nerve if they see the glint of the naked blades behind the Standard of Kaveh."

Manuchehr laughed when the scout related Tur's foolish words regarding his lineage. Everyone knew the legitimacy of his descent from Iraj. Manuchehr urged his troops to fight to the death in the righteous cause of avenging their martyred prince, Iraj. The battle was joined. For the first two days, the Iranian warriors dominated the field. As the sun set on the second day, Salm and Tur conspired to ambush the Iranians under cover of darkness.

Manuchehr, who had received the intelligence regarding the surprise attack, appointed Qauran to lie in wait for the raiders with thirty thousand men. Tur arrived at the Iranian camps with one hundred thousand troops to find an army ready to fight. The advantage of surprise was lost, but withdrawing was not an option, and Tur desperately hurled his army at the Iranian forces. The din of the battle was deafening as blades struck shields and lances broke on the barding of horses. After a short battle, the armies of Salm and Tur were routed.

The young prince scanned the field in search of Tur and found him trying to abscond. He gave chase as Tur brought his horse to full gallop. But Manucher's steed was faster. He caught up with his escaping foe and struck him with his javelin, causing him to fall off his horse. Manuchehr dismounted, swiftly executed Tur, and sent his head to Feraydun with a note:

> In the name of the God of nobility, purity, and justice, I greet the rightly crowned Feraydun, the wielder of the ox-headed mace. I came to avenge the death of Iraj and fought three battles in two days under the sun and the moon. Tur conspired to ambush us by night, but I set a trap for him. He tried to escape, but I gave chase and knocked him off his horse. He had sent Iraj's head to you as a trophy. Now that you have Tur's, the scores are half-settled. I am off to pursue Salm, whose chastisement is long overdue.

THE BATTLE WITH SALM AND KAKOUY

Salm was shaken by his brother's fate. But he did not fear for his life as he knew that in the event of danger, he could always retreat to the impregnable granite castle of Alanan, which was surrounded by the sea. Wishing to block this avenue of escape, Qauran asked Manuchehr for a contingent of warriors to deprive Salm of his last refuge.

For the success of his plan, Qauran needed the royal standard and the deceased Tur's signet. Manuchehr approved the plan and sent Shiruy to carry the required props. The commander kept Shiruy's forces back in the vicinity of the castle and approached the gate with his men. On the strength of Tur's signet, he gained entry, convincing the gullible gate master that he was sent by their king to help defend the castle. Once safely in the fortress, Qauran climbed up to the ramparts and unfurled the royal standard. This was Shiruy's cue to storm the castle. The defenders were caught between the invading forces and the Iranian troops inside.

By sunrise, the castle of Alanan was captured and torched. Qauran went to the commander in chief and reported the success of his mission. Manuchehr commended him. But there was new trouble brewing, as one of Zahhak's grandsons, Kakouy, had come to the aid of Salm with one hundred thousand troops. "He has the reputation of a fearsome warrior and is a powerful demon at war," Manuchehr said. "I have not tried his mettle, but I will surely do so in the coming battle."

"Kakouy will never be a worthy opponent for my prince," Qauran assured him. "Let's ferret him out and see how good he is at the battle."

Blood flowed when the army of Iran stormed the gates of Kakouy's castle. Kakouy emerged shouting his battle cry and struck Manuchehr with his lance. The blow undid the avenging prince's chainmail. In response, he hit his opponent's neckpiece, causing his entire armor to fall. Finally, Manuchehr took Kakouy off the saddle, threw him to the ground, and slashed him. With the death of their commander, Salm and Kakouy's confederated forces fled from the battlefield.

Manuchehr removed his horse's barding to lighten the animal's burden. Then he searched the field for Salm, found him, and gave chase. Cutting the distance between them by leaps and bounds, the spirited prince came within the earshot of Salm and taunted his treacherous great-uncle: "Why are you running away? Did you not murder your brother for the sake of a crown? Well, here I am to bring you the crown you coveted. The sapling that you planted has borne fruit. You have only yourself to blame if that fruit is bitter."

Manuchehr continued his taunts until his steed ran directly alongside Salm's. Animated by his righteous rage, he sliced through Salm's neck as if his sword encountered no resistance as it moved through the air. This feat of swordsmanship astonished the onlooking soldiers as Salm's head went flying. They picked it up and carried it aloft at the tip of a lance.

With Salm's demise, the enemy armies asked for quarter. Their envoy came to the Iranian side and declared: "We are farmers dragooned into this war against our will. We have no hatred toward Manuchehr, and now we are at his mercy. If he wants to kill us, we are ready for the gallows. But if he will let us live, we will bring him our leaders for punishment."

"I prefer a good name to garnering worldly advantages," said Manuchehr. "Your love or hate is immaterial to me. When victory is achieved, the victor must refrain from bloodshed. Now drop your weapons and return to your homes in peace."

The surrendering men approached the king and dropped their arms, forming a mound of armor, shields, lances, and swords. Manuchehr sent another letter to Feraydun, apprising him of the completion of the mission to avenge Iraj. Then he returned to Tammisheh by way of the Caspian Sea. In the region of Saury, Feraydun's standard was spotted. The great king had come with his massive army and a vast contingent of the brave, Gileh-mard* tribesmen to welcome his triumphant great-grandson home.

Manuchehr dismounted and kissed the ground to greet his great grandfather. The king took him by the hand and motioned for him to step up and join him on the throne. Feraydun prayed to the heavens: "You are a just God. You hear the sigh of the oppressed. You have brought me justice and ensured that my progeny will rule this land."

King Feraydun passed away soon after this triumph, and Manuchehr was enthroned. The new king saw to the construction of a worthy crypt for his ancestor and laid him to rest on a bed of ivory, his crown hanging above his body.

Another leaf withered and fell, a royal branch broke
Death carried off a glorious king who ruled in justice
This world is full of delusions, mirrors, and smoke.

* Gilan was and is a region near the Caspian Sea. Gileh-mard means "men of Gilan."

CHAPTER 3

The Love That Triumphed: Zaul and Rudabeh

Manuchehr mourned for a week, and then reclined
On the throne as the sovereign of the seven realms
Possessed of the divine halo, he was inclined

To comfort the weak, humble the proud
Stand for righteousness and roar
Against injustice like a thundercloud.

After this royal declaration, Saum, who was the first among the knights at the court of King Manuchehr and bore the exalted title of Champion of the World, rose to speak on behalf of his colleagues: "You are the king of justice and generosity, a lion on the battlefield, and a shining sun at any banquet. If I am a knight, it is because of the honor your ancestors bestowed upon my clan."

Saum shone on that day, but his tale of woes
Had just begun, as he was led astray
By fate as well as the wrong path he chose.

ZAUL IN THE WILDERNESS

Saum, the son of the famous knight Narimon, was the most prominent knight of Iran. A musk-haired* consort whose face was fresher than flower petals bore him a male heir. The newborn was happy and healthy, but his hair was white. The nurses called him Zaul, meaning old. For a whole week, no one dared to break the news to Saum. Finally, a brave attendant went to him.

"May this day be auspicious for the great knight, and may his ill-wishers

* Musk, a dark substance secreted by the male musk deer, was used in making a perfume by the same name. In poetry it is used as a metaphor for hair that is dark and fragrant.

be cursed," she said. "You are blessed with a boy who is perfect in every respect. He has only one flaw: his hair is white. Such has been your fate, my master."

Saum rushed to the women's quarters. His spirits sank when he looked upon the face of his son. "My God, you are above wrongdoing," he said, lifting his head up to the heavens. "I offered you contrition for my sins. I hoped that you would punish me for my infractions. How am I going to face my noblemen when they ask me about this demon boy? They're going to mock me in public and gossip behind my back. How am I supposed to live with the shame?"

Saum could not bear it. So, he neglected his parental obligation to unstintingly care for his son and ordered his attendants to leave the helpless infant on a mountain.

A lioness nursing her cub whispered with a sigh
"You don't owe me for this milk, nor would you
Be indebted to me if you bled me dry.

The attendants did as they were told, leaving the baby on the high, desolate rocks of a mountain. Zaul lay there on the cold stone, unaware that he had been abandoned. Naturally, he soon started to cry—but he was not alone.

The mountain range was home to a magical bird, the Simorgh, who was flying overhead when she spied the helpless, naked baby kicking up the dust below. She had taken flight to fetch food for her hungry hatchlings. And when she scooped up Zaul and brought him back to her nest, the chicks welcomed him with kindness and even shared their food. From that day on, the Simorgh loved Zaul as her own and raised him into adulthood.

In time, travelers in the caravans that passed would tell stories about an agile, silver-headed young boy who leaped over the impossible peaks of the mountains.

ZAUL IS FOUND

When the foundling had grown into a strong young man, Saum had a dream in which a stranger on a horse gave him good tidings that his son was alive. Upon waking, the knight called the wise men who could interpret dreams and asked their opinion of his vision. They were unanimous in the judgment that one of them expressed: "Beasts of the wild and fish of the sea care for their young. You alone have cast out your innocent child in breach of the rules of morality. Now you must repent to God, for He is our guide to what is good and bad."

The next night Saum had another dream. Again, a handsome young man galloped from the mountains, flanked by a cleric and a sage. This time, he berated Saum. "You are a shameless man of impure thoughts," he said. "How can you call yourself a knight while a bird rears your child? If you consider white hair a defect, look upon your own white hair. Do you fault God for this, too? The Almighty has appointed one of his wild creatures to foster your son. You need not worry, for she is kinder to him than you were."

Saum roared like a lion caught in a trap as he woke from that dream. He had to do something. The knight left the capital with a handful of his lieutenants, and they trekked to the foot of the mountain range, overgrown with a thick blanket of intertwined trees. High above the valley, on the soaring rocks, was the nest of the mighty Simorgh. Saum attempted to scale the cliff in vain, and knelt to ask for divine assistance.

Seeing the commotion below, the Simorgh knew that the visitors had come for Zaul and that it was time to bid farewell to her ward. "Your father has come to fetch you," she said. "Let me take you to your real family."

But Zaul was hesitant. "Are you sick of me? This nest is my home, and I'm proud to wear your plumes in my hair."

"Soon, you will be at Iran's royal court," she said. "Soon, you will have forgotten this nest. But don't worry. I've taken you under my wing and will never deny you my protection. Take these feathers of mine. Burn one if you ever need help. I will come to your aid like a black cloud and take you back whenever you wish."

With her human ward on her shoulders, the Simorgh flew off the nest, and alighted on the ground. Saum bowed before the marvelous bird and offered his humble thanks. The father and son embraced. Zaul was given clothes to cover his nakedness and a horse to ride. The company was flushed with excitement and sang joyful songs as they returned home.

The saga of the abandonment and the recovery of Zaul was related throughout the kingdom. Manuchehr was elated that the story had come to a happy end and sent his crown prince, Nowzar, to invite Saum and his son to the court.

On the appointed day, King Manuchehr reclined on his ivory throne, flanked by his high-ranking knights Saum and Qauran. Zaul was ushered in wearing the golden helmet of knighthood and holding a javelin of glittering gold. He was breathtaking. The courtiers were astounded, and the king was duly impressed as well. He turned to Saum with these words of advice: "Take good care of this lad whom I appoint as a knight at my court. Enjoy the company of your new-found son. He possesses a wise man's heart and a lion's quiet swagger. He has a halo of divine sanction around his face."

Then the king called on his astrologers to cast Zaul's horoscope. They informed the king that the stars were kind to the young man of the mountains. He would be a great knight and a prodigious hero. Manuchehr was delighted by the news and endowed the clan of Saum with their own kingdom of Zabol. Scribes prepared the deed of the endowed realm that extended from Kabul and Dunbar to the river Sind and the sea of China.

Father and son kissed the royal throne and traveled to Zabol, loaded as they were with the lavish gifts of the king. But after a short stay in their new home, the great knight was summoned to Bactria to crush an insurrection. Before leaving, he called the noblemen: "As a young man, I made a reckless choice to abandon my son," he told them. "But the noble Simorgh found and raised the boy that I had rejected. I thank God, who forgave my sin and restored my child to me. Now that I am commanded to leave, I entrust him to your care. Keep him close and offer him your good counsel."

"If anyone was ever born under an ill star, I am that person," Zaul told his father. "There are many flowers in the world. But I only get their thorns. I grew up on a bed of dirt, drinking blood with the hatchlings of a bird while you lived in comfort. Now I'm being abandoned again."

"I have been derelict in my duties toward you," Saum agreed. "But the astrologers have determined that this is the realm where you will thrive. Stay here and surround yourself with learned men. Let them teach you in every field of knowledge. This is your new home. Rule this realm in justice and serve its people. But continue to gather knowledge and be merry."

Zaul went along with Saum's departing army to see him off. They rode together for two milestones. Then Zaul embraced his father and wept as he bid him farewell. From there, he returned to his palace, donned his golden torque and belt, and sat on his turquoise throne. Zaul invited equestrian and martial arts trainers, diviners, and scholars of all nations to his court. He studied day and night and absorbed his lessons until he gained a reputation as a wise man.

FALLING IN LOVE WITH THE PRINCESS OF KABUL

One day Zaul decided to tour his eastern provinces with some of his companions. Mehraub, the vassal king of Kabul, who had descended from Zahhak, came forward to welcome this famous knight of Zabol. The young nobleman hosted a lavish banquet in honor of the local king of Kabul. The host was impressed by his guest's heroic build, handsome features, sartorial splendor, and refined manners.

After this gathering, an attendant approached Zaul and told him about Mehraub's daughter, Rudabeh: "She is possessed of a skin whiter than ivory. Her hair is blacker than musk, her lips are redder than pomegranate seeds and her dazzling eyes are framed by eyelashes that compete in blackness with a raven's feathers. Her eyebrows are shaped like a long bow at rest. Her breasts are the image of unripe pomegranates breaking through a smooth, silvery surface. The princess of Kabul is also very well spoken and refined." The description ended here, but the image of the lovely princess was so seared in the young man's heart that he could hardly sleep that night.

The next day Mehraub came to pay his respects. Zaul asked him if there was anything he needed, adding that his request would be granted regardless of its magnitude. The vassal king replied, "My only wish is to host you in my palace so that you can shed your light upon my humble abode."

This was the only request that Zaul could not grant. Saum and the king would frown on his going to the house of an idol worshipper to drink and get drunk with him. "Ask me something else."

Mehraub had no other wishes, so he took his leave. Zaul was surprised by his guest's abrupt departure. And yet, he found himself compelled to give expression to his deep admiration for the noble Mehraub. The company thought it odd that their leader was flattering the king of Kabul. But when they realized he was serious, they too praised the man for his manly stature and quiet dignity.

Meanwhile, the love Zaul felt for Mehraub's daughter had continued to consume his soul. Of course, he knew that marriage to the royal house of Kabul, which was reputed to follow a different religion and whose members traced their lineage back to Zahhak, would cause a scandal. Zaul did not want to get embroiled in such a sordid affair. But his heart was set, and love had conquered reason.

The morning after the banquet, Mehraub went to his inner quarters and was dazzled by the resplendent beauty of his queen, Sindokht. He was so struck with the loveliness of his daughter, Rudabeh, that he praised God for His masterful handiwork. The fair Sindokht asked him about this new knight of Iran. She had heard that a wild bird had raised him. Did he seem human? Was he more suited for the throne or the lair of a wild beast?

"Zaul is peerless among the knights of the world," said Mehraub. "Blessed with an elephant's strength and a lion's heart, he's generous on the throne and brave on the battlefield. He is a sprightly young fellow with a complexion that puts the flowers of a redbud tree to shame. His only flaw, if one might call it that, is that his hair is white."

That was all the description Rudabeh needed to fall in love with Zaul. Her cheeks flushed, and a sweet melancholy filled her heart. All desires, save the wish to be with her beloved, vanished from her mind. The princess felt like an entirely new person.

Later she would trust her five attendants with her secret: "You are my confidantes. So I'll confess to you my consuming love for Zaul, the knight of Iran. Will you be my allies?"

The attendants were confounded. "Your beauty is admired from India to China," one of them said. "You can bring down suitors from the fourth sphere of the heavens if you wish. Why then fall for a man spurned by his father and brought up by a bird? To make matters worse, he has white hair, like an old man!"

Rudabeh was enraged. "Your opinions don't interest me. Nor do I fancy the emperors of China or Rome for my husband. I want Zaul, and I don't care if you call him old."

The attendants saw Rudabeh's determination and pledged their loyalty to her. "Forgive us," another said. "We are your servants. Command us, and we will fly with the birds, roam with the deer, learn sorcery, and go down the caves of the world to bring you the man you love."

Rudabeh smiled, and her sallow cheeks regained their rosy color. She accepted their pledge and charged them to use all their wiles to find Zaul and bring him to her. The attendants happily dressed in Roman silk, wore blossoms in their hair, and set off on a jaunt to collect flowers. It was March, so wildflowers bloomed along the riverbed of the plains around Kabul.

Zaul noticed the group of girls strolling near his camp and asked his young squire about them. He replied that they were attendants from the court of Mehraub and had come to pick flowers. This was intriguing. Zaul picked up his bow, jumped on his horse, and rode out to the riverbank where the girls were. As luck would have it, a flock of ducks glided along the river. The young man quickly notched an arrow in his bow and shot a duck as it attempted to soar. The attendants were enchanted by the young man who had performed this feat. One of the girls turned to the squire and asked: "Who is this charming young man? We have never seen a more splendid hunter."

The squire chided them for not observing proper decorum. "Don't speak of my master in such familiar terms. This is Zaul, of the house of Saum and Narimon. He is no ordinary hunter but an unrivaled knight."

The attendants teased him. "You think so highly of this Zaul," one of them said, "but that is only because you don't know our mistress, who is far superior to your master. She's the daughter of the king of Kabul. Her name is Rudabeh, and she is tall, with beautiful ivory skin, and possessed of eyes so sad and sleepy that they rival a pair of narcissus flowers. Rudabeh's ruby-red lips burn in expectation of a kiss from Zaul. What do you think your master would say to that?"

The squire demurred and said he would never convey such a crass message. Of course, he rushed back to his master, with laughter on his lips, and related the entire conversation. Zaul's heart leaped with joy when he learned that his secret love had been reciprocated. He resolved not to miss this opportunity, and sent a request to the attendants that they should linger near the camp for a little while. Then he prepared a small package of precious jewels wrapped in embroidered Roman silk as a gift for his beloved.

The squire took the package to the attendants so they could deliver it to Rudabeh. He also swore them to secrecy, despite the old wisdom that so many people could never keep a secret:

Cut the numbers to two to keep a secret down
For at three, it becomes a rumor
And at four, it's the talk of the town

Rudabeh's attendants had no such worries. They giggled, and one whispered to the group: "Trust me. The lion is caught in the trap. Soon Rudabeh's hopes will be realized."

Zaul was so excited that he could not let them go. He rushed out and interrogated them about his beloved's attributes, and with every description, his love grew. Finally, he said: "I want nothing more than to meet your mistress. Tell me. Can you arrange an assignation?"

"Your wish is our command, sire," they replied. "We will stoop to every lie and deception to help you snare our lovely mistress in your noose."

They left, and the lovelorn Zaul returned to his camp to spend another sleepless night, a night that seemed longer than an entire year.

Rudabeh's attendants returned to Mehraub's castle with their flowers. The gatekeeper chided them for staying out so late when strangers were camping so close to the castle. But the girls teased him and laughed the matter off. They went to their mistress to bring her their good tidings, and Rudabeh asked: "So, how was your encounter with the son of Saum? Tell me every detail. Is he handsome? Do his looks and manners match his reputation?"

The attendants responded by singing Zaul's praises. One of them gushed: "Built like a lion with charming white curls, he has the complexion of a crimson flower, the heart of a mage, and the charisma of a king. We promised to arrange a tryst. Now make haste and prepare to receive him. And tell us what message to take back, since he is awaiting your reply with bated breath."

Rudabeh laughed and chided them. "Suddenly, the wild, feral boy turns into a winsome prince with white curls and the complexion of a redbud tree! You certainly have changed your tune on my Zaul. I bet you promised to deliver me into his hands for a handsome reward, haven't you?"

They all laughed and went to work preparing a room for the meeting. They brought golden vessels filled with wine, musk, ambergris, and rosewater and arranged them on a spread of Chinese silk. Heaps of violet, hyacinth, and jasmine were brought to freshen the air.

The next evening, an attendant brought word to Zaul that everything was ready. Rudabeh went out to wait on the battlements. At long last, he appeared, and she watched him come to the castle walls. Then she addressed him, calling out, "Welcome, my gallant knight! You are as striking as my attendants described. Thank you for crossing the long, arduous road on foot to come here."

Zaul looked up at the exquisite form of Rudabeh on the high ramparts and thought she was like a rising sun peeking from an eastern mountain range. "I have spent many nights praying to be united with you," he said. "I have watched the moon go through its stations in the sky dreaming about you. Now, at long last, I am hearing your sweet voice. But what good does it do us if I'm down here and you're high on the ramparts? Come and let us find a way to be close. We've waited long enough for this tryst."

Rudabeh untangled the dark coils of her hair and dangled one of her long braids off the wall, inviting Zaul to climb. Not dreaming of hurting his beloved in this manner, the dauntless young man looped his lariat around one of the teeth of the ramparts and scaled the forbidding, sixty-fathom high wall with ease. At the top, Rudabeh kissed the ground and led her secret caller down the stairs to the room she had prepared for their visit. Zaul was as stunned by the beauty of Rudabeh as she was by his kingly radiance. They drank wine together, kissed, and caressed. They spent the night in this manner but remained chaste.

At the approach of dawn, Zaul said: "I know that neither Saum nor King Manuchehr will approve of our union. But I pledge my life to your love, and I will get my father and the king to consent to our marriage."

Rudabeh replied, "I, too, take God as my witness that you will be my one and only king."

They said goodbye with tears in their eyes before the dashing knight rappelled down the wall. Back at his pavilion, Zaul called the magi and reminded them that every young man must marry and procreate. Then he entrusted them with the secret of his love for Rudabeh and asked for their opinion. Knowing that Mehraub was descended from the Serpent King Zahhak, the magi were afraid to approve the union. Instead, they suggested that Zaul write Saum to solicit his approval.

THE SON PLEADS WITH HIS FATHER

Following the advice of the magi, Zaul wrote to his father:

> In the name of the God of Venus, Saturn, and the sun, the Creator of all that exists. This is a letter from Zaul, a devoted and humble servant to Saum, who wields the mace and the blade. In court, the great Saum is a kingmaker, and on the battlefield, he sustains the scavenging birds that feed on the carrion he leaves behind.
>
> You know well that I was born in adversity. Such was my fate, and I will not complain. But now I have a problem of a different sort: a self-inflicted one. I have become enthralled with the daughter of Mehraub. But love has not made me insolent. First, let me remind you that you swore an oath before the king to grant my every wish. Now, command me, and I shall follow.

Zaul sent this letter with a messenger, providing him with two additional horses lest his steed prove unable to withstand the long journey. The messenger rode day and night until he reached the mountains of Bactria, where Saum was hunting, using cheetahs and falcons. The envoy came forward, kissed the ground, and submitted the letter. Saum descended from the hunting ground to his pavilion to read Zaul's dispatch. Then he sighed and muttered, "What is one to expect of a boy raised by a wild bird?"

Saum brooded on this quandary. If he were to oppose his son's choice, he would be blamed for breaking his oath to the king. But he could not agree to the marriage of Zaul and Rudabeh, either, as he was leery of what would result from the union of a man reared by a bird and a woman descended from the Serpent King.

Saum slept on this matter and the next day called the magi and said: "I'm uneasy about the union of Zaul and Rudabeh. Water and fire don't mix. Good will not mix with evil. Feraydun cannot make peace with Zahhak. Allay my great fear. Go and look into the future of this troublesome marriage."

The wise men took their astrological tables, charted the stars and the movement of planets, and cast the horoscope of the proposed marriage. After a day and night, they returned, smiling. One of them said: "Good tidings, our lord. Mehraub's daughter and your son will produce a hero who will humble the enemies of Iran. Happy is the king to have your grandson among his knights."

Saum rewarded his wise men and entrusted Zaul's envoy with a message:

> Yours is indeed an odd whim. But since I have pledged to grant all your wishes, let me see what I can do. I will have to go to the king to disentangle this knot.

TROUBLE IN KABUL

Happy to receive his father's approval, Zaul sent a courier to Rudabeh, apprising her of the good news. The courier delivered her message, but she was caught on her way out by Sindokht. The queen interrogated her with some severity. "I keep seeing you around the palace, but you deliberately hurry past my chambers. Who are you, and what is your business here?"

Upon further questioning, the queen suspected that her daughter was having an affair. She ordered the gates of the palace closed and called on Rudabeh to come explain herself. The princess appeared with her head hung low.

"I have not denied you a single thing throughout your life," said the queen. "So why have you chosen the path of wickedness? Who is this courier, and who is the man who has stolen your heart? Remember that we have descended from the Arabs. The crown of Zahhak has been a mixed blessing for us. And yet, there is no blemish on the reputation of the house of Mehraub. You are throwing all that to the wind. I have been cursed with a daughter like you."

"The truth is that I am in love," Rudabeh said, staring at the ground. "I adore Zaul with all my heart and consider everything that does not pertain to him as expendable. He and I have taken an oath of loyalty, sending word to his father and convincing him to give his blessings to this union. The woman that you just abused was bearing Saum's letter."

The queen of Kabul fell silent. She approved of Zaul, of course, but she also knew that this was a weightier matter than her daughter realized. She knew this union would enrage the king of Iran and imperil the kingdom of Kabul. The queen allowed her daughter to retire to her chambers. Then she anxiously went to her quarters and stayed there until her husband returned.

Mehraub asked what was wrong, and Sindokht replied: "I was thinking of the ways of the world. Everything appears so untrustworthy. Powers wane, people get old and die, and this palace of ours and all our precious possessions are destined to decay and crumble."

The king of Kabul dismissed his wife's concerns. "But this has been the way of the world since time immemorial."

Sindokht replied that her musings were meant to prepare him for some news. The truth was that Zaul had seduced their pure daughter. Rudabeh was pale with the misery of love and deaf to the voice of reason.

Mehraub jumped to his feet, trembling with rage. Grasping the hilt of his sword, he shouted, "I'm going to make a river of blood flow from Rudabeh's veins."

Sindokht put her arms around her husband and implored him to calm down and hear the rest of the story. But Mehraub threw her down, on the ground saying: "I should have killed her at birth, as my ancestors would have done. I took pity on her, and this is how she repays me! If Saum and King Manuchehr hear this, they will lay waste to our land and sack our city."

Sindokht enjoined her husband to rein in his anger and listen to her. Then she said that Saum not only knew of the matter but indeed had approved it. And the king was likely to be persuaded as well. But Mehraub did not believe a word of this.

"Why are you lying to me? It is not that I resent the idea of this marriage. Who wouldn't want to be related to Saum? The point is that such a marriage is inconceivable, and Saum and Manuchehr would never stand for it."

Sindokht argued that the connection between different lineages was neither unwise nor unprecedented. Hadn't Feraydun sought the daughters of Sarv, the king of Yemen, as brides for his sons? Nature combined opposites all the time, and marriage between strangers would make a clan strong.

Mehraub was not moved. He listened silently to Sindokht's words and then commanded her to fetch Rudabeh.

Fearful for her daughter's safety, Sindokht made her husband swear an oath not to harm her. She went to Rudabeh and instructed her to put on her finest clothes and go to her father. Rudabeh protested that she was unable to dress up in her misery. But she obeyed her mother nonetheless and went to her father, radiant as the rising sun. Mehraub was silenced by his daughter's splendor and praised her in his heart. Then he proceeded to berate her for intending to marry a man so utterly unsuitable. Rudabeh remained silent.

THE KING'S DECREE

The story of the love of Zaul and Rudabeh had reached King Manuchehr before Saum could intercede on his son's behalf. The king consulted the magi and decreed that such a connection would spell disaster. "I did not rid Iran of the talons of the lions and leopards to lose it to a silly love affair. If the son of Rudabeh and Zaul inclines to his mother's clan, he might attempt to restore the house of Zahhak to the Iranian throne."

The magi concurred. The king then commanded the crown prince Nowzar to go to the battleground of Bactria and summon Saum to court.

Saum warmly welcomed Nowzar, and they spent a night drinking and merrymaking. The following day they took off for the capital, passing through many cities until the glittering weapons and colorful standard of Manuchehr's sentries were in sight.

Saum entered the court, kissed the ground, and reported his pacification of Bactria. King Manuchehr was pleased by the report. He replied: "You have nearly finished off the rebels of the north. Now go south and burn Kabul to the ground. Bring me Mehraub's head and slaughter his whole clan. Cleanse the land from the spawn of Zahhak before they rise again."

Saum was horrified by his new charge but had no choice. He kissed the ground in obedience, gathered his army, and set off for Kabul the next day.

When this intelligence reached Zaul, he jumped on his horse and set off in a cloud of gloom to confront his father and declare: "The raging dragon Saum would first have to separate my head from my body."

When Zaul's standard appeared on the horizon, a company of elders from Saum's camp greeted him. They paid their respects, and one of the elders said: "Your father is offended by you. Offer your apologies, and don't be stubborn."

"Then don't let him start a quarrel," Zaul replied. "Don't let him speak to me in anger, or I will shame him into tears." He then proceeded to Saum's camp, dismounted, kissed the ground, and addressed his father with tears in his eyes.

"May the heroic Saum be content," Zaul began. "May his mind be disposed to justice. When you charge the enemy on your pale horse, the world submits to your blade. An army that feels the waft of your mace does not last long. The whole world benefits from your justice. I alone seem to have no share of it. I have committed no sin that I am aware of unless being your son is a sin. You abandoned me at birth and denied me your love. You should have taken up your quarrel with God, for he created me the way I am. The Creator saw to my care, restored me to the world, gave me a kingdom and a soulmate in Kabul. I stood in the eastern frontier of Zabol and kept faith with you in hopes of one day being helpful to you.

Now you bring me this gift. You come here with a ruthless army to wreck my house and home. Is this the way you repay me for all my suffering? Now, look at me. Here I stand, exposed to your rage. Cut me in half if you want. But I will not allow you to invade Kabul, while I live."

"You are right," Saum agreed, hanging his head. "Everything I did was unjust. But don't be hasty in your judgment. I am with you, not against you, in this matter. Let me remedy the situation by sending you to the king with a letter. If the Creator helps us, everything will work out."

Saum's letter started with a list of his heroic labors. He had slain the legendary dragon of the Kashaf River with one blow of his mace, earning the title of One-Blow-Saum. And he had crushed the rebellions of Bactria. Saum pleaded with the king to be kind to his son and ended his letter drolly:

> My son has come to me now saying that he would rather be hanged than witness the invasion of Kabul.
>
> Well, what can we do? The lad is in love. Is it any wonder that a boy who grew up in the wilderness is smitten by the first girl who happens to cross his path? The ward of the bird is shedding a torrent of tears enough to turn the dirt under his feet into a patch of mud. He is so miserable that passersby take pity on him. I am sending the youthful lover to you as a supplicant. Treat him with the benevolence that befits a king.

Zaul took the letter and set off to King Manuchehr's capital. A company of dignitaries came out to welcome the young knight and ushered him into the palace. Zaul prostrated himself before the king and remained in that position. Manuchehr ordered his attendants to raise the young man and perfume his face. He bowed and presented Saum's letter. As the king read, his humor changed to joviality. "I was deeply concerned about this marriage," he said, laughing, "but this pleasant letter from the old Saum has moved me. So, despite my misgivings, I am prepared to grant you this favor. Go forth and marry your beloved."

Manuchehr engaged the royal astrologers to determine the fate of Zaul and Rudabeh's union. After three days, the prognosticators returned with the good news that a peerless warrior would be born from this union. The king charged the magi to test the young man's intelligence with their difficult riddles, and Zaul proved equal to this challenge. Then he asked for leave to return to Zabol, since he missed his father.

"It's not your father whom you miss, but the fair daughter of Mehraub!" the king retorted. "I am sure your tryst can wait a day or two."

The next day, the sound of drums, trumpets, and cymbals announced elaborate games arranged by the king. Zaul shined as a hero in contests of shooting and fighting, and he bested all his challengers. After the games, the king sent the young man off along with a letter addressed to Saum:

> You are my dear companion in fighting and feasting. You are pleasant in looks and wise in consultations. I have examined your son and found him courageous and wise as well. I have granted all his wishes.

PANIC IN KABUL

Meanwhile, Mehraub's reaction to the news of the departure of Saum's army was even more frenzied than Zaul's. Rumors of an army on the move had caused panic in Kabul. The vassal contemplated slaying his wife and daughter to appease King Manuchehr and thus save the people of his capital city. But Sindokht had a better idea. She said: "Be patient, and this dark night will pass. The dawn is about to break."

Mehraub retorted: "Don't ply me with old platitudes. Show me a solution or prepare to pay for this scandal with your life and that of your daughter."

"Shedding my blood would not solve your problems," said the queen. "I suggest you open your treasure houses instead and allow me to go on a mission of reconciliation to Saum. Give me your word that you will not harm Rudabeh in my absence."

Having secured Mehraub's promise, Sindokht got to work donning an extravagant jewel-encrusted silk gown. Then she collected the lavish offerings that she intended to bring to Saum.

Ten golden bridled horses carrying thirty thousand dinars, a crown, a torque, bracelets, and a pair of earrings led the caravan of gifts. Fifty slaves in golden belts walked behind the horses, followed by thirty more Persian and Arabian horses, each flanked by two slaves carrying golden chalices full of musk, camphor, sugar, and rubies. Then walked a line of one hundred red-haired she-camels and one hundred hinnies carrying forty bolts of gold-embroidered silk and two hundred Indian swords, thirty of them laced with a deadly poison. At the end of the convoy, four war elephants carried the disassembled pieces of an enormous golden throne. When all was prepared, Sindokht led the procession to Saum's camp, riding a swift horse. She had disguised herself and told the heralds not to announce her arrival.

Saum was surprised to see an elegant woman as the ambassador of the king of Kabul, and he was also astonished by the lavish gifts she had brought along. The enchanting Sindokht went to Saum with three of her most beautiful attendants, each carrying a goblet of gems, and said: "You are a legendary knight, and your fame for valor and justice precedes you. If Mehraub is guilty, why should the people of Kabul pay for his sins?"

"First tell me how Zaul was enthralled by the beguiling daughter of Mehraub," Saum replied with a smile. "And pray describe the looks and the wisdom of Rudabeh, who has stolen my son's heart."

Sindokht asked for immunity to speak freely, and once approved, replied: "I am Mehraub's wife and Rudabeh's mother. I have indeed descended from Zahhak, but we are loyal vassals of the king. Now I have come to see what you intend to do with Kabul. And I come to you in humility. Kill me if you wish, or bind me. But spare the people of Kabul, for they are your loyal subjects."

Saum was impressed by her sophistication and reached out to hold her hand. "Rest assured that you and the people of Kabul are safe," he comforted her. "I have already given my consent to this marriage. You are our equals, although you have descended from a different race. This is the way of the world. One cannot quarrel with God for creating different races. And I have sent a letter to the king by the hands of Zaul. I am sure the king will smile when he reads the letter, and all will be fine. Now, show me the face of this angel descended from Zahhak and receive a king's ransom!"

Sindokht was all smiles. "We will be most honored if you deign to enter our palace on your steed."

Then she sent a swift messenger to her husband, apprising him of the success of her mission. The next day she asked leave to join her husband in Kabul.

Shortly after Sindokht's departure, Zaul arrived at Saum's camp, unannounced, from the court of King Manuchehr. He had galloped so fast that Saum's scouts had not been able to precede him to the camp. He brought the good tidings that his marriage to Rudabeh had been approved. Saum was happy, but Zaul was so excited that he could not sleep that night. The next day he sent a missive to Mehraub, saying that the king no longer opposed his marriage to Rudabeh and they should prepare for the festivities.

THE WEDDING

When Mehraub learned of the success of Sindokht's mission to Saum, he showered his wife with praise and gifts. A few hours later, his happiness was complete as he received word from Zaul that the king, too, had approved of the proposed marriage.

The happy queen of Kabul went to her daughter and said: "You sought to be united with your beloved and did not vacillate in your determination. Rise and rejoice, for all your dreams have come true."

Sindokht attended to the details of the upcoming royal wedding and issued orders to decorate the city, while the vassal king went out to welcome Saum and Zaul. When the father and son came through Kabul's decorated gates, Sindokht headed a procession of three hundred slaves, each holding golden chalices of wine and goblets of jewels. They rested and drank. Then Saum addressed the queen: "For how long are you going to hide the fair Rudabeh from us?"

Sindokht smiled slyly: "And where is the king's ransom that you promised to offer for a glimpse of the sun?"

All were merry as they went to the palace. Saum was speechless when he saw the heavenly beauty of Rudabeh. The wedding celebrations commenced, and all were gay for three weeks. Then Saum and Zaul returned to Zabol as Rudabeh followed them in her splendid litter. The newly married couple remained in Zabol, but Saum, who had unfinished business in the battle against the insurgents of Bactria, bid them farewell and set off for the north.

Zaul crowned Rudabeh with a golden crest;
His heart brimmed over with abundant love
For his heavenly consort. He felt utterly blessed.

CHAPTER 4

A Hero Is Born: Rostam

The young sapling of love took root.
And as time passed, the tall,
Proud poplar was laden with fruit.

THE SIMORGH'S GIFT

Not long after Rudabeh and Zaul's wedding, the princess became heavy with child. She felt like she was carrying a boulder in her belly. Her complexion turned from rose to saffron, and she despaired of surviving her pregnancy. Sindokht tried to comfort her in vain. With the first pangs of labor, Rudabeh lost consciousness. The queen scratched her face in grief, and Zaul kept to her bedside, tears streaming through his silver beard.

In the depths of his desolation, Zaul recalled the carefree days he had spent in the Simorgh's nest. Suddenly a ray of hope shot across the clouds of his despondency. He remembered the solemn promise of the Simorgh at the moment of their farewell that she would come to his help whenever he summoned her. Zaul only needed to burn one of her feathers, and she would come to the rescue. The silver-headed knight set to work fetching the feather and lighting charcoals in a brazier. Then he sent word to Sindokht that perhaps all was not lost. A fire was kindled, and Zaul extended the long, multi-colored plume to the flames.

The feather was not fully singed when the sky grew dark, and a massive cloud gleamed above with coral rainbows. Just the sight of those familiar colors brought Zaul great comfort. The Simorgh landed and gathered her wings before approaching with delicate steps, lowering her head in deference to the great knight. Zaul humbled himself to his benefactor and praised her in a tremulous voice. Then the Simorgh spoke: "Why this sorrow, why these tears in the eyes of my brave knight?

Your beautiful wife is blessed with an auspicious child. He is destined to humble the beasts of the wild and the kings of the world. Tall as a cypress tree and mighty as an elephant, your child will inherit the wisdom of his grandfather Saum. But this birth is not destined to be an ordinary one. Call a skilled mage with a sharp dagger. Induce the mother into a stupor with wine and instruct the able practitioner to slice open her side and deliver the baby. Once he has sutured her up, mix this medicinal plant with musk and milk, and apply the balm to the mother's wound. To complete the cure, pass a feather of mine over the scar, and its shadow will heal her. Be content and praise God, for your happiness is of divine origin."

With these words, the Simorgh shed a feather from her wing and took to the skies.

Those who witnessed the scene were awed by this spectacle. And yet Sindokht had reason to feel uneasy. None had ever heard of a baby born as described by the Simorgh. But they followed the advice of the enchanting bird, and all went well. After the ministrations of the skilled mage, a prodigious baby was born, with a face radiant as the sun. Within one day, he was as big as a one-year-old.

It took a long time for Rudabeh to wake, but upon coming to consciousness, she rejoiced to see her healthy son, who was as full of color as a heap of lilies and roses. She called him Rostam. Ten wet-nurses could hardly keep up with the appetite of the extraordinary infant. When he had been weaned, he consumed enough bread and meat for five men.

Zaul and Sindokht were proud, and had a silken likeness of Rostam made and sent to the noble knight of Bactria. Saum's delight was boundless, and he could hardly contain his desire to see his grandson. When Rostam had grown as tall as his father's belt, he was said to resemble his grandfather in appearance, grace, and intelligence. It was then that Saum embarked on a journey back to Zabol to finally meet him.

Zaul and Mehraub went out to greet the elder knight. The hosts dismounted and prostrated themselves. The child Rostam was presented to his grandfather riding a war elephant. Saum praised his grandson as one praises a grown man—nay, a great knight worthy of a crown.

"I am your servant, great ancestor," said Rostam after dismounting. "I will seek my steed and armor. I will take a quiver of arrows to the battlefield so as to send forth my greetings to our foes. I pledge to humble the enemy with the king's and God's blessings. It is said that my countenance resembles yours. I only wish to be your equal in courage."

Saum took him by the hand and kissed his face and head. They all retired to the terraces of Zaul's palace, and a month was spent in merrymaking.

One day, as Saum admired Rostam's broad shoulders and slender waist, he thought about the child's magical birth and the intercession of the Simorgh. He declared: "No one is the equal of this child, nor has there been one born like him in one hundred generations. So, let's have a drink in his honor, for the habit of this fleeting world is to bring forth the new and carry off the old."

Mehraub drained many chalices of wine. Then he made an outlandish jest: "I will no longer fear Zaul, Saum, or even their hallowed King Manuchehr. When I ride with Rostam on a worthy steed, holding a well-honed blade, not even the clouds will dare cast a shadow on us. Together we will bring back the ways of our common ancestor, the Serpent King Zahhak."

Old Saum laughed with abandon, recalling the false misgivings that he and King Manuchehr had harbored for this good-natured and loyal vassal.

The next day Saum prepared to return to Bactria. Before departing, he left his son with a few words of advice: "Walk only in the path of righteousness and obey the commands of your king and the edicts of reason. Hold your hand from doing evil, and follow the path of God, for no one lives forever. I tell you these words knowing I don't have much longer in this world."

Zaul and Rostam escorted the elderly knight for three milestones then returned to Zabol, where Zaul saw to his son's comfort and education. From the surface of the earth to the constellation of Aries, the world was suffused with hope.

A HERO'S FIRST ADVENTURES*

One night, after much merrymaking, young Rostam heeded his father's advice and presented his companions with gifts of gold, garments, and horses. All retired to their quarters drunk with wine and heavy with riches. They had not rested for long when their slumber was marred by the din of Zaul's war elephant, which had broken its chains and was running amok.

None of the warriors dared approach the fuming beast. Suddenly Rostam roared into the melee. Some attendants tried to stop him, but the spirited boy pushed them aside and stood before the beast wielding a large mace. The furious elephant rushed him like a moving mountain, but he held his ground, swung the mace, and dispatched the vicious elephant with one blow. Then, as if he had performed a simple chore, the young hero turned around and went back to bed. The following day Zaul heard of his son's daring feat and was proud of him, despite having lost a good war elephant. Now he knew he could set his son on the path of glory.

Zaul's first mission for Rostam was to conquer the impregnable Arab castle on Sepand Mountain. Zaul's grandfather, Narimon, had lost his life laying siege to that stronghold. Unlike his ancestor's direct approach, the wily Rostam's path to breaching the citadel involved subterfuge. He would disguise himself as a salt merchant since the castle was sufficient unto itself for all things except salt.

Rostam took a few brave warriors with him. They hid their weapons in their loads of salt and quickly gained access to the castle. Rostam gave two loads to the lord of the fortress as a gift and sold the rest to the castle's denizens. When night fell, they attacked the guards, and by morning they had taken the castle.

Upon inspecting the premises, Rostam came across a well-hidden

* The following two stories are listed as later interpolations in our reference copy of *Shahnameh* (edited by Khaleghi-Motlagh et al.). But we have included them as they help set up the character of the hero Rostam.

chamber made of solid granite. He smashed the iron gate of the room with his heavy mace and found that the room was filled to its dome with gold coins and precious gems. It was as if the mines of the world and the bottoms of the oceans had been scraped clean to fill that chamber.

Rostam sent a missive to his father, reporting that he had avenged their ancestor and garnered untold treasures. Zaul shed tears of joy, sent the good tidings to Saum, and dispatched thousands of camels to carry off the booty. Indian trumpets blared in Zabol, and the town's enormous drums pounded to announce the return of the triumphant hero. Rostam dismounted and prostrated himself before his father, then he went to his mother's quarters and rubbed his forehead in the dust at the threshold. Fair Rudabeh kissed his shoulders and praised him. The son of the white-haired knight was already prepared to serve his king as a paladin.

THE NEW KING

Astrologers had foretold the day of King Manuchehr's passing. As it did not befit a wise king to be ambushed by death, he called the noblemen, the high clergy, and his firstborn to a final audience. Then he turned to the crown prince and spoke: "Heed my words, Nowzar. Don't let this throne bewitch you, and don't be seduced by its comforts and glory. Like wayfarers resting at an inn, we all linger for a spell in this caravanserai. Let not the love of this fleeting world run deep in your heart. All that remains from us are our deeds, so do not deviate from the path of righteousness. I have suffered much, fought great battles, crushed enemies, and avenged my grandfather Iraj on his evil brothers. For six score years have I served the throne of our forefather, Feraydun. I cleansed the land from enemies and erected entire cities of abundance.

I must leave all of this to you now. Meditate on this lesson and know that great evil awaits you from Touran, the land ruled by the children of Tur. Be wise in weathering the storm; attack and parry, now as a wolf and later as a ram. Seek the support of your knights Saum and Zaul in this hardship. Ah, and I see a scion has been born to the mighty Zaul, a hero at whose assault the Touranians will drop their shields. Rely on him, for he is the one to avenge you."

With these words, the king's eyelids fell for the last time, and he passed into legend.

A propitious day was chosen for Nowzar's crowning ceremony. All were merry at the coronation of the new king of Iran. Gifts were bestowed upon the army, and the knights pledged their allegiance. But as the ceremonies concluded, the king disappeared into his opulent chambers and did not emerge for two months. He gave into sloth, gluttony, and avarice away from the public eye. Nowzar had abandoned his father's ways all too soon. To fill his coffers, he burdened the farmers with taxes, impelling them to take up arms and rise in rebellion. External threats menaced Iran as enemies realized the sovereign power was weak and unpopular. God had withdrawn his sanction from Nowzar, and the divine halo had left his face. Terrified, the king sent an urgent dispatch to Saum, reminding him of Manuchehr's final words and asking for his help in restoring calm and order to the land.

Saum was swift in obliging his king. As he approached the palace, a delegation of Iranian knights welcomed him. They were disappointed with Nowzar and proposed a plan to raise Saum, who was the most exalted among them, to the throne. But noble Saum would not contemplate rebellion against his king. Instead, he persuaded the assembly to return to court and plead with His Majesty to mend his ways. Together they went to Nowzar and expressed their dissatisfaction, and the king, aware of his lapses, listened to their counsel. He was contrite and pledged to be just from that day forward.

THE INVASION FROM TOURAN

King Nowzar did attempt to restore order to his land, but it was simply too late. Tidings of disarray had reached far and wide. King Pashang of Touran called his knights to assembly, recited Touran's old grievances against Iran, and lamented that Manuchehr had spilled the blood of his grandfather Tur. His son, the gallant Afrasiab, stood up and girded his loins in a pledge to exact revenge on Iran. He proudly opened the treasure houses and decreed that an army be assembled for the invasion, turning a deaf ear to the sage advice of his other son, Prince Aghrirat, who said: "Weak as it has grown, Iran still has many brave defenders, not the least of whom is the noble Saum."

Not long after this pronouncement, the great warrior Saum passed away. When news reached Afrasiab, he knew that Zaul and his entire clan would be distracted by his funerary rites. He surmised that the whole of Iran was ripe for conquest.

With the coming of spring, the armies of Touran gathered. One glorious morning, Afrasiab's war drums sounded from atop armored war elephants, and his mighty army crossed the Oxus River, which had separated Iran and Touran since Feraydun.

Afrasiab sent one prong of his army toward Zabol, as he was sure of a swift victory against Saum's bereaved clan, and led a second prong toward Nowzar's capital. The king brought out an army against the Touranian force, and the two sides met at the fields of Dehestan on the eastern shores of the Caspian Sea.

In the grim battles that ensued, Afrasiab lost some of his best warriors. He fought fearlessly, but several of his deeds were despicable. His most significant victory was the defeat and capture of King Nowzar. When news arrived that some of his kinsmen were slain at the battle of Zabol, Afrasiab bellowed with rage and ordered Nowzar to be hauled to him in rags.

Afrasiab reminded King Nowzar of the vendetta between their ancestors before decapitating him. This regicide did not sate his fury, so he called for the massacre of all the Iranian captives. The monstrosity of this edict dismayed Afrasiab's righteous brother Aghrirat, and he pleaded for a stay in mass executions and took the prisoners into his custody. Later, fearing for their lives, he would allow them to escape. Afrasiab was so enraged by this act of defiance that he rushed his own brother and cleaved him in half with one blow of his sword.

With the death of King Nowzar, the throne of Iran belonged to Afrasiab, but he yearned to possess and control the entire nation, from the Oxus River in the east to the deserts of Arabia to the west. His campaign in Zabol had not succeeded in dislodging Saum and Zaul's clan from their stronghold. King Pashang of Touran issued fresh orders for Iran to be subdued in its entirety. Afrasiab launched new waves of invasion, leaving the Iranians vulnerable and terrified.

After Nowzar, neither of his warrior sons, Tous and Gostahm, were deemed worthy of ascending Iran's throne. It was assumed that the divine sanction had been withdrawn from the entire line of the late king. So the knights appointed a very old man named Zav, and later his son, Garshasp, to the throne. But their rule was too anemic to save Iran from further disintegration. After Garshasp's death, Iran was utterly helpless in the face of the ferocious armies of Afrasiab.

Disheartened Iranian knights went to Zaul and bitterly lamented the impending demise of their nation. The kings were inept, enemies were at the gates, and Zaul was too old to save the day.

STANDING AGAINST AFRASIAB

The ancient land needed a new hero, and Rostam had proven himself in battle against beast and man. Keenly aware of the crisis, he went to his father shortly after his victory at Sepand Mountain and asked permission to confront Afrasiab. The idea had occurred to Zaul, but he was torn between paternal love and patriotic duty. On the one hand, his brave son, his prodigious strength and agility notwithstanding, was still too young to face such a strong opponent. On the other, Rostam was already an exceptional fighter, and he very well could be the savior of his homeland.

The decision was made easy for Zaul when Rostam declared that he preferred the life of a hero to the comforts of childish games. The boy was consumed with the need to win glory in combat. Zaul finally relented and solemnized his approval by presenting his son with the ox-headed mace of their great ancestor Saum. The boy's joy upon receiving the legendary weapon was boundless. He proudly accepted it and then asked his father, "Now, where is the steed to carry me?"

Zaul smiled and called on his aides to gather all the herds of Zabol and Kabul. The herdsmen rustled up the horses for Rostam to survey. He searched for a long time but could not find a steed with the strength to carry him. They all buckled under the pressure of his right arm as he pushed down on their backs. Finally, he saw a brawny pinto colt, the color of rose petals dappled in saffron. The colt was following a feisty mare. He was a splendid specimen, keen enough to track a distant ant on the blackest night. Seeing that it was not branded, the young hero prepared to capture it, but the herdsman remonstrated that it was not right to steal a horse that belongs to another. Rostam protested: "But I don't see a brand on that horse."

The herdsman replied: "This untamable fiend goes by Rakhsh, meaning 'the bright one.' He is not branded because no one has been able to approach him, although he has been long ready for taming. We have heard stories of a legendary hero, a giant named Rostam—so we call this wild stallion the Rakhsh of Rostam. Beware of him and his fire-breathing mother."

Rostam was delighted to hear the description, but to capture the colt, he had to scare off his fiercely protective mother with a roar. Then he walked up to Rakhsh and pushed down on his back with all his might, but the horse stood its ground. Rostam knew that he had finally found his worthy steed, and asked the herdsman, "What is the price of this horse?"

"If you are Rostam, then the horse is yours," he replied. "Ride him well and defend the land, for the price of this horse is the safekeeping of Iran."

Rostam smiled and said, "All good things come from God."

The young hero saddled Rakhsh and, giving in to fantasies of combat, brought him to a full gallop. Yes, this horse could carry him in full battle gear. This was a magical gift, a robust and clever stallion with round haunches and an elegant gait. Beautiful as a deer and pleasant to touch, Rakhsh had a neck softer than a thick layer of goose feathers. Rostam burned clouds of incense for Rakhsh to ward off the evil eye.

Zaul's heart bloomed when he saw his gallant son riding a steed that resembled a dragon. As was the custom, he generously gave a fortune to the company of the attending noblemen to celebrate Rostam's new stature. Then he sounded the bell from atop his war elephant to initiate the march toward the forces of Touran.

The army of Zabol moved forward until it reached the Touranian front lines at the plain of Rey. When Afrasiab heard that two miles south of his front lines, Iranian troops were gathering under the command of Zabol's men, he lost all desire for food and was struck by insomnia.

On the Iranian side, all appeared ready for battle. But Zaul knew that something was amiss. Rostam and his troops needed a royal commander, and Iran needed a monarch hallowed by divine grace. Zaul consulted with his advisers, who informed him that a young descendant of the magnificent Feraydun named Kay-Qobaud lived in obscurity in the nearby Alborz Mountain Range. Without delay, Zaul dispatched his son to fetch the prince who could occupy Iran's empty throne. Swift as the wind, Rostam rode his stallion into the heart of the forbidding range. Fighting fatigue and scattered groups of Touranian foes, he did not rest until he returned with the man who would be the next king of Iran.

According to tradition, Zaul convened a gathering of the high clergy and noblemen to name Kay-Qobaud the new king of Iran. They chose their new sovereign by acclamation and rejoiced for seven days and nights. On the eighth day, Kay-Qobaud sat on the throne and admitted the assembly of knights, who pledged their loyalty and called on their new king to cleanse the homeland of foreign hordes. Kay-Qobaud unfurled Kaveh's crimson, yellow, and purple standard, and promised to reward bravery on the battlefield. He then charged the knights to take down the marauders of Touran.

As the armies prepared for battle at the decisive hour, Rostam asked his father to point out the standard of Afrasiab. Zaul warned that the commander of the Touranian forces was no easy prey for an inexperienced warrior. But Rostam was aware of Afrasiab's reputation, and that was precisely why he wanted to fight him. Afrasiab was a worthy opponent. Spotting the enemy commander's black flag, the hero cued Rakhsh to a charge, thundering his battle cry. Afrasiab turned to his advisers and asked, "Who is that?"

"That's Rostam, Zaul's son," an attendant replied. "Don't you see that he's wielding Saum's mace? Don't you see that he has come to seek glory?"

Locking gazes, the opponents spurred their horses into a furious gallop.

Rostam gripped Rakhsh under his thighs and lifted his mace. Afrasiab unsheathed his sword. As the combatants grappled, Rostam returned his mace to its holder and grabbed onto Afrasiab's belt, lifting him off his saddle with ease. He wanted to carry his royal captive straight to King Kay-Qobaud. But Afrasiab's belt snapped, and he was saved by the ignominy of falling to the ground. A few soldiers rushed in to help him regain his composure. Afrasiab added to his humiliation by running from the field and leaving his troops to their fate.

Distraught that he had lost his captive, Rostam snatched the crown off the dishonored prince as he fell. Kay-Qobaud was encouraged by this event, and ordered the Iranian troops to charge under Rostam's command. The hero wielded his ox-headed mace, and wherever he turned, heads fell like autumn leaves in a gust of wind. The victory went to the Iranians, and what remained of the crushed Touranian throngs retreated behind the Oxus River in shame. The knights of Iran returned to their capital weighed down with booty. The young king sat upon the throne flanked by Rostam and Zaul, the father and son who had made him king and saved Iran.

SUING FOR PEACE AFTER THE DEFEAT

Afrasiab left his defeated army at the banks of the Oxus River and went to his father's court to harangue him for breaching his covenant of peace with Iran. "You relied on wild rumors instead of investigating the strength of your enemy," he seethed. "Iran's throne did not stay empty for long. Nor was Iran ever devoid of courageous defenders. One among them is Rostam, a wonder of nature who humiliated me by lifting me off my horse as if I weighed no more than a mosquito. You know my courage and cunning in war. And yet, in his grasp, I was like nothing but a weed pulled from the ground with its root.

"You treated war like a sport and let our best knights and ten thousand soldiers die in battle. Worst of all, we now must live with the embarrassment of a defeat that will never be forgotten.

"I, too, erred in slaying my brother Aghrirat. I lived to learn a hard lesson about the wages of injustice. I was ambushed by legions of knights, each flying a different flag. I regret my evil deeds and hope to be forgiven by you. But we must forget the past, as the only way forward is to sue for peace. This powerful enemy will no doubt vanquish us if this war continues."

Pashang was staggered by the wisdom of his once impetuous son. With tears in his eyes, he called for a scribe and dictated a careful letter. The missive began by praising God and the divine Feraydun, who divided the world among his three sons. If Iraj met treachery at Tur's hand, he was rightly avenged by his grandson, Manuchehr. Feuds should have ended there and then. The king of Touran finished his message by pledging that his side would never cross the Oxus River again, unless in peace and brotherhood.

The letter was sealed and entrusted to Viseh, the king's wise brother. A great peace offering was sent along with the message of peace, including heaps of jewels, crowns and daises, as well as golden-belted slaves. There were also Arabian horses adorned with elaborate bridles and silver scabbards.

King Kay-Qobaud graciously responded to Pashang's offer.

> You know very well that we did not start this conflict. Tur was the one who betrayed and murdered his brother, Iraj. And it was Afrasiab who initiated this war and slew our King Nowzar in captivity, an act so egregious as to offend even the wildest beasts. Nor did he spare his own brother, the wise Prince Aghrirat.
>
> But if the children of Tur are inclined to peace, I will not deny them this wish. I will not hold a grudge, for I have withdrawn my passions from this ephemeral world. Let the Oxus River remain the border between us, as the olden kings decreed it.

Rostam protested that the proposed peace was disingenuous, that it rose not from a sudden Touranian thirst for justice but from the impact of his mace on the battlefield. King Kay-Qobaud's magnanimity was greater than the impetuous knight's worldly reckonings.

At the conclusion of the peace, Rostam and Zaul returned to their domain in Zabol, and King Kay-Qobaud retired to the Winter Palace in Pars, where he ruled Iran in prosperity and justice for the next century. When the time came for the king to pass on, he called his firstborn, Kay-Kavous, and advised him to be just and generous.

"Time has come for me to leave this world and for you to inherit the throne," he said. "Be mindful of the fickleness of this world. It feels like it was yesterday that I arrived from the slopes of the Alborz range to become king. Only the unwise pass their time without reflection. If you rule with justice, you will be rewarded in this world and the next. But if you unsheathe the sword of injustice, you will be slain by it."

Then the king traded his palace for a wooden chest.
A coffin became his home after leaving this world
We come from dirt, and that's where we are put to rest.

CHAPTER 5

The Follies of a King: Kay-Kavous

When a crooked branch grows out of a tree
The root is not at fault, nor should
A father be blamed if a son stains his legacy.

A child who defies his teachers has none to blame
For the hard knocks he'll receive in the school of life
And his last lesson is that life was not a silly game.

THE MAUZANDARAN EXPEDITION

King Kay-Kavous sat on the throne wearing the bejeweled golden crown of his late father Kay-Qobaud. He was adorned in lustrous earrings and the torque of royalty. The national treasure houses were full, and the king's stables were teeming with Arabian horses. The land was safe and people submitted to the new sovereign.

One day, sitting in his pleasure garden drinking with his knights, the king was approached by a devil in the guise of a skilled musician. To turn him away from the path of righteousness, he sang a bewitching ballad about the ever-blooming orchards and the majestic green slopes of his homeland, the enchanted abode of the demons.

Now I will sing the praises of Mauzandaran for my king
The land whose mountains bloom with hyacinth and tulips
As a confusion of warblers serenade the eternal spring.

The lords of that land spend their days
In hunting and falconry, as they are served
By lovely attendants worthy of a king's praise.

The devil enthralled Kay-Kavous with his song, and left the king burning with the desire to possess the riches of Mauzandaran. "We are growing soft with merrymaking," said the king to his warriors. "I have surpassed my royal ancestors in fortune, divine grace, and justice. I ought to exceed them in conquests as well."

The knights were silent, their foreheads were furrowed. None among them relished the thought of waging war on the powerful demons of Mauzandaran. But they dared not oppose their sovereign's ambition. Instead, they intoned their humble submission and retired for the night.

Later they gathered, to discuss the predicament. "We are in great danger," said one of the knights. "Was it the wine, or did I hear right that the king plans to invade Mauzandaran? Jamshid, Feraydun, and Manuchehr were mighty kings who knew how to subdue demons, and even they did not set out to conquer that enchanted land. This conceited king, who has inherited the windfall riches of his predecessors, intends to squander the royal treasury and forfeit our lives.

Only one person can save us from this calamity: Zaul. He and his son, Rostam, saved this land from the disaster caused by Nowzar. All those efforts will have been in vain if this king gets his way."

A swift messenger was dispatched to Zabol, asking Zaul to come to the court without delay. Zaul shuddered when he learned that the novice king had chosen the path of recklessness. He knew that Kay-Kavous would probably ignore his counsel, but he was duty-bound to warn the king.

The knights came forth to welcome Zaul and ushered him into the palace. The old knight of Zabol bowed his head to the king and advised him against stumbling into a war with the demons. He warned that it would be an unnecessary and bloody conflict—and that previous kings had avoided such a risk. Kay-Kavous boasted that he was superior to all past kings. Then he solemnly thanked Zaul for his concern and commanded him to stay behind in Iran and protect the land in his absence.

Having spoken his piece, Zaul pledged his submission and expressed his hope that the venture would be successful and that the king would not regret his decision. With these words, he left the royal court with downcast eyes, bid farewell to the knights, and traveled back to Zabol.

Soon the drums of Kay-Kavous's war sounded, and an army gathered under the leadership of two prominent knights: Tous, the late King Nowzar's son, and Gudarz, Kaveh the blacksmith's great-grandson. The armies of Iran marched from the capital to the slopes of Mount Esprouz, just at the border of Mauzandaran. They set up the royal camp in a beautiful meadow and prepared for the invasion. The following day the king commanded Geav, Gudarz's gallant son, to select two thousand warriors skilled in wielding the mace and the blade.

"Exterminate man, woman, and child—don't even spare the old," he ordered. "Burn every house. Turn medicine into poison and day into night. Let the arch-demons who dominate this land hear of our might."

Geav unsheathed his sword and carried out the king's orders. The rampage went on for seven days. Great treasures were found, and dazzling cities were plundered. Thrilled by his success, Kay-Kavous praised the musician who had sung of this rich land of the demons.

On the eighth day, intelligence of the Iranian invasion reached the king of Mauzandaran. In anguish, he called on the chief guardian of his realm, the White Demon, to rid the land of the invaders. The fearsome White Demon swiftly engulfed the Iranian soldiers in a noxious, pitch-black cloud that blinded them. Arrows and javelins rained down from the poisonous cloud onto the warriors for one whole week. Helpless, wounded, and blind, the Persian army staggered, cursing their king.

"You are to the kings what the willow is to the fruit trees," said the White Demon, appearing amid the dark cloud to taunt Kay-Kavous. "You followed the path of pride and coveted the throne of Mauzandaran. Like a musth elephant run amok, you only thought of power. Now you have lost your throne and earned this captivity—and the death that will soon come for you and your companions."

The White Demon appointed twelve thousand minions to guard Kay-Kavous and his troops. They were kept in darkness and fed meager rations. The king sat in the company of his defeated knights, recalling Zaul's sage advice. "A good adviser is better than a full treasure house," he muttered ruefully.

The king recovered from his apathy long enough to secretly dispatch a message to Zaul, confessing the utter foolishness of his endeavor and asking for Rostam's aid. Zaul was devastated that his vision of disaster had come to pass, but he did not gloat. Instead, he urged his son to ride out to rescue the arrogant king. Rudabeh watched her son mount his steed with tears streaming from her eyes.

"A wise man does not willingly go to the gates of hell or offer his flesh to a raging lion," Rostam told his mother. "But it is my destiny and duty to slay the White Demon and rescue my king. Pray for me, Mother, and please grant me your blessings."

With these words, the young hero set off. There were two routes to Mauzandaran: a long, safe road and a shorter but far more dangerous path. Rostam was forced to take the faster route.

THE SEVEN LABORS OF THE HERO

Rostam rode out of Zabol in such haste that he did not pause for two days. Finally, he stopped at a thicket, where he hunted an onager for his supper, and allowed Rakhsh to graze. Then he lay down to rest. Unbeknownst to the hero, the thicket was the lair of a ferocious lion, which returned while he was fast asleep. The lion spied the stallion and considered him an easy prey, but when he went in for the kill, Rakhsh sprang from his clutches and managed to dispatch the predator with a few blows of his front hooves. When Rostam woke and saw the lion's carcass, he chided Rakhsh for risking his life. "I forbid you from fighting," he commanded his steed. "In the future, wake me up if you're in danger." The next day, when the sun rose above the mountains, Rostam rubbed down and saddled his loyal horse.

In front of them lay a seemingly endless desert devoid of vegetation. They rode on until Rakhsh was too thirsty to go on. Rostam dismounted and staggered ahead, leaning on his lance. Parched and exhausted, he collapsed and prayed for divine intervention. Suddenly a beautiful ram leaped into his range of vision. Delirious, he crawled after the ram, using his sword for support, and Rakhsh followed close behind. The ram led them to a lovely spring, where they all drank. Indeed, this was a divine sign. Rostam thanked God and praised the ram that had saved his life: "May the grass grow on your field aplenty, my ram of well-formed haunches. May cheetahs never be sated on your flesh. May the bow that aims at you snap. May arrows coming at you miss their mark. The formidable knight of Iran would be lost and dead without you."

Rostam drank deeply and bathed. He saw to the needs of his horse, hunted another onager to sate his hunger, and made his bed to rest. Before falling asleep, he warned Rakhsh once again not to endanger himself needlessly.

This time, the rider and his steed had unknowingly chosen to rest in the den of a magical dragon, which returned while Rostam slept. The beast was amazed that a man had dared to venture into his realm, let alone fall asleep there. The dragon rushed Rakhsh with great ferocity. Not wanting to disobey his master, the stallion retreated and stomped the ground to wake him. But when he awoke, the magical creature had disappeared. Rostam scolded his steed for interrupting his rest and went back to sleep. Then the dragon reappeared and attacked again. Rakhsh neighed and raised a cloud of dust to wake his master, whereupon the dragon vanished again. This time Rostam more sternly warned his horse against disturbing his sleep. When the dragon attacked for the third time, Rakhsh was torn. He feared the dragon's claws as much as his master's wrath. Finally, he decided to awaken Rostam, but this time a divine light flashed, and the dragon appeared as an expansive shadow against the sky.

Rostam took in the sight of the beast, drew his sword, and asked the dragon's name. The creature breathed out a dark cloud, flickering with sparks, and replied: "What is your name, and who shall cry over your lifeless body?"

"My name is Rostam, the son of Zaul, the son of Saum, the son of Narimon. I am the destroyer of armies and the master of Rakhsh."

At this, the dragon rushed Rostam and wrestled him with all its might for a long time. Recognizing that his master might be overcome, Rakhsh joined the battle and tore at the shoulder of the dragon with his teeth. Rostam used this respite to swing his sword and behead the dragon, whose blood turned the dry earth into a field of red mud. The hero washed the blood off his garments in the nearby stream, thanked God for his victory, and rode on.

The journey to Mauzandaran was long and arduous, but the valiant rider pressed on until the sun started its descent. Suddenly the landscape changed, and Rostam found himself at a pleasant spring in the middle of a lush garden. A delectable meal of lamb and bread, along with garnishes, desserts, and cups of wine, was set out, along with a lute next to a golden chalice. Unbeknownst to Rostam, he had walked into a gathering of witches who had scattered as he approached. In great astonishment, he dismounted, filled a cup, picked up the lute, and sang:

This is the song of a vagrant hero who is branded
By a life that only brings him grief and sorrow.
Fate leads Rostam on and leaves him stranded

In strange lands, entangled in clashes.
My gardens are barren mountains, and my orchards
The desolate wastelands, ruins, and ashes.

Dragons and lions confront me in every labor
And I am attacked by the demons of the desert
Whom I slay by my unsheathed saber.

Fate doesn't grant me companions or wine.
And my portion of the pleasures of life is
A parched wilderness and an ocean of brine.

Rostam is ever contending with the crocodiles of the sea
Or else he is in a dense forest, entangled
With ferocious leopards one, two, or three.

Lured back in by Rostam's song, one of the witches transformed herself into a fair maiden and came forward. He offered her a cup of wine and bid her drink it in the name of God. The witch, who could not bear the divine name, relapsed to the shape of the hag that she really was. Rostam slew the witch and set off on the road again.

The hero trekked on through a gloomy realm that was dark as night. He dared not stop until he finally emerged into sunshine. Exhausted, he stopped at a wheat field, lifted Rakhsh's bridle, and allowed him to graze. As he slept, a farmhand rushed in and struck at his feet with a stick. Gravely insulted, the hero rose and meted out swift and rough punishment to the rude man who had awakened him. The anguished guard ran away to inform his master about the dangerous trespasser in his fields. The owner, whose name was Oulad, gathered an armed posse to capture and punish the trespasser. But in the ensuing battle, Rostam slaughtered the gang one by one and captured their leader.

Oulad pleaded for his life. The hero said he would allow him to live if he acted as his scout. He would have to lead him to the Iranian army and then to the White Demon's den. He promised to make Oulad king of Mauzandaran if he served efficiently and in good faith. The choice between certain death and the promise of becoming the king of his realm was not difficult. With this agreement, Oulad led Rostam to Mount Esprouz, where Kay-Kavous was imprisoned.

Once they arrived at the edge of the encampment, the hero tied Oulad to a tree and asked him for the name and a description of the head demon guarding Mount Esprouz. The name of the demon commander was Arzhang. Rostam packed his ox-headed mace in his saddle, heart racing with excitement. He brought his steed to a full gallop, screamed his terrible war cry and waded into the demonic army—straight for Arzhang's tent. Demons scattered from his path, falling over each other. In the pandemonium, fathers trampled sons to escape. Even the leader of the demons was terrified. As he rushed out to see what calamity had befallen his troops, Rostam grabbed him, tore off his head, and flung it at the throngs of his minions.

Through his prison walls, King Kay-Kavous recognized the sound of Rakhsh's neighing. "Our sorrows are over, my worthy knights," he said, elated. "I can hear Rakhsh, and I remember this sound from the wars Rostam fought under my father."

Once freed, the king and his warriors greeted Rostam in gratitude and humility. Kay-Kavous embraced his knight, shedding tears of joy, and enquired about Zaul's well-being. He also asked for an account of Rostam's recent adventures and advised him about what he needed to do to bring about their rescue.

"Be on your guard. Once the White Demon hears that Arzhang has been killed, he will bring another army against us. To prevent this you must go to his lair beyond the seven mountains. There you will find a great pit, where he sleeps. As you can see, we are all struck with the curse of this blindness caused by the White Demon's sorcery. Slay him and bring back a vat of his blood—it is said to be the only cure for our affliction."

Rostam bid the king farewell, untied Oulad, and set off on the road again.

When they reached the pit of the White Demon, the hero asked his scout for the key to overcoming these creatures. It was best to attack them at noon, said Oulad, since they were nocturnal and at their weakest at midday. Rostam rested for a while, preparing to attack as the sun rose high. Then he bellowed his battle cry and charged into the camp. Only a few sentries were posted, all sluggish and disoriented from the bright sun. Rostam had no trouble fighting his way to the opening of the pit, but he was forced to stop at the mouth of the cave until his eyes adjusted to the dark. Only then could he make out the massive form of the White Demon filling the enormous cavern.

Suddenly the beast awoke with a fearsome growl and rushed the intruder like the sliding side of a mountain. Rostam quickly drew his sword and lopped off the beast's leg. The monster threw himself on the hero, and they wrestled through the dark. With supreme effort, Rostam finally sunk his dagger into the White Demon's heart. The monster went limp, and the cave filled with a torrent of blood.

THE FINAL BATTLES OF THE VICTORIOUS HERO

Rostam emerged from the cave carrying the enormous, bloody liver of the monster. He untied Oulad for the last time, and they headed back to Mount Esprouz. The excited scout ran beside Rakhsh, carrying the White Demon's blood-dripping organ and reminding the hero of his promise to grant him kingship. It would be unseemly if such a famous paladin as himself failed to honor his word.

Back at the Iranian camp, they cured the king, his companions, and soldiers by dripping the blood of the White Demon into their eyes. Kay-Kavous drafted a letter to the king of Mauzandaran, urging him to come to court and pay tribute immediately. Having lost the support of the White Demon, Arzhang, and their minions, Mauzandaran could not fight off the armies of Iran.

But the king refused to surrender. Instead, he prepared for war. Gudarz and Geav commanded the Iranian army's right and left flanks, and Rostam was put in charge of the center in the ensuing great battle. Victory went to the Iranians, and the king of Mauzandaran lost his land and life. To reward the services of his loyal scout Oulad, Rostam interceded with Kay-Kavous to grant the kingship of the region to him. The king called the noblemen of Mauzandaran together and asked for their endorsement of Oulad before naming him the new king of their realm. With this, the hostilities in Mauzandaran ended, and the Iranian troops returned home.

After a triumphal procession, Kay-Kavous sat on his throne and called on Rostam to reward him for his valor. Honored with a gem-encrusted crown, he was seated on a turquoise throne next to his king. Kay-Kavous lavished him with garments, bracelets, a magnificent torque, and a hundred purses of gold. He was given a hundred mares and a hundred Arabian horses loaded with Roman fabric and festooned in golden bridles. The hero's caravan included a hundred slaves wearing golden belts. The king also renewed the royal grant of Zabol and its vast environs to the clan of Zaul and Rostam.

It was known throughout the world that Kay-Kavous had subdued the demons of Mauzandaran. The world seemed to have returned to peace and tranquility.

THE LOVELY PRINCESS OF HAMAUVARAN

To celebrate his victory, Kay-Kavous embarked on an expedition to the territorial borders of Iran. Everywhere rulers greeted him with generous gifts and tribute. The news of the conquest of Mauzandaran had awed the lesser kings, who were keen to show their respect. Only the defiant ruler of Barbary was unimpressed, and he came forward with a massive army whose lances resembled a dense thicket. Offended by this show of insolence, Kay-Kavous charged the knight Gudarz to subdue the rebellious king. With the backing of one thousand brave soldiers, the chosen commander savaged the heart of the army of Barbary and routed them. As Kay-Kavous entered the defeated city, the town's elders greeted him in humility and pledged to pay more tribute than he had demanded. The king forgave their impudence and announced his plan to go to Zabol for a month of rest. But this sojourn was interrupted when word of a new revolt in the provinces of Egypt and Hamauvaran arrived. The treacherous Barbars had joined this revolt despite their previous pledge of loyalty to the king of Iran.

Kay-Kavous launched a massive naval expedition to crush the new insurgency. Once the Iranians emerged from the sea of Zereh, they found the troops of Barbary and Egypt on their right and left. The army of Hamauvaran occupied the center of the battlefield. The war began in full force as the Iranian knights kissed their saddles and rushed the allied armies of the three kingdoms, wading into a sea of blood. The din of clashing lances and battle-axes was deafening. The Iranian army proved unstoppable. The king of Hamauvaran was the first to drop his sword in surrender. He asked for quarter and pledged to pay a heavy tribute in horses, arms, gold, and jewels. Kay-Kavous accepted the terms of his surrender, and when the two remaining armies fell, he took all three realms under his protection.

After the provinces were pacified, the king set up camp near the battlefield of Hamauvaran and took a respite to celebrate his victories. During an evening of merrymaking, an attendant told him about the king of Hamauvaran's daughter Sudabeh. Tall as a cypress, the princess was exquisitely beautiful, with a magnificent crown atop her raven-black hair that set off lips sweeter than sugar. Burning with desire, Kay-Kavous sent a messenger to her royal father to ask for her hand.

Having lost the battle to Kay-Kavous, the king was loath to give his favorite daughter away to his victorious enemy. But he had little choice. In desperation, he asked for his daughter's advice and was surprised to learn that Sudabeh was agreeable to the marriage proposal. She said: "The fact is that we don't have any other option. A king is entitled to whatever he has conquered. Besides, why would one spurn good fortune? Union with the Iranian royalty could serve us well. This connection should be cause for joy."

For a week, the king prepared his daughter's wedding procession. After the requisite ceremonies, he reluctantly sent Sudabeh to Kay-Kavous along with a train of slaves in golden belts carrying an abundance of royal gifts.

The princess of Hamauvaran was happy with the union, and as time passed, she grew to love the king and her position as the queen of Iran. When her father invited the royal couple back to his realm to celebrate a festival, Sudabeh advised her husband against going; she knew that her father resented Kay-Kavous, and suspected foul play. But the proud Kay-Kavous, who was not disposed to listen to wise counsel, ignored this warning and went to the banquet, accompanied by his queen and his three favorite knights.

The king of Hamauvaran warmly welcomed Kay-Kavous and his retinue. But in secret, he was plotting with the kings of Barbary and Egypt. On the eighth day of festivities, he locked up his royal guests in an impregnable castle. Sudabeh was furious with her father's treachery and refused to leave her husband.

With Kay-Kavous nowhere to be found, chaos descended on Iran. Enemies breached the borders on all sides and often fought for the spoils of their raids. Sensing an easy victory, Afrasiab also crossed the boundaries of Touran, laying waste to the western borders of Iran, enslaving its population and winning a three-month battle against the Arabs, who had also penetrated Iran in the king's absence.

As Iran became a battleground of foreign marauders, fugitives from various wars fled to Zabol to ask Rostam for help. It was at this time that the king managed to send a secret missive appealing to him for help. Rostam responded that he was ready to come to the rescue of his king. But there was a chance that the king of Hamauvaran would become angry about this fresh invasion and take it out on the king. What would be the use of the thrones of Barbary and Hamauvaran if any harm came to the king? Kay-Kavous sent his response:

> I am not the center of the universe. Pain and pleasure, poison and panacea are mixed in the bowl of life. Do not worry for me, as God is my protector. Ride your noble Rakhsh. Aim your spear at the enemy's heart. Annihilate them all.

Rostam gathered an army and, after many battles, succeeded in crushing the forces of the three defiant kings. This was now the second time that Rostam had restored the king to his royal seat. Kay-Kavous returned to Iran, hauling the treasures and tributes of the three defeated kingdoms. Queen Sudabeh, who had defied her father, traveled back to the Winter Palace of Pars with her husband in a dazzling litter.

Now it was time to expel Afrasiab from the Iranian soil. Kay-Kavous sent him a letter, advising that it would be best if he withdrew his troops to avoid war. But Afrasiab refused, citing flimsy arguments that his grandfather Tur was a descendant of King Feraydun and that he had a right to the Iranian land. He also claimed that he had not taken the territories from the Iranians but won them fairly from the Arab invaders. It was obvious that dislodging Afrasiab would not be possible without another conflict.

Rostam was dispatched to subdue the army of Touran. Afrasiab found himself on the losing side of the great battle that followed. In desperation, he promised to marry his daughter to anyone who would kill Rostam.

But his efforts came to naught, and he was forced to redeploy back to his ancestral land beyond the Oxus River.

Kay-Kavous lavished praise on Rostam again and named him the Champion of the World. Then, he reasserted his sovereignty and built a castle in the Alborz Mountains, where many nations would come to pay tribute.

THE KING WHO REACHED FOR THE HEAVENS

Iblis, the archdemon, was displeased that Kay-Kavous was steering close to the path of righteousness. So, he sent a fiend disguised as a lad to tempt the king. Holding a bouquet of flowers, the devil's spy kissed the throne and said:

"A sovereign with your divine halo deserves to ascend to the heavens. You've conquered the world. You are the shepherd, and all the world's potentates are your flock. Only one thing remains. You must discover the hidden secrets of the heavens above. What causes the sun to rise and set? Why do the heavenly bodies climb to their zenith and descend to their nadir? What manner of thing is the moon? Wherefore is this day and night? Who oversees the revolution of the heavens?"

Not recognizing that it was an offense to God to break into His heavenly realm, Kay-Kavous gave in to the temptation of ascending to the skies. He devised a scheme whereby eagles would be attached to the four corners of his throne, and lift him into the sky. A piece of lamb dangled at each of the top corners of the platform, beyond the reach of the eagles' beaks, tempting them to fly higher to reach the meat. The throne of Kay-Kavous was raised to the clouds. People were amazed by the spectacle. Rostam, Geav, and Tous ran to follow the path of their high-flying king. But the eagles grew tired, and the ill-conceived flying contraption crashed in a thicket near Amol.

The Eagles took off, and the flight looked stupendous
But the birds were exhausted tying to reach the bait.
Among the sins of man, greed and ambition are the most horrendous.

The knights were furious when they spotted the wreckage of the flying machine. Gudarz grumbled to Rostam: "Of all the kings I have seen, none has been so bereft of common sense and judgment."

"The insane asylum is more suitable for you than the royal palace," Gudarz scolded his king. "You keep endangering your life and the safety of this country. You have done this three times now, and you don't seem to learn your lesson. Do you remember what disasters ensued following your foray into Mauzandaran? Then you decided to go and feast at your enemy's house. Only God was not harangued by you. And having finished with the earth, you got it into your head to set the affairs of the heavens in order! People will mock you as the king who wanted to manhandle the sun and the moon and impose a census on the stars. You should stop this once and for all. You ought to humble yourself and follow the way of the wise kings of the past."

Kay-Kavous was contrite. He meekly accepted the knights' rebuke. Back at the palace, he locked himself in prayer for forty days to repent and ask forgiveness for his impudent adventure into the heavens. Once more, God forgave him.

I've spoken of the way this king behaved
He tried to be just, but a truly just king
Would not have to be so frequently saved.

POACHING GAME IN TOURAN

A measure of recklessness is needed in strife
Prudence and piety have no place there
Bring a sword to the fight, not a dull butter knife.

One beautiful day Rostam called his fellow knights to a hunting party in Navand, near the fire temple of Azar-Borzin in northwestern Iran. Aside from his brother Zavareh, the most prominent members of the company were Tous, Gudarz, Geav, Gorgin, and Gorazeh.

After several days of merrymaking, Geav guzzled a goblet of wine and said to the hero: "The hunting grounds across the Touranian border are teaming with game. What do you say we take our hounds, falcons, and cheetahs and shoot ourselves a few deer and onagers?"

Rostam thought it was a capital idea. "Let's do it," he said. "We'll wipe Afrasiab's hunting grounds clean of game!" The following day the Iranian knights galloped through the lands stretching from River Shahd to the plain of Sarakhs, looking for victims. Lions fled, and birds flew from the wild hunters who had invaded their realm. The knights hunted in this manner for a week without a moment's respite. Between kills, they laughed, ate, and drank.

"Afrasiab must have heard of our poaching by now," Rostam said on the eighth day. "He's sure to send an army after us. Let's post a sentry to watch the horizon." Gorazeh, from the Gudarz clan, volunteered for the task while the others went on with their hunting and feasting.

Afrasiab had indeed heard of the encroachment, but he considered it more of an opportunity than a border violation. This could be his chance to kill the seven most prominent knights of Iran and pave the way to future victories over his old rival kingdom to the southwest. He quickly raised an army of thirty thousand warriors and set off in the direction of the Iranian camp within his borders. They moved stealthily, choosing desert plains instead of trodden roads.

When Gorazeh spotted the Touranian army, he rushed to Rostam and advised him to call off the feast. There was a large plume of dust indicating an approaching army, and he had seen the standard of the Touranian king Afrasiab through the cloud of dust raised by the army of Touran. Rostam laughed heartily. "There's no need to fear that dust puff or the king of the Turks," he said, holding up his goblet. "He can't have more than a hundred thousand warriors, and there are enough knights here to take care of them all. I don't even need the knights. I can vanquish them all riding Rakhsh. Come and drink another cup of this Babylonian wine."

The knights all suited up for battle, refusing Rostam's bid to continue drinking. A battle was afoot, and they knew they could not keep up with the hero in drinking bouts. Rostam drained his cup to Zavareh's health, then the brothers kissed the ground in preparation for combat. Rostam wore his singlet, armor, and leopard skin surcoat, and led his six companions on his steed. They moved in unison as one body. Afrasiab was impressed by the show of the shining Iranian knights. He hung back at the heart of the army, encouraging his comrades to confront the seven Iranian knights. But they fell one after another in single combat. Afrasiab turned to Piran, his trusted viceroy and advisor. "Our paladins are no match for these roaring lions," he said. "You are the most famous of our knights. Go and fight them. I pledge to give you the Iranian kingdom if you win this battle, for without these men, Iran would be lost."

Having received his marching orders, Piran led his ten thousand crack troops in a broad attack against the brave seven. Rostam readily destroyed two-thirds of Piran's army and was busy dispatching the rest. Afrasiab then called upon Kalkus, a knight who was always bragging about how he could vanquish such Iranian knights as Geav and Rostam. He kissed the ground in front of Afrasiab and launched a fresh attack riding his black horse ahead of his one thousand strong, lance-bearing soldiers. It was his dream to kill Rostam and win everlasting glory. And he thought his goal was within reach when he engaged Zavareh, thinking he was Rostam. The two fought valiantly until their lances and swords broke. But Kalkus was the victor of the battle of maces when he unhorsed his opponent with a powerful blow. He had joyfully dismounted to behead his enemy when he heard a roar that scared him out of his skin. Rostam had come to the aid of his brother. Zavareh slinked away as Rostam skewered the hapless Kalkus by his lance and threw his body in front of his troops. Panic ensued and Kalkus's men fled, followed by the rest of the Touranian army. Rostam tried to capture Afrasiab in his lariat, but the adroit king slipped off the noose and escaped with his life.

The Iranians did not bother to strip the dead of their armor and weapons. Instead, they gathered the richly caparisoned Touranian horses that had lost their masters and returned to the hunting ground. Then the brave seven wrote a letter to their king appraising him of their adventure and the stunning victory they had won. The only casualty was that Zavareh had been knocked off his horse but had not suffered an injury. They spent another two weeks in the same spot before returning to the royal court.

We stay at this worldly lodge for three or five days
Some win at its betting tables and others lose
And then, we all have to leave the lodge; no one stays.

CHAPTER 6

A Tragedy of Errors: Rostam and Sohrab

When a green orange is torn off the branch
And falls to the ground, never ripening
To shine at its own corner of the ranch,

Or when a young boy's life is snuffed
Before he could grow into a young man,
What do you call this without being rebuffed?

If you claim its justice, then explain what
Example you would offer for injustice.
Such sophistry is surely easy to rebut.

THE CHAMPION OF THE WORLD FALLS IN LOVE

Rostam packed his quiver full of arrows one day and went hunting on the border of Touran. Soon he had a spitted onager roasting on a great fire, and Rakhsh was happily grazing in the fields. While he slept, sated, a band of horse thieves invaded his camp, and he woke to find that his steed had vanished. It was considered a disgrace for a knight to allow his horse to be stolen.

Holding his empty saddle, Rostam tracked Rakhsh until his hoofprints faded near the city of Samangan, within the borders of Touran. The local king, who had heard that the great knight of Iran was in his realm to look for his horse, came out on foot to welcome him. A prominent stallion like Rakhsh would not remain hidden for long, the king said to comfort the hero, before inviting him into his palace for a night of rest. Rostam accepted the invitation, as there was nothing to be done about his predicament that evening. After the festivities, when Rostam had drunk his fill of wine, he was led away to his quarters, where a fragrant bed awaited him.

One watch of the night had elapsed, and Venus had completed its pass over the vault of the heavens when Rostam was wakened by soft whispers. He opened his eyes to the delicate beauty of a tall girl standing at his bedside, and an attendant carrying a perfumed candle. Instantly captivated, the hero stammered, "What is your name, and what do you want from me?"

"I'm Tahmineh," said the girl. "I'm the daughter of the king of Samangan. No one else has ever seen my beauty, nor will anyone see it after tonight. I have heard the legends of your heroic deeds and bitten my lips in longing. Now I stand before you, having traded reason for desire. I want to be the mother of your son."

Charmed, Rostam opened his arms, and they spent the long, dark night in the glow of their passion. At dawn, he gave her an armband.

"If our child is a daughter," he said, "she should tie this in her braids as an amulet of good fortune. But if we have a son, suffer him to wear it on his arm as a sign of his father."

In the morning, the local king greeted the hero with the excellent news that Rakhsh had been found. Happy to be reunited with his loyal companion, Rostam quickly saddled his steed and said farewell to the king of Samangan. Tahmineh watched him depart with tears in her eyes. When Rostam disappeared over the horizon, she returned to her chambers with an aching heart.

COMING OF AGE

After nine months, a son, bright as the full moon, was born to Tahmineh. She named him Sohrab. The infant had Rostam's large frame but resembled Saum in appearance. At one month, he was bigger than a one-year-old child. He continued to grow quickly, and came to excel at polo and hunting. At ten, no one could match him in wrestling. Aware that he was different than his friends, the boy went to his mother. "What should I say when I'm asked about my father?" he demanded. "Who is he? Tell me the truth."

"Don't be harsh with me," Tahmineh replied. "You should be proud.

You are the son of the gallant Rostam, who descended from the illustrious Zaul, the son of Saum, the son of Narimon. Hold your head higher than the clouds. You are from an exalted lineage."

She showed Sohrab a letter his father had written and three gold-encrusted rubies he had sent along. The boy was pleased to learn of his noble pedigree, but Tahmineh had two requests for her son. First and foremost, he had to hide the secret of his paternity from Afrasiab, the king of Touran. Being known as the son of an Iranian knight would expose him to mortal danger. He also would have to keep his precocious maturity from his father. Tahmineh feared that if Rostam knew that his son had surpassed his peers in size and strength, he would take him away for heroic adventures and break her heart. Sohrab granted the first wish but thought it was absurd to hide away from his own father.

So, the ambitious Sohrab started to chart his plans. He would raise an army of Touranian warriors, wrest the crown from Kay-Kavous, and bestow it upon his father. Then he would throw Afrasiab off his throne and unite the two countries. Father and son were destined to rule the united kingdoms of Iran and Touran, he mused, and Sohrab and Rostam should be the kings of Touran and Iran. Why would the stars sparkle in the sky while the sun and the moon dominate the heavens? Tahmineh consented to the plan on the condition that he take along her brother, Sohrab's uncle Zende-Razm. He had met Rostam and could point him out to his nephew. With this, Sohrab announced his plans for an invasion of Iran, and gathered his army.

Afrasiab's informers had learned of the famous Sohrab's noble lineage, and of his plans to invade Iran. As the king of Touran after the passing of Pashang, Afrasiab was delighted by this intelligence. With some deceitful planning, he could use Sohrab as an instrument of eliminating Rostam. Afrasiab quickly dispatched his trusted knight Houman with an auxiliary army of twelve thousand warriors to Samangan to assist Sohrab in his plan to invade Iran.

Houman carried the king's message of support along with his army to Sohrab. But the general's main task was to misdirect Sohrab and prevent him from identifying his father on the battlefield. This way, the son would challenge his father to a duel and kill him. Thereafter it would be easy to dispose of Sohrab by some plot.

Sohrab was emboldened at the approach of the forces of Afrasiab. And he was delighted to read the king's letter, which promised him the crown of Iran if he was successful in his conquest. Sohrab marched his vastly augmented forces toward Iran until they came to the first Iranian outpost, the White Fortress. Hojir, the guardian of the fortress, and one of the sons of the Iranian knight Gudarz, rode out of the castle to confront the young commander who was leading the forces of Touran.

BATTLES AT THE WHITE FORTRESS

In front of the fortress, the opponents taunted each other. Sohrab harangued Hojir for having come to the arena alone and expressed sympathy for his poor mother, who would mourn him that night. Hojir retorted that the Touranian who could defeat him in battle was not born yet and that he looked forward to sending the impertinent young Touranian's severed head as a trophy to King Kay-Kavous. But when the combat got underway, Hojir was knocked off his horse by a single thrust of his foe's lance. Sohrab dismounted to sever his head, but Hojir asked for mercy. His plea was granted, and soon the defender of the fortress was being pushed toward the enemy ranks with tied hands.

Those who watched from the ramparts of the White Fortress were appalled by the duel's quick and rather shameful course. But none was more dismayed by the scandal of Hojir's easy defeat than Gordafarid, the daughter of the lord of the fortress, Gazhdaham. She was a formidable equestrian and worthy warrior in her own right. Enraged, she hastily donned a coat of chainmail, hid her long, flowing hair under a helmet, and rode out of the castle like a lioness. Upon reaching the enemy's ranks, she called on the warriors of Touran to come out and defend their honor.

"Another victim walks into the hunter's trap," Sohrab said, chuckling to himself. But as he put on his helmet, Gordafarid showered him with a torrent of arrows. Only fear of disgrace compelled the young hero forward, holding his shield against the barrage. When he came closer, Gordafarid slung her bow on her shoulder, directed her horse to stand on its hind legs and thrust her lance at her opponent. Sohrab turned aside to evade the lance and simultaneously hit the disguised warrior with his own lance, causing her chainmail armor to come unfastened. She broke the lance with her sword and turned to flee, but the agile foe gave chase and lifted her helmet to reveal a cascade of lovely hair.

Sohrab was astounded. He caught her in his noose and said: "Why would a creature like you come to the battlefield? And now that I've got you, don't even dream of escaping my noose. I've never trapped a game comelier than you. So, give up your struggle—I will never let you go."

Gordafarid knew she could not escape her enemy but by deception. So, she turned her exquisite face to her opponent and softly suggested they keep her identity a secret; Sohrab would be disgraced if his peers realized that he had been fighting a woman. "Besides," she said, "I'm at your mercy, and if you let me go, I will open the gates of the White Fortress to you."

Gordafarid allowed her hair to fall onto her face and gazed at Sohrab with the soulful eyes of a captured doe as she spoke. Enamored by her beauty, the young man boasted that he would not need her help to conquer the castle. Pointing disdainfully at the fortress, he said he could bring down the puny edifice on his own. Gordafarid used this moment of distraction to loosen the noose that bound her. Having freed herself, she turned and galloped back toward the castle gates, Sohrab chasing closely behind. Gazhdaham, alert to his daughter's actions, quickly opened the gates and slammed them behind her before Sohrab could get through. Soon the beguiling warrior appeared on the ramparts and taunted her opponent.

"It's time for you to go home, my dear commander," she called down. "Don't regret losing me, for fate did not decree that you find a companion in Iran. If you stay here, the news will reach our king, and he will dispatch Rostam. It would be a pity for him to defeat your army and kill a young man like you."

Sohrab turned around angrily and laid waste to the areas near the fortress on his way to his camp. That night Gazhdaham prepared to abandon the castle. But first, he dispatched a letter to King Kay-Kavous, apprising him of the significant threat the young Touranian warrior posed to Iran. He wrote that an extraordinary young man named Sohrab, who resembled the noble Saum, had come forth against the White Fortress. He had easily trounced Hojir in battle and taken him captive. The warrior was sure to breach the fortress walls, so they were forced to abscond under the cover of night.

The following day Sohrab took over the deserted castle, where he set up camp and waited for the arrival of the armies of Iran.

THE RAGE OF THE KING

Gazhdaham's letter caused a great deal of anxiety at court. Kay-Kavous was beset by fear when he considered what could happen if this formidable new adversary led the forces of Touran. He called a council of the knights, and they agreed that Rostam should lead the charge against this new menace.

The king dispatched Geav to fetch Rostam from Zabol, insisting that he be swift in this mission and not linger in Zabol for more than one night. Geav carried a letter from the king that began by extolling Rostam for his service in the Mauzandaran and Hamauvaran campaigns. It concluded by stating that the hero's services were needed to cope with the new threat on the borders of Touran.

Rostam read the letter and put it aside dismissively. Scorning the speculations about the appearance of a new warrior with the qualities of Saum in Touran, he said: "Well, I doubt any Touranian would resemble my noble grandfather. I have a son with the princess of Samangan. He might resemble Saum one day, but his mother wrote recently. He is still a child. Now, let us drink to the sound of these pleasant singers. In due time we will investigate this matter."

Rostam and Geav lingered in Zabol, drinking and carousing before returning to court. Four days later, they finally set off. Upon their arrival at the royal palace, the fuming king ordered Geav to take Rostam out to the gallows and hang him for insubordination. Geav was too stunned to move. Kay-Kavous took this as defiance and ordered Tous to hang them both. This command was even more absurd.

"Muzzle your wrath, Kavous," roared Rostam. "You don't deserve to be king. All your deeds have been evil, one worse than the next. You say you want to hang me. Why don't you hang Sohrab if you are so quick to anger?"

Tous rose not to execute Kavous's command but to lead Rostam out of the court to calm him. But Rostam sent him flying with one blow of his arm, and stomped out. He mounted Rakhsh and said to those who had followed him: "I am the kingmaker of this dynasty. Kavous is nothing to me. Why should someone like Tous dare lay hands on me? The earth is my slave; this horse is my throne; this mace is my royal staff, and this war helmet is my crown. I light up the dark night with my blade. The sword and the lance are my confederates. I am no one's slave and obey only God. Let Sohrab come and lay waste to Iran. It will be none of my concern. Contrive a way to save yourselves, for I have left you. I am taking wing like an eagle high above this land."

With these words, Rostam brought Rakhsh to a gallop and disappeared into the horizon. The noblemen and the knights were dismayed. They advised that old Gudarz should speak to the king. He reminded Kay-Kavous of the services Rostam had rendered, how he had twice rescued them all from captivity. Did such a hero deserve to hang in ignominy? Kay-Kavous was contrite.

"You are right," said the king. "Words of wisdom issue from old lips. A king must be impervious to anger. Go talk to Rostam and wash his heart of the poison of my words."

Gudarz immediately went in pursuit of Rostam. Upon reaching the hero, he praised him and said what was common knowledge among the knights: that Kavous was reckless and impetuous. He was notably devoid of reason when he was overcome by rage. Rostam declared that he had had his fill of the foolish king. He had no fear of Kavous. Nor did he need him in any way. "True," Gudarz agreed, "but Iranians need you. Why should they be deprived of your help for the folly of their king? Besides, leaving the battle while Iran is under attack would leave the impression that you are afraid of this new Touranian warrior."

This last remark seemed to clinch the matter. When Rostam returned to court, Kay-Kavous rose and apologized for his conduct. "You know that I am quick to anger. This is a flaw in my God-given nature. I was so distraught over this young adversary that I lost my temper. If you have been offended by my outburst, it is my duty to beg your pardon."

Rostam accepted the apology and pledged his submission to his sovereign. Kay-Kavous rejoiced and called for a lavish feast. The next morning, he opened the treasure houses and ordered his knights to prepare the army for departure.

THE GREAT CONFRONTATION

Geav and Tous, who were charged with organizing the troops, brought a hundred thousand cavalrymen to the royal camp. The earth turned ebony, and the sky grew darker than lapis lazuli. The massive army marched toward the White Fortress to the beat of battle drums fastened to the backs of war elephants. Golden shields and silver lances glittered in a dark cloud of dust that enveloped the immense procession. The news reached the White Fortress that an army of vast proportions had appeared in the distance. The commanders of Touran ascended to the ramparts to view the approaching phalanxes of the army of Iran. Sohrab turned to Houman and swept the horizon with the curve of his hand. "Don't be afraid," he said, "no one out there can match me on the battlefield. There are many weapons and many hands. But I don't see any heads daring to rise above the crowd. I will vanquish this army in the name of Afrasiab." To show his lack of concern, he called for a chalice of wine to celebrate the coming war.

When night fell, Rostam asked Kay-Kavous's permission to go on a scouting mission. He wanted to catch a glimpse of the young warrior who had struck such fear in the hearts of the Iranians. The hero wore a disguise and slipped into the occupied fortress with the skill of a lion tracking a deer. He followed the sounds of a banquet and arrived at a hall where

Sohrab was sitting on a throne, flanked by Houman and his maternal uncle, Zande Razm.

Rostam was amazed by the young hero's enormous size. Radiating the vigor of youth and endowed with a solid and muscular frame, the field marshal appeared to fill the throne. One hundred warriors and fifty attendants surrounded him. As Rostam watched this scene, Zende-Razm got up for what appeared to be an important errand. "Who goes there?" Zende-Razm suddenly demanded from behind Rostam, having spied him in the shadows. "Come out and show your face!"

Rostam rushed the man and struck him a mortal blow. Then he quickly left the fortress and slinked back to the Iranian side. He told King Kay-Kavous that the Touranian hero was superior in stature and charm to those around him—and to anyone on the Iranian side.

Back at the White Fortress, the body of Zende-Razm had been found. Sohrab terminated the festivities, appointed sentries to guard all entrances, and swore an oath to avenge the death of his uncle.

The next day, as the sun fastened its noose on the high wheel of the heavens and began its ascent, the young commander of the Touranian army donned his armor, climbed to the roof of the fortress, and looked out over the massive Persian army that filled the horizon. Without his uncle to point out Rostam, he would have to rely on the captive Hojir. Sohrab threatened dire consequences for lies before ordering Hojir to identify the Iranian standards. He started his report: "The mark of an elephant belongs to Tous. An embroidered lion on a flag signifies Gudarz. The likeness of a wolf appears on Geav's standard."

Sohrab pointed at the center of the camp and asked, "But who is the mammoth warrior at the heart of the army flying a flag with the image of a dragon? Is that Rostam?"

Hojir was surprised at his captor's accurate guess. But he also feared that Sohrab would challenge Rostam to a duel and kill him. If this happened, the Iranian defeat would be inevitable. This would also bring about eternal shame, since no one would be strong enough to avenge Rostam. What would be the value of life after Iran was humiliated—or his father, Gurdarz, and his entire clan were killed? Hojir resolved to lie. "No, that's not Rostam," he said. "The Champion of the World is in Zabol this time of year attending local festivities. The hero you have pointed out must be a Chinese mercenary. I can't remember his name."

Sohrab did not believe him. It was unlikely that Rostam would sit out such an important campaign. He made threats and then tempted his captive with untold riches if he would point out the standard of the man he was seeking. Hojir replied: "If I don't tell you that hero's name, it is because I don't know it. Besides, why would you want to challenge Rostam? Don't you know that only those with a death wish go against him? Don't you know that he has the strength of a hundred men and can slay an elephant just as easily as he kills a man?"

Sohrab was sickened by Hojir's mendacity and cowardice. "What a shame it is for a great knight like Gudarz to have sired an unworthy son like you! You lack the might to fight and the wisdom to think. Nor have you the right to compare anyone's strength to mine after what you have suffered at my hand."

When Hojir repeated that Sohrab was no match for Rostam, he received a blow that knocked him off his feet. And yet, the young hero had come to believe Hojir's lies. He was disappointed that he would not encounter his father in the upcoming campaign. But he had to go on as he was obligated to avenge his uncle Zende-Razm.

FATHER FIGHTS HIS SON

Sporting a Chinese helmet, the impetuous Sohrab mounted his steed. With his feet firmly in the stirrups, he held a lance with a tempered tip and galloped through the fortress's gates toward the Iranian army. Haranguing Kay-Kavous, he roared: "What brings you to the battlefield, Kavous? And why have you tagged the royal title of "Kay" to your name? Last night I swore an oath to avenge Zende-Razm by impaling you on my lance. Is there one among your men who can stop me?"

There was silence in the ranks, as no one had ever seen such a fearsome fighter. Receiving no answer to his challenge, Sohrab charged the Iranian troops, reached the royal camp and cut the ropes of seventy tents. Kay-Kavous was scared. He sent Tous on an urgent mission to call Rostam to the front.

Upon receiving the summons, Rostam complained bitterly. "Other kings would occasionally call me to feasts and festivities. But Kavous summons me only to suffer the miseries of war."

Rostam issued orders for his steed to be prepared for war. But as he watched from his tent, he saw that the stable hands did not discharge the menial tasks of caparisoning his horse. Rakhsh was being prepared by such high-ranking knights as Tous and Gorgin, hurrying each other and fussing over every detail. This unsettled the hero. "This is the doing of the devil," he murmured. "Why should the fate of Iran revolve around one person?"

Rostam tightened his belt, climbed onto Rakhsh and galloped toward the frontlines. He could make out Sohrab's horned helmet in the distance, its plumage fluttering in the wind like a lion's mane. He had to admit that the warrior cut a mighty figure reminiscent of the noble Saum.

Rostam approached his opponent and proposed that they choose the ground for their combat. Sohrab agreed. But as they headed to the appointed dueling place, the young warrior mocked his Iranian foe: "Impressive as you may have been in your prime, you no longer appear as a worthy opponent. Are you sure you want to take me on?"

"The young should be modest in their speech," Rostam shot back. "The mountains, the seven seas, and the stars above bear witness to how I have crushed the armies of Touran."

"In that case, I have a question and expect an honest answer. Are you Rostam, the son of Zaul, the son of the legendary Saum?"

"I am not Rostam," he claimed. "I'm a subordinate without a pedigree."

Sohrab's bright day turned into a black night. He was not destined to find his father after all. His grand plans to unite Iran and Touran had come to naught.

The two warriors fought with lances until they broke, with Indian swords until they shattered, and with maces until they tired. The barding was torn from their horses, and the parched warriors riding them were soaked in sweat, dust, and blood. In utter exhaustion, father and son separated to regain their strength.

This is a capricious world that makes and breaks
Love and common sense forsook them both
Neither one stopped to correct his mistakes.

Fish, onager, and beasts of burden in their mangers
Know their own. But greed so blinded the filial pair
That they faced each other as utter strangers.

Tired of the stalemate, Rostam attacked the troops of Touran, causing disorder in the ranks. Houman stood his ground with orders not to move before Sohrab's battle with Rostam was complete. The young Touranian retaliated by tearing into the heart of the Iranian lines with his mace. Tous was injured, and great knights fled behind a buffer of the infantry. Rostam looked back and saw that his powerful foe was nearing Kay-Kavous's standard. Fearing for the king's life, Rostam called out: "Why are you fighting the Iranians, you bloodthirsty wolf!"

"You tore into the ranks of Touran first, attacking those who were not a party to our duel!

"The sun is setting, and it's getting late," huffed Rostam. "You've brilliantly demonstrated your skills with a blade. This example will live forever. Let us rest now and see what God decrees tomorrow."

THE LAST DAY

With these words, they parted for their own camps. Rostam went to Kay-Kavous with a heavy heart and reported his difficult battle: "This warrior is strong. I have never failed to lift an opponent off his horse. But this man sits like a mountain of granite upon that saddle. We have agreed to wrestle tomorrow, but I am not confident I will win."

The king prostrated himself to God and asked for divine intervention.

Rostam went to his brother, Zavareh, and shared his forebodings, adding: "Tomorrow, follow me to the front, carrying my standard. If I am victorious, I will not linger on the battlefield, but if I am defeated, keep your composure. Do not try to avenge me. Go back to Zabol and console our mother. In this life, I have killed my share of men, demons, and beasts. Death comes for all of us sooner or later. Advise our father, Zaul, that he should continue to obey the royal house of Kay-Kavous."

Sohrab had a more festive night, as he had dominated the battle. But in the morning, he shared his misgivings with Houman. "This lion who fights me has all the characteristics of Rostam, described by my mother," he said. "He is as strong as I am. I am mysteriously drawn to him, and although he denies it, I have a strange feeling that he is my father, that I ought not to fight him."

Houman misled Sohrab, agreeing that the warrior and his horse were indeed reminiscent of Rostam and Rakhsh, whom he had encountered in previous battles. But he was convinced that the horse was not, in fact, Rakhsh, as the beast lacked the stamina of the famous steed.

Although it had been thrice confirmed that his opponent was not his father, Sohrab was still not persuaded. Grave misgivings had gnawed at him throughout the night, and in the morning as he put on his armor. Later that day, he once more demanded that his opponent identify himself, adding: "It's my hope that you die in bed, old man. I don't want you to meet your end on this battlefield. Let's sit down together and drink wine, leaving the fighting to others. My heart calls for your companionship, and I have a sense of shame in fighting you. Maybe you can tell me about your knightly lineage."

Rostam scoffed at the idea, which he considered frivolous. He said they had better begin the contest by wrestling.

The two warriors dismounted and began an hours-long hand-to-hand combat. Finally, at a stalemate, Sohrab tackled Rostam into the dust like a lion catching its prey. As he sat on his opponent's chest to sever his head, Rostam spoke deceitfully: "But this is not the custom of Iranians. Among us, the loser of the first round always gets a second chance."

Sohrab relented and walked away. Confident that he would always have the upper hand, the young man went on a leisurely deer hunt in the nearby thicket. Houman, who had been monitoring the wrestling match, was dismayed that Sohrab was so easily deceived, and reprimanded him after for being so naïve.

Rostam used his respite to take a much-needed rest. He bathed in a nearby stream and asked God to give him victory. When he returned for the second round, he found Sohrab wielding his lariat to hunt. Rostam was amazed by the vigor and confidence of the young man who had gone searching for deer in the middle of their deadly combat. The haughty Touranian cast an indifferent look at his opponent and said: "I see that the game that barely escaped the talons of the lion has come back to his lair."

They tethered their horses and started the second round of wrestling. But fortune had deserted Sohrab. It was as if the heavens were holding him back. After a short while, he was brought down by Rostam. Knowing that his opponent would not stay down for long, Rostam acted decisively. He drew his dagger and deeply slashed his young opponent's side.

Sohrab sighed, realizing the wound he had received was mortal. "My peers are still playing in the sand as I lie here dying on the battlefield," he said, panting. "I don't blame your treachery, for I've been slain by my own fate. You will not escape the hand of destiny either. Soon my father, Rostam, will find you and avenge my death, even if you turn into a fish and hide in the sea, even if you become a star and escape to the heavens."

Rostam's head swam, and the world darkened in front of his eyes. After a few moments, he regained his composure and realized the enormity of the disaster that was engulfing him. He asked his victim if he had a sign to prove that he was Rostam's son. Sohrab said: "So, you are my father, after all. Why did you lie to me? Why did your parental tenderness desert you when I was pleading to learn your real name? Here, look at the badge that my mother placed on my arm. Little did she know that you would see it only after you killed me."

When Rostam saw the badge, he pulled his hair in anguish and wallowed in the dirt. Sohrab said that it was too late for tears. He had only one wish: that Iranians do not attack the army of Touran after his death: "This war was my idea, and the defeat is mine alone." Rostam agreed that enough innocent blood had been spilled for one day. He then walked back to the Iranian side. His return meant that he had survived the duel, but his state was not that of the victor. Rostam told the stunned knights what had happened and asked them to respect Sohrab's wish. Then he rode back to his dying son.

Tous, his brother Gostahm, and Gudarz followed behind Rostam. They consoled and even prevented him from committing suicide in that moment of utter desolation. Rostam remembered that Kay-Kavous had a magical potion, a panacea that could save his son. He charged Gudarz to plead with the king for the miraculous remedy he had in his possession. "Tell the king that I have grievously wounded my son in battle," he ordered. "If I have ever rendered him a service, let him take pity on me now and send along the elixir of life. If Sohrab gets well, he too will serve the king, as I have done for all these decades."

But the king had not forgotten Rostam's harsh words before the conflict, when he had accused him of incompetence. He also remembered his leaving his court in defiance. What would such an arrogant knight be capable of if he were to join forces with someone like Sohrab? Who could resist the combined forces of father and son? Thus, Kay-Kavous refused Gudarz the panacea. Gudarz rushed back to Rostam with these words: "Kay-Kavous is a tree hung with bitter fruit. He withholds the magical potion. Rush to him yourself if you want to change his mind."

Rostam prepared a bed for his wounded son, appointed an attendant to care for him, and set off on the road to the king's pavilion. He had not gone far when someone came from behind to tell him that Sohrab was dead. The bereaved father sighed and closed his eyes. He dismounted, wallowed in the dirt, and wailed:

"Who has suffered this misfortune before me? What kind of father kills his own son? How will I plead my case when Zaul and Rudabeh denounce me? The knights of Iran will curse Saum's progeny for this monstrous act. And how can I tell the fair Tahmineh that I have killed our innocent son? Who could know that this precocious child would so quickly grow into such a formidable warrior?"

Rostam ordered Sohrab's body to be adorned in kingly brocade and placed in a casket. Then he went to his encampment and set fire to it. The luxurious tent and its golden, silk-covered throne burned to the ground as he stood there and decried his fate for its malice. The knights of Iran kept him company. When Kay-Kavous came to extend his condolences, the knight conveyed the only wish of his son that there should be no war against the Touranians. The king reluctantly agreed.

In tattered clothes, Rostam led Sohrab's funeral cortege back to Zabol. A great crowd of mourners had gathered at the gates, where Zaul dismounted and said, "The world will never see a young man like this."

Rostam opened the casket and showed his father the face of the grandson he had never met. Everyone could see that Sohrab bore an uncanny resemblance to the noble founder of their clan. They all wept. The young scion was entombed in a magnificent crypt.

Tahmineh heard of the death of her son and died of sadness in less than a year.

Sohrab's tale brings tears to the eyes
One cannot help being angry at Rostam
Who was reckless and most unwise.

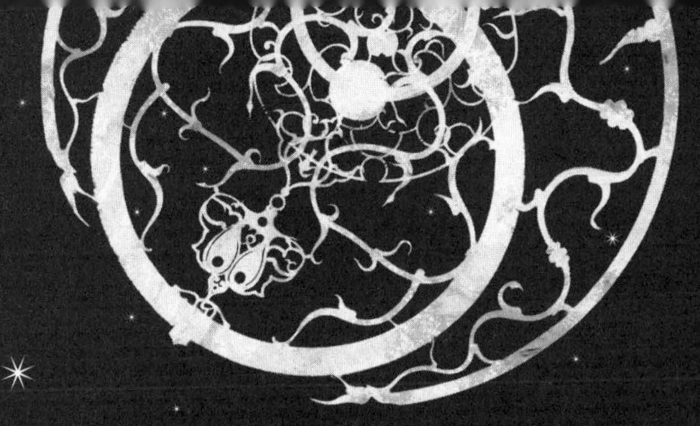

CHAPTER 7

The Prince of Sorrows: Siavosh

I'm versifying these ancient tales at the age
Of fifty-eight for I'm sure they'll be one day read
With great care and attention, page by page.

THE MAIDEN OF THE WOODS

At the crowing of the cock one morning, Tous, King Nowzar's son, led a hunting expedition of the Iranian knights to the plains of Daghuy, near the border of Touran. Using hunting cheetahs and falcons, the group spread out across the lush grounds on their horses. Tous and Geav rode off into a dense thicket in pursuit of wild boar. Instead of the game they were chasing, however, they came upon a radiant girl hiding among the bushes.

Tous asked the maiden to explain how she had come to be alone in such a wild place. The girl told them she was a Touranian princess of the house of Garsivaz—the brother of the Touranian king, Afrasiab. Her father had come home drunk from a feast the previous night and had pulled a dagger on her. She had no choice but to run for her life. Having lost her horse to exhaustion and her jewels to a band of thieves, she sought refuge in the thicket.

To Geav and Tous, the beautiful maiden was not a princess in need of care but just a slave girl, an object of desire to be possessed. When they could not settle the matter of her ownership, they returned to the capital and took up their dispute with their king. Kay-Kavous's self-serving advice was that the worthy knights would do well to busy themselves with the stories of their hunt and leave the lovely catch of the day in the care of His Majesty. "Would you prefer to be a king's consort or a knight's slave?" he asked the girl. The matter was settled to the king's satisfaction.

The following day the maiden was in the king's seraglio reclining on a sumptuous seat decorated in yellow silk and studded with rubies, lapis lazuli, and turquoise. In due time she grew heavy with child. But she did not survive the birth of her son, who was more beautiful than an idol that is worthy of worship. The king was saddened by the death of his consort but rejoiced at the sight of his son, whom he called Siavosh, meaning rider of a black stallion. Royal astrologers cast his horoscope but found little happiness in the stars of the newborn, only that the boy was expected to sire a magnificent king. Kay-Kavous was disheartened with the prediction but could do little but entrust his son to divine protection.

A few years had passed since Rostam had retired to Zabol after the tragic death of his son. He thought it was about time he paid his respects at the royal court. It was during this visit that he saw Siavosh for the first time.

Upon seeing the marvelous child, Rostam expressed a desire to take him to Zabol and see to his proper education. The king happily delegated the training of the crown prince to his able knight, and thus his education started in earnest. Rostam treated his young ward like his son, caring for his every want and desire. Under his watchful eye, Siavosh mastered the arts of riding, combat, and archery, as well as the ways of justice and the finer points of decorum. At the completion of his education, the adolescent prince expressed a desire to return to the capital and display his skills at his father's palace.

Rostam prepared a grand celebration, and the city of Zabol was decorated for the prince's departure. People lined the streets, and a mixture of gold coins and rare fragrances such as ambergris and musk rained on them from atop the walls and domes of the city. Well-groomed horses marched in the parade to the rhythmic beat of the musicians. Siavosh rode out with Rostam, sad to leave his teacher but thrilled at the prospect of being reunited with his father. The Persian court welcomed their impressive prince with lavish festivities that lasted a whole week.

For the next seven years, Siavosh busied himself with refining and perfecting the royal and martial arts he had learned in Zabol. He tried his best to be a good son and a perfect crown prince.

THE QUEEN'S GAMBIT

Unbeknownst to the prince, Queen Sudabeh had developed a secret admiration for him as he grew into a handsome young man. Her heart melted at his sight, and she felt a sweet melancholy in his presence.

One day Siavosh received a message from the queen indicating that a visit to her private chambers would be welcomed. He judged this an inappropriate invitation and sent word that he was not in the habit of frequenting the women's quarters. Sudabeh tried another approach, telling the king that the prince had sisters in the harem who longed to see their gallant brother. The king thought that this was a grand idea and suggested it to his son. But he demurred, contending that visiting the harem would be a waste when his time could be more profitably spent in the company of learned men and great warriors. The king praised his son's good judgment but did not relent on the idea of his stepmother's invitation. The prince eventually gave in despite his misgivings.

The king issued orders for a glorious welcome for his son at the seraglio on the appointed day. The doors opened, and the young prince was ushered in, across a spread of Chinese silk lined with musk, saffron, and wine bowls. Handfuls of gold coins, agate, and lapis lazuli were thrown at his feet. Sudabeh, alluring as a garden of paradise, descended from her bejeweled dais, and embraced the prince, kissing his eyes and face. Siavosh sensed that there was no innocence in that lingering embrace. He cut short his discourse with the queen and walked to where his sisters were sitting. He spoke to them for a spell and left.

Siavosh went to the king and pronounced that His Majesty's good fortune had exceeded that of the glorious kings of yore. Kay-Kavous was pleased by these words of praise. The prince hoped that he had done enough to appease his father, and that it would be the end of Sudabeh's invitations.

Later that night, the queen visited Kay-Kavous's chambers, extolling the virtues of the crown prince, and proposing to arrange his marriage to her daughter. The king was delighted by this idea, recalling that the royal astrologers had prophesied that a magnificent king would be born to Siavosh.

The young prince agreed to wed anyone his father chose but begged to be excused from another visit to the queen's chambers. The king laughed at the awkwardness of his son and insisted that Sudabeh was like a mother to him and that her opinion was crucial in his marriage. Kay-Kavous was confident that he was offering Siavosh sound advice.

False confidence leads a foolish man to slaughter
He thinks he's stepping on solid ground, but it turns out to be
A layer of straw floating on a puddle of water.

The prince had no choice but to smile and bow his head in acquiescence as a great storm raged inside him. He returned to the queen's quarters, where he was presented with a bevy of nubile virgins, including the queen's chosen daughter. Although they were shy, none of the girls could take their eyes off the young prince. Then the queen dismissed them, turned to Siavosh, and said: "Stop hiding your thoughts. What is your pleasure? As you see, those who behold your angelic face can't resist you. Which one of these beautiful girls is worthy of your companionship?"

Siavosh could not find the words to speak. During this moment of pause, Sudabeh threw off her veil. "I understand your hesitation," she said. "Why would anyone look at the moon when the sun is high in the sky? Why would you choose another when I stand before you in all my splendor? Pledge your loyalty to me, and I will choose a pretty bride for you. But I will be the one to love you and sate your desires. And when the king passes from this world, you will become my protector. You will love me and spoil me just as he has. Look at me: I am yours, body and soul."

With these words, Sudabeh approached the handsome prince, shamelessly held his head, and kissed him with parted lips. Siavosh flushed like a rose. With tears in his eyes, he prayed for strength against evil temptations. He would never betray his father. But he also knew that his stepmother would not relent. "You are as exquisite as the moon in the sky," he said, trying to placate her. "You are unmatched in the entire world. Only a king deserves to be your companion. It's honor enough for me to wed your daughter. Ask the king for her hand on my behalf, and I pledge not to divulge what transpired between us today. You are the queen, and I see you as my dear mother."

The prince hurried out in confusion. Assiduously following her plans, the queen went to the king with the good tidings that the crown prince had chosen her daughter as his future wife. The king opened his treasure house and piled up a heap of gifts for the wedding. Sudabeh watched on, absorbed in reveries of terrible vengeance if the young prince continued his defiance.

The next day the queen called for Siavosh and told him that the king had given him his daughter. "Two hundred elephants can hardly carry her trousseau," she said. "I, too, am giving you my daughter, so I will give you more gifts than the king has. Now, look at me and tell me what possible excuse you could have to turn your back on me. I have pined for you for seven painful years. My sun has been blotted out, and my days have been dark for long enough. Come and make me happy; revive me! But let me warn you: I will ruin this kingship for you if you scorn me. I will turn your father against you."

"May I never lose my head for a matter of the heart or be so dastardly as to betray my father," Siavosh replied in exasperation. "You are the queen, the sun upon the throne. You are above committing a sin like this."

Sudabeh screamed that he did not deserve her trust and wanted to defame her. Then she tore her clothes to shreds and clawed at her cheeks. The palace reverberated with the sound of her wailing. The king rushed to her chambers. But she continued to cry and pull at her hair, screaming that her stepson had lusted after her, and that his assault had to have injured her unborn child. The bewildered prince turned to his father, pleading with him not to believe the lies of his treacherous wife.

TRIAL BY FIRE

To ascertain the truth, the king sniffed his wife. He found that she was redolent of rosewater, musk, and wine but that there was no trace of these scents on his son. Siavosh had not touched Sudabeh. She was lying, and the king had no choice but to take his son's side.

Of course, she deserved the edge of the sword for her calumny, but the king thought of the dire consequence of executing the daughter of a neighboring king. Besides, how could he kill a woman who had been loyal to him and shared his prison cell at her father's castle? What would come of their children after the execution of their mother? Above all, how could he kill a woman he still loved? These thoughts assailed Kay-Kavous one after another. Instead of punishing Sudabeh, he advised his son to keep the matter to himself and try to forget the sordid affair altogether.

But the vengeful Sudabeh was not content with the peaceful resolution of the dispute. She knew a hoary sorceress who was having a difficult pregnancy. To win back the king's sympathy and corroborate her version of the events, the queen convinced the witch to end her pregnancy. Then she placed her twin fetuses in a golden basin on display and took to bed, feigning a miscarriage.

Suspicious of Sudabeh's claims, the king called on astrologers to determine the identity of the stillborn infants. Again, the definitive judgment was against the queen: far from being children of royal parents, the infants were the devil's spawn. Kay-Kavous considered the matter for a week and then broached it with his scheming consort. She refused to admit her guilt and insisted that Siavosh had suborned the astrologers. She bitterly wept and said: "There will be no love between us if you take the fate of your perished infants so lightly. This matter shall be decided at the divine tribunal after we die."

Kay-Kavous wept. Bewildered by the whole ordeal, the king turned to his high priests. They advised that the ultimate test of truthfulness was the trial by fire. The contenders had to go through the flames and emerge unscathed to uphold their claim. Sudabeh refused, arguing that the aborted fetuses were her evidence. Siavosh welcomed the occasion as a chance to prove his innocence once and for all. The king was reconciled that he would lose either his son or wife to the fire's judgment.

On the appointed day, a hundred caravans of red-haired camels brought firewood to the palace, and the servants piled the wood into two mountains, separated by a path that could accommodate four horsemen riding shoulder to shoulder. Siavosh appeared on his beloved black stallion Behzad and bowed in front of his father. According to custom, his white shirt was sprinkled with camphor to imply that he was clad in a shroud and was prepared to die. The king was ashamed that his favorite crown prince faced death over his bad decisions. But the prince comforted him, saying that this was his fate and that he was sure of vindication.

The crowds that had gathered to witness the event hailed the white-clad prince who galloped on a black horse toward the immense, scorching fire. A hush fell as the mouth of the inferno swallowed him. Sudabeh watched from her balcony, full of anxiety and hatred. She cursed and prayed that the prince would never emerge. Time seemed to stand still. People began to shed tears.

Suddenly Siavosh rode out of the blazing wall unharmed. His face was flushed, but there was not a speck of ash on his white shirt. A loud cheer went up from the crowd, and the city rejoiced. Again, Sudabeh tore her hair out and clawed her face. The king embraced his son and begged his pardon for doubting his honesty. Lavish festivities commenced, and the courtiers drank with the king and his son for three days.

On the fourth day, the king sat on his royal throne, holding his ox-headed mace as he prepared to mete out justice against his devious wife. He summoned Sudabeh and ordered her to put a stop to her lies. The queen confessed that Siavosh had told the truth and that she had earned her just deserts. She only begged the king to forgive her before she was put to death.

Kay-Kavous consulted with his advisers and announced their unanimous recommendation: Sudabeh was condemned to die. As soldiers entered to take her away, the king blanched. Realizing that he would be blamed for the execution, one way or another, Siavosh interceded with his father, asking him to forgive the queen. The king immediately granted this wish as if he had been waiting for an excuse to spare her. The prince kissed the throne and left the court as the queen's attendants cheered her for her narrow escape from the gallows.

As time passed, Sudabeh bewitched the king with her love despite her past treachery. Judging from his adoring gaze, Kay-Kavous had forgotten the entire affair. It was only a matter of time before she resumed her seduction of Siavosh.

THE VICTORIOUS PRINCE

Kay-Kavous was enjoying his new-found peace in the royal palace when Afrasiab, the king of Touran, sent a hundred thousand soldiers across the Oxus River to occupy the adjacent provinces of Iran. Kay-Kavous called his knights to the council and announced that he would lead the charge against the enemy. The royal advisers did not endorse this plan. Kay-Kavous had twice allowed himself to be taken captive, endangering the country's safety. The king asked his knights, "Well, which brave knight will rise to this worthy challenge?"

When no one spoke up, Siavosh stood and declared that he would expel the Touranian invaders. He was seeking the glories of victory, but he also wished to get away from the royal palace, rife as he found it with Sudabeh's deadly plots. The king embraced his brave son and praised him. Then he wrote Rostam, appointing him commander of the new campaign. The hero accepted the charge, as he had nurtured the crown prince and loved him like a son.

Twelve thousand shield-bearing infantry and as many Baluchi, Parsi, and Gilani cavalry gathered under the command of Siavosh. Five priests carried the Standard of Kaveh in front of the army. Kay-Kavous traveled one milestone of the journey and embraced his son at the moment of his departure. Father and son cried aloud as if they knew this would be their last embrace. From there, the young prince drove his army to the realm of Zabol and stayed for a month until the troops of Kabul and India converged with Rostam's army.

When all was ready, the forces of Iran marched to the city of Balkh, where they faced the army of the Touranian general and Afrasiab's brother, Garsivaz. What followed was a lengthy and intense campaign. Siavosh fought two pitched battles in three days against superior numbers and succeeded to defeat and rout the enemy. Thrilled by his first military success, he wrote Kay-Kavous about his decisive victory and asked for further instructions. The king took pride in the triumph of his son but advised caution. Chasing the enemy would risk dissipating the forces of Iran. The prince was commanded to sit tight and await another Touranian incursion, whereupon he could wipe them out.

Garsivaz redeployed his forces behind the safety of the Oxus River and rushed to Afrasiab's court. Wildly exaggerating the numbers of the Iranians, he tried to justify his defeat. Afrasiab shot a severe look at his mendacious brother and dismissed him with accusations of cowardice and incompetence. Then he called a thousand of his elite warriors to a feast where he shared his plans for a decisive counterattack. They ate and drank until sleep overcame them.

A TERRIFYING VISION

One watch of the night had elapsed when Afrasiab woke from a nightmare with a deafening scream. The attendants were startled, and Garsivaz rushed to the king's chamber. Interpreters were called, and Afrasiab related his dreadful dream to them: The king found himself in a snake-infested field under a sky swarming with eagles. A wind toppled his standard, and the Iranians slaughtered his troops. He was captured and taken to the Iranian court, where a young prince took a sword and cleaved him in half. It was the pain of this execution that had awakened him.

The dream's meaning was not difficult to decipher, but only one among the interpreters dared to reveal it. First, he asked to speak without fear of punishment reserved for those who cast bad omens. He said the dream was a warning against war with the Iranians under the command of Siavosh. Touran would be doomed if the young prince were killed.

Afrasiab was disturbed to hear the news, and soon convinced himself of the wisdom of the path of peace. He halted the preparations for war and called a council of knights. In the gathering, the king spoke in praise of peace and reconciliation. He said he abhorred war's depredations, misery, and senseless bloodshed. The council approved of this sentiment and endorsed the king's peace plan.

Afrasiab sent a substantial settlement offer to Siavosh, including rich offerings and a nonaggression pact. Garsivaz acted as the king's emissary and led a caravan of lavish gifts on camelback, accompanied by long trains of Arabian horses and formally attired slaves.

When the caravan reached Balkh, it was received in accordance with protocol, and Garsivaz was hosted in luxury. Then a scribe read the royal missive in which Afrasiab had extolled Feraydun, the common ancestor of the peoples of Iran and Touran. He stressed that the Oxus River was the eternal border between the children of Iraj and Tur. He also denounced war and urged Siavosh and Rostam to convince the king of Iran of the wisdom of his proposed peace.

The Iranian prince and his military commander sent word to Garsivaz that they needed time to consider the proposal. The offer of gifts was satisfactory, and the pledge to withdraw from the territories west of the Oxus River was acceptable, but Afrasiab could not be trusted, given his habit of violating his covenants. To ensure compliance, Rostam drew up the names of one hundred relatives of Afrasiab that were to be delivered to Iran as hostages. If Touran were to violate the peace treaty, the hostages would pay with their lives.

Garsivaz returned to his king and conveyed Siavosh's demand. Afrasiab was hesitant, but knowing he had no option, he sent the hostages to Balkh, feeling some relief that he was close to concluding the peace treaty. Garsivaz returned to the Touranian court and sang the praises of the Iranian commander, whom he described as a prince unmatched among the princes.

Flushed and happy with the extraction of a strong treaty, Siavosh dispatched Rostam with a letter to his father, explaining the new offer of peace backed by the guarantee of prominent hostages to be held in Iran.

The Iranian king welcomed Rostam at the court and asked why he had come to visit. Rostam delivered the letter to the scribes. As the document was read, Kay-Kavous's mood darkened, and his face twisted in anger at the suggestion of ending hostilities with Touran. He accused Siavosh of naïveté, saying that he had been deceived. Surely hostages would be worthless in preventing someone like Afrasiab from carrying out another invasion; he would easily forfeit the lives of his lowborn relatives. Kay-Kavous commanded that the gifts of Touran be burned on the spot. The hostages had to be shackled and sent to the Winter Palace of Pars for decapitation. War had to commence immediately.

Rostam reminded the king of the policy he had detailed in his previous letter—that they not blunder into a reckless war. He added that the king of Touran had sued for peace and that his final proposal was fair and sound. Besides, Siavosh would never go back on his word or allow the execution of hostages, while Afrasiab maintained his side of the peace treaty.

Kay-Kavous unleashed his fury on Rostam and accused him of being complicit—nay, of masterminding the peace proposal seduced by the promises of comfort and blinded by the greed for the enemy's trifling gifts. Then he threatened to relieve him of his command if he refused to carry out his bellicose policy.

Grievously offended, Rostam resigned his commission and left the court. Kay-Kavous appointed Tous in his stead and ordered him to wage war on Afrasiab immediately. He also sent a scathing letter to his son, berating him for his indolence and commanding him to return if he did not have the spirit to immediately burn the gifts, behead the hostages, and wage war on Touran.

THE PRINCE IN EXILE

When Siavosh read his father's letter, he whispered, "Would that my mother had never given birth to me, and, having been born, would that I had died before this day."

To disobey his father's commands would be tantamount to sedition. But obeying his father was inconceivable. Allowing the execution of a hundred innocent men was morally repugnant. Siavosh could not bear the thought of returning to the royal palace to face the king's wrath and his queen's intrigues.

Torn by this dilemma, Siavosh finally resolved to go into exile and spend the rest of his life in obscurity. His trusted friend and lieutenant Bahraum advised against this course. He urged the young prince to remonstrate with the king, ask for the return of Rostam, and, if it all failed, to obey and carry out the king's orders. But Siavosh, who had made up his mind, expressed his defiance in his last letter to Kay-Kavous:

> I have sought the path of virtue since I came of age. But that woman—your wife—plotted against me and turned your court into my prison. I had to go through an inferno to prove my innocence, but the torments continued. When I could no longer bear the misery, I went to war, won glory, and brought peace to two nations. But it was all to no avail. You have no love for me. I wish you happiness as I walk into the mouth of the dragon. I do not know what the stars have in store for me.

Siavosh sent a message to Afrasiab asking permission to pass through his realm in search of refuge. He returned the hostages and the goods offered for peace as well. The king of Touran was dismayed to learn of the new Iranian position and was shocked that the prince requested safe conduct through the enemy territory.

Piran, Afrasiab's cousin, and trusted adviser, offered him guidance. He echoed Garsivaz's earlier praise of the Iranian prince and said the king would do well to offer him asylum in Touran. Graced with divine sanction and possessed of courage and righteousness, Siavosh deserved to be treated as a royal guest. Kay-Kavous was getting old, and his son was sure to return to the throne of Iran. Then the two countries would be united by the friendship that they had extended at that crucial moment.

Afrasiab listened to Piran and found his words worthy of reflection. But he offered that when all was said and done, one could hardly trust a son of Kay-Kavous. Piran disagreed. Siavosh had disobeyed his father on the matter of the hostages at the expense of the throne of Iran. This was proof that he had not inherited his father's selfish nature and impetuous temper. Afrasiab was persuaded. He wrote back to the young prince, extending a paternal invitation to come to Touran and remain there as his revered guest.

Siavosh was relieved to have found a way out of his predicament. But he was also heartbroken that he would spend the rest of his life in exile. The young prince delegated the army's command to Bahraum and ordered him to await Tous's arrival. Then, with a heavy heart, the prince mounted his black stallion Behzad and rode out toward the Oxus River at the head of three hundred of his loyal warriors.

Piran crossed the Oxus River to welcome the famous prince and accompanied him as they rode toward Kang, the capital of Touran. Four white elephants and a thousand attendants heralded the welcoming delegation. Cheering crowds thronged the streets of every town they passed, plucking on the strings of harps and lutes and singing songs of welcome. All this reminded Siavosh of his joyful return to the Winter Palace of Pars from Zabol. Piran noticed the melancholy of the young prince and the sorrow he was trying to hide. In their final rest before arriving at the capital, Piran said: "Among the highborn, you are unrivaled for three reasons. You are from the seed of Kay Qobaud. You are utterly truthful. And your luminous face commands love and respect."

Siavosh smiled. "Your reputation for loyalty and kindness precedes you," he said. "I know that you will never betray a friend. So, allow me to ask you a question. Can I rest assured that I will be safe in this country? Otherwise, I am prepared to cross Touran and settle elsewhere."

Piran assured his guest that he would be protected in Touran. Although Afrasiab had a bad reputation, deep down, he was a godly man. As the king's blood relative, his knight, and his adviser, the old warrior claimed to be in a position to judge Afrasiab's character. Besides, Piran assured Siavosh that his army of one hundred thousand warriors would be on hand should the slightest threat to his security arise.

The sad prince took comfort in these heartfelt assurances and trusted Piran like a father. When they arrived at the gates of Kang, Afrasiab came out on foot to welcome them, and Siavosh quickly dismounted. "From now on, there will be no wars," said the king, embracing him. "The ram and the tiger will drink from the same fountainhead. The world has had enough of the discord unleashed by Tur's slaying of his brother Iraj. But in you Iran and Touran will finally be reconciled."

The king took Siavosh by the hand and allowed him to share his throne. He looked at the face of the young prince and marveled at the foolishness of old Kay-Kavous, who had spurned such a virtuous son.

Elaborate games were announced in honor of the royal guest, and the entire city came out to watch. The companions of the Iranian prince excelled at polo to the point that he asked them to go easy on their Touranian competitors. At archery, none could string the young prince's bow. Even Garsivaz failed at the task. Afrasiab, who thoroughly enjoyed Siavosh's athletic performance, laughed and said: "Once I had a bow like this. None could string it. But those were the bygone days of my youth."

For the next year, Afrasiab spent more time with his charming guest, to the exclusion of his advisers, including Garsivaz. Despite this attention, Siavosh could not shake the sadness of being separated from his homeland, so Piran offered his young daughter Jarireh as a suitable companion to relieve his solitude. Siavosh bit his lip when he cast eyes on the lovely girl. Shortly after this arrangement was made, Piran suggested Afrasiab's daughter, the stunning Farigis, as the royal consort for his Iranian protégé. Marrying the king's daughter would ensure his success at the court and help him adjust to his new life in Touran. Siavosh demurred at first, but Piran insisted that Jarireh would continue to serve him as a loyal companion.

Afrasiab had some reservations when Piran broached the subject of a marriage between his daughter and the Iranian prince. Astrologers had foreseen that the fruit of such a connection would be a king who would destroy Touran. Piran, who was in the habit of dismissing such prognostications, convinced Afrasiab to give his consent despite the superstitious forewarning. An extravagant wedding was arranged, and Siavosh settled into his new life in comfort and good standing. Another year passed, and the young prince's memories of Kay-Kavous and Rostam began to fade.

The king offered his new son-in-law the vast territories between Touran and China. Leaving Jarireh behind in her father's care, Siavosh traveled to his new realm with his wife, where he built the city of Siavoshgerd. The walls of this city measured three miles by three miles. Its cobbled streets were lined with beds of tulips and hyacinth. At the heart of this new city, a magnificent palace was built for Farigis, topped with high domes. In his throne room, the prince commissioned lavish frescoes on opposite walls portraying the knights and heroes of Iran and Touran feasting and fighting. Kay-Kavous, Zaul, Rostam, and Geav were portrayed on one wall, and images of Afrasiab, Piran, and Garsivaz graced the opposite wall. At this time, a letter arrived from Jarireh. Despite her tender age, she was proud to have produced a son for her noble husband Siavosh. The boy was named Forud. The prince was delighted to see a saffron handprint of the infant at the bottom of the letter.

On a visit to Siavoshgerd, Piran was dazzled by the wealth and luxury of the city. Everything seemed to be going well, but the prince had a foreboding sense that he would be haunted by ill fortune. Siavosh had a strange premonition that his blood would be unjustly spilled on foreign soil. He shared with Piran the chilling vision of his death and the disaster that would befall Touran after his passing. This prophecy shocked Piran, despite his skepticism of visions and fortune-telling. He thought to himself: *What have I done? What if he is right? Afrasiab had also spoken of this dark future. I'm the one who brought the prince here. I may very well have been the cause of his demise.*

Upon his return to the capital city of Kang, Piran told Afrasiab of the grandeur of the city of Siavoshgerd. To learn more about his son-in-law's disposition, the king dispatched his brother, Garsivaz, to the new city with many gifts. His task was to find out whether the young prince had acclimated to his new homeland.

THE WICKED EMISSARY

Garsivaz rode out to Siavoshgerd with one thousand cavalrymen. He was awestruck by the beauty of the newly constructed city. The more Siavosh showed him around the city, the more envious Garsivaz grew. The excursion ended at Farigis's palace, where she descended her throne and greeted her uncle. The royal envoy looked around, begrudging the wealth and power the upstart Iranian prince had been allowed to amass in Touran. Give it a year or so, he thought, and this man will not regard any native of this land as his equal.

Garsivaz's resentment was augmented during the welcoming games arranged in his honor. First, he challenged his host to a contest, but Siavosh refused because it would be improper for a young prince to engage the king's brother in a contest. Instead, he called on his guest to designate a substitute. The Touranian knight appreciated the propriety of the young prince and called on his troops for a volunteer. A soldier named Goruy claimed he would be a proper match for the Iranian prince. Siavosh frowned at the impudence of this simple soldier. But Garsivaz said he approved the match, as Goruy was a good warrior. The prince disagreed. "Since I won't be engaging a knight, not one but two from among your men must join forces against me."

A second warrior was chosen to assist Goruy, and the two approached their Iranian opponent in an equestrian armed contest. The prince did not lay hands on his arms, but quickly clutched Goruy's belt and threw him off his horse into the dust. Then he shamed the second warrior by snatching him off his saddle, carrying him by the neck, and depositing him at Garsivaz's feet. Siavosh dismounted and climbed his throne with a triumphant gesture and a derisive laugh.

The royal emissary did not relish the taste of that humiliation. He continued his brooding, and thought Afrasiab had made a mistake in elevating a foreign prince above the best of his noblemen—especially to have allowed Siavosh to shame Touranians in their own land.

When Garsivaz returned to Kang, he went straight to the court to report to Afrasiab. He spoke of Siavosh as a prince who trafficked with Iran, China, and Rome to foment rebellion. Afrasiab was troubled by this intelligence and said he needed three days to think the matter over.

On the fourth day, the king called Garsivaz to a private consultation. Despite their numerous misgivings, the fact remained that Afrasiab had invited Siavosh into his realm and given his daughter to him in marriage.

Neither the heavens nor the world would look kindly upon a king who would turn on his son-in-law without just cause. It would be best to summon his Iranian protégé to the court and encourage him to return to his country.

Garsivaz disputed the wisdom of this plan. He argued that Siavosh would never accept such an invitation, as he was not the young prince Afrasiab remembered. Nor was Farigis the shy princess of the past. From what he had seen in Siavoshgerd, they now had ambitions of sovereignty. Besides, Garsivaz warned, the Iranian prince could not be trusted to go back to Iran, as he knew all the military secrets of Touran. He urged action before the arrogant prince charmed the entire army and reduced Afrasiab to a vassal in his own land.

At long last, the king decided to invite Siavosh and Farigis to the capital to study the matter more closely. He wrote a mildly worded invitation expressing a desire to see his daughter and hunt in his son-in-law's company. Garsivaz was charged with taking the royal invitation to the Iranian prince. He set off immediately and did not pause until he reached the vicinity of Siavoshgerd. From there, he sent a messenger ahead:

> Exalted Siavosh!
>
> Under no condition should you trouble yourself by coming out to welcome me. I ask you in the name of the love you have for our king to forgo this cumbersome formality.

This show of false modesty puzzled Siavosh. But when Garsivaz arrived with Afrasiab's message, he was delighted. He said that he would be honored to go to the capital. The deceitful envoy then put on a mask of sympathy. He looked away, sighed, and wiped fake tears from his eyes. Siavosh asked for an explanation.

"Afrasiab is hatching a murderous plot against you," Garsivaz told him. "Do not assume that being related to him would guarantee your safety. Remember that this king murdered his brother, the worthy Prince Aghrirat, by his own hands!"

Trusting Garsivaz, the prince decided to refuse the king's invitation. He wrote to Afrasiab that he could not travel because Farigis was unwell and pledged to visit the king when she was better. Garsivaz praised Siavosh's prudence and assured him that he was a true friend and would send word once he had managed to douse the fires of the king's wrath. With these words, he took additional horses to avoid delays in conveying the Iranian prince's response to the capital of Touran in Kang. The envoy then explained his speedy return to the king with a false account of what had transpired in Siavoshgerd:

"I have returned in haste because the conditions do not warrant dithering. The brazen Siavosh has used a flimsy excuse to refuse your invitation. He's grown so arrogant that he did not even come out of the city to greet me. And he assigned me an inferior seat below his throne at his palace. His city is full of Iranian, Roman, and Chinese troops. Lack of decisive action at this juncture will lead to a war against a coalition of nations under the command of this Iranian interloper."

Afrasiab was so angry that he did not reply. Instead, he commanded that the drums and trumpets of war be sounded for the immediate departure of his army.

SORROWS OF THE PRINCE

As Afrasiab was gathering his troops, Siavosh had another nightmare. In the dream, he was in a boat floating on a river that touched the sky on one side. The other bank of the river was lined with lance-holding soldiers, and behind them, a mountainous blaze of fire reached for the heavens. The river flowed toward Afrasiab, seated on a war elephant, furiously regarding Siavosh and blowing on the fires to increase their intensity. The prince woke with a start and anxiously shared his vision of doom with Farigis. She tried to decipher the dream as an omen against his enemies, but her interpretation did not ring true.

Siavosh alerted his troops of the danger posed by the approaching army and donned his armor, awaiting word from Garsivaz. As Afrasiab's army approached the walls of Siavoshgerd, Garsivaz sent ahead a message saying: "All is lost. My words did not affect the king. Save yourself if you can."

Still trusting the treacherous Garsivaz, Siavosh informed his wife that Afrasiab was coming to kill him. Farigis cried, clawed at her cheeks, and said: "Don't worry about us. Get on your fastest horse and save yourself. My only wish is that you remain alive."

"My dreams of doom have come to pass," he said. "Men are fated to die, and my time has come. I will be beheaded. My body will not be honored with a burial. No one will weep for me. The king's henchmen will march you off, poorly clad and debased. But you will find a protector in Piran. In four months you will give birth to our son. Name him Kay-Khosrow. In time, an Iranian knight named Geav will come and take you both beyond the Oxus River. Our son will be king, and he will avenge my death. Be strong and prepare yourself for hardship until the appointed day."

Farigis rushed to her husband, held him for the last time, and sobbed.

Siavosh went into the stables and lifted the collar and bridle off his favorite black stallion Behzad on whom he had crossed the fire at the great trial at his father's palace. He hugged his neck, and whispered: "Run away, my loyal Behzad. Abandon the comforts of the stable and suffer no one to ride you until Kay-Khosrow rises to avenge me. Be his steed as he crushes the cobra's head."

He released his horses and rode out ahead of his trusted warriors toward the borders of Iran, tears streaming down his cheeks. Soon they came against the army of Touran that filled the horizon.

Siavosh addressed the king: "Why have you brought these troops, Afrasiab? Why do you intend to kill an innocent man and sow vengeance and animosity between nations?"

"Silence, you unworthy man!" said Garsivaz. "If you are honest, why have you come to welcome the king in your armor?"

At that moment, Siavosh realized that the wicked Garsivaz had been deceiving him. Afrasiab ordered his troops to attack the prince and his armed guard, and the Iranians prepared to fight to the death. The prince declared that he would surrender to avoid senseless bloodshed. But it was to no avail. Afrasiab's men attacked and massacred the Iranian troops.

Siavosh was wounded in the confrontation. Goruy, who had led the charge, captured the prince, tied his hands, put a packsaddle on his back and brought him before the king.

Afrasiab decreed that Siavosh must die. One of Piran's brothers, Pilsam, tried to prevent the inevitable by urging patience. He pleaded with the king to wait for Piran, who was away but was expected to arrive there by the break of the next day's dawn. But Garsivaz insisted on immediate execution, adding that it was unwise to delay killing a wounded snake. He threatened to resign from the king's service if the execution was stayed.

Afrasiab knew that Siavosh's guilt had not been proven. He also remembered his dream prophesying that killing the Iranian prince would doom Touran. But things had gone too far to change course. Releasing Siavosh after all that had happened would also lead to war and disaster.

Farigis, who had learned of the bloody confrontation, arrived in a state of desperation. "Why do you want to lower me to the dust?" she pleaded with her father. "Why have you surrendered yourself to lies? Heaven shall not abide killing a righteous prince who turned his back to his father and his country to live under your protection. Haven't you heard what happens to the unjust? Haven't you heard how Feraydun dealt with Zahhak? Aren't you afraid of what will happen to this land when Rostam and Geav gird their loins to avenge their prince?"

With this, she looked upon her husband's bloody face and pulled at her own hair. Afrasiab pitied Farigis as she sobbed and wailed. He could not bear to see his daughter in that state, so he had her sent to a castle in Kang before Siavosh's execution. He stipulated that the beheading take place on barren land where nothing grows.

Goruy dragged the doomed prince to the place of his execution. Siavosh turned to the heavens and prayed that his blood would be avenged. He said goodbye to Pilsam and begged that he convey his affections to Piran. "And be sure to ask him: 'Where were your one hundred thousand troops to protect me when Garsivaz's henchmen dragged me into the dust?' Tell him that there was no one to mourn me as I was slain."

The shameless Goruy hurled his victim to the ground. He was

instructed to prevent the blood of Siavosh from trickling into the soil, lest it invokes the wrath of the heavens. So, he placed a golden basin under his victim's head. Garsivaz handed him a dagger, and Goruy beheaded Siavosh. A dark wind blew, and dust storms covered the sun.

This hoary world is rotten to the core
It takes the breast from the infant's lips
And tramples he who's deceived by its false splendor.

The steed of the poet's life is at the milestone of fifty-eight
With old age, he trades the reins of his stallion
For an old man's cane and tempers his gait.

His only hope is that providence gives him time
To finish his poem, so the Legends of Yore
Are versified and saved in perfect rhyme.

CHAPTER 8

Return of the King: Kay-Khosrow

Now listen to the old farmer's tale of Iranian rage
When they heard what had befallen their martyred prince
And the wars of revenge they pledged to wage.

TOURAN AFTER THE MARTYRDOM OF SIAVOSH

When Farigis heard that her husband had been murdered, she clipped her braids, scratched her face, and cursed Afrasiab in public. Outraged at this insolence, the king ordered his men to beat her and show no mercy. He didn't care that she was with child. He was heard saying: "I want no sapling from that tree. Destroy it, branch and root."

Dreading what could befall Farigis at her father's hands, Pilsam, along with his two brothers, Lahauk and Farshidvard, rode out to meet Piran, who was on his way back from a mission to the eastern regions of the empire. When the old knight heard about the beheading of the prince, he ripped his clothes and wallowed in the dirt in a gesture of mourning. Pilsam advised that there was no time for lamentations, as Farigis's life was in danger.

Piran galloped for two days without rest to reach Kang, arriving not a moment too soon. He wrested Farigis from Afrasiab's minions and brought her to court to admonish the king, saying that killing his daughter would bring him infamy in this world and damnation in the hereafter. Thus, Piran was allowed to take Farigis away on the condition that her baby be brought back for the king's final judgment. He heaped blame on Afrasiab for his evil deed and cursed the wicked people who had deceived him into committing such a monstrous crime, which would engage Touran in interminable wars of revenge. He then took the bereaved princess into his protection, took her to his palace and entrusted her to the care of his wife, Golshahr.

On a moonless night a few months later, Siavosh appeared in a dream to Piran. He emerged from the sea, holding a sword. In his other hand he held a candle lit by the sun. The martyred prince turned to Piran with a smile and said: "Wake up from your sweet slumber. This is an auspicious night. A son is born to me, and I name him Kay-Khosrow!"

Piran stirred to awareness and roused his wife, urging her to attend to Farigis. Lady Golshahr went to the princess's chambers and found that she had given birth to a beautiful boy. She ran back to her husband and said: "Come and see the handsome child. He is a veritable king in the cradle."

Piran set his eyes on the beaming infant and bitterly wept for Siavosh and swore an oath to protect Kay-Khosrow from his vengeful grandfather. The following day, he went to the court and declared: "My glorious king, last night your daughter, Farigis, gave birth to a son. He has your looks, and your divine grace is reflected in his face. He resembles his ancestors Tur and Feraydun. Dispel all evil thoughts from your heart on this blessed day."

Afrasiab sighed with regret. He had not forgotten the prophecy that a king from the lines of Tur and Kay-Qobaud would spell his doom. But that day, the king was in a fatalistic mood. The mortals, he thought, can't undo the decrees of heaven. What is the use of killing an infant?

Thus, Afrasiab ruled that the baby must be sent away to the countryside, where he would never learn of his lineage. Piran arranged to have him sent to the shepherds once he was weaned.

Being confined to a rural environment did not snuff the light of Kay-Khosrow's royal heritage. At seven, he fashioned a crude bow and arrow and practiced deer hunting. At ten, he was hunting wolves and boars, and at twelve, he went after lions armed with nothing but a club.

Worried that the lad would be injured in such reckless adventures, the shepherds complained to Piran that they could not cope with their young ward's ambitions. Piran smiled, for he had always known that the royal lineage of the son of Siavosh would eventually shine through. He rode out to see the shepherd boy who hunted like a king. The boy found it odd that a knight would deign to treat him with affection. Piran smiled and told him about his royal lineage. Ignoring Afrasiab's instructions, he provided the boy with a worthy steed and a proper outfit and took him back to live in his palace.

Around this time Afrasiab had another disturbing dream that reminded him of the dark prognostications about Siavosh's son. He ordered his trusted knight to bring Kay-Khosrow to court for an audience. Piran feared for his ward's life as he knew that Afrasiab would not hesitate to kill him if he sensed the slightest threat. Thus, the child was advised to act the part of a foolish farmhand. On the appointed day, the young Kay-Khosrow was brought to court in the company of his benefactor. The king looked at him with suspicion and asked:

"How do you care for your flock, shepherd boy?"

"There is no game. And I have no bows and arrows to hunt with."

"Do you believe in fate? Do you know the difference between right and wrong?"

"If there is a leopard, it is sure to maul people."

"Who are your parents? What do you know of Iran?

"Even a ferocious lion can't overcome a good dog."

Afrasiab laughed at the palpable stupidity of Farigis's son. Piran's ploy had worked, and the king's fears about the future of Kay-Khosrow were allayed. He exiled Kay-Khosrow and his mother to Siavoshgerd, the city that Siavosh had built many years before. In the absence of its founder, the magnificent city was overgrown with thornbushes. The people who still revered their beloved prince came out to welcome his son.

A tall tree had grown in the place of Siavosh's slaying, where his blood had trickled on the parched land. It had a fragrance like musk. Its leaves bore the pale image of the martyred prince. It was called "the feather of Siavosh" (maidenhair fern) and to this day it is believed to have medicinal properties. People routinely gathered in the shade of that holy tree to pray and rest.

A FEW YEARS BACK AT THE IRANIAN COURT

Kay-Kavous was beside himself with grief when he heard the news of his son's martyrdom. None dared to console him. Everyone was in a state of shock. Tous, Gudarz, and Geav tore their garments and sobbed. When Zaul and Rostam heard the news, they mourned for one week. Rostam swore not to take off his armor, put down his weapons, or even wash until he had avenged Siavosh. Then he traveled to the royal palace at the head of a great army and went straight to the chambers of Kay-Kavous and harangued him.

"The seeds of your evil deeds and intemperance have borne fruit," he said. "You have forfeited your royal charisma to your reckless infatuation with that woman, Sudabeh. Lack of wisdom and excessive power is a deadly combination. You have brought disaster upon our heads. Our prince was heroic on the battlefield and generous in feasts. I will not rest until I have avenged him."

Kay-Kavous was too ashamed to return Rostam's angry gaze. He just sat on his throne and sobbed, staring at the floor. He did not move when Rostam pulled Sudabeh out of her chamber and slew her in full view of the court.

When the Iranians concluded their mourning, Rostam led the army that was going to avenge their fallen prince. Tous, Gudarz, Geav, Faramarz, son of Rostam, and Fariborz, son of Kay Kavous, led the army. Rostam gave Faramarz the command of the forward division, composed of twelve thousand warriors, as they marched toward the Oxus River.

On the borders of Touran, Faramarz's army came against the troops of a vassal king named Varauzad. In a great fury, Faramarz tore into the enemy and killed hundreds of warriors until he came face to face with the vassal king. Varauzad asked him to identify himself. Faramarz said he would not deign to reveal his name to a lowly servant of Afrasiab and felled him with a blow of his javelin. Then he dismounted, beheaded him, and set fire to the border territory.

Alarmed by the news of this invasion, Afrasiab responded by sending his son, Sorkheh, with thirty thousand sword-wielding cavalrymen to stop the forces of Faramarz. The king said to him: "You are my favorite son and the pillar of my kingdom. No one in the army of Iran is your equal in combat. You can lock swords with Faramarz if you wish but stay away from Rostam."

With his thirty thousand swordsmen, the Touranian prince engaged in a furious battle with Faramarz. The two sides fought to the sound of massive tin drums, as their bloody swords glittered in the cloud of dust that arose from the battlefield. Spotting Faramarz's standard, Sorkheh left his bow with his son, grabbed a lance, and went forward to challenge him in a duel. But it didn't take him long to realize the foolishness of that decision. Faramarz struck him with his lance with such force that he was knocked off his saddle. Grabbing onto his horse's neck, he tried to escape, but Faramarz caught up to him from behind, lifted him off his horse, bound his hands, and sent him back to the Iranian lines as a captive. Rostam praised his son and curtly ordered Tous to execute the young, handsome prince. Sorkheh pleaded with Tous: "Why do you want to spill my innocent blood? I'm the same age as Siavosh, and we were friends. I cried day and night for him after that calamity. I cursed his murderers."

Tous took pity on his captive and begged Rostam to spare him. But this was in vain, since the hero's rage knew no bounds. He commanded his brother, Zavareh, to carry out the gruesome execution, adding: "Afrasiab must suffer the loss of his son just as Kay-Kavous had."

When news of Sorkheh's demise reached Afrasiab, he displayed great sorrow and called on his troops to avenge the blood of their son. Pilsam volunteered to bring down Rostam in a duel if Afrasiab granted him an excellent horse and a set of well-made weapons from his treasury. Piran objected, pleading with the king to release his brother from the deadly mission. But Pilsam insisted, and upon receiving his commission, rode to the Iranian lines and shouted: "Where is Rostam, who claims to be a dragon on the battlefield?"

Geav drew his sword and roared, "The great hero Rostam does not duel any upstart who happens to show up in the arena."

Pilsam threw his lance, causing Geav to lose his hold in his stirrups. Faramarz rode out to help Geav, and Pilsam managed to ward off two of Iran's greatest knights. Rostam saw the power of the Touranian warrior from his position in the center of the army and knew that the opponent was none but Piran's legendary brother. The hero told the army commanders to hold their ground and galloped to the center of the battlefield, shouting at Pilsam: "Here I am, if you seek me." Then, without delay, he ran him through with his lance, lifted him off his horse and dropped his corpse before the Touranian lines. Piran was dismayed at the quick demise of his mighty brother. He was in deep mourning as the trumpets and the drums of war sounded, and the general battle commenced.

In the confrontation that followed, both sides suffered huge losses. In one of his forays, Afrasiab succeeded in forcing Tous to flee. But Rostam rallied the knights and mounted a counterattack to push back the warriors of Touran. When Rostam spotted the black standard of the king, he charged and struck him with his lance, sending Afrasiab flying off his horse. His trusted brother Houman came to his rescue, pounding his mace on Rostam's shoulder. The blow didn't cause any damage. It merely distracted the hero long enough to let Afrasiab escape once again from his clutches. Soon the army of Touran followed its leader away from the battle, and victory went to Iran.

THE RAGING KNIGHTS OF IRAN

With Afrasiab's flight, Touran belonged to Rostam, who reclined on his adversary's throne and delighted in his triumph. He gave away the royal treasures to his warriors and divided the kingdom between Tous and Geav. To Fariborz, he offered Afrasiab's golden crown and said: "You are our crown prince and Siavosh's brother. Do not rest until you have avenged him." Then he declared an amnesty on those who withdrew their loyalty from Afrasiab and submitted to the Iranian conquerors.

For several years, the Iranian knights remained in Touran. They enjoyed the spoils of battle and the comforts of victory. One day, Zavareh was on a hunting expedition and heard his scout say that it had once been the favorite hunting ground of Siavosh. Reminded of the martyrdom of his beloved prince, he lost consciousness and fell off his horse, letting go of the falcon he was carrying. Upon waking, he swore to forsake all the comforts he had been enjoying and to rededicate himself to avenging the prince's death. Despite the amnesty they had granted to the people of Touran, Rostam and the other knights joined Zavareh in his renewed campaign to exact revenge for the blood of Siavosh. Thus they waged indiscriminate war, laying waste to the land, pillaging, and killing man, woman, and child.

When this carnage had gone on for a while, the elders of Touran went forth and pleaded with Rostam. One of the elders said:

"We had nothing to do with Afrasiab. We are not guilty of the innocent blood that he spilled. Nor do we know where he might be hiding, in the clouds or in a dragon's mouth. We humble ourselves at your threshold. Shed not the blood of the innocent in victory. Do not wage war on the heavens."

Rostam felt ashamed of what he had done, ceased his indiscriminate massacre, and called for a war council. Having stopped their senseless behavior, the knights gathered and discussed the troubling rumors that had reached them: Afrasiab was regrouping to attack Iran. With Rostam and the knights languishing in Touran and the inept Kay-Kavous at the helm, Iran was vulnerable.

The return of the Iranian troops from Touran was a sound decision. But Rostam was not convinced of this until a mage came forward with a piece of ancient advice:

Sate your passions but temper your greed
Rein in the demon of excess and remember death
That turns pleasures of life bittersweet.

Rostam held his head in shame.

In short order, the knights gathered their booty and returned to Iran. As Rostam and his army of revenge were retreating to Iran without capturing or punishing any of the perpetrators of the crime against their prince, Afrasiab returned to his capital city of Kang that had turned into a devastated wasteland. To avenge the destruction of his kingdom, he crossed the border and laid waste to Iranian territory, burning cities and demolishing villages. Iran had already been suffering from a seven-year drought. War and natural disasters compounded the misery of the ancient land.

THE DREAM OF GUDARZ

One night, the angel Sorush appeared to Gudarz in a dream, riding on a rain cloud. He intoned: "If you want to escape the clutches of misery and the depredations of this foreign invader, seek Kay-Khosrow, the son of Siavosh, whose maternal ancestor is Tur. When he sets foot in Iran as king, heaven will fulfill his wishes. He will not rest until he avenges his father. From among the knights of Iran, only your son Geav is destined to find him."

As the sun started to peer through the raven wings of the night, Gudarz summoned Geav and shared his dream with him. He warned his son: "Finding Kay-Khosrow is a dangerous and difficult assignment. But what would be greater for a mortal than the everlasting glory of enthroning a righteous king?"

Geav accepted the mission and set off on his lonely quest to the borders of Touran. For seven years, he searched the land and kept his identity a secret by living in obscurity, and killing those who might inform on him. He hunted onager for food and wore their skin as his garment. As a gaunt, wild man he came so close to despair that he doubted whether his father's vision about Kay-Khosrow was divine or demonic.

Finally, the wandering knight made his way to the region of Siavoshgerd and drifted into a garden. He was musing on the futility of his mission when he came across a charming lad wearing a garland of flowers and holding a chalice of wine. There was a divine light about the young man's face as if he were sitting on a royal throne, wearing a torque and crown. Geav knew instantly that this was none other than his future king. He eagerly dismounted and ran to the young man, who turned and smiled. The disheveled knight kissed the ground and said: "My lord and master! I am convinced that you are the son of Siavosh, who was the crown prince of the kings of Kay. We have long awaited your arrival in Iran."

"And I suppose you are Geav, the son of Gudarz," he said.

"May you live a long and happy life. Who told you about Geav, the son of Gudarz?"

"My mother told me of you, as she heard it from my father. She promised me that you would come from Iran to take us back to my father's homeland where I will be king."

Geav asked to see the mark of Kay-Qobaud on the young man's arm and praised God when he saw it. Then he begged his future king to lead the way back to his mother's house. As happy as she was to see Geav, Farigis urged great speed as well as stealth in their upcoming escape. The slightest lapse or delay would alert Afrasiab and bring the armies of

Touran upon them. As they prepared for the long journey, the banished princess urged her son to ascend to the high meadow beyond the mountains and find Siavosh's black stallion, Behzad.

"My royal son, listen to my instructions," she said. "There is a catchment where wild horses drink. Behzad runs with that herd. Hold this saddle and bridle over your head when you approach and speak to him softly. No mortal has been able to ride him since your father was killed."

As Kay-Khosrow approached the meadow, Siavosh's noble steed neighed. But he did not move from the spot at the edge of the watering hole. Kay-Khosrow enfolded Behzad's neck in his arms, kissed his face, and whispered the sorrows of his father's last day in his ears. Then he saddled and mounted the stallion and returned to Siavoshgerd. Farigis presented Geav with Siavosh's armor as a token of her respect, and the three of them slipped out of town swiftly as three ghosts riding the winds.

ESCAPE FROM TOURAN

The fugitives from Siavoshgerd rode hard for many hours, and when they could go no further, stopped at a small oasis to rest. Geav kept watch on his horse until he detected the dust of the approaching warriors of Touran.

Having received intelligence of Kay-Khosrow and Farigis's escape, Piran had dispatched three hundred cavalries under the command of his brothers Golbaud and Nastihan, authorizing them to kill Geav and Farigis on sight and bring Kay-Khosrow back in chains. He hoped this would prevent a new wave of revenge wars by Iran.

Geav drew his sword, brought his horse to a full gallop, and fearlessly tore into the enemy lines. The warriors of Touran that surrounded him appeared like a thicket of lances. But Geav moved like a great sickle cutting a path through that thicket. Golbaud was incredulous. He consulted his brother, and they agreed that the only wise course was to withdraw their troops and return to Piran for reinforcements. But Piran dismissed his brothers as inept and cowardly and told them they had brought shame upon their clan.

"How could a single man vanquish two knights and three hundred equestrian warriors?" he asked. Piran then formed his battalion of one thousand cavalry and went in pursuit of the fugitives himself. He forbade rest until the objects of their chase were killed or taken captive.

Having repelled the first wave of attacks, Geav was keenly aware of further peril. He and his companions rode at top speed until they crossed a deep but narrow waterway. Exhausted from their long journey, they stopped to rest. This time Farigis stood watch as the two men slept. When she spotted a colossal army approaching under the banner of Piran, she anxiously woke the men. Geav assured her that he would be equal to the challenge.

Kay-Khosrow offered to fight along with him, but Geav refused his assistance. "I am a knight, one of the seventy-eight sons of Gudarz," he said. "There are many knights like me, but there is only one king. If you are killed, my seven-year search will have been in vain. Don't worry. I can handle this army. Just get to the top of that mountain and watch over the battlefield."

Geav rode out to the river and challenged the army of Touran to send forth their best warrior. Piran cursed him as an inferior man of low birth who was doomed by his false pride. How did he hope to overcome a thousand soldiers by himself? Geav replied to the boastful fulminations of the Touranian knight: "You are a lionhearted commander indeed. So, why don't you cross this stream and see how a single man of low birth contends with a highborn knight."

Piran stormed across the river. But the bold Iranian who had taunted him did not rush to battle. Hiding in a nearby thicket, he was quietly holstering his mace and deploying his lariat. Suddenly, the Touranian general found himself ensnared by the neck and dragged down to the ground. Geav quickly tied his hands, and relieved him of his clothes and armor. Donning them himself, the wily knight mounted his captive's horse, and crossed the river to the cheers of Piran's men, who mistook him for their leader coming back in triumph. They realized their mistake only when Geav tore into their ranks, wielding his mace and killing anyone who was not quick enough to escape.

When Touran's forces were thoroughly routed, the triumphant knight crossed the river back and dragged the helpless Piran to his future king, calling him a faithless wretch who had richly earned his impending death for deceiving Siavosh. The old Touranian commander kissed the ground when he saw Kay-Khosrow and begged him to spare his life. Farigis interceded with Geav: "You have seen many hardships and traversed long distances for us. But know that this old man is righteous and wise. After God, he is the only one who stood between us and certain death."

Geav replied: "But, my lady, I have sworn an oath to the moon to paint the earth crimson with his blood."

"Keep your oath, then," said Kay-Khosrow. "Pierce his ear and let his blood run."

Piran had escaped death. But he begged for his horse, or else he had no hope of catching up with his men. Geav agreed but bound his captive's hands to the saddle and made him swear that he would allow none but his kind wife Golshahr to untie him. With this promise, the Touranian knight crossed the river back to his side for the last time and followed the tracks of his retreating soldiers.

When Afrasiab heard of Kay-Khosrow's escape and the disastrous skirmishes that had ensued, he gathered an army to pursue the fugitive prince himself. First, he came to the battlefield where Golbaud and Nastihan had been defeated. Disheartened, he demanded to know how an entire army had been allowed to cross into Touran without notice.

A commander answered that this was not the work of an army. One single knight, named Geav, had fought against and annihilated the forces of Golbaud and Nastihan. Afrasiab said: "May no one ever rely on Piran's advice. I would not have seen this day if I had killed and buried that impertinent son of Farigis. And who, I wonder, brought the intelligence about the existence of Kay-Khosrow to this son of a demon, Geav?"

Moving forward, Afrasiab came to the second battlefield and found Piran leading his army. First, he rejoiced thinking they were returning in triumph. But as they came closer, he saw Piran's bound hands and blood-spattered face. The dejected general explained what had happened, and Afrasiab dismissed him with a disdainful bark, telling him to return to his wife.

Then the king of Touran gave full rein to his rage and swore an oath to bring down Farigis and Kay-Khosrow even if they ascended to the clouds. He pledged to mince their flesh and feed them to the fish of the sea.

He then appointed Houman commander of the pursuit and reminded him of the urgency of the chase, adding that there was a prophecy that when a mixed-blood king from the seeds of Kay-Qobaud and Tur rises, Touran would be destroyed and its cities would turn into fields of thorns.

CROSSING THE OXUS

The three refugees from Touran beat their enemies to the shores of the Oxus River. Geav asked the boatman for a ship with new sails fit to carry a king. The boatman replied that the river did not know king from servant. The knight insisted he would pay the price, whatever it might be. Sensing their desperation, the boatman demanded a heavy ransom for rides across the river, swollen as it was by the angry torrents of spring. He wanted to keep either the prince or his mother, or, failing that, he demanded the black stallion or Siavosh's armor worn by Geav. "You are a thief and a brigand, although you don't carry weapons," Geav retorted. "You ask a heavy price for your meager services. Keep your boats. We shall cross the river on our horses."

Turning to the prince, Geav said: "If you are truly Kay-Khosrow, you will gain from challenging the waves as a testament to your divine sanction. King Feraydun won his crown only after he had humbled the mighty waves of the Arvand River. We will follow in your wake, but you must not care if we survive the crossing. Farigis and I were put on this earth to usher in the day of your ascending the throne."

To the shock of the boatman, Kay-Khosrow said a prayer and rode his black stallion into the angry waves, Geav and Farigis following not far behind. When the three safely emerged on the Iranian side of the river, the troops of the chasing battalion appeared on the Touranian side of the river. Afrasiab was harsh with the boatman for his assistance to the fugitives. He defended himself, saying: "I had nothing to do with it. They defied the river on their own. Nobody has ever seen horsemen in full armor cross the Oxus in the height of the spring flooding."

Afrasiab ordered the boatman to prepare his ships. He wanted to chase the fugitives into Iran, but his brother, the cautious Houman, dissuaded him. Going into Iran would be interpreted as an invasion, and they were unprepared for that.

Once on Iranian soil, Geav escorted Kay-Khosrow and Farigis to Isfahan, the realm of his clan. He sent letters ahead to his father and King Kay-Kavous with the good tidings of their safe return. Gudarz rode eighty miles to welcome the new prince, saying: "May your father rest in peace. As God is my witness, I would not be so happy if I saw Siavosh alive."

In Isfahan, they celebrated for seven days, and on the eighth, they set off to the Winter Palace of Pars. The city of Pars was decorated in honor of Kay-Khosrow's arrival, and King Kay-Kavous cried tears of joy as he descended his throne to place kisses on his gallant grandson's eyes and face. Then he asked about his exile in Touran and the adventures involved in his rescue.

Kay-Khosrow told his stories and denounced his maternal grandfather, Afrasiab, for killing his father. Then he related Geav's heroic deeds in rescuing them from the land of Touran.

All the knights, except for Tous, pledged their allegiance. Tous favored Fariborz as the crown prince and the next king of Iran, for he was Kay-Kavous's son born to an Iranian mother. He considered Kay-Khosrow impure, for his mother and grandmother were Touranian princesses.

Geav and the clan of Gudarz, however, firmly stood by Kay-Khosrow. The confrontation between the two knightly families over who would climb the throne of Iran brought the country to the brink of a civil war, and neither side was willing to compromise.

To end the stalemate, Kay-Kavous declared a contest. The contender who would succeed in opening the enchanted Castle of Bahman in Ardebil would be king. Fariborz and Tous launched the first invasion as the August sun rose in the constellation of Leo. Tous led the vanguard and Fariborz followed carrying the Standard of Kaveh, the symbol of the Iranian sovereignty. But the magical forces of the castle turned the environs of Ardebil into a veritable hell. The armaments got so hot that the soldiers could not lift them without burning their hands, and their chainmail armor scorched their bodies. After a week of surrounding the enchanted stronghold, Fariborz gave up and returned in defeat.

When the clan of Gudarz heard of the return of Fariborz, they paraded their war elephants in the direction of Ardebil. Knights of the clan, wearing golden slippers, rode at the head of various divisions. They were all led by Kay-Khosrow in his crown of garnet and torque of gold. Near Ardebil, he changed into his gambeson and armor and called a scribe to take down his declaration of war written in ink that was infused with ambergris.

> This is a message from the servant of the God of Saturn, Mars, and the sun, who gives us power and prosperity. He endowed me with a prodigious body and the halo of divine sanction. I rule the expanse of the earth and heavens from Taurus to Pieces. I do not consider sorcerers worthy opponents at all, as their delusional power is nothing compared to the dominion of God in whose name I shall vanquish you. A single angel such as Sorush can destroy an army of demons. I command you to leave this castle in the name of the Almighty.

He then attached the letter to the end of a long lance and commanded Geav to lean it against the wall of the castle, utter the name of God, and return as fast as he could. As soon as this was done the walls of the castle cracked and a dark wind turned the world black as pitch as the sound of thunderclaps reverberated everywhere. Kay-Khosrow then ordered his men to shower the castle with their arrows. Some of the demons were killed and many died of fright. Then the sun came up and a refreshing breeze started to blow. Kay-Khosrow and the old Gudarz rode into the castle of Bahman in triumph. Kay-Khosrow ordered the building of a fire temple topped with a massive dome that was ten lassos wide and tall. He richly endowed the holy compound so it could support a staff of priests, scholars, and astrologers and named it the Azar-goshasp temple. He lingered there for a year of meditation and prayers before returning to the Winter Palace of Pars, where he was graciously received by his uncle and erstwhile rival Fariborz, who kissed and then seated him on a turquoise throne. Tous also came to offer his apologies for opposing him. He then resigned his position as the carrier of the Standard of Kaveh. Kay-Khosrow said that apologies were unnecessary. What he had done was express his opinion about who would be the best candidate for kingship and that was no treason. He then reappointed Tous to the post of the highest knight at court and the bearer of the Standard of Kaveh.

Then King Kay-Kavous confirmed his grandson as the next king, offering him his crown and his seat on the throne.

Kay-Kavous recognized his glorious grandson as king,
Placed the prince on his ivory throne, and endowed him
With a plethora of gems and the royal ring.

Rostam arrived from Zabol to pay his respects. Thrilled to meet his father's beloved mentor, the young king sent Geav, Gudarz, and Tous in their ceremonial golden boots to welcome him. Trumpets blared, and drums beat as the hero was ushered in. Rostam kissed the ground and wept at Kay-Khosrow's remarkable resemblance to his lost friend Siavosh. Kay-Khosrow descended the throne and tearfully embraced his father's mentor. They stayed up, drank wine, and told stories, both bitter and sweet, of times past.

Soon after the festivities Kay-Khosrow revisited the mountaintop fire temple of Azar-goshasp that he had established to engage in solitary prayers for a year. Then he came back to the Winter Palace of Pars to reside, naming his mother, Farigis, the Queen of the World.

The mercurial fate haphazardly grants
Favors and inflicts undeserved pain.
Fortunate is he who supplants

Worries for serenity of the heart, calms
His avaricious nature and shares his wealth
Most generously and without qualms.

CHAPTER 9

The Wrong Path: Forud

Four things are required for excellence in ruling
Noble birth, talent, acquired skills, and wisdom.
The highborn and gifted prince must undergo schooling

In royal arts but above all he must work hard
To acquire wisdom which means the ability
To tell good from evil and guard

Against selfish desires. Only at this stage
Could a prince reign like a perfect king who is
At once, noble, talented, skillful, and sage.

THE SECOND INVASION OF TOURAN

Kay-Kavous was worried that Kay-Khosrow would go easy on his maternal grandfather, Afrasiab. Thus, he made him swear an oath to avenge his father, regardless of blood ties. Kay-Khosrow made a solemn promise to do so and immediately opened the treasure houses to prepare for war. He gave generously to all the knights who vowed to bring down the house of Afrasiab, but Geav, Gudarz, and Bizhan got the lion's share of the gifts because they undertook greater responsibilities.

Kay-Khosrow watched his knights march past the throne in a display of might. His uncle Fariborz led the procession at the head of one hundred ten knights from the royal house of Kay. Tous's son Zarasp led eighty knights of the house of the late king Nowzar. Then Geav and his seventy-eight brothers marched behind the standard of their father, Gudarz. One prong under Faramarz, the son of Rostam, was sent to the southeast to recapture a Touranian province beyond Zabol. As the forces gathered to leave, Kay-Khosrow admonished Faramarz against waging war on noncombatants and urged them to protect the poor and the weak: "Be generous and resist the temptations of avarice. Remember that a good name is our only lasting legacy."

THE NORTHERN PRONG

After the departure of the first army, Kay-Khosrow appointed Tous, who had earlier opposed his kingship, to head the second prong of his army that would head north, to where Afrasiab was laying waste to Iranian land. Before dispatching the expedition, the king again issued strict orders against harming ordinary Touranians. Peaceful peasants and artisans were not to be abused or harassed. "Such is the way of ruling as a just king: people must be protected from harm as an army marches to war."

The king also warned Tous to avoid the mountain path toward the enemy lines, which would lead him to the impregnable castle of Kalat ruled by the king's half-brother, Forud, who was born to Jarireh, the daughter of Piran. There was no reason for the Iranian army to confront the mighty son of Siavosh. Forud held no animosity for Iran and might even be disposed to help Kay-Khosrow avenge their father. Tous promised to follow these instructions and set off for battle.

A few days into their journey, the army reached a fork in the road. On one side lay an expanse of rugged and parched terrain. On the other stood the lush mountain path that passed by the castle of Kalat. Tous chose the easier route against the advice of King Kay-Khosrow.

As the Iranian legions climbed the mountains approaching the castle of Kalat, Forud's scouts brought him news of an advancing army, and he swiftly herded back his flocks of sheep, camels, and horses and locked the fortress's gates. Then he sought his mother's counsel, who had long mourned Siavosh and resented Afrasiab for killing her beloved husband.

"Your brother is the new king of Iran, and he knows you well," Jarireh advised. "Siavosh asked Piran for my hand and took me as his first Touranian bride. As the elder brother, it falls upon you to seek revenge for your father. Put on your armor and pick up your weapon. Join your brother. Be a new avenger at the service of a new king."

She further advised her son to seek out Bahraum, Siavosh's trusted lieutenant. As Forud did not know the Iranian knights, she appointed a guide named Tokhwar to accompany him on the expedition. Commander and guide rode up to the peak of a crag to inspect the approaching forces. The valley of Kalat was filled with thirty thousand warriors whose golden helmets, maces, shields, and belts glimmered as they marched to the sound of heavy drums. From this position, Tokhwar identified the standards of all the knights leading the legions. The standard of the elephant belonged to Tous, and that of a shining sun signified Fariborz. Geav's flag bore the likeness of a black wolf, and Bizhan flew a banner with the image of a horned moon.

Down in the valley, Tous espied the two equestrians on the lookout point and roared orders to Bahraum. "Go see who dares spy on my army? Let them be punished with two hundred lashes if they are from our side. But if they are locals, kill or bring them to us in chains."

Forud asked Tokhwar about the identity of the knight who was boldly approaching them. He said that judging from the appearance of his helmet and armor, he was a knight from the clan of Gudarz.

"Who goes there on that peak?" Bahraum shouted. "Do you not see an army approaching, do you not hear the drums and horns? Are you not afraid of the field marshal who commands that army?"

"Speak softly," Forud retorted, "for we have not meant to offend you. Do not speak to me like a lion ready to pounce on an onager! You are in no way superior to me. Let us speak as equals. What is this army, and who is its commander?"

"This is the army of Iran, led by Tous and such knights as Gudarz and Geav," Bahraum replied. "Bizhan and Gostahm also belong to this army."

"Why have you not mentioned Bahraum, who is also of the house of Gudarz? He would be a delight to my eyes if fortune allowed us to meet. My mother, Jarireh, told me of him. She advised me to seek him out, since he was like a brother to my father, Siavosh."

"Then you must be Forud, the exalted son of Siavosh."

"I am Forud, a branch of that mighty trunk that was felled by treachery and deceit."

"And I am Bahraum. But to prove your claim, show me the birthmark that distinguishes your father's line."

Forud bared his arm to display his birthmark. The two warriors dismounted, embraced, and rejoiced to see one another. Forud explained that he wished to greet the commander of the army of Iran and invite him and his troops to a banquet at his castle.

Bahraum said he would convey this message to Tous. "But Tous is not a man of reason," he added. "Proud of his wealth, skills, and nobility, he is disdainful of the directives of his king. Not long ago, he disparaged Kay-Khosrow, preferring instead to enthrone Fariborz because he was of pure Iranian blood. The clan of Gudarz stood against him and won the dispute. Tous is still resentful. He commanded me to come to this peak and speak to you only in the language of the mace and the dagger. I will return to him with your message but beware that he will likely turn his back on you. If I do persuade him, I will come back with the good news. But if he sends another man, know that he means you harm. If this happens go back to your fortress and close the gates."

As a parting gift, Forud presented Bahraum with a mace covered in gold and studded in turquoise.

Bahraum returned and reported to Tous that the man on the mountain was none but the king's brother and the castle's lord, accompanied by a lieutenant. "Know that it is indeed Forud, the son of our martyred prince, Siavosh," he said. "I have seen his resemblance to his father and his birthmark."

Tous was livid. He had no interest in the identity of the men who had insulted him by daring to scout his army from their high position on the mountain; and he was furious that Bahraum had neither fought nor brought the men down for questioning. Tous reprimanded him for insubordination and heaped scorn on the house of Gudarz for what he considered to be Bahraum's cowardice. Tous commanded his brave warriors to go to the lookout point and behead the men who spied on the armies of Iran.

FORUD FIGHTS FIVE KNIGHTS

Tous's son-in-law, Rivniz, was the first to volunteer for the mission. Bahraum warned the volunteers that they would be fighting Forud, a task that was at once dangerous, dishonorable and offensive to their king. "If you ever wished to see Siavosh, you must look upon the face of his son, who stands on that mountain. He is the brother of our king. One hair on his head is worth a hundred knights."

Forud knew Tous had rejected his overture when he saw that a stranger was approaching. He pulled an arrow from his quiver and asked his guide to identify the man. "His name is Rivniz, and he is a servile man, the only brother to forty sisters," he said.

Forud was not moved to compassion. "I will not take pity on this warrior of Tous. I will send him to lie with his sisters."

Tokhwar agreed that Rivniz didn't deserve to be spared, as he had forfeited his life by accepting the mission, and Tous had to be taught a lesson for his disrespect. Forud pulled his bowstring and loosed an arrow that went straight through Rivniz's head, piercing his Roman helmet on both sides. He collapsed from the saddle in full view of the army.

Astounded, Tous ordered his son to avenge his fallen brother-in-law. But Zarasp, too, was dispatched as a formidable arrow split his armor below the waist. As Zarasp fell, a collective cry went up from the Iranian troops. Consumed with rage, Tous donned his armor and rode out to seek revenge for his son and son-in-law. Tokhwar identified Tous as the field marshal himself and suggested that they go back to the castle. But Forud would have none of it: "I don't care if it is a host of wild elephants, tigers, and crocodiles. When the battle is raging, you must feed the fire of the warrior's courage, not smother it in mud!"

Tokhwar said that killing Tous would mean challenging the entire army of Iran. "Thirty thousand men will descend on your fortress and raze it to the ground," he warned. "Besides, this would divert them from their main mission, which is avenging your father's death."

This was good counsel, but it should have come earlier.
Poor advice led Forud to forfeit his castle and his life
One should not take advice from a foolhardy courtier.

It appeared too late to withdraw. Forud could not turn back and run in full view of the entire army of Iran, not to mention his eighty attendants and consorts, cheering him from the ramparts of his castle. Tokhwar's next piece of advice was that his lord shoot Tous's horse—a knight would not fight without his steed. So Forud notched another arrow in his bow and proceeded to unhorse Tous. Another roar went up from the ramparts as the proud commander was sent staggering back to his troops on foot.

The Iranians were happy that their commander had not lost his life, but Geav was scandalized by the scene. The loss of Rivniz and Zarasp and the disgrace of Tous returning on foot was too much to take. So now he suited up to go against Forud.

As the formidable Geav rode out, Forud sighed in despair and said: "It appears that this pugnacious lot is bereft of common sense. I am afraid they will not succeed in their mission to avenge my father unless Kay-Khosrow comes to Touran himself. Then the two of us will join forces to defeat our enemy. Tell me, who is this horseman whose fate will soon be sealed?"

"He is the man who brought your brother, Kay-Khosrow, out of the land of Touran, singlehandedly annihilating entire divisions that were sent to chase them," Tokhwar said. "He is the one who tied the hands of your grandfather, Piran, and crossed the Oxus River on horseback. He wears Siavosh's armor, which deflects arrows and blades. None dares confront him. Don't shoot him. Target his horse instead."

Forud pulled an arrow from his quiver and shot Geav's horse through the heart. A roar of laughter from the battlements followed as the second Iranian knight made his way slowly down the slopes on foot. At the camp Bizhan reproached his father for turning back, but Geav said he had no choice but to retreat—that it was not fitting for a knight to fight on foot. Bizhan grew furious. He said he would personally see to it that Forud was punished for this insolence and turned around to walk away. At that moment he felt the sting of his father's horsewhip on his head.

Geav said, "Have you not heard that discretion is the better part of valor, you insolent boy?"

Bizhan was too angry to heed the pain and humiliation of his father's horsewhip. He swore an oath not to take off his armor until Zarasp's death had been avenged. Acquiring a worthy and well-armored horse from one of the commanders, Bizhan prepared for battle. Geav realized that Bizhan was determined to fight Forud and gave him Siavosh's armor for protection.

As the fifth Iranian warrior made his way up the mountain, Tokhwar informed his master that the new challenger was Bizhan, the audacious son of Geav, who was liable to pursue combat even without his horse. Indeed, the young warrior continued his climb wielding a glittering sword even after losing his horse. Forud then loosed a second arrow that pierced Bizhan's shield but did not go through his armor. As Bizhan rushed forward on foot, the young lord of Kalat turned his horse around to gallop toward the castle. A desperate cry went up from the ramparts. Bizhan gave chase and slashed at Forud's horse, sending it crashing to the ground, but the rider managed to slide through the gates that were cracked open for him. The sentinels quickly shut the doors and rained rocks down on the bellicose Iranian knight.

Now it was Bizhan's turn to taunt: "So, where is your courage now? Mounted on a horse, you ran away from a man on foot. You should be ashamed."

Bizhan returned to the Iranian camp in triumph. Tous swore an oath to raze the castle and paint the rocks of the mountain crimson with Forud's blood.

THE LAST STAND AT KALAT

That night Forud's mother had a dream in which a fire devoured their fortress. Troubled at the meaning of her vision, she ascended to the ramparts and found the entire surrounding mountains crowded with enemy soldiers. Then she went down and told her son that their fate was sealed.

"We cannot fight fate," Forud said. "My time has come. My father died unjustly at the hands of Goruy. I will be killed by Bizhan. But I will not beg for mercy. I will die a proud man." At this, he suited up for war and led his men out the gates of the castle. They fought a desperate but heroic battle as trumpets of war blared.

When the sun reached its zenith, the men of Kalat had all fallen. Forud attempted to gallop back to the castle entrance but ran into an ambush. He fought Bizhan head-on this time, but a knight named Roham slashed at him from behind, severing his arm. In great shock, Forud somehow managed to slip through the gates of the castle. There he collapsed off his horse in a pool of blood.

Jarireh came to her son's side. As he took his last breaths, she lamented that he was dying at such a tender age. The prince looked up at his mother and whispered his last request: "Nothing should go to the enemy as the rewards of their victory. Don't let Bizhan gloat over our treasures and women."

Following their master's request, the loyal consorts and attendants of Kalat flung themselves from the battlements. Jarireh burned all the treasures in a great fire and hamstrung the horses in the stable. Having denied the enemy the spoils of that unjust war, she stumbled back to Forud's side, rested her face on her son's cold cheek, and split her side with a dagger.

When the Iranians entered the castle, they found the bodies of mother and son. There was no one to enslave and nothing to plunder. Bahraum wept at the scene of the senseless carnage and rebuked his companions. "Forud died more tragically than his father," he said to Tous, Gudarz, and Geav. "Are you not afraid of the curse of the heavens? Are you not ashamed of disobeying your king's strict orders? How will you face him now that you have murdered his brother?"

They were all contrite, although Tous tried to justify the misadventure as revenge for the deaths of Zarasp and Rivniz. Bahraum responded that they were all the victims of Tous's pride and insubordination to the king's direct orders. Tous fell silent, and later ordered a royal burial for Forud. After three days of rest, the army of Iran moved forward to discharge its mission of avenging Siavosh's death.

DEFEATS AND THE RETREAT

Once the Iranian army left Kalat, a weeklong blizzard impeded their advance. Then Tous locked horns with a Touranian general named Tazhauv, who was married to Afrasiab's daughter Espanouy. After a brief skirmish, the Touranian general escaped, carrying his wife on the back of his horse. Bizhan gave chase, and Tazhauv managed to evade capture but only once he had lost his crown and abandoned his wife to be taken by his pursuer. Espanouy was known for her beauty and was considered one of the most valuable trophies of the war even before it started.

Tazhauv returned to the Touranian capital and reported the invasion to his king. Afrasiab appointed Piran to lead the counterattack. With thirty thousand battle-hardened warriors, the general moved stealthily toward the Iranian lines with the aim of waylaying the invaders. His spies arrived with the intelligence that the Iranians were drunk and asleep. Based on this information Piran managed to completely surround their camp. Tous's army had spent the night drinking and carousing to celebrate their easily won victory against Tazhauv. In their hubris, they had not posted sentries to protect them from a raid.

Thus, the entire army was caught half-naked, disarmed, inebriated, and generally unprepared when the deadly raiders struck in the middle of the night. Fortunately, Fariborz, Geav, and Gudarz were sober, and they valiantly fought back against the night raiders of Touran. The younger knights Bijan and Gostahm also gave a good account of themselves by performing prodigious acts of valor in the middle of the chaos. By the morning, the scale of the massacre was evident. The plain was littered with the corpses of the Iranian soldiers. Tous was driven to the brink of madness by the enormity of the disaster. Gudarz had lost most of his sons to the slaughter.

When Kay-Khosrow heard of the catastrophe, he relieved Tous of his command and ordered him and the clan of Nowzar to return to the capital. Instead, he dispatched his uncle Fariborz to carry the Standard of Kaveh, which was the sign of the supreme commander. Upon the return of Tous and his kinsmen, Fariborz proposed a truce to the

Touranian commander. Piran replied that the Iranians were the invaders. Nevertheless, he gave them one month to leave Touran or prepare for war. Once the truce period had elapsed, the two sides were ready for another confrontation.

In the bloody and heavy battles of Pashan and Lauvan that ensued, the Iranians were defeated again. Fariborz withdrew to higher ground, and a rout was avoided only because of the heroic determination of the knights of Gudarz's clan. Bizhan heaped shame on Fariborz for failing to stand his ground and claimed he should surrender the Standard of Kaveh to be used in the counterattack. Fariborz refused this demand as it was tantamount to abdication. Bizhan ripped the flag in two and carried his half with his clan's counterattack. Fariborz's brother Rivniz joined this heroic assault. Geav, Bizhan, and Gostahm the son of Kazhdaham pushed forth and saved the army from a disgraceful collapse, but the casualties were heavy, and the battle was lost. Only eight warriors of Gudarz's clan survived the conflict. The worthy Bahraum, who had lost his horse, fought for three days on foot, and refused Piran's offer of quarter. Finally, he was ambushed and killed by Tazhauv, who was later captured and killed by Geav. Fariborz's brother Rivniz was also among the casualties. Nor was he the only victim of the house of Kay. They had lost eighty knights and princes in one battle. The victors also suffered enormous casualties. Piran lost nine hundred of his children, grandchildren, and kinsmen, and Afrasiab lost three hundred.

The Iranian expedition that had started with the misadventure of Kalat and the killing of Forud had foundered at Pashan and Lauvan. After this disaster, the Iranian morale was so poor that they retreated in shame. Piran received a hero's welcome at the Touranian court. Afrasiab celebrated the triumph for two weeks, and lavish festivities were arranged in honor of the victorious general.

The knights stood before their king at the Iranian court with folded arms and hung their heads low in shame. They had disobeyed the king, killed his brother, been caught in a shameful ambush, and lost two battles in the most ignoble way. Kay-Khosrow cried tears of sorrow and fury, reprimanded his defeated generals, and said that a thousand of them deserved public execution for insubordination and incompetence.

But he had spared them out of pity for the sake of God. Kay-Khosrow averred that none among the knights deserved beheading more than the villainous Tous.

"Have you no shame before God and the assembly of knights?" the king excoriated him. "Did I not warn you against taking the mountain path? After your senseless murder of Forud, you continued your march of folly and allowed yourself to be waylaid. Why would you treat the battlefield like a banquet, drinking to excess and leaving yourself vulnerable? Your evil deeds have brought immense loss to the clan of Gudarz. You are a fool. You belong in a madhouse. Indeed, you are the mad son of your inept father. You are lower than a dog in my eyes. Only your white beard and lineage save you from beheading. Be gone from my sight, and let your house be your prison."

Then the king addressed the assembly:

"I can't tell friend from foe anymore. I was mourning my father. Now I must mourn my brothers. I dispatch a great army headed by forty knights in their golden boots, and I reap nothing but disaster and humiliation."

With this, the great king contemptuously dismissed the knights and barred them from his palace. He forbade himself a life of leisure and happiness.

Such is the enigmatic nature of war
One finds a narrow grave and another
Victory and all one could ever wish for.

CHAPTER 10

The Great War of Nations: Iran Besieged

Before the battle of Kamous, let us say grace
To our Creator and honor the great Rostam
Whose heroic deeds deserve our humble praise.

Splendid mansions decay by the dint of time
Even a house of flint is tarnished by the elements
But the poetic edifice I erected in rhyme,

Shall endure damages of the rain and the sun.
For decades have I suffered to restore and versify
These legends and now my work is almost done.

THE THIRD INVASION

When Rostam heard about the failed invasion of Touran and Kay-Khosrow's dismissal of the assembly of his knights, he left Zabol for the Winter Palace of Pars and requested an audience with the king so he might speak on behalf of his fellow knights.

"I beg the king, who brings honor to the throne, the crown, and the royal ring, to forgive Tous's faults," he said. "The confrontation with Forud was an unfortunate blunder. Tous is reckless by nature. Witnessing the demise of his son and son-in-law by Forud's hand drove him over the edge. Such was the decree of fate."

At this, Tous came forward to offer his apologies. "I am ashamed," he said with humility, "in the sight of the king, as the guiltiest among the knights. Forud, Rivniz, Zarasp, and Bahraum were all slain for my sins. But if it pleases the king, I shall redeem myself by avenging Siavosh's death. I wager my life on it."

Kay-Khosrow said that the battles of Pashan and Lauvan were a stain on Iran's reputation, and that he aimed to set the accounts straight and take revenge for the fallen. The knights pledged their commitment to the new campaign, and Tous was once more appointed to lead the invasion, on the condition that he consult Geav in all his decisions.

Drums rolled, and the army moved behind Kaveh's standard toward Touran's borders. Piran was distraught when he heard that a new invasion had been launched, as he knew his Touranian armies were not prepared for war. In desperation, he sent a message to Tous: "After all my care and mourning for Siavosh, and after the services I rendered to Farigis and Kay-Khosrow, is this the bitter harvest I deserve to reap?"

Tous took pity on Piran and sent word that, should he leave with his troops and come to the Iranian side, he would be forgiven and rewarded with knighthood and a crown of honor.

Piran responded deceitfully, indicating that he needed time to persuade his clan to defect. At the same time, he dispatched a messenger to Afrasiab, asking for reinforcements.

Afrasiab sent an army so enormous it nearly blotted the sky and sun. When the Iranians were outnumbered two hundred to one, Piran put aside all pretense of seeking peace and charged forward in full force. Tous had been deceived.

As the two sides faced off, Houman rode up from the Touranian front to challenge the Iranian army, and Tous came forward. Houman expressed his surprise that a commander would come in person to fight, to which his Iranian opponent responded: "I am both commander and warrior. You and your brother Piran should come over to our side. The king has advised me to protect the clan of Piran, the son of Viseh."

"Piran's hands are tied," Houman replied. "He does not fight this battle of his own accord. He is loyal to his king just as you are to yours."

As they continued the discourse, Bizhan rode out and harangued Tous for fraternizing with the enemy rather than speaking in the language of the sword. Houman addressed Bizhan: "It is true that your clan of Gudarz was nearly wiped out in the battle of Pashan. You have every right to be angry with us over the death of your brother Bahraum as well. But you have no right to tell Tous what to do. If you are so eager to fight, let us draw our swords. Death is our inevitable fate, and it is best to die on the battlefield."

Bizhan accepted the challenge, and the two fought with spears, swords, and bows and arrows. They were too equally matched for one to emerge the victor. Both warriors returned to their sides, and the general battle commenced in full force.

As valiantly as the Iranians fought, they could not prevail, and the number of casualties swelled. Gudarz lamented his fate as he watched what remained of his relatives and members of his clan fall. Tous was heard saying: "Would that my royal father, Nowzar, had not planted my seed, so I would not witness so many friends and kin lying lifeless on the battlefield."

Tous had no choice but to withdraw his men under cover of night to Hamauvan Mountain. From there, he sent word to his king for reinforcements and, above all, for Rostam's assistance.

When Piran heard of their withdrawal, he knew it was only a matter of time before Rostam arrived—now was his only chance to crush the Iranians. Houman rode out to the retreating army and scolded Tous and Geav. "You came from Iran with war elephants and a great army to avenge Siavosh's death. Are you not ashamed to run to the mountains like a flock of sheep?"

Once they had fully retreated, Piran decided to surround the Hamauvan Mountain to starve the Iranians into surrender. To implement this plan, he asked Afrasiab for massive reinforcements. The auxiliary forces came in the form of a coalition of ten nations; kings from India and China and champions from Kushan, Sind, and Rome joined the armies of Touran, filling the horizon with their various flags.

The disaster seemed to be upon them, and Tous was unsure if his own reinforcements would make it in time. Provisions were in short supply, and morale was low. All attempts to break the siege had failed. That night, Tous dreamt of Siavosh, whose face was luminous. He reclined on an ivory throne enveloped in the glow of a candle that strangely emerged from watery depths. The martyred prince addressed him: "Keep your troops here, for victory is yours. Do not mourn for the fate of those lost to the clan of Gudarz. We are drinking wine in a bower of flowers, and we shall drink forever."

Tous interpreted the dream to mean that Rostam was coming to rescue them. He shared this vision with Gudarz, and the two knights took heart.

But the next day, the enemy had multiplied and tightened the siege. Gudarz climbed to a high peak and saw the enormity of the coalition assembled against them. "Bitter misfortune is my lot," he wailed. "My chalice is filled with poison. I had an army of sons and grandsons. They have all been killed to avenge Siavosh's death. I have lost hope, and my day has turned to night. Would that I had never been born."

Gudarz ordered his horse to be saddled and his grave to be dug. He prepared to wade into enemy lines for a heroic death. But at that very moment, a lookout spotted an army approaching from the west, flying a standard that bore the image of a dragon.

THE HERO AT THE HAMAUVAN MOUNTAIN

Having heard of the plight of his army at Hamauvan Mountain, Kay-Khosrow dispatched Rostam and Fariborz to bring reinforcements. Rostam sent an envoy ahead of him to the besieged Iranians, advising that they refrain from desperate attempts to break the siege before his arrival. Tous and Gudarz rejoiced. With Rostam on their side, the tide would undoubtedly turn in their favor.

Piran was disheartened to hear of the approaching Iranian forces. He said to his knights: "I am filled with dread. I truly hope that it is not Rostam who has come to the aid of the enemy."

But Rostam, too, was disappointed to hear that one of the champions of the Touranian alliance, Kamous of Kushan, had just unhorsed and humiliated Tous and Geav. As he arrived on the front lines of Hamauvan, another Kushanian champion, Ashkebous, was taunting the Iranians. Scandalized by the failure of his fellow knights to rise to the challenge, Rostam picked up his bow and a quiver of arrows and walked out into the arena on foot. Rakhsh was too tired from the long journey, so he could not go to battle in full gear. "Speak your name and tell me, who shall cry over your headless body?" sneered the overweening Ashkebous.

"You will not last long enough to benefit from knowing my name. But if you must know, my mother named me 'Your Death.'"

"Then where is your horse? Is this a joke? What kind of knight comes to war on foot?"

"Tous sent me here on foot to take you off your horse," said Rostam. "Surely someone of your strength will fight much better with his boots on the ground."

"Where are your weapons? You are making a mockery of battle."

"This bow is all I need. Allow me to show you how it works."

With this, Rostam loosed an arrow that struck Ashkebous's horse and brought him to the ground. "You were so proud of that horse," Rostam laughed. "Go mourn your companion somewhere away from the battlefield."

Badly shaken, the Kushanian warrior sent a barrage of ineffective arrows at his opponent. Rostam kneaded the string of his bow with relish as he advised his opponent not to fatigue himself in a useless exercise. Then he chose an excellent shaft from his quiver. No sooner had the arrow kissed Rostam's fingertips than it went through Ashkebous's backbone, killing him on the spot.

The Chinese king, one of Afrasiab's allies in the grand coalition of nations, looked upon this scene with amazement and sent someone to retrieve the unknown Iranian warrior's arrow. Upon examining the missile, he turned to Piran and said, "You disparaged these people, calling them a ragtag army of worthless warriors. This arrow is longer than a lance. What kind of a ragtag warrior uses such arrows?"

Piran's heart sank, as he knew that arrow could only belong to Rostam. But Kamous of Kushan had not lost his confidence. He swore an oath that he would vanquish the owner of the long arrow that had killed his compatriot.

At the next day's dawn, Rostam put on his helmet and donned his leopard skin surcoat over two layers of chainmail, and rode up to the front of the Iranian army. He advised the troops to forget their ties to this world and seek glory on the battlefield.

Kamous came forward and, in the first battle of the day, slew one of Rostam's chosen lance holders. The hero unfurled his lariat and roared, challenging the Kushanian to a duel.

"Why are you haranguing us?" Kamous replied. "Lower your voice and explain what you intend to do with that string wrapped around your arm."

"How can a lion not roar when he sees a herd of onager? As for this string, don't be hasty. I will demonstrate how it is used."

Kamous rushed Rostam and threw a javalin aiming for the neck of Rakhsh, but the blade did not break through his barding. Rostam ensnared the Kushanian warrior in his lariat, fastened it to Rakhsh's saddle, and in one swift movement unhorsed and captured him. Thus, he lost the gamble on which he had wagered his honor and his life.

The Chinese king called for a warrior to avenge Kamous. A man named Changash rose to the occasion. He donned his armor and rode to the Iranian side with much bravado, shooting arrows and calling for Rostam. The hero came forward and presented himself. Rostam's pose struck such fear into the heart of Changash that he fled the scene. Rostam gave chase to his opponent, riding so quickly he was able to grab his horse's tail. The Touranian army watched in amazement as Changash threw himself on the ground and begged for mercy. Ignoring this pitiful gesture, Rostam dismounted and beheaded him.

The battle's tide was turning in favor of Iran. The Chinese king told Piran that it was time they spoke to the confounding warrior to see whether he could be appeased in any way. Houman was charged with learning the identity and intentions of the man.

EMBASSIES OF PEACE

Houman rode out to Rostam incognito, gave him a false name, and professed to be on the verge of defecting to the Iranian side. Then he asked the mighty Iranian warrior his name and intentions. "You don't need to know my name," Rostam replied. "Suffice it to say that I am here to wreak havoc on those who spilled the blood of our innocent Siavosh and annihilated the clan of Gudarz. To end this war, you must surrender the wicked Garsivaz, who plotted against Siavosh, and the shameless Goruy, who beheaded our prince. Then you must surrender five children of Viseh: Houman, Lahauk, Farshidvard, Golbaud, and Nastihan—all except the noble Piran, whom I love and pity. He alone is moderate among the Touranians. He was the only one to mourn Siavosh. Send me Piran as your ambassador and be quick about it."

Houman swiftly went to his brother. "Our days are numbered, as this hero is without doubt Rostam," he said, trembling. "He knows us all by name and demands our surrender. My name is at the top of his list. You are the only one for whom he has respect. He wants to have a word with you."

Piran reported to the Chinese king that the man who had killed Kamous was indeed the great hero Rostam. Then he went to the Iranian side and addressed Rostam.

"Exalted commander!" he shouted. "Here I am."

"State your name and business."

"I am Piran, the son of Viseh. I was told that you wish to see me. What is your name?"

"I am Rostam of Zabol."

At hearing this, Piran dismounted, kissed the ground and asked about the health of Zaul, Zavareh, and Faramarz. He also inquired about Farigis and Kay-Khosrow.

"If you will indulge me," Piran said after the pleasantries, "I wish in all humility to share my troubles with you. I planted a tree, but its leaves have turned into poison, and its fruit is blood. Siavosh loved me like a father, and I was his shield against all evil in the world. It is true that I failed him. But I was the one who saved his wife, Farigis, and held her in my own house. I was the one who protected her son, Kay-Khosrow, from the wrath of Afrasiab. Hardships have been visited upon me since that day. For all my labors, I am now caught between two kings. I have already lost my dear brother Pilsam and many of my kin to these wars of revenge. The soldiers standing here have nothing to do with Siavosh's death, yet their lives have been forfeited. I cry tears of blood. What is the point of living if I cannot prevent this bloodbath?"

"I have seen nothing but honesty from you," replied Rostam. "I offer you two solutions. Either Touran should send us those responsible for spilling Siavosh's blood, or you can personally defect to our side, in which case King Kay-Kavous will compensate you tenfold for all you will lose in this move."

Piran despaired, knowing that he could not deliver Afrasiab's close relatives to expiate the blood of Siavosh. Nor could he hand over his own five brothers as a ransom for the brothers Gudarz had lost in the previous battles. So, he asked for a reprieve on the excuse that he needed to consult his peers and the king of Touran on the Iranian offer.

Piran conveyed Rostam's conditions to his clan. Then he met with the war council of the Touran coalition. Neither the Chinese king nor the commander of the Indian contingent, King Shangol, seemed concerned. Shangol displayed some bravado, saying that he would slay Rostam in the next day's battle. These empty boasts did not hearten Piran.

I could picture this day when I advised Afrasiab against alienating Siavosh, an unrivaled prince brought up by Rostam, Piran mused to himself. *But he listened to the worthless Garsivaz instead of me. Rostam has come to avenge his beloved prince, and none can stop him. I pity my brothers who will be killed in this conflict and my homeland, which will be devastated.*

On the Iranian side, Rostam had similar presentiments about the demise of Piran's clan. He said to Gudarz: "An impeccable warrior must avoid acts of injustice and take the path of righteousness. Piran protected Farigis and Kay-Khosrow. My heart goes out to him. I know he and his brothers will be slain before this affair ends. But I will not stain my hands in the blood of this honorable old soldier."

Gudarz reminded Rostam of Piran's earlier treachery when he had asked for time to surrender while dispatching messengers to Afrasiab for reinforcements. Rostam agreed that Piran was a cunning warrior but again insisted he would not wage war on him unless he rejected his terms.

The next day's battles confirmed Piran's suspicions. King Shangol came to the arena riding his war elephant, decked out with a colorful parasol. A massive army followed him in well-ordered flanks. Rostam mounted an immediate frontal attack, and the king panicked and turned back, causing his men to flee from his elephant in a disgraceful rout.

The Chinese king sent a messenger to invite Rostam to a parlay so they could discuss peace. He replied that it was too late for negotiations as Iran was the decisive victor of the war. The messenger begged to differ and claimed that the Iranian commander was too self-confident. At this, Rostam broke off negotiations, galloped to the Chinese king sitting on his elephant, caught him in his lariat and pulled him down.

With this final move, the coalition of Touran unraveled. Piran and his brothers were reduced to flight. The remainder of the armies milled about like a flock of sheep who had lost their shepherd. After a while they all surrendered. Rostam declared victory on the fortieth day of his arrival at Hamauvan Mountain and claimed the enormous booty left behind by the Touranian alliance for his king. The hero allowed the enemy soldiers to disarm and leave in peace. He also sent Fariborz to King Kay-Kavous with the good tidings of the total defeat of Touran. The king praised his powerful knight: "He who has Rostam at his right hand will be forever young." Kay-Kavous rewarded his uncle Fariborz with a crown, a throne, a bejeweled torque, and golden slippers. Then he sent a caravan of handsome and richly attired slaves and camel loads of jewels to Rostam to express his appreciation for the victory at the battle of Hamauvan.

Only one battle remained: The conquest of the castle of Bidad, whose master was the notorious cannibal Kafoor. Many Iranians were killed in that ensuing battle. Gostahm was frightened when he saw the visage of the giant, demonic man in his full armor and sent Bizhan to call Rostam to the front. Kafoor threw his sword at the hero but Rostam deflected it by his shield and lowered the demonic man to the ground with a powerful blow of his javelin. At this, the defenders pulled back behind the ramparts of the castle. Rostam ordered digging under one of the walls of the fortress, causing it to collapse. The Iranians poured in, killing the defenders and laying waste to the place. Geav was sent to pursue the escaping warriors of

Bidad all the way to the borders of Khotan. Rostam declared three days of rest to be followed by an invasion of the capital of Touran, Kang.

A DESPERATE CONTEST

Dismayed by the crushing defeat of his armies, Afrasiab mounted a frantic counterattack under the flag of a local king by the name of Puladvand, who was famous for his prodigious talents with the lariat and the mace. He brought a mass of warriors to where the Iranian army was camped and challenged them to a new battle. Rostam ferociously tore into the right flank of this army, killing many of its officers.

Puladvand rode up to the front and unfurled his lariat. Tous responded to the challenge but was immediately captured in the enemy's noose. Geav, Roham, and Bizhan went to rescue their friend, but they, too, were ensnared. To further aggravate his offense, Puladvand breached the Iranian lines where the sacred Standard of Kaveh was raised and managed to tear it in half.

A wave of panic shot through the Iranian camp as Puladvand caught Tous in his noose. Gudarz was forced to personally appeal to Rostam when Roham, Geav, and Bizhan too were caught by the indefatigable enemy. The hero beheld Puladvand's massive frame and knew why he inspired so much fear among the Iranians. With four of their best fighters in bondage, Rostam said a prayer and stepped up to challenge this new enemy.

After exchanging taunts, Rostam and Puladvand pounded each other with their heavy maces until it was clear that they were in a stalemate. They agreed to settle the contest by wrestling on the condition that both the Iranian and Touranian sides refrain from interfering in the contest.

Afrasiab worried for his champion and intended to violate the rules of the contest by sending someone to assist Puladvand. His son Shideh opposed this unchivalrous act. At the arena Rostam lifted his opponent high upon his neck and slammed him to the ground. He remained motionless and all assumed that he died of the impact.

The sound of drums and trumpets rose from the Iranian camp to celebrate the victory, and Rostam rode to join them. Realizing that his foe was gone, Puladvand nimbly jumped to his feet and ran away. Afrasiab, too, dropped his standard and escaped. The Iranians saw the army of Touran escaping and prepared to give chase. Rostam forbad it. "Let them go," he commanded. "Stop the killing. It is time for peace." And thus concluded the third cycle of Iran's wars of vengeance.

The lengthy tale of Kamous has ended at long last
I've succeeded to preserve it in minute detail
In the grand frame that I've cast.

CHAPTER 11

A Curious Foe: Akvaun the Demon

Ponder the world we inhabit and the mysteries thereof.
Think about your own body and what quickens it to life
And behold the dome of the starry heavens above.

Getting stuck on the surface of fairy tales is demeaning
To reason. If one calmly sounds the depths of these stories
Judgments will give way to a comprehension of their meaning.

CONTENDING WITH A CONTRARIAN DEMON

During a hiatus from the wars of revenge, Kay-Khosrow sat in a pleasure garden drinking wine in the company of his knights. Suddenly a shepherd happened upon the gathering and delivered a bewildering report: "A strange creature has appeared in my herd. It looks like an onager with the mane of a lion and the color of the golden sun. It's taller than a horse, and a black line runs from its head to its tail. The creature runs amok like a demon on a rampage."

Kay-Khosrow knew that this was no onager. He charged Rostam with investigating the matter, advising him to be cautious. The hero obliged his king and headed out to where the creature had been sighted. After three days of hunting onagers, he spotted the strange beast. Bringing Rakhsh to a gallop, he attempted to capture it in his lariat, but it vanished into thin air.

The hero concluded that the beast had to be the notorious demon called Akvaun. Rostam kept looking for the golden mane of the beast for three more days and nights until he came to a fountain. Hungry, thirsty, and in desperate need of sleep, he dismounted, relieved Rakhsh of his bridle and saddle, and lay down to rest.

Akvaun was monitoring Rostam from a distance. Once he was sure Rostam was asleep he crept up and lifted him high above his head. The monster had discarded his disguise and reverted to his true form as a fearsome giant, so tall that his head scraped the heavenly spheres. Rostam awoke and found himself in the air, about to be hurled from incredible heights.

"Now I shall grant the great knight of Iran one wish," Akvaun spoke. "Which way do you prefer to be thrown? I could hurl you far away into the sea or against the boulders of that mountain."

It was evident that Rostam would not survive a fall on land from that height. But there was a chance of survival if he were thrown into the sea. Knowing the demon's contrarian nature, he responded: "It is said that the one who is drowned at sea will never attain salvation. So, now that you grant this wish, throw me on the mountain so I can show its leopards and the lions how courageous men fight."

To spite Rostam, the demon turned toward the sea, roared, and flung him to the farthest blue horizon. Upon splashing into the water, Rostam unsheathed his sword to defend himself against any predators as he swam toward the land. When he reached the shore, he dried his clothes and searched for his steed.

With his master gone, Rakhsh had been taken in by Afrasiab's stable hands. Rostam stole close to the herd and spotted his trusted stallion cavorting with Afrasiab's mares. Quickly he roped his horse in, saddled him, and galloped away. Several shepherds gave chase, but Rostam unsheathed his blade and attacked the posse, killing two-thirds of them. The rest ran back to Afrasiab and reported the theft of the horse they had captured.

"This is humiliating, Your Majesty," one complained. "Have we been so degraded in the world that a single man dares to raid your herds and ride away with his choice of the stallions?"

Afrasiab gathered an army along with four white elephants to give chase. Realizing that he was being followed, Rostam confronted his pursuers with a torrent of arrows, forcing them to retreat. He then took Afrasiab's prize war elephants and returned to the fountainhead, where he had first encountered the demon.

When Akvaun saw Rostam approaching, he taunted him. "I see that you escaped the perils of the sea to come here for fresh torments."

This time Rostam was ready. He swiftly caught the demon in his lariat and pounded his face with a heavy mace, cut off his head, and packed it along with the booty he had won from the Touranians for the pavilion of his king.

Kay-Khosrow was delighted to see Rostam return triumphantly and offered thanks to God for having such an able knight. They feasted for two days. Rostam asked leave to visit his father, Zaul, promising to return, as the task of avenging Siavosh's death was still incomplete. Kay-Khosrow endowed Rostam with many gifts and went with him for two milestones before bidding him farewell.

This was a pleasant labor as Rostam overcame
A monster and won glory for his friends and kin
Alas this mutable world doesn't remain the same.

CHAPTER 12

A Daring Love: Bizhan and Manizheh

It was a black night that swallowed the stars
The moon was anemic and dim
As were Mercury, Saturn, and Mars.

Not even the cry of a distant bird broke
The heavy silence. I felt oppressed
Under the night's black cloak.

I rose in tears and asked my beloved for a light
She lit a candle and tended to me with caresses
To soothe my anxieties and allay my fright.

I partook of wine, quinces, and pomegranates that night
And she told me the story of a foreign princess
Who fell for Bizhan, the gallant Iranian knight.

On the condition that once she was through
I would render the tale in Persian verse.
This was the pleasant task that I agreed to do.

With the triumph against Touran, Kay-Khosrow once again celebrated his victories in the company of his knights. During the revelries, the court chancellor presented petitioners from Armenia who lived close to Touran's border. The envoys kissed the ground and complained of an infestation of wild boars that had ruined their cultivated lands and decimated their herds. Unable to cope with the savage beasts, they had come to seek the assistance of their king. Kay-Khosrow took pity on the petitioners and challenged his brave company of knights. "Who among my knights volunteers to rid my subjects of the wild boars that plague them?"

The king ordered a spread of precious jewels to be laid out, to induce volunteers to step forward. Ten horses with golden bridles were also added to the prize. Bizhan volunteered for the dangerous mission, to the chagrin of his father, Geav, who said: "Why would you recklessly set foot on an unknown path beset by all kinds of peril?"

Bizhan reminded his father of his past heroic deeds and said to the king: "I may be young in years, but I am a seasoned warrior. I shall wipe out these beasts. Am I not the son of Geav, the destroyer of armies?"

Kay-Khosrow entrusted the mission to him and said: "The king who has a knight like you will never fear the enemy."

A knight named Gorgin, who was familiar with the Armenian plain, was appointed to accompany Bizhan as a guide. The two embarked on their mission in high spirits, taking falcons to hunt partridge and pheasant and cheetahs to catch mountain sheep and onager. In this manner, the two knights jauntily rode out to the Armenian border. As they approached the thicket of boars, they heard strange noises as it was heaving with the sound of the unseen beasts.

Bizhan suggested that his companion collaborate in the hunt by accompanying him into the woods or else stand outside with his mace and dispatch any boars that tried to escape. This did not sound fair to Gorgin: "This is not my business. You are the one who took the kingly gifts to exterminate the boars of Armenia. I am only a lowly guide." Offended by this remark, Bizhan tore into the thicket alone, holding a single dagger. A large swine attacked him, slashing his armor with its tusk, but he stabbed it and cut off its head. He then slaughtered the entire sounder and returned to his camp with a sack full of tusks. He said he would present them as a trophy of his victory to the king.

Gorgin pretended he was happy about the success of his companion, but his heart was dark with evil thoughts. He knew that if Bizhan returned in triumph, everyone would learn of his refusal to assist in the hunt, which would diminish him in the eyes of the king and the knights.

"Swine tusks are hardly a good idea for a royal gift," he told Bizhan. "I have a better suggestion. There is an annual Touranian festival that is about to commence in a gorgeous meadow not far from here. Afrasiab's daughter, Manizheh, presides over the festivities in the company of a hundred of her elegant attendants. Don't you think capturing a few of these beauties for the king's harem would make for a better trophy than a heap of worthless tusks?"

THE LOVELY FESTIVAL OF THE WOODS

Bizhan was fascinated by the descriptions of the festivity and decided to make the one-day journey to the lush plain where it would be held.

Upon arriving on the border of Touran, the knights busied themselves with hunting for a couple of days until the tents of the revelers were erected in the distance. Wishing to go to the event alone, Bizhan donned his favorite golden crown, decorated with a lammergeier feather, a torque, earrings that he had received from his king, and a bracelet that was a gift from his father. Then he fastened the golden buckle of his belt and rode his black stallion to the festival grounds where he dismounted under a cypress tree to rest. His intention was to recoonoiter the event and decide his next move.

But, Princess Manizheh, the daughter of Afrasiab, espied him first from her pavilion. Smitten by the handsome knight, she sent forth her lady-in-waiting with this command: "Go to that young man and find out who he is. He looks like Prince Siavosh incarnate, if he isn't some angel in human form. Find out why he has come this way and invite him to honor us with his presence for I have never seen another more handsome than he."

Manizheh's emissary went to Bizhan and conveyed her mistress's message. The dashing paladin replied: "My fair lady, I am neither Siavosh incarnate nor an angel. My name is Bizhan, the son of Geav and a knight of Iran. I came here to rid the locals of the plague of wild boars, and I have succeeded in that labor. I have heaps of boar tusks as proof of my success at the task entrusted to me by my king. The reason I came further was to catch a glimpse of the beauteous daughter of Afrasiab. I will offer you a crown, a belt, and earrings of gold if you lead me to her."

She took this message back to her mistress and sang Bizhan's praises. Manizheh sent her back with this message: "Rejoice, for you have found what you came here to seek. Come to me this instant and fill my dark life with the light of your presence."

The lady-in-waiting led the young knight to the princess's pavilion. As he entered her chambers, Manizheh embraced him and graciously suggested that he might undo his ceremonial belt and be at ease. "Why are you marring your handsome visage by this formal outfit?" she asked. "And why are you carrying a mace? You have no enemies here. Eat and drink and be merry as our guest of honor."

As Bizhan sipped fine wine served in crystal chalices, he was overcome by the joy of being in the company of the seductive Manizheh. For three days and nights, they ate and drank to the sound of skillful musicians until sleep and inebriation overcame them. But the young lovers had a sense of melancholy, knowing the time of their departure was approaching.

The princess of Touran found herself unable to let her handsome companion go. Thus, she had her attendants lace his drink with a soporific substance. When the potion took effect, she ordered her attendants to wrap the sleeping Bizhan in soft sheets and place him in her litter, which was carried atop an elephant. She hid him under a blanket and arranged the trip so they would enter the capital of Touran at night. In this manner, the bold princess spirited her beloved man into her quarters at the heart of Afrasiab's palace.

Bizhan woke from his slumber to find himself still in the embrace of the lovely Manizheh. Frightened to be without a weapon in enemy country, he cursed Gorgin for ensnaring him in such a trap. Manizheh put his mind at ease, saying: "Don't worry, my love, over what has not happened yet. Be merry, for the future is no more real than the wind. There is a time for pleasure and a time for war. Let us fully enjoy the time we have together."

Bizhan surrendered to Manizheh's temptations. At her command, beautiful girls from every corner of the earth entertained the couple with their songs and music for the remainder of the day and many more days and nights that came and went.

BIZHAN BOUND

All went well until the gatekeeper at Manizheh's palace heard the rumors that a stranger was being kept in the princess's quarters. After investigating the matter and learning the identity of the secret visitor, he went to the king afraid for his life. "Permission to report," he said, "that His Majesty's daughter has been hiding an Iranian knight in her chambers."

Afrasiab was outraged. He would have acted precipitously had it not been for the advice of a wise counselor who enjoined him to probe the matter first. After all, relying on rumors had served the king poorly in the affair of Siavosh. Afrasiab turned to his brother Garsivaz and said: "Fate torments me with disobedient children. Now I must contend with both of these crises at once. Go to Manizheh's palace and investigate this sordid business. If you find an intruder, bind and bring him to me immediately."

Garsivaz surrounded Manizheh's palace with three hundred soldiers. But when they tried to enter, they found all the doors locked. The air filled with music of a harmonious harp and lute, and sounds of merriment. Garsivaz tore the main entrance door off its hinges and burst in to find three hundred servant girls with instruments and chalices of wine surrounding the presiding princess of Touran and her special Iranian guest.

When Bizhan saw the intruders, he jumped to his feet in great anguish. *How can I defend myself without my horse and weapons?* he thought. *Now only God can help me.*

He pulled out the dagger he always carried in his boot and addressed Garsivaz: "I am Bizhan, the son of Geav. None will lay hands on me unless his body has tired of the company of his head. Nor will anyone see my back in flight. You know the reputation of my warrior clan. Many of your men will die by my dagger. And yet this could be avoided if you spare my life and advocate my cause before the king."

Garsivaz knew that the Iranian paladin meant what he said. So, he pretended to agree to his conditions. Thus, the young knight was disarmed, bound, and brought to Afrasiab. "Greetings to the great king," said Bizhan. "If you ask me why I am here, I will say I did not come of my own accord. Nor is anyone to be blamed for my presence at your palace. I came to Armenia from Iran on a boar hunting mission from my king. I lost a falcon and followed it until I fell asleep under a cypress tree. A genie spread its wings over me and spirited me away. Then we flew over a Touranian caravan with an elephant on which a litter had been fixed. A beautiful lady was asleep in the litter. The genie invoked the devil's name, dropped me in the litter, and recited an incantation over the lady to keep her from waking. That is how I entered your palace without my volition or the awareness of the princess Manizheh. I have not offended you. Your daughter is innocent of this affair. I blame the accursed genie for everything that has happened."

"Your luck has run out," replied Afrasiab. "You came here to spread mischief and make a name for yourself. Now you stand before me with shackled hands and tremble like a woman. Worst of all, you are trying to save your skin by a string of outlandish lies."

"Now listen to a sober assessment, great king," said Bizhan. "Boars and lions fight with their tusks and claws, and warriors need their swords and maces to fight. I am disarmed and my hands are tied. To examine my mettle, let His Majesty provide me with a horse and a mace. I shall take on a thousand Touranians and win."

Afrasiab was incredulous. He turned to Garsivaz and asked: "Can you believe that this devil of a man thinks I am obliged to provide him with the means of glorious combat so that he can kill my men? Does he suppose he hasn't done enough evil already? What else can we expect from dishonorable Iranians? Take him out and hang him from the gallows. Let this be a lesson to those who covet what is ours."

As they dragged Bizhan out to the gallows, he cried out: "I don't complain of my fate if an early death is written for me. I'm afraid of what the knights of Iran will say when they find out that I was hanged with a body unscathed by battle wounds. I dread the disgrace this will bring to my clan and my noble forefathers."

But the impetuous knight's luck had not entirely run out. As they dug the holes to erect the gallows, the wise Piran arrived on the scene and asked the reason for such activities. Garsivaz said that the man intended for execution was Bizhan, the son of Geav, and his crime was crossing the borders of Touran and violating the sanctity of the royal palace. The old Touranian knight took pity on the victim and asked him his side of the story. Bizhan told him everything, including Gorgin's disloyalty. Piran stayed the hand of the executioner and went up to the king to plead for the victim's life.

In Afrasiab's palace, the old knight was received according to protocol. The king commanded him to state his purpose and pledged to grant his wish. "All I have is due to your generosity, great king," said Piran. "I am here not to ask favors for myself but to advise you on a matter of great importance. I warned you over the matter of Siavosh. I said that killing the son of Kay-Kavous would spell disaster for us, and it did. You have seen what they have done to the land of Touran to avenge Siavosh's death. Rostam's sword is still dripping with blood over that affair. No one knows the power of Geav and Gudarz on the battlefield better than Your Majesty. Shedding the blood of their scion would bring a fresh calamity upon us. It is not wise to create new causes for strife with Iran."

This enflamed Afrasiab's anger. "But you have no idea how this man has shamed me in my own land," the king said. "He has dishonored my daughter and made me a laughingstock among nations. If I let him live, wagging tongues would never stop, and my honor would never be restored."

Piran recognized that the king had a right to be angry but continued to advise prudence. "Then punish him. Put heavy chains on this sinner and suffer him to serve as an example to the world. This imprisonment will be a living death for him. Lock him up and let his name be wiped from the annals of time."

Afrasiab accepted this advice, and charged Garsivaz: "Fix chains on Bizhan and lower him into a deep well in the middle of the Khotan desert, where the rays of the sun and the moon never reach. Cover the well with the boulder that Akvaun hurled from the bottom of the ocean onto that desert. I give you Manizheh's palace to plunder to recompense you for your troubles. Convey my rebuke to that insolent girl: 'You have ruined my good name. You do not deserve the golden wreath of a princess. Be content, for if you look deep inside the darkness of the well, you can behold the man you once placed on a golden dais.'"

Garsivaz did as he was told. He brought the unfortunate princess, wearing tattered rags, to Bizhan's well and mocked her: "This is your home now. You are now the servant of your pitiful lover."

She lay beside the opening, pushed her arms through the crack between the boulder and the edge of the well, and wept for Bizhan all night. When the sun rose on the horizon she wandered around the close by villages and begged for leftovers. At night she came back, pushed the meager morsels through the well's opening, and wept. Thereafter this was how Manizheh spent her days and nights.

RETURN TO COURT

Gorgin kept waiting for his companion to return to the thicket of boars. He was beginning to feel the pangs of guilt for his disloyalty. Returning to the site of the festival he found Bizhan's unkempt black horse. He lingered there for a few days vaguely hoping for the return of Bizhan. Finally, he roped in Bizhan's horse and went back to Iran.

When Geav learned that Gorgin was returning alone, he rushed out to demand an explanation. Gorgin dismounted at the sight of the prominent knight and humbled himself, saying: "I am so ashamed that an exalted knight like you has come out to welcome a lowly servant like me. I am even more ashamed that I have returned without your son. But do not worry. He is alive, and I will give you a full account of what happened."

Geav knew something had gone terribly wrong as his son's horse had been brought back without his master. The knight dismounted, ripped his garments to pieces, and wallowed in the dirt, crying: "God, please take me to the abode of the blessed souls if I am to endure life without my son." Then he demanded Gorgin's report: "Tell me where you lost track of my son. Did he leave you? Did you see what manner of evil overcame him? Where did you find this abandoned horse?"

"Open your ears and listen to my full account," he replied. "When we got to Armenia, we found a deforested land that had become a breeding ground for wild boars. We went to work clutching our lances and flushed them out of their lairs. They attacked us in droves, but we overcame the innumerable beasts and heaped up a hill of their tusks as the trophy of our triumph.

"Then we happily set off on our way back to Iran, hunting as we trekked back. Suddenly an onager appeared whose chestnut hide resembled that of Gudarz's horse. Its head, ears, and tail were reminiscent of Bizhan's black steed. The creature had the muscular legs of the fabulous Simorgh, a lion's neck, and bright steel hooves. It was swifter than the wind. One would think it was descended from Rostam's famous Rakhsh.

"Bizhan caught the head of the powerful creature in his noose, but it pulled the rope, and the two of them disappeared in a cloud of dust. I tracked them for a long time but could only find my friend's black horse. I assume the onager was a demon."

The account sounded hollow. Gorgin was pale, and his eyes were shifty as he stammered through the story. Geav was so sure that the entire report was a fabrication that he contemplated killing the mendacious man in revenge for whatever he had done to his son. But a dead man could not help him find Bizhan.

"Enough of these lies," he roared. "You have stolen the sun and the moon from my sky. You have betrayed your companion. How can you sleep with the weight of this betrayal? I will search the world for my son. But I will be sure to report your treacherous misdeeds to the king and claim the right of a father to avenge his son."

Geav went to Kay-Khosrow, related Gorgin's transparent lies, and demanded justice. The king listened somberly, and comforted Geav with these words: "Stop your worries and rejoice in a prophecy I heard from a learned man. There will come a day when I will avenge my father in the land of Touran. Bizhan's name is on the list of my companions on that day. So, he is sure to survive this ordeal."

Geav retired, still worried and troubled for his son.

When Gorgin entered the royal court, he found it empty. The knights had all gone to comfort Geav. He sheepishly approached the throne carrying the sack of boar tusks and stood before the king. Kay-Khosrow asked him about his adventure and the story behind Bizhan's disappearance. Gorgin lost his composure in the king's presence and confabulated, producing an even more incoherent account than he had provided Geav.

"Have you not heard that even a lion shall not escape harm if he should nurse ill will for the clan of Gudarz?" Kay-Khosrow seethed. "Were it not for fear of my salvation and good name, I would have you beheaded for this treachery."

Kay-Khosrow ordered blacksmiths to fashion iron chains for Gorgin and had him locked away in a dungeon. He told Geav: "Wait until the arrival of the vernal equinox. When the flowers bloom, and the green blanket of vegetation is unfurled at the holiday of Nowruz, I shall stand before God and ask for his sanction to use my enchanted grail. I shall then reveal to you Bizhan's whereabouts." Geav thanked the king and left the court with renewed hope.

When Nowruz arrived on the first day of spring, the king called Geav back to his presence. Arrayed in his ceremonial garb and cap, Kay-Khosrow sat on the throne, praised God, and denounced evil. Then he picked up his magical grail, filled it with wine, and peered into it. The twelve constellations, from Aries to Pisces, were etched on the higher register of the chalice. Images of the seven realms of the world, the sun, the moon, and the planets Saturn, Mars, Venus, and Mercury appeared in lower registers. The king looked into the grail and saw Bizhan languishing in a dark jail in the Khotan desert.

"Let your heart be glad, for your son lives," said the king, smiling. "He is in a dark prison, cared for by a princess who weeps for his plight. Your son has grown thin as a switch of a willow tree, and he has despaired of the help that might come from friends and kin. Bizhan prays that death delivers him from his torments.

"It seems that his rescue is a task for Rostam alone. Now, rise and go to Zabol and beg Rostam for help. Do not breathe a word of this to anyone."

The king dictated a letter addressing Rostam as the subduer of the Mauzandaran demons and the seeker of vengeance for the blood of the innocent Siavosh. He then asked him to rise to the occasion once more and help a dear friend in his hour of need. Rostam promptly obliged this request and accompanied Geav to the royal palace of Kay-Khosrow. At court, the hero greeted the king and prayed that the angels shower their blessings on him: "I was born to serve an exalted king like you and it is an honor to be of assistance to the clan of Gudarz." All were merry and drank to the glory of the blooming flowers of spring.

Gorgin, still languishing in prison, also heard of Rostam's arrival. He sent word to the hero, complaining of his fate and expressing regret for betraying Bizhan. "I will go into the flames to restore my name. If you solicit the king on my behalf, I will come with you to fight for you and grovel at the feet of my unfortunate friend to beg his pardon."

Rostam felt pity for the wretched man. He sent word to Gorgin that the monstrosity of his deeds was evident to all but that he would plead for him before the king and Geav. He added: "You had best pray that we find Bizhan alive. If we don't, Geav is sure to seek the right of revenge for your betrayal of his son."

The hero waited for two days without mentioning Gorgin's case to the king. He asked for a special audience on the third day and broached the subject. Kay-Khosrow scowled. "You are making matters difficult for me," he said. "I have sworn an oath on my crown to mete out nothing but harsh punishment to that malevolent man. Ask me anything else, and it shall be granted. But not this."

Rostam insisted that the king forgive Gorgin as a special favor to him. Not wanting to turn down such a direct request from his most prominent knight, the king relented and issued orders for his release.

THE RESCUE

Kay-Khosrow proclaimed that he would spare no expense for the emancipation of his young paladin. Rostam preferred a covert mission as he feared that Afrasiab would be enraged at the suggestion of an invasion and kill his captive. Kay-Khosrow opened his treasures to Rostam and let him choose a large quantity of precious stones to be carried by one hundred red-haired camels. The plan was to take a few knights through the Touranian borders in the guise of merchants. A contingent of one thousand soldiers, and seven knights, including Gorgin, volunteered for the stealth mission. Rostam stopped the soldiers at the border and ordered them to stay on alert in case they were needed. He and his knights donned the outfits of merchants and crossed the border near Bactria.

The parched desert air chimed with the bells of the camels. The caravan stopped in Khotan where Piran had a hunting lodge. When he returned from an expedition, Rostam took a goblet of precious gems and two well-caparisoned purebred Arabian horses and went forth to meet him. Luckily for Rostam, Piran did not recognize him in disguise and addressed him as a merchant: "Who are you? Identify yourself."

"I am a simple merchant carrying a load of gems," lied Rostam. "This would be an excellent place to set up my business for a while if I could garner your protection."

With this introduction, Rostam presented the prominent knight with his generous gifts. Piran was pleased and offered the merchant his protection and his son's house. Rostam said that he preferred living close to his merchandise and chose a spacious house near the market with plenty of room for displaying his wares. Once he settled in, a great number of people were attracted to the merchant of Iran, turning the corridors of the showhouse into a virtual bazaar.

Manizheh, too, heard of the Iranian caravan and came searching for news. The tearful princess, still clad in rags, entered Rostam's chambers and pleaded with him.

"You have ventured far from your home, and I pray that your fortunes increase," she said. "May you return in success to the beautiful land of Iran. Tell me the news of the king and his knights. Do they not seek their long-lost knight? Does the clan of Gudarz not miss their young scion, who vanished on the borders of Touran? His hands and feet are bruised by the heavy chains that he wears. I do not cry for my own poor soul. All my tears are for Bizhan."

Rostam did not trust the young woman who spoke to him so boldly. "Stop your rambling and be gone," he yelled, "for I know no king and have never heard of the clan of Gudarz. Away with you, woebegone woman!"

"It is not becoming of a man like you to be so callous," she sobbed. "If you don't wish to speak to me, at least don't throw me out in such an insulting manner. Is it the custom of Iranians to abuse the unfortunate?"

Rostam paused, reconsidering his words. "I was harsh because you interrupted my business. I am afraid I was too preoccupied with my trade. To answer your question more properly, I don't live in the city where the king resides. Nor have I gone to the realm of the clan of Gudarz. I simply don't know them."

Rostam ordered his cook to set a delectable spread in front of the strange woman. Then he asked about her interest in the king and knights of Iran.

"Now you are interested in my story?" she asked. "I had nursed the hope of being treated with kindness by this Iranian caravan. But you spurned me. I had traversed such a distance from the well of my miseries to seek refuge in your protection. But you yelled at me as if I were a warrior on the battlefield.

"I am Princess Manizheh, the daughter of Afrasiab, if you must know. The sun had never seen me unveiled before I met Bizhan. Now, I am naked and exposed to the world. I am reduced by harsh fate to beg door-to-door for a crust of bread smeared with whey. But my pain is nothing next to that of my beloved Bizhan. He languishes at the bottom of a well, bound by heavy chains and unable to tell day from night.

"I request you convey Bizhan's predicament to the clan of Gudarz. Try to find Geav or Rostam and tell them to do something if they want to see him alive."

Rostam shed tears for the princess's fate and advised her to seek help from her father's friends. He added that he would have helped her if he did not fear Afrasiab's wrath.

Then he ordered the attendants to wrap a roasted chicken in bread for Manizheh to take back to her lover. Rostam gave the package to the unfortunate princess, but not before slipping his signet into the belly of the chicken.

Bizhan was surprised by the rich offering and asked where she had gotten it. She told him about the Iranian caravan. Then he found the signet. A wave of happiness washed over him once he could make out Rostam's name on the ring, and he exclaimed in delight. Manizheh feared for his sanity.

"How can you be so giddy in your dark misery?" she asked.

Bizhan said that he would tell her the reason for his happiness but that she had to swear an oath to keep the secret. Manizheh was offended.

"There is no end to my wretchedness. I have abandoned my father and my fortunes for you. I have offered you my body and reputation, but you still do not trust me to keep a secret."

"Forgive me," Bizhan apologized. "I should have known that you would keep this important matter hidden. I need your guidance, for suffering has diminished my wisdom. The truth is that the merchant of jewels has come here for the sole purpose of rescuing me. God has taken pity on me, and it seems that the day of my liberation is nigh. Now, go to the man whose cook gave you this roasted chicken and ask him: 'Are you the master of Rakhsh?'"

Manizheh sprinted back to the merchant and conveyed her lover's question. Rostam knew that Bizhan had entrusted the girl with his secret and said: "Yes, my fair lady. Tell your friend that the master of Rakhsh has come from Zabol only for him. And tell him that we have missed him and suffered in his absence. Soon I will fling that boulder that blocks his well to the cluster of the Pleiades in the sky."

Then Rostam gave her these instructions: "Once you deliver this message, go and collect firewood. When night falls, light a bonfire at the well so I can find you. And be discreet until then."

Manizheh flew back to the well and told Bizhan that the merchant was the one he had suspected. She also told him about his instructions to light a fire by which the men of Iran could find their location.

Bizhan said: "Carry out your instructions. By the glow of that fire, we will escape our perpetual darkness. And know, my lovely girl, that I will reward your loyalty. When we return to my ancestors' land, it will be my turn to serve you as a slave."

Manizheh set to work gathering firewood. She climbed trees like a bird and scurried about in search of kindling as she monitored the sinking sun on the western horizon. At dusk, she breathlessly awaited nightfall. Finally, when it was dark enough, she stoked the fire that illuminated the desert like a sun. And then she heard the approaching hooves of Rakhsh.

FREE AT LAST

Rostam rode out into the desert with his seven knights, guided by Manizheh's fire. The knights were charged with removing the great boulder that blocked the well. They applied themselves to the task but could not budge the stone.

Rostam dismounted, hitched up the edges of his coat of chainmail under his belt, lifted the boulder over his head, and threw it away. The impact of the rock shook the ground like an earthquake. Then he shouted into the well: "Your share of destiny was a goblet of wine. Why did you sip from the chalice of poison then?"

From the unseen depths, Bizhan responded: "When I heard your voice, the poison of fate turned into clear wine in my veins. With chains of iron below and a mountain of stone above, I had given up the desire to live."

"God has taken pity on you. You are all but restored to the world. But I have a request before rescuing you. Forgive Gorgin for my sake and forget his treachery."

This was a hard request. "But you don't know what he has done to me. I have the right to seek revenge."

"In that case, I will saddle Rakhsh and leave you in this hole."

"Friends, kin, and knights have abandoned me. I have suffered so much, but I give up. I forgive Gorgin and cleanse my heart of his hatred."

At this, Rostam lowered his lariat and pulled Bizhan out of the well. His body was naked and smeared in blood. His unkempt hair was overgrown, and his nails had grown into claws. He still had chains on his hands and feet. Rostam tore the chains off his body and led him and Manizheh back to his headquarters. The young couple related their tale of woe to Rostam as they traversed the desert to safety. When they reached Rostam's camp, Bizhan and Manizheh bathed and dressed themselves in fitting garments. Then Gorgin came forward and groveled before his former companion, begging to be pardoned for his act of betrayal. He rejoiced when his wish was granted.

THE LAST RAID

Rostam announced that it was time for the couple to return to Iran. Camels were loaded with what they had brought, and one of the knights took the responsibility of the returning caravan. Rostam advised Bizhan and Manizheh to go with the caravan back to Iran, as he and the rest of the knights had unfinished business in Touran. "We will not sleep tonight until we make a laughingstock of Afrasiab before his nation," Rostam proclaimed. Bizhan dispatched his beloved to go ahead of him, for he was the main cause of the conflict and wanted to be a party to the raid.

Rostam and his knights rode to the palace of Afrasiab, forcing their way through the gates and into his inner chambers. Rostam harangued the Touranian king. "I am the son of Zaul. Rise and fight those who have entered your palace. For many nights you slept on your soft bed and let our friend languish in a well. Now I have broken him out of your prison."

Bizhan joined in. "Do you remember how you preened yourself on the throne as I stood before you with shackled hands? Now I am free to roam your land, and none dares stop me."

Afrasiab attempted to rally the palace guards to drive away the marauders who had breached the sanctuary of his palace, but they were all killed in the attempt. Afrasiab was reduced to escaping his quarters through a secret passage, leaving behind his concubines, who would later walk out of the palace holding hands with the Iranian knights.

The Iranian war party made haste to escape the enemy's land with its spoils, as Afrasiab was sure to gather an army and give chase. They galloped west and made it across the border, joining their troops that had stood at the ready. As they turned around, a cloud of dust was rising on the eastern horizon.

Afrasiab was giving chase, having appointed Piran as the commander of his army. Rostam was not concerned by the prospect of being outnumbered. He stood before his men and addressed the king of Touran. "For how long do you intend to hide behind huge armies? Time and again, you have learned the painful lesson that numbers do not make a victory. A lion does not fear a horizon filled by herds of onager."

The armies lined up against each other. Piran and his brother Houman commanded the left and right flanks, and Garsivaz and Shideh, the son of Afrasiab, held the center. Rostam and Bizhan stood at the heart of the Iranian army. The battle began, and the Iranians emerged victorious. Again, Afrasiab fled the scene, and Rostam chased him for two miles before returning to the site of the Touranian defeat to distribute the booty.

RETURN IN TRIUMPH

When King Kay-Khosrow heard of the success of Rostam's expedition in rescuing Bizhan and defeating a Touranian counterattack, he prostrated himself before God in a gesture of thanksgiving. Geav and Gudarz welcomed the hero with a vast army that marched to the sound of trumpets and drums. Colorful standards were carried behind the two prominent knights of the house of Gudarz. Upon reaching the returning army, they dismounted and addressed Rostam. "You have rendered a great service to our family. From now on, consider this clan as your humble servants."

The king, too, delighted in welcoming the triumphant Rostam. The hero took Bizhan by hand and delivered him to the king, along with a thousand Touranians captured in the skirmish.

"Your father, Zaul, and the people of your town, Zabol, are surely proud of you," said Kay-Khosrow. "But they can't possibly be as proud as I am of having such a worthy knight. Geav must be happy to be reunited with his son, thanks to your bravery. Rejoice that the Creator chose you for the deliverance of this young knight from his dungeon."

Geav agreed and praised Kay-Khosrow as well as his friend, and fellow knight, Rostam. The king called for a banquet, and the company spent a delightful night in merrymaking. The next day, when Rostam came to ask royal permission to leave, he was provided with lavish gifts, including ten lovely consorts and ten slave girls to attend them. All wore golden belts and coronets. Kay-Khosrow endowed the couple with rich gifts in appreciation of Manizheh's loyalty. He told Bizhan: "Be kind to your enchanting bride and do not break her heart. As you have seen, fate can elevate one to the revolving heavens or lower him to the depths of a lonely well. Do not chase worldly goods and wealth. A man should avoid harming a fellow human while he lives on this earth."

Thus, ends my adventurous love story.
Now, to the clash of Piran and Gudarz
And a bloody duel soaked in gore and glory.

CHAPTER 13

The Fall of a King: Afrasiab

Any man who desires a good life must feed
And support his family and have enough left
To be generous to his friends in need.

Beyond this, one must abhor
Worldly goods and dreams of grandeur
That rot the tree of his life to its core.

THE LAST WAR AND THE BATTLE OF THE ELEVEN CHAMPIONS

When Afrasiab brought an army of three hundred thousand warriors to the Oxus River, he set in motion the fourth cycle in the wars of revenge between Iran and Touran. Kay-Khosrow sent Tous to stand against him; then he dispatched three armies into the eastern borders of Touran and entrusted the central force of one hundred and ten thousand soldiers to Gudarz to confront the army of Piran. The king advised his general to be merciful with noncombatants and temperate in his decisions.

When Gudarz arrived at the Zibad River near the Iranian eastern borders, he sent his son Geav to deliver an acerbic message to Piran:

> We aim to avoid bloodshed. Cleanse your heart of the love for Afrasiab. If you want peace, send us the murderers of our martyred Prince Siavosh in chains and submit your horses, weapons, and treasures of gold. You must surrender your son and his two brothers to serve as hostages. Comply with these demands before it is too late.

Piran received the message just as thirty thousand sword-wielding reinforcements reached his camp, with a charge from Afrasiab that the goal of the current war was to wipe out the forces of Iran once and for all. Feeling reassured by the arriving phalanxes, Piran sent Geav back with a terse response that he was not in a position to deliver the culprits. Nor would he surrender his relatives or belongings.

Expecting this answer, Gudarz deployed his army on the higher slopes of Gonabad Mountain, intending to draw out a frontal attack.

Piran had arrived later and arranged his forces on the flat plain. Although he had more troops than the Iranians, he was reluctant to initiate hostilities, given the enemy's superior position. He wanted to fight on an open field that would allow him to encircle Iran's smaller forces.

The two seasoned commanders bided their time and kept their armies in check for a week, each waiting for the other side to make the first move. The spirited Bizhan tried to dissuade Gudarz from maintaining his defensive posture on high ground, but to no avail. On the Touranian side, warriors were also pressuring Piran to attack until Houman finally broke rank. Disobeying the strict instructions of his commander and elder sibling, he rode out to taunt the knights of Iran, who refused to fight because they could not disobey their commander. The rogue Touranian knight turned to Gudarz with venom in his voice: "Is this what you promised your king? I thought you came to avenge Siavosh. So why are you cowering here like a ram hiding from a lion? What is your excuse?"

Gudarz did not want to waste time on individual contests; he wanted to draw the Touranians into general war, allowing him to exploit his superior position. Thus, he coldly refused Houman's challenge and told him to return to the Touranian side, claim victory, and collect his prizes. But refusing a direct challenge was more than some Iranian knights could take. They asked permission to fight Houman on his behalf, but the field marshal Gudarz forbade it.

Furious that the Iranians would not answer his challenge, Houman rode up the slope of the Gonabad Mountain and shot four Iranian sentries blocking his way to the top of a nearby mesa. Upon reaching the high, flat surface, he swung his lance around his head and called himself the uncontested champion of the two armies. Sweat appeared on Gudarz's forehead as his enemy rejoiced.

Bizhan heard of what was happening on the front lines and complained to his father that Gudarz had become senile. How could he allow such effrontery? Geav told him to be calm and forget the idea of fighting Houman. He had to respect his grandfather and his commander in chief to refrain from duels. But Bizhan ignored his father and rode straight to the front.

"I have heard an incredible story, my great ancestor and field marshal," he said to Gudarz. "Is it true that my superiors in this army have allowed a common Touranian to ride up and down these lanes, shaming our heroes and haranguing our commanders? If so, I hereby ask your permission to teach Houman some manners. Have you forgotten my prowess as I went against Forud? Have you forgotten that I saved this army at the battle of Pashan? I shall report this ignominy to my king if you don't permit me to fight today."

With this direct threat, Gudarz was constrained to give his grandson leave to engage the challenger. Bizhan joyfully rode away from camp to make arrangements.

Geav was extremely worried. He humbly begged God not to afflict him with the sorrow of mourning his beloved son. He regretted hurting his son's feelings by implying that he was too young to face the enemy knight in battle. Now that Bizhan had Gudarz's permission, Geav also needed to approve this duel against the man who had taken the lives of scores of his brothers. Thus, he called for Siavosh's famous horse and armor and took them to his son with some mild rebukes and apologies.

"Do not worry, father," Bizhan said, donning the famous armor. "Houman is not made of iron and tin. He is a warrior just like me. I will defeat him unless my destiny has written another end to my story." At this, he galloped through the ranks toward Houman's position, and caught up to the Touranian knight as he was descending the high mesa whence he had boasted victory. Houman saw Bizhan and laughed aloud.

"Has your body tired of the company of your head, young lad?" he asked. "I will send your corpse back to Geav and let him mourn you as he mourned your uncles that I have killed. I will snuff your life as a hawk snatches a pheasant from the branches of a cypress tree and picks it apart into a bloody mess of feathers. Alas, it is too late tonight. Come back tomorrow, and we will resume what you have started."

"For now, I will allow you to return to your men," Bizhan replied. "But when tomorrow comes, say farewell to your king and kinsmen, for that will be the last time you see them in this world."

The next day, Bizhan and Houman found a flat arena near the Touranian lines. The battle commenced, and the two warriors fought for a full day with lances, javelins, maces, and swords. Finally, tired of fighting, they took a break and decided to wrestle without weapons. Houman was stronger, but in misfortune, virtue becomes vice. As he lunged forward on his left foot, Bizhan pushed him on the right shoulder while pulling his left leg. The great Touranian knight lost his balance and collapsed like a heavy camel. Bizhan swiftly drew his dagger and beheaded his opponent. He paused to breathe, not believing that he had killed the man who had exterminated so many of his relatives. He then tied the severed head to his saddle string and galloped back to the Iranian lines as the westerly sun sank under the horizon. Geav, who had waited anxiously, cheered his triumphant return. Together with their army, they celebrated the demise of one of their most formidable opponents.

Meanwhile, Piran tore his garments and bitterly mourned the death of his brother. To exact revenge, he sent his other brother Nastihan on a night raid against the Iranian camp. Anticipating this attack, Bizhan set an ambush and waylaid the raiders, slaying them all. Piran was inconsolable. He had lost two brothers, who also happened to be his top commanders, in one day. In utter desperation, he sent his son Ruein as an ambassador to Gudarz with a letter:

> If it was revenge you sought, you have avenged yourself on my dear brothers, whose headless bodies you left on the battlefield. Why should so many lives be lost to redress the death of one man? Is it not time to end the bloodshed? If it is territory you are after, I will give you all you want, from Kashmir to Kandahar. Don't suppose I write this letter out of weakness, for I am superior to you in manhood and riches. But as our hair turns gray, it behooves us to avoid senseless carnage.

> If your bloodlust is insatiable, let us limit the war to a contest of champions. We shall designate ten mighty warriors from each side and suffer them to fight in close combat unto death. You and I shall meet as the eleventh pair. Let the side that wins these contests claim victory. But we must pledge that the conqueror let the troops of the conquered nation to return in peace.

Gudarz received Ruein with respect and affection, but his answer to Piran's overture was a harsh rebuke. The lands he had promised were already conquered by the three other prongs of the Iranian army, and the terms he offered fell far short of the campaign's goal to bring the murderers of Siavosh to justice. Further, Gudarz wrote:

> Your words are a mirage of falsehoods. Your side started the hostilities with the murder of Iraj and the execution of Nowzar. Siavosh walked into the Touranian trap because he listened to your lies. You speak of correct behavior in old age. My only regret in the hereafter would be to have left the deaths of Siavosh and my sons unavenged.

Piran sent a letter to Afrasiab describing the dire conditions at the front. He also begged forgiveness, for his compassion for Farigis and Kay-Khosrow had precipitated the successive wars of revenge. Afrasiab was gracious in absolving his general of guilt and chose instead to blame fate for what had happened. Regarding his current worries, Afrasiab advised him to take heart. Iran would be conquered, and that would put an end to the wars. Piran conveyed the king's message to his troops to restore their confidence, but still he had a feeling of impending doom. In his desperation, the old knight turned to God.

How strange is the fate you decree for us! he prayed. *Who would have thought that Kay-Khosrow would grow into such a powerful king? Why should there be such a bloody vendetta between grandfather and grandson? Armies face each other because kings want to settle scores. Grant that I die in my armor rather than live to see the day Afrasiab has been slain. It is better to perish than to see my homeland lost and the ways of my forefathers abandoned.*

Gudarz had initially rejected the idea of ten champions dueling in lieu of war, hoping for a decisive victory in open battle. But as he was sure of the prowess of his champions, after some contemplation he decided the confrontation of the best of the two armies was an excellent way to proceed. He sent a missive to Kay-Khosrow, boasting of his recent victories. Then he wrote that he had picked ten warriors who would go against their Touranian challengers in a final contest.

The battle of the ten champions ended with total victory for the Iranian side. Among the victors were Bizhan, who killed Ruein, Piran's son, and Fariborz, who killed Golbaud, Piran's brother. The only survivor on the Touranian side was Goruy, Siavosh's executioner. Geav, who had gone against Goruy, spared his life because death in combat was too good for him. He had to be kept until he would be executed as a criminal.

Finally, it was time for the battle of Gudarz and Piran, the field marshals of the two armies. The Touranian knight looked at the field dyed with the blood of his best warriors, including his son and brother. The end was nigh, he thought. But he had to be impeccable in discharging his duty as a soldier. His opponent had come, ready to fight.

The battle began with a shooting contest. Gudarz loosed a deadly arrow that pierced the barding of Piran's horse, giving his opponent no chance of disentangling himself from his mount. The horse collapsed and rolled over him, breaking his arm. Injured and without a horse, Piran fled from his mounted rival, knowing he would not live to see the end of the day. Gudarz was suddenly overcome with sadness. He wept to see the play of fate that had humiliated the exalted commander of Touran against whom he had fought so many battles.

"Famed warrior and pillar of Touran's strength!" he said with a tremulous voice. "Your might, manliness, arms, riches, and wisdom have deserted you. Destiny has brought you low. Where is your army? Why isn't someone coming to your aid? Don't you see that the time for battle is over? Why don't you beg for mercy, so I can spare your life and take you to my king?"

Piran staggered among the rocks, hiding behind his shield. He replied: "May that day never come that I beg the enemy for my life. Death is our destiny, and there is no shame in dying on the battlefield with honor."

With these words, he flung a dagger that sliced the Iranian knight's arm. A rivulet of blood poured from his wound. Moved to anger, Gudarz threw a javelin that penetrated Piran's armor and went through his liver; he fell, coughing blood, and let out a sky-splitting roar. He shook as he lay on the rocks until death made him still. Gudarz addressed Piran's corpse: "You were the best of the knights of Touran, a courageous lion. But this world has seen many like you, and it is never faithful to the likes of you and me."

The Iranian knight dismounted and dyed his face in his opponent's blood in a gesture of revenge. Vengeful as he was, Gudarz could not bring himself to sever Piran's head. Instead, he planted the fallen hero's standard by his body, placed his head in the shadow it cast on the ground, and rode back to the Iranian lines, drenched by the blood still streaming down his arm. Once on the Iranian side he issued orders that the body of the Touranian knight be brought back with due honors and be prepared for respectful interment.

The lookouts on Mount Gonabad brought the good tidings that the royal standard of Kay-Khosrow had appeared on the horizon. The king arrived at the scene and viewed Piran's corpse. Solemnly, he reminded the company of the fallen Touranian commander's good deeds.

"This is not the fate I wished for this kind man," said the king. "He mourned for my father with all his heart, took me under his wing in my youth, and gave me refuge. We tried to win him over to our side, but he was loyal to his king. Fate brought him low when he went against Gudarz and lost everything." Kay-Khosrow decreed that a royal crypt be built for Piran. His body was covered in tar mixed with rosewater, musk, and camphor. Clad in Roman silk, he was entombed with his belt and helmet.

Goruy was executed for his terrible crimes. The rest of the Touranian army came to ask for quarter, and King Kay-Khosrow graciously forgave them and allowed them to leave their arms and return home. Piran's two remaining brothers, however, refused to surrender.

GOSTAHM PURSUES THE FUGITIVES

The Iranian scouts on Mount Gonabad reported a small contingent of the Touranians leaving the battle scene under the leadership of Piran's sons, Lahauk and Farshidvard. Gudarz was troubled by this intelligence. If they were allowed to escape, they could raise an army to avenge the death of their brother.

Gudarz immediately called on the Iranian knights to pursue the fugitives, but they were either wounded or too tired to volunteer. Only Gostahm, the son of Kazhdaham, rose to offer his services:

"You appointed the other knights to fight legendary duels against their Touranian challengers," he said. "They all won fame and glory. I alone was left behind to protect the camp. Let this be my chance to seek renown." Gudarz assented with a smile, and Gostahm quickly turned in pursuit of the runaway knights.

Worried about sending one man to eliminate two of the most formidable warriors of Touran, Bizhan raised his voice in protest when he heard what had happened. Gudarz countered that Gostahm was the only choice for the mission and that he was equal to the challenge. Bizhan disagreed with his grandfather's assessment of the relative powers of the pursuer and the pursued. He pleaded to be allowed to join his friend on the daring pursuit.

"There is no need to endanger your life and worry your father again," Gudarz said.

Bizhan retorted: "Do you not remember how the two of us fought on the battlefields of Pashan? Our fates have been entwined ever since. I don't wish to live one day after Gostahm."

Gudarz was constrained to give his blessings to another one of his grandson's daring adventures. Bizhan wasted no time in setting off after his friend. Riding out all day and for part of the night, he finally came upon a thicket where he could hear faint moans.

Gostahm was lying supine by a fountain, having fallen off his horse and lost a great deal of blood. He weakly greeted his friend and said he had succeeded in his mission. He had killed Farshidvard with a single arrow but received grievous wounds in the fight against Lahauk, whom he had also killed.

"I know I am mortally wounded," he said, sighing. "But take me back to the camp so I can look upon the face of my king before I pass from this world. And bring along the heads of the men I slayed as trophies of my campaign." Bizhan ripped his garments to shreds to make tourniquets for his friend's wounds. Then he found Gostahm's horse, which had wandered away.

In his search for the corpses of the fallen Touranian knights, Bizhan captured an enemy soldier and coerced him into holding Gostahm up on his horse during their journey back. Upon their arrival, King Kay-Khosrow came to see Gostahm and offered him a magical healing potion that he had inherited from his royal ancestors. The king prayed for him, laid hands on his wounds, and appointed skilled physicians to care for him. Within two weeks, the brave knight had wholly recovered from his injuries. The speedy recuperation was a cause of great amazement. The king called the two brave knights to his audience, praised God for their spectacular success, and rejoiced at their loyalty.

THE FINAL BATTLES

Afrasiab was indignant when he heard about the defeat of his army and the slaying of Piran and his illustrious brothers. In short order, he regrouped and crossed the Oxus River, intending to avenge Piran's death. His brother Garsivaz and his sons Jahan and Shideh led the charge.

At the challenge of the Touranian troops, Kay-Khosrow, too, gathered a formidable army. Afrasiab was intimidated by the Iranian forces and apprehensive about the coming confrontation, so he desperately called on his fortune-tellers to foretell the war's end. He remembered the dreams he'd had many years before that Touran would fall to Kay-Khosrow. Shideh disapproved of consultation with soothsayers and astrologers, which he considered a show of weakness.

"You are an exalted king. A mountain of steel turns into a watery ocean when your name is mentioned. You treated Siavosh like your son but rightly turned on him when he became treasonous and nursed ambitions of grandeur. You reared his unworthy son instead of consigning him to the grave. Now he has fled Touran like a bird of prey. Forgetting the kindness of Piran, he has slain the exalted knight and brought an army against us. Iranians are not worthy of your concern. Why should you call on fortune-tellers rather than your warriors in this matter? Our troops are arrayed on the left and right flanks. Say the word and I will slaughter the Iranian enemy to the last one. I hope to confront Kay-Khosrow head on. I shall vanquish this upstart king and drag his body and good name in the mud."

Afrasiab advised his son to be calm and not underestimate the enemy's power. "Besides," he added, "if Kay-Khosrow wanted to fight a duel, he would pick his equal, and that is me."

"You have five sons," Shideh said, "and it is not proper in the eyes of God and the army that you fight while we are alive."

Afrasiab endorsed his son's proposal, sending him to the Iranian side. When the news arrived that a man named Shideh was challenging the king to a duel, Kay-Khosrow was overcome with sadness. He said to his entourage of knights with eyes brimming with tears: "This man is my maternal uncle, a splendid warrior, and my equal in battle. Proposing a duel in lieu of war means only one thing: Afrasiab regrets crossing the Oxus River to wage war."

The leaders of the army believed that the duel posed a great danger to the Iranians. Losing a king would throw their side into disarray, since Kay-Khosrow had no heir. The assembly was silent for a while. Then the king announced that his mind was made up. He would accept the challenge and send word to Shideh to prepare to lose his life.

When the appointed time came, the royal opponents chose a corner away from the armies to avoid interference. They fought on horseback until Shideh realized he could not win, and thus proposed that they wrestle. Although a king typically would not fight on foot, Kay-Khosrow accepted. Shortly after the hand-to-hand contest commenced, the king took Shideh off the ground and smashed him on the rocks, shattering his backbone. Then he drew his sword and killed him. Kay-Khosrow issued orders for the proper interment of his uncle: "This man was my kin, brash and reckless as he was. Honor him in death and bury him in a proper crypt with all the rites due to royalty."

In the next day's general battle, the Iranians routed their enemies and pursued them as they withdrew. After a few more skirmishes, Afrasiab realized the futility of fighting against the superior forces of Iran and sent his son Jahan with a peace proposal. Flattering Kay-Khosrow as the king of the world and reminding him of their filial bond, Afrasiab pleaded that he had been led astray by the devil in the affair of Siavosh. He proposed to remove himself from office and go into voluntary exile if the Iranians withdrew.

Kay-Khosrow's response was acerbic.

> Don't ply me with flattery and lies. I am a son bent on avenging his father's unjust murder. Regarding your filial rights, remember that you had my mother beaten to induce a miscarriage. Had it not been for the wise Piran, you would have killed both of us. Later you intended to behead me if you found me worthy of challenging you. And remember that you murdered your brother Aghrirat, the king of Iran, Nowzar, and my father, Siavosh. Your excuses that a devil misled you are not new. The Serpent King Zahhak and the haughty King Jamshid also made these excuses to justify their evil acts. He who is steadfast in righteousness never strays from the straight path. Stop this verbiage and prepare for war.

When the battle commenced, the Iranians overpowered their enemy with little effort, capturing both Afrasiab's brother Garsivaz, who had conspired against Siavosh, and his son, Jahan.

Kay-Khosrow took over Afrasiab's palace, but refused to enslave any of his women, disregarding the custom of the time. Wagging tongues accused the king of favoring his maternal grandfather despite his obligations to avenge his father. The magnanimous king explained his act of mercy to the females of the house of Afrasiab thus:

"We ought not to do unto others what we are unwilling to suffer. My mother and grandmother suffered such indignities. I shall not visit those horrors upon the womenfolk of my enemy. And to my soldiers, I say: 'Do not kill the innocent; stay away from defenseless women and keep your hands off the property of your enemy. This is how you turn an enemy into a friend.'"

Afrasiab's next desperate move was to send a message challenging Kay-Khosrow to a duel. The Persian king accepted, saying, "If it is a battle he seeks, let him have it. Why should we fill the battleground with dead soldiers when two kings can fight each other?"

A messenger returned to Afrasiab with this response, but he decided not to pursue the matter. Instead, he tried his luck at an ambush. Kay-Khosrow, who had foreseen this move, ordered the Iranians to douse their fires and lie in wait. Thus, the army that had come to waylay the Iranians was ambushed and routed. Afrasiab abandoned his family, fled to the wilderness of Barda', and sought refuge in a cave near the Sea of Chichast.

AFRASIAB'S LAST STAND

One night the divine angel Sorush visited a hermit named Houm, a descendant of Feraydun, in a dream to tell him where Afrasiab was hiding. The monk sent word of his vision to the royal court and traveled to the far-flung refuge in pursuit of the deposed king of Touran. As he stood at the mouth of that cave, he could hear Afrasiab lamenting the loss of his kingdom. Houm rushed in, captured the fugitive king, tied his hands, and led him out. But when the prisoner complained about the tightness of his binding, the hermit took pity on him and loosened the ropes. Afrasiab used this opportunity to slip from the grasp of the monk, jump into the waters of the Chichast, and escape yet again.

He was standing by the seashore, looking for signs of his captive, when the knights of Iran, Gudarz and Geav, arrived carrying the prisoner Garsivaz. Houm explained how he had caught and lost Afrasiab. Geav and Gudarz brought Garsivaz to the seashore and tormented him to lure his brother out of hiding. Unable to bear the thought of his brother in pain, Afrasiab emerged from his hiding place and addressed him: "I have taken refuge in this wilderness to avoid witnessing scenes like this. How dare your captors inflict pain on you, a prince descended from Feraydun?"

Garsivaz, too, was moved to tears when he saw that Afrasiab was reduced to a vagabond. "My royal brother and king of the world! What happened to all your power and glory? Your fortunes are reversed, and you have traded your throne room for a watery hiding place."

As the brothers were engaged in this discourse, Houm managed to capture them both in his lariat, delivered them to the Iranian knights, and returned to his hermitage.

The king arrived shortly thereafter. Afrasiab cried: "I have seen this day in my dreams. Tell me, you vindictive man, with what justification would you kill your grandfather?"

"Where do I start?" Kay-Khosrow replied. "With the blood of your brother Aghrirat, your regicide of King Nowzar or the murder of your son-in-law, Siavosh?"

"My king, the past is behind us," Afrasiab said. "Suffer me to see my daughter Farigis one last time."

"I was in my mother's womb when you killed her husband. Now the day of revenge is at hand, for God has decreed that those evil deeds be repaid in kind." With this, he drew his sword and beheaded Afrasiab. Garsivaz cried when he watched his brother's white beard turn crimson. Then it was his turn. Kay-Khosrow enumerated all his sins and what his ancestor Tur had done to Iraj before consigning him to the executioner's blade.

Kay-Khosrow and the other Iranian knights marched back to Iran after their final victory. Siavosh's death had been avenged, with Afrasiab paying the ultimate price for his sins. The old king, Kay Kavous, sequestered himself in the fire temple of Azar-goshasp and gave a fortune in alms, for God had granted his greatest wish. Finally at peace, Kay-Kavous passed from the world.

Kay-Kavous was solemnly consigned to his crypt
Death does not spare king or prophet, nor does it exempt
The sage most learned, the soldier well equipped.

Kay-Khosrow gave the throne of Touran to Jahan, Afrasiab's only living son and advised him to respect the boundaries set by Feraydun between Iran and Touran.

OCCULTATION OF THE KING

And thus Kay-Khosrow reclined on the Iranian throne and ruled in justice. But he grew uneasy as he approached the age of sixty. He was descended from Kay-Kavous on one side and Afrasiab on the other. These were impetuous men, given to violent passions, greed, and injustice. How could Kay-Khosrow be immune from their legacy of corrupted rule? Mighty kings like Zahhak, Tur, Salm, Jamshid, and Nowzar had all succumbed to selfish temptations and lost their divine sanction. Their names were blackened forever. Kay-Khosrow feared that he, too, might lose his way and lean toward iniquity.

With these thoughts, the king spent a week in solitary prayer. Then he emerged, called on his knights to pray for divine guidance, and went back to his private chambers for another five weeks. He was praying to pass from this world while his spirit was untarnished. He had grown pale, and his back had started to curve like an old man. Troubled, the knights consulted fortune-tellers and sent for Zaul and Rostam to come to the capital. Upon arrival, Zaul opined that the king had probably grown weary of his office and that good advice and companionship would help him recover from his malaise.

In his seclusion, Kay-Khosrow continued his fervent prayers to God, asking: "What good is this kingship to me if I lose Thy favor?"

Finally, he fell asleep and had a vision of Sorush, the divine messenger. The angel intoned: "You shall find all that you seek and a place by the supreme God if you leave this world. Don't linger in this darkness. Give away all you have and appoint a successor, for your day of departure is at hand."

Kay-Khosrow woke to find himself soaked in perspiration and tears. Swept up by a torrent of joy, he prostrated himself before God. He knew he had to make haste to receive all he had been promised. Thus, he put on a new garment, avoiding the crown and torque of his office, and sat on the ivory throne. The king admitted the noble knights in their golden boots and gave them the startling news of his imminent abdication.

The knights were dismayed. Rostam beseeched the king to reconsider, to which Kay-Khosrow responded, "You are the first among the knights and the Champion of the World. The kings of this land have been in your debt since the days of Kay-Qobaud. For five weeks, have I prayed to God to forgive my sins and take me from this world lest I turn to injustice. At dawn, Sorush came to me with the good tidings that my soul's dark night had ended. Time has come for me to abdicate the throne and unburden myself of the yoke of this life."

Zaul whispered to the knights: "This is not right. Reason has deserted this man. I must speak truth to him even at the expense of my life." The knights agreed to support Zaul, and he rose in protest: "Now hear the bitter truth from an old man, and don't quarrel with what is right. You were born in Touran to a daughter of Afrasiab, a man who trafficked with demons in his dreams. Your paternal grandfather was the malignant Kay-Kavous, who schemed to trespass the gates of the heavens. I admonished him then as I tell you the truth now. He did not listen to me or repent his sins until he crashed from the skies. You, too, were reckless in your battle against Touran as you went against Shideh, not caring that Iran would lose the battle if you were killed. God saved you and us from certain ruin. Now you bring this new disaster upon our heads. You stray from the path of God and endanger your divine sanction. If you persist, people will abandon you. Your office will be lost, and your name shall be blackened. Listen to me and come back to the path of God. Use your brain and let reason be your guide."

Kay-Khosrow sat silent for a spell before finally speaking. "It would displease God if I spoke to you with the harsh tone you have taken with me," he said softly. "Besides, I don't wish to offend my dear Rostam by insulting you. So, I will speak gently lest I break your heart. It behooves you to speak with caution and be mindful of your station. I swear I have not strayed from the path of God or been inclined to the ways of the devil. You disparaged my Touranian lineage. I am the son of Siavosh, the progeny of the kings of Kay. I am also from the seed of Afrasiab, the son of

Pashang and a descendant of Feraydun. His fear killed the appetite of Iranian knights, and his terror caused them to dread bathing in the waters of the Oxus River.

"Regarding the heavenly adventure of Kay-Kavous, know that kings are not faulted for their ambition to conquer the unknown realms. I avenged my father and slew the evildoers of the world. And if I went against Shideh, it was because I did not find a knight who would rise to confront him. That was a battle I won with the aid of my divine sanction.

"I have meditated for five weeks and importuned God to rid me of this world of misery. I have had my fill of this office and wish to relieve myself of these worldly concerns. You have suggested that the devil has misled me. I know not where and when you shall be repaid for this slander."

Zaul was shamed by the magnanimity of the king, and rose from his seat in the assembly. "You are pure and wise, my righteous king," he said. "Forgive me, for I was the one who was misled. If I appeared harsh and unjust, it is because I love my king and can't bear the thought of being separated from him."

Kay-Khosrow took Zaul by the hand, sat him on the throne, and accepted his apology. Then he ordered the knights to take the royal Standard of Kaveh and set up a pavilion outside the capital. Amid colorful tents and banners, the king gave away his worldly possessions. His gardens went to Gudarz, his garments to Rostam, his weapons to Geav, and his armor to Fariborz. He confirmed the stewardship of the lands of Zabol to the house of Zaul, and gave the lands of Isfahan and Khorausan, respectively, to the houses of Gudarz and Tous.

Then Kay-Khosrow called for a knight named Lohrausp to come forward and accept the crown as the next king. The company was shocked by this declaration. "He came with nothing but a horse from the ultramontane Alan tribes," Zaul objected. "You endowed him with troops, a standard, and a leadership belt. I see in him neither talent nor lineage. Who has known a king like this?"

The assembly of knights murmured in agreement, protesting that they would not recognize as king an obscure man bereft of a proper pedigree. Kay-Khosrow countered the charges and vouched for Lohrausp as a man of reason, nobility, and lineage, intimating that he was descended from King Hushang. Zaul and the rest of the knights appeared incredulous, but they had no choice but to relent. Zaul apologized for his objections and the assembly of court elders ratified the dynastic shift from the Kays to the house of Lohrausp.

After a week, Kay-Khosrow started his journey to the mountain that the divine messenger had signified. One hundred thousand Iranians accompanied their king to the slopes, which were covered in snow. The king advised his knights to return as he started his lonely ascent.

Three elderly knights, Gudarz, Zaul, and Rostam, followed these royal instructions and safely returned. But five knights refused to turn back. One of them was the king's son Fariborz. The others included two brothers from the house of Nozwar, Tous and Gostahm, and father and son of the clan of Gudarz, Geav and Bizhan. They followed Kay-Khosrow up the windswept inclines until they reached a fountainhead. The king bathed in the spring waters and advised his five companions once more that he would go into occultation the following day and that they must return as a snowstorm was approaching.

The following day the king disappeared. Astounded at this event, the knights searched for their king without success. They spent the next day there, reminiscing about times past and extolling the virtues of Kay-Khosrow. As they lingered, flurries started in earnest. The knights commenced their descent, but were buried in the fast-descending snow one by one. Each tried to dig his way out, but they all succumbed to the blizzard and perished.

Joy and grief come and pass in this den of strife
What remains after we're gone is a good name,
And that's the lesson of Kay-Khosrow's life.

Gudarz mourned his son and grandson, sprinkling ash
On his head for his clan was decimated
In attacks to avenge Siavosh and its backlash.

CHAPTER 14

Knightly Pride and Royal Ambition: Rostam and Esfandiar

After the kings of Kay it's time for us to purvey
The story of Lohrausp, a king who like Feraydun
Started his rule at Mehregan that was a holy day.

A DYNASTIC SHIFT

Lohrausp ascended the throne and remained loyal to the legacy of the saintly king he had replaced. His reign over Iran was long, and it would have been uneventful had it not been for his son's greed for power. Twice Goshtausp urged his father to give up the crown and declare him king. When Lohrausp ignored this brazen request, the impatient crown prince abandoned the court and took refuge in India.

After some years, Goshtausp traveled to Rome and married the daughter of the Caesar. With his status elevated, he sent a letter, threatening his father that he would invade and take the crown by force. Tired of his son's harassment, Lohrausp abdicated and retired to the Now-Bahar monastery at the city of Balkh to pursue a life of solitude and meditation. At long last, Goshtausp returned to the capital with his Roman queen, Katayun, and their sons, Esfandiar and Farshidvard, to receive his crown.

Over the years, a prophet named Zarathustra had come to prominence in Iran, calling people to worship the one God. King Goshtausp converted to the new faith and made it the state religion. His crown prince Esfandiar was also a devotee of the prophet and a missionary for the new religion. Zarathustra blessed the prince with a talisman to shield him from harm.

At this time, Iran had good relations with all the neighboring kingdoms except for Touran, which had prospered under a new king by the name of Arjausp. Indeed, it had grown so powerful as to levy a tax on Iran. Zarathustra was scandalized that Iran would pay a humiliating tax to the pagan king of Touran. At his urging Goshtausp refused to pay the annual levy and thus began another confrontation between the two countries that had lived in peace since Afrasiab's death.

THE NEW WAR WITH THE EASTERN ENEMY

Upon the rejection of their tax, Arjausp issued an ultimatum instructing Goshtausp to repent from the Zoroastrian heresy and spurn Zarathustra or else suffer the wrath of his Turkic and Chinese hordes. Goshtausp authorized his brother Zarir, his vizier Jamausp, and his son Esfandiar to draft a defiant response, daring Arjausp to launch his vaunted invasion. As neither side was ready for a compromise, their massive armies met on the battlefield. The Iranian side suffered immensely, and Goshtausp lost all his top commanders. Worst of all, the Touranian commander Biderafsh killed the king's own brother Zarir in this war. The situation appeared hopeless. In his desperation, the king asked Esfandiar to assume the supreme command, as he was heralded for his righteousness, invincibility, and extraordinary strength. If he defeated the enemy, Goshtausp promised, he would abdicate his royal office and appoint him the next king of Iran. Esfandiar was thrilled by the prospect of immediate kingship and readily routed the Touranian army, killing Biderafsh in vengeance for his uncle Zarir. King Arjausp was forced to withdraw.

Esfandiar returned to court expecting to receive the crown, but instead, Goshtausp had a new mission for him: to propagate the Zoroastrian religion. Esfandiar did as he was told, but the king was still disinclined to surrender his office. The royal court was alive with the gossip over the king's unfulfilled promises.

One day, in an attempt to forget his troubles, Esfandiar went hunting for game with his sons. They were out on the grounds when the king's trusted adviser and astrologer Jamausp ran out with an urgent letter calling the crown prince to court. Esfandiar confided in his sons that the king's heart was set against him; he would be walking into a den of intrigues.

"But why? What have you done to deserve the king's enmity?" his son Bahman asked.

"I have spent my life serving him," Esfandiar replied, "and I have cleansed the world of his enemies and propagated our religion of the righteous path. But he has been led astray by my enemies and wants to destroy me."

At this, Jamausp confirmed Esfandiar's suspicions about courtly plotters who had convinced the king that he had seditious intents. Despite this intelligence, Esfandiar went to the capital, as it was impossible to disregard the royal summons. When he entered the palace, the king turned to his courtiers with this question: "What is the appropriate punishment for an ungrateful son who repays his father's kindness by plotting to depose him?"

The crowd gasped. "Exalted king!" exclaimed one man. "How could a son dream of ascending the throne while his father lives? Such a thing would be inconceivable."

"Ah, but I have such a son, and he is my crown prince," said the king. "I intend to make an example of him. Soon he will find death preferable to his punishment."

The crown prince stood up with confidence and spoke clearly: "I am innocent. I have not hatched any plots against you. But if you deem me guilty, do what you want. Kill me or bind me as you wish."

The king's heart could not be softened. He ordered his son to be bound and banished to a faraway fortress, where he was fitted with heavy iron chains pinned to four steel pillars. The courtiers and most of Esfandiar's brothers and sisters kept silent as he was led out of the court and later as he was sent as a prisoner to the forbidding castle of Gonbadan. Only Farshidvard spoke out in his defense.

Goshtausp felt relieved. Having thus lain to rest all worries about honoring his promises, the king traveled to Zabol on a mission to spread the new Zoroastrian religion. For two years, Rostam and Zaul tended to every desire of their royal guest.

As word spread that Esfandiar was imprisoned and Goshtausp was distracted, Touran invaded the Persian city of Balkh. King Arjausp and his soldiers sacked the town, massacred eighty Zoroastrian priests, and extinguished the holy fire of their temple. Then they killed the retired king Lohrausp and carried off his daughters in chains.

Upon hearing the news of this invasion, Goshtausp was forced to call off his retreat in Zabol to prepare for a war that he would lose. The invincible enemy killed thirty-eight of his sons and severely wounded Farshidvard before taking him as prisoner. The king narrowly escaped to a mountaintop, knowing that only one person could save him from imminent disaster: the man he had falsely accused of treason. Desperate, he sent his trusted advisor Jamausp across the siege lines to the castle of Gonbadan where Esfandiar was imprisoned.

Jamausp slipped through the enemy lines in a Touranian disguise and reached the area of Gonbadan. Esfandiar's son Noush-Azar, who had accompanied his father to protect him from harm, spotted the strange equestrian sporting a two-feathered Touranian helmet. He rushed to his father with the news of his sighting. "Despite his appearance," Esfandiar opined, "it is a herald from Goshtausp."

Jamausp entered the prison, prostrated himself in front of the shackled crown prince and conveyed the king's greetings before beseeching him to come to help his father, who was desperate for succor, and was once more pledging to give up his crown and retire, just as his own father had done.

Esfandiar smiled. "Why would one humble oneself before a captive who is tied down like a beast of burden? You convey the king's greetings to me! You might as well have brought your greetings to Arjausp, who is roaming the land and inundating it in a pool of blood. I will never help a king who listens to worthless gossip and locks up his innocent son in a godforsaken castle. Instead of rewarding my services with treasures of gold, he has bestowed on me heavy chains of iron."

Jamausp implored Esfandiar to put aside his resentments. After all, he was obligated to seek revenge for his grandfather, Lohrausp, and the eighty temple priests at Balkh. The blood of his brothers remained unavenged, and his sisters languished in captivity. But the prince was unmoved.

"You speak of Lohrausp's blood?" he raged. "Avenging this death is the obligation of his son, Goshtausp. As for my brothers and sisters, I am not stirred by their plight. My brothers are already dead, and I can't bring them back. Nor do I recall either they or my sisters having cared one whit as I was falsely accused, bound, and sent to this filthy dungeon."

"What of your brother Farshidvard, who is grievously wounded and imprisoned? You know that he denounced this calumny against you at every banquet and battlefield."

Hearing Farshidvard's name stung. Esfandiar sat in anguish, and, after some tears, decided to go to war to avenge his brother. Blacksmiths were slow to remove his chains, so he scorned them and broke out of the remaining chains himself—an effort that caused him to faint. When he regained consciousness, the prince went to his noble black horse, which had been badly neglected during his imprisonment. Why, he asked, would his cruel captors stoop to mistreating a horse for the alleged crimes of his master? Then he bathed and called for princely garments, his armor, and weapons.

Once the gallant Esfandiar had gathered an army and was ready to embark on his journey to the battlefield, he beseeched God to give him the strength to avenge his grandfather and his thirty-eight brothers who had fallen to Arjausp. He pledged to build one hundred fire temples and as many hostels on every desert road. When they reached the frontline, Esfandiar went to say farewell to Farshidvard, who was on his deathbed. Moaning with pain, the moribund prince blamed Goshtausp for exiling the invincible Esfandiar and provoking Arjausp's disastrous invasion.

After burying his brother in a simple grave, without the condign royal ceremonies, Esfandiar shed tears for him and all the Iranians who had been killed there. At the battlefield, he found the body of one of his brothers: Gorzam, who had helped spread gossip of his disloyalty. He murmured: "A wise enemy is better than an ignorant friend. You wished to be the crown prince but paved the way to your own demise." Then he broke the siege to his father's mountaintop refuge. Goshtausp blamed Gorzam for his wrongful imprisonment of Esfandiar and repeated his pledge of abdicating in favor of his crown prince once the enemy was defeated.

Soon the Iranians had restored their lines of defense and formed a properly organized army. The king was ensconced at the heart of the army. Bastur the son of Zarir commanded the left flank and Gordoy stood at the head of the phalanxes of the left flank. Esfandiar led the vanguard. Arjausp had an equally well-organized army and was in great spirits for a proper battle. Esfandiar tore into the enemy lines, killing three hundred soldiers with his mace, and then he turned to kill one hundred sixty-five warriors on the Touranian left flank. In the ensuing duel, Esfandiar took Gorgsar, the Touranian commander, into captivity and presented him as a gift to Goshtausp. Arjausp, who knew the battle was lost, fled the scene on fast-running camels. Esfandiar urged his men to give chase. The Touranian troops who had witnessed their king's flight surrendered. Esfandiar granted them quarter and forbade revenge killing. Gorgsar also asked and received forgiveness for his role in the sack of Balkh where the retired king Lohrausp had been killed.

To prevent Esfandiar from demanding the fulfillment of Goshtausp's solemn promise to abdicate in his favor, the king claimed that the battle was not over until his daughters Homai and Behafarid, who had been taken captive in the sack of Balkh, were rescued from Arjausp's Invincible Castle. Thus, Esfandiar had no choice but to accept yet another mission.

THE LABORS OF ESFANDIAR

Before embarking on this journey, he selected a few capable warriors and put them under the command of his only surviving brother, Pashutan. He also called upon a high-ranking Touranian captive to provide him with intelligence for his journey. The scout revealed that there were three ways to the Invincible Castle. The easy but long road was lush with forests and meadows, and could be traversed in three months. The middle road was harsher but could be crossed in one month. And finally, the shortest route would take only one week. This path was fraught with rugged terrain, inclement weather, magical monsters, and dangerous beasts.

The Touranian guide also advised that there was a division of dedicated sentries guarding the castle. A turbulent river encircled the stronghold, which was sufficient unto itself—it had water, and its inhabitants grew crops and made flour in their mills. Having weighed this information, Esfandiar risked the shortest route.

On his way to liberate his sisters, the prince went through seven labors. He killed vicious wolves and lions, survived blizzards, and killed an evil sorceress. To contend with the teeth of a dragon and the powerful claws of an enchanted bird, he erected a wooden enclosure that he covered with spikes.

The taking of the castle itself was the last and the most difficult of his labors, as it required cunning. First, he disguised himself as a merchant to gain access. Then he persuaded Arjausp to allow him to host a banquet on the castle's roof. The fires of the feast were a cue to his brother Pashutan to rush the ramparts as the troops from inside took the castle, beheaded Arjausp, and opened the castle gates.

THE TRAGIC CLASH

Why does the nightingale alight
On the Narcissus flower to sing a ballad
Throughout a dark and stormy night?

It is for Esfandiar that the bird grieves
As Rostam roars in thunderclaps
Far above the shaking, wet leaves.

The Invincible Castle was torched, and its commanders who had murdered Goshtausp's sons were executed. Having freed his sisters and killed King Arjausp, Esfandiar sent a train of camels to his father's palace carrying the great treasures of Touran and many slaves, including Arjausp's sisters and daughters. With this triumph, the prince took the leisurely road back to the royal court, expecting to receive the long-promised crown.

Goshtausp welcomed his triumphant son with a large entourage, having invited many guests to the palace and arranged for lavish festivities. The king spoke about various subjects, but once again, there was no hint, in words or deeds, of fulfilling his solemn promise to abdicate in favor of his crown prince.

When the king requested that Esfandiar relate the story of his seven labors, he refused. "This is neither the time nor the place for such stories," the prince said curtly. "I will provide a full account of my exploits when you are sober."

The king's ominous silence proved that he had no intention of fulfilling his promise. More desperate and disappointed than ever, Esfandiar went to his mother, Katayun, and bitterly complained about Goshtausp's deceitfulness. He listed his victories against the enemies of the land and his brave service that had saved the crown several times. He had won two battles against Touran and killed its king, liberated his sisters, and propagated the religion of the righteous path. But his father, who had promised to make him king in exchange for each one of those missions, continued to deny him the prize. Esfandiar swore that he would ask Goshtausp one last time to fulfill his promise and then wrest the crown by force.

Katayun advised her son to bide his time and savor his position as the crown prince. One day Goshtausp would pass away, and he would be king through natural succession. But the impetuous Esfandiar rejected his mother's counsel, blaming himself for having confided in a woman. "I should have known better than to consult a woman on such an important matter. The ancients were right when they advised against taking women into one's confidence. They offer worthless advice and betray your secrets by idle gossip."

Katayun fell silent, deeply wounded by these words.

Esfandiar did not go back to the king. Instead, he retired to his quarters and sought solace in wine and the embrace of his consorts. The significance of this absence was not lost on Goshtausp. Distressed over the growing strain with his son, the king called on Jamausp to cast the horoscope of the crown prince. He wanted to know when and by whose hands his son would be killed if indeed his lot was to die a violent death.

The crown prince, Jamausp said that Esfandiar was destined to die at the hands of Rostam in Zabol. Stunned, Goshtausp asked whether that fate could be circumvented. Would, for instance, he be spared if the king were to abdicate in his favor? Jamausp answered that fate was ineluctable. The king brooded over this conundrum. At the crucial moment of decision, however, he allowed iniquity to guide his actions.

The next day, as the king took his place on the throne, Esfandiar came to the court and boldly protested that he had broken his promise again. There were no enemies, no infidels, no captives, and no contenders. What possible excuse was there to deny him the crown?

Goshtausp granted that Esfandiar had been unremitting in pursuit of his royal commands.

"But it is not true that there are no contenders left. Rostam, the son of Zaul, does not bow to the royal authority. It is reported that he has said: 'Goshtausp wears a new crown . . . but ours is ancient.' There are no external enemies left. But an internal enemy remains. Thus, one last labor awaits my brave crown prince: humbling the house of Saum. Go to Zabol, bind the impudent knight's hands, and bring him as a captive to the court along with his father, brother, and son. I swear a solemn oath before this court to give up my throne when Rostam is chastened."

"You have spurned the ways of our ancestors," said Esfandiar. "It behooves you to challenge such worthy opponents as the king of China. Why would you go after an old, honorable man who served many kings, from Kay-Qobaud to Kay-Khosrow? He has received royal titles of Kingmaker, World Conqueror, and Champion of the World for his services."

Goshtausp reminded his son of the importance of obeying the directives of one's king as if they were commands from God.

"Don't stray from the path of righteousness," the prince retorted. "You don't care for humbling Rostam. You mean to find an excuse to get me out of your way, as you are loath to surrender your royal office. And yet, you are my king and your wish is my command. I will do your bidding, but I will not need an army for this task. A few of my family members will suffice for this undertaking."

The prince left the royal chamber in despair. Katayun had heard from her grandson Bahman that Esfandiar had accepted the impossible mission of humbling Rostam, and that her grandchildren would go with him. She bitterly wept as she addressed her son. "This man is not an ordinary foe. Surely you have heard that he spilled rivers of blood to avenge Siavosh. He defeated legendary heroes and subdued fearsome beasts. Don't lose your head to gain a crown. I curse this royal ambition and all the butchery and bloodshed that it inspires. Heed my advice and save your life. Don't lower me to the dust of mourning for you."

Esfandiar was aware of Rostam's exalted station and nobility and knew that humbling him would not be an easy task. "But if you have to go," the queen begged him, "at least leave your sons—Bahman, Mehrnush, and Nushazar—behind. I can't imagine mourning them." Esfandiar refused. Boys were meant to see the battlefield and endure the hardships of war. Staying behind with women would corrode their character.

CAMPING AT THE HIRMAND RIVER

At the dawn's break, as the roosters' crowing filled the air, Esfandiar set off for Zabol with his three sons, his brother Pashutan, and a small contingent of priests and warriors. A caravan laden with supplies followed behind.

When they reached a fork in the road near the Gonbadan castle, the lead camel of the supply caravan lay down and refused to move. The prince took this as a bad omen and slew the beast to nullify the portent. At the bank of the river Hirmand, which marked Rostam's realm, Esfandiar ordered the company to set up camp and rest. He asked for wine and declared that he would not follow his father's injunction to treat Rostam with harshness. Instead, he would send an envoy and try to gently persuade him to come to the capital of his own accord. Thus, he sent Bahman, clad in his most splendid outfit, along with ten high priests to deliver a crucial message to the prominent knight of Iran:

Anyone favored by heaven must know that our destiny is death and that we receive our just deserts in this world and the next. Now, let us judge your deeds according to the rules of reason. You have lived long and seen many kings. You have earned worldly goods and won honors from my ancestors. But you have not paid your respects at the courts of Kings Lohrausp and Goshtausp.

My father has humbled the world from China to Rome, forced the desert Arabs and Indian kings to become obedient vassals. He defeated Touran and killed their king. You have chosen the path of pride, drunk as you are in your exalted position. This behavior cannot be tolerated. The king has commanded me to bring you to his court with your hands bound.

If you choose the path of repentance and obedience, I swear by the sun, my father's life, and the divine spirit that I will intercede on your behalf. As my brother Pashutan is my witness, I have tried to dissuade the king from this path, but I cannot help conceding that you are guilty as charged. My father is a king, and I am his subject. I have been given a mission. I want your family to hear my advice. This clan of yours must not be wiped out. Your land must not be divided among the gallant knights of Iran. If you let me take you to the king in bondage, I swear to take your side and quell his anger. I pledge my honor and give you my word that I shall not allow even a cold breeze to blow on you.

Bahman took up the royal standard and set off to deliver the message. When Zaul heard that a dashing knight with a golden helmet had crossed the Hirmand River on a black horse, he rode up to a vantage point, sporting a lariat on his saddle and a mace in his hand. On the peak, the silver-haired knight looked down to see the rider was from the royal clan of King Lohrausp and heaved a cold sigh. This would not bode well for his clan.

Bahman identified himself as the son and the emissary of Esfandiar, and asked the whereabouts of Rostam. Zaul dismounted, humbled himself before the prince, and said that his famous son was out hunting with Zavareh and invited him to rest and partake of wine until their return. Bahman replied that he was not permitted to rest before accomplishing his mission. Zaul bowed and sent a scout to point the way to Rostam's camp.

At the hunting grounds, Bahman climbed a hill with a commanding view of the surrounding lands. From there, he could see a colossal man who had uprooted a tree to use as a spit for an onager he had just hunted. Bahman's heart sank. It was evident that Esfandiar was no match for this giant of a man.

Compelled to do something before this powerful hero could overcome and kill his father, Bahman pushed a boulder off the steep incline of the mesa. As the boulder hurtled downhill loudly with increasing speed, it raised a cloud of dust that caught Rostam's eye. Instead of moving, he stood his ground until the rock reached him, and kicked it off to the side with remarkable nonchalance.

Bahman stood in wonder, shocked by Rostam's strength. After a while, he rode down the slope, introduced himself, and announced that he was carrying a message from Esfandiar.

Rostam expressed his pleasure at meeting the young prince and invited him to share a meal of venison and wine with him and his brother Zavareh. A delectable spread was prepared, and the hero teased his guest for how little he ate. Bahman retorted: "It is at the battlefield that a man proves his mettle, not at the table. Besides, it is not fitting for a prince to speak or eat much in public."

Once Rostam had finished his massive portion, Bahman conveyed his father's message in full. Rostam reflected on the graveness of the matter and gave his written reply to Bahman to take to Esfandiar:

> A man who is wise, noble in birth, and accomplished in the art of war must avoid greed and vain speech. You have surpassed your ancestors in virtue, and your name is known as far afield as India, Rome, and China. I have long wished to behold your countenance. Allow me to come and see you alone. We shall ponder my

covenants with the kings of Iran and reflect on all I have done for this land. I appoint you the judge. You decide if the reward of my long service to Iran is abject servitude. If you so judge me, then I will wear a packsaddle, put my own feet in shackles, and offer my neck to your sword.

Act as a prince and don't say what is unseemly. Banish wrath and the reckless judgments of youth from your heart. No one has ever seen me in chains. Come to my quarters instead and stay for a couple of months. Let this elder knight rejoice in hosting a gallant young prince like you. The hunting grounds are teeming with game, and I am eager to see how you hunt lions and tigers. After this respite, you will receive my parting gifts and return to King Goshtausp. I shall ride with you to the court and soften the king's heart with my apologies.

After Bahman left, Rostam and Zavareh went back to Zaul with a command to prepare the palace for a royal guest in the event Esfandiar accepted his invitation. Then he went to the shore of the river Hirmand and waited for his response.

Meanwhile, Bahman carried the dispatch to his father and prefaced it with words of praise for the hero. Esfandiar reprimanded his inexperienced son for flattering the foe in public and within earshot of the troops. But he confided to his brother Pashutan that these descriptions indicated that the passage of years had not diminished the old warrior.

THE CROWN PRINCE FACES THE OLD KNIGHT

Esfandiar ordered his black stallion to be fitted with a golden saddle and rode to the edge of the Hirmand. Rostam crossed the river, dismounted, and hailed the prince as a beloved friend whose arrival had made him as happy as he might have been to see Siavosh alive. The prince also praised Rostam and said he reminded him of his uncle, Zarir, who had been killed in the war against King Arjausp.

Rostam repeated his wish to host the worthy scion of the king, but Esfandiar could not accept that invitation. King Goshtausp had sent him to bring Rostam back in chains without delay. It would behoove Rostam to put shackles on his own hands and feet and present himself at the royal court in humility.

"If you came to court this way," Esfandiar insisted, "everyone would praise you for your modesty and blame the king for mistreating you. My heart aches for you, and I wish to be your humble servant. I pledge that your confinement will not last beyond nightfall. And when I wear the crown, you will return to Zabol in the season of blossoms. You will come back satisfied and laden with my gifts."

"I have long wished to see you," said Rostam. "I hate to be disagreeable. Young or old, we are both proud warriors. But I am afraid some demon has come between us. I can see that your heart is obsessed with assuming royal office. It would be an indelible stain on my honor if a commander of your rank refused my invitation to be a guest in my land. If you banish the demon of hatred from your heart and come to my humble abode, I will do anything you want. But I cannot accept the disgrace of bondage. No one shall see me in chains while I live."

"You are the last of the race of heroes," Esfandiar lamented, "and everything you have said is true. But I cannot come as a guest to your house, for that would be tantamount to disobeying my king, which would be an impious act. Besides, should you refuse the royal command, I have no choice but to fight you. And I cannot shed the blood of one who has hosted me at his home. However, we can eat and drink together tonight at my encampment. Let us be merry for one night. Who knows what tomorrow will bring?"

Rostam accepted this invitation. But as he had been hunting for a week, he asked leave to refresh himself and come back later. They agreed that a messenger would come to escort him for dining at Esfandiar's camp. The hero returned to Zaul and confessed that he was worried about the outcome of the affair.

On the other side of the Hirmand River, the prince had started to regret inviting Rostam over for dinner. Of course, he had made the right decision when he refused to go to the knight's palace. But for the same reasons, he was wrong to invite the knight to his camp. Thus, Esfandiar decided to renege on his promise and refused to send a messenger to bring him to his base camp. Pashutan advised his brother to be more accommodating and to seek the path of peace rather than that of confrontation. The hero would naturally bristle at the idea of humiliation and bondage. Esfandiar replied that he could not compromise on that issue, for disobeying the king was a sin. He thus called for the stewards to serve dinner, raised a chalice of wine, and called on the bard to recount his own famous seven labors.

As the evening wore on, it became clear that no one was coming to collect Rostam. Finally, he ordered his horse to be saddled and took Zavareh as a witness to the appalling behavior of the prince. At Esfandiar's camp, he derided him for neglecting to observe the most elementary obligations of a host: To disinvite a guest. The prince laughed and said that he did not intend to insult Rostam. He simply did not want to trouble him as the trek was long and the evening too hot for a comfortable ride. Instead, he had planned to go to his palace in the morning, apologize, and seek an audience with Zaul. "But now that you have taken the trouble of coming here," he added, "pick up a chalice of wine and put aside your anger."

The prince offered Rostam a seat to his left. The hero protested that he was a highborn knight descended from the exulted Saum, who traced his ancestors back to King Hushang. Only when a golden seat was set for him opposite his host did the knight deign to sit down. In response to this outburst, Esfandiar made a snide remark about Zaul being an outcast abandoned by his father and brought up in a wild bird's nest. Rostam replied that without his exploits, from saving King Kay-Kavous to the conquest of Touran in the vengeance wars, there would be no Iran to speak of and no throne to be passed down to Lohrausp and Goshtausp. "And by the way, who told you, 'Go and tie Rostam's hands?' The high vault of the heavens cannot put me in shackles."

Esfandiar advised his guest to lower his voice, drink his wine, and await the next day's events.

"I will tie your hands and take you to the king. But I am firm on my promise to advocate your cause and relieve you of all your sorrows."

Rostam laughed. "You are about to have your fill of fighting. You are yet to see how a true champion fights. But do not worry. I will take you off the saddle and bring you in my embrace to the noble Zaul. I shall open my treasure houses, enrich you with gifts, and make you king."

There was nothing else to say. The two drank wine in tense silence and parted ways. Rostam worried. If captured alive and taken to court as a slave, he would be shamed forever. If he were killed in battle, his entire clan would be wiped out. And if he were to emerge victorious, people would curse him for shedding the blood of a noble prince. His only hope was to capture the prince alive.

"I will not bare my blade or draw my heavy mace on him," Rostam told his father. "Rather I will lift him off his saddle in a friendly contest and carry him to the palace. I will serve him as an honored guest, take him to the capital and make him king just as I did with Kay-Qobaud."

Zaul bitterly laughed at his son's wishful thinking. "Don't speak like that if you don't want to be a laughingstock. Iran was in disarray, and the throne was empty when you enthroned Kay-Qobaud. You cannot rebel against a sitting king of Iran. Nor can you take Esfandiar off his saddle with the ease you describe. This is a man who has vanquished great kings of the world."

In utter desperation, Zaul prostrated himself and fervently prayed to God so the coming disaster would be turned away from his clan. He did not rise from his position all night.

THE FIRST BATTLE

The next day Rostam suited up for war. He donned his leopard skin surcoat over his armor, picked up his heavy mace, and set off for the shore of the Hirmand River on Rakhsh. Zavareh followed, but was instructed to hang back with Rostam's son Faramarz and the rest of the troops—the contest was between the two champions. Esfandiar, too, asked his brother Pashutan and his sons to stay back with their forces.

Rostam announced his readiness while beseeching his opponent to reconsider the matter. "If it is vengeance and bloodshed you desire," he said, "I will bring my armies in Zabol and Kabul to fight against your troops."

Esfandiar was offended. "How dare you suggest that I desire to shed innocent blood? If you wish to bring help, that is your affair. But I am sufficient unto myself. Let us see whose horse will return without a master at the end of this day."

With these words, a pitched battle between the two champions commenced. They fought with lances, javelins, swords, and maces until their weapons, shields, and armor were in tatters, and their horses were exhausted. Then they engaged in a contest to lift each other off their saddles, but they were equally matched at this as well. Finally, caked in mud and drenched in sweat and blood, they separated to rest.

Farther from the scene of this contest, the troops of both sides faced each other. After a while, Zavareh grew impatient and used foul language to taunt Esfandiar's men. Why, he chided, were they standing idle instead of fulfilling their duty to put his brother in chains? Nushazar replied in kind and added that they did not have permission to fight but would defend themselves if attacked. Zavareh decided to teach the brazen intruders a lesson. Leading the charge, he killed many of the opposing troops. Nushazar joined the fray and killed Rostam's lance holder in a swordfight. Moved to anger, Zavareh struck Nushazar with a lance and killed him. Mehrnush went forth to avenge his brother's death, but he came face to face with Faramarz. The young prince and the son of the great knight crossed swords. Mehrnush swung at Faramarz's neck, but missed and struck his own horse. He jumped off and tried to fight on foot but was killed by Faramarz. Distraught by the succession of these bewildering events, Bahman galloped in great speed to his father and told him of the calamity that had befallen them.

Esfandiar was livid. Turning to Rostam, he said: "Is that how you keep your promise, you scoundrel? Did we not pledge to keep our troops at bay while we fight? Where is your shame before God and man? Two worthless men from your side have slain my royal sons."

The knight of Zabol was dismayed by what he heard. He swore by the sun, the sword, the battlefield, and the king's soul that he had not authorized his troops to attack and pledged to bind and surrender the culprits, even if they were his brother and son. He gave Esfandiar the right to execute them in retaliation. This did not seem like a fair exchange to the prince. "Kings act justly when they seek revenge for their kin. But there should be parity between the victims. No one sheds the blood of a snake to avenge a peacock. Think of saving your miserable life as I stitch you to your horse with my arrows. If you survive, I will drag you away like a slave. This will teach you to rebel against your superiors."

Rostam sighed, realizing that talking no longer served a purpose. Soon thereafter, a shooting contest began in which the mighty Esfandiar ran circles around his opponent, showering him with diamond-tipped arrows that pierced his armor and Rakhsh's barding. But none of Rostam's arrows seemed to find their target due to Esfandiar's excellent armor, speed, and agility. Rostam dismounted and let Rakhsh, who was severely wounded and visibly diminished, walk back to his stable. He chose to climb a rocky knoll for protection from Esfandiar's arrows.

"What happened to your legendary strength, my great hero?" Esfandiar mocked him. "Once upon a time, demons wept at your approach. Terrible beasts were flayed alive at the glint of your sword. But now you act the part of a scared fox running to high ground from hunters."

Zavareh, who had traced Rakhsh's footprints back to Rostam, could see that the battle had gone poorly for his brother. He took the bad news back to Zaul, knowing that the existence of their entire clan was in peril.

Back on the battlefield, Esfandiar kept taunting his opponent. "How long are you going to hide up there? Who do you think is coming to your rescue? Put down your weapons and suffer me to tie your hands and save your life. I am still willing to plead your case before the king and ask him to absolve your sins. But if you wish to continue this duel, appoint someone to fight in your stead. Settle your accounts with God as your death is nigh."

"Darkness is falling, and no one fights at night," Rostam replied in desperation. "Return to your camp and allow me to return and dress my wounds before conveying your commands to Zavareh, Faramarz, and Zaul."

Esfandiar called Rostam a man of many wiles but added: "I accept your words, duplicitous as they might be. I don't want to see you dishonored, and thus I offer you safe conduct this night. But be sure to live up to your word and stop your trickery."

Relieved, the defeated hero staggered back across the river, wading through the waves of Hirmand despite the arrows embedded in his flesh. Astonished at the strength of the old champion, Esfandiar praised him as a wonder of creation and went back to his camp, where Pashutan was mourning the deaths of Mehrnush and Nushazar. The prince gravely dismounted and mourned over the bodies of his young sons but did not linger there for long. He commanded the company of mourners to moderate their lamentations. "I see no profit in shedding bloodstained tears or clinging to life. Young or old, we are all destined to die. The point is to live in the light of reason while we are alive."

Esfandiar ordered his sons' corpses to be placed in gold-encrusted teak coffins and sent back to his father with this message: "You schemed to humiliate Rostam. The evil tree you planted has borne fruit. Behold the coffins of your grandsons and muzzle your greed. Their fate is sealed, but their father's destiny remains unsettled."

THE FINAL BATTLE

When the hero returned to his palace, he found his father, mother, brother, and son in despair. He pleaded that they find some cure for Rakhsh's wounds before tending to himself. Zaul lamented that he had lived to see his brave son in such a state. Rostam called on his kinsmen to be calm and submit to the decree of fate.

"Nothing seems to mollify this impudent man," he said of Esfandiar. "My humility inflames his pride. In a life of contending with demons, beasts, and champions of the world, I have never seen the like of this man. My arrows, which used to pierce even an anvil, are rendered harmless by his armor, and my blade, which caused tigers to hide under rocks, can't even tear his silken headband. My only reprieve was the darkness that descended and saved me from that dragon of a man. Now my best option is to leave my horse behind and escape. Esfandiar is sure to sack our land. He will eventually tire of it, but perhaps it will be too late for us."

Rostam's family had accepted their impending fate. But Zaul had a plan, and snuck off to a nearby hill with three braziers of glowing coals to implement it. There, he singed a feather of the magical bird who had reared him and saved the life of his infant son. He crouched by the ambers and waited for the Simorgh. Suddenly the night seemed to grow darker as the Simorgh flew over the silver-headed old knight.

"What has driven you, my gallant champion, to call upon me?"

"This wretch of a lowborn man, Esfandiar, has brought us much suffering," Zaul lamented. "Rostam's wounds are fatal, and Rakhsh, with so many arrows in his flesh, is at death's door. Not satisfied with the fruit, Esfandiar wants to uproot the whole tree, root and branch. He wants to destroy our entire clan."

The Simorgh consoled Zaul and called for Rakhsh and Rostam. First, she scolded the hero for clashing with the invincible prince, who had been blessed by the prophet Zarathustra. The hero explained that he had to fight because he preferred death to the dishonor of captivity. The Simorgh countered that captivity to Esfandiar would be no dishonor.

Using her powers, she then extracted six arrowheads from Rakhsh's neck and healed his wounds. The injured horse neighed with the vigor of a healthy beast once again. Turning her attention on Rostam, she removed four arrowheads from his body and extracted the foul blood from him with her beak. Then she passed her feathers over his wounds and healed them.

With Rostam fully recovered, the Simorgh advised him: "Pledge to repent from challenging Esfandiar and implore him to accept peace. He will refuse your overture only if his time has come. For that occasion, I shall provide you with a weapon that will make you a hero of legends."

Rostam was relieved that the dreadful prospect of his captivity had been lifted. "But," the Simorgh continued, "the killer of Esfandiar will be harried by fate in this life and tormented in the hereafter. If you are reconciled to this, you shall be brave on the battlefield. Now take a glittering dagger and ride Rakhsh, following the path of my flight in the sky."

At this, the marvelous bird led the son of Zaul to the edge of the sea of China, where she landed, filling the air with the scent of musk. There she pointed at the shaft of a tamarisk tree and said: "This shaft shall seal the fate of Esfandiar. Cut it down, straighten it with fire, marinate it in wine, arm it with an ancient arrowhead, and fasten feathers to its end. Use it only after you have pleaded for peace. Your words might rekindle in him remembrances of your past service to Iran. But if he insists on despising you, notch this arrow in your bow. You must aim only at his eyes, for the rest of his body is in an impenetrable armor. Shoot the arrow and allow fate to guide it to its target."

After completing these instructions, the Simorgh bid farewell and soared away. Rostam went to work, preparing the arrow as he had been instructed.

The following day the reinvigorated hero returned to the Hirmand camp and roared that it was time for the prince to rise to the challenge of the day. Esfandiar turned to Pashutan, astonished, and said: "I did not expect this man to live to see the sunrise, covered as he was with my arrows. I had heard that Zaul was a formidable sorcerer. Alas, I didn't believe it."

Then he came forward and addressed Rostam. "Have you forgotten the chastisement of my arrows? Have you come back for more? Zaul has revived you with his sorcery; otherwise, you would be halfway into your grave by now. Today I shall pound you so hard that even Zaul will not be able to help you."

"I have not come to fight you," Rostam replied. "I have come to ask for your indulgence and to beg your pardon. You have treated me with inequity and unreason. I beg you in the name of the sun, the moon, the holy fire, and the sacred books of Zarathustra to turn this harm from me. Forget the past, and let me enrich you with the treasures of Saum and accompany you to the royal court. I will submit if the king wants to kill me or tie my hands. I will do anything for peace."

"Stop this peacemaking talk, as the time for speeches has passed. If you want to live, prepare the chains of your captivity."

Rostam renewed his entreaties, but Esfandiar insisted that nothing would tempt him away from his king's command. The old knight's choices were limited to war or bondage. At long last, he saw that supplication was useless. He pulled the shaft of the tamarisk arrow from his quiver and looked toward the heavens, asking for forgiveness.

Esfandiar took his opponent's delay as a sign of hesitation and said: "It seems you have not had your fill of my arrows yet, you worthless man. Behold the arrow of the house of Goshtausp and Lohrausp."

Rostam pulled at the bowstring, training his choice arrow at his opponent's eyes. The tamarisk shaft shot through the air and found its target. Esfandiar dropped his composite bow, bent over his saddle and clutched the mane of his horse. Blood streaming from his eyes painted the ground crimson.

"The sapling of your pride has borne fruit," Rostam taunted. "You boasted of being invincible. I did not cry in pain once when I was wounded by your arrows yesterday. Now you slump over your horse and turn away from battle because of a single arrow! Soon your head will be lowered to the ground, and your gentle mother will mourn you."

Esfandiar's world grew dim, and his awareness waned. He fell off his horse and lay still for a moment. Then he propped himself up and pulled the bloody arrow from his eye.

Bahman, who had sensed a lull in the battle, rushed to the battlefield and saw his father on the ground in a pool of his own blood, and ran to the camp to tell his uncle what had happened. Pashutan came to his dying brother's side and lamented his demise: "Providence and the evil eye conspired to doom our flawless prince. My curses on the crown and the throne of Goshtausp and on that sycophant Jamausp."

"Don't cry for me," Esfandiar muttered, "as this was the result of my lust for the crown. Death is written for us all. Glorious kings like Hushang, Feraydun, and Jamshid were also mortals. This was my fate. I have done good deeds, and I hope that I shall be rewarded in paradise. Rostam did not kill me in honest combat. Look at this shaft that I hold in my grasp. It is from the Simorgh. It is proof of Zaul's sorcery."

At this, Rostam arrived at the side of Esfandiar and confessed. "I have seen many champions in my time, but none as worthy as this dying prince. I could not match him, so I looked for help in the shaft of the tamarisk. We are all destined to die. Although I stand here laden with the guilt of killing the prince, it was destiny that spelled his doom. The tamarisk shaft and I were mere instruments of fate."

"My days are at an end, and my views have changed," said Esfandiar. "You were not the one who killed me. You were the tool, as were the Simorgh, the bow, and the arrow. It was my father who killed me. He commanded me to lay waste to your land and abandoned me to sorrow so he could keep his crown and treasures.

"It causes me pain that your knightly name will be henceforth stained because of this affair. This one evil act smears all your service to the previous kings. But this was the will of the heavens. Now I leave my remaining son, Bahman, to your care. Keep him in Zabol, and be his benefactor in my absence. Teach him the arts of war, hunting, and courtly conduct. Jamausp, that accursed diviner, has foreseen that he will be my heir."

Rostam stood up, held his hand on his heart, and swore an oath to instruct Esfandiar's son as if he were his own. Zavareh would advise him against accepting the charge. Bahman, he contended, would one day grow up and seek to avenge his father's death on their clan. But the hero was honor-bound to take the son of the man he had slain under his wing.

Zaul came out crying for the prince's death as if he was grieving for the fate of his son. He, too, knew that misfortune and torments would hound the slayer of Esfandiar in this world and the next.

Pashutan listened to his brother take his last breaths. Esfandiar said that he no longer desired anything from the world except a shroud, and charged him to relay a final message to their father:

> Don't look for alibis as all of this was the result of your schemes. The world is to your liking. All royal seals are still in your name. Your share is the throne, the crown, and the army. Mine is the shroud and the casket. I did not expect this from you, yet I should have. I cleansed the world of your enemies and spread the religion of the righteous path by my sword. In public, you praised me with lofty words, while secretly plotting my demise. Now you will take the blame for my death. Don't look at my face in the coffin, for this will increase your torment. Nor must you gloat in your victory, for soon you will join me on my eternal journey. There I will bring you to the presence of the Almighty and let Him judge between us.

At this, the fallen prince asked Pashutan to convey another message to his sisters and wife: "Fare you well, my dear ones. It was the desire for the crown that brought me low."

He inhaled one last time and uttered his final words: "What Goshtausp did to me was unjust."

Rostam tore at his clothes in mourning. He wished his victim an abode in paradise and echoed him: "Goshtausp has sullied my good name."

Four black horses carried the prince's iron casket. Pashutan led the funeral cortege back to the capital. Esfandiar's mother, wife, and daughters surrounded his horse, laden with his weapons. Its tail and mane had been cropped as a sign of mourning. They stroked the horse and asked him why he had forsaken his gallant master.

The king wept for his son. But the noblemen of Iran questioned his sincerity and accused him of knowingly sending the crown prince to his death. Pashutan did not mince words with Goshtausp either. One of Esfandiar's sisters addressed the king: "Esfandiar avenged your brother Zarir, your father, Lohrausp, and all of your sons and daughters. He saved your kingdom, liberated us from captivity at the Invincible Castle, and killed Arjausp, who had routed your army and forced you into hiding. But you sent him to his death in Zabol. Rostam and Zaul did not cause this. You were the one who killed your son for the sake of your crown. Shame on you and your white beard."

Thereafter an annual wail would arise
From the public squares of Iran
As people mourned Esfandiar's demise.

They sang of a wicked king, an old knight,
And an ambitious prince whose time came
When a fateful tamarisk shaft took flight.

CHAPTER 15

A Tragedy: The Demise of the House of Saum

An erudite man who hailed from the city of Merv
Told me this tale of Rostam. The man was of the clan
Of Saum and was known as the noble Azaud-sarv.

THE ILL-STARRED CHILD

In the good years before the calamity of Esfandiar, Zaul had a beautiful consort skilled in the arts of singing and playing the lute. She gave birth to a boy who was lovelier than the moon in the sky. Saum's clan was pleased, as the infant resembled their founder in stature and appearance. Astrologers and diviners of many religions were called upon to cast the horoscope of the newborn. Bewildered at the disastrous future that awaited the infant, they went to Zaul and declared their shared judgment: "The verdict of the heavens on your son is severe. He will destroy the house of Saum and bring about the ruin of this realm. Then he will perish in the calamity of his own making."

Zaul sought solace in God and prayed for divine protection. He chose to call the infant Shaqaud.

When the boy had grown into a winsome young man, he was sent to the court of the vassal king of Kabul for further education and refinement. There, he matured into a lethal warrior skilled in the lariat and the mace. The king was charmed by Shaqaud and gave his daughter to him in marriage, along with a rich dowry.

According to custom, every year, vassal kings paid a cowhide full of gold pieces as tax to Rostam, the reigning knight of Zabol. The king of Kabul presumed that taking Rostam's brother as his son-in-law would exempt him from the annual tax. To his surprise, the tax collectors arrived as usual and demanded the tribute without much ceremony. Shaqaud was embarrassed and offended. He kept his peace at first, but when the emissaries of Zabol left, he confided in his father-in-law.

"I am tired of this world," he said to the king. "Rostam dishonors me and treats me more as a stranger than a brother. This business we just witnessed is an example of his poor opinion of me. Who does he think he is? Let us lay a trap for him. We shall gain repute if we bring the Champion of the World low." They conspired through the night to slay Rostam and bring grief to the old Zaul:

A wise man once said: He who sows the wind
Shall reap the whirlwind. Harsh punishment
Awaits the treacherous man who has sinned.

The vassal king of Kabul and his son-in-law agreed to stage a public charade whereby the king would heap insults on Shaqaud, forcing him to return to Zabol and seek redress. Rostam was sure to come out to help an aggrieved brother, making him an easy target for their dishonorable plot.

THE PLOT

The king called the dignitaries of Kabul to a feast, and they came in droves. They ate, and copious amounts of wine were served to the pleasant song of the lute. Shaqaud drank to excess and started to boast of his grand lineage. "Who among you can surpass my nobility? I am from the house of Saum. My father is Zaul, and my brother is the world-renowned Rostam!"

The king of Kabul sneered: "Truth be known, you are not from the seed of Saum. Zaul never mentions you by name. Nor does his wife, Rudabeh, recognize you as a brother to Rostam. At best, you are a servant at Rostam's gate."

At this, Shaqaud dramatically sulked and left the feast in protest. In the eyes of the dignitaries present at the banquet, the king's son-in-law left in anger because he had lost face. He rode out toward Zabol with a contingent of his close allies.

Before leaving, however, Shaqaud had left instructions with his father-in-law to lay a trap for Rostam. Wide and deep pits were to be dug in the hunting ground, whose bottoms bristled with javelins, sharp swords, and lances. The ditches were then to be covered by false roofs made of branches, fabric, vegetation, and dirt.

When Shaqaud arrived in Zabol, he was greeted by Zaul. Happy and proud to see his younger brother, Rostam gushed. "Descendants of the noble Saum are all handsome, mighty, and brave. How fares Kabul, and what does its king say of Rostam?"

"Don't mention the name of that vile man to me," Shaqaud replied. "At first, he treated me respectfully, but now he holds me in contempt. He resents his obligation to pay tribute to you and considers himself your equal in lineage and power. He insults me, denies that I am a son of Zaul, and claims that I am of no consequence in this family, I have turned my back on Kabul with a broken heart and sallow cheeks."

Rostam was furious. "Such talk from that man will not remain hidden. And for that reason, he has forfeited his crown and his life, and I shall bestow his crown upon you."

The traitorous brother was quartered in luxury as a guest of honor while Rostam gathered an army. When all was ready, Shaqaud went to the hero and said: "There is no need to invade Kabul with a real army. I am certain that the king has sobered up by now and that he is terrified of confronting you. He would never lock horns with you. Once we appear, he is sure to humble himself before us and beg your pardon for his past behavior."

Rostam agreed that the affair was not worth deploying an army. Instead, they set off for Kabul ahead of a hundred equestrian warriors and infantrymen under the command of Zavareh.

Shaqaud dispatched a secret runner to his father-in-law, informing him of Rostam's imminent arrival. When they reached the vicinity of Kabul, the king came out, displaying signs of contrition. He approached Rostam's horse bareheaded and barefoot. Prostrating himself and crying tears of remorse, he appealed for forgiveness and implored: "If a slave gets drunk and speaks unwisely, is it not fitting for the master to forgive his folly?"

The hero took pity on the king and confirmed him as the ruler of Kabul. Grateful for this kindness, the king invited Rostam to a feast.

As the matter of the king's insolence appeared to have been resolved, he accepted, and the company retired to a pleasant meadow outside Kabul, where delectable food and a variety of wines were set in front of decorated daises. The company dined while listening to the musicians. Then the king volunteered that the grounds were teeming with mountain sheep, deer, and onager. The pleasures of a hunt lured Rostam. He picked up his bow and ordered his horse to be saddled.

The fate of Rostam was sealed, for he received
All that hospitality without once suspecting
The possibility that he was being deceived.

THE HERO'S END

The hunting party took to the plains as their trained hawks and falcons flew above. The men spread out over the grounds, and many of them, including Zavareh and Rostam, rode in the direction of the hidden pits. Shaqaud anxiously trailed behind.

Rakhsh approached one of the ditches, smelled the freshly overturned dirt, and reared up, stomping the ground. Rostam urged him forward with irritation. Rakhsh found a narrow passage of firm ground between two pits and gingerly ambled. Furious with the unruliness of his steed, Rostam cracked his whip. As Rakhsh tried to jump, the ground gave way, and his hind legs sank into the edge of one of the ditches. In vain he tried to hold on to the brink with his front legs. Seconds later, horse and rider crashed through the false cover of the pit. Rostam and Rakhsh were mortally impaled by the weapons planted at the bottom of the ditch.

Zavareh perished in an adjacent pit, another victim of Shaqaud's treachery, and the rest of the men accompanying Rostam also died in the trenches, except for one who made his way back to Zabol with the news of the monumental betrayal.

Despite his grave wounds, Rostam made a heroic effort to pull himself up to the edge of the pit, realizing that he was the victim of his brother's dastardly assassination plot. When he saw Shaqaud coming to inspect the result, he said: "You have ruined our ancestral home, you wretched man. You shall regret this evil deed before your impending death."

The conniving Shaqaud replied: "You have finally received the due meed of your wicked deeds. How long did you think you could plunder and murder? You have preened yourself as the first knight of Iran for long enough. Now taste death at the hands of the demons."

At this point, the king of Kabul had arrived on the scene. Pretending to be surprised, he feigned concern for Rostam and offered to bring a healer to tend to his injuries. It was a cowardly lie, and Rostam knew it. "Give up the pretense. Shed no false tears for me, you wretch of a worthless man. No physician can help me now. I am dying, and in this, I am joining the kings and heroes of yore. I am surely not more exalted than Jamshid, whose body was cleaved in two by Zahhak's henchmen. Nor am I better than the late kings Feraydun and Kay-Qobaud. Prince Siavosh's neck was slashed by Goruy when his time came. They all departed and left us behind. But rest assured that my son, Faramarz, shall come to avenge me. Your days on this earth are numbered."

With these words, Rostam turned to his brother and said: "Now that it has come to this, at least bring me my bow and arrow so I can defend myself against the scavenging lions that might want to attack me while I am still alive."

Glad that the death of his famed brother was imminent, Shaqaud came forward carrying Rostam's bow and two arrows. He put them by the side of the pit and snickered, gloating over his success. Rostam picked an arrow, notched it in the bow, and pulled the string. The shameless Shaqaud panicked and ran to seek the cover of an old plane tree. The tree bore green leaves but its trunk had been hollowed out by the passage of time. Despite the pain that rankled him, Rostam gathered all his strength to pull the bowstring tighter, and he shot a mighty shaft that pierced the tree and the man hiding behind it. Pinned to the ancient trunk, Shaqaud heaved a sigh and died. Rostam praised God for letting him avenge himself before the sun set on his death.

Back in Zabol, Zaul was beside himself. He wallowed in the dirt and lacerated his face, "From now on I shall wear a shroud and spend my time mourning for my sons Rostam and Zavareh. The accursed Shaqaud has uprooted this majestic tree. How could an ill-omened fox ensnare these elephants in that faraway land? Who has heard of such a thing? What reason do I have to live after this day? What comforts can life offer me now? Alas, my valiant, world-conquering son who is no more!"

AVENGING ROSTAM'S DEATH

Zaul sent his grandson, Faramarz, with an army to retrieve the bodies of the dead heroes, but he found Kabul deserted of its leaders. The noblemen had fled, and the ordinary people were bewildered over the disaster that had befallen its guests. Faramarz went to the hunting grounds, threw himself on the earth, and cried for his father and uncle. "I curse the wretched man who did this to you and swear by the soul of our ancestor Saum I shall avenge you both. I shall not take off my armor until I bring everyone who was connected to this vile plot low."

Then he ordered his men to attend to Rostam's body. He was carefully laid on two bejeweled slabs, as one was not enough for his mammoth size. They sutured his wounds with golden thread and gently washed the blood away. While a mixture of saffron and gray amber burned close by, they rubbed his skin with camphor and rosewater and combed his white beard. Finally, they draped the body in perfumed silk and placed him in a coffin fashioned out of ivory inlaid teak planks joined together with golden pegs. The casket was sealed with pitch infused with the essence of musk and rosewater.

Zavareh's body was prepared and placed in a coffin made of the root of an elm tree. At last, Rakhsh was hauled out of the pit, washed, draped in silk, and put on the back of an elephant, a task that lasted two days.

The funerary cortege traveled for two days and one night to reach Zabol. Crowds of people thronged the procession and helped carry the dead. Not once were the caskets put down. Nor did anyone hear a voice unless it was a wail of lamentation. In Zabol the bodies were taken to a garden and put on two golden platforms for display. The people, free-born and slave, brought flowers and musk. They mourned their fallen hero with these dirges:

> What has befallen you? Why, of all the perfumes of the world, are you wearing musk and ambergris? Why are you no longer shining on the battleground and at the center of the banquet? Why don't you generously give away worldly goods as you used to do? Alas, you are gone from us. Live forever in paradise, for your soul was the essence of justice and valor.

Once Rostam and Zavareh were consigned to the darkness of the luxurious crypt that was prepared for them, Faramarz gathered an avenging army. At dawn, he led his men through the gates of Zabol to the sound of trumpets and drums. The king of Kabul also gathered a massive army to defend himself. A dark wind rose as the two ironclad armies clashed on the battlefield. The jangling of steel and the throbbing of drums dominated the arena.

Faramarz penetrated the heart of the enemy with a small contingent of brave warriors and captured the king alive. At this, the army of Kabul panicked and ran, but Faramarz's men set upon them like wolves, turning the dirt into red mud with the blood of the escaping enemy. Those who were not killed fled without care for the families and homes they left behind.

The king of Kabul was brought to the hunting ground in a trunk hoisted on an elephant, as blood streamed from his mouth. He was tied up, suspended over one of the pits and executed along with forty of his relatives. Firewood was piled on the plane tree where Shaqaud remained pinned by Rostam's arrow. The corpse and the tree burned in the flames.

Faramarz appointed a king for Kabul as the entire clan of the old king had been annihilated. Then he went back to Zabol, but there was no joy in this victory. The public lamentation for Rostam lasted a whole year. No one was as stricken by the death of Rostam as Rudabeh. In her grief one day, she told Zaul: "No one has ever suffered a darker day than this since the world began."

Zaul reproached his wife, saying that extreme hunger alone was harder to bear. Rudabeh was offended and swore an oath to abstain from food. For a week, she fasted and mournfully communed with her departed son.

As her eyes grew dim and her body became feeble, her attendants monitored her carefully, afraid that she would harm herself. In her grief and hunger, she was beset by delusions. As night fell, she found a dead snake in a stream and attempted to bite off its venomous head. An attendant caught her in time and led her away to be nursed back to health.

Later, when she recovered, Rudabeh agreed with Zaul that sorrow and happiness would become indistinguishable in extreme hunger. She had grown wiser about the tragedy of losing her heroic son. "Rostam is gone," she said, "and we, too, shall join him. We shall all be one with the Creator of the universe. Oh God, forgive the sins of my son, admit him to paradise, and reward him for his good deeds."

THE REIGN OF BAHMAN

When King Goshtausp knew his time of departure from this world was nigh, he called his adviser Jamausp and confided in him. "I was so heartbroken by the death of Esfandiar that I have not had one good day since then. Now I pass from this world entrusting the crown to his son Bahman. May he reign in justice. Let him appoint my brother Pashutan as his royal adviser."

Rostam had groomed Bahman for the royal arts, according to the pledge he had made to Esfandiar. When his training was complete, Bahman returned to his grandfather's court on the condition that the old animosities be set aside. At his grandfather's deathbed, Bahman received the keys to the royal treasury. Reflecting on his own shortcomings, Goshtausp advised Bahman in the art of ruling as a righteous king. "Keep the wise close at hand and eschew the wicked. As a dying king who dominated the world for one hundred twenty years, I give you my throne and my treasures."

After a royal funeral, the old king was consigned to a magnificent crypt in a coffin made of ivory and ebony.

Bahman took the throne and generously endowed his army with worldly goods. Then he addressed the assembly of knights and noblemen:

"You all remember what Rostam and that old sorcerer Zaul did during the terrible events that led to the martyrdom of my father. Now his son, Faramarz, continues his insolence. I can think of nothing but avenging Esfandiar and my brothers, Nushazar and Mehrnush.

"Honor demands that I even the score and slay those who killed my father. King Feraydun went against the Serpent King Zahhak to avenge the slaying of Jamshid. Manuchehr exacted revenge for the murder of his father, Iraj, on his dastardly uncles Tur and Salm. Kay-Khosrow killed Afrasiab and extinguished his hearth as punishment for the murder of his father, Siavosh. My grandfather, Goshtausp, sought justice for his father Lohrausp's death, when he went to war with King Arjausp of Touran. Even Rostam's son, Faramarz, killed his father's murderers and desecrated their bodies on the plains of Kabul. I, too, claim the right to exact revenge for the peerless Esfandiar. Now advise me. What is your counsel?"

The knights and noblemen pledged their obedience to Bahman. One of those assembled stepped forward and said, "When it comes to past affairs, you are more knowledgeable than us. We are all your servants. Do what you wish to win fame and glory in the world. None of us will disobey your commands."

These words further inflamed Bahman's desire for revenge. Soon the drums of war were sounding, and the air was thick with the dust kicked up by an army of one hundred thousand soldiers leaving the capital for the banks of the Hirmand. A messenger from Bahman went across the river and into the realm of the clan of Saum with a message for Zaul:

> The yearning to avenge Esfandiar and my brothers is ablaze within me. I shall dye the Hirmand with the blood of the wrongdoers.

Zaul's heart burned when he heard this message. He sent back a response:

> The affair of your father was a matter of ineluctable fate. Not even dragons and lions can escape the verdict of destiny. I grieved

> for Esfandiar like my own son. He entrusted your care to Rostam and we raised you as our own. You did not suffer harm at our hands.
>
> You ought to remember the services Saum and Rostam rendered to the kings of Iran. Your ancestors owe a debt of gratitude to our line of heroes. Come now and let us assuage your rage. I will give you all the riches of Rostam and Saum's treasures. We will turn a new page; you will be our shepherd, and we will be your docile flock.

Zaul enriched the messenger with a horse and gifts and sent him back with his plea of reconciliation. But Bahman was not mollified. He rode into the city of Zabol and looked down on Zaul, who had come out on foot to plead with him again.

"This is the time for forgiveness," Zaul told him, "the time of cleansing the heart of the resentments of the past. You grew up among us. Pardon us our sins in exchange for the services we have rendered you. Leave the past behind, and don't seek to punish the dead. Leaning on a cane and broken by age, this is the son of the great Saum begging you for mercy."

Ignoring the advice of his councilors, Bahman rejected this gesture of humility and ordered that Zaul's feet be placed in shackles. He ransacked the treasury of the house of Saum, sending back caravans loaded with gold and silver, Arabian horses with golden bridles, jewel-encrusted weapons, sacks of rare spices, and many slaves. Whatever Rostam had gathered over the years was carried off. The treasury was plundered to the last coin.

Faramarz was in Bost when he heard of Bahman's sacking of Zabol and the mistreatment of his grandfather. Outraged, he gathered his generals. "Zavareh told my father more than once that Bahman would one day seek vengeance for his father's death. At his peril did my father ignore that advice. Now Bahman's army has come from Iran like a rising black cloud. He has put my grandfather in bondage and plundered our treasury. Advise me, my lords: What is your counsel?"

The leaders of the army pledged their obedience to Faramarz as they had obeyed his forefathers. His head full of memories of Rostam's exploits,

Faramarz donned his armor and led his men into battle against the enemy. Bahman, too, brought his army to the front for confrontation. The two sides lined up on the plain of Gourabad as the dust of their horses swirled around them. The trumpets sounded, and the drums rolled. Arrows poured from the sky like raindrops. Maces and blades grew out of thin air.

The battle raged for three days and three nights. On the fourth day, a wind blew against Faramarz's forces, and Bahman saw his opportunity to take to the field. With the wind on his back, the young king drew his sword and led an attack, routing the armies of Zabol and Kabul. So many had been killed on both sides that their tangled corpses resembled a range of grisly hills. A brave lion descended from brave lions, Faramarz fought along with a small band of his followers until they were dead and he was injured and captured. He was brought to the king in chains. Bahman took no pity on his captive. He had Faramarz suspended upside down from the gallows and killed in a torrent of arrows.

THE DEMISE OF THE CLAN OF HEROES

Appalled by Bahman's cruelty, Pashutan addressed Bahman. "King of truth and justice, if it was vengeance you sought, now you have it. Don't condone the continuation of bloodshed and plunder. Fear God and have shame. Beware of the play of fate that wantonly raises some high and lowers others to the dust. Didn't our willful father come to his final rest in a casket? Didn't the legendary Rostam meet his end at the bottom of a pit? Keep your hand from harassing noble souls while you are king. Free Zaul from captivity. The stars have favored you, but the old, silver-haired knight's sigh could incur the wrath of the heavens and reverse your fortunes. Do not forget that you, like your forefathers owe your crown to the labors of the house of Zaul and Saum. Indeed, you are more indebted to him than to your own father and grandfather."

Regretting his excesses, Bahman released Zaul from captivity, arranged for a proper funeral for Faramarz, and issued orders for decamping and preparing for a quick return to the capital.

When Rudabeh was reunited with Zaul, she lamented once more for her dead son. "Woe is me, my brave, departed Rostam. You were descended from a line of exalted knights. You outshined Goshtausp on his throne. Now your treasure houses are robbed and your son is murdered in a hail of arrows. Your old father has been humiliated like a slave. May no one share your fate. May the land be cleansed of the seed of Esfandiar."

The clan of Saum hummed with the sounds of weeping. Bahman, frightened by Rudabeh's curses, hurried to depart. As the mountains were painted red with the setting sun, the army of Bahman left the land of Zabol.

Pashutan urged his king to make haste
And leave the plain of Zabol as Rudabeh
Started to curse Bahman and lambaste

The ungrateful man who had razed
The city of his upbringing and enslaved
The benefactors by whom he was raised.

Having destroyed the house of Saum, King Bahman returned to his palace. He resumed his rule gratified that he had avenged his father.

At the approach of his final hours Bahman considered his legacy and who would replace him on the throne. The obvious choice seemed to be the lionhearted crown prince Sassan. But the king's favorite was his daughter, the wise and beautiful Homai. The affection between father and daughter went beyond the bounds of filial love, so much so that the king married her in a union that was sanctioned by their Pahlavi religion. After six months the moonlit princess bride was with child.

King Bahman gathered his advisors and said: "The chaste Homai has not known happiness since she was born. I hereby pronounce her my crown princess and place the royal succession in her line. Her child, boy or girl, will rule my kingdom."

Prince Sassan was utterly devastated by this strange decree that deprived him of the office that he considered his birthright. He mounted his horse and left the royal palace in haste, riding for three days and two nights without rest until he arrived in the city of Nishaupur. There he settled down and decided to spend the rest of his days in anonymity. He married the daughter of a local landowner and gave his son his own name. Thereafter the elder sons of his progeny were all given the name of Sassan to keep their royal lineage alive. Deprived of wealth and a trade, the sons became shepherds who tended the flocks of their local vassal king.

Part II

Historical Traditions

CHAPTER 16

Prelude to Calamity: Homai to Dara

Bahman ruled for sixty years, but when he died
None dared climb his throne but Homay,
The late king's beloved daughter and graceful bride.

THE CROWNING OF A QUEEN

Homay unlocked the royal treasure house and generously spent its riches to establish order throughout the land. During this period, she developed a taste for her office as the glorious sovereign, and by the time she gave birth to Bahman's son, she neither wished to abdicate nor act as his regent. Instead, she told those who knew of her pregnancy that her infant was stillborn. Only a trusty wetnurse knew that the prince was alive and well.

After eight months, as the infant was growing to resemble his father, Homai had a beautiful wooden box made for him. One could mistake it for a coffin, but it was a well-built boat covered with a mixture of musk, tar, wax, and resin. On the inside, it was lined and richly padded with Roman silk and filled with golden coins and precious gems. The infant was fitted with an armband studded with a kingly ruby and placed inside the box, where he was then covered in Chinese silk fabrics.

As instructed by the queen, the wetnurse and two male servants sealed the box shut and floated it on the waves of the Euphrates. Their task was to follow the precious box as it sailed down the river and report on its progress. At dawn, the box floated into a rivulet that was partially dammed for laundering clothes. A fuller fished the box out of the river and opened it to find the baby surrounded by treasure. In great excitement, he left the riverbank, carrying the box and a load of his half-washed laundry. Having witnessed this scene, the servants returned to inform their queen that her son was in safe hands. Homai commanded the servants to keep the matter in strict confidence.

THE PRINCE AND THE FULLER

The fuller's wife was baffled by the early return of her husband. How did he expect to be paid returning with a load of damp and unwashed clothes?

The fuller laid down his load and opened the box. She beamed with delight when she saw the baby, and listened to her husband with rapt attention.

"I will tell you everything that happened, but you must not tell a soul about this. I was laundering the clothes near the boulder on which I beat my wash when I saw this box floating toward me. We just lost our own infant. Now, look at how the heavens have favored us with a child blessed with nobility and good looks."

The husband and wife stared in amazement at the beautiful baby. He held golden coins in his left hand, and the fingers of his right squeezed a fistful of rubies. The recently bereaved mother pressed the baby to her breasts, which still flowed with milk. With joy, the couple named the child Daraub, as he was water's gift.

The new-found riches the couple had discovered in the box could improve their lives. But such a change would raise suspicions, so they packed their bags with their treasure and set off for a faraway city that lay sixty miles away, near the Roman border. There they exchanged some of the gold coins and gems for garments and household items and, in time, bought a house and a garden. The fuller, however, continued to ply his trade. When his wife protested that he did not need to work as hard, he said, "This is what I do. Nothing is nobler than working at one's trade."

As Daraub grew up, he excelled his peers in wrestling to the point that they feared him. This did not help the fuller's business, as the boys' parents were his clients. He admonished his son to be humble and learn how to beat clothes against the rocks at the river's edge. But Daraub did not heed this advice.

One day the fuller happened upon his son wielding a bow and arrows, pretending to be on a hunt. He scolded the boy for wasting time on such frivolous games instead of learning a worthwhile trade. Daraub protested that he needed to be educated before choosing a profession and begged to be allowed to learn the Zoroastrian scriptures of Zand and Avesta. So, the fuller took his son to a learned cleric, who taught him the arts of reading, writing, and quoting the scriptures. Then the boy expressed interest in equestrian skills. The father indulged his son again and hired a coach to train him in horsemanship and polo.

Finally, Daraub confessed to his father that he had higher ambitions than becoming a fuller. "And what's more, I don't feel like I belong here, despite all the love and care that you lavish on me. I don't even look like you. Who is my real father, and where is he?"

The fuller advised him to consult his mother. Confounded, Daraub suspected his mother had lain with another man and rushed home to confront her. Locking the door, he motioned to his sword and threatened her to confess the truth. As she related the long story of how he was found, everything started to make sense. Now Daraub knew the fountainhead of his lofty ambitions and his desire to lead a nobleman's life.

He asked his mother if anything was left of the treasure. She gave him the last of the gems and gold but kept the big ruby from the armband hidden. Daraub bought a good horse. But he didn't have enough to properly caparison it.

Then he went to the border of Iran with Rome and asked the military commander in charge to be enlisted as a soldier. The request was speedily granted, as a skirmish with the Romans was looming, and the border needed better protection. The young man was accepted and quickly promoted to the equestrian guard. Shortly after that, Daraub's commander perished in a battle. When the news reached the capital, Queen Homai replaced the fallen leader with one of her well-respected paladins named Rashnvaud and accompanied him to the border to review the troops. At the parade, Daraub appeared tall and proud, shining like a star in the cavalry ranks. Impressed by the gallant but poorly dressed young man, Homai inquired about him. Rashnvaud told her he was a local recruit who had distinguished himself in combat. The queen was strangely drawn to the young man but did not know why. She dismissed the feeling, wished the troops good luck, and returned to her palace from where she monitored the rising tensions between Iran and Rome.

COMMANDER AND THE BOOMING RUINS

A storm of torrential rain descended on the Iranian camp as they prepared for a crucial battle with the Roman army. Daurab, who was outside the camp for a chore, sought shelter in a ruin and fell asleep due to extreme exhaustion. Rashnvaud was riding through the tempest to make sure no one was left outside the tents. At that time a flash of lightning illuminated a gloomy but impressively domed building. It was followed by a loud thunderclap. The general thought he heard a sonorous voice from the direction of the magnificent ruin saying:

"Oh, degraded dome, protect the king of Iran, who has taken refuge in thee."

Was the booming thunder deceiving his senses? But then he heard the voice coming from the ruin again.

"Beware, crumbling dome. You are sheltering the son of King Bahman."

The portentous warning echoed three times. Rashnvaud sent his lieutenants inside to investigate. There, on the wet dirt, they found a sleeping young soldier in old garments. They shook him awake and informed him that he was being summoned by the field marshal. As soon as the group left the gates of the building, the entire edifice crumbled with a tremendous sound.

There was no mistaking the gravity of the signs Rashnvaud had witnessed. He brought the young man to his camp, dressed him in luxurious clothes, and ordered a bonfire to be lit. The following day, he was given a magnificent and richly caparisoned Arabian horse and well-forged weapons. The knight asked the bewildered soldier about his name and lineage. Daraub related the entire story as he had heard it from his adopted mother. Orders were issued to bring the fuller, his wife, and all the relevant evidence to Rashnvaud. But the full inquiry had to wait as a clash with Rome was imminent.

Daraub was given the command of the vanguard, and when the battle was joined, he readily decimated the Roman army like a raging lion riding a dragon. The ground turned into a sea of blood, and the Iranians emerged as the victors of that day's campaign. Rashnvaud praised his daring commander and assured him that the queen would richly reward him. The next day's confrontation was another remarkable success. The Iranians crushed the enemy, killed forty chaplains and captured the enemy's standard, which was in the shape of a cross.

At the conclusion of the battle, Rashnvaud sent a messenger to inform the victorious Daraub that he could take whatever he wanted as his share of the booty. But he took only a well-made lance and brought the rest to his commander. In the third battle, the Iranian army chased the enemy back into Rome, burning cities and laying waste to the land along the way. At long last, the Caesar sued for peace, sent forth slaves and gems to mollify the Iranians, and pledged to pay an annual tribute.

Back at camp, Rashnvaud directed the fuller and his wife to come forward and relate their story. A written version of the wondrous tale was sent to the queen along with the special ruby. Upon reading the story and viewing the gem, Homai knew that the young soldier who had impressed her in the ranks was her long-lost son.

Overcome with sympathy for her abandoned son, she declared that she would abdicate in favor of him. "I was young, inexperienced, and scared when I entrusted my one and only son to the waves of the Euphrates. It was a sin to spurn the divine gift of a worthy son. He has had a difficult adolescence, growing up in obscurity. But now he has been restored to me, unworthy as I am."

To celebrate the crowning of the new king, Homai declared nine days of celebration. She gave alms to express her gratitude to God and sent a rich donation to fire temples where the holy scriptures of Zand and Avesta were recited and where the fire rites of the day of Sadeh were celebrated.

When the celebrations ended the queen admitted Rashnvaud and Daraub to the throne room. Holding goblets brimming with rubies and yellow sapphires in each hand, she sat her son on the turquoise throne and crowned him king of Iran. She then begged his forgiveness. The long-lost son praised his mother for ably ruling the land and graciously accepted her apology. He further consoled the queen by stating that an error, regardless of its gravity, would never blot out all the good she had done in the thirty-two years of her reign.

As Daraub sat on the throne wearing the crown of the olden kings, the fuller and his wife came to offer their respects to their new sovereign. The king attired them in regal garments and enriched them with gems and gold coins. With a smile, he told the fuller, "Now you are fabulously wealthy. But this doesn't mean that you should abandon your profession. After all, you may never know if you will receive another surprise package floating to you on the waters of the Euphrates."

DARAUB'S REIGN

The new king declared that he had not gained his crown by hard work or ambition. It was a serendipitous, divine gift and a wonder for the world to behold. He announced that he did not wish to unduly tax people to fill his royal coffers. "The wealthy should prosper, and the poor must be raised as our justice suffuses the land."

He sent emissaries to the four corners of the world with gifts to make friends out of enemies. But he did not abandon prudence. Troops were stationed at the borders to secure the homeland.

One day, when he had gone to oversee the shepherds rounding up their colts, the king discovered a wide and deep river. He called experts from Rome and India to dig tributaries to irrigate vast tracts of land from that water. Then he founded a new city in the center of the cultivated areas named Daraub-gerd and brought skilled artisans to reside there. Daraub-gerd was famous for its graceful fortifications and the awe-inspiring fire temple erected on its highest hill.

At this time, an Arab commander named Shoa'yb from the tribe of Qotayb attacked Iran with a hundred thousand lance-wielding warriors. Daraub's forces won a three-day campaign against the enemy, during which Shoa'yb was killed, and many noble Arabian horses and well-forged armaments were taken as booty of the war. The king appointed another Arab leader as commander of the region to collect its overdue taxes and future tributes.

Having subdued this insurgency, Daraub brought his victorious army to the borders of Rome to provoke a confrontation. Caesar Philqus,* apprised of the troop movements, brought a large army from Amorium to the border. After three days of battle, the Iranians crushed the enemy and entered Roman territory, laying waste to the land and enslaving residents. Philqus asked for terms and sent an envoy carrying two chests full of precious gems as tribute and reparations. The emissary conveyed the message of peace, enjoining King Daraub to emulate his royal grandfather Bahman in magnanimity and agree to sign a new treaty.

Daraub responded that he would accept Philqus's peace initiative if also sent his daughter Nahid to be his wife. The Caesar gladly acceded to these terms and sent Nahid to the Iranian king in a golden litter, accompanied by Roman philosophers, monks, and a line of beautiful slave girls each carrying a golden goblet full of gems. A trail of forty camels carrying Roman silk and the back taxes of Rome followed. The treasure included one hundred thousand jewel-encrusted golden eggs, each weighing slightly less than half a pound.

Unfortunately, the marital union between the royal families failed, as the princess suffered from bad breath. Roman healers recommended a bitter herb called eskanadar, but Nahid was cured too late. The king had grown cold toward his new bride, and the sad princess was sent back to her father. She hid the fact that she was with child. When her son was born, she named him Eskandar after the herb that had cured her. Shortly thereafter, Daraub married a princess who gave birth to a son slightly younger than his unknown brother in Rome. They named the Iranian prince Dara.

ESKANDAR AND DARA

The young prince of Rome possessed a king's golden heart and eloquent speech. He was diligent in learning the intricacies of courtly and martial

* In *Shahnameh* Philqus assumes the role of Alexander's father (whereas he is his maternal grandfather). It is reasonable to assume that Philqus is a corruption of "Philippos" (Φίλιππος), or Philip, the famous Macedonian king (382–336 BCE), who was Alexander the Great's father.

arts. Dara, by contrast, was infamous for his supercilious ways, impetuous temper, and brash tongue.

Twelve years into his reign, King Daraub had a premonition that his time of leaving this world was approaching. Soon he was on his deathbed, surrounded by his courtiers. As the pallor of death drained the color from his face, the king sighed and advised his son: "Remember that our worldly sojourn is brief. It would behoove you to stay on the path of justice."

After a period of respectful mourning, young Dara, adorned with the crown of the olden kings, ascended his father's throne and issued a short declaration. "I will not lower he who is riding high, nor will I make it my business to raise the ones who have fallen. Disobey me, and I will cause your head to part company from your body. I will not tolerate the prosperous among you to blithely enjoy their wealth while my coffers remain empty. And don't fancy that I keep courtiers to benefit from their advice. I keep my own council. Everything belongs to me, for I have been given dominion and kingship in this world."

Dara sent acerbic letters to the kings of the world, warning them to remain obedient and avoid arousing his wrath. Soon gifts, tributes, and taxes flowed to his treasury, enabling him to be generous to his commanders, the rich, and the poor.

Meanwhile, Philqus also passed away, and Eskandar became the Caesar of Rome. Hoping to edify the new king and guide him to the right path, a sage by the name of Aristotle came to the royal court and addressed him.

"Hark my advice, oh prosperous sovereign!" he said. "The most ignorant person in the world is he who thinks he knows everything. The throne on which you rest is a fickle friend. It is sure to desert you, as it has the previous kings. We reap what we sow, and a good name is all that we leave behind. From dust we come and to it we shall return."

Eskandar honored Aristotle, followed his advice, and allowed him to recline on the throne when he was away on his campaigns. One day as the Caesar presided over his audience hall, an ambassador arrived from Iran to demand the tributes and taxes pledged by Philqus to King Daraub. The young Caesar was furious. "Go back and tell Dara that the goose that laid golden eggs has died." Frightened by this outburst, the ambassador left Rome in haste.

Eskandar had a passion for traveling. Drawing on Roman treasuries, he gathered a formidable army, heralded by a standard on which the words "The Lover of the Cross"* were emblazoned, and set off to see the world.

Eskandar's first destination was Egypt. He expected to be welcomed by the Egyptian king and his retinue, but he found the gates closed and the armies arrayed to fight him. Thus, he issued orders to his troops to open the borders for his expedition. In the ensuing battle, the armies of Egypt were crushed, and countless horses, shields, armor, and armaments were taken as booty. Many Egyptian soldiers also switched sides to join the Roman host.

Eskandar then moved his army to the borders of Iran. Hearing this, Dara left his summer palace for the Winter Palace of Pars with an army so numerous that their lances blocked the wind. The two armies camped two miles apart at the western shore of the Euphrates.

The Caesar, who had heard of the legendary size of Dara's army, decided to ascertain the enemy's strength in person. To accomplish this task, he disguised himself as an envoy, picked an interpreter, and rode with ten of his elite commanders to the Iranian camp, where he announced his mission to the court: "Caesar Eskandar sends his greetings to the Great King Dara. He says his purpose is to travel and see the world, not wage war. He recognizes you as the sole sovereign of Iran. But if you refuse him passage and agitate for war, he is not one to demur from such a challenge. If you are determined to deny him passage, prepare for battle and name your day."

Impressed by the appearance and eloquence of the envoy, Dara asked him to state his name, that is, if he was not the Caesar in disguise. The envoy protested: "With so many able attendants at his camp, why would the Caesar come here as an envoy?"

* In the *Shahnameh* version of the "Alexander romance" one finds many anachronisms. Among them is the supposition that Alexander the Great, who died in 323 BCE, was a Byzantine Caesar and a Christian.

That night the Roman mission banqueted with the king. As they were draining their cups of wine, Dara's ambassador, who had been rebuked by Eskandar while trying to collect the Roman tributes, recognized the Caesar. He stole to the king's side and whispered in his ear: "This man is no envoy. He is the Roman king in disguise who has come to spy on your troops." The king nodded, for he had guessed as much.

Eyeing this exchange, the Caesar realized that his disguise had been blown. He finished his wine and asked permission to retire to his tent. But instead, he jumped on his horse and fled with the speed of the wind, followed by his companions. The good news he brought to his commanders was that the enemy's army was not as powerful as he had supposed. Both sides knew that war was inevitable. They were standing in battle formations as the sun came up.

THE FOUR BATTLES OF ROME AND IRAN

The shore of the Euphrates shook with the blaring of horns and throbbing of drums as the Roman phalanxes crashed into the Persian ranks. Both sides fought valiantly, and the carnage did not subside for seven days.

A strong black wind rose against the Iranian side on the eighth day. Soon thereafter, they suffered heavy casualties and were forced to pull back to their side of the river. Eskandar gave chase but stopped short of crossing. The first battle had gone to the Romans, but war was far from over.

Within a month, the defeated king had gathered another army and crossed the Euphrates again with vengeance in his heart. The second battle lasted three days but ended with another defeat for the Iranians. Dara abandoned his failing campaign and fled to the city of Jahrom, the seat of his treasure house. The forsaken Iranian soldiers were left to roam the battlefield like a flock of sheep without a shepherd. They asked for quarter, which Eskandar granted, and many defected. Over the next four months, as the Roman army rested, Dara returned to the Winter Palace of Pars, having exhausted his treasures to equip a new army. The past defeats had damaged the Iranian army's confidence. The king addressed his troops, admitting that there had been a traumatic reversal of fortunes. "The balance of power has changed between us and the Romans. The prey has become the predator. But the worst is yet to come. It is time to prove your mettle and defend your homeland."

"Death is better than life with dishonor," the army chanted. "Long live the king." But the temporary rush of patriotism did not last. On the day of the battle, the Iranians were routed, and Eskandar marched into the Winter Palace of Pars and occupied it. He repeated his pledge to protect the Iranian side from death and despoilment if they surrendered. This gave rise to another wave of defections, further swelling the Roman ranks. Even more crushing, the royal family was taken into captivity during this battle.

After his third defeat, Dara fled to the easternmost city of Kerman. "Our fate is sealed," he lamented to his weeping commanders. "None has ever heard of such bad luck. Our battles are lost, and our wives and children are enslaved. Only divine intervention can save us now. What is your council?"

The commanders conceded. "We must accept our fate, surrender, and beg him for mercy. It is only speech. After all, uttering the word 'fire' does not burn the tongue."

Following this advice, Dara wrote a letter to Eskandar, promising to send him the riches of Goshtausp and Esfandiar and to become a vassal king. He begged the Caesar to act honorably toward his family, who had become his slaves. A gracious response was brought back by a messenger riding a swift camel. The letter stated that members of the royal family were safe in Isfahan, and no one would dare treat them with disrespect. And if the Iranians ceased their hostility, he would be honor-bound to maintain Dara as the king of Iran.

But doubts gnawed at the humiliated king. Groveling before the Roman Caesar was worse than death. He had to fight one final battle, come what may. In his hour of desperation, Dara sent a pitiful letter to Foor, the king of India, promising him rich rewards in exchange for military help. But this plan, too, was doomed from the start.

When Eskandar received the intelligence that Dara had changed his mind and was preparing for war, he quickly moved his well-disciplined armies to Kerman, where the Iranian king was planning to take his last stand. The situation was so hopeless that Iranian commanders defected to the enemy, and the army disintegrated before the battle was engaged.

Dara fled with his top advisors, Mahyar and Janushyar. But even they had lost respect for the defeated king. Wishing to ingratiate themselves to the enemy, they stabbed their sovereign, left him for dead, and rushed to Eskandar expecting a reward. Horrified by the news, the Caesar put the perpetrators in chains and demanded to know where they had committed their heinous crime.

Rushing to the appointed place, he found Dara mortally wounded and barely breathing. He lifted the dying king's head and said: "Last night, I heard from elderly advisors that you and I are the fruits of the same branch. Please don't die. I won't begrudge you your land. We will share the command of the world like the brothers that we are. Why should we let greed divide us?"

But Dara knew his hour had come. He kissed the palm of Eskandar's hand and told him that it was too late for such talk and added that it behooved the victor to take his untimely death as an object lesson and refrain from pride and avarice. His final request was for his conquering opponent to marry his daughter, Rowshanak, so his progeny would practice their Zoroastrian faith. Eskandar promised to carry out these wishes and arranged a royal funeral for him. Then he sent an envoy to the female companions of the departed king who were honorably sequestered at Isfahan. He advised:

> Let no one celebrate the demise of the king. Nor should you scratch your faces in grief. Death is our inexorable lot. Although your king has departed this world, Iran is what it was. I am the new Dara in the world.

The Caesar sent another letter to the righteous overseers of Iran:

> This is a missive from Eskandar, son of Philqus, to the noble administrators of Iran. Praise God, who created the world by the two letters of the word: "Be." We are all bondsmen, and He is the most exalted king of the universe. God knows that I wished no evil to befall Dara. He was my brother. Oh, inscrutable fate! His enemy was hiding in his own house.
>
> I will maintain you in your dominions, castles, and palaces if you pledge to obey me as your king and mint your coins in my name. Be secure wherever you are, and keep your markets and borders safe. Send beautiful female companions as concubines to my seraglio, but only if they are willing to come. Attend to peaceful travelers, and especially the mendicant mystics. Register their names in a special roster and give them a share of your wealth. Be generous to the poor. Comfort the afflicted and afflict the comfortable.

Having made these arrangements, Eskandar left Kerman for the Winter Palace of Pars, styling himself as the latest in the line of the kings of Iran.

Don't attempt to unravel the world's mystery
For it punishes those who pry into its ways
And throws them into the dustbin of history.

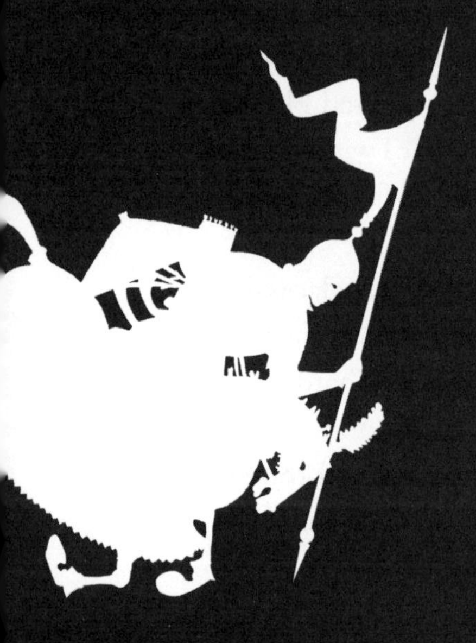

CHAPTER 17

The Roman King of Iran: Eskandar

Eskandar climbed the Persian throne and professed
That a king must be guided by justice and wisdom
If he wishes his reign to be blessed.

To express his care and generosity, Eskandar forgave five years' taxes and forbade his sentries to turn away petitioners, even if they came in the dead of night. He asked for Chinese ink and Roman brocade to pen a letter to Dara's widow, the queen mother, Delaraum:

> You know that I am innocent of your husband's blood. I tried my best to make peace, but he rejected my overture. He fell victim to a dastardly plot hatched by his advisors. May God elevate his soul and punish his disloyal servants in the hereafter. At his deathbed, the king asked me to marry princess Rowshanak. I gave him my word that I would. Send her to me, along with her companions and servants. She will comfort my forlorn soul. Forget your sorrows, for I, too, am Dara.

Eskandar sent a separate letter to his future bride:

> Come to me, my queen, and rule my house! This was your father's wish. I have also asked Queen Mother Delaraum for your hand. The magi of Isfahan will solemnize our union.

Rowshanak's eyes brimmed with tears. She heaved a cold sigh, read the letter, and generously rewarded the messenger before giving him this reply:

> The heavens sealed my father's fate. I wish you success in this world, as I know that you sought peace with him and rightly avenged him on the regicides Mahyar and Janushyar. We seek delight in the moon when the sun sets. You are the moon in my dark sky after

Dara. I bow my head to my father's wish and accept you as my king and companion for life.

On the occasion of the royal wedding, Eskandar called his mother, Nahid, to come from Amorium to the Winter Palace of Pars with a caravan of riches to pay a visit to the queen mother and Rowshanak.

On the Iranian side, knights showered the Roman Caesar with lavish gifts when the royal bride arrived from Isfahan. She was heralded by three hundred handmaidens holding goblets of gems, two hundred camels laden with golden vessels, jewel-encrusted Indian daggers, swords, shields, saddles and harnesses. The queen mother also accompanied the caravan with ten interpreters and counselors. The newlyweds enjoyed a week of marital bliss in seclusion. The conquest of Iran was complete.

With the conclusion of his Persian adventure, Eskandar set his eyes on India and called his advisors to plan his expedition.

THE TWO KINGS OF INDIA

At this time, the wise King Kayd of western India had a series of disturbing dreams. Only the skills of a brilliant oneiromancer could unravel their meaning, so Kayd went to a hermit named Mehran, who eschewed human company and lived on berries and the seeds of mountain shrubs. Before interpreting the king's enigmatic dreams, however, the holy man warned him of a more immediate peril: India was about to be overrun by the world conqueror Eskandar. "But" he modified his portent, "You can protect yourself and avoid the destruction of your country by offering him the four things you hold most dear in this world: your peerless daughter, your charmed chalice that never runs low, your philosophical advisor, and your skilled healer."

Shortly thereafter, Kayd received the famous conqueror's summons to drop everything and present himself at the Roman camp that had been established within his borders. Kayd sent back a respectful reply indicating that it would be discourteous of him to come to the august Caesar in his unkempt state. Instead, he would prove his obedience by sending him four gifts so marvelous that no one in the world could match them. Only then would it be proper for him to pay his respects in person.

Intrigued, Eskandar dispatched a commission of nine wise men to appraise the offerings before they were sent. The committee was speechless as they beheld the charms of the princess of India. They unanimously ruled that she alone was worth a king's ransom and sent back word that Kayd's offer should be accepted. The Caesar consented, and King Kayd sent a caravan of five hundred camels laden with gold, silver, and dazzling gems. Ahead of the procession tromped a decorated elephant carrying the litter of King Kayd's beloved daughter.

One look upon the tall and slender princess, whose eyes rivaled narcissus flowers, was enough to stun Eskandar into silence. In a daze, he mumbled prayers to the Lord for His wondrous creation and commanded his chaplains to wed them on the spot.

After the conclusion of the wedding period, the Caesar proceeded to examine the other three gifts. First, he tested the Indian philosopher by sending him a tub of oil with instructions that he rubs some of it on his body. The philosopher refused to do so as the oil would penetrate the body, and rubbing it in would be tantamount to recognizing the superiority of the Caesar's knowledge. Instead, he dropped one thousand needles in the oil to symbolize that his knowledge was sharp enough to penetrate the oil.

Eskandar had the needles melted into a lump of black iron to communicate that he was impervious to needles like a block of iron. The philosopher had the metal chunk cut, ground, burnished, and buffed into a mirror and returned it to convey that with the wise instruction of an advisor, even a leader's rough, black soul could become smooth as a reflective mirror. The world conqueror laid the mirror in a damp place and suffered it to be covered with rust, meaning that a king's worldliness darkens the soul. The philosopher received the ruined mirror, polished it back to its pristine clarity, and sent it back to underline the corrigibility of a corrupted soul.

Satisfied with the philosopher's wisdom evidenced in their symbolic exchange, Eskandar interrogated the healer about the causes of health and illness. The wise physician said culinary moderation and sexual restraint were keys to health. The Caesar agreed that this advice made perfect sense and gifted the healer with a black horse caparisoned with gold-laced leather.

Finally, it was time to try the bottomless goblet in a banquet. The courtiers were astonished by the miraculous quality of the vessel that remained full; despite being repeatedly drained to the last drop. The attending astrologers opined that the vessel probably had a magnetic quality that converted the vapor of the air into liquid.

Eskandar rested his troops in the realm of Kayd for a month, amusing himself with his enchanting bride. But the time had come to continue the voyage deeper into India. Thus, the Roman army marched to the border of the realm of Foor, a proud ruler who would not yield to foreign invaders. Eskandar sent his usual, terse summons ordering the Indian king to come to his pavilion. The response was just as short and decisive:

> It does not behoove a king to engage in self-aggrandizement and bluff. Don't preen yourself on vanquishing Dara, for he was killed by his men, not by you. You will find us waiting in thick formations behind our war elephants if you come for war.

But the insolence of the Indian king was not the only problem Eskandar was facing. There was discontent in the Roman ranks. Some commanders thought the morale was low, and the troops were too fatigued to give a good account of themselves in battle. The protest bordered on insubordination. The Caesar was stern with the malcontent and continued to press for war until his soldiers relented, and the protests subsided.

However, when the battle was joined, it proved bloody and inconclusive, even though the Romans had found ways to neutralize the Indian war elephants. Eskandar had to find a way out of the stalemate that harmed his side more than the enemy, as they were on their turf. Thus the Caesar challenged his counterpart to single combat. In his letter, he argued that a duel between the kings was the right choice as it would decide the fate of the war without further bloodshed. Foor accepted the challenge as he deemed his opponent too slim to be a match to his muscular frame. But he had miscalculated. Being light and agile enabled Eskandar to exploit a momentary distraction, and lunge at his enemy and slash his neck. The incredulous army surrendered once they saw that their king was slain. The Caesar soothed the defeated army with honeyed words, assuring them that he would not plunder their riches. He then settled the conquered kingdom by appointing a vassal king and instructing him to be generous and eschew worldly temptations.

After resting for two months at Foor's palace, Eskandar fixed his sights on Andalusia, whose path went through Arabia and Egypt, a land he had already conquered. Thus, he retraced his path out of India and set a course for the Arabian city of Mecca.

The din of war drums and red, yellow, and purple flags of the Roman army intruded into the sleepy Arabian desert at the break of dawn. Eskandar was heading to the place called "the house of Abraham" in the city of Mecca. It was also known as the "house of God." The designation implied that the place was holy, as God could not be said to have an earthly abode.

A local chief named Nasr-e Ghutayb came forward at the head of a host of lance-bearing warriors to receive the Caesar. He had descended from Ishmael, the son of Abraham. Nasr explained that Abraham had bequeathed the holy land of Mecca to his ancestor Ishmael. The current ruler of the area was a usurper by the name of Khaza'eh of the Qahtani clan.

Eskandar waged war, expelling the clan of Qahtan from the land, and restored Mecca to the house of Ishmael. Then, with his army, he crossed the remainder of the Arabian desert and arrived at the port of Jeddah on the Red Sea. From there they sailed to Egypt, which was ruled by his vassal king.

Eskandar rested in Egypt as he contemplated a plan for a swift conquest of Andalusia. He assumed this would be easy as the kingdom was ruled by a woman. He would be proven wrong in this respect.

THE JUDICIOUS QUEEN

Qaydafeh, the queen of Andalusia, was not one to be surprised. As a precaution against the threat posed by the notorious Eskandar lurking in the neighboring land of Egypt, she gathered intelligence in various ways, including sending a skilled painter to draw sketches of the famed world conqueror who coveted her realm. Upon receiving the imposing images drawn by her spy, Qaydafeh felt admiration for her worthy foe. But she was also overwhelmed with dread. In due course the weary queen received the dispatch that she expected: Eskandar was demanding that she choose between war and vassalage.

The queen responded that she was impressed neither by Eskandar's threats nor by his fortuitous conquests of Iran and India. The lesson he should have drawn from the fates of Dara and Foor was that pride could bring down a kingdom.

Angered by this impertinent letter, the Roman army laid siege to the fortified city where one of the queen's sons, Qaydrush, ruled. The city resisted the besieging army's catapults and crossbows for a week before opening its gates. Ordinary denizens were spared, but prominent leaders were taken captive. Among them were Qaydrush and his wife, the daughter of the castle's lord.

Eskandar plotted to use the captivity of the prince as a ploy to persuade the queen to exchange her sovereignty for vassalage and pay an annual tribute to Rome. He called his top advisor, Bitaqun, and shared his intricate plot: the advisor was instructed to wear royal robes and pretend to be the Caesar. In this role, he would condemn prince Qaydrush and his wife to summary execution. At this point, the real Eskandar disguised as Bitaqun would enter and beg that the convicted couple be spared as a personal favor to him. Once the request was granted, the noble couple would owe their lives to the good will of the advisor. Then the false Bitaqun would accompany the prince and his consort to the Andalusian court to submit his terms of peace. Queen Qaydafeh was sure to be more amenable toward a man who had saved the lives of her son and daughter-in-law.

The clever charade nearly worked. The queen was initially taken in by the ruse as she welcomed her son, her daughter-in-law, and the kindly envoy. As predicted, Qaydrush gratefully presented the friendly Caesar's advisor Bitaqun, who had saved his life. The queen was unsettled as she found him to be vaguely familiar. To give herself time to consider the matter, she sent the ambassador to a luxurious residence and invited him to return the next day. Only when she consulted her sketches did she realize that this man was none other than the Caesar in disguise.

The following day, as the overconfident Eskandar went to see the queen, he was utterly unprepared for the unraveling of his plot. She calmly welcomed the false ambassador as the son of Philqus. He protested, but the denial was futile. She knew who he was, what he had done, and to what purpose. Beaten at his own game, Eskandar confessed that his only mistake was to come there without his trusty dagger, bragging that he could fight off the queen's guards and her entire army by himself. Qaydafeh smiled.

"Hubris is and has always been your downfall. You still take full credit for defeating Dara and Foor as if fate had nothing to do with it. You preen yourself on your cunning, but then, disregarding your fame, recklessly pretend to be someone else. And now you boast that you can fight my entire army with a knife! A smart man never underestimates his enemies."

Having scolded the hapless Eskandar, the queen proceeded to allay his fears. "I am not a regicide and have no intention of killing or harming you. I will not reveal your identity even to my son Tinush. You should know that he is married to the daughter of King Foor, whom you killed in a duel, and he is sure to avenge his father-in-law if he learns who you are. So, I will continue to call you Bitaqun. In return for my goodwill, you must agree to respect my sovereignty and pledge not to harm my family."

Eskandar was deeply touched by the queen's munificence and swore an abiding oath to all that was holy in the Christian faith that he would be loyal to the queen and her family. Then it was time for the queen to summon her attendants to court so they could hear the message sent by the Caesar.

The man known as the ambassador read the prepared letter, which amounted to an ultimatum for the subjugation of Andalusia. Tinush was enraged by the naked intimidation, cursed the Roman invader, and threatened to kill his insolent envoy. The queen reprimanded her son for breaking protocol. She then ended the public meeting. When all had left, she told her guest to be careful as his life was in danger, even as the Roman ambassador. Eskandar said he knew how to mollify Tinush.

"Call back your son," he said. "I want a word with him!"

When the queen reconvened the meeting, the false Bitaqun declared that he was just a messenger. He did not share the bloodthirsty designs of his king and was willing to betray him. Holding Tinush's hand, he added, "What would you give me if I brought Eskandar unarmed to you and put his hand in yours, just as we hold hands now?"

"You do that, and I will make you rich beyond your wildest dreams. I would even appoint you as my advisor. But I doubt you can deliver on your lofty promises!"

Eskandar explained his plan as the prince listened with rapt attention. Qaydafeh watched on with an inscrutable expression, secretly admiring the wiles of her royal accomplice. The envoy proposed that the two men ride out to the Roman camp leading a host of one thousand elite warriors and a rich train of offerings. They would stop outside the Roman camp, where Tinush and his men would hide in a thicket. The envoy would lure his king into their ambush by claiming that the Andalusian prince had come to deliver his country's tribute. But he would do so only on neutral ground. Eskandar would have to go and collect the tribute in person. Thus, he would be ensnared in their trap and killed by Tinush's men. The prince was charmed and he agreed to the plan.

The next day, as the dawn raised its flag upon the eastern horizon, and the mountains glowed like yellow resin, Tinush led the army of Andalusia toward the designated location. The prince and his men waited with great anticipation as the envoy went to bring his Caesar. After some time, Tinush saw a great army setting siege to the thicket. He was shocked that the man pretending to be Bitaqun was leading the troops dressed as the Caesar. It was clear that he had been tricked. Trembling with fear, he kissed the ground and begged for his life. Eskandar guffawed: "You need not fear me. I have pledged an oath to the queen that I would never harm her family. Nor have I lied to you. When I held your hand, I was putting your hand in that of Eskandar."

Tinush heaved a sigh of relief. The world conqueror called for a feast to celebrate his friendship with the kingdom of Andalusia and sent the prince back, saying: "Go in peace and tell the queen mother that nothing will mar our friendship as long as I live."

WILD PEREGRINATIONS: FROM A BRAHMAN HERMITAGE TO THE CITY OF WOMEN

From Andalusia, Eskandar set a course for the realm of the austere Brahmans, hoping to benefit from their wisdom. The hermits of India were puzzled when they heard that the famous Caesar was approaching their borders. They sent him this message:

> Why is Eskandar coming to see us? We have nothing but patience and knowledge. These are precious treasures, but they cannot be pillaged! We are naked but for a grass skirt. We do not have any victuals for him and his army, as we are always fasting.

This letter further piqued Eskandar's interest. Leaving the army behind, he took a few of his philosophers and followed the Brahman envoy to their monastery to discover the ways of the hermits. They were greeted with a paltry offering as a token of the community's respect. The Caesar asked them about their tattered garments and wondered how they defended themselves in battle.

"Why should we bother about sartorial splendor as we come into this world naked and leave it in the same state?" asked one hermit. "And regarding warfare, we need not prepare for it. Potentates of the world see nothing to covet here."

"Who is asleep in this world and who is awake?" Eskandar asked the hermits.

"The most deluded is he who is beset by hatred and avarice. Cleanse your mind of these demons. Two tyrants rule the human mind: need and greed. Steer a middle course and follow the golden mean."

The Caesar was impressed and wished to offer the ascetics a boon. "Ask me a favor, and it shall be granted."

"It would be lovely if the Caesar would exempt us from old age and death."

"But I have no dominion over these evils."

"Then why are you coveting worldly gains? Once you are dead, others will reap what you have sown. Why toil to benefit another man? Don't you know that white hair is the herald of death?"

The sobering conversation left Eskandar uneasy. It was as if they could read his mind. He bid the hermits farewell and returned to his army. They continued their trek and soon set up camp by the sea where men spoke a strange tongue, survived only on fish, and dressed as women. As Eskandar looked out at the sea, he noticed a yellow mountain swelling up from the surface toward the sky. Excited that a new adventure was afoot, he ordered his shipwrights to build a craft to explore the strange island. Since the royal counselors deemed such an adventure too risky for their leader, the ship was staffed with Persian and Greek sailors and sent off while he waited on shore. Eskandar watched with great interest as the vessel approached the landmass. But then the island appeared to move. To the onlookers' bewilderment, it turned out to be the hump of a sea monster. Before the sailors could turn around, the leviathan opened its enormous jaws and swallowed the ship whole.

Relieved to have listened to his prudent advisors, Eskandar decamped and led his army across a dense thicket of tall bamboo and sojourned in a place with sweet-smelling earth and freshwater. However, the pleasant surroundings proved too good to be true. As they slept, poisonous snakes and scorpions crawled out of their holes to bite many of the soldiers, killing most of them before help could arrive.

In the morning, the rest of the crew woke from their slumber to another calamity, as savage boars and lions as big as cows descended on them. By this time, the soldiers had found their feet and managed to fight back and kill many of the beasts.

After this perilous adventure, the army moved toward Ethiopia, where they were attacked by a tribe of naked warriors with bloodshot eyes who wielded sharpened bones for weapons. Then they encountered a race of enormous, soft-footed savages who hurled stones and attacked in great numbers. Shocking as these strange enemies were, the brave soldiers of Eskandar proved equal to their challenges.

Finally, the troops arrived at a friendly city built on the slopes of a mountain, where they were welcomed graciously. Comforted by the city's hospitality, the Romans rested in the safety of its walls. When they were ready to cross the mountains in pursuit of their travels, they were told that a double-maned, fire-breathing dragon was blocking the road to the other side. To keep it from slithering over the peak and destroying them, the citizens appeased it with five freshly slaughtered cows daily.

Eskandar undertook the challenge of vanquishing the dragon. To this purpose he filled the carcasses of the cows with poison, and fed them to the dragon. When the beast swallowed them down, their toxicity pierced its innards and caused it to violently bang its head against the rocks. The troops showered a rain of arrows to finish it off, and the people of the city were immensely grateful.

Further down the unmarked path that connected east and west of the world, the army came across another mountain. Legend had it that at the summit laid a corpse that could foretell the future. The carcass was said to present so hideous an aspect that many died of fright as they came close enough to see it. But Eskandar's curiosity got the better of him, and he hiked up the mountain to find the body lying on a golden slate. Without moving its lips, it intoned:

You've won battles and overthrown kings
You've enjoyed your easy victories to the hilt
It's time to prepare for destiny's arrows and slings.

Upon hearing the prophecy, so much blood rushed to Eskandar's face that it glowed like a lantern. As a young king who had not even reached the halfway point of his life, he was ill-prepared for such a portent. He turned and descended the mountain, trying to disregard what he had heard.

Eskandar's next destination was Harum, the legendary city of women warriors. In place of a left breast, they had hard, scaly skin like armor. Men were not allowed to pass through their gates. As Eskandar approached, he sent a message as the king of Iran and Rome, indicating that he was coming to converse with their leaders and observe their city's wonders. A philosopher who had taken the letter was treated well in Harum and charged to take back their response:

> If you invade our city, you shall find it full of women who sleep in their armor and defend their home with ferocity. We are virgins,

> and anyone of us who wishes to take a husband will be expelled and not admitted again unless she has given birth to a girl. The only way to the city is by the deep sea, and our harbor is defended by ten thousand fierce virgins. If one of our warriors kills a man, she is honored with a golden coronet. We have thirty thousand of these battle-worthy champions. We are aware that you are a great warrior. But consider this: If you vanquish us, it will not redound to your glory, for no one would brag about defeating women. But your infamy will be eternal if you fail to subjugate us. People will say that the famous world conqueror lost to an army of women.

Eskandar continued the respectful correspondence by indicating that he was no longer seeking martial victory in the world, as the smell of a camphor-laden shroud and the black dirt of the graveyard had dulled the sharp edge of his greed.

The city accepted this message as sincere and opened its gates. As the army marched toward Harum, they traversed through freezing cold climes, followed by intolerable heat. When they arrived at the immediate surroundings of the city of Harum, they found a race who foamed at the mouth and had red eyes. The extreme climates were their protection against would-be invaders.

Once they arrived at Harum, however, they were surprised at the glorious welcome arranged by the Amazon warriors of that kingdom. Two thousand girls, all refined and capable of intelligent discourse, marched to offer Eskandar the tribute of their city. Another two thousand female warriors followed behind, carrying golden coins that filled the Roman coffers to the brim. The army rested for one month at Harum before resuming their trek.

PORTENTS ABOUND: FROM THE KINGDOM OF DARKNESS TO THE TALKING TREE

The wonders of the City of Women had whetted the world conqueror's appetite for new adventures. Now he wished to find where the sun sets and discover the famed Fountain of Eternal Youth in the Land of Darkness.

As he neared the western edge of the world, Eskandar saw a robust and blond race who told him about a nearby lake where the sun sinks at night, a sight that was too wondrous to miss. They also spoke of the Fountain of Eternal Youth that originated in paradise and bubbled up deep in the Land of Darkness to the north of their city. "But," asked the world conqueror, "how could one travel in utter darkness on horseback?"

They responded that travel in darkness was possible only on four-year-old colts. Determined to reach the famed fountain, the Caesar took provisions for forty days and rustled up ten thousand colts for his journey.

Embarking upon such an adventure without a guide was perilous, even for the bold Caesar. But fortune smiled on him as he encountered the legendary Green Prophet, Khezr, in the vicinity of the city and persuaded him to accompany his expedition. Eskandar had two luminous orbs to guide him in the darkness, and offered one to Khezr. It was agreed that the prophet would lead the way and act as the group's scout.

Thus, the Green Prophet led the army through the curtain surrounding the dark world. Initially, they made good progress as the Green Prophet went ahead and left provisions for the army at set distances. But at a fork in the road, the army could not see the scout's orb and chose the wrong path. Khezr reached the Fountain of Perpetual Youth and attained immortality, while the Romans wandered away. When Eskandar emerged into the light on the other side of the Land of Darkness, he saw a glowing mountain covered in aloeswood trees. Upon each tree sat a magnificent green bird with the power of speech. One of them addressed the leader of the army in his Roman tongue, saying:

"What do you seek in this world, oh lover of suffering? Even if your head scrapes the high vault of the skies, you will still be a beggar."

With this strange introduction, Eskandar and the bird engaged in a long conversation. The curious creature asked about the wonders of the human race: the abodes of the poor and wealthy, and the habits of the hermits and the worldly. At the end of the conversation, the bird recommended that his interlocutor scale the mountain, if he wanted to discover something marvelous was at the summit.

Leaving his army at the aloeswood forest, the undaunted king climbed to the mountain's peak. There he saw the angel Seraph holding a trumpet to his lips, ready to announce the end of the world upon receiving God's command. The angel turned to Eskandar with misty eyes and said:

Stop wandering about, you slave of greed
Your life is over. It's time to prepare
A coffin for that's all you will need.

Dismayed to hear yet another haunting prophecy about his death, Eskandar stammered. "But I was born a wanderer, and I only wanted to explore the world." He said this and descended the mountain, calling on the name of God and shedding tears. He took command of his army and led them back through the Land of Darkness.

This time, they heard a sonorous voice coming from the direction of a black mountain: "He who takes stones from this place shall regret it. He who does not take stones from this place shall also regret it."

Some soldiers filled their saddlebags with rocks and some put a few pebbles under their belts. But most did not bother to pick up anything. As they crossed back into the world of light, they realized that the stones they had picked up were rubies, emeralds, lapis lazuli, and diamonds. Those who had picked nothing regretted having missed out on the treasure, while those who had taken some reproached themselves for not taking more.

Having reached the end of the world, Eskandar turned back toward the east, traversing a northerly route. The first city he encountered was populated by people who lived in dread of the savage hordes of Gog and Magog. One among them described the terrifying features of these creatures:

"They have faces like camels, black tongues, and bloodshot eyes. They are possessed of bodies as big as elephants, with wider ears and boar-like fangs. Their females give birth to a brood of a thousand hatchlings. Their numbers swell in the spring and thin out in the winter. In the cold season, their bodies shrink, and they sound like so many pigeons cooing."

The city begged the Caesar to protect them, so he built two walls five hundred fathoms tall and a hundred fathoms apart. In the middle, he deposited a mixture of iron, copper, crude oil, and sulfur. Then he set the mixture on fire. Aided by the bellows of a hundred thousand blacksmiths, the molten mixture welded the two walls together and provided them with an impregnable metallic core. Enormously grateful, the people of the city brought rich offerings to Eskandar. But he refused to accept the generous gift and continued his adventures.

For the next month, the Caesar and his army continued on their path, until they came upon a blue mountain made of lapis lazuli. Curious, Eskandar left his army and climbed to the summit. There he found a topaz-domed crystal palace where a saltwater fountain bubbled. A sparkling ruby illuminated the palace from its stand that was blacker than a raven's feathers. Under the high dome, an enormous human corpse with the head of a wild boar lay across two golden beds. It was wrapped in a camphor-infused shroud of brocade. A sound coming from the saltwater fountain reverberated in the palace.

Eskandar will cease his travels. The seeker
Who's met many strange creatures is about
To meet the most terrible of them all: the grim reaper.

Eskandar was heartbroken as he had little doubt that his death was at hand. He took his place at the head of his columns again and rode across a vast desert until he reached a pleasant city whose inhabitants had never seen either an army or a king. The Caesar asked about wondrous things in those parts, and they responded that there was an enchanted tree possessed of two trunks that conjoined at the root. This tree knew all the secrets of the world and it was capable of speech in a strange language, understood only by the attending priests.

The ground around the speaking tree was littered with pelts of sacrificial animals. The female trunk became redolent and spoke at night, while her male counterpart spoke during the day.

"And what lay beyond the tree?" Eskandar asked.

"Nothingness," they replied. "You have reached the eastern edge of the world."

When the next day's sun was high in the sky, a frightening sound issued from the male trunk. A priest translated the message that was meant for Eskandar:

The world bent to your willfulness and wanderlust
You have had a life of glorious conquest, but now
You are about to rest upon a heap of dust.

The blunt prophecy shocked the Caesar. The trunk had emphasized the impending end of his wild life. He shed tears of blood and remained silent until midnight. Then, the female trunk pronounced its divination:

The world could not cope with your cupidity
You should've known that coveting
What you cannot carry off is pure stupidity.

In desperation, Eskandar begged the female trunk to reveal if he could embrace his mother once more before his death. The trunk intoned:

You shall not see your mother again
Death shall overtake you in a strange land
Your demise is nigh, as is the end of your reign.

The Caesar returned to his camp. He accepted the enchanted city's rich offerings, which included an indigo-colored armor, two enormous ivory tusks, sixty cubits of gold coins, and life-size golden statues of a rhinoceros and a lion.

RETURN FROM CHINA TO BABYLON

China was the final destination in Eskandar's world peregrinations. As was his wont, Eskandar went to the emperor disguised as his own ambassador. Overwhelmed by the opulence of the royal palace, he conveyed his message: "The Caesar of Rome comes in peace. But it would be unwise to try the patience of one who has vanquished Dara of Persia, Foor of India, and many other potentates."

He threatened that the emperor would be well advised to appease the Roman conqueror with rich gifts that included ivory thrones and silken fabrics of China.

The emperor appeared infuriated by the audacity of the message. But then he fell silent and smiled. He offered his guest a chalice of wine and asked him to describe his king. The envoy said Eskandar was like none other in stature, strength, generosity, and speech.

The envoy left the royal court somewhat inebriated, holding a fragrant orange. The following day the emperor called him back to his audience, smiled, and kindly enquired if he had a hangover. Then he asked for pen and paper to dictate his response to the Caesar, starting by praising God and attributing all, including the Roman victories, to the will of the heavens.

> The world is ephemeral. Where are Feraydun, Zahhak, and Jamshid now? I am not afraid of your might! Nor am I haughty like you. I choose to send you much more than you have demanded, and no one will blame me for excessive generosity.

Eskandar was ashamed by the tone of the emperor's speech and pledged to never again resort to these games. He returned to his army, leading a caravan of China's tributes accompanied by a representative of the emperor. Upon reaching the Roman camp, the Chinese envoy discovered that the Roman envoy was none other than the Caesar in disguise. He was bribed to keep the secret to himself.

Finally, after another month of rest, Eskandar was ready to head back in the direction of his homeland. The troops were excited to go home. Their penultimate destination was Babylon. The path took them first through Jeghwan, a realm too poor to invade. Then they had to pass the headstrong people of Sind, who put up stiff resistance aided by the veterans of the vanquished army of King Foor of India. The army of Sind was defeated, their land was plundered, and their women and children were enslaved. This was their punishment for waging war on the Roman army. The captives of Sind abjectly begged to be set free. But their entreaties were not heeded.

The returning army rested for two months in Yemen, where Eskandar was presented with camel loads of saffron, delicately woven silken fabrics, and chrysolite, and lapis lazuli goblets filled to the brim with sapphires and rubies. After another month of traveling toward Babylon, they found their path blocked by a granite mountain whose peak was lost in black clouds. Scaling it was difficult, but from the summit, the army beheld a pleasing blue sea surrounding a glimmering island city. Their descent was easy, as the slopes of the seaward side were full of lush vegetation and game. Along the way, the soldiers encountered a hairy giant with elephantine ears, whom they brought to the presence of their king.

Amazed by the strange humanoid, Eskandar asked what his name was and if he knew anything about the island city. He said his name was Ear-Cocoon, as he would use his large ears for bed and cover. Regarding the island city, he said that it was like a veritable paradise devoid of dirt. The island dwellers ate fish. Buildings were made of fish skin and bones, and their monuments were graced with images of Afrasiab and Kay-Khosrow. He volunteered to go to the island as an envoy. Permission was granted, and Ear-Cocoon returned with eighty citizens of the island. They bowed to the king and presented him with golden crowns. Satisfied with this encounter, the army left for Babylon.

Aware of his impending demise, Eskandar dispatched a letter to his mentor Aristotle to appraise him of his plan for protecting Rome after his death. He was most afraid of an uprising in Iran, and thus intended to invite the leaders of the powerful clans of Persia to a fateful repast and kill them all. The philosopher was appalled when he read the missive and sent a reply urging him not to go through with the plot:

> It would not benefit Rome to exterminate the influential leaders of Iran. On the contrary, such an act would tempt people in the east to cross Iran and threaten the borders of Rome. The best way to protect Rome is to keep the potentates of Persia as independent rulers in his realm. Powerful but disunited, they

would be a buffer against invaders from India, China, Touran, and Mokran.

The Caesar acknowledged the wisdom of his mentor's advice and chose to maintain the Persian chiefs as rulers of their clans.

As the army arrived in Babylon, Eskandar was confronted with the last sign of his imminent death: a woman gave birth to a baby with the head of a lion, which died shortly after his birth. Astrologers were summoned to decipher the event. This was an easy task. The Caesar was born when the sun was in Leo. Now, a child with the head of a lion was born and prematurely died. The death of the king was imminent.

The world conqueror advised people to be moderate in mourning for him and dictated his last will and testament to his mother, naming her as his heir:

> If my Iranian wife Rowshanak gives birth to a son, he will be my successor. If the infant is a girl, she must marry the son of Philqus, allowing their son to inherit his empire. King Kayd's daughter should be allowed to respectfully return to her father along with her dowry. Annual alms should be distributed from a bequest to the peasants. Let my body be wrapped in a shroud infused with perfumes and placed in a golden casket sealed in a mixture of pitch, camphor, musk, and ambergris.

When the king died, the sound of weeping and wailing filled the barracks. His army set fire to their deceased commander's tent and cut off the tails of ten thousand horses.

Our worldly sojourn is brief. You cannot afford
To rely on the splendor of your possessions
Or carry away the treasures that you hoard.

Persians and Romans alike mourned their departed king. But they debated whether he should be buried in Iran or Rome. Unable to come to a consensus, they agreed to seek advice from an enchanted mountain in the nearby meadow of Khorm. The magical mountain sonorously echoed its answer: "The dust of Eskandar belongs to the city he founded: Alexandria."

The Caesar's casket was placed on the funerary pedestal. His mother and Aristotle, who had heard the prophecies of Eskandar's impending death, had arrived in Babylon along with philosophers and sages of Rome. Aristotle spoke:

I lay my hand on a coffin bearing a young king
And wonder what lured him away to the underworld
From life's pleasures in the fullness of his spring?

Then the sages came forth one by one and spoke:

We miss his refined mind and manners.
Who vanquished our noble king?
Who toppled his fluttering banners?

When you lived none escaped your whip,
Now tell us how it feels to be
In the grim reaper's grip.

You are about to finally own,
Standing before the divine tribunal,
That you reap what you've sown.

The worst sin on the other side
Of death is to have killed a king.
Prepare to be treated as a regicide.

Behold, the mighty Eskandar has perished.
Avoid avarice for even he had to leave
The possessions he so cherished.

Why did you leave the women you embraced
For a golden sarcophagus, diaphanous silks
And its cold comforts in such a haste?

Why did you toil so in your brief life,
When you knew only an adorned chest
Would be your abode after all that strife?

After the sages had had their say, Eskandar's bereaved mother approached his coffin and intoned:

You are here, and yet you're so remote
From me, your army, and court. I feel as if
I speak to you across an impassable moat.

Finally, Rowshanak spoke to her husband:

You slew kings like Dara and Foor
You were full of thunder and hail,
I thought you would forever endure.

You could make a name and gain repute
Instead of making war and spreading chaos
The tree you planted has borne bitter fruit.

When there was nothing left to say, the mourners consigned Eskandar's coffin to the black earth.

We cannot unravel the mystery of death
But as we live in its shadow, let's be caring
And kind to one another until our last breath.

CHAPTER 18

A Dynastic Shift: Ardavan to Ardeshir

"Destiny favored me as a youth, only to denigrate
And scorn me as a broken, old man," I wailed,
"You faithless stars! You fickle fate!"

"Don't blame us," I heard the heavens intone
"Man is superior to nature as he is given
The gift of free will among all creatures alone."

"We each have a rank in the divine chart,
Go to God if you wish to complain, but speak
In humility and from the depth of your heart."

After Eskandar's death, Iran was ruled by a confederacy of brave horsemen for hundreds of years. It was the Caesar Eskandar's wish that Iran remain strong but divided. This way, the land would provide a buffer against invasions from the east without posing a direct threat to Rome.

These ruling clans called themselves the Ashkanian, or Arsacid, dynasty, as they traced their origin back to a descendant of King Kay-Qobaud named Ashk. They also counted Arash, the legendary bow master, among their ancestors.

I've heard of this dynasty's name. But few are the remarks
Made about them in the ancient sources. Nor could I find
A trace of them in the old Book of the Monarchs.

The Ashkanian dynasty ruled their pasture lands while obeying a nominal king.

But the dynasty of the olden kings had not been obliterated. One of King Dara's sons, Sassan, had fled to India after the defeat and murder of his father.* He made a living as a shepherd but kept the memory of his royal line alive by giving his eldest son the name Sassan and the moniker of Ardeshir, meaning sacred king. This became their custom. Every generation passed on the secret knowledge that they were descended from Dara, the last of the kings of Kay.

THE SHEPHERD AND THE KING

Upon his coronation, the Ashkani king Ardavan moved his capital from the city of Pars to the northern city of Rey, entrusting the governing of Pars and its environs to his vassal King Baubak.

A young man named Sassan came from India to the city of Pars to seek employment at Baubak's court. He was hired as a shepherd, but given his strength and skills, it didn't take him long to become the chief shepherd.

One cold night Baubak had an extraordinary dream about Sassan, in which he wielded an Indian blade and rode a magnificent elephant. People paid him obeisance, and he treated them with magnanimity. The next night Baubak had an even stranger dream in which the magi presented Sassan with flames lit at the three main Zoroastrian fire temples of Iran. Baubak called oneiromancers to interpret his night visions, and they all agreed that either Sassan or his son would become king.

Baubak summoned the shepherd and demanded that he come without delay. Sassan anxiously hurried to the court wearing a cassock that was covered in snow. Baubak took him to a private chamber, allayed his fears for being summoned so suddenly, and encouraged him to reveal who he truly was.

"I am Sassan, the great-grandson of King Dara, who was the great-grandson of King Bahman, the sacred king," he said, his voice trembling. "I am the last link in the dynasty of King Lohrausp and Prince Esfandiar."

* There are two versions of the origins of the Sassanian dynasty in *Shahnameh*. In the first version Sassan is the son of King Bahman. This is mentioned in chapter 15. In the second version related in this chapter and maintained throughout the rest of the poem, Sassan is the son of King Dara, who fled to India after his father's defeat by Eskandar.

Baubak wept with joy upon hearing this and ordered a great bonfire to be lit.

"Bathe and perfume yourself before you dress," he told Sassan, gesturing to the rich garments he had specially ordered. "You will ride a well-caparisoned steed and live in the comfort of your own quarters in this palace, adequately attended by retainers and servants. And you will marry my daughter."

Nine months after Sassan and his lovely bride retired to their quarters, the beautiful mother was blessed with an infant whose brilliance rivaled the sun at high noon. They named him Ardeshir Baubakan, which denoted his paternal and maternal ancestors. As the boy grew, he excelled in the royal arts of hunting and courtly etiquette, and soon became the master of every gathering. Baubak expected that the king would eventually hear of the reputation of his grandson, and he was right. One day, a letter arrived from Rey, the capital of King Ardavan. As it had been brought by a royal messenger, there was no doubt that the author was the king himself.

> I have heard that your grandson Ardeshir is an impressive young man who has mastered the martial and the royal arts. Thus, I wish him to come to the capital as a companion to my four sons. Rest assured; he will not be treated as a stranger at my court.

Baubak was both elated and deeply sad by the prospect of separation from his beloved grandson. He sent him off with gold-plated weapons, a well-caparisoned steed, and cash, along with gifts to bring the king, including gold coins, silk brocade, musk, and ambergris. Ardeshir also brought the king a perfumed note written by his grandfather:

> I send you my cherished grandson. It befits a king to treat such a dear guest with tender care.

Thus, the young, provincial nobleman became a peer to the royal princes. One day, during a hunt, an onager appeared on the horizon. The young men were all eager to be the first to shoot it, but it was Ardeshir's arrow that found its target. King Ardavan was impressed as the shaft of the arrow had penetrated the rump of the onager all the way to the fletched end. Ardeshir basked in the king's praise, but the Crown Prince Bahman resented his success. He claimed that the arrow was his, to which Ardeshir rashly retorted: "The plain is as vast as arrows and onagers are plentiful. If you shot this onager I am sure you can repeat the feat! Lying is a sin, especially by a prince."

"What a disgrace!" roared the king. "How dare you insult my son? I should never have let a brazen lowborn like you into my court. Go back to the stables and attend to my Arabian horses. Live there and associate with your kind."

Ardeshir was mortified, but he had no choice but to obey. He retired to the stables and wrote a letter to his grandfather appraising him of what had happened. In his response, Baubak scolded the young man for forgetting his place and advised him to seek forgiveness and make amends. As the old man did not wish for his grandson to live on the wages of a stable boy, he had also sent him money to build a house near the stables and live in comfort. After that, Ardeshir led a simple life.

ELOPING WITH THE ROYAL CONSORT

King Ardavan's favorite companion was a beautiful slave named Golnar. She was so loved and trusted that she resided in her mansion within the royal compound and held the keys to the king's treasure house. One day, Golnar saw Ardeshir strolling by and fell in love with him at first sight.

Impatient to meet him, she waited until the trumpet that announced the palace's nightly curfew sounded. Then, she tied knots in a rope, rappelled down from her room, stole across the grounds, and broke into Ardeshir's bedroom. She crawled into his bed and wrapped her arms around him as he slept.

"From what lucky horizon did you arise, oh beloved full moon, to brighten my dark night?" he said upon waking.

"I am the favorite consort and the treasurer of the king. I was his slave, but I want to be your's if you will have me."

The couple spent the night together and exchanged vows of love. The secret affair completed the happiness of Ardeshir at the margins of King Ardavan's royal court. But his happiness did not last long.

Baubak died shortly thereafter, and the king gave away his lands in the Pars region to his eldest son, Prince Bahman. Deprived of his grandfather and his birthright, Ardeshir felt he had no prospects. Nor did he have any fealty to the king who had so grievously mistreated him.

At this time King Ardavan called the astrologers to chart his horoscope. They were housed at Golnar's quarters, where they conducted their research using astrolabes and elaborate charts. For three days, Golnar was constrained to stay home and see to the needs of her guests. But she used the opportunity to eavesdrop and hear that they predicted that a highborn subordinate would rebel and establish himself as a rival to King Ardavan.

Golnar ran to Ardeshir as soon as the astrologers left. He was unhappy about her long absence. She explained that the astrologers had detained her, and that there were prophecies about the rise of a new king. Ardeshir's heart beat wildly in his chest.

"I no longer have any doubts," he said. "I'm leaving for my ancestral home in Pars. Will you share this adventure with me? Or do you prefer the safety of your mansion? If you come with me, you will be a queen and a jewel in the crown of this nation."

"Of course, I will come. I love you."

"Then meet me back here at the break of dawn."

That night, Golnar stuffed her purse with gold, rubies, and other gems from the treasury and waited. When the dawn broke, she found Ardeshir ready for her with two well-caparisoned royal horses that he had stolen from the royal stable. One was white and the other black. The stable hands were in a drunken stupor due to the copious amounts of wine they had been given to drink by Ardeshir. And thus, the couple headed south.

King Ardavan woke up in an empty bed just as the fugitives were crossing the outer reaches of Rey. He demanded to know why Golnar was not at his bedside. His attendants, who had gone to look for her, found that she and Ardeshir were both gone, as were two of the best royal horses.

A search party followed the fugitives' tracks, headed by the king and his prime minister. When the posse reached a hamlet, the king questioned its residents: "Did you hear or see horses pass by earlier today? We are looking for two equestrians riding a white and a black horse."

"Indeed, we did," a villager responded. "But we also saw a magnificent wild ewe galloping behind them, kicking up as much dust as a horse."

Puzzled by this response, the king asked his vizier, "What is the meaning of this? Why would a wild ewe follow a fugitive stableboy?"

"I am afraid the wild ewe is the embodiment of the young man's divine sanction," said the advisor, "his kingly halo of sovereignty, his God-given *farr*. We must call off the chase if the beast catches up with him, for then we will be facing a much bigger challenge."

The runaway couple had reached a pleasant catchment. Ardeshir intended to recuperate from the exhaustion of their perilous escape, but two young men witnessing the chase from higher ground cautioned them against dismounting. They disguised their warning as a song:

You've just escaped the dragon's maw
Keep running lest your fortunes are reversed
And you're caught in his outstretched claw.

Heeding the advice of the righteous bystanders, the couple continued on, remaining a tad out of sight of their pursuers.

The next day at noon, King Ardavan arrived at a prosperous city, and again asked the residents if they had seen two riders crossing their town at night.

A merchant responded, "Indeed we have. Two riders galloped past our city, covered in the dust and sweat of their travels. One of them was carrying a splendid wild ewe on the back of his saddle."

The grand vizier's demeanor changed. "Your Majesty! The time has come for us to call off the chase because the wild ewe that embodied Ardeshir's *farr* has now caught up with him. Write to Prince Bahman and appraise him of the situation. He must be discrete. But he should be prepared for a confrontation with this pretender. Now, let us return and prepare our army for battle."

Ardeshir and Golnar did not relent until they reached the blue expanse of a vast river. The boatman, who had sensed the *farr* of Ardeshir as a halo around his head, offered to help him and his companion across the river. As they emerged on the other shore, they were welcomed by the noblemen of Pars, who had heard the news of Ardishir's approach and had come to greet him.

"You all have heard how Eskandar wrecked this country," he addressed the crowd. "He killed my ancestor, King Dara, and laid waste to Iran. Why would you let a lowborn like Ardavan recline on the throne when a direct descendant of prince Esfandiar is among you? Let us reclaim the crown for Iran's rightful king."

The crowd cheered for the restoration of the ancient kingdom of Iran under one, powerful king. Prominent among the well-wishers of Ardeshir were two groups who had descended from his maternal and paternal grandfathers: the relatives of Sassan who had flocked to Pars after he married into the family of the vassal king Baubak, and the descendants of the vassal king himself. A magus emerged from the crowd and advised the Sassanian prince to unify Iran before standing against Ardavan, the scion of the Ashkanian kings. But it was too late.

The next day Ardeshir arrayed his small supporters for an assault on the city of Pars. Crown Prince Bahman, however, was well-prepared for the confrontation as he had received the warning about Ardeshir's escape from his father. All Ardeshir had was a ragtag collection of poorly armed if enthusiastic followers congregating at the edge of the river. Luckily for the Sassanian contender, a powerful nobleman came from the city of Jahrom to pledge his allegiance. His name was Bonak and he had seven sons, each commanding a well-equipped division. This was good news indeed, but

Ardeshir was hesitant to place his trust in a total stranger. Sensing this reluctance, Bonak declared: "I swear by the holy scriptures of Zand and Avesta that I am sincere in my support. As soon as I heard that you have rebelled against Ardavan I knew that I belong on your side." It took a leap of faith, but Ardeshir decided to trust Bonak and integrate his followers into the troops of Jahrom. And thus, he brought his new army to the gates of Pars, awaiting the inevitable confrontation.

Both sides gave a good account of themselves as the battle commenced. Prince Bahman's forces fought valiantly throughout the morning. As sun reached its zenith in the sky an indecisive but hard confrontation was in progress under a cloud of dust. But the army of Bahman broke ranks and ran when Bonak mounted a brutal assault in the late evening. Bahman managed to escape with his life as Ardeshir chased him past the city of Pars. When he returned the liberated people of Pars opened their gates to welcome their victorious hero. There Ardeshir found Bahman's hidden treasures and dispersed them to his army. But he knew that it was only a matter of time before King Ardavan would come down with a great host to avenge his son's defeat.

And indeed, within days the royal army appeared on the horizon. Ardavan and Ardeshir stood at the heart of their armies. The distance between the battlelines was about twice the length of the flight of an arrow. The cacophony of war trumpets, battle drums and cymbals mixed with the neighing of the horses and the clanging of the armaments. The din was loud enough to wake the snakes burrowed deep inside the earth.

The two sides were so equally matched that the battle lasted forty days, until a black wind blew against the forces of the Ashkani king, to the horror of his commanders. When an earthquake shook the ground beneath them, Ardavan's forces lost heart, convinced that the heaven's decree was against them. They were routed and their king was captured and brought to the presence of Ardeshir. The badly wounded Ardavan slowly dismounted, knowing that he had lost everything. Ardeshir commanded his executioner to decapitate his archenemy.

Destiny is ineluctable, this much is clear
Living creatures are allotted a time and when it arrives
Neither Ardavan can escape his fate nor Ardeshir.

Prince Bahman fled to India with one of his brothers. Their two remaining brothers were captured and imprisoned. Bonak saw to it that the body of the last Ashkani ruler was interned with the funerary honors due to a king.

PACIFICATION OF IRAN

The first act of King Ardeshir was to travel to Ardavan's capital Rey to take inventory of his treasury. At Bonak's advice, he married the daughter of the fallen king to gain access to his hidden riches. After two months he returned to his headquarters at Pars to construct two new cities of Khorreh-ye* Ardeshir and Shahr-e Gur. They were provided with elaborate waterworks and irrigation tunnels. Their wide, cobbled streets were lined with trees and fragrant gardens. Holidays of Sadeh and Mehregan were annually celebrated in their dazzling fire temples that towered upon their hills.

Ardeshir then took his army to the Zagreus Mountains to subdue the Kurdish rebels. He was defeated at the first encounter as his troops were outnumbered thirty to one. But after regrouping at Khorreh-ye Ardeshir, the young king launched a night ambush that wiped the rebels out. As the western regions were pacified, a strange menace was slowly rearing its head in the east.

* "Khorreh" is a variation of "Farreh" or "Farr," i.e., the divine sanction. The ruins of these Sassanian cities that are mentioned in several sources lay in the plain of Firuzabad in the central state of Fars.

THE MONSTER WORM

In the town of Gajaran by the Persian Gulf lived a man and his family. Though he was known by most as Haftvaud, which meant father of seven sons, he also had a willful daughter that he doted on. Like every girl in that impoverished city, she spun cotton to help with the family's finances.

To make the best out of their monotonous life, the Gajaran girls gathered by the town's gates each morning to commute to a pleasant hillside. They nattered and laughed along the way. But there was no resting, laughter, or idle talk during the day, except when they broke for lunch. The spinning girls of Gajaran were fiercely competitive when it came to yarn production.

One morning as Haftvaud's daughter was carrying her cotton to work, she found an apple under a tree, which she picked up and saved for lunch. But when she bit into it, she found a tiny worm. "This is my lucky charm," she told her friends, holding it up. "With its magical power, I will win the yarn contest today."

The company laughed at this amusing challenge. But at the end of the day, she did win the contest by a considerable margin. Her mother was amazed by the amount of yarn she brought home that evening. And with each day thereafter, her production continued to increase. Haftvaud was happy for the increase of his household income. "What is happening?" the girl's mother asked, "Have you found a fairy to help you spin?" The girl confessed that the cause of her success was the good luck of her tiny worm.

Haftvaud, who had become wealthy on his household's yarn production, declared that the worm was a talisman of good luck, and soon the whole town took pride in it. Together they nourished it, and soon it morphed into a beast with a black head and a dazzling body flecked with saffron patches. They built a special tub to accommodate it.

The greedy governor of Gajaran learned of this windfall and tried to extort money from Haftvaud. But he rebelled against this overlord with the help of his seven sons and his comrades. They defeated him and confiscated his treasury. It was obvious that as the magical creature grew larger and became famous, it would pose a threat to the people of the town. To be on the safe side they transferred the worm to an impregnable citadel with an iron gate built on a high mountain. A fountain bubbled inside the enclosure, which made its inhabitants immune to thirst in the event of a siege.

By this time, the worm had outgrown his tub and was transferred to a large basin made of mortar and smooth rocks. He was fed rice, milk, and nectar from a bronze caldron and had his own vizier and scribe. Soon word spread, and armies from the Indus valley to China attempted to conquer the worm's stronghold. Haftvaud, assuming the role of the castle's commander in chief, along with his sons and their armies, defeated all the invaders.

Ardeshir took umbrage that his authority was being challenged by a corpulent worm. But he attempted to invade just as Shahuy, Haftvaud's eldest son, returned from overseas. Shahuy's army blocked Ardeshir's forces from behind, cutting off their supply lines. Just as Ardeshir thought things could not get worse, news arrived that the king's palace at Pars was plundered by Mehrak-e Nushzaud, an aristocrat from the city of Jahrom who traced his pedigree back to the kings of Kay. Ardeshir regretted his rash decision to attack the citadel of the worm while his home front was exposed. As the humiliated king and his commanders sat down to supper, an arrow shot from the citadel—which was two hours' walk away—pierced the roasted lamb in the middle of their spread. A message was wrapped around the shaft of the arrow:

> This comes to you as a warning from the citadel of the worm. We could have sent this through the torso of your king if we so wished. Let this be a sign to your king that he must abandon the dream of subjugating the worm.

By morning, Ardeshir had decided to retreat back to Pars, but the army was ambushed by Haftvaud's forces, who were chanting slogans in praise of the worm. Soon the withdrawal turned into a rout, and the king, who was isolated from his troops, escaped into the wilderness. When night fell he took refuge in an abandoned house. Two young men in the vicinity came over to Ardeshir's makeshift shelter and asked who he was. "I am following Ardeshir," he told them, "the unfortunate king who was defeated by the ragtag militia of the lowborn Haftvaud."

The men treated the stranger with kindness and prepared a meal for him. As they sat down to eat, one of them assured him, "Don't worry. Injustice will not triumph. Recall what came of tyrants like Zahhak, Afrasiab, and Eskandar. They all died, leaving behind nothing but a bad name. The same fate awaits Haftvaud."

Ardeshir then revealed his identity, sensing that he could trust the strangers. He asked for their advice regarding his predicament, and they told him the creature was not an overgrown worm at all but a malignant demon who could only be conquered by deceit.

In the morning, they escorted the king to his stronghold in Khorreh-ye Ardeshir where he gathered an elite force, rode to the city of Jahrom, and executed Mehrak-e Nushzad and his entire clan. It was said that only a girl escaped the massacre.

With this nuisance out of the way, Ardeshir could once again focus on Haftvaud. But this time, he would be more cautious. "I will use deception, just like my great ancestor Esfandiar did when he conquered the Invincible Castle of Arjausp."

He appointed one of his knights by the name of Shahr-geer as the commander of an army of twelve thousand soldiers for the final assault on the citadel of the worm. They would hide in a forest and attack only when they saw smoke rising from the ramparts.

Ardeshir then went to the citadel with a train of donkeys and seven of his paladins disguised as traders. He presented himself as a merchant who had made a fortune thanks to the good luck bestowed upon him by the worm. He said he had come back to express his gratitude with a devotional offering. The commander of the guards opened the iron gates for the caravan to enter.

"I have pledged to feed the worm for three days," Ardeshir announced to its sixty attendants. "You need not worry about performing your duties during this time. Come to my banquet instead, eat, drink, and be merry."

As night fell, they feasted in grand style. Once the guards fell into a drunken stupor, Ardeshir went to the worm, who looked up, waiting to be fed. But he poured molten tin into the varmint's maw. A sound like that of an earthquake rumbled within the monstrous creature as it burst open in a terrible explosion. The king emerged from the grisly chamber, gathered his paladins, and massacred the servants of the worm as they slept. Then they ascended to the ramparts to light the bonfire. At the sight of the flames, the troops of Shahr-geer charged the citadel shouting their war cries. Haftvaud and his son Shahuy, who happened to be outside as these events unfolded, hurried back, trying to win back their headquarters from Ardeshir. The king went up on the ramparts and declared with a loud voice that the worm was dead and that whatever good fortune it emanated had ceased. Haftvaud and Shahuy were captured shortly thereafter and hanged at the gallows for their rebellion.

Ardeshir-e Baubakan returned to Pars in triumph. He visited some of the cities that he had founded but chose Ctesiphon, which was on the western bank of the river Tigris, as his capital. From this date, his forty-two-year reign of a reunited Iran commenced.

Such are the mysterious ways
Of the ever-revolving heavens
They hide their secrets from your gaze.

If your road is uneven, don't be vexed
Adapt to its roughness, though it might be
Uphill one day and downhill the next.

THE REIGN OF ARDESHIR-E BAUBAKAN

The new king sat on the ivory throne in Baghdad, a city neighboring Ctesiphon. He wore the royal cummerbund and the crown of the kings of Kay. Iran was unified under a real king for the first time since Eskandar's conquest. Gone were the days of nominal kings and local potentates of the Ashkanian confederacy. "I treasure justice," the king announced upon his accession. "God is my protector as I am the protector of my people. Let no one who works for me be discontent with his lot. Let the gates of this palace be open to those who have suffered."

But all was not well in the state of India, where the exiled Prince Bahman was rankled by the memory of the execution of his father and the death and imprisonment of his brothers. Thus, he hatched a plot to assassinate Ardeshir and return to Iran as king. The former crown prince secretly sent a vial of poison to his sister, who had become Ardeshir's favorite consort, with a note:

> It is indecent of you to choose the enemy over your flesh and blood. As you indulge in a life of luxury, your brothers are suffering in exile or in the king's dungeons. Take this vial and put it to use to save your clan from this misery.

Ardeshir's consort took pity on her brothers and determined to kill her husband. She made the potent potion into a paste and mixed it with sugar and fragrant nectars in a topaz goblet of iced water. When the king returned from an onager hunt, she offered him the chalice with trembling hands. This caused the chalice to slip out of her grasp and shatter on the floor. Suspicious of what had happened, the king ordered his hens in to peck at the paste, and they all dropped dead. Ardeshir was outraged at his wife's betrayal. He called on the royal advisors and chaplains to judge the case.

"Suppose you take pity on the enemy's daughter and bring her into your household," he said. "And then she gets so intoxicated by your kindness that she decides to plot your demise. What is the punishment for such a crime?"

"Anyone who attempts regicide must be punished by execution."

Ardeshir ordered his vizier Geran-khaur to take the guilty woman into custody and see to her immediate execution. When they left the hall, the terrified girl told her would-be slayer:

"Exalted Geran-khaur! I know that your orders are to kill me. But I am carrying the king's baby. My child is innocent. Wait until he is born and then do with me what you will."

Geran-khaur returned to the king with the news that the girl was with child. But Ardeshir's heart was not softened. "Your orders were to take this woman out and hang her. You were not authorized to converse with her. Carry out your mission."

The vizier left the royal court, considering the king's cruelty. *It's an inauspicious day when a king issues such a cruel decree,* he thought. *And besides, he has no heir. The country would plunge into chaos if he were to die. And what if he regrets his precipitous decision in the future and blames me for carrying it through?* Thus, Geran-khaur decided to spare Ardavan's daughter. He took her to his wife with strict orders to hide her.

But doubts continued to gnaw at him. *What if the affair came to light? What would wagging tongues say? What if they accused the vizier of taking liberties with the royal consort? How could he prove his innocence?* The solution was as obvious to him as it was unthinkable. To defend himself against calumny of being disloyal to his king he had no choice but to castrate himself.

Stepping into a side chamber, the vizier cut off his testicles and put them in a box of salt. After treating his self-inflicted wound, he returned to ask the king to consign the sealed and dated container to his treasurer for safekeeping.

In time Ardavan's daughter gave birth to Ardeshir's son, whom the vizier named Shaupur, meaning son of the king.

Seven years passed. One day, Geran-khaur entered the royal chamber to find the king in a pensive mood. He inquired why such a prosperous and successful king would give himself to despondency. After all, he had the seven realms under his signet, and the world brought him tributes from near and far.

"I'm fifty-one years old and I have no heir. A father without a son is like an orphan without a father. Who will inherit my throne when I die?"

"If His Majesty gives me immunity," Geran-khaur replied, "I will dispel his sorrows."

"Granted."

"May the king order the treasurer to bring the box I deposited with him seven years ago?"

"Of course. What is in the box?"

"I will tell you what is in the box. My shame! My manhood! That which I sacrificed to protect myself, my king, and his royal consort from calumny. The truth is that I did not kill Ardavan's daughter. As you recall, she was with child. I took pity on her. I considered the possibility that you might one day regret your precipitous decision. She lived and gave birth to your son. She is mother to your crown prince Shaupur. And none can accuse me of betraying your trust."

The king was torn among conflicting emotions of joy, regret, sorrow, and pity. He said after a long pause: "I have suffered so much in the last seven years. Bring me my son. But wait. Don't bring him to me. Let me find him myself. Gather a hundred boys, all wearing identical garments. Arrange a game of polo. I want to pick my son out of that crowd."

Geran-Khaur gathered the sons of the courtly staff for a game of polo. The king, viewing the group from his hunting chair, pointed to a boy and said: "There goes my son. There goes the new Ardeshir." Then he commanded one of his retainers to take his mallet and hit the ball toward the king's pavilion. The kids galloped after the wooden ball, but they all stopped short of the pavilion when they saw who was sitting there. Only the boy Ardeshir had singled out dared to come close and hit the ball back to his playmates. This was proof that the child did not merely look like a king. He had the spirit of one.

Thereafter, Shaupur was entrusted to royal tutors to be trained in the arts of writing, wielding a lance, and other martial arts. He was also instructed in courtly etiquette. He learned, for instance, to maintain a regal demeanor at formal and informal occasions such as drinking wine and practicing generosity. In celebration of finding his son, the king minted gold coins that featured his visage on one side and that of his dedicated vizier Geran-khaur on the other. He gave liberally to the needy and established the city of Gondi-Shaupur. As time passed, son and father became very close to the point that they were inseparable.

But the affairs of the country were continuously in turmoil. Trouble followed trouble, and the king seemed embroiled in fighting an endless series of insurgencies and rebellions. To figure out if there was a snag in his stars to bring about such bad luck, he sent an envoy to the renowned astrologer and soothsayer of India, Kayd. He diagnosed the problem and prescribed a solution: To end his string of bad fortune, the king needed to mix his blood with that of Mehrak-e Nushzaud, the rebel who had plundered his palace. This meant that Shaupur should marry the daughter of Mehrak, who had escaped the massacre. Ardeshir was not amused. He considered the remedy to be worse than the disease.

"May I never see the day that someone of Mehrak's blood reclines on my throne. Why would I bring the enemy into my house? Instead, I will make sure that this girl is found and executed just to prevent such an inauspicious union."

Despite their efforts, however, Ardeshir's spies could not find the girl. One day as the crown prince was out hunting he came across a pleasant farm where an elegant young woman was hauling water from a well. She offered to draw some for the equestrian and his steed, adding that water from other wells was brackish.

"Why should a beautiful girl like you draw water? I have many men in my company who can take care of that chore!"

She nodded and calmly stood by as one of the prince's attendants came forward. Hard as he tried, he was unable to pull up the bucket. Shaupur mocked his assistant and stepped forward to draw the water himself, a task he accomplished with some difficulty. He was amazed at the girl's strength. She, too, was impressed by the looks and demeanor of Shaupur. "A prince of the blood is surely able to turn water into milk," she praised him. Shaupur was taken aback by her statement.

"How did you know who I am?"

"Your visage and kingly demeanor gave you away."

"Now it's your turn. Tell me who you really are."

"I'm nobody, just the daughter of the farmer who owns this well."

"It is a sin to lie and a crime to lie to a prince of the blood! There is no way a woman like you could be a commoner."

"May I have permission to speak freely?"

"Granted."

"My father is Mehrak-e Nushzaud. I have become adept in drawing water because I have lived here since I was a little girl, hiding from the king's henchmen."

Utterly besotted, Shaupur called the farmer and asked him for the hand of his adopted daughter. In short order, clerics of the Zoroastrian faith were called in to solemnize the simple marriage. After nine months, the charming mother gave birth to a luminous child. Shaupur named his son Urmazd, derived from the supreme God of their faith. Knowing his father's feelings regarding the house of Mehrak, however, the prince hid his son for seven years.

One day as Ardeshir was hunting in the vicinity of the farm of Shaupur's secret family, he came across a gaggle of children playing a polo-like game and fixated his attention on a child holding a bow and two arrows. At the same time, one of his playmates shot the ball in the king's direction. None of them dared to come and pick it up, except for the boy carrying the bow and arrow. He boldly stepped up, picked up the ball, and threw it back to his playmates. The king was startled by the child's audacity. Remembering that Shaupur had performed a similar feat, he asked his chamberlain to bring the child to his presence.

"Who are you? What is your pedigree?"

"I am your grandson," said the boy. "My mother is the worthy daughter of Mehrak-e Noushzaud."

Impressed by the looks and spirit of the child, the king sent for Shaupur. "This child has descended from the line of kings, hasn't he?"

"He has, Your Majesty. He is my son, and his name is Urmazd."

Then he related the story of how he met Mehrak's daughter. The king ordered his treasurer to bury his grandson in gold coins and jewels up to his neck, distributed alms and sent large contributions to fire temples. He also noted that ever since the boy's birth seven years ago, the land had calmed down, as Kayd had predicted.

ARDESHIR ON MILITARY AND STATE FUNCTIONS

At the height of his power, when he was receiving tributes from Rome, China, and the Turks, King Ardeshir shared his wisdom with the people of Iran.

- A well-ordered army is the essence of a state. Universal military training for young boys should be established. The courageous should be exalted and the cowardly punished. He who deserts his post or runs from the enemy deserves imprisonment, if not execution.
- Commanders should see to the proper communication between the left and right flanks of the army so that it can move as a unified body. In the event of an enemy retreat, the army should keep its composure. The heart of the army must stay put except on rare occasions. Nor should the commanders be tempted to pursue every retreating foe, discounting the dangers of feigned retreat and ambush.
- Capable civilian administrators must accompany the army so the military does not act impetuously. Nothing should be taken from the local population during military operations without pay. Nor should soldiers be billeted in domiciles without compensation.
- Quarter ought to be given should the enemy wish to surrender. Under no circumstances should prisoners of war be killed. Instead, they must be brought to one of the cities I have built, where they can work and prosper.
- Educated officials and well-trained scribes are my kin. State bureaucrats should be respected as if they are each a king worthy of obedience. State administrators should be vigilant lest bribes and emoluments corrupt them.
- Emissaries to foreign lands are forbidden to take their family and

relatives along. They must keep company with the troops and guards provided for them.

- When an ambassador is sent by a foreign power, he must be received and closely monitored at the border. Then he should be brought with an honor guard to the royal court. The protocol must be observed regarding their monitoring as well as respectful treatment, and no amenities should be denied them.
- A poor man who comes to the royal court to seek redress for injustice must be attended to by aides. All complaints must be taken seriously. Further, they must be questioned about the nature of their case and the conditions at their place of origin. This way, the needs of people in remote regions will be known to the state. The royal treasury must provide housing for the needy.

There was no king like Ardeshir
While he lived and after his death
None could be considered his peer.

I am the proud poet who revived his name.
May Ardeshir receive favor and copious rewards
In the Hereafter as in this life he attained fame.

ARDESHIR ON PERSONAL MORALITY

- Leave nothing but a good name behind, for possessions will be of no use when you are dead and gone. Obey God's commands and be just and humble in His sight. I have taken no more than a tithe as taxes from you, and I have forgiven even that when the treasury was full. I have spent the tithe due to me on public projects. Nothing has been wasted on luxuries. I did not seek glory, for I have seen what happens to those who are deceived by this world's false glitter.
- Believe in God, respect knowledge, admire wisdom, fear sin more than its punishment, and hold your tongue from vicious talk. Be frank in

your speech but speak softly. Avoid boasting. Frankness and moderation in speech are conducive to happiness.

- Muzzle your greed. Be honest. Pay your tithe. I do not squander your taxes but spend them on your safety and well-being.
- Never stop learning and ensure that your children are educated. Take care of your health and obey your king and your God.
- Provide for yourself and your family. Attend to your own affairs and don't pry into other people's business. Don't be greedy, and avoid unnecessary strife.
- Banish fear of the future and sorrow of the past from your mind. Attend to your own well-being for it falls on the king to worry about the common weal.
- Only just kings will succeed in running the affairs of the state. A tyrant is more dangerous than a ferocious lion.

When the king finished his proclamations, an old man by the name of Khorrad rose to speak. "May you live a life of happiness and contentment. Even wild beasts and birds of the air humble themselves to you. We thank the Lord that we live at a time when you are king. You have made our lives safe within our borders and saved us the ignominy of plunder and enslavement. May you rule this land for a long time. May your ways last forever."

ARDESHIR'S LAST WORDS TO THE CROWN PRINCE

When the king reached the ripe age of seventy-eight and sensed that he was sick unto death, he summoned Shaupur and said: I leave you with these words of advice as I leave this world:

- Destiny is a wild and recalcitrant horse. There is no telling if it will behave, and when it does, no one knows for how long.
- Know that religion and state are conjoined twins. They cannot come into conflict. Nor can they be separated. A religious man cannot

possibly oppose his king. Nor is it conceivable for a legitimate king to despise religion.

- The three enemies of the state are injustice, the promotion of untalented men, and greed. Greed is the worst among these blights.
- Don't begrudge the farmer his treasure, for his wealth is the nation's wealth.
- Shun anger like the plague and keep generosity within the bounds of reason.
- Don't be reckless in entertainment. Don't mix drinking and hunting if you wish to avoid terrible accidents.
- Don't procrastinate, and don't be naïve in trusting the common people, for they are often faithless.
- Don't share your secrets with anyone, not even your trusted friends, for every trustworthy companion has a trustworthy companion of his own who will be privy to your secret.
- Be merciful to a man who has violated the law but regrets his act.
- When a ferocious enemy appears on the horizon, don't hesitate to lavish money on your army and ask for help from friendly neighbors.
- Keep my advice and follow the path of righteousness. The good fortune of this dynasty will last for five hundred years. In time my progeny will forget my advice. They will treat the powerless with disdain and incline to injustice. We will be the authors of our demise.

I founded a dynasty having unified the realm.
For forty years, have I subdued Iran's enemies
And now it's your turn to take the helm.

CHAPTER 19

Sassanian Glory: Shaupur I to Shaupur II

Praise the One who's praised by all creatures. Love
Him who is loved by everything from the thornbush
Underfoot to the revolving heavens above.

SHAUPUR I

Whereas Ardeshir had cut the high taxes of his time to a simple tithe, Shaupur reduced them to one-thirtieth of his subjects' annual income. As a frugal king, he managed to keep the army on a tight budget while achieving huge victories.

Although everything seemed secure at home, trouble had started to brew on Iran's borders. The Queen of Andalusia and the Roman Caesar conspired to provoke the Iranian king into a conflict by refusing to pay their annual tributes. Shaupur launched a formidable army to enforce these financial obligations, and he met their combined forces on the plain of Cilicia.

Shaupur gave the command of his forces to Karzasp. The other side was led by the able Roman commander Baraunush. The armies clashed in a deafening clamor, both sides fighting with determination. But as the war dragged on, the Iranians managed to break through the enemy formations and cause a general flight. In the ensuing chaos, the allied armies of Rome and Andalusia were decimated. Baraunush and sixteen-hundred members of his elite guard were taken captive. The Caesar sued for peace by sending an envoy to Shaupur with this message:

> It is unseemly to shed blood over money. What excuse will you bring to the divine tribunal when you are questioned about this carnage? If it is about taxes, we will pay them as well as war reparations. We will also send hostages to assure you that we will not violate the terms of this agreement.

Shaupur remained on the battlefield until the enemy sent ten cowhides filled with gold coins, a thousand slaves, and a considerable quantity of Roman brocade as restitution. Highborn Roman hostages heralded the train of tributes. Only then the king returned to Ahvauz.

In Khuzestan, he founded the city of Shaupur-gerd. Further along in the state of Pars, he founded a city named Kohan-Dejh, whose name meant the Old Castle. The king charged his Roman captives to design and build an elegant bridge over the turbulent Shushtar River as a condition of their release. This act was the culmination of his victorious campaigns.

The exemplary rule of Shaupur lasted thirty-two years. There was no flaw in his wise management of the country. On his deathbed, he called his Crown Prince Urmazd and advised him to avoid pride and reflect on the life of King Jamshid, who lost his divine sanction and forfeited his good name to hubris.

Amass not the wealth of this world nor presume
That those who inherit your wealth will do more
Than come to your wake to put a flower on your tomb.

REIGN OF FIVE KINGS

Urmazd was a perfect king, but alas, his reign lasted only a year and four months. The same fate awaited his successor, Bahraum I, who ruled for three years, three months, and three days.

Bahraum II ruled for nineteen years. As Iran was prosperous and calm, no significant events marred his rule. He was replaced by his son, Bahraum III, who carried the moniker of Kermanshah, but he died after only four months. The subsequent kings Narsi and Urmazd II each ruled for nine years.

Don't rack your brains over this enigma
That king and pauper are equal in the tomb
All mortals are branded with the same stigma.

Urmazd II died without an heir. There was great consternation over the possibility of a succession war among various factions at the court. After forty days, a magus discovered that a lovely concubine of King Urmazd II was in late pregnancy. The court celebrated that an heir had been found. Within weeks, the mother gave birth to a radiant boy possessed of the halo of divine sanction. He was crowned in the cradle as Shaupur II.

SHAUPUR OF THE SHOULDERS

A magus named Shahruy was appointed as regent. But his rule did not last long, as the child king was precocious. At the age of five, he presided over a gathering of the high-ranking courtiers at the palace of Ctesiphon. The child king heard a great din of shouts and screams from the direction of the narrow bridge over the river Arvand, where the Tigris and Euphrates joined. Shaupur II asked his advisors about the cause of the commotion, and he was told that people were hurrying to cross the crowded bridge and go home at the end of the workday.

"Then build another bridge to accommodate the traffic both ways," said the king. "My subjects should not fall into difficulties just because they want to go home after a day of honest work."

The courtiers were impressed by the astuteness of the boy who was their king and toasted each other, observing that the cub was growing a luxurious mane. The plans of the young Shaupur were put into action and soon a double bridge across the river was built to accommodate the workers. As time passed Shaupur II matured, excelling his teachers in every subject. At seven, he mastered polo, and at eight, he chose the Winter Palace in Pars* as his seat of power.

While the young king was in Pars, the Arab chief Tauyer of the Ghassanid tribe raided Ctesiphon. In the ensuing plunder, princess Nusheh, an aunt of the young king, was carried away to the Ghassanid territory as a captive. After a year, the abducted princess gave birth to Tauyer's daughter, the beautiful princess Maulekeh.

* Called Estakhr by the Iranians and Persepolis by the Greeks.

Shaupur II was enraged by this brazen act of aggression, but he was too young to chastise the perpetrators. So, he harbored his resentment until he reached the age of eighteen, when he could avenge the sack of Ctesiphon. The young king took an elite force of twelve thousand camel-riding warriors and invaded the Ghassanid territoy beyond the western borders of Iran. Tauyer withdrew to an impregnable castle in Yemen, and Shaupur besieged the stronghold, aiming to starve his enemy into surrender.

Maulekeh, who had no great love for her father, stood on the ramparts and watched as the Iranian army laid siege to the castle. When she saw the illustrious Shaupur atop his steed, commanding the troops, she fell in love. Later that night Maulekeh secretly sent her handmaiden with a letter to the Iranian king.

> We both are the progeny of King Narsi and our common enemy is the man who abducted my mother, Nusheh. Take me first and pledge your love to me. Then the castle will be yours to take.

The night was black as pitch, and stars hung from the sky like icicles. Terrified of getting caught by the night guards of Tauyer, the slim handmaiden stole across the castle, found a crack in the walls, slipped out with some difficulty, and ran to the Iranian camp. She asked a soldier to take her to the king's tent. Shaupur was ecstatic when he learned that the princess of the castle was in love with him. He rewarded the daring messenger and asked her to convey his mutual feelings:

> I swear by the sun, the moon, Zoroaster's belt, and my crown that I will soon hold you in my everlasting embrace. None shall surpass you in my heart. Nor will your station be diminished at my court.

The handmaiden rushed back and gave Shaupur's letter to Maulekeh, adding: "My princess, the sun and Jupiter have aligned in your sky. The handsome king returns your love and agrees to your plans for the conquest of the castle."

That night the princess treated the courtly retinue and defenders of the castle to a feast. She appeared as the gracious cupbearer, filling everyone's goblet with strong wine laced with a soporific potion. Once the guards fell into a drunken stupor, the princess and her maids opened the gates, allowing the king and his troops to enter. The guards woke and fought with valor until they were all killed. Tauyer was taken captive.

The next day, when her father entered the hall, Maulekeh was sitting on a throne beside Shaupur.

"Do you see, oh great king, what my daughter has done to me?" said Tauyer. "How can you trust someone who betrays her father?"

"You have no right," replied the king, "to appeal to morality when you raided a king's city, abducted a princess of the blood, and forced her to carry your child."

Tauyer was executed for his crimes. His commanders were subjected to strappado, which caused the dislocation of their shoulders. Thereafter, the king became synonymous with this gruesome act and earned a fearsome new title: Shaupur of the Shoulders.

THE KING'S ROMAN ADVENTURE

Having avenged himself on the rebellious Arab chief, Shaupur II called his astrologers to study the stars and divine what was in store for him. He was hoping for a long and prosperous rule. The astrologers studied the path of the star Regulus at the heart of the Leo constellation, as it represents royal fortunes. They could not ignore a shadow of evil lurking in the king's horoscope. But there was little Shaupur could do to avoid the impending calamities. Thus, the royal councilors advised him to pray to the Almighty for protection during the inevitable misfortunes. Shaupur was resigned to his fate.

Shortly thereafter, the king craved an adventure. He decided to travel to Rome and gather intelligence on the Caesar's personal characteristics and military strength. This would be vital information if their relationship were to sour. He entrusted the country to an administrator and set off for the western borders disguised as a merchant. Shaupur led ten caravans, each with its string of camels and caravanner. They stopped at a village on the outskirts of the capital, where the disguised king asked the headman to represent him to the royal court as a seller of rare jewels and armaments. He was willing to offer the Caesar kingly gifts in exchange for a writ that would enable him to conduct business in the Roman marketplace.

The effort was successful. The caravan was let into the city, and Shaupur was invited to an audience with the Caesar. But he was instantly recognized by an Iranian outlaw who had fled to Rome. The man casually approached the Caesar to avoid alarming the royal guest, and whispered into his ear: "This man is no merchant. I know for a fact that he is the king of Iran."

The Caesar kept his composure until his guest, inebriated, rose to leave. Then he grabbed the false merchant with the help of his guards and said: "What a surprise to meet Shaupur, the son of Narsi, in such a bad disguise!"

He ordered the hapless king taken to the women's quarters and sewn inside the rawhide of a freshly skinned donkey. As Shaupur's torturers were completing their revolting task, servants mocked him: "There goes a jackass with the head of a king!" said one of them. Another interjected: "What I see is a man who left his palace and traveled a long way only to become a preposterous donkey." Then Shaupur was taken out and imprisoned in the basement of an adjacent house that belonged to the queen of Rome. She charged a handmaiden to give the prisoner enough water and bread to keep him alive.

Having ensconced Shaupur in his dungeon, the Caesar decided to invade Iran, as he was sure the land would be vulnerable without its leader. And he was right. There was no resistance on the Iranian part. He sacked many cities, enslaved their population, and laid waste to the land. Then he camped in the southwestern hunting grounds of Iran to spend his time in leisurely pursuits.

Back in Rome, the hapless Shaupur moaned in the donkey's drying hide that was crushing him to death. The maid, who happened to be of Iranian descent, took pity on her charge and asked: "Who are you? For what crime are you being tormented like this?" He promised to tell her the truth if she took an oath to keep his confidence. She solemnly swore to God, the seventy knots of the deacon's sash, the suffering of Jesus on the cross, and the passion of the saintly martyrs to keep his secret.

The king revealed his identity, shared the story of his capture, and added that she would be exalted over all ladies of the world if she helped him escape. But first, he had to break out of the revolting hide that was slowly killing him. The maid brought a jug of warm milk every day for two weeks and massaged the drying skin to make it supple enough for her ward to slither out. Bloody and slimy as he was, Shaupur could not believe his sense of relief as he was freed from his confines. But this did not prevent him from planning his next step: Slipping out of his house prison and escaping to Iran.

"Tomorrow will be a perfect opportunity to make our getaway," the handmaiden suggested, "it is a holiday, and people will leave town at dawn to go to the open fields." As soon as the revelers left the town, the maiden came back leading two horses laden with provisions, weapons, and some money. The king and the maid jumped on their horses, galloped away and didn't look back until they had crossed the southwestern borders of Iran. There, they stopped to knock on the gates of the first orchard that they saw. The owner opened the door and asked, "What are you doing here so late at night? Who are you, and what do you want?" Shaupur responded: "Why would you ask questions of people who have lost their way? I don't know where I am, but I know that I am an Iranian escaping from the Caesar of Rome. I wager that you will be well compensated if you offer me and my companion hospitality."

"Far be it from me to fail in my duties as a host," the man responded. "Consider my house, my garden, and my table as your own. I beg you to stay at my humble abode for at least three days."

After the lady of the house served a delicious dinner, they lingered to drink wine. The stranger bid his host drink the first goblet as he was older. But the farmer deferred to his guest, saying that nobility precedes age.

Shaupur took a sip and sighed. "So, tell me about the state of the country. What is happening to Iran and Iranians?"

"What can I say? The land is in ruin, and nothing remains untouched by this invader, the Caesar of Rome. Cities are sacked, and people are massacred. Huge numbers have been hauled away as slaves, and some have converted to Christianity in exchange for better treatment. Sash and tiara of the Christian clerics are common in public places. We are a conquered people."

"Where is King Shaupur? Why doesn't he defend his people?"

"He is missing in action," said the man, choking back a sob. "The entire nation has been brought to its knees before Rome, and no one knows where the king is."

The following day the host came to his guest's quarters to see if he needed anything. Shaupur made him swear an oath to tell the truth, and then asked him about the whereabouts of the chief of the magi. The host said his house was so close that it could be seen from where they were sitting. The king asked for some seal clay, impressed his signet on it, and said: "Take this to the grand magus."

Upon seeing the king's seal, the mage wept with joy and asked where the ring's owner was.

"He is a guest at my house," said the farmer.

"What does he look like?"

"He is tall as a cypress on a riverbank and muscular as a wild lion. He is enveloped in a halo of divine sanction."

There was no doubt in the holy man's mind that the orchard owner spoke of the king. He quickly sent word to the regional knight that the king had returned. The knight sent envoys to the neighboring lands and instructed them to gather their troops. Once they had a strong army, the magus and the knight went to the orchard where the king was residing. The knight kissed the ground and said: "Welcome back, my king. My army is ready to carry out your orders."

Shaupur embraced them both, told them of his ordeal in Rome and introduced the brave handmaiden who was the cause of his liberation and in whose everlasting debt he was. Regarding military action, however, he urged caution. The forces of the Caesar were in Ctesiphon, and the Iranian regional troops were not sufficient for a confrontation. He ordered the knight to discretely gather additional soldiers and prepare for a fierce battle.

When the army of Iran swelled to six thousand properly armed and well-disciplined men, the king sent spies to report on the enemy's position. Secure in his supposition that the Iranian king was imprisoned in Rome, the Caesar had indulged in a life of laziness and dissipation. He was drinking and hunting without a care in the world. He had not even bothered to post sentries around his camp.

Based on this intelligence, the king selected three thousand elite cataphracts from among his troops and stole across the desert and mountain ranges to arrive in the vicinity of Ctesiphon at the break of dawn. The Caesar's entire camp was in a deep sleep, unprotected by guards. Shaupur pulled his mace out of its holder as a sign to attack. The troops galloped their horses at maximum speed as the drums of war pounded and tin trumpets blasted. The night raid was a brilliant feat of military success. The segment of the Roman army that was still alive surrendered. The Caesar was among the captives.

Shaupur ordered a census of the prisoners of war. One thousand one hundred ten Romans were in bonds. Those who had commanded the sack of the cities, massacres, and enslavements were severely punished. The rest were imprisoned. The Caesar bent a knee when he was brought to the king's presence. He wept and abjectly apologized for his cruel treatment and begged forgiveness for his crimes.

"You follow a false religion and address God of the eternal universe as 'the Son,'" Shaupur said with derision. "You call yourself a Caesar, but you have no shame and no nobility. I had not come to Rome to make war. I was your guest. For what crime was I sewn into a donkey's hide? Why did my people deserve to be mistreated after you jailed me?"

"Oh, great king," the Caesar begged, "What can I say? Who can escape the fate ordained by God? I blame destiny for my spurning of reason and allowing evil spirits to commandeer my soul. You can take revenge on me. But, consider this: You can also win everlasting fame in the world if you reward bad deeds with good. Allow me to serve you as a slave and be an ornament to your royal court."

"I will grant this wish if you return my people to me, pay reparations, and rebuild every house you have demolished. You must also replace every highborn person you have killed with ten prominent Roman citizens and replant every tree you have cut down. Your hands will be bound, but I will not wrap you in a rawhide. I am not a cruel man like you."

As further punishment, the king ordered the Caesar's earlobes sliced, and his nostrils pierced as is done to beasts of burden to be commandeered by ropes. In Rome the news of the humiliating defeat and captivity of the Caesar was treated as the great scandal that it was. Yanis, the Caesar's brother, was crowned and charged to avenge him. But in the ensuing fight his army was routed by Shaupur.

Finally, the Romans elected Baraunush, who had both Iranian and Roman ancestors, as Caesar. He sent a letter of reconciliation to the Iranian king:

> May divine favors shower on the eternal king of Iran. You know that plunder and bloodshed are grave sins, whether they occur in Iran or Rome. Why are you insisting on attacking us? This cannot be an old grudge, for King Manuchehr avenged the blood of Iraj on his brothers Salm and Tur. Nor can you be seeking revenge for Dara. As you know, he was not killed by Eskandar but by his own lieutenants. And if you are furious at the ill-treatment you received in the hands of this Caesar, well, he is in your prison. There has been enough plunder and enslavement of women and children. It is time we snuffed the fires of your wrath and did what pleases God.

Shaupur welcomed the Roman overture and responded:

> Speaking of immorality and sinful acts perpetrated between our nations, you have omitted to mention those who torture their guests by sewing them into a donkey's hide. But if you are sincere, come to me with your wise philosophers. You are all in my protection, and no harm will come to you.

Baraunush humbly went to the Iranian court with a hundred wise men carrying thirty thousand dinars of gold as tribute. Shaupur commanded them to restore the cities and orchards captured in the Roman invasion. Annual indemnities were set at three million dinars to be delivered three times a year. The king also demanded the annexation of the border city of Nisibis.

Baraunush agreed to the terms of peace. But Nisibis did not open its gates to the Iranians, calling them followers of a demonic religion. The people claimed it was improper for an infidel to rule a Christian city. The king was enraged at the Christians and said that a religion whose prophet allowed himself to be killed by Jews was not worthy of respect. The insurgency was crushed with great brutality and Nisibis was subdued. At the end the elders of the city begged for mercy and the king granted them quarter.

Upon his return, the king showered the owner of the orchard with gold. He also honored the servant girl who had helped him escape with the royal titles of "the one who gladdens the heart" and "the one with auspicious footfalls."

Iran thrived for a quarter century after this great victory. Shaupur ruled peacefully alongside the worthy consort who had liberated him from bondage. The Caesar died in prison, and the king sent his remains to Rome for burial. The king founded three cities in this period: Khorram-Abaud, where the Roman captives were settled; a city near Ahvauz featuring a hospital and a palace; and a city called Pirouz-Shaupur, built in the Levant.

At this time, a painter named Mani arrived from China claiming to be a prophet of God. Shaupur respected the prophet and advised the magi to listen to what he had to say, but they considered the man a dangerous heterodox. The king then arranged for a theological debate between Mani and the chief of the magi. Mani lost, and his teachings were deemed blasphemous. The clerics pressured the king to have him executed, and he was. Mani's skin was filled with straw and hanged at the city's gates to deter others from following his teachings.

When Shaupur reached his seventies, he called an audience of magi and courtiers and requested that his brother Ardeshir take the reins of power as a regent for his young son Yazdegerd. Ardeshir took an oath that he would perform his duties, and the king advised him to rule in justice and be generous and forgiving toward his subjects. "Above all," added the dying Shaupur, "a king should be zealous for religion, take good care of the army and keep their armaments in good order. And remember that death will arrive without warning. So, keep an eye on your behavior in the sight of the Lord."

*It's the twentieth of January, a Friday**
I have finished the tale of Shaupur
Earning the right to enjoy this day.

So, I drink wine without caring
One whit that I've turned sixty-three
And am an old man who's lost his hearing.

* Because the poet has provided the date and the day of the week, we can surmise that this line was written on January 20, 1003 CE.

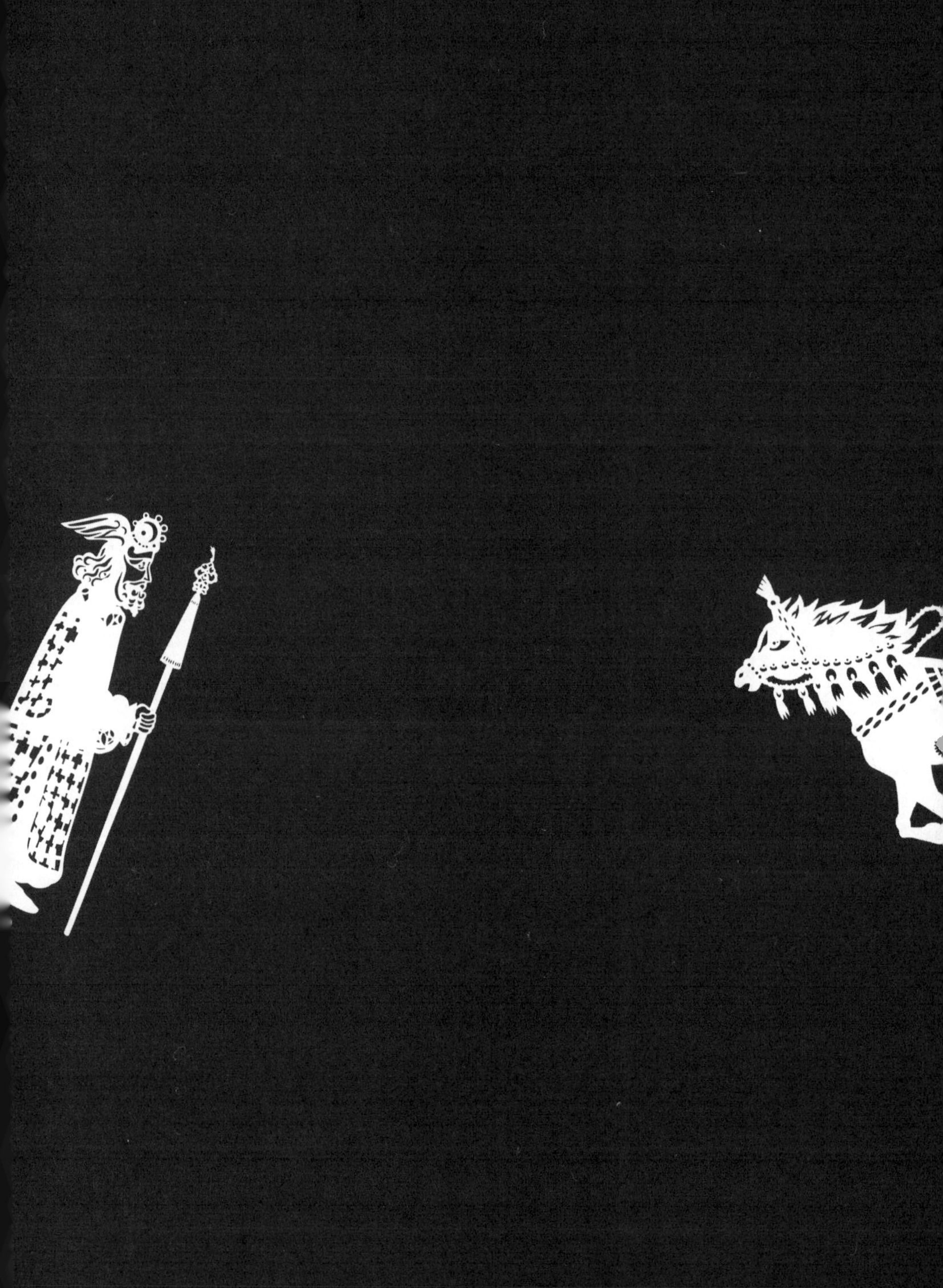

CHAPTER 20

A Tyrannical Ruler: Yazdegerd the Sinner

Shaupur's brother went by "Ardeshir the Benign."
He was a gentle soul who honestly discharged his duties
As regent and withdrew when it was his time to resign.

Ardeshir refused to collect taxes during his ten-year regency, as there was enough in the treasury to run the affairs of the government. In accordance with the pledge he had made to Shaupur of the Shoulders, Ardeshir crowned Shaupur III as soon as he reached maturity.

After reigning just five years and four months, Shaupur III was killed during a hunting expedition. He died of head injuries caused by a falling tent pole during a storm. His uneventful rule was followed by the equally quiet tenure of his son Bahraum IV, who ruled for fourteen years. He had five daughters but no male progeny. Thus, his brother Yazdegerd ascended the throne.

Quit wine, oh poet, and atone for your indiscretions
Repent and hope that the wisdom of your poetic works
Will earn you the Lord's mercy and divine concessions.

I have lived a good life in the sight of God
And versified an epic to honor my benefactor
Whom the world will know thereby and applaud.

THE SINNER KING

Young King Yazdegerd did not attempt to hide his pleasure at the occasion of his brother's untimely death. He directly climbed the throne and declared himself king. In his declaration he praised the just, warned the rebellious, and threatened to severely punish anyone who provoked his wrath. Over the subsequent years, his pride waxed, and his compassion waned. Yazdegerd rarely forgave an infraction and rushed to harsh punishments that grew crueler over time. Petitioners were turned away from his gates, and a general climate of fear pervaded the royal court. Thus, people called him "Yazdegerd The Sinner."

On the eighth anniversary of the king's rule, a son was born to him. He was named Bahraum, the fifth Sassanian prince to receive that name. Astrologers were sanguine about his prospects, as he was born on an auspicious day. It was predicted that the reign of the crown prince would be long and that he would preside over the seven realms of the world. But the courtiers were hesitant. How would they protect the impressionable crown prince from the corruptive influence of his selfish and tyrannical father? They had to gently persuade the king to send his son abroad to be educated.

Yazdegerd accepted the plan and invited the courts of Rome, China, India, and Arabia to send their envoys and plead their cases for taking the Iranian crown prince under their tutelage. They all came and presented their merits in various sciences and practical skills. Monzar, the king of Yemen, was the last to rise.

"We are simple folks," he said. "Unlike the august royal families in this hall, we know neither philosophy nor geometry. Nor do we count the stars or predict the future. But I will say this for Yemen: we know how to ride our noble Arabian horses, and we know how to love our king."

With this simple plea, Monzar gained Yazdegerd's favor and won the honor of bringing up Bahraum in his desert tradition of hunting, fighting, and enjoying the pleasures of a simple life. Upon the return to Yemen, Monzar hired four wet-nurses to feed the infant. Two of them were descended from the kings of Kay, and the other two were the progeny of the most gallant tribes of Arabia.

At seven, Bahraum came to his benefactor and said: "Do not treat me as a babe in the cradle. Appoint qualified tutors to teach me all I need to know as a grown-up. I do not want to be idle." Monzar demurred. The child was too young for such instruction. But in time he relented and engaged three tutors, one to teach him reading and writing, one to make him proficient in hunting with falcons and cheetahs, and the third to train him in polo and the use of bows and arrows. The prince proved a diligent student of every branch of the royal arts and excelled in all of them.

At eighteen, Bahraum asked the Yemeni king to provide him with a worthy steed that could gallop down a sharp incline without fear. One hundred noble horses were rustled up from the four corners of Arabia. The prince chose two horses: a handsome chestnut and an elegant bay horse sporting a copper-colored body and a black tail. The king paid for these noble horses from his treasury.

Bahraum was also ready for female companionship. At his request, Monzar commanded the slave master to present him with forty girls, all slender and gleaming like ivory statues. The prince chose two: one was a gorgeous harp player named Azaudeh, and the other was an exquisite beauty with prominent cheekbones and skin more delicate than rose petals. She stood out among her peers like the beautiful, rarely sighted Canopus.*

The prince had found happiness. His face had a healthy color reminiscent of the rubies of the Badakhshan mines. . . . He did not spare lions and ostriches, but nothing excited him like chasing onagers. Thus, Bahraum V came to be known as "Bahraum the Onager Hunter" or "Bahraum-e Gur."

The talented prince was a trick shooter, able to hunt with a combination of slingshots and arrows. He could target and hit any part of a game in any position. But he did not brook criticism. One day, he took Azaudeh on a jaunt. She played a small harp while riding behind her master on a horse equipped with two sets of gold and silver stirrups. Bahraum allowed Azaudeh to set up a challenge so he could demonstrate his skills.

As a male and female deer appeared on the horizon, she dared Bahraum to shoot off the stag's antlers and plant two arrows on the forehead of the doe, thus making each appear like the other. The prince succeeded in the difficult task. Then she demanded that he nail the head and foot of another deer with one arrow. Bahraum hit the third deer with a slingshot in the ear, and as the animal tried to scratch its ear, he shot an arrow stitching the foot of the deer to its ear.

But instead of praising the stunning expertise of her lover, Azaudeh shed tears of compassion for the victims of the hunt, which she had set

* Canopus (or Soheil) is a bright southern hemisphere star that is rarely seen in lower latitudes of the northern hemisphere. Canopus is in the Carnis constellation, which is in the vicinity of the famous Southern Cross constellation.

up herself. The prince was vexed by the inappropriate reaction. "What if there was a witness here?" he hissed. "What if I failed in the difficult challenge and lost face because of a slave girl's whim?" He furiously threw her off the horse and trampled her. She died of her injuries, and the prince pledged never to take a concubine along on a hunt again.

THE CROWN PRINCE AT HIS FATHER'S COURT

Monzar sent a report of the prowess of the prince to the Iranian court along with a painting of one of his hunting feats. The king was pleased and said he longed to see his son again. After many years of separation, Bahraum, too, missed his father.

Thus, the prince returned to the Winter Palace of Pars accompanied by No'man, the son of King Monzar. They brought King Yazdegerd gifts of Arabian horses, Yemeni Bord fabric, and jewels from the mines of Adan. Yazdegerd welcomed them graciously.

After a month, No'man returned to Yemen with worthy gifts for his father, along with a letter from the Iranian king thanking him for all he had done for the crown prince. Bahraum secretly begged his friend to take another letter to Monzar expressing his disappointment about his life at the Iranian court:

> This is not the welcome I expected at my father's palace. I am not treated properly here. I am neither a favorite son nor an honored courtier. Despite my title, I feel like a man in limbo.

Monzar was glad to receive the king's gifts and his kind words. But his mood dampened when he read Bahraum's letter. Secretly, he dispatched ten thousand dinars and a comforting letter of advice to his protégé:

> You ought to obey your father and serve him to the best of your ability. Endure the hardships, as one must bow to one's fate. Freely spend the money I have sent you. You need not ask your father for amenities. I will replenish your purse when you run out. Your

father's temperament is set in stone. Accept him for who he is, and don't fatigue yourself trying to change him.

Bahraum was starting to calm down by the letter and the gifts of his benefactor when the situation worsened. One night the young prince felt exhausted at one of his father's feasts that had gone too long into the night. Yazdegerd took offense when he caught Bahraum dozing and ordered him out. Thereafter the prince was forbidden from attending court except during the holidays of Nowruz and Sadeh.

Life had become so intolerable at the palace that the prince appealed to the Roman ambassador Tinush to help him return to Yemen. He used his influence, and finally, the king permitted his son to return. To express his gratitude, he gave away some of his wealth to the needy, gathered his servants, and left for Yemen at nightfall.

King Monzar came out of his palace to greet Bahraum and ask after King Yazdegerd's health. The prince was so annoyed that he did not want to even speak his father's name. It took a while for him to forget his ordeal at the Iranian court and get back to enjoying his old pleasures of hunting and merrymaking.

THE SINNER KING'S DEATH

Yazdegerd had reached the age when one begins to think about death. He asked astrologers to chart his horoscope and determine where he would die. His prospect was grim. He would die near a healing spring in Tous known as the Sue Fountain. Thus, the king determined to never set foot in that region. But then he suffered a series of nosebleeds, and the healers prescribed partaking of the healing waters of the Sue. This, they contended, was the only cure for the king's ailment. He made the journey with much trepidation. The treatment paid off and Yazdegerd's nosebleeds stopped. But it didn't take him long to revert to his old, boastful ways: "This is how kings do it. I recline on my throne, cured of my ailment and unaffected by the curse of this fountain."

As the king spoke, a magnificent white horse with blue eyes rose from the waters of the healing spring. Admiring the wild steed, the king commanded his lieutenants to capture it, but none was able to approach it. The king mounted his own horse and gave chase, only to be promptly knocked off by the white horse, who killed him with a double barrel kick and dived into the Sue's depths. The demise of the king was instantaneous. After twenty years of tyrannical rule, Yazdegerd the Sinner had been dispatched by a horse.

Once the funerary ceremony of the royal internment was complete, the noblemen and knights gathered at court to discuss the issue of succession. The consensus was that no one from the seed of the Sinner King should rule again. They especially opposed the candidacy of the crown prince, leery of his ties to the Arab confederates of Iran. Unable to agree on who should replace Yazdegerd, the magi decided to appoint Khosrow, a pious and well-respected prince, as a provisional king.

When Bahraum learned of his father's demise, he mourned for one month, as was the custom of the court. Then he consulted his Yemeni benefactor about regaining his birthright. How would he confront those who had stolen his crown? Monzar knew that changing dynasties would challenge his position as the friend of the deposed line. He told the prince that he had a plan. "I will show Iranians who their real king is."

Monzar ordered his troops to plunder Ctesiphon and lay waste to Mesopotamia. In the ensuing chaos, the Chinese and the Roman armies mobilized to attack Iran to carve out their own choice parts. The Yemeni potentate called upon the Ghassanid and Sheybanid tribes of Arabia to prepare their fighting men for a general campaign.

Alarmed by these developments, Iranian knights and noblemen sent a magus by the name of Javanuy to carry their message to Monzar:

> In the past, you protected Iran's borders and were a great source of our comfort. Can you imagine our surprise when we see you as a menace to our sovereignty? Where is your fear of God? Where is your regard for justice?

Monzar listened to the ambassador as he read the message and advised Javanuy to meet with Bahraum first. The Iranian envoy was so amazed by the handsome face, athletic frame and authoritative demeanor of the prince that he forgot his question. He felt that he was in the presence of a king. They conversed for a while, then Javanuy returned to meet with Monzar and receive a response for his message:

> I did not start this strife. You started it by spurning your legitimate crown prince, who is possessed of divine sanction. He is a virtuous young man with prodigious powers and an army. He who pulls a snake from its hole should be prepared for a deadly bite. Javanuy has seen the magnificent Bahraum-e Gur and heard his speech. Ask him if he considers this prince worthy of reclining on the throne of Iran.

The envoy, who was dazzled by Bahraum, proposed that Monzar and the prince accompany him to Iran as a friendly hunting party. This way, the Iranians would not be alarmed. The suggestion was accepted, and soon the crown prince and the vassal king of Yemen set up camp near the city of Jahrom. Although they had thirty thousand lance-wielding warriors and were ready for combat, Monzar was hopeful that a war would be unnecessary. Once the Iranians looked upon the face of the shining prince, all their objections would melt away.

Javanuy brought a delegation of Iranian courtiers to the Yemeni camp. Bahraum sat on a turquoise throne flanked by No'man and Monzar in a magnificent pavilion. The Iranians were bidden to make their case against the coronation of their crown prince. After all, he was the only direct descendant of the line of kings who had ruled Iran for centuries. They said they hated his tyrannical father and did not wish to see anyone from his progeny on the throne. The crown prince responded that opposing him was their right.* But on what grounds did they exclude him from the consultations? At the very least, he was a member of the Iranian nobility. They agreed that Bahraum had the right to participate in the succession process and was within his rights to nominate himself.

* This process demonstrates the role of the ruling aristocracy in choosing a king when succession was in question. See the Translator's Note.

As all agreed to the fairness of the procedure, a three-day period of deliberations commenced, during which they made a short list of one hundred candidates. Bahraum garnered most of the votes and secured a place at the top of the roster. The same results were obtained as the list was shortened to fifty, thirty, and finally, four. Once the chances of the crown prince improved, the nobility loudly voiced their objection to the kingship of a son of Yazdegerd. Why would they accede to the sovereignty of the scion of a violent and brutal king who had the limbs of thousands of people lopped off on a whim? To dramatize their point, they brought a group of the former king's maimed victims to the assembly.

Monzar advised the young prince to speak frankly with the Iranians. Bahraum stood tall in front of the assembly of noblemen and said: "You are right about my father; he was even worse than you described. I condemn the evil that he did. He made my own life a veritable hell as well. I was liberated from my house arrest at his palace only because of the intercession of the Roman ambassador Tinush. My father showed no kindness to me. Why else would I spend my entire adult life as a refugee at Monzar's court? I thank God, who granted me the wisdom to tread the path of righteousness. I ask for His help to restore whatever my father has wrecked. I have proven my manhood and am willing to demonstrate it again. Let us put the crown of the kings of Kay on the throne and tie a wild lion on a long leash on each side of it. Let us see who among the remaining four contenders for the royal office is brave enough to take the crown." They agreed that the ordeal would be a good way of choosing the rightful king of Iran, and that the crown prince had already demonstrated that he had the temperament and charisma of a king.

The next day all was prepared for the great contest. The lions were brought in by attendants and tied down on each side of the royal throne. Upon seeing the scene, Khosrow, the meek nobleman who had been appointed provisional king, withdrew from the contest, as did the other candidates. The court chamberlain addressed Bahraum. "There is a consensus that you are fit to be king. We do not have another contender for the office, and there is no need for this perilous ordeal."

"Do not worry for me. I absolve you of my blood if I fail to secure my prize," Bahraum responded. "But I am more than a match for these lions."

Having said this, he pulled his ox-headed mace from its holder and approached the lions. One of them tore its chain and attacked the intruder. Bahraum dispatched it with a blow of his mace. The second beast was killed with another mighty blow. The prince climbed the throne and placed the crown on his head. The first to congratulate him was the old prince Khosrow. Then the entire assembly came forward and saluted their new king. The coronation of Bahraum V occurred on the twenty-sixth day of December.

CHAPTER 21

The Onager Hunter:
Bahraum-e Gur

Gathering rainclouds covered the moon
Hail blasted the crops as a myriad of arrows from the sky
Heaven and the earth swirled in a typhoon.

I've nothing left at home, not even firewood,
Salt-cured meat, or barley until the next harvest.
The coming tithe is sure to ruin me for good.

But not if Hoya-e Qotayb gives me a chance*
And forgives my past debts and the tithe I owe
So, let me regale you with the Hunter King's romance.

On each of the first nine days of his rule, Bahraum-e Gur issued advice and moral guidance to the noblemen and knights of his court. On the tenth day, he charged Javanuy to issue a general amnesty for those who had agitated against him during his campaign to become king. Some of the more prominent noblemen who had opposed the crown prince took refuge with Monzar. He interceded on their behalf, and the king forgave them as well. Those who had been mistreated by Yazdegerd the Sinner were given reparations and domiciles in a new city that the king built for them. Monzar and his son No'man returned to Yemen laden with legendary riches. Goshasp the keeper of accounts and the high official Javanuy reported that ninety-three million dirhams were left in the treasury. This enabled Bahraum to forgive all the taxes and debts owed to the state. To dramatize this act of generosity, he ordered the public burning of all the account books related to people's financial obligations. He also sent donations to fire temples and distributed alms among the needy. Finally, the

* Hoya-e Qotayb was the Samanid tax collector in Tous. Besides repeatedly exempting Ferdowsi from taxes, he seems to have extended other help to the poet. He is thanked in the poem's conclusion as well.

king appointed his younger brother Narsi to the post of supreme commander of the army.

Thereafter Bahraum-e Gur's life was defined by adventures, not unlike those he once had as a young prince in Yemen. People of Iran loved to relate stories of his escapades. Some of the stories detailed his prowess in hunting and success in romance. Others described his penchant for traveling incognito to observe his subjects. These stories gave the foreign leaders the impression that the new king of Iran was a frivolous man, incapable of defending his borders, a reputation that would have dire consequences for the king later in his rule.

WRECKING A VILLAGE WITH BAD ADVICE*

One day, the king arrived at a lush village after a hot day of pursuing game. Residents came out to view his hunting party, but they failed to show proper etiquette. When nobody rushed forward to invite the king to dismount and rest, he murmured, "This is an ominous place and its residents are uncouth! May their homes become the haunt of beasts of prey. May tar, instead of water, run in their streams."

The court chamberlain Ruzbeh took it upon himself to cause Bahraum's curse to become a reality. Thus, he went to the public square and told the residents that the king was impressed by them and had decreed that everyone in the village were equal in his eyes. "Let every man, woman and child be a headman," he said. It didn't take long for this decree to cause strife in the village. In the ensuing brawls, the village headman was killed. Nobody stooped to everyday tasks like plowing the fields, tilling, or harvesting the crops. None cared to maintain the irrigation channels or take the sheep to pasture. Beasts of burden died of neglect, and personal bickering turned into a war of each against all. Soon, most of

* None of the stories of this chapter of *Shahnameh* have been cut in this abridgement. However, their order has changed and a classification (of the romantic adventures and tales of the generous and the miserly) has been introduced by the translator. In the original *Shahnameh* the following thirteen stories appear without any order.

the population abandoned the village, and the once prosperous hamlet became a ghostly ruin.

The following year the king passed by the same village, empty of people and partially overtaken by vegetation and wild animals. He was amazed at how quickly his curse had come to pass. He got off his horse and asked an old man what had caused such decay.

"This is all the work of that foolish chamberlain who traveled in your retinue," said the man. "He was the one who told us that we are all equals, that there was no inferior or superior among us. "

The king regretted his curse, and called Ruzbeh to come forth and commanded him to undo the damage. He kissed the ground and said the king's wish was his command. Then he went to the old man and appointed him headman to replace the last one who had been killed in the skirmishes of the previous year. He also told him to seek funds, beasts of burden, and seeds from the king's treasury to replace what had been lost. The new headman was also put in charge of collecting taxes once crops, animal products, and other goods were produced. Within three years, the village was rebuilt to its previous glory. On his third visit, the king was astonished by the village's quick recovery. He asked Ruzbeh for a full account of what had happened to wreck and revive the village. Upon hearing the whole story, he rewarded Ruzbeh with a bag of gold coins and said he was as wise as any king.

HOW THE PROHIBITION WAS LIFTED

There was a man named Kay-ruy who supplied the royal court with fresh flowers, apples, quinces, and pomegranates from the farms near the capital. After delivery one day, he noticed a basin filled to the brim with wine. He lifted the heavy basin and, toasting to the king's health, drank it to the dregs. He downed six more cups and boasted that he could easily ride home to his village despite being drunk.

Although he was famous for holding his wine, Kay-ruy felt sleepy on the way back, so he dismounted by a tree and passed out. He appeared so inert that ravens descended on him and plucked out his eyes. Those who had gone to look for Kay-ruy the next day found his lifeless and disfigured body by his horse. The gruesome affair so disgusted the king that he issued a decree banning wine. From that day forward, people stopped drinking because they feared incurring the king's wrath.

The prohibition had gone on for a year when a young cobbler married a beautiful girl from an affluent family. Unfortunately, the man could not perform his husbandly duties on his wedding night or any night thereafter. The cobbler's mother lost face because of her son's impotence. So to help him, she gave him a jug of wine that she had hidden away, saying: "A pickaxe made of felt cannot break the rock. Drink this wine and break that seal." The boy drank the wine and walked out in great spirits, confident that he would accomplish the task, and he did.

It just so happened that as the cobbler stepped out of his father-in-law's house, he came face to face with a wild lion that had just escaped the royal menagerie. Still giddy, the drunk cobbler jumped on the back of the lion as if it was a horse and grabbed on to its ears. The zookeeper who had gone chasing the lion was speechless when he saw the incredible spectacle of a man riding a wild lion. He ran back and related the story to the king.

"Such courage," the king declared, "cannot be expected from the son of a cobbler." He charged his courtiers to investigate who the real father of the cobbler was. But the investigations did not turn up evidence of high birth. Hearing of the inquiries, the cobbler's mother went to the king and revealed that the cause of her son's heroics was not noble lineage but wine. The king laughed with delight and lifted the prohibition. "Drink enough to be able to mount a lion but not so much that blackbirds pluck out your eyes," he declared.

HOW A KING'S THOUGHTS AFFECT THE WORLD

After slaying a fearsome dragon one night, the king found himself outside the closed gates of a nearby castle. He had no choice but to ride along the road until he reached a small hamlet. He stopped and asked the farmer's wife if he could stay there for the night. Modestly covering her face from the stranger, the woman invited the exalted guest to treat her humble abode as his own. Then she took the rein of Bahraum's horse, woke her husband, and told him to tend the stranger's horse.

"Get up and look sharp," she ordered. "Spread the straw mat and put bread, watercress, and vinegar on the spread. Then kill the lamb so I can prepare dinner for our noble guest."

The husband grumbled: "Why would you invite guests if you don't have salted meats, and firewood? Suppose we killed the lamb and fed your guest. What would become of us when we are hungry later in the season?"

The farmer's wife didn't argue with her husband. Suffice it to say that the mat was spread, and the lamb was killed. The fare included porridge of well-cooked meat and cereal grains. The grilled lamb was garnished with fragrant herbs and eggs. Then the host brought out a gourd of wine and a plate of oleanders. When Bahraum had eaten and drunk his share, he said:

"Tell me, my gentlewoman, a story from the olden days to pass the time as I drink your good wine. And if you don't know such stories, tell me what you think of the king that rules our country."

"He is a good man, you know, everything else being equal," she said. "But I have to say that I see some of his minions who pass through this village. They abuse us. One accuses a poor peasant of petty theft and gets him into trouble over a few coins, and another dishonors an innocent woman with inappropriate language and brings shame upon her. We suffer at the hands of these men who do what they wish in the name of the king."

Bahraum was offended. He thought to himself, *No good deed goes unpunished. This is the thanks I get for spreading justice and providing safety for these ingrates. I will be harsh with them for a while so that they appreciate the value of what they have.*

When Bahraum went to bed he could still hear the old couple bicker.

"Get up, old man, and soak the grains and beans that I've put in the cauldron for tomorrow. I will milk the cow while you do that."

But as she squeezed the cow's teat, she gave a little cry. "The cow has no milk. No doubt the king is planning to do something evil."

Her husband brushed her off. "What are you talking about, woman? Why would you cast bad omens and accuse the king of injustice?"

"I am not speaking in vain. It is well known that when a king turns away from justice and allows inequity to prevail, the moon loses its luster. Crops stop growing, and milk dries up. Eggs rot under hens, musk dries in the navel of the wild deer, and pastures desiccate and die. Wolves devour people upon the plain. Soft hearts turn to flint, and adultery and usury abound. Darkness descends on everything, and evil consumes the world."

Bahraum was shaken by what he heard. He repented from his previous determination to be harsh with people and pledged: "May this kingship not endure one day if I become a cruel king."

As he said this prayer, the old woman squeezed the teat of the cow to see if it had filled with milk, and indeed it had. "In the name of the God of the prophet Zarathustra who changed the heart of a willful man. The king has repented, and now he intends to be just. Look at the flow of the milk into the basin! Be cheerful, for God is smiling upon us again."

The following day, the couple brought their guest a bowl of rice pudding. In return for their hospitality, Bahraum gave them his jewel-encrusted whip and recommended they hang it from the apple tree in front of their house. The couple watched in amazement as a division of the army stopped, dismounted, and genuflected themselves before the whip.

They realized that the whip belonged to the king. They went to their guest with great trepidation to apologize for their lapses. Bahraum laughed and rewarded them with the gift of the entire village. They could end their hard life of farming. Instead they were told to set up a hostel and offer hospitality to strangers passing through.

TALES OF THE GENEROUS AND THE MISERLY

"Lonbak and Barauhaum"

Lonbak was a water carrier with a reputation for extreme generosity. He sold water in the market and would invite a guest to share his evening meal with whatever funds he had earned that day. To examine the extent of the day-laborer's liberality, the king sent a secret order to his agents to warn the people in the market against doing business with the water carrier. Thus, Lonbak had earned nothing when Bahraum appeared at his door pretending to be a king's servant who had lagged behind the hunting party. The poor water carrier welcomed him with open arms. "Please honor my humble hut by entering," he said. "I wish you were here with your friends in the hunting party, for that would bring me even greater pleasure."

Lonbak treated the stranger to a lavish dinner followed by a game of chess. In the morning, he begged Bahraum to extend his stay to three days, and he accepted. Lonbak sold his robes and even his cups and water-skin to buy food. After three days, with nothing left to sell, he was still begging his guest to stay." Bahraum said: "The three days I've spent at your house were dearer to me than any I spent at the palaces of kings. Rest assured that one day you shall be rewarded for your hospitality."

After saying goodbye to Lonbak, the king set off to hunt lions. An old man approached the hunting party and told the king about a wealthy, but miserly Jewish merchant named Barauhaum. Despite his legendary wealth, however, the man was notoriously stingy. As the night approached, the king sent his valet to Barauhaum with this message: "My master is one of the king's huntsmen, and he has fallen behind the retinue. Could he spend the night at your house?" The merchant sent word flatly refusing the request and professing that he was a penniless old man who could not afford to host anyone. But Bahraum insisted. The merchant finally relented and let him come but only on the condition that he make no demands for hospitality.

That night Barauhaum provided no bedding for the disguised king, so he slept reclining on his saddle and its blanket. The host ate and drank without inviting his guest to share the meal. To justify his unseemly behavior, he said: "Such is the wisdom of the ancients: He who has, eats, and he who has not, looks on." He sipped his wine. "The ancients have said that the wealthy are protected by a chainmail of coins. But the poor suffer from the slings and arrows of thirst and hunger."

In the morning, Barauhaum insisted that his guest clean after his horse before leaving. Bahraum-e Gur, who was hungry and tired, offered to leave some money for another man to clean up the mess, but the demanding host would not allow it. The king had to wrap the horse dung in his silken kerchief and carry it out himself.

The next day the king sent for Lonbak and Barauhaum and sat in judgment. To Barauhaum he said:

"Last night you stated he who has, eats, and he who has not, looks on. I have measured your property. Twelve hundred camels could hardly carry it. I am confiscating your wealth. It will be distributed among the poor. The water carrier Lonbak will received ten camels' worth of it. I have left you four dinars to start a new business. The wisdom of the ancients still applies. I think now it's your turn to look on as Lonbak eats."

"Farshidvard and the Milkvetch Peddler"

On his way home after a successful hunt, Bahraum encountered a man named Farshidvard, who lived in a grimy shack. The king asked him if he could stay there for the night. The man moaned that he could not provide even the most rudimentary hospitality—including a drink of water. "Why would anyone want to linger in my dirty hut," he asked, in self-pity. Unable to endure the pathetic man's destitution, the king left.

Later that day, Bahraum came across a man named Delaraum digging milkvetch shrubs that he sold as fuel. He asked the laborer who the most prominent man in the village was. Delaraum said: "Surely it must be Farshidvard who owns a hundred thousand sheep and many horses and camels. He's extremely wealthy but lives alone like a beggar. His lowliest shepherd boils meat in milk for dinner while he survives on millet bread smeared with cheese."

The king deputized Delaraum and one of his lieutenants to assess Farshidvard's total worth. Countless sheep, oxen, cows, and all kinds of animal products stored in underground silos were discovered. But that was still just a fraction of the hoarder's possessions. Bahraum ordered all the property to be redistributed among the poor. Farshidvard was allowed to keep only his hidden underground treasures. After all, he had not stolen from anyone. His sin was being ungrateful to God and ungenerous toward himself and others.

"The Miserly Merchant and His Valet"

After spending a week at the hunting grounds, Bahraum was afflicted with a stomachache. Thus, he decided to return to his palace and seek medical attention. At a nearby town, he sojourned at a rich but stingy merchant's house. The merchant invited the tired hunter to stay. Bahraum, who needed to treat his stomachache, gave the merchant money and asked him to bring him wine and prepare almonds and aged cheese to be served with his dinner of chicken and bread. The merchant had almonds but did not provide them to his guest, nor did he bother to procure cheese and wine. He gave some of the money he had received to his valet to buy chicken and bread and told the king he should be happy with what he had.

The king was offended by the vulgarity of his host and went to bed without touching his food. Obviously, he thought, the crafty merchant had given the servant a fraction of the money to buy the chicken. The suspicion was confirmed when he overheard the merchant berate his valet for paying too much for the chicken. If he paid less for the fowl, the merchant quibbled, he could save a quarter of a coin to buy some cheese. The servant felt that such trifles were not worth discussing and said he could take the price of the chicken off his salary.

In the morning, the king rubbed down his horse and saddled it. Before leaving, he told the miserly merchant: "Greed is your downfall. Last night you sold me out for a quarter of a coin and then blamed your servant for your failure of hospitality."

The merchant's valet took pity on the guest who was unwell, and invited him to his house. The king accepted the invitation and the poor servant proved far more generous than his rich master. He treated his guest to cheese and almonds in warm bread served with plenty of eggs and wine. He also served grilled lamb and other dishes with ingredients like sugar, saffron, and rosewater.

The next time the king ascended his throne he summoned the merchant and his servant, and rewarded the servant with a bag of gold coins and said to the merchant: "From now on, you will treat your servant as your master. You will give him sixty gold coins every month so he can arrange a feast and invite guests to eat and be merry at your expense."

"Discovering the Hidden Treasure of Jamshid"

One day a farmer carrying his shovel burst into Bahraum's hunting lodge and insisted on speaking to the king in private. The farmer told Bahraum about a curious cavity he had discovered while irrigating his crops. He had excavated the hole with his shovel to discover several structures that bore the name of the legendary King Jamshid. They were full of coins and various golden objects, like statues of bulls, lions, peacocks, and pheasants studded with jewels. The king went to the buried mansions but did not touch a penny of the treasure. Instead, he distributed it among the orphans, widows, and the destitute of the nation. He explained that the only wealth he was interested in was what he had earned on his fast horse and by the edge of his sharp sword. "Possessiveness," he averred, "is the attribute of shallow souls. The world is transitory, and no one can carry wealth through the gates of death."

Bahraum-e Gur looked down on greedy and possessive souls and admired people who worked for a living and were generous with what they earned.

THE AMOROUS ADVENTURES OF THE HUNTER KING

Bahraum-e Gur was famous among kings for his erotic conquests. He had hundreds of women in his seraglio, but was always looking for more. Those around him did not look favorably on this, but since he was the king, he did what he wanted.

"The Dancers at the Mill"

One day, while on one of his incognito jaunts to the countryside, the king arrived at a mill. He was mesmerized by four beautiful girls singing and dancing to a song praising their Hunter King. When the miller returned carrying the carcass of a game, the king asked him about the dancers at his establishment. He confided to the noble stranger that they were his chaste daughters. But the maids had no prospects of marriage due to his penury. Bahraum had the perfect solution to his problem: the miller could send them to the king's seraglio to be his consorts. The miller kissed the ground and complied. "You don't have to be concerned with these four anymore," the king said, smiling. "But please, don't have any more girls if you cannot afford to properly marry them off!"

"The Lost Falcon"

Once, the king lost his falcon and went off to find it. As his search radius expanded, he came across a wealthy farmer named Borzin, who had seen the bird perched on a nearby walnut tree and led Bahraum to it. The bird flew to his master, and the farmer invited the king to a feast where his three beautiful daughters played the harp, danced, and sang to celebrate this success. Impressed by their looks and talents, Bahraum asked for their hands in marriage, and Borzin was honored to accept the noble suitor's proposal. He offered rich dowries for them, but the king refused. Soon the freshly acquired brides were in their golden litters heading toward their well-furnished chambers in the king's seraglio.

"Mauhyar the Jewel Merchant"

After a day of spectacular feats at the royal hunting grounds, the king saw a shepherd leading a large flock. He wondered why anyone would risk bringing sheep to a place full of predators. The shepherd said that he could protect his herd, and besides, the sheep belonged to a wealthy jewel merchant named Mauhyar who was not overly concerned about occasional losses. He only cared about his beautiful harp-playing daughter, on whom he doted. Upon hearing this story, the king asked for directions to the jewel merchant's house. Then he bathed, changed, and rode away, leaving his retinue behind. The royal chamberlain Ruzbeh was most chagrined, not because the king already had nine hundred thirty women in his seraglio, but because he was dissipating his vital energy on amorous excess. The chamberlain believed that intercourse should be conducted no more than once a month. In his opinion sex was for procreation, not recreation.

Soon Bahraum was drinking wine with Mauhyar to the accompaniment of his daughter's strings. Her name was Aurezu. The king let it slip that he wished to take the lovely prodigy as his wife that night. The old merchant was not sure this was a good idea, as inebriated men often regret their decisions upon sobriety. The king insisted, and Mauhyar consulted his daughter about the matter. The attraction was mutual. That night the lovestruck couple consummated their marriage, and, in the morning, the new royal bride set off with great fanfare toward the king's palace.

THE KHAGAN OF CHINA INVADES

When the king's reputation as a philanderer reached the khagan of China, he concluded that Iran lacked proper leadership and that time was ripe for him to invade his western neighbor. There were also rumors that Rome was amassing troops in preparation for war. Many at the Iranian court openly criticized the king for being an imprudent man who spent the nation's wealth on his pleasure palaces and hunting excursions.

The king responded that he was indeed a capable and effective leader and would, with God's help, repel all enemies and keep the borders safe. But he was tightlipped about his plans. Bahraum preferred to conduct the defense of his border with discretion and subterfuge. He appointed his brother Narsi as regent, selected an elite cavalry force of six thousand, and hastily departed Ctesiphon for the high temple of Azar-goshasp in northwestern Iran.

The leaders of this elite force were legendary in their spirit, prowess, and love of the land. They consisted of nine knights: Gostahm, the minister to the king, Piruz, the son of the previous king Bahraum III, Mehr-Piruz, the son of Bondad, Mehr-borzin, the son of Khorrad, Khazarvaun, the son of Roham, Qauran, the son of Borz-mehr, Daud-borzin the Pugnacious, Daud-borzin of the Rueful Countenance, and the Armenian knight, Andian. The kings of Gilan and Rey also joined the Hunter King's strike force.

Bahraum was aware of the rumors that he was an inept king. But rather than fighting those allegations, he seemed to play up to them. As he left the capital heading northwest rather than east where the enemy was, rumor spread that he had absconded. Even the king's brother Narsi didn't seem interested in defending his brother against the accusation of cowardice.

Confirmed reports that the king of Iran had fled reached the khagan of China. This gave him added confidence in his invasion. Some Iranian noblemen who thought their worst fears had been realized wrote a letter to the khagan asking for terms of peace. They pledged to pay a lavish tribute to keep the invaders out. An Iranian cleric by the name of Homauy took this offer to the enemy camp. The khagan was happy to have subdued Iran without a fight and said he would come to the border to await the swift arrival of the promised tribute. Thus, the khagan brought his army to the city of Merv and gave them a holiday while abandoning himself to merrymaking at the Koshmahin hunting grounds.

Bahraum, monitoring the situation through his spies, knew that the khagan had let his guard down and planned his attack accordingly. His elite force moved with lightning speed as they wore minimal armor and carried no provisions. From the high temple of Azar-goshasp, they took the backroads, past the northern towns of Ardebil, Amol, Gorgan, and Nesa, to arrive at the vicinity of Merv across the eastern border of Iran. The king gave his forces one day of rest and then they crept toward the hunting grounds of Koshmahin.

The khagan's forces were utterly unprepared for the predawn attack. Most of them were massacred where they stood. The khagan and three hundred notables were taken into captivity. The king pursued those who escaped for sixty miles and returned in triumph.

Chasing his victory in Merv, Bahraum occupied the city of Balkh and the area formerly called Touran that was taken over by Turkic raiders from the eastern expanses of the Oxus River. The rebellious tribes surrendered and pledged to pay tribute and reparations. The king built a turret made of rocks and plaster to mark the border of Iran on the eastern side of the Oxus. Then he appointed one of his knights, Shamr, as the king of the Touranian plains, and returned to Iran.

Having inflicted crushing defeats on the Chinese and Turkic

insurgents, the king wrote to Narsi and the noblemen and knights of Iran, many of whom had assumed Bahraum was escaping when he left Ctesiphon. Regretting their shameful conduct, those who had approached the khagan for terms begged Narsi to intercede on their behalf. The king forgave all.

The war booty amounted to eleven hundred and sixty cowhides filled with gold coins. Bahraum sent generous donations to fire temples and pavilions where the holidays of Sadeh and Mehregan were celebrated. The jewels recovered from the khagan's crown were hung on the walls of the fire temples. The remainder of the windfall was spent on repairing bridges all over Iran, supporting widows, orphans, the disabled, the indigent old, people of high birth who had been reduced to penury, and the travelers who had fallen on hard times but were loath to beg.

Having proven his mettle in battle, the king returned to the olden capital of Ctesiphon. Narsi led a procession of the knights, noblemen, and courtiers who humbled themselves in front of the king and paid their obeisance. Bahraum announced a tax break for seven years, as his coffers were full of plunder from the wars he had won. Narsi received the governorship of the prosperous region of Khorausan, with the advice to be humble and serve the people.

"I give you this realm," said the king to his brother. "Make it prosper. Conquer the hearts of its people on my behalf. Be just, for the unjust will end up like a naked man exposed to the cold winds of autumn. Remember the fate of our father, Yazdegerd the Sinner, who pursued the path of pride and tyranny."

It was known that the Romans had also contemplated an attack on Iran. But they had not followed through. Now that the malicious rumors about Bahraum were proven false, they sent a platonic philosopher to restore friendly relations with their victorious neighbor. Bahraum honored the emissary and admitted him to the royal court with fanfare. The envoy said he had come to learn and exchange views on worldly affairs and ask questions about the meaning of life. A conference was arranged between him and Ruzbeh, the chamberlain. The Roman philosopher was impressed with the answers he received about physics and metaphysics. He congratulated Bahraum for having such learned advisors and on behalf of Rome pledged a considerable annual tribute to be paid to the Iranian king.

With the end of the war, Bahraum had time to reflect on the principles of efficacious kingship. He shared his thoughts with his knights and noblemen.

"Let us consider what led such kings as Jamshid and Kay-Kavous astray, and what caused my father, Yazdegerd, to lose his way," he said. "Their glory has vanished, but their evil reputation remains. Death is our common destiny regardless of whether we are Arabs, Romans, or Persians. Peasants, landlords, rulers, and the ruled all die. Where are the heroes and heroines of the past? They are all gone and forgotten.

"After these wars, enough has flushed into my coffers to enable me to be generous. I shall compensate a poor man who has been robbed of his bedspread with a length of Roman brocade. I will replace the stolen sheep of a poor husbandman with a horse. Injured soldiers will receive a generous pension so that their children will not suffer the pangs of poverty.

"Don't despise the oxen who have worked for you their entire lives, and don't slaughter them when they have grown old.

"Honor orphans.

"Don't tax the poor to enrich the wealthy—as did my father. I hope to compensate for the evil that he has wrought.

"Let the young enjoy their lives instead of hindering them. Don't break their hearts. When you get old, refrain from indulging in pleasures and prepare for the everlasting peace of the hereafter."

THE KING'S INDIAN ADVENTURE

The world was pacified, and every king paid tribute to Iran, with only one exception. King Shangol of India did not merely refuse to pay tribute. He had levied taxes on the Indian region of Sind and China. Bahraum dictated a letter to him:

> May God be generous in endowing wisdom to people, especially the kings. You fail to appreciate your station and transgress

> your bounds. Your ancestors were vassals of our kings, but you are rebellious. Look at the fate of the khagan of China, for that is what awaits you, should you insist on your intransigence. Honor my envoy who brings this letter. You have two choices: Pay tribute or prepare for war.

But Bahraum did not send an envoy. Instead, he picked thirty elite equestrians and rode to India himself, pretending to be his own envoy. He wished to personally assess the character of Shangol and the strength of his forces.

When he arrived in India, Bahraum was impressed by the royal palace's luxury and well-armed guards. He was ushered in and treated with respect due an ambassador of a great king. But Shangol frowned when the ambassador's message was recited in court.

"Your king is too proud, as is his envoy," he said. "If killing ambassadors were allowed, you would lose your head for this insolence. I am an eagle, and other kings are but a flock of storks. I am an ocean, and the rest are lower than dirt. Eighty kings pay tribute to me from the Indian lands of Kannauj and Sind to the lands of the Slavs and the Romans. My consort is the daughter of the Chinese emperor, the son of heaven. She has borne me a courageous son who is tougher than a mountain. Iran has not dreamed of dominating us since the kings Kay-Qobaud and Kay-Kavous."

"It is not proper for a king to engage in hyperbole," Bahraum retorted with indignation. "My king challenges you to one of two things: a war of wits between your wise men and ours or a contest of martial prowess between one hundred of your soldiers and one of ours. We will exempt you from all taxes and tributes if you win in either contest."

"Let us be reasonable," said Shangol. "Why don't you rest instead of uttering such absurdities? We will continue this discussion tomorrow."

A luxurious pavilion was prepared for the ambassador's rest, and as the sun rose to its apogee the next day, he was called to lunch with the king. After the food was served, they sipped wine and enjoyed the spectacle of wrestling. Bahraum drained his crystal chalice and asked permission to compete. Shangol laughed. "Rise and suit up," he said. "And don't hesitate to kill my champions if you can bring them down."

The ambassador entered the arena, lifted his opponents off the ground, and slammed them down with such force that one could hear their bones crack. Impressed, the king drank to his health and offered him higher seating in the hall.

The next day Shangol invited the ambassador to join him in the polo arena. Then a shooting contest was arranged. The gifted ambassador shone brightly in these contests, which made Shangol suspicious. Was this a mere envoy or a member of the royal family? Was he perhaps the king's brother? The envoy laughed at these speculations. He said his name was Borzuy, and he was a simple servant of the king without a drop of royal blood. "At any rate," said King Shangol, "Whoever you are, don't think I will let you leave my court so easily. Drink and let us have a good time."

King Shangol was determined to seduce the envoy to change alliances and stay in India as the governor of Kannauj, a magnificent city in northern India ruled by Shangol. Attracting him would be a significant boon for the Indian military, while his return to Iran would constitute a present danger in case a war broke out between the two countries.

The ambassador proved impervious to Shangol's temptations and insisted that he wanted to return home. The king frowned and denied his request for departure. He was afraid of sending back such a powerful champion to Iran in case the two had to fight a war. He would rather get rid of him by sending him on a number of dangerous labors. This way, he would be killed without implicating Shangol.

The first labor was to kill a rogue rhinoceros, who was the cause of much dread. The brave ambassador accepted the mission and asked for a scout to show him and his companions the way. The guide took Bahraum and his men to the edge of the thicket where the rhinoceros lived. Upon seeing the beast, his companions grew apprehensive and asked their leader to return without fighting. They even concocted an excuse for Bahraum so he would not lose face. All he needed to say to Shangol was that he was not authorized to perform feats of valor without his king's permission. But Bahraum was fatalistic: if his fate was to die in battle with a wild rhino, no one could stop it. If not, he would win glory and add the prodigious victim to his long list of trophies.

Then he took out a sheaf of arrows from his quiver and sent a volley of deadly shafts that deeply penetrated the hide of the beast, causing him to collapse. Unsheathing his hunting knife, Bahraum cut off the monster's head, and called for oxen to carry it to the royal court. All those who saw the evidence of the hunt were amazed. The king was glad that his countryside was safe. But he was not entirely pleased that the remarkable Iranian had survived his first trial.

The next labor was to slay a dragon. Shangol assured the ambassador that he would give him leave to go back to Iran if he completed this labor. Bahraum readily accepted the challenge, once more defying his companions. He started with a volley of his unerring arrows again and did not relent until the creature fell. Then he drew his sword and beheaded it.

While pretending to be pleased, King Shangol felt threatened by this victory. He contemplated having Bahraum assassinated. But his advisers offered that such a deed would be shameful as well as dangerous, as it would lead to an Iranian invasion. The king slept on the matter, and by morning, he had developed a new plan.

Shangol called the ambassador to a private audience. "You have achieved great victories," he told him. "But I advise you against pride. I will give you one of my daughters in marriage. Stay with me for a while and accept a high office at my court."

Bahraum pondered this proposal: On the one hand, there was no shame for the king of Iran to marry a princess of India. On the other, this would forestall his return. In the end, he decided in favor of the proposal. "I will be honored to marry one of your daughters. You choose the one you consider to best match for me."

The king called his three daughters and allowed Bahraum to choose for himself. He selected Sepinud, whose beauty illuminated the room like a candle. She was exceedingly alluring but also coy. King Shangol gave her the keys to one of the treasure houses as a dowry. The wedding festivities lasted a week.

The interest of the emperor of China was piqued when he heard that King Shangol had given his daughter as wife to an Iranian ambassador. Thus, he sent a letter to Bahraum:

> This is a missive from the world-dominating Emperor of China to the Ambassador of Iran to India. It has come to our attention that you have slain a rhinoceros and a dragon and married King Shangol's daughter. I hereby invite you to come to China and spend time with us. I have no quarrel with the king of Iran. So, your travel should not displease your king. Nor would I hinder you should you wish to return. I promise that when you leave China, it will be with parting gifts of such value that you cannot imagine.

Bahraum-e Gur, disguised as his own ambassador, sent back his response:

> It does not behoove you to call yourself the king of the world when King Bahraum is on the throne, for the title is his. Whatever I have achieved in India is due to the fortune of my king and the fact that Iranians possess all skills and are endowed with enough courage to dismiss a rogue rhinoceros as an unworthy opponent. I thank God who has made me sufficient unto myself. I do not covet the riches of China that you so generously offer.

As the love between the young couple blossomed, and their trust deepened, he revealed that he was planning to escape to Iran. Sepinud said she would accompany him wherever he went.

The best among the wives is the beguiling,
Compliant one who feeds her husband
And caresses him while smiling.

The princess helped plan their escape. They could make a run to the border during a festival that would be held for five days at the temple of the idols, which was a twenty days' walk away from the capital city. Sepinud's mother could be trusted to find an excuse for their absence by telling the king that their son-in-law was indisposed because of illness. After the king's departure, the couple and their thirty companions could set off for Iran without alerting anyone.

The plan was implemented, and the refugees galloped to the border with great speed. But as fast as they were, Shangol was faster. Once informed, he left the festivities and gave chase with his troops, reaching the couple by the river's edge as they were boarding a ship.

"You ungrateful daughter!" he exclaimed. "How dare you abandon me? You have tasted my kindness all your life. Now you will feel the sting of my javelin."

Bahraum stepped in. "Why have you come here to challenge me? Haven't you seen my prowess in battle? Don't you know that I am equal to one hundred thousand of your soldiers, even without the assistance of my thirty companions?"

"I treated you as a son," said Shangol. "But you have betrayed me. Is this how an Iranian repays a good deed? It is true what they say about nursing a lion cub. Once it grows up, it will devour his master."

Bahraum was no longer willing to be addressed as an underling. He chose that moment to reveal his identity. "Don't dare to take that tone with me. I am not some ordinary man to be obliged to a king. I am Bahraum-e Gur, the king of Iran and the commander of its vast armies. I have done you honor to marry your daughter, whom I will love and honor as long as I live. I will also keep faith with you as my father-in-law. All of your taxes and tributes will be forgiven as your daughter is now the queen of Iran."

The sudden revelation changed everything. Shangol rode into the shoals and embraced Bahraum. He apologized for his behavior and called for a feast to celebrate their reconciliation. Then, he bid farewell to his daughter and son-in-law and returned to his throne.

Iranians welcomed Bahraum-e Gur back to his palace. The king's brother Narsi and his crown prince Yazdegerd joined the chief of the magi to lead the procession of the knights and noblemen who had come to welcome their king.

After a while, Shangol came to visit his daughter in the land where she had become a queen. Eight vassal kings accompanied the exalted king of India on this visit. Bahraum welcomed his royal father-in-law at the Nahrawan canal. The two kings embraced and entered the gates of Ctesiphon hand in hand. The entire capital had been decorated for the visit of the king of India. At the palace a table that was longer than the throw of an arrow was set to accommodate Shangol and his retinue. The fare included delicious dishes of fowl and lamb, and wine was served to the accompaniment of musical performances. Shangol was dazzled by the opulence, and asked Bahraum for a private visit with his daughter.

Upon receiving permission, Shangol went to Sepinud's chambers and beheld her reclining on an ivory throne wearing a golden crown. Rows of ladies in waiting attended her. He kissed her head, presented her with jewels, crowns, and priceless garments and said: "My dear Sepinud, you have escaped the temple of idols for this veritable paradise."

The next day the two kings went to the royal hunting grounds to amuse themselves. Shangol returned to his daughter's quarters and wrote his will and testament in both Indian and Persian script, advising his realm to remain loyal to the king of Iran and his queen Sepinud. After two months, Shangol left Iran for India, followed by a train of camels that carried the parting gifts of the Iranian king. Bahraum went along for three milestones and provided all the necessary provisions and feed for the elephants, camels, and horses of King Shangol's caravan.

Once Shangol had departed, Bahraum asked astrologers and soothsayers to determine how long he would rule. They told him that he would rule for three times twenty years and leave the world sometime in the fourth period. The king determined that the first period was for enjoying himself and the second for spreading justice and enriching the world with his generosity. He would set aside the third period for meditation and religious practices, preparing to leave the world.

Bahraum forgave all taxes for the remainder of his rule, as he still had sufficient funds in the treasury. People stopped working as hard as they had because taxes were forgiven. But as it turned out, living without work did not agree with the mental state of the people. Young men became indolent and turned to vagrancy and agitation. So, the king reinstituted the daily routine of mandatory work for the young people. They were required to till the land and drive the oxen for a living. The idle were punished and even hanged. Soon, the deviant behavior ceased.

To ensure everything was functioning in Iran, the king sent his emissaries to see whether there were any grievances in the provinces. What he heard made him laugh. The poor complained that, unlike the rich, they could not afford to hire musicians to perform at their drinking parties. The king agreed that it was not right to drink wine without musical accompaniment. To remedy this, he wrote his father-in-law to send a cast of musicians and dancers that would come to be known as the Luries.*

When they arrived, the king provided them with seeds, donkeys, and oxen to make a living so they could entertain the masses for free. But they proved unwilling to become farmers and wasted the money they had been given. Thereafter the Luries roamed the land with their dogs and quails and worked odd jobs, playing music, dancing, and occasionally resorting to some less honest means of survival.

At Bahraum's sixty-third regnal year, the treasurer informed him that national coffers were empty and suggested that it was time to tax the people. But the king refused to issue the requisite orders as he knew that he was past the sixty-year period the astrologers had determined for his rule. His time to leave this life was nigh.

After the treasurer left, the king went to his bedchamber, his head swimming with the thoughts of his impending demise. The next day he called an audience and formally endowed the crown prince Yazdegerd II with the royal crown, torque, and bracelet. Then he engaged in private prayers and remained in seclusion until the sun dipped below the horizon.

* The group known in Europe as the Gypsies.

The king went to sleep that night but did not wake from his slumber. As the next day wore on, the chamberlain asked the crown prince to inquire about the cause of the king's delay. He went to his father's bedchamber and found his cold body.

I've glorified this king as he was noble,
Just, liberal, humane and kindhearted.
He lived a praiseworthy life and he died well.

CHAPTER 22

The Hephthalite Intrigue: Yazdegerd II to Qobaud

Yazdegerd II wore the crown and greeted
His knights with the sage advice to treat others
In the manner that they wished to be treated.

YAZDEGERD AND PIRUZ

Unlike his grandfather and namesake, Yazdegerd II was a just, amiable, and competent king who ruled the land in justice and peace for eighteen years. But his last decree on his deathbed was controversial. He passed over his crown prince Piruz to name his middle son Hormazd as his successor. "My crown prince is outstanding in every respect," he said, "but he tends to be impetuous. Hormazd outshines him in prudence. He will make a better king."

Piruz flew into a rage at the loss of his birthright. In great agitation, he fled the capital for the kingdom of the Hephthalites on the eastern border of Iran. Eager to insinuate himself into Iranian politics, the new chief of the Hephthalites lent thirty thousand warriors to the disinherited crown prince. This army, whose galloping horses rose enough dust to darken the sublunar sphere, fought many battles against Hormazd's army. Piruz led his borrowed Hephthalite army to victory and took Hormazd captive. But fratricide was avoided. The victorious prince embraced his brother and overlooked his royal ambitions. Hormazd renounced his right to the throne and thereafter lived as a loyal subject of his elder brother.

EASTERN EXPANSION

On the day of his formal coronation, Piruz declared that he would restore the social hierarchy of superiors and inferiors that had crumbled over time. He also pledged to reward the virtues of courage, good judgment, and humility.

All appeared to go well, but a devastating drought descended on Iran only a year after his coronation. The king responded by suspending all taxes and tributes. By the fourth year of the drought, hunger was endemic. The king threw open the state granaries and distributed grain among the needy. He made hoarding and food profiteering capital crimes. A day of prayer for rain was announced as well. The drought continued through the eighth year and then the skies opened in the month of March, and the parched earth was saturated with blessings from the heavens. Redolent gardens were speckled with rosebuds and rainbows adorned in the sky. To celebrate the end of the hard times, the king established two new Iranian cities: Piruz-Raum, also known as Rey, and Bauzan-Piruz, later known as Ardebil.

It appeared that things were returning to normal. But the national tranquility was once more disturbed by Piruz's decision to expand Iran's eastern frontiers. During his last campaign, Bahraum-e Gur had built a turret of rocks and plaster to mark the border of Iran at the east shore of the river Oxus in Central Asia. Neither Iranians nor any of the Turkic and Chinese tribes of Touran dreamed of advancing beyond the turret. But King Piruz wanted to push the border of Iran all the way back to the river Barak that marked the border between India and China, the distance of about two months' ride to the east.

Thus, he gathered an army and set off to the eastern border. Hormazd was given the command of the vanguard, and the crown prince Qobaud was appointed to command the rearguard.

The king's youngest brother Balaush was to remain at the capital as regent. As he was too young to run the country's daily affairs, Sufrai, a prominent knight from Shiraz, was engaged to assist him. He was a worthy warrior who had governed the eastern regions of Zabul, Kabul, Bost, and Qaznein.

King Piruz left Ctesiphon at the head of his army. Upon crossing the Oxus, King Bahraum's turret came into view. All knew that the exalted Bahraum V had meant for all sides to respect his marker. Piruz was scheming to honor the letter, but not the spirit of that ruling. He ordered the turret to be dug up and carried ahead of his armies to be set down at the shores of the river Barak.

"Let no one say that I have violated the turret rule," said Piruz. "As I move, it is still ahead of me, carried away to be set down in its proper location. We will tell the Hephthalites that their border is at the shores of the river Barak, and that's what King Bahraum intended. Their chieftain might object to this, but that would be a costly mistake."

Piruz's crossing of the Oxus and his violation of King Bahraum's borders incensed the new Hephthalite chief, Khosh-navauz. He dispatched an angry letter of protest to the Iranian king:

> It is shocking when a young king tramples on the borders established by his royal grandfather. Now that you have torn up our border agreement, I am justified to unsheathe my sword and defend my people.

The messenger who brought the letter also carried many gifts to signify the respect of the Hephthalite kingdom for the Iranian king, notwithstanding his hostile actions. Piruz shot back: "Go tell that upstart chief that Bahraum-e Gur gave you the land up to the shores of the Barak, not the Oxus. I have come to set things right, and I will wipe your shadow off this land if you stand in my way."

Prepared for the inevitable confrontation, Khosh-navauz advanced with a great host. He suffered a lance bearer to carry aloft the parchment on which King Bahraum V had marked the eastern bank of the river Oxus as the border of Iran. He tried one more time to reason with Piruz by sending the following letter:

> I have brought forth the treaty that His Majesty King Bahraum granted to my grandfather. Disrespecting this sacred document will not redound to your glory. Nor can my defensive war against your invasion be considered a rebellion. My cause is just. Consider this my last attempt to reach an amicable resolution with you.

Piruz growled at the envoy bearing this message. "Tell that old man to stop his jabbering and go back to his old capital of Chauch on the shore of the Jaxartes River. I have not come all this way to enter into border negotiation with the likes of him. There will be hell to pay, should he take a single step from the Jaxartes toward the Oxus."

The emissary went back and reported to the Hephthalite chief. "This king is hell-bent on war. He has no fear of God. Nor does he appear to have wise mentors to enjoin him to act justly."

Khosh-navauz retired to his private chamber and said a prayer as he prepared for the final confrontation. "Oh, just Lord, who created the sun and the earth! You know that the unfair Piruz is in no way superior to the righteous Bahraum-e Gur. He is rash in speech and pugnacious in conduct. Help me rid the earth from this abomination of a king."

Khosh-navauz ordered his men to dig a trench in front of his army as deep as the length of a lasso and ninety feet wide. He covered the pit with thin reeds, straw, shrubs, and dirt until it was hidden under the false surface. Battle commenced with the beating of war drums from both sides. Khosh-navauz cautiously brought his army to the edge of the concealed ditch and watched as the Iranian king and his top brass blithely galloped into his trench. Piruz, Hormazd, and three other princes were killed when they fell on the sharp blades and sticks planted at the bottom. Only the crown prince Qobaud and Ardishir, the chief of the magi, survived the fall. They were pulled out and put in chains, and the Hephthalites plundered the defeated army. It was an ignominious defeat for Iran.

A great king must be wary and wise
Enough to know that destiny appears
Most obliging while it's plotting his demise.

Balaush was inconsolable when he received the news. After a month of mourning, the young king took his seat upon the throne. He declared that the edicts of a king should never be countermanded, and he who opposes a king must humbly apologize and submit himself to be punished. Balaush was inexperienced and ill-prepared in such matters. Yet he was honor-bound to avenge his father and uncle and to liberate his brother from captivity. His advisor, Sufrai, was aware of this and sent a letter of condolence to the bereaved king and suggested that avenging Iran on the Hephthalite chief and freeing the royal captives would be best handled by himself. Balaush concurred.

Sufrai then gathered the remainder of Piruz's rambling army and integrated them into his existing ranks. With a true commander's skill, he organized his army into standard-bearing formations that resembled a pheasant's bright feathers as they paraded. Soon, one hundred thousand sword-bearing warriors were marching to the border of Merv. The beating of their war drums was loud enough to cause the dust of the desert to rise to the heavenly spheres.

Sufrai declared war on Khosh-navauz:

> You have broken faith with your king and started a new vendetta between our peoples. You have committed regicide. Didn't King Bahraum make your grandfather a king? Is this the way you repay a favor? Why didn't you approach King Piruz in humility if you had a disagreement? Now that you have chosen the path of rebellion, prepare for your punishment. I have come to destroy your kingdom and exterminate you and your clan.

Khosh-navauz responded without delay:

> A pious man who is obedient to God would never break faith with his king. Piruz was the one who broke the Hunter King's sacred pact. I wrote several letters warning him against tearing up our treaty. But he chose to attack me, and his destiny took care of the rest. The same fate awaits you should you seek a confrontation. My powers have not diminished since I defeated your king. And I will not run from war if you are determined to wage one.

Sufrai cursed the Hephthalite chief when he read this letter. Tin drums throbbed, and brass trumpets blared as the Iranian army made its stance at the plain of Koshmahin, near Merv. The Hephthalites brought their troops to Bikand near the city of Bokhara that lay about ten days' ride to the northeast of Merv. Sufrai moved his army toward the enemy and engaged them in a fierce battle. Flying arrows made the air unsafe for the buzzards circling above, and the ground turned into a basin of blood. Sufrai broke the enemy lines and delivered a blow to Khosh-navauz's helmet. He survived the blow and managed to escape with a few of his guards to the castle of Kohan-Dez that was at the center of the Hephthalite capital in Bactria. From the ramparts of that fort, he beheld the battleground, strewn as it was with the corpses of his soldiers. He had lost the battle, but not the war.

Khosh-navauz sent an offer for cessation of hostilities with Iran:

> Why can't two reasonable commanders agree to an honorable peace instead of damning their souls to hell in an inglorious bloodbath? You know very well that I am not responsible for Piruz's death. He was the one who quaffed the chalice of hemlock instead of sipping from the goblet of ambrosia. He was the one who reneged on our time-honored border arrangement and turned a deaf ear to my entreaties.
>
> But that is all in the past. Let bygones be bygones. I will surrender the spoils of our victory: all the gold, silver, jewels, and horses will be returned. Above all, your captives, including the royal family's prominent members, will be released. This way, you can return to Iran loaded with the spoils of war and crowned with the honor of having liberated your prisoners. As for me, I will never cross the Oxus. I will honor King Bahraum's turret and continue to rule over what lies on the eastern bank of the river Oxus.

Sufrai consulted with his commanders. Putting aside the benefits mentioned in the request, there was a danger that Khosh-navauz could execute the crown prince Qobaud and the chief magus Ardeshir if his offer were rejected. The commanders considered the peace proposal fair. Sufrai sent word that he agreed with the peace terms, and the Hephthalites promptly returned the captives and the riches they had promised.

The Iranian forces crossed the Oxus back to Iran, and jubilant crowds greeted them in every city as they made their way back to Ctesiphon.

The crown prince Qobaud and the chief of the magi received a lavish welcome at Ctesiphon. Balaush embraced his brother and ushered him into the royal court. But Sufrai was the true hero. His popularity grew, and ballads were written throughout the nation to praise him.

Although the crown prince Qobaud had returned, Balaush continued to function as king, an office he had arisen to due to the long absence of his brother. Unspoken tensions developed, and gossip spread at court. Four years passed, and it was increasingly apparent that Balaush was no more than a boy luxuriating on the throne. Sufrai wanted to minimize the friction, so he took Balaush aside and gently suggested he was not cut out to be king and would be much happier as the honored brother to the king. The young man agreed and resigned in favor of his brother. This was the second time that Sufrai had saved Qobaud's throne.

THE SHORT REIGN

The first act of Qobaud after his acclamation was to move the capital from Ctesiphon back to the city of Pars, the seat of the ancient kings of Kay. Although the new king was older than Balaush, he was still just a callow sixteen-year-old without much experience in ruling the country. Thus, Sufrai continued to serve as a virtual regent until Qobaud reached the age of twenty-three. Once the commander was confident that the king was mature enough to handle his duties, he asked permission to return to his hometown of Shiraz and take up his previous role as governor.

Of course, given his unique position at court and immense popularity, there was the danger of palace intrigue if Sufrai left the capital. But he did not worry about plots in his absence as he was confident of Qobaud's friendship. After all, the king owed him a debt of gratitude.

But this confidence was misplaced. The young king had already begun to resent the power and glory of his governor in Shiraz. He was willing to listen to the courtiers' backbiting against the advisor who had served him so well. Intelligence indicated that Sufrai had boasted of being a kingmaker and had collected taxes from foreign lands, an act reserved for the sovereign. His treasures were said to surpass those of the king. Instead of being grateful for his general's service, Qobaud petulantly complained that he felt less in charge than he did under the rule of his brother Balaush. Finally, Sufrai's enemies asked the king: "Why have you settled for the title of a king while someone else has usurped your authority?"

Although he had come to hate his former advisor, Qobaud had no intention of openly challenging the formidable knight. Such a confrontation would be difficult to win and damaging to the country. Thus, it was suggested that the task be entrusted to Shaupur of Rey, an ambitious knight who had descended from Mehrak-e Nushzaud. This man, who also loathed Sufrai, could be relied upon to do their bidding. Shaupur was summoned to the capital and sent to Shiraz with an army to arrest the famous governor. The conspirators hoped he would submit to the king's wishes without resisting. And their gamble paid off.

Sufrai went forward with his army to welcome Shaupur, not knowing the nature of his mission. The two knights engaged in a friendly conversation. Then the guest confronted his host with the king's warrant for his arrest, saying: "As you see, the king has charged me with the chore of bringing you to him in chains. We both know that this king of ours is quite willful. I am afraid I have no choice but to put you in chains."

"The king knows me," Sufrai said. "I was the one who rescued him from the dungeons of Khosh-navauz and then went out of my way to restore him to his throne by asking Balaush to abdicate. The king is in my debt. So, I will neither plead for a respite nor beg for mercy. If my reward for all I have done is to be bound and transported to the capital like a criminal, then let it be so.

"Nor am I ashamed of allowing myself to be arrested. God and the people know I am no coward. My hand was welded to the handle of my sword, which was red with the blood of those who had imprisoned my king. Chains are ornaments on an innocent man's limbs; I will wear them with pride."

And thus, the hero was dragged to the capital and thrown into a dungeon. Even so, his enemies were not satisfied with his imprisonment, and they told the king that as long as the former advisor was alive, the royal throne was in danger. So, the reckless king ordered his henchmen to kill the hero who had saved him from captivity and made him king.

The people of the capital were outraged by the summary execution of the victor of the Hephthalite campaign. Disgusted by their king and his sycophants, they rose up in rebellion, deposed Qobaud, and slaughtered the courtiers who had prevailed on him to kill Sufrai. Their final act was to appoint Jamausp, Qobaud's ten-year-old brother, as king.

The rebels released the deposed king into the custody of Sufrai's son, Zarmehr, expecting that he would avenge his father. But Zarmehr was sure that such an act would throw the country into another crisis. Jamausp was too young to rule, and there was no doubt that another regency would harm the country's stability.

Thus, the virtuous Zarmehr forgave his father's killer in order to preserve the peace. Profoundly moved by this magnanimity, the disgraced king humbly asked him to pardon the wrong he had done and swore that he was deceived by the connivers at court. Zarmehr assured Qobaud that all was forgiven.

Trusting his unlikely new ally, Qobaud asked him to facilitate his breakout so he and five of his trusted companions could escape to the Hephthalite kingdom and ask for help. Zarmehr bribed the jailers, notified the king's friends, and procured the horses and provisions necessary for the long journey. And thus, Zarmehr, Qobaud, and five of his friends stole out of the dark city and waded into the desert as dawn broke over the horizon.

Their first stop was at a small farm near Ahvauz. It was supposed to be a brief sojourn, but as fate had decreed, Qobaud fell in love with the farmer's raven-haired daughter. He sent his trusted new friend Zarmehr to act as an intermediary.

"If your daughter is not attached," Zarmehr said to the farmer, "I have a perfect match for her. My companion here is an honest and noble man, and I promise he would be a good husband. If you accept him as your son-in-law, don't be surprised if one day you find yourself the governor of Ahvauz."

"My daughter is not engaged," the farmer replied. "I trust you, and if you approve of this young nobleman, I, too, consent to this match."

Zarmehr went to Qobaud with the good news. "May your love, at first sight, be the auspicious beginning of a happy union." When the girl visited her betrothed's quarters, he placed her on his lap and gave her his priceless ring as a sign of his everlasting devotion. After a brief ceremony, the young couple spent a blissful week together, and then the group took off riding in an easterly direction.

Qobaud and his companions crossed the Oxus and went straight to the Hephthalite court to meet with the chief. Qobaud declared that he needed help to regain his crown. The chief smiled and said that he was glad the tree of Khosh-navauz's peace was still bearing fruit. He then granted the refugee prince an army of thirty thousand riders. In exchange, the Iranians agreed to support him against the claims of the rival tribes to the Hephthalite kingdom.

With the conclusion of the Hephthalite agreement, Qobaud returned to Iran at the head of his new army. When his men reached Ahvauz, he heard the good tidings that his wife had given birth to a radiant son. With overflowing sentiments of love and excitement, he embraced her and held the infant, whom he named Kasra Nushin-ravaun. He then asked his father-in-law about his ancestors. It turned out that the family had descended from the ancient King Feraydun, who had subdued the Serpent King Zahhak. All rejoiced that the royal pedigree of the infant was secure on both sides. Qobaud then placed his queen in a resplendent litter and brought her ahead of his army to the gates of Ctesiphon.

The Iranians had no appetite for civil war. It was clear to all that the path of diplomacy was preferable to that of a fratricidal war that would weaken the nation and expose it to invasions from abroad. At the suggestion of the courtiers, Jamausp was brought to meet his brother. Qobaud embraced the child and forgave him. He also pardoned those who had overthrown him. To celebrate his restoration, the king, who had been restored to his throne, founded two new cities near the Roman border and thereafter dedicated himself to the education of his crown prince.

THE CURIOUS REFORMER

Toward the end of Qobaud's reign, a highly learned but somewhat arrogant cleric named Mazdak rose to prominence. The newcomer advanced in courtly ranks to become the vizier and treasurer of King Qobaud.

At this time Iran was suffering from another drought, and hungry crowds often loitered about the palace gates, hoping for charity. One day Mazdak came out and told the crowd to put their worries aside. The king had the solution to their problem. But they would have to wait a little while to receive their bounty.

He then went inside and asked the king, "What would His Majesty's judgment be if a man has plenty of antidote for snakebites but refuses to share it with one who is about to expire due to a bite from a snake?"

"I judge that although he has not killed anyone by his own hands, he is nevertheless a murderer," the king answered. "His refusal to share his medicine caused a man's death, and I rule that he should be executed."

Mazdak went back to the starving people at the gates. "I have spoken to the king. There is good news. Come back tomorrow to hear it."

The crowd left and returned at daybreak to hear what the king's friendly minister had to say. Upon seeing the desperate crowd, Mazdak ran to the king again and asked: "How would you judge, oh great king, if a jailor of yours denied his prisoner a crust of bread knowing that he was dying of starvation?"

"I judge that he should be uprooted from this world the way a weed is pulled out of the ground," the king said. "Such a man is no better than a murderer and must be executed at once."

Mazdak kissed the ground and strolled out to give the crowd the good news: "Go forth and plunder the royal silos. Distribute the grains equally among the hungry population. Everyone should have a share of the wheat."

The king's informants brought him the news of the plunder instigated by Mazdak. Qobaud summoned and commanded him to explain his behavior.

"I have done nothing but heed the letter and spirit of the king's advice," Mazdak replied. "You twice ruled that inaction in the face of grave injustice is criminal, and I didn't want my inaction to cause the death of the pitiable people standing at your gates."

The king was astounded by the simplicity of his minister's logic. Nor could he disagree with his conclusions. Thereafter Qobaud listened to his minister's words and eventually became one of his disciples. Mazdak became enormously popular with the poverty-stricken masses and the day laborers, despite the unorthodox nature of his teachings. He taught that the wealthy were equal to the poor and that the two groups were interdependent. He also decreed that no one was allowed to hoard women, houses, and property. Mazdak didn't claim to have brought a new religion as much as he had distilled the essence of the old, Zoroastrian faith.

"Didn't the scriptures say that the twin evils of jealousy and avarice are the conjoined roots of all sins?" he asked his audiences. "Well then, what is the cause of these two evils, if not private property and exclusive possession of women by the rich and the powerful? Once these two are held in common, possessiveness will vanish along with jealousy and avarice."

Such talk united the poor behind the new radical, egalitarian creed. Of course, Mazdak was less popular at court, especially among the orthodox Zoroastrian clergy who considered his views heretical. But none dared contradict the prophetic figure while he commanded the king's respect and sat at his right hand, a place formerly occupied by the chief of the Zoroastrian magi.

One day, after the king had addressed a mass of one hundred thousand Mazdakites on the palace grounds, he came inside to converse with the radical priest. Mazdak told the king that the crown prince did not believe in their new faith: Kasra needed to sign a pledge that he shared their interpretation of the scriptures and would continue to serve their new creed when he became king.

Qobaud summoned Kasra. Mazdak declared: "The crown prince must agree that the five evils of envy, hatred, anger, need, and greed are humankind's worst enemies. Unless we rid ourselves of these cardinal sins by holding everything in common, we will never attain salvation. Sharing women and property is the best way of removing the causes of these evil sentiments."

Then he reached over to hold Kasra's hand. The crown prince angrily withdrew his hand. The king smiled and asked his favorite spiritual teacher: "What do you think of my son's faith?"

"He is not one of us, Your Majesty," Mazdak replied bluntly.

Qobaud asked his crown prince why he rejected the new faith. Kasra said he needed time to compose a proper response to that question. "How many days would you need, my son?" asked the king. Kasra said that he needed five full months before presenting his case.

To prepare his argument, Kasra sought the help of two learned magi: the elderly Daud-Hormazd, who hailed from Khorreh-ye Ardeshir, and Mehr-Auzar, who came with his thirty disciples from the Pars region. Once he felt prepared, Kasra set the conditions. He told the king that he would convert to the new religion if he lost the debate. But if he won, he should be allowed to decide the fate of the prophet and his followers. The king agreed, and a day was set.

This was a terrible day for Mazdak. He was showered with questions and accusations by the clerics around Kasra:

"You have fabricated a new and most pernicious religion. If women are held in common, what would happen to paternity? How would the son know his father?"

"If people are equal, how would the world's affairs be managed? Who would be the ruler, and who would be the ruled?"

"Pray tell, what would happen to inheritance rules after someone dies? How would the estate of the deceased be divided?"

"What you expound is not a religion but the ravings of a lunatic. You will lead people straight to hell with your dangerous doctrine."

The king and the crown prince joined the chorus of the challengers, and the audience turned on Mazdak. There was a consensus that he was a corruptive influence that should be banished from both the temple and the state.

As Mazdak was vanquished, Kasra demanded that he and his followers be placed under his power. The king responded: "Do with them what you want. Just never mention them to me again."

Kasra dug three thousand holes in a lot surrounded by low walls. He then stuck the Mazdakites in the holes headfirst, in the manner of planting saplings. When this was done, he invited the prophet to come into the garden and see how the seeds that he had planted had come to fruition. Mazdak fainted at the macabre garden of his dead followers. Kasra ordered the prophet to be strung up, hanged upside down from the gallows, and dispatched in a hail of arrows.

Qobaud cursed the false prophet. To expiate the sin of associating with Mazdak, he gave generous donations to the fire temples. Thereafter the king consulted his son on matters of religion and state. Their bonds were strengthened with time.

After four decades, the king knew that his reign was ending. Thus, he wrote his last will and testament on a silk canvas, praising the Lord and appointing Kasra as his rightful successor. The document was sealed in gold and left in the care of the magus Raum-Borzin. The king's body was consigned to an opulent vault according to the funerary rites reserved for the kings.

No one saw the face of Qobaud after that;
He blew through the world like a breeze.
Your fate will treat you the same, 'tis your caveat.

CHAPTER 23

A Just King: Kasra Nushin-ravaun

The tall cypress bends over like a willow
Redbud flowers turn into saffron. My bones
Are brittle, my rosy cheeks, sallow.

Kasra reigned for forty-eight years;
What awaits this poet who's passed sixty,
But autumnal winds and streaming tears?

THE ROYAL REFORMS

Reclining on the ivory throne wearing his resplendent crown, Kasra praised the Lord. "I submit to the will of God, who is judge above all earthly judges. He is the One who created time and space, and kindled the sun and the moon to illuminate the earth." The new king urged his subjects to remain truthful, industrious, and wary of the wicked demon of procrastination. He also noted, "Subjects will thrive under a just king who is humble and ever-mindful of the transience of this world."

Kasra Nushin-ravaun began his rule with radical reforms. First he subdivided Iran into four administrative quadrants: the eastern region of Khorausan, the northwestern areas stretching from Isfahan and Qom to Azerbaijan, Ardebil, and Armenia, the central lands of Pars and Ahvauz, and the western environs of Iraq and Rome.

He then simplified the tax system by replacing payments in kind with cash imbursements. Previous kings had levied a tax of one-third or one-fourth of the crops on farmers. Qobaud reduced this to a tithe and had intended to reduce it further when death overtook him. The new king's scheme of cash payments brought predictability to state finances and allowed better planning. Of course, taxes were waived in such cases as frost, locust, and drought damage. The king ordered the measurement of the arable areas and levied the tax of one dirham for each acre of cultivated land. Fallow fields and summer fruits were exempt, but autumnal fruits were taxed. Poor peasants could borrow seeds and beasts of burden from the royal bureaus. Vineyards and date farms paid six dirhams per acre. Fruit growers were charged one dirham for every ten olive or walnut trees. If a farmer died and there was no one to maintain the land, the state would take it over to prevent waste of resources. Merchants, too, were obliged to pay between four and ten dirhams in annual taxes.

The lucrative business of tax farming that allowed widespread exploitation and abuse of the peasants was replaced by the centralized state administration of taxes. All revenues were collected three times a year. To ensure the accuracy of accounts, payments were recorded in three ledgers. One of these was kept at the local bureau, and the other two were sent to the central treasury and the high clerical commissionaire of finances. To check ill-treatment of farmers, peasants, and husbandmen by overseers, formal and anonymous royal agents were sent to supervise and monitor all transactions and report irregularities.

"I do not collect taxes to fill my own coffers," the king declared. "Tax income belongs to the nation and will be spent on public projects and the standing army. I will remain diligent, for it is well known that a lazy shepherd will lose his flock to the wolves. Not an inch of Iran will be abandoned to lawlessness while I rule. Lamb and wolf will drink from the same fountainhead. Nor will I tolerate graft and corruption. I swear by the Almighty who crowned me king that I will cleave in half anyone caught extorting a farthing from a peasant."

None among the kings of the world
Surpassed Kasra in wisdom and justice.
Not one was as humble, erudite, and bold.

The king's participation in military parades illustrates his fairness and humility. Kasra appointed a gifted magus named Baubak as master of parades. The young cleric designated an arena for parades and called the entire army to a formal procession at an appointed date. The army assembled, flying their bright colors. Baubak, sitting erect on his horse atop a podium, did not see the commander in chief leading the parade. Thus, he canceled the event and ordered the troops back to their barracks with these words: "I had explicitly ordered the entire army to come to this event!" The army returned the next day, but the king was still missing. Baubak canceled the parade again, pointedly declaring: "Leading the royal army does not diminish the crown's glory. Let the entire army march again at the rising of tomorrow's sun."

The king smiled when these words were reported to him. On the third day, he obliged Baubak and led his army in full royal regalia. Kasra performed an equestrian commander's feats, pulling his horse's reins to the left and right to demonstrate his readiness to draw his weapons and fight while mastering his steed. Baubak bowed, saying: "May His Majesty's fame be everlasting."

The master of parades then rewarded the elite troops with one thousand gold coins. The knights received two thousand pieces of gold each, and the king received the knight's reward plus one gold coin. Kasra had a hearty laugh at his minimally favorable treatment. After the event's conclusion, Baubak went to the royal court, prostrated himself before the throne, and offered his abject apologies for his impertinence. The king responded that no offense was taken. "Far from being diminished, your stature has increased in our eyes. Discipline in the ranks is of utmost importance. It is impossible to win a victory against a determined enemy unless the entire army, soldier, knight, and king act in unison."

The king advised Baubak to ensure every young man in Iran would receive military training for forty days to create a reserve army for use in national defense emergencies. Then he issued a public invitation to hear all grievances:

> Don't be intimidated by the grandeur of my palace or the glitter of my court. I am at your service day and night, rest or labor. I may be feasting in the company of friends or playing polo with my knights, but it is always a joy to right a wrong or address an injustice committed against an ordinary man. I am accountable before God for the slightest infraction of the law or the embezzlement of a penny of taxes.

When the king made these announcements, the clouds let loose, and the earth became a paradise of verdant fields and ruby-red roses. Gardens shone like the sun, and the fields glittered like the face of the full moon. Rome and India, who had learned of the power and prosperity of Iran, were swift in sending their rich tributes.

THE ROYAL TRAVELS IN IRAN

Given the news of minor disturbances and pockets of insecurity, the king launched an expedition to pacify the country. He led his army to Khorausan and then to the beautiful rainforests of Gorgan, Saury, and Aumol. Kasra was dazzled by these areas, where woods gradually faded into rolling green hills and open horizons. "No wonder," he exclaimed, "that King Feraydun chose this land as his capital." The people of the region came to venerate the king. They had been prosperous since the days of the legendary kings of yore. But there was danger of increasingly frequent incursions by the marauding Turkic tribes. Kasra shared his subjects' concern for Iran's borders. Thus, he halted the progress of the expedition and commanded the construction of robust, defensive fortifications on that part of Iran.

Next, the royal army advanced to the areas north of the river Araxes that was made unsafe by the Alan brigands of the northwestern borders of the country. The king sent an envoy with the message that their days of filibustering in Iranian lands were over:

> I have heard that you don't think much of my power. You have boasted of being able to face my armies. I am here now, and you have the home advantage. Let us see if your deeds back up your bold words.

The Alans, however, did not want a battle. Instead, they made their apologies and surrendered. The king accepted their submission and promised not to punish them on the condition that they refrain from banditry, rebuild the public works and private property that they had wrecked, and pay their taxes. They humbly accepted the king's terms and withdrew to their own territory.

The royal retinue and army then set course for India, where they were hosted by the local rulers in the style befitting the great king. But as Kasra turned back to head toward his capital, he learned of marauding bandits of Baluchistan in the southeastern parts and the rebellious brigands in Gilan and Deylaman in the north.

Kasra was furious. Foreign armies withdrew in fear of his advancing forces. How could a few outlaws dare spread chaos within his borders? The first to taste his wrath was the Baluchi bandits of the Kufchi Mountains who had occasionally made the area unsafe since the times of King Ardeshir. Kasra was determined to end the nuisance once and for all. He captured the bandits and their families and put them all to the sword. Their flocks were left roaming the mountains without a shepherd.

Then Kasra and his army moved north to confront the rebels of Gilan and Deylaman, who suffered total defeat in their first encounter and threw themselves at the king's mercy. To dramatize their submission, they tied their own hands and presented themselves and their families to be either beheaded for their crimes or forgiven by the king's grace. Kasra forgave them. But he took two hundred hostages from their leading families to ensure their future obedience. He also urged them to pay their taxes and obey the knight he had appointed as their ruler.

With his tour completed, the king turned south to return to his capital. Before he reached the gates of Ctesiphon, however, a single rider appeared on the horizon. The Arab tribal chief Monzar had come to pay his respects and to complain. "If you are the king of Iran and the benefactor of its knights, why are the Romans roaming the land and lording it over us? We are a race of warriors who know how to wield a lance on our swift horses. We are not afraid of Roman armored soldiers and their cataphracts. But we can't stand up to their numbers without the support of our king."

The king was angry at Rome's meddling in Arab affairs. He sent an envoy with a harsh message to the Caesar:

> Have you lost your mind? Are you incapable of knowing where your borders lie? I will not tolerate your filibustering in Arabia or harassing Monzar while he is in my protection. I am the master of the eastern and western horizons, and I rule the heavens from Taurus to Pisces.

The Caesar responded by weakly accusing Monzar of spreading falsehoods and denying that he had overstepped the Roman boundaries. Kasra was annoyed by this diplomatic double-talk. He sent a final message threatening an invasion unless Rome stopped its incursions into Arabia. The Caesar did not deign to speak to the king's envoy. He just handed him a written reply:

> You are free to consider yourself a king who is superior to the planet Jupiter. But don't esteem me an inferior. Remember that the Romans never paid tribute to the kings of Kay. If anyone must demand payment, it's me, not you.

Kasra's reply was a full-scale invasion of Rome. He led his army to the mountaintop fire temple of Azar-goshasp to bring a splendid devotional offering and humbly beseech the Lord to make him victorious. Then he appointed various knights to their posts in the different sections of the army. The king would remain mobile, visiting the various segments of the troops at will. He was adamant that the army should not impose upon or violate the rights of the people they encountered as it marched to the battlefield. He called all the commanders and declared: "If I catch a soldier harming a peasant, trampling his crops, or plucking his fruits without pay, I swear to the God who gave me this crown that I will put him to the sword. Beware that I am omnipresent in my army when I am at war."

Kasra sent his herald to announce his decrees to the rank and file. If a soldier died of disease or by accident, he would be honorably interned with his weapons. Commanders were obliged to give the enemy a chance to surrender before using lethal force. Roman cities would be treated with respect, and no harm would come to those cities that opened their gates.

Thus, some cities were peacefully annexed. But the fortified cities of Sura and "the Glory of Rome" defied the king. The walls of these cities were knocked down with the use of mangonels. The inhabitants were spared, but their treasuries were carried away.

BATTLE WITH THE ARMIES OF ROME

When the two armies finally clashed on the battlefield, the Iranians handily defeated the Roman forces and advanced to the fortified city of Gallienus. The Romans closed their gates, climbed the ramparts, and bombarded the Iranian forces with missiles and incendiary flagons, until the city fell. Kasra ordered his troops to stay out as he did not wish the city to be sacked. The next day as the summer sun rose from the constellation of Cancer, the citizens of Gallienus came out and declared that they did not condone the Caesar's offensive behavior. They asked for quarter, which was granted.

The prize among the Roman cities and the king's next target was the well-fortified city of Antioch. A fierce battle that raged outside the walls of the city lasted for three days, and on the fourth, the Iranians emerged victorious. The city's gates were thrown open, and the Caesar's treasures were carried away to Ctesiphon.

Kasra was so impressed by the beauty of Antioch that he ordered an exact copy of it to be built in Iran. He named this city Zeyb-e Khosrow (The Glory of Kasra) and had all Roman captives, including those of Antioch, moved there. Then the king appointed a Christian mayor for the city and advised him to fear God and to dedicate himself to the people entrusted to his care.

After the settlement was complete, a cobbler came to the king complaining that his house in the new city did not give him the same pleasure as the one he had in Antioch. He missed the mulberry trees that adorned his former home. The king accommodated the cobbler by ordering one hundred mulberry trees to be planted around his property.

Meanwhile, the Roman general Porphyrus, who had withdrawn from his battle with Kasra, advised the Caesar to stand down. He argued that given the lightning victories of the Iranian army and the threat to the sovereignty of Rome, capitulating to Kasra was the best course. "The Iranian army is so vast that it fills the sea and the land. Your armies are no match to such a host."

Convinced of the wisdom of this advice, the Caesar sent a delegation of philosophers to ask for terms. The king was impressed by the ambassadors' knowledge and accepted their gifts. Rome surrendered and pledged to pay an annual tribute of ten cowhides full of gold coins.

Kasra deputized the commander of his armies to stay at the front to receive the peace offerings and the first installment of Roman taxes. Then, he triumphantly returned to the plain of Arzhan in Pars to recuperate from his arduous campaign.

THE STORY OF NUSHZAUD

Every man, king, or commoner deserves a beautiful wife.
A raven-haired soulmate, slender, tall, and soft-spoken.
Kasra had such a consort, the solace of his life.

King Kasra had a lovely queen who happened to be a Christian. She gave birth to the king's firstborn son, Nushzaud. When the handsome prince came of age and studied the paths of Ezra, Jesus, and Zarathustra, he chose his mother's faith over Judaism and the Zoroastrian religion of his father. The king wondered why his beloved rosebush had borne thorns instead of flowers. He tried to convince his son to change his religion, but Nushzaud was firm in his convictions. Thus, the king ordered him confined to his palace in the city of Gondi-Shaupur.

While Kasra was engaged in his Roman campaign, he was taken ill in the vicinity of the River Jordan, which led to the rumor that he had died. Nushzaud believed the rumor and rejoiced at the news of his father's demise. Instead of mourning, the brash young man broke out of his confinement and joined a gang of ruffians that included a few Christians, to sack Gondi-Shaupur. To add insult to injury, he forged a letter from Caesar, appointing himself Rome's vicegerent in Iran.

Kasra was enraged at Nushzaud's actions and ordered the local knight, Raum-Borzin, to crush the rebellion. However, because his son was leading the uprising, he cautiously delineated the governor's authority. "A king can hardly hear worse tidings that I have. My son has incited a rebellion to take the throne. Nushzaud has taken leave of his senses. He professes an alien faith, cheers his father's death, and joins the riffraff to wreck a city. It is vulgar to celebrate anyone's death. A wise man once said: 'If you plan to rejoice at another man's death, first make sure that you will live forever!'

"Don't take pity on the mob who has joined this cause. But refrain from harming or cursing my son, as he is from my seed. Do your best to end this peacefully. Take him alive and keep him under house arrest along with his women. However, if this cannot be done and my son is impossible to restrain, I authorize you to do what it takes to quell the insurgency. A son who takes delight in his father's death has forfeited his life."

Raum-Borzin gathered an army and marched to the gates of Gondi-Shaupur to suppress the rebellion. One of his senior knights, Piruz, approached Nushzaud to admonish him. "Why have you turned your back on your ancestral religion of Gayumart, Hushang, and Tahmuret? The swindler Christ was killed because he turned his back on God. He would have lived if he had the halo of divine sanction.

"It would be a pity if a brave and splendid prince like you were to revolt against the mighty Kasra, who has defeated the Caesar and is sure to beat you. Don't break your father's heart and spoil your birthright. Dismount and ask for mercy."

"I don't need the intercession of an old fool like you," Nushzaud retorted. "Nor do I need the old religion of Kasra after I have found solace in my mother's faith. The death of Christ was no ignominy. It was a voluntary act inspired by his loathing of this world and his desire to join his heavenly father. I hope to join him if I am killed in this battle. Death is not the true believer's poison, but his panacea."

With the end of this exchange, the war commenced in a hail of arrows from both sides. Nushzaud annihilated the left flank of the Iranian army, killing many of its commanders. But he was struck by an arrow as he fought. Realizing that his wound was fatal, the prince returned to the heart of his army and declared that his death was nigh. He asked that his body be buried according to Christian funeral rites. His mother heard the news and ran to the front only to find soldiers bearing away her son's lifeless body. There was no dry eye among the Christian population of the city that had come to mourn their prince.

Don't smell the flowers of this life
For they are soaked in poison. Be merry
And above all, avoid greed and strife.

There's no harm in partaking of wine
If you avoid drunken excess. Happiness
Is not a sin in God's grand design.

A CURIOUS DREAM

A dream is not the mind's plaything.
Visionary dreams can be prophetic,
Especially when they occur to a king.

Kasra dreamed he was at one of his banquets, enjoying his musicians and wine, when a boar entered, insisting on drinking from his cup. In the morning, the king called on his oneiromancers to reveal the meaning of this enigmatic vision. They listened carefully to the dream and declared that they were confounded by it.

Admitting your ignorance is a mark
Of honesty. Professing to know what you don't
Is as foolish as pretending to see in the dark.

The king dispatched envoys to the empire's four corners, promising a purse of ten thousand gold coins to anyone who could interpret his dream. One of these messengers, Azaud-sarv, came upon a school on the outskirts of Merv where a stern magus was teaching the Zoroastrian texts of

Zand and Avesta. A student stood in front of the class, enthusiastically reciting the scriptures. The envoy asked the teacher if he could interpret the king's dream. The teacher replied that he was a simple instructor of scriptures, not a practitioner of the secret arts. The standing pupil interjected, claiming that he knew what the king's dream meant. The teacher reprimanded him for speaking out of turn, but Azaud-sarv urged the student to speak up. The pupil said that the meaning of such a dream was for the king's ears only.

The envoy had a sense that the extraordinary student, whose name, he learned, was Buzarjmehr, was in fact able to unravel the dream. Thus, he supplied him with a horse and wages to go with him to Ctesiphon for an audience with the king.

Together they left Merv for the capital, spending their time in pleasant conversation. The student used the opportunity to learn about the king's personality and the protocol of the royal court. At dusk, they stopped by a bubbling fountain for supper and rest. The boy fell asleep under a blanket. Shortly thereafter, Azaud-sarv noticed a spotted snake sliding around in the young man's bed. He was paralyzed with fear. But the snake did not seem threatening; it only smelled Buzarjmehr from head to toe and slithered away. The envoy took the visitation of the snake as a sign that mysterious forces favored the prodigy.

At Ctesiphon, Azaud-sarv left his young companion outside the audience hall at the royal court. He went in and gave an account of how he had found the student, and also added the story of the snake. Buzarjmehr was then called in to stand before the throne. "The ominous dream can only mean one thing," he said. "The king is betrayed by a man hiding in his seraglio. He is disguised as a woman. Let the king command his women to parade in plain view to find the culprit."

Astonished by this interpretation, Kasra cleared the audience hall and commanded his wives and concubines to present themselves. The exquisite procession of women of the haram did not yield the result Buzarjmehr had promised. They all looked like women. The interloper would be found if the women disrobed, said the student.

When this was done, a handsome man, redolent of musk and jasmin, was discovered among the women. He looked terrified. When questioned, he confessed that he gained access to the seraglio as a servant of the princess of the city of Chauch at the banks of the river Jaxartes. The ivory-white and statuesque princess claimed that the man she had smuggled in was her half-brother, who had come in disguise because he could not bear being separated from her. The king did not believe this story and ordered his executioner to take them both away and slay them.

This event established the young man's acumen, but this was not the zenith of his career at the Iranian court. He continued to impress the king with his erudition and wisdom. The king had a council of seventy sages and magi whom he consulted from time to time. Excited by the discovery of his brilliant young advisor, Kasra called upon this group to convene once a week for seven weeks. In these sessions, many topics ranging from the etiquette of individual conduct to statecraft and politics were discussed. Among Buzarjmehr's wise declarations were the following.

THE FIRST MEETING

- Speak sparingly and when you do, say nothing but the truth.
- Don't say what does not bring benefit. Don't say what might cause harm.
- Strength in a man breeds honesty. Weakness leads to duplicity.
- Don't fall in love with your own knowledge. Remain skeptical of your certainties and walk in the light of sound judgment.
- Tolerance is the brother of reason, and reason is the crown of a moral man.
- Be moderate in your spending. Avoid stinginess and profligacy.
- An educated enemy is better than an ignorant friend.
- An educated king will always be humble.
- One must obey the king, for he is the shepherd, and we are his flock.

THE SECOND MEETING

- Learning from one's mistakes in war or trade is the mark of prudence.
- Wasting favors on the unworthy is the way of an imprudent man.

- Be judicious on picking those whom you choose to benefit.
- A man of inferior nature will not smell good even if you bathe him in musk.
- Avoid sin and do not do unto others what you don't wish to be done unto you.
- Four things are unseemly in a king: timidity on the battlefield, lack of generosity, refusing to take counsel during the war, and being hasty in decision-making.
- A good king's voice comforts the virtuous subjects and frightens the wicked.

THE THIRD MEETING

- A good king needs to be diligent in learning and mastery of skills. Noble birth is not enough for a king, just as bright colors are not enough for a flower. Fragrance is the essential quality of a flower.
- Correct action is rooted in wisdom. If one is not born with that innate light, one must acquire learning taught in schools. If he does not have the aptitude for school learning, let him choose the military path.
- Avoid the seven vices: Uncontrollable rage, generosity to the mean-spirited, impiety, sharing of secrets, garrulousness, gullibility, and, above all, lying.
- Avoid potential danger like the game avoids a trap.
- Beware of the transient pleasures that lead to sorrows.
- Eschew laziness, for nothing in this life is achieved without great effort.

THE FOURTH MEETING

- A king must fear God, move with prudence, be truthful, value a knowledgeable advisor, and turn a deaf ear to malicious gossip.
- People who are in the state prison must be given a chance to appeal their case.
- An army commander must lead his men with intelligence rather than intimidation.

- Princes should receive proper education and measured discipline.

THE FIFTH MEETING

- In response to the king's request to enumerate ten evil deeds, the sage tallied them: lying by a judge, hoarding by an army commander, worldliness of a learned man, ill health of a healer, ostentation of a poor man, encumbering a favor by frequent mentions, quick temper and acquisitiveness of a learned man, putting a lazy person in charge of one's business, careless speech that entails later regret, and finally, lofty dreams that consume the heart of the ignorant the way fire ignites sulfur.

THE SIXTH MEETING

- Neither envy your superior nor oppress your inferior.
- Avoid rumormongering.
- Protect yourself in battle. Don't fight against a superior foe when you can withdraw.
- Avoid gluttony. Withdraw from the spread before you are full.
- Educate your child. He who learns the arts of a scribe will stand before kings.

THE SEVENTH MEETING

- A pious man knows that worshipping the king is an act of devotion. Conversely, he who hates the king is an agent of the devil. Love your king more than your child, for his love wards off need and privation.
- A wealthy man must assign the credit for his success to the king and gladly pay the tithe due to him.
- Be humble if the king shows you kindness and be silent and remorseful if he is displeased with you. He can read your mind, for he is given the power of perception.
- The king is like a sea, and you are a sailor on the ship of your learning. Let reason be your sail and anchor.

❧ The king is like a mountain of fire that illuminates when he is calm and burns when he is angry.

Whenever the king liked what was uttered in these meetings, he would say, "Zeh!" This meant the speaker could collect four purses, each filled with ten thousand coins. When the king said "Zeha-Zeh!" the speaker was entitled to forty such purses. Buzarjmehr received several of these accolades during these sessions.

THE TALE OF MAHBUD AND ZARVAUN

Don't cease learning, for when you claim
To have mastered a field, fate will roll its dice
To show you up as a novice at life's game.

Now hark to a most curious tale
Related by the old and wise farmer
Who remembers ancient stories without fail.

Kasra had a confidant named Mahbud, who also acted as his taster. His wife oversaw the kitchen, and his two sons served as stewards at the royal table. The king loved and trusted this family.

The closeness of Mahbud to the king aroused the envy of courtiers, and none among them was more resentful than the court chamberlain, Zarvaun. As the jealousy of the official became known around town, a man who had mastered the black arts saw an opportunity to exploit the situation. He approached the chamberlain with the excuse of asking for a loan and let it slip that he was a sorcerer and that he could poison milk by merely glancing at it. Zarvaun admitted his hatred of the king's taster, and thus they became accomplices in a plan to poison the king and let Mahbud take the blame.

Zarvaun learned from his spies that milk was among the items in the royal repast. So, one day, he stopped Mahbud's sons on their way to serve the king and asked if he could view the sumptuous dishes they had prepared. The request was unusual, but the boys saw no harm in obliging the chamberlain, and this was enough for the sorcerer, lurking nearby, to cast his deadly spell on the milk. As the king sat to eat, Zarvaun rushed in to declare that he had discovered a plot: the king's enemies had poisoned his drink. He should by no means sip it without having it tried by his taster. As Mahbud was not in attendance, his sons, who were confident of the integrity of the food, drank a quantity of the milk. A few seconds later, they both fell to the ground and died after terrible convulsions. Furious at the assassination attempt, Kasra ordered Mahbud and his entire clan to be executed.

Thereafter Zarvaun replaced the royal taster as the main companion of the king. One day, as Kasra was preparing to go wolf hunting, he noticed Mahbud's brand on a few horses. He was saddened by the memories of his friend. Tears streamed down his cheeks as he wondered how the devil could have deceived such a good-natured and honest man. With this thought, the king also entertained the possibility that Mahbud might have been set up.

Later in the day, while Kasra was riding with his retinue, he casually opined that sorcerers were all charlatans. How could they possess occult powers while the omnipotent God was the only Lord and master of the universe? Zarvaun volunteered that sorcery was real and that he had personally witnessed its formidable powers. He added that a master of the demonic art could poison a bowl of milk by merely glancing at it. This unintended revelation had confirmed the king's suspicions. He brought his horse to a gallop and outpaced the group to hide his agitation. Overwhelmed by the treachery that had doomed Mahbud and his entire family, he felt guilt for his own role in the tragedy.

When the hunting party arrived at a river, the king ordered his tent to be set up. Then he sat on his royal dais, summoned Zarvaun, and commanded him to speak the truth about Mahbud's fate. Was he the victim of a conspiracy? The chamberlain's pallor gave him away. With trembling lips, he confessed that he had a hand in the plot but that the real culprit was the sorcerer. The king had the sorcerer immediately arrested and brought to the court. He, too, confirmed the conspiracy but blamed the chamberlain for masterminding it.

The king had two gallows set up at the riverbank, where both men were hanged. A search for living members of Mahbud's kin turned up a girl and three men. The property of the sorcerer and Zarvaun was distributed among them.

An evil act may seem easy at first
But secrets will not remain hidden for long;
The culprit will be caught and forever cursed.

A king who is brutal and unjust
Is eternally despised, and his reign
Will be remembered with disgust.

But a just king like Kasra Nushin-ravaun
Is praised by poets and adoring subjects,
From the highest lord to a humble peon.

During his reign, King Kasra built many cities with palaces, plazas, and gardens nearby. He was so impressed by the Roman city of Andiv-Shahr that he built a replica of it—calling it Surestan. To ensure the perfection of his urban masterpieces, he invited skilled architects and masons from Rome and India. He also lavished attention on the surrounding villages of his cities, as they were essential for the provisions of the urban areas.

BATTLE OF THE KHAGANS

The khagan of China was the only rival of Kasra in the eastern expanses of Asia. He resided near the city of Chauch and was the son-in-law of the great emperor of China. Having heard of the magnificence of the king of Iran, the khagan decided to send him a goodwill mission composed of ten camels carrying thirty thousand gold coins, painted canvases, and delicate silk fabrics. A wise and eloquent ambassador led the delegation of friendship.

The caravan had to cross Sogdiana, which was under the control of the Hephthalites. Upon hearing of the purpose of the goodwill mission, the Hephthalite chief Qautfar decided that a rapprochement between his eastern and western neighbors was not in his interest. Thus, he ordered the confiscation of the caravan's goods and the beheading of the Chinese ambassador.

This act of sabotage infuriated the khagan of China. To punish the Hephthalite chief, he called the descendants of Afrasiab and Arjausp to join his forces on the shores of the Jaxartes. Meanwhile, Qautfar also prepared for war by gathering a ferocious army at the city of Bokhara.

The Hephthalite army was ready when the khagan's forces crossed the river Barak. A bloody and savage battle ensued, which lasted for a week. On the eighth day, the Chinese side broke through the Hephthalite ranks and routed Qautfar's forces. They seemed unstoppable and indefatigable at the long battle.

Qautfar took the blame for the defeat and was replaced with a man from the Chaghani tribe named Foghanish. He wanted to appeal to Iran for help but was reduced to the vassalage of the Chinese khagan.

The unification of Iran's eastern rivals worried Kasra Nushin-ravaun. After all, the Chinese khaganate traced its progeny to the ancient Touranian enemies of Iran. And he had not forgotten that King Piruz had been killed on an eastern campaign.

Kasra contemplated a preemptive strike to neutralize the newfangled Chinese-Hephthalite entity, but his council of advisors was not keen on the idea. They offered that such a war would divert forces from the western frontier and expose Iran to Roman adventurism. Kasra dismissed this argument and treated it as an expression of his generals' timidity. Maybe they had gotten accustomed to the life of feasting and laziness. Faced with this accusation, the generals gave up their opposition and fell in line behind their king. Soon the formidable Iranian army marched to Gorgan in north eastern Iran to confront the khagan's forces in greater Sogdiana.

Given his recent victory over the Hephthalites, the Chinese khagan had spoken of his dream to conquer Iran and Arabia. But he found the arrival of the vast army of Kasra to be a sobering reminder that his plans might have been too ambitious. His war council was equally worried that a defeat from Iran would wipe out the glory they had just gained. They concluded the best course was to send a peace mission to Iran and explore their options.

The khagan entrusted a letter to ten wise courtiers. It stated that he was the mighty lord of the east, as evidenced in his recent victories against the Hephthalites. He had not come to attack Iran but to avenge the unjust plunder of his goodwill mission and the murder of his peace ambassador to Iran.

Nushin-ravaun was pleased by the khagan's diplomatic overture and hosted the envoys in grand style for a month. He arranged a military parade and a contest of strength to display his military's prowess. As the delegation watched the display, a whispering was heard among them. They were wondering why the king was not among his elite soldiers, exhibiting his might. Hearing of this, Kasra rode into the arena, excelled the commanders in every contest and challenged his paladins to carry his armor and weapons. None of them was able to rise to the challenge. The delegation was stunned by his martial prowess and physical strength. They were also impressed by the generosity and affability of the king.

Upon their return to their khagan, the delegates sang the praises of the Iranian warriors and their king. The khagan concluded that the best course of action was to make peace with Iran and cement the accord with a royal marriage between one of his daughters and Kasra.

This time he sent three high-ranking ambassadors with the proposal of marriage. The king accepted and appointed an elder sage named Mehran-shetaud to choose a bride from among the khagan's five daughters. His mission was to find out who among the princesses was the famed daughter of the queen consort, the daughter of the emperor of

China. It would not do for the king of Iran to marry the progeny of an ordinary concubine.

The khagan and his queen were attached to their only daughter, and planned to marry off one of his other daughters. They dressed them in beautiful garments and adorned them in luxurious torques, colorful sashes, and glittering crowns. Their daughter, meanwhile, was kept on the sidelines, unadorned and dressed in rags. But Mehran-shetaud was wise to this deception. Having detected the nobility of the true princess, he turned to the queen and said: "I choose the girl in plain clothes who wears no crown. Adornments are plentiful at the king's court. My purpose is to choose a noble bride for my king, not a well-dressed one."

Trying to dissuade the envoy, the queen said, "But you are making a grave mistake, old man. How can you choose a mere child over such noble princesses?"

Mehran-shetaud was firm and declared that opposing him would constitute defiance of the king. The queen asked for time to consider the matter. The royal couple consulted prognosticators and astrologers and were told that the marriage between their daughter and the king of Iran would be auspicious and that a great king would be born to them.

Thus, the matter was settled, and the highborn princess was sent to Iran. One hundred mules, one hundred horses, and one hundred camels laden with royal fabrics, jewels, torques, crowns, and ivory thrones accompanied the golden litter of the princess bride, who was carried atop an elephant. Three hundred ladies and their servants attended the bride as well. Before the caravan, an enormous standard was carried by a hundred men. When Kasra saw his beautiful bride for the first time, he was speechless. All he could do was call upon the name of God and thank him. The princess was tall, elegant, and lovelier than the crescent of a new moon.

Thereafter, Iran was tranquil and secure for a long while. Justice of the king pervaded the land. The country was prosperous and peaceful. The Hephthalites and the Romans paid tribute, and nature was generous to the peasants and husbandsmen. If a man coveted another's wife, he would be severely punished. If a knight allowed his horse to wander into a peasant's field, he would be reprimanded and obliged to pay damages.

During this peaceful hiatus, the king continued to benefit from the wise council of his advisor, Buzarjmehr. Once, he asked the sage to rank the demons representing the universal evil among men. He enumerated ten demons ranked according to their malignity: Greed, Need, Envy, Anger, Dishonor, Hatred, Gossipmongering, Deceitfulness, Heresy, and Ingratitude. The first three, Greed, Need, and Envy, were the worst among the minions of the universal evil because they were at the root of our unhappiness. But, the sage added, God has also given us a formidable armor against these demons: Kherad, or practical reason, which is innate to humankind.

CHALLENGES OF CHESS AND BACKGAMMON

One day a dazzling train of a thousand elephants carrying a variety of souvenirs arrived from the Sind region of India. They were decorated with embroidered fabrics and colorful parasols. Leading the caravan rode an ambassador who humbly presented Kasra with the Indian king's offerings: jewels, luxurious fabrics, well-forged Indian swords, and elephants festooned with gold earrings. The ambassador had also come with a friendly challenge: "This is chess, a game of strategy featuring pawns, castles, elephants (bishops), knights, viziers (queens), and kings. We challenge the king's advisors to figure out this game. What moves are assigned to each piece? How is this game won or lost?

"You have one week. Should you succeed in unraveling the mysteries of chess, we will pay your tribute as we have done in the past. But if you are confounded by it, you should pay us a tribute whose amount will be determined."

Kasra was intrigued by the delicately carved ivory and teak pieces and wondered how they would wage war upon the black and white squares of the board. He was confident that his advisors and magi would decipher the rules of the game. But after a few days, they returned with downcast eyes and confessed that they had failed at their task.

The king summoned Buzarjmehr and asked him if he could take on the challenge. The sage returned after only two days to explain the game:

the king of each side was settled at the heart of his army, flanked by his vizier, elephants, knights, and castles. Pawns lined up in front, ready to engage the enemy. Then he described the moves assigned to each piece.

The Indian ambassador was astounded. How could a man who had never seen the game played discover its rules? Kasra asked for wine to celebrate his advisor's success and presented him with a bag of gold coins and a luxuriously caparisoned horse.

Now it was the Iranians' turn to dare the king of Sind to a similar challenge. The task was entrusted to Buzarjmehr, who designed a game of strategy and fortune. It, too, was played with teak and ivory pieces on a rectangular board representing the battlefield. The two armies arranged themselves in eight vertical rows moving in flanking directions. Isolated warriors would be easily eliminated. The roll of ivory dice determined the player's move, underlining the role of luck in every war. The question was how a commander would play with the possibilities allotted to him by the rolling dice of fortune. King Kasra was impressed with the new game, which they called Nard (backgammon). A luxurious set was fabricated and sent back with the ambassador of Sind. Two thousand camels laden with the riches of the royal treasury followed the envoy's litter. Buzarjmehr was also sent to pose the challenge of discovering the rules of backgammon to the king of Sind. If they could solve the riddle, they could keep the two thousand camels and their cargo. But if they failed, they would have to return double the amount of those riches to Iran.

Much as they tried, the clever men of Sind could not unravel the secrets of the game of backgammon. Thus, the king's ambassador returned to Iran with treasures consisting of incense, ambergris, camphor, gold, jewel-encrusted goblets, and silken garments. "I thank the Lord for the gift of recognizing and appreciating the talents and virtues of my subjects," said Kasra. "Kings of the world pay me obeisance even as knowledge bows down at the gates of Buzarjmehr."

THE ORIGINS OF CHESS

"The game of chess was invented to assuage
A mother's grief after her sons fought a tragic battle,"
Thus spoke our narrator, Shahuy the elder sage.*

Once, a king named Jamhur ruled eastern Indian lands stretching from Kashmir to China. He resided in the city of Sandali with his beautiful queen and their infant son Gav. The king dedicated his life to learning and the welfare of his subjects. But he was not destined to linger long in this world. After the king's precipitous death due to a severe affliction, the nobles of Sandali invited his brother Mauy to come from Dunbar and ascend the throne. Mauy was a righteous man as well as a good king. In time, he married the dowager queen, and they were blessed with a son whom they named Talkhand. But misfortune struck again. Mauy also died young, when Gav had reached the age of seven and Talkhand was only two.

While Gav and Talkhand were children, the twice-widowed queen acted as regent. She entrusted the education of each son to a learned magus. The brothers often quarreled over which one of them would become king. If one of them went to their mother and asked this question, she would mollify him with firm promises. But when they were both present, she prevaricated: "You both have a right to be king. Prepare by being humble, just, and reasonable, for that office requires these qualities." She wanted to keep both of her sons happy, but her evasion increased their rivalry until childish bickering turned into a fierce conflict over the question of royal succession.

Thus, the brothers went to the queen mother one last time to resolve their dispute. Gav spoke first, requesting the queen appoint one of them as the next king. He pledged to abide by her judgment, although as the elder son, he had the right to succeed his father. She demurred again and

* Shahuy Khorshid, the son of Bahraum, is one of the four scholars who gathered the prose archetype of *Shahnameh* commissioned by the Samanid ruler Abu-mansur Muhammad bin Abd al-Rasszaq-e Tousi.

said they should not be in such a hurry and warned them against worldly ambitions. The headstrong Talkhand rejected his brother's seniority claims and argued that talent and ability trump age in matters of succession. After all, he averred, some in his army were older than ancient vultures, and they had no claim to leadership! He ended his harangue by accusing his mother of partiality toward her firstborn.

"On what ground do you accuse mother of favoring me?" Gav retorted. "Regarding the issue of seniority, remember that your father respected that principle. He never made a claim to the throne while Jamhur was alive, and unlike you, he considered it an honor to be the younger brother of a king."

"I refuse to choose between you," the queen said. "I hereby resign from the regency, surrender the keys of the royal treasury, and leave this matter to the elders."

The brothers tried to let their advisors resolve the matter. But the advisors could not come to a decision either. People knew that splitting kingship was untenable and hoped an assembly of the elders could resolve the issue as the queen recommended. They ended in a deadlock as well.

As the nation hurtled toward civil war, Gav and Talkhand met for the last time. "Mauy obeyed Jamhur," said Gav. "If you were older, I would not have disputed your seniority."

"You can't win the crown by sophistry," the younger brother replied. "This matter should be settled by the sword."

Shortly thereafter, the brothers faced each other on the battlefield. Talkhand initiated the attack, galloping ahead of his troops in full armor. Gav met the challenge, and the two armies clashed amid the deafening sound of war drums, cymbals, and trumpets. Two flags fluttered on each side—one with an image of a tiger, the other a lammergeier. The armies appeared equally matched. As the war dragged on, senseless carnage continued. Gav sent a message to his brother:

> You alone are responsible for this mayhem. I never wanted a war that would divide our nation and pave the way for a foreign invasion.

> I will give you whatever land you wish. Take it all from here to the borders of China. Don't stain your hand in this pool of blood.

Talkhand responded:

> Words are improper in the middle of a war. I no longer consider you a brother or even a friend. Your advisors have given you false confidence. Regarding your promises of giving me land, death is preferable to taking your charity. We will continue this conversation when you are brought to me in manacles.

Gav had no choice but to prepare for another battle. But his advisor cautioned him against aiming for a crushing defeat: "I have cast Talkhand's horoscope. He is predestined to perish in this war, and there is no point in becoming the instrument of his inevitable death. Offer him anything he wants except for the crown. Let posterity know that you did your best to avoid fratricide."

Following this advice, Gav sent another envoy cautioning his younger brother against shedding blood within the family. The envoy hinted that people's destiny was written in the movements of the sun, moon, and planets within the constellations of the zodiac. Talkhand replied: "Since you are so interested in the stars, I will make tomorrow so dark that you will be able to follow them at midday."

The next day Gav arrayed his forces for a final assault, advising his troops against initiating hostilities, plundering the enemy, or killing his brother. The younger brother, too, had forbidden his soldiers to kill Gav.

In the final battle, Gav's forces dominated the field. He extended an amnesty to the retreating enemy, and they surrendered. Isolated with a handful of followers, Talkhand withdrew to the city of Margh to regroup.

Gav sent an envoy inviting his brother to a peaceful resolution, "But," he added, "If you insist on war, let us go to the seashore, dig a moat around the battlefield and fight a final time. Retreat would be impossible, the vanquished party would have to accept defeat, and the victor would refrain from plunder and massacre. The kings will be safe, no matter what happens."

Talkhand accepted the terms, and both armies went to the appointed place; together they dug the moat and filled it with water, before getting in formation against each other. The contending brothers were nestled at the heart of their armies, wearing their crowns. They were flanked by their viziers, elephants, knights, and infantry.

The two armies gave a good account of themselves. But the superiority of the army of the older brother was evident. To make matters worse, a black wind blew against the forces of the younger brother. Pushed to a corner and feeling despondent, Talkhand watched as his army was decimated. He sighed, bent over to put his forehead on the horn of his saddle, and died not of a fatal wound, but of sadness. As hostile action ceased, Gav sent his knights to retrieve his brother's body. They found the uninjured yet lifeless corpse of Talkhand sitting on his elephant.

The queen cried tears of blood when she heard the tragic news. She set fire to the palace of her younger son and intended to immolate herself on Talkhand's pyre. Gav prevented her from this act and tried to convince her that he had not killed his brother. But the grief-stricken mother refused to believe him.

Gav consulted with his advisors about the best way to prove his innocence. A council of sages was convened, and they designed a game to demonstrate to the queen how the final battle was fought. They represented the battlefield delimited by a moat as a checkerboard of black and white squares. The opposing armies were carved in miniature statues of teak and ivory. The pieces represented two armies on opposite sides of the board. Each king was served by his vizier, knights, elephants, castles, and infantry. Each would move on the board according to set rules. The formidable castles moved straight with such force as to forbid resistance. Elephants moved diagonally, and knights moved in twisted ways in every direction. The lowly pawns moved one step at a time. But if one was brave enough to penetrate the enemy lines and reach the back of the battlefield, he was promoted to a vizier. Kings moved slowly and deliberately, one square at a time. The cardinal rule of the conflict was that a king could not be killed. He would only be warned—checked—to move out of danger's way. The game was won when a king was cornered with nowhere to run, just as Talkhand was checked and mated on the battlefield.

The queen sought solace in the game of chess. Now she knew how her son had lost the battle for his life without suffering a violent death.

THE WISDOM OF PANCHATANTRA

Our narrator Shaudan-e Borzin has revealed*
The story of a man who sought the elixir of life
But found a fabulous book of advice that healed.

Among King Kasra's council of sages and learned advisors was a physician by the name of Borzuy. One day he told the king that he had read an astonishing thing in a book on medicinal plants. There was a magical herb in the mountains of India whose colorful flower resembled Roman brocade. If properly harvested and prepared, it would yield a potion that could revive the dead. "With the king's permission, I will go to India and bring back this wondrous plant," he said.

Kasra was skeptical but agreed that the story merited an investigation. He dictated a letter of introduction to Rauy, the king of India, and sent along a train of three hundred camels bearing rich offerings, including gold coins, fur, silk, musk, and ambergris. The Indian court honorably received the mission of the Iranian healer in pursuit of knowledge. Rauy pledged to facilitate the research. A team of Indian healers joined Borzuy to comb the mountains in search of the magical plant. After a while the plant was found, harvested, and prepared according the instructions of the book. But the potion proved ineffective when sprinkled on

* Shaudan, the son of Borzin of Tous, was another one of the four sages who gathered the prose archetype of *Shahnameh*. All are mentioned in the introduction to the prose archetype, which is the only part of it in that volume that is extant. The other two are Elder Maukh, son of Khorausan of Herat, and Yazdandaud, son of Shaupour of Sistan.

the dead. Borzuy was disheartened. How would he return to Iran empty-handed, having wasted the riches entrusted to him? He asked his Indian colleagues if they knew someone who could explain why such a falsehood was written in a respectable book of Indian medicine. They took him to their grandmaster, who told Borzuy, "We, too, read about the magical plant in that book and took it literally. We, too, were disappointed by the results. But then we discovered that the passage had a deeper meaning. The dead, in that context, stands for ignorant men. The plant represents the knowledge in the book of wisdom known as Panchatantra that is kept in the king's vault."

Borzuy returned to King Rauy and asked if he could examine the book of wisdom that could cure ignorance. The king was surprised that the Iranian envoy knew about the precious book kept under lock and key. He said that none had ever asked him for such a favor, but he would not withhold anything from the envoy of King Nushin-ravaun. There was only one condition: the book would be brought to him in the king's audience hall. Borzuy could read it in the presence of the king. But he was not allowed to copy it.

Borzuy accepted the terms. Every day Panchatantra was brought out from the treasury for his perusal, and every day he read a portion of the book—but only as much as he could commit to memory. Upon returning to his quarters, he immediately translated the portion he had memorized into Persian, a task that would take all night. In this manner, he managed to copy and transmit the book of wisdom to Iran, where it was called *Kelileh and Demneh* after the names of two of its main protagonists.

Nushin-ravaun felt that his soul was rejuvenated when he read the book. To reward Borzuy, he gave him permission to go to the treasury and take whatever he wished. But he brought back only a robe once worn by the king. Kasra asked why he had taken so little, and the sage responded that he had indeed taken a lot. It would be a great honor to wear a royal garment; it would gladden his friends and rankle his enemies. His only request was to be allowed to add his own introduction to the book so future generations would know that he was the one who had brought it to Iran. The king granted this wish.

THE GREAT ADVISOR'S MISFORTUNES

Buzarjmehr was tormented with travails
Ranging from house arrest to jail, dungeons
And finally, an Iron Maiden spiked with nails.

On a countryside jaunt, Kasra rested in the shade of a tree with his head in the lap of a concubine. He was also attended by Buzarjmehr, who had risen to the position of the grand vizier. While the king slept, a raven alighted nearby and used his beak to undo the stitching of his bejeweled armband. As the loosened jewels rolled off the king's arm, the bird swallowed them one by one and flew away.

When the king woke, he saw Buzarjmehr shaking his head and biting his lower lip. The wise vizier, adept in augury, was astonished at the enormity of the misfortune portended by this event. But Kasra, who had misunderstood the meaning of this gesture, asked himself: *What could have happened to produce such a reaction?* He falsely supposed that his digestive system had betrayed him as he slept and that his vizier was expressing dismay at the undignified sound that had issued from him.

"Who told you, mangy dog, that a sleeping man could control his gastral functions?" Kasra questioned. "Did you presume that I am a God or an angel? Is my body not composed of the common elements of wind, water, earth, and fire?"

The grand vizier was stunned by the speed with which the bad fortune he had foreseen was descending on him. He stood speechless as the king fulminated. In great agitation, the king mounted his horse, galloped to his palace, and issued orders that the vizier be confined to his mansion.

After a few days, one of Buzarjmehr's nephews, who was allowed to visit him in confinement, asked him for advice. He was a personal servant of Kasra and feared that he had offended the king while pouring water for him to wash his hands. Buzarjmehr asked the boy to demonstrate how he had performed the task, and instantly knew what he had done wrong. The attendant needed to increase the volume of water and stop only when the king commanded him.

Nushin-ravaun noticed the improvement in his attendant's performance and asked who had instructed him. Upon learning the source of the advice, Kasra sent word to his vizier asking if house arrest had served him well. Instead of apologizing or explaining his behavior, Buzarjmehr sent back an obtuse message that implied he was much better off than the king. Furious at this impudence, Kasra sent him to a dark dungeon and put him out of his mind.

After a while, the king sent another messenger to inquire if his vizier had changed his tune. Buzarjmehr maintained that even in his dark and damp chamber, he was better off than the king. This time the poor vizier was stuffed in an iron stockade standing up. The chamber was studded with sharp spikes protruding from the sides to increase the torment.

A few days later, the king sent his executioner along with his envoy, with orders to decapitate the prisoner if he gave the same blunt answer as he had in the past. The long-suffering man felt it was time he explained himself. He said to the king's envoy: "I have been saying this not to be intransigent, but because I believe that holding the grave responsibility of a king makes his position harder than being confined and tortured." With this explanation, the king took pity and commuted his sentence to house arrest.

THE MYSTERY OF THE SEALED CHEST

While Buzarjmehr was still restricted to his mansion, an envoy arrived from Rome with a riddle. The Caesar had sent a closed box challenging the Iranian sages to divine what was inside. He would reward Iran with riches if the king's wise men succeeded. Otherwise, Rome would have to be exempted from all taxes and levies due to the Iranian king. This was not the kind of challenge Kasra could resist. He asked for a week to unravel the mystery, but his wise men, seers and soothsayers failed to solve the riddle. The king was forced to send for his ostracized vizier.

Buzarjmehr presented himself at court freshly bathed, still weary of the king's wrath. The king did not mention the past and just asked him to solve the mystery of the Roman box. Buzarjmehr required an assistant as he had lost his sight due to the prolonged imprisonment in the dark dungeon. Having consulted the celestial charts, he asked his assistant to take him to a bazaar. There he stood on a corner, and had his assistant ask the first three women who passed by about their marital status. The first said that she was married and pregnant. The second said she was married but was not with child. The third confessed that she was a virgin and had no interest in marriage.

Buzarjmehr returned to the court and said that he knew what was inside the sealed box. The king noticed his former advisor's blindness and offered a brief apology for his cruel treatment before asking him to speak about the mystery box.

"The chest contains three pearls," Buzarjmehr replied. "One is fully polished and pierced. The second one is somewhat polished, and half pierced. The third one is neither polished nor pierced."

The box was opened to reveal what the vizier had prophesied. The Roman philosophers were speechless as they witnessed the perspicacity of the blind man. The king rewarded him with riches and fully expressed his sorrow over what he had suffered. Buzarjmehr related the story of the blackbird swallowing the jewels of the king's armband, which was the cause of his expression when the king woke up. He added that his fate was ineluctable and that the king had no reason to burden himself with guilt on his account.

TENSION WITH ROME AND THE AFFAIR OF THE COBBLER

The last significant event of Kasra's reign was the death of the Caesar of Rome. The king sent a letter of condolence to the Roman crown prince and assured him of Iran's continuing friendship and goodwill. But the letter achieved the opposite effect. The young Caesar was offended that he was not addressed as an equal sovereign but only as the bereaved son of the late Caesar. He offered the Iranian ambassador a lower seat in his hall, gifted him with cheap garments, and proceeded to dictate his response to the scribes:

> It does not behoove you to consider me your inferior. Nor am I less important than the chief of the Hephthalites whom you treat with deference. Disrespecting me is like attempting to cover the sun with a patch of cloud. Be just in your speech and mend your ways. I prefer to consider you what you were: a friend of my father than the enemy of the Roman nation.

The envoy hastily rode back to the capital, refusing to take the customary rest at the royal waystations. Kasra was shocked by the missive and thought the breach of etiquette grave enough to justify a military response. "I do not consider the new Caesar a man devoid of sense. The problem is that he thinks he is a king among kings. I swear by God, the moon, the sun, my throne, my crown, and the eternal fire at Azar-goshasp that I will not rest until I have wrecked his nation and plundered his treasures."

Once these words were uttered, trumpets and cymbals of war were sounded, and drums were fastened to the back of war elephants. The streets of Ctesiphon resembled a river of stars as knights in shining armor marched through the city gates in their golden boots.

The Caesar sent his chief chaplins at the head of an army of three hundred thousand from Amorium to the walled city of Aleppo. Kasra invested the city and pounded its walls with mangonels from across the moat that surrounded it. Bloody but inconclusive skirmishes were fought at the gates of the city. After two weeks, the battle turned in Iran's favor, though their victory was not a decisive one. Many Roman commanders were killed, and thirty thousand soldiers were taken captive. Iranians also suffered losses and were short of provisions and armaments.

Kasra needed financial resources to break the stalemate and launch a new offensive. Thus, he ordered Buzarjmehr to travel to the royal treasure house of Mauzandaran and bring the needed funds for the prosecution of the war. But the vizier countered that this would take too long and that it was best to borrow from local farmers and merchants.

Buzarjmehr and a learned assistant were sent off to solicit loans from the nearby Iranian districts. In this expedition they met with a prominent cobbler who asked how much money was required. The answer was four million dinars. The cobbler said that he could supply the entire amount by himself. To expedite accounting, instead of counting the coins, he ordered sacks of gold to be placed on scales. Soon the whole amount was weighed and piled up, ready for delivery to the king's coffers at the front. As the envoy was preparing to leave, the cobbler asked for a favor in exchange for the loan. Would the king issue a decree allowing his beloved son to be educated as a scribe? Happy to have secured the entire amount in one transaction, the envoy promised to convey the message. He was fairly confident that the king would grant the favor.

The king, too, was delighted that a single cobbler could provide the entire amount. He decreed that he be given one hundred thousand coins more than what he would be due at the time of the loan repayment. But his demeanor changed when Buzarjmehr mentioned the cobbler's request. "You have made a grave mistake. Load the money back on the camels and return it to the impertinent sender. How dare a mere shoemaker subvert the order of our ranked estates? Do you imagine my son would one day become king only to take advice from the son of a laborer? Won't posterity curse us for such an impious breach of tradition?"

The cobbler was disappointed to hear that the king had refused his loan.

But, as it turned out, the funds to continue the war were unnecessary. Soon after the affair of the cobbler, a mission consisting of forty Roman philosophers, each carrying an offering of thirty thousand pieces of gold, arrived at the pavilion of Kasra and asked for an audience with the king, which was granted.

"Our Caesar is a callow youth grieving for his father," said the leader. "He does not know the ways of the world. We apologize for his insolence and beg the king's pardon. We know that Rome has always paid tribute to Iran and wish that this tradition will be continued. "

Kasra smiled and agreed that the Caesar was a young and indiscreet man whose speech is unbecoming of his station. But, he added, it was fortunate that the great Alexander's wisdom was still preserved by the Roman philosophers. The delegation kissed the ground and fixed ten cowhides full of gold coins as the annual Roman tribute. Kasra accepted the offer but relegated the details to his bursar. The tribute and taxes were received, but the treasury officer stipulated that a thousand lengths of Roman brocade had to be added to the peace offering. The request was accepted, and the entire amount was delivered to the treasury. And thus, a treaty of peace was concluded, and the king's triumphant army returned to Ctesiphon.

KASRA NOUSHIN-RAVAUN ON MATTERS OF STATE

Kasra was not only a king but a sage
Ruler whose edicts could enlighten
The kings of every nation and every age.

The magi were the clerics of the Zoroastrian faith who helped administer Iran. They took every opportunity to consult their king on matters of state. His responses were preserved for posterity.

THE MAGI: The king treats some criminals who confess their crimes with leniency while others are severely punished. What accounts for this inconsistency?

THE KING: The guilty to the king is a like a patient to the healer. The constitutions of patients vary, and different patients require different medicines.

THE MAGI: Why has the king neglected to help the commander of Gorgan, who was robbed by Gilak bandits as he slept in a thicket?

THE KING: What use is a commander to me when he can't even protect himself?

THE MAGI: What does His Majesty think of a merchant who is wealthier than the king?

THE KING: It gives us pleasure to have subjects who are wealthier than us for it denotes that we have a prosperous nation.

THE MAGI: There are some children among the Roman captives. At what price should they be ransomed?

THE KING: Send them to their mothers without delay. Children should not have been enslaved.

THE MAGI: Rich Romans are ransoming their relatives on the cheap. What would the king advise on the price for manumission?

THE KING: Go easy on them. Let them buy the freedom of their relatives for the price of a sow. There is glory in conquest and plunder. There is none in ransoming captives.

THE MAGI: There are two affluent men in the capital. One of them is a moderate subject. The other is a profligate man who indulges in pleasure-seeking day and night. What says His Majesty?

THE KING: As long as he does not harm others, let him do what he wants with his money.

THE MAGI: The king of Yemen faults His Majesty for praising the dead more than he honors the living.

THE KING: Those who forget their dead are deficient in loyalty.

THE MAGI: It appears that the youngest of the king's sons spends much money to develop land for which he has paid less than the asking price.

THE KING: I condemn this practice. No one should be forced to sell his land under fair market value. Rectify this matter immediately.

THE MAGI: The king is, of course, above blame. But we wonder why he was more reticent as a young man and so outgoing later in his life.

THE KING: An infant does not need teeth. It is a different story when he becomes an adult and must bite into meat.

THE MAGI: The king has surpassed us all in judgment and knowledge. Naturally, his behavior should not be compared to that of his subjects. But why does His Majesty not emulate the previous kings?

THE KING: The previous kings only saw appearances while I see the essence of things.

THE MAGI: The royal falcon has brought down an eagle. What shall we do?

THE KING: Punish him for challenging his superior. Hang him from a high place and let him be a lesson, lest a knight takes it into his head to challenge his king.

THE MAGI: When the knight Borzin departed the court with a great army, advisers predicted that this would not bode well for the king should the knight turn rebellious.

THE KING: A competent king blessed by heaven is not afraid of such trifling matters.

THE MAGI: Goshasp, the old knight, is needy, and it would be a great help if he were given a governorship.

THE KING: Choose another. A man who does not have personal wealth is open to the temptations of corruption in a position of power.

THE MAGI: The royal chef complains that he goes out of his way to prepare extravagant dishes for the royal table. But the king gives the food away to his guests.

THE KING: Gluttony turns pleasure into pain.

THE MAGI: Courtiers are worried when the king ventures out without the proper protection of the guards.

THE KING: A righteous king's justice is all the protection he needs.

THE MAGI: Commander Khorausan alleges that the king has fired Karzasp. Why was that?

THE KING: He was sacked for disobeying our command. He failed to distribute the riches of our treasury among the needy.

THE MAGI: What was the guilt of old Mehrak, the servant? Why was he sacked?

THE KING: Carelessness and excessive drinking! He made a habit of coming to the court drunk.

THE MAGI: In the campaigns against Rome, the king only takes soldiers of Iranian descent. What is the reason for this?

THE KING: Motivation! There is an old enmity between Iranians and Romans.

THE MAGI: Who is an ideal soldier?

THE KING: He who does not tire of combat. A real soldier enjoys the arena as another might enjoy a pleasant feast.

THE MAGI: The caretaker of the fire temple at Fasa is at the gates. He says he has gone through his budget of three hundred thousand gold coins. The temple staff is worried about their daily expenses.

THE KING: Give him the money from the treasury. Don't question him on the matter.

THE MAGI: A disabled veteran injured on the Roman front has died. Four children survive him, and they are destitute.

THE KING: Give each child a thousand dirhams. Every disabled veteran should be registered and given a quarterly salary. After their passing, their children are entitled to the same stipend they received.

THE MAGI: A knight has extorted great wealth from the people of Merv. People are reduced to penury, and many have migrated to other cities.

THE KING: Confiscate his wealth and give it back to the people. Set up gallows in the middle of the city and hang the miscreant from it upside down. Let him be a lesson to all knights who might consider such despicable acts.

THE MAGI: There are many people at the gate, and they are praising the king for his justice.

THE KING: Thank heavens that none of us live in fear of the consequences of our unjust acts. We must continue to look out for the people.

THE MAGI: There seems to be too much carousing in the city. The poor and the rich drink and amuse themselves with music.

THE KING: It is my wish that all people, regardless of their rank, are merry while we rule this land.

THE MAGI: Some blame the king for his excessive generosity.

THE KING: What good are riches if we fail to distribute them among the poor?

THE MAGI: Jews and Christians consider Your Majesty their enemy. These are hypocrites who follow demonic religions.

THE KING: No king is considered excellent unless he is magnanimous and tolerant of diverse peoples.

THE MAGI: One of the king's administrators appears to have been too liberal with His Majesty's money. He has dispersed three hundred thousand coins to compensate day laborers.

THE KING: Money spent on the working poor is never wasted.

THE MAGI: But the treasury is nearly empty due to the king's generosity.

THE KING: Pruning a shrub causes it to grow back thicker. Miserliness breeds misery.

THE MAGI: Qara-khan, the cruel governor of Merv, has forced the people to pay excessive taxes.

THE KING: Far be it from us to benefit from the hardship of our subjects. Such wealth topples mansions and dooms lavish palaces to ruin. Return the monies to Merv and distribute them among the people. Make sure to add to it if people are still needy. And cross this enforcer's name from our servants' list. Never appoint someone of his ilk to high office.

THE MAGI: Why does His Majesty often relate the stories of King Jamshid and King Kay-Kavous?

THE KING: Because I don't wish my own deeds to be forgotten.

THE MAGI: Why doesn't the king share his secrets with his advisor, Bahman-e Sarfarauz?

THE KING: Because he is guided by impulse rather than reason. He is unreliable.

THE MAGI: Sometimes, the king appears hard to approach.

THE KING: I am the same that I have always been. I get along with the clerics, and people who are guided by reason. But I have no time for those who are inspired by evil.

THE MAGI: His Majesty has stated that the world will continue without religion but not without a just king. What is the meaning of this?

THE KING: The world is never devoid of religions. There are many religions; some are false, and some are true. The fact is that falsehoods uttered about God do not affect the world. But the world will fall apart if there is no king on the throne. The world goes on without religion. But everything falls apart if there is no king.

THE MAGI: The king has said: "I am the essence of the age. He who praises the world has praised me." Is this true?

THE KING: Indeed! Kings are the crown of the world.

KASRA NOUSHIN-RAVAUN ON MATTERS OF ETHICS AND FAITH

There was an old man from a knightly line
Who compiled a record of Kasra's ethical advice
And quoted them when he wished to opine.

THE MAGI: How should a supplicant ensure that God hears and fulfills all his prayers?

THE KING: Be moderate in what you ask God. Too many yearnings darken the heart.

THE MAGI: What is the foundation of wisdom?

THE KING: Learning, restraint, modesty, and nobility of birth.

THE MAGI: What are the signs of a good king?

THE KING: Generosity, knowledge, royal deportment, divine sanction, wisdom, and piety.

THE MAGI: What is most important among the requirements of a king? Is it divine sanction (farr) or learning?

THE KING: Farr alone does not guarantee a successful reign. Learning is more important than the inherited right of kingship that is endowed by God.

THE MAGI: What blights life?

THE KING: Need, avarice, and associating with mean-spirited people.

THE MAGI: Why should one eschew evil if death wipes the slate clean, equalizing good and bad deeds?

THE KING: We leave behind a reputation that outlives us for a long time.

THE MAGI: What is the greatest treasure in life?

THE KING: An easy conscience and a life free of worries.

THE MAGI: What are the cardinal virtues?

THE KING: Modesty for a woman and knowledge for a man.

THE MAGI: What conduct is pleasing to God?

THE KING: Humility and being guided by practical reason. Associating with the wise and avoiding the quarrelsome and idle. Working hard, as there is no shame in working. Always being patient and compassionate toward the poor.

THE MAGI: Why does the king appear indifferent when he is praised?

THE KING: Because I am not sure that the praise is pure and sincere. People might honor a king out of fear or greed.

NOMINATING THE NEXT KING

At the age of sixty-one, I ought to repent
From wine. Imbibing for an old man is like
Wearing a summer shirt at the winter's advent.

I pray that the Lord grant me enough time
To finish this poem that extols the great kings
From Kayumart to Yazdegerd III in rhyme.

On the sixth day of the festival of Nowruz, King Kasra chose Hormazd from among his six sons as the crown prince. He enjoined him to rule in justice, keep the company of learned men, and eschew hasty judgments, lying, and false promises. He warned him against arming the lowborn mercenaries to fight his wars, for they often turn against their benefactor.

"Do not go back on a promise nor utter a falsehood," Kasra advised his crown prince Hormazd. "To deserve the crown, a prince must acquire learning, master the arts, and above all, act wisely. He must eschew unnecessary bloodshed in wars and be generous as long as it does not shade into profligacy."

LAST WILL AND TESTAMENT OF THE KING

When Kasra reached the age of seventy-four, he wrote his last will and testament, which included exact instructions for his internment.

> Build my tomb on the forbidding heights of a mountain. After blood is drained from my corpse through an incision in the belly, let it be perfumed with camphor and musk, wrapped in Roman brocade, and placed on an ivory pedestal. Let my crown

hang above my body. Arrange basins of rosewater, wine, saffron, musk, camphor, and ambergris around my mausoleum. After the entrance is sealed, let people mourn me for two months. Then it will be time for them to obey Hormazd as their new king.

Once the cup of his life was filled to the brim
The king quaffed it and yielded to his fate.
This world won't be kinder to us than it was to him.

CHAPTER 24

A Contested Kingship: Hormazd

You can glimpse the apple blossom's spring flair
On the summer fruit that glitters like a pearl . . .
Too bad all colors will fade in autumnal despair.

I asked Maukh, resplendent in his white mane,*
To speak of King Hormazd, and he related
The story of that sovereign's troubled reign.

On the day of his inauguration, King Hormazd wore the crown of the olden kings and pledged to comfort the poor, promote the gifted, and spread justice throughout the world. But he concluded with a harsh warning: "I will smite anyone who dreams of rising above his station. I will pulverize he who aspires to rival the king in power or wealth."

The young king was suspicious of his late father's top advisors, as he had a sense that they were not entirely loyal of him. So he decided to liquidate the leadership of the court. His first target was Izad-goshasp, who had been one of Nushin-ravaun's highest ministers. The poor elderly man was falsely accused of a crime and thrown in jail. His friends and family were barred from visitations. In despair, Izad-goshasp sent a note to his companion, Zarathustra, who had risen to the office of the chief of the magi.

> Help me, old friend. They are starving me in this dungeon. Everybody has forsaken me. You are the only one left. Give me the gift of a warm repast now and promise to have me properly interred when I die.

Zarathustra's heart broke. Although he was aware of the danger of fraternizing with the king's enemy, he had his cook prepare a meal and

* One of the four collectors of the prose archetype of *Shahnameh*.

went to the prison. The warden, who had strict orders to keep the prisoner in isolation, did not dare to interfere with the prominent cleric's call, but he did inform the king of the unusual visit.

The old friends began their meal with the solemn Zoroastrian ceremonies of holding a bundle of holy twigs, called Barsom, and reciting the mantras of Bazh. After the dinner, Izad-goshasp appealed to Zarathustra to remind the king that he had served his father with distinction and nurtured him as a child. To make a loyal servant suffer such ignominy in his old age was an affront to decency. Zarathustra was sad as he knew remonstrating with Hormazd would only make him angrier. And indeed, soon after his visit, Izad-goshasp was slain by the king's henchmen.

Thereafter the priest lived in fear of his own life. So, it was with much trepidation that he accepted an invitation to a private visit at the court. Given his high office, he knew that the method of his execution would likely be subtle.

Zarathustra entered the royal audience hall. After a brief conversation, the king invited him to stay to appreciate the culinary skills of his new chef. The priest feigned a lack of appetite and watched the king eat from a delectable spread. Then a dish made of bone marrow was presented. Hormazd scooped up some choice parts of the stew and made a wrap for Zarathustra. The priest protested that he was full, but the king persisted. There was no way to reject such a direct request, so he reluctantly took a bite knowing that it was laced with poison. Shortly thereafter the toxin started to take effect, and Zarathustra limped home in pain. He tried an antidote, but it was ineffective, so he laid down and awaited death. As he was taking his last breaths, a royal envoy arrived to check on him. With great effort, the saintly man lifted his head and mouthed these words: "Go tell this king that his days are numbered. I doubt he will fare well in this world. And, when we stand before the divine tribunal of justice, I will charge him with my murder."

The envoy's eyes welled with tears as he delivered the message. When the king heard this message, he, too, was sad and even shed a few tears. But his great purge continued. The next target, Simauh-e Borzin, was to be eliminated without a royal indictment. Instead, Hormazd pressured one of the victim's close friends to denounce him. The chosen accomplice, Bahraum-e Azarmehan, readily accepted to play his part in the diabolical plot.

When the sun of a late spring day rose in the constellation of Gemini, the king climbed the ivory throne and addressed Bahraum. "Tell me," he urged, "What do you think of your friend Simauh-e Borzin? Is he a scion of Light or a descendant of Darkness? Does he deserve honors and accolades or the agony of chastisement?"

Bahraum-e Azarmehan knew that he was expendable once he had denounced his friend. So, he took it further: "Let His Majesty not utter the name of that treasonous wretch. Simauh-e Borzin is an inveterate liar, intent on destroying the land of Iran!"

"Why would you bear false witness against me?" Simauh responded. "What have I done to deserve such calumny?"

"He who sows the wind shall reap the whirlwind," Bahraum responded. "Surely you recall the day we joined such luminaries as chief of the magi Borz-Mehr and Izad-goshasp to advise the late king on the matter of his succession. King Kasra Nushin-ravaun was contemplating who among his six sons should inherit the throne. That council unanimously rejected Hormazd's candidacy, since he had descended from our enemies on his mother's side. He even resembles his mother, the daughter of the khagan and the granddaughter of the emperor of China. You were the only one who rose in support of this cruel man. The time has come to taste the bitter fruit of the tree you planted, for on that day you wrecked this nation and doomed yourself in the bargain."

Hormazd was stunned by this revelation and mortified by the utter failure of his scheme. He quickly dismissed the assembly and sent both men to prison to await their fate. Simauh-e Borzin was killed in his cell after three days. Knowing that he was next, Bahraum-e Azarmehan sent an urgent message to the crown asking for a brief stay of his execution so he could bring a crucial matter to His Majesty's attention. The wish was granted, and he was brought to the court in chains. Bahraum said that he knew of a letter written in King Kasra Nushin-ravaun's hand. It was kept in a locked and sealed box in the royal archives and would be of great interest to the king. The chest was retrieved, and the letter was read aloud:

> Hormazd will rule in peace and prosperity for a dozen years. Then enemies will appear on every side, and chaos will reign. He will be blinded and murdered by his own relatives.

The king tore up the letter. His complexion turned sallow as he glared at Bahraum-e Azarmehan with bloodshot eyes: "Why would you bring this accursed letter to my attention? What good will this do other than troubling my mind?"

"I wanted to mar your macabre pleasure in shedding the blood of innocent men," Bahraum explained. "You are the spawn of our enemies. You don't deserve to wear the crown of the kings of Kay."

Bahraum was sent back to jail. When the moon rose over the mountains the following morning, he too was put to the sword.

By the end of these bloody purges, the royal court was bereft of sage advisors. But Hormazd was considerate of his ordinary subjects. For instance, he decreed that cultivated land should never be trampled by the horses of the noblemen or soldiers. As punishment for this infraction, the ears and tail of the offending horse would be cut off, and its owner would be obligated to compensate the farmer for his loss. Not even the crown prince Khosrow-Parviz was exempted when his favorite horse wandered into the crops of a peasant.

On another occasion, a knight whose cook was preparing a savory dish took a bunch of sour grapes from a vineyard. The farmer threatened to report the theft. In a great panic, the offending knight undid the buckle of his bejeweled cummerbund and gave it to the farmer as reimbursement. Although this was a rich payment for a bunch of unripe grapes, the farmer said: "I am doing you a favor by accepting this for my stolen property. You know well what would happen to you if I were to press charges."

SHATTERING INVASIONS

In the twelfth year of Hormazd's reign, news of various border incursions reached the royal court. The most threatening army was that of Saveh-shah, an Eastern king, whose four-hundred thousand men had crossed the Merv River and were approaching the city of Herat. He sent an insulting message to the Iranian king:

> Hurry up and prepare your realm. Pave your roads and repair your bridges for the arrival of my army. Stock up on feed for my horses. I am about to cross your eastern frontier, pass through Iran and invade the lands of the Romans and the Arabs beyond your western borders.

Saveh-shah was treating Iran as a vassal state rather than an enemy worthy of invasion. But this was not the only threat to Iran's territory. Another army of Khazar tribes was advancing from Armenia and Ardebil in the north. A third invasion was mounted by the Arab chiefs Abbas and Amr, and they were encamped at the southwestern borders. The fourth threat came from Iran's old enemies, the Romans. The Caesar appeared to be marching with an army of one hundred thousand soldiers to take back the cities they had lost to Kasra Nushin-ravaun.

A war council was formed to advise the king. Although no one remembered such a convergence of enemies in the history of the country, the committee was sanguine on the prospects of all but one of the invasions. The chief of the magi summed up the committee's consultations.

"We can mollify the Romans by letting them take back the cities they lost to Kasra. Khazars and Arabs can also be managed with our existing military forces. But the threat from the east is serious. Alas, we don't have a hero like Esfandiar, who saved Iran from the scourge of Arjausp of Touran at the time of King Goshtausp. We must work with what we have. Let the scribes take account of the total infantry and cavalry that we can call to service."

The accounting revealed that the entire army of Iran amounted to just one hundred thousand soldiers. Fortunately, the Romans withdrew after recovering the territories they had lost, the northern invasion was defeated by the able knight Khorrad-e Borzin, and the Arabic threat faded away. Saveh-shah's army, however, continued to present an immediate and insurmountable threat.

A PROVIDENTIAL SAVIOR

As the king's advisors were fumbling for a solution to the eastern peril, a knight named Nastuh went to Hormazd with the news that his father, Mehran-shetaud, had intelligence that could be conducive to a solution. Upon receiving an audience, the old knight related the story of his journey to the Chinese khaganate.

He was the ambassador of the late king Kasra, charged with choosing his queen from among the daughters of the khagan. Once he had selected the bride, the khagan charged his soothsayers to determine if the union was auspicious. Promising as that royal marriage appeared, there was trouble in the future for the son who would be born to the couple. Of course, he would become the king of Iran. But then, he would face a shattering invasion from the east. At that moment, a fierce warrior would emerge to save Iran. He would come from a distant land, and he would be called Bahraum-e Chubineh. Tall and possessed of a big nose and curly hair, this man was destined to keep Kasra's son from ruin.

Mehran-shetaud fell to the ground and died upon finishing his story. The old knight had performed his last duty by rekindling hope in Hormazd's heart.

Hormazd asked his courtiers to find the hero described by the old knight. The royal groom in waiting said he knew a man who matched those descriptions. He was Bahraum, the son of Bahraum, and grandson of Goshasp, a marvelous equestrian from Rey. His family had governed that region for generations, and he was currently in charge of the districts of Barda' and Ardebil. The king sent a message to this man to drop everything and come to Ctesiphon. Bahraum-e Chubineh jumped on his horse and did not dismount until he was at the gates of the royal palace.

The king gladly welcomed the awaited guest and commanded him to rest for the night and return to him at sunrise.

When the musky cape of darkness fell off the night's shoulders, Hormazd called upon Bahraum-e Chubineh to attend the assembly of knights and answer his questions.

"Should we fight or negotiate with the eastern khagan Saveh-shah?"

"It's not wise to negotiate with someone who has come for war," advised Bahraum-e Chubineh. "Talking to such a foe will be seen as weakness, which will only embolden this enemy and encourage others to launch their invasions."

"Shall we wait or give battle immediately?" asked the king.

"Aggression must be met with aggression. We should not fear defeat, for death is not shameful after an honorable war. It's the humiliation of surviving such a defeat that should scare us."

With every bold reply of the confident knight, the king seemed surer that he had found his providential savior. But the army commanders looked down on the newcomer and considered him a provincial braggart. After the meeting, they approached Bahraum and cautioned him to be careful when dispensing advice in the king's presence.

"Do you know this enemy is so numerous that it covers the eastern horizon?" asked one of the imperious commanders. "And pray to tell, what kind of a fool would accept the command of our meager forces against such overwhelming odds?"

Bahraum's answer was stunning in its simplicity: "With the king's permission, I will be that commander, and I don't have the slightest doubt that I will crush this enemy."

Hormazd was pleased when this conversation was reported to him. He immediately appointed the impetuous Bahraum field marshal of the army and authorized him to select his top brass and requisition his needed weapons from the arsenals of Pars and Ahvauz. Bahraum-e Chubineh appointed a knight by the name of Bahraum-e Siavoshan as his chief of staff. Yalaun-sineh was put in charge of the vanguard. Izad-goshasp was given the left and right flanks, and Bonda-goshasp took command of the rearguard.

Bahraum's cavalry consisted of only twelve thousand crack troops chosen for their courage and riding skills. And it was composed entirely of forty-year-old warriors. People were puzzled about the eccentric commander's choice in the numbers and the age of his troops. But none was more curious than the king.

"You know that Saveh-shah has amassed an immense army," he said. "Why on earth would you go against him with only twelve thousand middle-aged warriors?"

"His Majesty knows that smaller numbers can be an advantage in battle when the winds of good fortune are at an army's back," said the brash commander. "Consider the cases of Rostam rescuing King Kay-Kavous from Haumavaran, Gudarz avenging Siavosh's murder in the Battle of the Eleven Heroes, and Esfandiar defeating Jamausp in the Battle of the Invincible Castle. All these heroes had only twelve thousand warriors at their disposal. Too many men can complicate command. Regarding the age of my cavalry, I will say that men at that age have experience in war and a reputation to defend. They have families whom they must protect from slavery. Overall, a man of forty combines all the attributes I seek in a good soldier. He is at the peak of his strength, courageous, motivated, and level-headed in combat." Impressed by the sober mind of his laconic general, Hormazd decided to dispatch his armies to the front without delay. The next day, when Bahraum came to court in full armor to formally accept his commission, he was thrilled to also receive Rostam's legendary standard that featured the image of a dragon on a purple backdrop.

"This is the flag of the knight who served my ancestors with distinction," Hormazd declared. Carry it with pride, for you are the Rostam of our age!" The new field marshal of the Iranian armies rode out of court holding the standard of Rostam and waded into a sea of his admiring warriors.

Bahraum-e Chubineh requested that a scribe be appointed to record the heroic deeds of his army. The king appointed Mehran-Dabir to the position.

As the king watched the army depart through the gates of Ctesiphon, he turned to a high clerical advisor and said: "What do you think of this scene? It seems like the stuff of legends, doesn't it? And we have such an extraordinary commander!"

"I, too, wish for a crushing victory. But this general was too bold as he spoke with His Majesty. I am afraid this hubris might one day turn into royal ambitions."

"Don't lace my panacea with venom," said the king. "The only way Bahraum-e Chubineh would be a king is if I make him so. And I am not above appointing him my crown prince if he rids me of this arrogant foe."

The priest wilted and bit his lips in silence. But the conversation had unsettled the king. He thought it prudent to monitor the man on whom he had lavished so many resources. To this purpose, he appointed an agent with the gift for intelligence gathering and soothsaying to follow the army and report back.

The first report was sent shortly after the army's departure. A sheep's-head peddler was watching the army march past his stand. Bahraum approached the peddler's large wicker basket, picked out a sheep's head with his lance, and flung it in the air, saying: "This is how I will handle Saveh-shah."

The agent relayed this act as an example of Bahraum's haughtiness and interpreted it as a bad omen. Hormazd agreed with both assessments and sent a herald urging the commander to halt the army and return to the capital for consultations. Bahraum disobeyed, reminding the king that such a move would be both inauspicious and harmful to the army's morale. "Let me return to you only after I have crushed your enemy," he wrote. The king liked this answer and sent a message countermanding himself.

When the army reached Khuzestan, a woman brought a grievance against a soldier who had taken her sack of hay without pay. She said that the soldier was wearing a distinctive iron helmet. The guilty party was found and executed as an object lesson to the army. Bahraum reminded his army that it was forbidden to abuse or exploit ordinary folk.

As the army was approaching the plain of Herat, Hormazd decided to help his commander with a bit of strategic deception. He sent Khorrad-e Borzin to mislead the enemy into thinking that Iran had chosen the path of appeasement.

The idea was to allow Bahraum time to slip in from the west and place himself between the enemy coming from the north and the city of Herat. The city would have been a source of supplies and offer Saveh-shah the higher ground. Blocking Saveh-shah's access to Herat would afford the Iranians a superior position on the battlefield and deny the enemy fresh provisions.

Khorrad-e Borzin bypassed Bahraum-Chubineh's camp and went directly to Saveh-shah, humbling himself before the powerful khagan. He declared that he had come to offer a peaceful resolution to the conflict. But the deceptive mission was jeopardized when heralds reported a small force of Iranians between their encampment and Herat. The khagan asked Khorrad who they might be. He insisted that the force that was seen on the hills could not possibly be the Iranian army:

"My king would not be so foolish as to send such a small contingent against you! This is probably a mutinous faction of the army or a bunch of bandits on the run. They are certainly small enough to be mercenaries hired to protect a merchant's caravan passing through."

The khagan believed Khorrad's explanation. But to ascertain the identity of the newly arrived armed men, he sent his younger son, Baghpur, to investigate. He found a small army bivouacking on a strategically favorable slope surrounded by rocky hills. Baghpur approached Bahraum-e Chubineh and asked what business he had to come before his father's formidable army. Were they a rebellious army faction, highwaymen, or mercenaries?

"We are neither criminals nor mercenaries," Bahraum responded. "And may God not bring the day that I rebel against my king. I am here on a mission from Hormazd to crush Saveh-shah's army and cut off his head."

Baghpur was taken aback by this blunt reply. When the story was reported to the khagan, he reacted with fury and sent for the Iranian who had deceived him. But Khorrad-e Borzin had escaped under cover of night. "How," shouted the khagan, "did he get past our sentries? Were they asleep at their posts?"

Of course, the invaders had a vast advantage in numbers. But the khagan knew that strategic disadvantages could neutralize superiority in numbers on the battlefield. He seemed to be facing an uncommonly brazen and confident adversary in the Iranian commander who had occupied the higher ground and blocked his access to Herat. Thus, he sent three increasingly solicitous letters trying to cajole Bahraum to switch sides. In the first, Saveh-shah implied that Hormazd had sent him on a suicide mission to get rid of him. Bahraum replied that it was no suicide mission and even if it were, dying in the cause of one's king was an honor. The khagan then tried to entice him with riches. Bahraum said that the only prize he would consider taking was the head of the enemy king. Finally, the khagan sent his last and most desperate letter:

> Only a doomed man turns a deaf ear to good advice. Open your ears and listen to me. Kings compete to call themselves my slaves. Only two are deserving of the royal name: I and my son Parmudeh. Your King Homazd scoffs at this fact, but he is a fool.
>
> As you see, my well-armed cavalry covers the horizons. My troops are so numerous that they will form an unbroken line on their march from here to Ctesiphon. Your troops will simply be arrow fodder if they are not trampled under the feet of my one thousand armored war elephants. Some demon must have deceived you into thinking that your puny army is a match for the might of the great khagan. Give up this mad fantasy and come to me. I will conquer Iran and make you its king before advancing to conquer Rome and Arabia.
>
> Don't get me wrong. I do appreciate your valor and military skills. It is evident that you are descended from a line of heroes, and it would be a waste of good military talent to kill you. If you stop this obstinacy, I will give you my daughter in marriage. We will be kin and rule the world together. Think before you respond, as this is my last offer.

Bahraum's reply was swift and characteristically terse:

> Those who can, act. Those who can't, blather. Stop boring me with these tedious letters. Your delusions of grandeur are pathetic.

> How dare you offer me terms? It reminds me of the saying that the one thrown out of the village always claims he was its headman.
>
> I find it odd that you offer your daughter as my bride. I would respect this proposal if you did not covet the crown of Iran. Indeed, I would be proud to be your son-in-law if you extended that offer before you found me blocking your army. But such a bid is worthless when the tip of my lance is close enough to pierce your ear. Once I've killed you and crushed your army, your daughter will be mine if I deign to take her.
>
> You keep boasting of the superiority of your army just as a dog running after a mirage barks louder the closer he gets to his imaginary lake. You accuse me of delusions. But you are the one who is delusional as you fantasize about giving the crown of a land you have not even conquered as a gift to your would-be accomplices.
>
> We are losing time. Let's get on with this war. I am in a hurry because I have promised my king to bring him your head within three days, and I am running out of time. One last warning: Watch out for my dragon flag, for it will be the last thing you see in this world.

Baghpur was outraged when this message arrived. He berated his father's dithering. "No more letters," he barked. "Stop groveling. It is unseemly to hesitate while this formidable army is at your disposal."

Recognizing that he had no option but to engage the enemy, the khagan ordered the drums and cymbals of war to be sounded. The forces of the east were arrayed in four segments of thirty thousand soldiers each. The left and right flanks positioned themselves behind the row of one thousand elephants, while the center and the rearguard lined up behind them. But this was just a fraction of the khagan's army. Most of them were left behind in the mountains as they could not fit in the theater of war. The dust of the moving divisions turned the sky the color of ebony.

The Iranian war formation was like that of the enemy, but with only three thousand warriors. Leaders of the four divisions were assigned new positions. Hamdan-goshasp led the vanguard. Izad-goshasp and

Bonda-goshasp took the right and left flanks, and Yalaun-sineh was in charge of the rearguard. As the westerly sun sank low, both sides lit huge bonfires.

Bahraum spent one watch of the night in conference with his commanders, and then retired to his tent to sleep. But he awoke with a start after a terrible nightmare where he was standing alone on the battlefield, unhorsed, and defeated. He called on his commanders, but none responded. The next morning, he went about preparing his men for war while keeping the portentous dream to himself.

At this time, Khorrad-e Borzin arrived, having just escaped Saveh-shah's camp. The intelligence he brought about the numbers and armaments of the enemy was not encouraging: "I can't fathom your confidence, Bahraum. Why do you suppose you can win this war against the formidable Saveh-shah? None has ever seen an army this immense. Don't walk into this trap. Pull back. Pity yourself and save the lives of your soldiers."

Bahraum-e Chubineh blew up in a ferocious retort. "You come from the city of fishmongers, and that's all your people do up there, all year long. You are still a petty fishmonger at heart. Stick to hustling fish and leave the business of war to real men. We trade in the currency of lances, maces, and javelins. When the sun climbs over that black mountain, I'll show you how a true warrior handles the likes of this pitiful enemy."

By dawn, the two narrow pathways on the hills behind the Iranian army had been walled in by the masons of Bahraum. The intrepid commander spoke to his troops as the August sun rose in the constellation of Leo. "On this day, you have only two choices: win glory or die. Withdrawal is not an option. I swear I will personally behead anyone who is caught trying to desert."

As the final preparations were made, the scribe, Mehran-Dabir, approached the commander. "This is madness. We are going to lose this war. We will be disgraced, and Iran will be ruined. Don't you see that the enemy has covered the horizons of the land and the sea? Compared to them, we are like a single white hair on the back of a black cow!"

"Out of my sight, you worthless pen pusher!" said Bahraum. "Your job is to write down what happens. Who told you to count soldiers for me?"

The scribe went to Khorrad-e Borzin, who was similarly humiliated by Bahraum and said: "This man is possessed by a demon." Then the two of them climbed to the safety of a hill to view the battlefield.

Bahraum's last act before combat was to prostrate himself before God and supplicate. "If you deem this war unjust and favor Saveh-shah, then give me a calm heart as I fight to the last drop of my blood. But if I am on the right path, steel my heart, give me victory, and make the world prosperous by my conquest."

The khagan commanded his sorcerers to create fire, smoke, wind, and clouds. Bahraum ordered his men to disregard the insubstantial magic, charge into the storm and engage the enemy. As the Iranian troops fearlessly rushed forward, Saveh-shah realized that his sorcery had failed, and commanded his right flank to attack. They crushed the left flank of the Iranian army and were about to break into the heart of their formation when a group of Iranian warriors hastily pulled back to redeploy. Bahraum noticed the breach and rode to the middle of the fight, where he swiftly knocked down three of the khagan's top warriors with his lance. "You call this fighting?" he snarled at his men. "Aren't you ashamed of this pathetic performance? Is this how you defend the integrity of your lines and your honor?"

Then he turned and attacked the right flank of Saveh-shah's army so violently that their standard fell. Having performed these feats, Bahraum rode back his troops, shouting. "There is no retreat from this war. The only path that leads to security is through the iron wall of the khagan's shields. Break through that wall. Give it all you have, my fearless men. You'll be home before you know it."

With this charge, the Iranians slammed themselves against the enemy's lines and broke into the heart of their opponent's army. The khagan sent his elephants against them, and at Bahraum's instruction, the Iranians showered their trunks with their poplar arrows. The elephants turned back and tramped through the khagan's forces in panic. Bahraum's warriors exploited the ensuing chaos and cut a wide path of devastation through the thick rows of the enemy. The advantage had switched to the Iranian side. Bahraum roared:

"Take the battle to them. They are on the run. Don't relent. Send them a hail of arrows and finish them off, for this is the day of action. There will be time enough for rest and leisure."

As disorganization turned into an all-out rout, Saveh-shah jumped off his golden dais and rode his dun horse down the hill.

But it was too late. The hunter had spotted his prey. Bahraum dismounted, bent his right knee, stretched his left leg, and chose a well-fletched messenger of death from his quiver. Calmly notching the arrow in his composite bow, he rubbed the grip and pulled the string back to his ear. The horny sinews of the bow groaned to the high heavens. No sooner had the arrow point kissed the fingertips of his left hand than the shaft went through Saveh-shah's spine. His body fell with an ominous thump. Saveh-shah's golden crown rolled across the ground while his soul departed the mundane world.

Such are the fickle ways of this revolving dome
Don't be seduced by its comforts for it lulls you
Into a sense of security and then wrecks your home.

Bahraum took Saveh-shah's head as a trophy. The body of the fallen leader was carried away by his soldiers, singing dirges and lamentations. Baghpur, who was commanding the army that was left behind, was puzzled by the sorry scene of the returning soldiers. Apparently things had not gone well for his father's army. He asked the officers about the reason for their defeat at the hands of such a small force. They gave an account of what happened and praised the Iranian commander's singular leadership. Baghpur remained stoic as he reviewed the rambling march of his father's vanquished soldiers, telling himself that the spectacular loss was the will of the heavens. Who would have thought that half of his father's massive army would be trapped behind the battlefield while the other half was trampled under the feet of his own elephants?

When the bad news reached the crown prince Parmudeh, he wept bitterly and threw off his crown. He asked the officers to explain how they had succumbed to such a puny foe. They extolled the superlative Iranian commander who surpassed the legendary Rostam in courage, might, and skills. He had won the war hardly losing any men.

Parmudeh had no choice but to avenge his father. He still had one hundred thousand soldiers, which vastly outnumbered the twelve thousand forces of the Iranians. But the recent defeat had wreaked havoc on their morale. Parmudeh, who was now the khagan, brought his army to the edge of the river Oxus in preparation for war.

Back at the Iranian front, Bahraum assigned Khorrad-e Borzin the task of taking a headcount of the Iranian leaders. This was a difficult task as the ground was soaked in blood and covered with the corpses of the enemy. All the warriors were accounted for except for Bahraum-e Siavoshan. But as they were looking for his corpse, the commander appeared on the horizon dragging a captive.

The field marshal greeted his commander and took charge of the strange, redheaded man whose irises were vertical, like those of a cat. "State your name and pedigree! You look like a demon from the depths of hell."

"I am a sorcerer," said the stranger. "And yet, as a manipulator of dreams, I could be of use to any commander. I am the one who sent that nightmare upon you last night. Fate was against Saveh-shah. He lost the war, but if you pity me, I will be an asset to you."

Bahraum-e Chubineh was tempted to keep the sorcerer and make use of him. But then he thought better of it and had him executed. After all, he had not been much help to Saveh-shah! And besides, why would one align himself with sorcerers instead of asking the Almighty for help?

As the soldiers were mopping up the battlefield and reorganizing themselves, Mehran-Dabir asked for an audience with the commander to express his admiration: "I declare that neither King Feraydun nor the late Kasra Nushin-ravaun could have hoped for such a stupendous hero. You are a commander descended from commanders and the sole savior of Iran. Proud is the father who sired you. Kudos on the mother who gave birth to you."

The next day Bahraum-e Chubineh charged the scribes to draft a report of the war he had won. The account was given to an official accompanying the caravan of the captives heading to Ctesiphon. The spitted heads of

Saveh-shah and his son Baghpur, who was captured and executed shortly after the battle, went ahead of the triumphant procession.

Back at Ctesiphon, the king was anxiously complaining that he had not heard any news of the war for two weeks when a herald rushed in with the good tidings of an Iranian victory and the impending arrival of the procession of war slaves and camels loaded with the plunder of the battle. Hormazd descended the throne and prostrated himself before God in a gesture of gratitude. The remarkable victory was not due to good generalship or the troops' bravery, he declared. All credit was due to God.

Feeling grateful to fortune, the king forgave taxes for four years and distributed one hundred thousand gold coins equally among the courtiers, the needy, the Zoroastrian fire temples and the caravanserais that had fallen into disrepair. After a week of lavish celebrations, the king sent Bahraum-e Chubineh a missive thanking him for his service and awarding him a silver throne, golden slippers of knighthood, and dominion over the territory that started from the land of the Hephthalites to the River Barak. He ordered his commander to share the remaining plunder with his warriors, and then count, seal, and dispatch Saveh-shah's entire treasure house to the capital. Bahraum's charge was to prosecute the war with Parmudeh in the enemy territory until he surrendered.

CONFRONTING THE YOUNG KHAGAN

On the way to confront the Iranian forces, the crown prince Parmudeh deposited his treasury at Avauzeh castle for safekeeping before crossing the Oxus. He set up camp with his army near the city of Balkh, where the young khagan set eyes on Bahraum for the first time. He turned to his commanders with grudging admiration for his opponent.

"There goes a lion of a commander. After this victory, he is the leader of a confident army. I don't suppose we would want to engage him in combat on the battlefield. But if God is with me, I will ambush this proud man and avenge my father."

The next day was a Wednesday, and Bahraum-e Chubineh planned to heed the warning of his astrologers and avoid bold adventures. Thus, he arranged a feast to unwind and drink with his friends.

While Parmudeh was preparing for a night raid, his scouts informed him that Bahraum could be surprised and slain at this banquet. The khagan sent six thousand elite warriors to surround the garden where the feast was in progress. But Bahraum was not one to be so easily surprised.

As soon as the commander got wind of the surrounding army's approach, he charged Yalaun-sineh to punch a hole in the garden wall just big enough for him and Izad-goshasp to escape. This was done with lightning speed. The rest of the party exited through another hole, dug in another wall, and joined the first group. Then they snuck to the back of Parmudeh's war party and mounted a counterattack. Wielding a javelin, Bahraum led the charge pushing Parmudeh's cavalry back to their camp.

On that dark night of long blades, the ground was drenched with blood, and rocks resembled the red coral of the warm seas. As the khagan's forces turned to flee, Bahraum cornered Parmudeh near his pavilion. "What do you think you are doing here, boy? Shouldn't you be back home suckling milk at your mother's breast?"

"Haven't you done enough, you ferocious lion?" Parmudeh asked. "The blood you have spilled could quench leopards of the land and the crocodiles of the seven seas. You killed my crowned father, who was beloved by the heavens. You butchered our army so savagely that the sun and the moon had to avert their eyes. Suppose you killed me. Then what? Death is the common fate of everyone, the Persians as well as the Turks. But you cannot kill me unless my hour of death has come. Remember Bahraum! Great generals are not stubborn. Give me safe conduct to get back to my camp where I can write a letter of surrender and ask your king to spare my life."

The Iranian commander nodded and allowed Parmudeh to retreat. He spent the rest of the night decapitating enemy soldiers and piling their heads up so high that thereafter the area was known as "Bahraum's Mound." In the morning, he dispatched a messenger to King Hormazd informing him that the new khagan had surrendered.

Meanwhile, Parmudeh dashed back to Avauzeh castle and bolted the gates against the Iranians who had given chase. To induce him to come out, Bahraum had the enemy soldiers brought in full view of the castle and executed. Parmudeh turned a blind eye to this scene and refused to come out, so Bahraum taunted him with a letter.

> Why would the great king of the Turks and the Chinese hide behind fortress walls like a woman? What happened to your father's plans to march through Iran and conquer the Romans and the Turks? Where are your war elephants, armored cavalry, and sorcerers? Be reasonable. You have lost. Send me your treasure, as you won't need it anymore. In return, I will write to my king and plead for mercy on your behalf. Otherwise, I'll be here waiting for you, if you wish to come out and face me like a man.

Parmudeh sent back the following reply:

> Hubris has blinded you. Rest assured that the euphoria of victory will pass. This sort of arrogance never pays. Think about my father's fate, who was brought low by his ambition. Witness how my fortunes declined in the blink of an eye. Don't take pride in the number and prowess of your soldiers. The heavens' revolving dome can turn your chalice of ambrosia into a cup of poison. He who spills blood dies in a pool of blood. You kill the Turks today, and they will kill you tomorrow. No good will come of the vicious circle of vendettas.
>
> I will not fight you without an army, for I have not lost my mind. But if your king grants me amnesty, I will surrender my treasures and forfeit my sovereignty.

Bahraum-e Chubineh forwarded Parmudeh's plea for vassalage to Hormazd. The king thanked God that he was in a position to extend his protection to the khagan of the east. To reward his competent field marshal, he sent him a bejeweled belt and regal garments along with the writ accepting Parmudeh's surrender:

> I do solemnly declare that the great khagan is now my friend. I take God as my witness that no harm will come to him while he is in my protection.

In a separate message, he commanded Bahraum to treat Parmudeh with respect and send him along with his treasures to Ctesiphon. He was also to cleanse the area of pockets of resistance. Finally, the king declared that he would send funds to reward prominent warriors and promote those who had distinguished themselves with gallant conduct.

Much relieved to have received the protection he sought, Parmudeh released the treasures of Auvazeh castle and rode out of the gates behind an honor guard. He seemed oblivious to his reduced rank as he steered his horse haughtily through the throngs of his subjects. He did not deign to recognize Bahraum as he passed his station. Infuriated by this haughty attitude, the general sent an aide to stop the caravan and drag the khagan back to him.

"I have fallen from the zenith of glory to the nadir of disgrace," Parmudeh complained. "I used to be somebody. Now I am reduced to begging your king for mercy. I gave you the treasures. What else do you want from me?"

Bahraum whipped Parmudeh, as one beats a lowly servant, and threw him in prison. Witnessing this scene, Khorrad-e Borzin told Mehran-Dabir: "This man has less sense in his head than the wing of a mosquito. He is his own worst enemy." They went to their commander and advised him that he was ruining his reputation. Bahraum agreed it was unwise to mistreat and imprison someone who was under the king's protection. To mollify Parmudeh, he released and set him back on the road to the capital on a horse caparisoned in gold. Accompanying the khagan along part of the way, Bahraum gently asked him to be discreet about what had happened between them.

"I am not the kind of man who whines about his fate," Parmudeh replied. "Though I am puzzled about the providence that has lowered me in this world, I would never talk about such matters to mortal men. But rest assured that what happened here will not remain hidden. Hormazd will have heard of it by the time I meet him at Ctesiphon. The king who does not know what is happening in his realm does not deserve his title."

Bahraum bitterly regretted his outburst. He tried to remind Parmudeh that he had treated him with kindness and was instrumental in obtaining amnesty for him.

"It is best not to hash out the past," Parmudeh said. "I do recognize that war requires harshness. But one must exercise forbearance in a time of peace. You don't seem to know the difference between war and peace. We must let bygones be bygones."

"Fine," Bahraum said. "I don't care to cover it up anymore. Say whatever you want to the king, for you can't harm my reputation no matter how hard you try."

"Only a foolish king fails to distinguish between good and evil acts of his men," Parmudeh retorted. "Only an idiot would tolerate the bad behavior of his underlings."

Khorrad spoke up, fearing Bahraum was about to kill the khagan. "Control your fury, commander. The khagan is right. Just listen and think about what he is saying."

Bahraum snarled. "This lowborn coward holds a grudge against me because I killed his father!"

"You will ruin what you have accomplished," the khagan interjected. "Don't be belligerent. I am not afraid of your king. He is my equal in every respect. I ask you in the name of your king to end this bitter exchange before something regrettable happens."

At this, Bahraum relented and let the caravan leave. He headed back to camp, still agitated, and ordered his colleagues to accompany him to the treasure house of Auvazeh castle. The accounting lasted from dawn until the third watch of the night. The treasury was filled to the brim with precious objects. It contained everything Afrasiab and Arjausp had left behind, including Prince Siavosh's bejeweled belt, two pairs of earrings, and two pairs of boots embroidered with gold thread. These had been passed to his son, King Kay-Khosrow, and then to Kings Lohrausp and Goshtausp. King Arjausp of Touran had plundered them, and that is how they had ended up in Saveh-shah's treasury. Two bolts of Yemeni Bord interlaced with gold, each weighing sixty pounds, were also discovered. Bahraum put aside a pair of Siavosh's earrings and golden boots and a bolt of the Yemeni Bord for himself before they were counted by the scribes. Time would show that this irregularity was reported to the king. The rest of the great treasury was loaded on thirty camels and sent along to catch up with the caravan of Parmudeh heading to Ctesiphon. A thousand soldiers commanded by Izad-goshasp were put in charge of the cavalcade.

THE AFTERMATH OF THE EASTERN WAR

Hormazd rode out of Ctesiphon's gates to welcome the khagan. Once the leaders had dismounted and warmly greeted each other, the king rode back to his audience hall while Parmudeh, who was no longer a sovereign, was commanded to enter on foot in accordance with the court protocol. And yet he was received as an honored guest and allowed to rest for a week.

Six thousand men carrying the wealth of the east could not finish the job of counting it in one day. What remained was hauled in by fifty thousand men the next day. Tallying the treasures required dividing them into one hundred different collections. As the accounting continued, an emissary from Mehran-Dabir arrived to inform the king that Bahraum-e Chubineh had taken two bolts of the Yemeni bord and pairs of Prince Siavosh's earrings and boots for himself. Hormazd had the report confirmed by other witnesses.

"Bahraum has lost his way," said the king, outraged. "First, I received news that he dared to thrash the khagan, who was under my protection, and now I learn that he has stolen from the royal treasury. What does a soldier want with a king's regalia if he doesn't have ambitions of royalty? He has forfeited his honor."

That evening Hormazd dined with the khagan. They drank wine until the night spread its musk-black hair over the sky. Then the king took the khagan by the hand and said: "Promise me on your honor that you would never renounce this alliance." Surprised by this personal appeal, Parmudeh took a solemn oath—on the crown, the throne, the sun, the moon, the eternal fire at the Azar-goshasp temple, and the Almighty who created the planets Jupiter and Venus—to remain a friend as long as he lived.

When the sun climbed the eastern range, Parmudeh prepared to leave. The parting gifts he was given included a crown, a bejeweled Indian sword, a noble horse caparisoned in gold and silver, and such regal accouterments as a headgear, a torque, earrings, and bracelets. The king accompanied the caravan for two milestones, bid the khagan farewell, and returned to his palace. The news of the favorable reception of the young khagan at the capital spread far and wide.

Parmudeh had to cross Balkh's realm on the way back to his homeland. As his caravan neared Bahraum's camp, the commander rushed out to ingratiate himself. He left feed for the caravan's horses at several locations and brought gifts of gold and slaves to accompany his offer of humble apologies. Parmudeh ignored this gesture. He did not stop or let his horses partake in the animal feed. He neither touched the gifts nor deigned to look at the commander as he followed the caravan for three milestones. Finally, the khagan sent a polite message asking Bahraum to stop troubling himself on his account.

Shortly thereafter, Hormazd expressed his displeasure with Bahraum's impudence by sending him mock gifts. These consisted of women's garments, some makeup, an old spindle, and wool. The letter sent along with these insulting items read:

> You have turned into a ruffian, insolent to your superiors and to God. Pride has corrupted you. Wear this garment and use the accompanying gifts as you don't deserve better.

To further express his contempt, Hormazd chose a lowborn courier to deliver an insulting verbal message: "How dare you disrespect me by abusing the man who was under my protection? I will throw you off the high horse of your pride!"

Bahraum's initial reaction to this development was resigned acceptance. Maybe, he thought, he deserved the ridicule of the king. Then he entertained the possibility that his enemies had poisoned the king's mind against him by augmenting his faults. Finally, he decided that his sins had to be balanced against saving Iran from destruction and enslavement. How could the king only look at his faults and forget that he owed his crown, let alone his life, to him? Thus, after some deliberation, he wore the tattered female garments, placed the spindle in front of him, and invited his commanders and lieutenants to comment on the king's offensive gesture.

"These are the garments and gifts that our king has seen fit to send me," he said. "What can one do? He is the king, and we are but his slaves. We must love and respect him, right? What else can we do?"

Bahraum's commanders were scandalized. "If this is how the king treats his highest commander and savior, just imagine how he would treat those who serve under him. We must be lower than a pack of dogs in his eyes. We renounce a king who treats us with contempt!"

"Don't say that," Bahraum protested. "We owe everything to our king."

But the commanders were adamant. "Our mind is made up. After this insult, we no longer consider Hormazd our king. Nor will we respect anyone who grovels to such a man."

Two weeks elapsed, and Bahraum and his top brass were still in limbo. Nobody knew where they stood with their king or what they should do.

THE ETHEREAL LADY

One day Bahraum-e Chubineh was riding in a thicket looking for game. Two of his commanders, Izad-goshasp and Yalaun-sineh, were following him in the distance. Bahraum spotted a strange onager that was wending its way through the thick shrubbery. He gingerly tracked the animal until it left the lush grove and emerged into a sunny patch that led to the desert. Once in the open air, the onager set off running. Bahraum gave chase without being able to catch up to the bolting onager. The hunter and the game were drenched in sweat as they continued to gallop through the open expanse of the desert. Gradually a magnificent edifice came into view. Now, it appeared that the beast was leading Bahraum to the edifice that turened out to be a regal palace.

The onager slowed its pace and stopped at the gates. When Bahraum dismounted, he turned around to see that Izad-goshasp had followed him. The master gave the reins of his horse to his commander and entered the vestibule of the palace. After a while, Yalaun-sineh also arrived. Still gripping the reins of Bahraum's horse, Izad-goshasp said: "I am taking care of one horse. Let me hold yours as well, so you can go inside and find out what is happening at this strange place."

Yalaun-sineh stepped into the palace's main hall and found himself under a high dome. He had never beheld such a luxurious audience hall. A plush, Roman carpet covered the floor. At the center, an elegant queen reclined on a jewel-encrusted dais of gold. She was tall as a cypress tree and redolent as the spring. Bahraum sat on a lower podium surrounded by the queen's attendants. She glanced at Yalaun-sineh and commanded one of her women to go to him saying: "Tell the brave paladin that this is not a place for him. Lead him back to his friend and assure them that Bahraum will soon come out."

Yalaun-sineh and Izad-goshasp were ushered by the attendants to a gallery where they were treated to a sumptuous repast presided over by a priest who solemnly mumbled the Bazh mantras over a ceremonial Barsom bundle. Their horses were taken to the stables to be rubbed down and fed.

After a while, they heard Bahraum and the queen bidding each other farewell at the gates of the audience hall.

"May Jupiter adorn thy crown, young man."

"May victory be thine, Your Majesty."

Yalaun-sineh and Izad-goshasp stood in attention to greet their commander. Bahraum's demeanor had visibly changed. His sharp, sparkling eyes were dreamy, as if he had been through an extraordinary encounter. As soon as he jumped on his horse, the mysterious onager reappeared and led the group back to where they had entered the thicket. Khorrad-e Borzin, who was waiting there, asked what had taken them so long in the enchanted woods. Bahraum simply glared at him with bloodshot eyes and returned to his palace without a word.

The next morning, as the sun rose from the eastern horizon and made the colors of the desert as vibrant as Chinese silk, Bahraum sat on a golden dais in a public pavilion, wearing a tiara suggestive of a crown. The significance of the moment was not lost on anyone, least of all on Mehran-Dabir and Khorrad-e Borzin. They later met to discuss the matter. The scribe confided in his companion what he had heard about Bahraum's visitation with an ethereal lady at the desert palace. The old knight said that the event and the recent public appearance of Bahraum in a headgear resembling a crown meant that he was nursing royal ambitions.

"This is not a trivial matter," he said. "We must be discrete, but the king should be informed of this development. After what has happened, we ought not to stay at the camp. Otherwise we will be implicated in the coming mutiny."

The pair slipped out of Balkh under cover of night, but only Khorrad-e Borzin made it to the capital. Mehran-Dabir lagged behind and was arrested by Yalaun-sineh, who had been sent with one hundred soldiers in their pursuit.

"Why were you leaving without my permission, you demon?" Bahraum interrogated the scribe.

"Khorrad-e Borzin put me up to this," he replied. "He convinced me that staying with you was dangerous."

"I can see how one might think that way. So, I forgive you this time. Go back to your tent and reclaim your possessions. Just don't try this again."

Meanwhile, Khorrad-e Borzin had submitted his report to the king. He told him all that had transpired in Balkh, including the affair of the Ethereal Lady and Bahraum's simulated coronation. This report was disheartening to the king, as he recalled his father's dark prognostications about an ominous rebellion and his own demise. He summoned the chief of the magi to shed light on the situation.

"What say you of the thicket, the onager, the desert palace, and the crowned lady?" he asked. "It sounds like a dream, or an old legend!"

"The onager was a demon sent to lead Bahraum astray," the magi responded. "That palace was conjured up by the sorceress who appeared as its queen."

The king asked what Bahraum-e Chubineh's warriors thought of the story. Khorrad responded that they did not consider the encounter to be demonic at all. On the contrary. They thought it was an auspicious event proving their leader was chosen to wear the crown of Iran. Realizing that a popular rebellion was afoot, Hormazd regretted having mocked such an influential commander with his insulting gift.

Shortly after this meeting, Bahraum sent a basket full of blunt daggers to the palace. The king had the tips of the blades broken and returned them in the same basket. Bahraum showed this to his commanders and said: "Our king has regaled us with another one of his gifts. He might as well have hurled obscenities at us."

"He is not our king!" they said in unison, and in a mutinous mood. "And we will denounce you if you ever call him king again."

Bahraum was ready to make his final move. "Your lives are forfeit given the report Khorrad-e Borzin must have filed at Ctesiphon. We either make a pact and stay together, or we are all dead."

And thus the seed of rebellion was planted.

REBELS HOLD A WAR COUNCIL

A meeting was convened in Balkh to weigh the prospects of overthrowing Hormazd and installing Bahraum.

"I am no longer able or willing to hide my deep sorrow from you, who are the ablest and most courageous commanders this land has ever seen," Bahraum said, initiating the discussion. "Nor is it wise for a patient to conceal his pain from the healer. Tell me which path I must take. I defeated Saveh-shah and Parmudeh, who posed an existential threat to Iran. If they had succeeded, this land and its king would not be worth a wooden coin. But I crushed them both. Once the king had used me to get rid of his enemies, he turned against me. We made him rich beyond the dreams of avarice, and he repaid us with insults, mockery, and threats. I have spoken my piece. Don't hold your peace."

Bahraum-e Chubineh's sister, Gordieh, who was an able warrior and a close confidant, addressed the commanders. "This is a crucial moment for you and your country. Don't keep your light under a bushel now. Speak."

"You are the best warrior among us, Bahraum," Izad-goshasp said. "Your words are divine. Your wish is my command. I am not a warmonger. But I will be an obedient soldier if you declare war.

"You have been given an army, a throne, a crown, and enough wealth to rule," Yalaun-sineh said. "Only the ungrateful spurns such divine gifts. Accepting your good fortune shall increase your blessings."

Bahraum-e Siavoshan laughed and threw his ring in the air. "The career of a commander who wants to be a king will last as long as this ring stays aloft. But think hard. Aspiring to royalty is not a joke."

Bonda-goshasp raised his voice. "A wise magus of Rey once said: 'It's better to be king for a day than live for a year in poverty.'"

Then Bahraum-e Chubineh turned to Mehran-Dabir and said: "Speak, you gray wolf. What say you?"

"He who seeks shall find, but only if fate allows him to do so," he said. "God's will shall be done."

"The timid will never attain the crown," said Hamdan-goshasp. "He who fears thorns will not taste the sweetness of dates. Don't hesitate. Do what you must and leave the rest to God."

Gordieh was infuriated by these opinions but held her tongue until Bahraum asked her to speak. She started by denouncing Mehran-Dabir. "Tell me, you clumsy old wolf, what commoner doesn't dream about becoming a king, wearing a crown and reclining on the royal throne? Who doesn't fantasize about spending the wealth of the treasury and commanding the national army? You deserve our pity if you are so naïve as to think that Bahraum is the first man to have such ambitions."

Mehran-Dabir replied meekly. "I was asked to share my views. I merely expressed my opinion. People are free to take or leave my advice."

"Dreams and fantasies aside, no common Iranian has ever deemed it possible to become a king, not even when the throne was empty," Gordieh said, addressing the entire assembly. "Recall what happened under the frivolous King Kay-Kavous, who ascended to the heavens on his flying contraption only to crash and become a laughingstock to the world. Rostam and Gudarz took the trouble of collecting him in Saury. But they did not depose him. And when he foolishly let himself be taken captive in Hamauvaran, Rostam responded to suggestions that he declare himself king by saying: 'How can I ascend the golden throne while our king lives?' Instead, he chose twelve thousand soldiers and rescued his king from captivity. Nor did Sufrai covet the position of the king after he ruled as regent for Qobaud. And when Qobaud unjustly killed this excellent man, his son, Zarmehr, did not seek revenge because he knew the nation would be lost without a king. He forgave the murderer of his father for the good of the country.

"My brother, you have bravely defended Iran against Saveh-shah. God willed that you garner the accolades for saving the nation. Don't ruin your good deed with mutiny. Don't covet the crown. Ignore Yalaun-sineh, who claims that he can make you a king. The elders of this nation and an army of three hundred thousand stand behind Hormazd. They remember him as the beloved son and heir to King Nushin-ravaun.

"The king chose you as his commander, and his father chose our father to rule in Rey. One does not repay benevolence with ingratitude. Don't allow greed to cloud your reason. I am younger than you and a woman at that. But allow me to warn you that you are tarnishing our patrimony."

The assembly was spellbound by this bold speech, and they knew she had a point.

"Honorable lady," Yalaun-sineh responded, "you need not rise in support of this king. Your brother deserves a crown, not a spindle. Surely, he has the skills and the mind of a ruler. And don't speak of pedigree, for the breed of the kings of Kay has long been diluted. Hormazd is half Iranian, anyway. Don't be afraid of the crown prince Khosrow-Parviz either, for all his top lieutenants are loyal to Bahraum. They will deliver him to us with tied hands if they are called upon."

"You are walking into the lair of a demon," Gordieh retorted. "My father was a loyal vassal in Rey before you insinuated yourself into my brother's company and seduced him into coveting Hormazd's crown. I wash my hands of this affair. He is blindly following you, and you are sure to lead him to his ruin."

With these words, Gordieh departed the gathering with tearful eyes. The company praised her eloquence and compared her to Jamausp, the wise vizier of King Goshtausp. Bahraum, unhappy about the way the council had derailed, ended the meeting and ordered a feast. That night, bards performed the story of the seven labors of Esfandiar and his conquest of the Invincible Castle.

The next day Bahraum dispatched a letter to the khagan apologizing for his past behavior and pledged that he would consider himself Parmudeh's younger brother if his rebellion against the Iranian king was successful. He then embarked on an elaborate scheme to foment confusion in the capital and undermine the Sassanian dynasty.

To sow discord between the king and his crown prince, Bahraum went to Rey, minted a coin in the name of Khosrow-Parviz, and sent a quantity of it to be circulated in Ctesiphon. As minting coins was done only by kings, Hormazd would suspect the crown prince of having declared himself king. To complete the deception, Bahraum wrote Hormazd a letter declaring that henceforth he recognized only Khosrow-Parviz as the legitimate king of Iran.

Hormazd was thus deceived into thinking that his son had started a revolt. After consultations with his confidant, Ae'in-goshasp, he appointed an assassin to lace Khosrow-Parviz's wine with poison. A quantity of a deadly potion was requisitioned from the royal apothecary for the purpose. But the court chamberlain had already informed the crown prince of the plot against his life.

THE GREAT ESCAPE

That night, Khosrow-Parviz fled Ctesiphon for the northwest state of Azerbaijan. As news of the attempted murder and escape of the crown prince spread, Hormazd became an object of hatred in the capital. Several prominent noblemen and knights gathered at the fire temple of Azar-goshasp and swore allegiance to the crown prince. Secure in his new powerbase, Khosrow-Parviz sent secret agents to gather information on his father's plans.

When the king heard of his son's escape, he jailed his maternal uncles, Gostahm and Benduy, suspecting them of plotting against him. In another meeting, Ae'in-goshasp and the king concluded that it was impossible to fight on two fronts against Bahraum-e Chubineh and Khosrow-Parviz. Thus, they determined to focus their efforts on the defiant crown prince. For the time being, the rebellious general had to be mollified.

"This man considers me his enemy," Ae'in-goshasp said. "I suggest you send me to him as a captive to prove your friendship."

"I am not the kind of a king who betrays his friends," Hormazd replied. "Instead, I will send you at the head of an army to negotiate with him. If you find him open to compromise, I am prepared to offer him land and a knighthood. But if he settles for nothing but the crown, we will have to fight him. Go in haste."

THE ILL-FATED MISSION

As Ae'in-goshasp prepared to leave, he received a strange letter from the royal prison.

> I have been imprisoned in the king's dungeon awaiting death. I hail from your city, and you must know me. Get me out of this jail and allow me to ride ahead of your army. Give me a chance so I can prove myself as a loyal servant. I will give my life for you.

Taking pity on the prisoner, Ae'in-goshasp requested a royal pardon for the prisoner. The king wrote back, warning that such a ruffian could hardly turn into an honorable soldier. But he granted his general's request as a favor to him. Shortly thereafter, the released criminal had joined the army as it left the gates of Ctesiphon.

Ae'in-goshasp advanced in a rapid clip to rest at the city of Hamedan. There, he asked to see a famed local soothsayer who could help him avoid bad fortune in his perilous venture. An old woman was brought out, and after a few preliminary questions, Ae'in-goshasp asked her to whisper in his ear if he would die in battle or in bed. At that moment, the discharged prisoner happened to pass by them. The old woman whispered in the commander's ear: "Who was that man? He is the one who is destined to kill you."

Ae'in-goshasp was shocked by this revelation. He recalled previous oracles that had predicted that he would be killed by a villainous neighbor. It was suddenly clear to the commander that he had made a terrible mistake. In great agitation, he wrote a letter to the king, praised his discernment and requested the immediate execution of the carrier of the letter. He then gave the letter to the released criminal and commanded him to go to the king in haste and bring back the response as soon as possible.

The herald departed with alacrity. But he was assailed by apprehension as he approached Ctesiphon. After all, he had been jailed there, awaiting execution. Why would he go back to such a place? What if something went wrong and they tried to imprison him again or even kill him? Soon, his gnawing suspicions spread to the nature of the letter he was carrying. The man broke the seal and shuddered to find out that he was carrying his own death sentence.

Why would the man who had saved his life condemn him to death? Was this because of a dream or a portent? Anxiously, he rode back to the camp and arrived at night, when the commander was in his tent, unarmed. Seeing that there were no sentries posted at his pavilion, the man unsheathed his sword and entered. Ae'in-goshasp begged for mercy and reminded the intruder that he had saved his life. The man responded, "Indeed. You did save my life. So, what did I do in the last couple of days to deserve execution?"

He then cut off his head, put it in his saddle sack, and fled to Balkh under cover of darkness, hoping to curry favor with Bahraum-e Chubineh.

The rebel commander was puzzled by the strange man's arrival.

"This is the head of your enemy," the scoundrel told him.

"I don't know him."

"This is Ae'in-goshasp, my master. He was coming with the king's army to fight you."

"You are a fool," Bahraum said. "This man was not coming to kill me but to negotiate on behalf of the king. You will be punished for betraying your benefactor."

The murderer of Ae'in-goshasp was hanged from the gallows in front of the army as an object lesson to those who might consider assassinating a commander. When the king's army learned of the demise of their general, they broke up into three camps. Some returned to Ctesiphon, some went to Khosrow-Parviz, and the rest joined Bahraum-e Chubineh.

THE UNHINGING OF THE KING

Upon receiving news of the failure of Ae'in-goshasp's mission, Hormazd was so despondent he became unmoored. He shut himself in his palace and spent his days in great agitation, pacing around and shedding tears. Knowing that Khosrow-Parviz and Bahraum were preparing to invade the capital, he could not eat or sleep.

Hormazd had lost his mind, and Ctesiphon was rife with rumors of his madness. People mistrusted the king for alienating his successful general and trying to assassinate his crown prince. A crowd that was furious at the unjust imprisonment of Banduy and Gostahm broke them out of jail. The released uncles of Khosrow-Parviz led the rampaging mobs to Hormazd's palace and set it on fire. As the guards fled, the crowd broke in, tore the crown off Hormazd's head, and hung him upside down above the throne. After letting him swing in this manner for a long time, they blinded him with hot irons and threw him in jail.

The high wheel of destiny is always in motion
Nothing remains of us but the sum of our deeds
Everything else sinks in history's dark ocean.

Benduy and Gostahm sent a fast envoy to inform Khosrow-Parviz that it was safe to return to the capital. The crown prince arrived leading the armies of Barda', Ardebil, and Armenia. People were relieved and delighted to welcome their new king. The royal ivory throne, the bejeweled crown of the kings of Kay, and the glittering royal torque awaited Khosrow-Parviz at the throne room of the royal palace. But this was far from a triumphal return for one who was preoccupied with his father's sad fate and the brewing rebellion.

Hope not for justice in this world, nor wish
To learn why it saves one man from the waves
While tossing another overboard to feed the fish.

CHAPTER 25

The Rise and Fall of a King: Khosrow-Parviz

When the prince ascended the royal throne
The noblemen showered their young king
With golden words and many a precious gemstone.

"I follow the way of righteousness," he declared at his coronation, "for I know that the reign of an unjust king ends in disaster. Mine is not the path of conflict but that of peace and harmony. Nor is it my place to sit in judgment of others, even if they desire the ring of prominence and the crown of glory. But let me advise you against three things: harming he who fears God, disobeying the king, and coveting what is not yours."

The king spent his first night as leader of Iran brooding over his father's destiny. When the new day's roosters sounded their clarion, he went to visit Hormazd in prison. He was now a disfigured old man wracked with pain.

Khosrow-Parviz bowed and said: "I would never have let anyone harm you if you had allowed me to be your guardian. I am prepared to renounce this crown and lay down my life for you."

"Do not worry about me," Hormazd said. "Hard days shall pass. But grant me three wishes. I want to start my day with a pleasant song at dawn, so send me a singer. I yearn for the company of a knight to regale me with his tales of conquest, and a man to read me the book of the olden kings.* Lastly, I long for revenge. Blind your uncles as they blinded me."

"How could a loyal son not mourn the loss of his father's sight?" asked Khosrow-Parviz. "Your first and second wishes shall be granted. Regarding your third request, remember that we are in a terrible bind. Bahraum-e Chubineh has raised the flag of rebellion and is coming at us with a formidable and loyal army. It is impossible to dispense with such able commanders as Benduy and Gostahm. Do not poison your mind with revenge. People are but instruments of our preordained destiny. I wish you fortitude in these dreadful times."

* This is a reference to prose versions of *Shahnameh* that were recited to the kings.

The son was kinder and had a softer tongue
In his head than his father. A pompous old fool
Is inferior to a wise man, even when he's young.

Bahraum-e Chubineh kept up with the developments in the capital. He knew that the right time to challenge the new Sassanian king was amid a troubled royal transition. Thus, he sent his army to rush like a flood of molten iron from Balkh to the western shores of the Nahrawan canal between the River Tigris and Ctesiphon.

Khosrow-Parviz, who had heard about the troop movements, posed three questions to his advisors: how popular was the rebel commander? Did he stay at the heart of his army or move around the formations at will? And did he hold court and hunt in the manner of kings?

The intelligence provided by the spies was unsettling. "Bahraum-e Chubineh is admired by his soldiers," they told the king. "Everyone loves him, regardless of age and rank. He does not hide at the heart of the army but freely moves among his men without the slightest fear. His soldiers trust him, and he trusts them. He does not need a foreign contingent to provide security. The man emulates the kings in every respect: he hunts, holds court, and listens to the recitation of Kelileh and Demneh."

Khosrow had feared as much. The rebel commander was well-liked, ambitious, and self-assured. He was determined to usurp the crown and abolish the Sassanian dynasty. The king called a council of advisors comprised of Benduy, Gostahm, Khorrad-e Borzin, and Gorduy, Gordieh's brother. Shaupur, Andian, Raudman, the vassal king of Armenia, and a few magi were also in attendance.

"Reason is to the mind what armor is to the body," the king declared. "I am younger than you and a novice at statecraft. Don't deny me the benefit of your advice."

"At creation," a magus replied, "God assigned half the sum of wisdom to the king, and the other half went to all his advisors and ministers. We humbly offer our advice. But you are the arbiter of what is good and bad."

Khosrow-Parviz listened intently before responding. "Those words must be written in gold letters. So, here is what I think. The best course is for me to go ahead and invite Bahraum to parley. I will try the path of reconciliation. If the overture is successful, we will make peace. We shall give battle only if he refuses to compromise."

The council ratified the plan, and the army left the gates of Ctesiphon. The vanguards of the two sides met as the night's pitch-black mane snuffed the celestial candle. The armies rested until the break of the dawn. As the sun came up war drums rumbled on both sides. The king commanded his uncles to suit up and accompany him across the bridge to the western bank of the Nahrawan.

When the arrival of the small delegation was reported, Bahraum-e Chubineh too came out with his top brass, Yalaun-sineh, Hamdan-goshasp, and Izad-goshasp, along with three intrepid Turkish warriors sent by the khagan to capture or kill the king should the opportunity arise. The two armies watched as their leaders approached on both sides.

Bahraum was flushed with rage when he saw Khosrow-Parviz in his sartorial splendor. "This son of a whore imagines he is King Feraydun redux just because a shadow of hair has appeared above his lip. But I see not one worthy opponent in his vast army. The bastard wears a crown and holds an ox-headed mace as if he embodies King Kasra. He will learn his lesson when I drown him in a sea of blood. Soon he will have seen how real men wield the sword and swing the mace on a charging horse. Soon he will have heard my pulverizing battle cry."

At this time the king, who was regarding the ranks of the rebel army, asked his companions to identify the rebellious general.

"He's the one on the piebald horse wearing a black baldric over a white cape," one responded.

The king followed the man with his eyes. "You mean the tall, dark one with the hook nose and drooping eyelids? He looks intransigent. And yet I will have to try my best to placate him. As the saying goes, if the donkey doesn't come to the bundle, the bundle should go to the donkey. Peace is better than war, and commerce is preferable to bloodshed."

Gostahm praised the wisdom of his king and endorsed his decision to give negotiations a chance. Encouraged by the backing of his top lieutenants, Khosrow-Parviz went forth and addressed his opponent with gracious words:

"What brings you to the battlefield, righteous general?" he asked. "Why would you want to fight me when you could be the ornament of my court and the brightest candle at my feasts? Having studied your deeds, I consider you an invaluable military asset. Allow me to host you and your troops. I will honor you as the commander in chief of my armies."

Bahraum greeted the king with a nod but remained silent. After a brief pause, he spoke. "I am doing well, but far be it from me to wish you a good day. You don't know the first thing about being a king. What else can one expect when the king of the Alan tribesmen* aspires to be the king of kings? I, too, have studied your life and works. And I have concluded that I must tie your hands and hang your inverted body from the gallows on this battlefield."

Khosrow-Parviz turned pale. It was clear that the love of the throne ran deeper roots in Bahraum's heart than he had supposed. But the king kept his composure and spoke softly: "Don't be churlish. I have crossed the river in search of peace. As your guest, I am entitled to respect. Arabs, Persians, and Turks abhor rudeness to a guest. It is especially shocking to hear this language in response to my respectful words of reconciliation. The road you have chosen leads to perdition. You abuse me with the title of the king of the Alans while you know that I ruled the Alans at the command of my father. You claim that I don't deserve to wear the crown of my ancestors. It was Zarathustra who endowed my ancestor Lohrausp with the crown of kingship. If the son of Hormazd and the grandson of Kasra Nushin-ravaun does not merit the crown, then who does?"

"You're neither a guest nor a king," fired Bahraum, "neither an exceptional fighter nor a learned nobleman. I'm the one who was acclaimed king. People love me as much as they hate you and your defunct dynasty. I will flay your skin and throw your bones to the dogs. Your Sassanian clan stole the crown from my Ashkani ancestors. Your forefathers

* The derogatory title probably refers to Khosrow-Parviz's post as the ruler of the northern parts of Iran. Apparently, this was a Sassanian custom that the crown prince would exercise the arts of leadership in that post.

were not the kings of Kay or disciples of Zarathushtra! Your forefather is that shepherd boy Sassan who killed his king and moved the capital from Rey to Pars. I intend to restore the ancient Ashkanian dynasty to power."

"Nothing good ever came out of Rey," retorted the king. "You are a true son of that accursed land that was home to Mauhyar, the regicide who stabbed King Dara in the back. I advise you for the last time to hold your tongue. Such speech is unbecoming of an Iranian commander. Despite everything that has passed between us, I am still reluctant to kill you, for your loss would be a waste of military talent. I feel the same way toward your brave companions and soldiers. Mend your ways, obey God, and make reason your guide. Thorn bushes do not bear flowers. These ambitions will be your undoing. Whoever planted these ideas in your head was not your friend."

Bahraum-e Chubineh remained silent and inscrutable. The fate of Khosrow-Parviz, not to mention the Sassanian dynasty, depended on the outcome of the confrontation that now seemed inevitable. So, the king removed his crown, dismounted, knelt and closed his eyes in a gesture of prayer:

Oh, great light of the universe, you are my only hope. It is a dark day when a king confronts such an unworthy foe. If this dynasty is destined to end today, I will be happy to serve you as a humble servant at a fire temple. I will wear rags and survive on milk. But if my reign is to continue, give me victory. If I triumph, I pledge this horse, my garments, earrings, and torque of royalty, along with ten bags of gold coins, to the Azar-goshasp fire temple as my devotional offering. I will also dedicate the revenue for the manumission of the captives to the temple.

Then he climbed back onto the saddle, having resolved that war was unavoidable, and addressed Bahraum-e Chubineh:

"You live in a fantasy world. Nature allocates a place to each creature. A crab cannot fly like an eagle. Nor can an eagle soar above the sun. Since you don't respect the divine will and the proper order of things in this world, I will have to teach them to you on the battlefield."

Bahraum bristled at this challenge: "You are the one suffering from illusions of grandeur. You advise me to piety, and yet, you are the one who blinded and jailed your father. I will take the crown off your head and give it to Hormazd."

And thus, what had started as an attempt at parlay turned into an exchange of taunts before a battle. Khosrow-Parviz roared: "You are a windbag without a shroud to your name, which, by the way, you will need before the sun sets on this day. How can a commoner from Rey with not a drop of royal blood in his veins claim to be a king? You owe everything to a story the old Mehran-shetaud told my father. He brought you out of your obscurity because of that old prophecy. But my lineage goes back to King Lohrausp, who was appointed by Kay-Khosrow. Lohrausp was also blessed by the prophet Zarathustra before he bequeathed the kingship to his son Goshtausp. Dara was the great-grandson of Goshtausp, and Sassan was his son who fled to India and continued the line of the kings of Kay until the last of that line, Ardeshir-e Babakan, reestablished the old dynasty."

Bahraum answered with a skeptical sneer. "As I said, the founder of your dynasty was nothing but a lowly shepherd boy and a usurper. The five centuries of the Sassanian rule is based on a lie. Your authority is waning, and your crown has grown moldy. I will cleanse the earth of your kind."

"Even if the house of Sassan were to be wrecked, no one would make you king. You hail from the land of regicides and traitors. My father should never have sent you that silver throne that seems to have fed your fantasy of being a king."

"Only one part of your story is true: King Dara died," said Bahraum. "Nobody believes the tall tale of Sassan and his children! Nor am I a commoner who has just arrived from Rey. I am from the clan of the legendary knight Gorgin, the son of Milad, one of the heroes of the Battle of the Eleven. Like my ancestors, I have performed famous acts of valor. I defeated the four hundred thousand strong army of Saveh-shah, who had come with twelve hundred war elephants to put the yoke of servitude on the neck of Iran. My hat is redolent of the crown. The tip of my dagger points at the ivory throne."

"Even so," Khosrow-Parviz said sternly, "both Gorgin and Arash obeyed their kings. I advise you one last time to follow the example of your ancestors. Rebellion against a king is an impious act that, according to Zarathustra, is punishable by execution after a grace period of one year. You are an unhinged idiot and your medicine is a dungeon and plenty of chains."

"That is rich, coming from a simpleton who believes a shepherd boy was a prince from an ancient dynasty that had gone extinct for centuries."

With these invectives, Bahraum-e Chubineh guffawed and turned back to go to his troops. Swiftly, one of the three Turkish warriors managed to ambush the king and catch his head in his lariat. But Gostahm cut the noose with his sword, and Benduy sent a shower of arrows to repel the attacker.

Bahraum was furious at the Turkish warrior. "Who told you to meddle? Did you not see that I was in parlay?"

When the rebel commander retired to his tent, Gordieh came to him wondering if his conference with the king had gone well. "That man is no king!" Bahraum exclaimed. "Khosrow-Parviz can conduct himself as a sovereign neither on the battlefield nor at a royal court. Courage and leadership skills are more important to a king than pedigree."

"You must dispel this bitterness from your heart," Gordieh responded. "Who among our ancestors was a king? Have you not heard of the parable of the donkey who fraternized with the oxen hoping to grow horns and ended up losing his ears in that bargain? Mark my words. You will come to grief. For this mutiny, you will lose your life and earn everlasting torments in the hereafter. Your name will be blackened. Remember that the great knight Saum was offered the crown when King Nowzar lost his way, and the country fell apart. Some noblemen tempted him to declare himself king. Saum said: 'May the day never come when I recline on the throne while one from the line of the kings of Kay is alive.'

"It is true that you attained glory in the war against Saveh-shah. But instead of puffing yourself up with pride you should have credited God. You should have been patient with Hormazd. And now that he is dethroned, you ought to humble yourself before the young king. There doesn't have to be bad blood between us. He seems like a flexible man."

Bahraum listened to his sister in respectful silence and simply said: "God knows that you speak the truth. But it's too late to change course. I've chosen this path and will pursue it, come what may."

THE FIRST BATTLE AGAINST THE REBEL ARMY

Khosrow-Parviz crossed the Nahrawan bridge back to his troops, convinced that he had done his best to avoid war, and there remained no possibility of reconciliation.

"You obey me for the same reason that you followed my father," he said after gathering his commanders. "Unfortunately, I have had no chance to reward your loyalty. But I trust you enough to share my secret war tactic with you. I am planning to waylay the enemy at night. Do not talk about this to anyone, for it must be a surprise.

"Bahraum speaks much but thinks little. He preens himself on defeating Saveh-shah, brags about his ability to wield the mace and the sword better than anyone and tries to scare me as if I am a child. But he has yet to see my skills in an ambush. When the night washes its face with black ambergris, suit up and await my orders."

The army took an oath to protect the secret and prepared for war. But when the king discussed his plans with Gostahm, Benduy, and Gorduy, they unanimously opposed it. Myriad family ties connected the two sides. The army could make all the pledges in the world, but it was impossible to protect the integrity of the surprise attack. If it had already been leaked, it would probably provoke Bahraum to launch one of his well-practiced counterattacks. The collective advice of the war council was for the King to stealthily move away from the army to protect his person from harm. He followed their counsel and withdrew to a nearby hill with a few of his paladins.

As predicted, Bahraum tried to exploit the kinship between the two armies by inviting the relatives of the king's soldiers to join his rebellion. He had hoped to attract most of Khosrow's army, except for the divisions that he had brought from the faraway lands of Barda' and Armenia. But his envoy failed to convince the Iranian soldiers to defect. They refused to switch sides before a battle. They added that the rebel commander should not be so confident of the next day's victory as Khosrow-Parviz planned to cut them down under the cover of night.

The anticipated defections had not materialized, but Bahraum had gained valuable intelligence about the plans of Khosrow-Parviz to launch an ambush. Thus, he quickly organized a counteroffensive with an elite force of six thousand under the command of his fierce Turkish confederates. Their preemptive attack was launched with alacrity and continued throughout the night. By daybreak, Bahraum had devastated the king's army.

Khosrow-Parviz came down and fought with some success against one of the rebel divisions. But there was no doubt that the battle was lost, and a rout was at hand, so he issued an order for a general withdrawal. Once his commander Nakhar reported that their entire force had crossed the Nahrawan bridge and were heading back toward the capital, the king and his top ten warriors beat a hasty retreat to the bridge as well. Bahraum-e Chubineh pursued them on a horse stripped of its barding for increased speed. As his steed did not have armor, Gostahm was able to slow Bahraum down by shooting his horse. Yalaun-sineh, who had advanced as far as the middle of the Nahrawan bridge, was stopped when Khosrow-Parviz shot his horse, forcing him to jump over the side of the bridge into the river. This gave the king and his companions enough time to demolish the bridge and put some distance between them and the pursuing rebels. Utterly exhausted from the continuous warfare, they galloped into Ctesiphon, but the enemy was not far behind.

In the short respite they had before the rebels infiltrated the city, the young king went to his father's prison to ask his opinion about seeking help from Iran's Arab confederates. Hormazd warned against this plan and urged an alliance with the Romans instead. They would make more reliable allies. After all, Iranians and Romans had descended from King Feraydun. This sounded like good advice.

As Khosrow-Parviz and his companions fled the capital toward Rome, they could see the dragon-emblazoned standard of Bahraum, ahead of the cloud raised by his army's horses. The king taunted his warriors for fleeing their pursuers at such a leisurely pace.

"Don't worry about Bahraum," Benduy yelled his response over the stomping of their horses' hooves. "He's not chasing us. There is no doubt in my mind that he is heading to Ctesiphon to put Hormazd on the throne as a figurehead. He will then write to the Caesar of Rome in your father's name and demand your extradition."

Tightly pressing the reins of his steed in his fists, Khosrow-Parviz mumbled: "Who needs ferocious enemies when bad luck is nipping at your heels wherever you go?"

But his uncles Gostahm and Benduy had more practical plans than whining about their misfortunes. They had decided that the only way to scuttle Bahraum's plot was to kill Hormazd. Thus, they slowed their pace to lag behind the pack and turned around once the group had disappeared in the dust of their trotting horses. With great speed, they went to Hormazd's prison, garroted him with a bowstring, jumped on their horses, and fled the city moments before the rampaging rebels entered.

And thus ended the life of a once-exalted king.

The world is capricious; its logic most insane,
First it drips with nectar, and then with venom.
The wise will shun both its pleasures and its pain.

Khosrow-Parviz guessed what his uncles had done when they caught up with the group. They were drenched in the sweat of their ride and flushed in the excitement of their grisly deed. But, confronting them would serve no purpose. Nor was it prudent to admit complicity in patricide. So, the young king kept his peace, until the situation would change.

To evade the thirty-thousand-strong army that Bahraum-e Chubineh had sent in their pursuit, the king and his companions left the road to wend their way through the desert paths in their flight to Rome. After a while, they reached a dilapidated Christian monastery. The king asked the abbot for food, and he brought some watercress, whey, and a crust of bread. When the party dismounted and prepared to eat, the king insisted on observing the rites of holding the ceremonial Barsom twigs and humming the Zoroastrian mantras of Bazh.

After the meager meal, the king asked if there was wine at the monastery, and the abbot brought him a cup of delicious date wine. He drank it with pleasure and fell asleep on the sand floor resting his head on Benduy's thigh. But the group's sense of security did not last long. After an hour, the abbot rushed in with grave news: an army was approaching, and judging from the cloud that had risen, their number was substantial.

In great distress, Khosrow asked his companions what should be done. Benduy said that he would stay behind as a decoy. The king left his crown, earrings, belt, and cape at the monastery to facilitate the plan. As Khosrow-Parviz and his friends slipped out from the back of the compound, Benduy went up to the roof wearing the king's regalia. Bahraum-e Siavoshan, who had been appointed as head of the pursuing party, saw the king's crown and robes from afar and thought he had caught up with Khosrow-Parviz. After a while, Benduy came down from the rooftop, took off his disguise, and went up again, this time as himself. But now, the pursuers had come close enough to allow a direct conversation.

"I am the king's uncle Benduy," he declared. "Khosrow-Parviz was just up here watching you approach. His Majesty knows there is no way out of this monastery, but he wishes to rest until morning before surrendering himself. He swears on his honor that he will keep his word."

Bahraum-e Siavoshan agreed to the terms of surrender. He ordered his army to encircle the monastery, making escape impossible. He figured that the king was in his vice trap, a bit of rest wouldn't hurt.

In the morning, Benduy went up on the roof again and shouted down to the rebel soldiers. "The king stayed up all night praying. He is exhausted and wishes to sleep today. I beg you to let him have one more day of peace. I swear you can quietly take him into custody tomorrow at daybreak."

Bahraum-e Siavoshan was in a bind. He told his commanders that taking the king by force was not the solution; fighting him and his knights would not be an easy task. Besides, there was a chance that Khosrow-Parviz would be killed in battle, and his charge was to bring him back alive. Thus, he capitulated again and accepted the outrageous demand for another day of delay.

At the dawn of the next day, Benduy went up on the roof for the last time and declared: "The time has come for me to tell you the truth. The king and his companions left the monastery when we saw the dust of your army on the horizon. He is on his way to the Caesar of Rome and there is no way you can catch up to him. But if you give me immunity, I will lay down my arms, surrender and tell you everything I know. Otherwise, I will don my armor and fight to the death. The choice is yours."

Killing Benduy would not bring Khosrow-Parviz back. Nor would it mollify Bahraum-e Chubineh. The mission was a failure no matter what the hapless commander did. At the very least, bringing the ringleader of the deception back might produce some actionable intelligence. Once more Benduy had bent the enemy to his will.

Furious at the mess his chief of staff had made of his mission, Bahraum-e Chubineh snarled: "It is my own fault for sending an incompetent fool on such an important mission." He then excoriated Benduy for his dishonesty. He replied: "It is the duty of a subject to serve his king by any means necessary. I have not acted dishonorably. Nor am I ashamed of offering myself as a sacrifice for my king. I take as much pride in my bravery as I do in my cunning."

"I will not kill you for the harm you have done to me," the rebel commander replied. "But mark my words. The day will come when you will rue the sacrifice you made for this wicked man."

With this, he ordered Benduy's feet to be bound in chains and commended him to Bahraum-e Siavoshan's care as his prisoner.

THE CROWNING OF THE REBEL COMMANDER

Having consolidated control of the capital and treasury in Khosrow-Parviz's absence, Bahraum-e Chubineh called a meeting of the city's noblemen and his own paladins.

"Zahhak was the worst of men because he killed his father and usurped his crown," he declared, "and Khosrow did the same before escaping to Rome. Now you must choose a new king for Iran, and I will bow to your choice."

The response was quite mixed.

"You are our savior," said the old knight Shahran-Gorauz. "Without you, we would all be enslaved by Saveh-shah. None deserves to be king more than you."

Khorausan, the commander, said, "Sycophants are ingratiating themselves to you. Don't listen to them and don't forget Zarathustra's rule that rebels against the king should be decapitated if they refuse to repent after the grace period of one year."

Farrokh-zaud rose only to extend his greeting to Bahraum-e Chubineh and wish him a long life.

Khazarvaun rose in opposition and declared: "How can a soldier rule while a king is alive? I advise you to send a messenger and beg Khosrow-Parviz for forgiveness. But if you fear the king's wrath, then go to Khorausan and live out the rest of your days there."

"There is no justification to make a king out of an ordinary man," Zaud-farrokh concurred. "Khorausan was right, but he needn't have been so blunt. I agree with Khazarvaun that we must seek peace and reconciliation. There were periods when Iran had no king. We have lived through bad kings as well. Zahhak killed King Jamshid and spread chaos and injustice in the world. Afrasiab killed King Nowzar, and Eskandar slew King Dara. And more recently, the Hephthalite chief Khosh-navauz killed King Piruz. But this nation has never seen anything approaching the current disaster. It is hard to believe that a king of Iran has fled his own country to take refuge with our enemies!" Having spoken these words, he sat down weeping.

Then the old Sonbaud stepped forward. "Bahraum is a competent knight from a prominent, though admittedly not a royal, lineage. I propose we search for a real king from Sassan's seed and until then keep this commander as regent."

Bahraum-e Chubineh rose, having had his fill of these meandering comments. He lifted his unsheathed sword and said: "Like hell, I'll be the regent. You find me that real king from Sassan's seed, and I will slay him with this blade. No one deserves the crown more than I do."

At this, the Armenian knight Baubuy and his followers drew their swords and declared Bahraum their king. The rebel commander announced that the matter was closed, and engaged the scribes to prepare a writ, declaring that he had been chosen to the royal office by acclamation and that the Sassanian dynasty had been toppled. The writ would specify that a new dynasty was established on that day, the second of December. He then gave those who did not recognize his royal office three days to leave his domain and join Khosrow-Parviz.

ESCAPE FROM THE REBELS

Benduy, who had been kept in jail for seventy days, finally managed to speak to Bahraum-e Siavoshan in one of his visits to the jailhouse: "Mark my words! Khosrow-Parviz will be restored to his throne, as was Kay-Qobaud. He has found an ally in the Caesar, and I promise within two months he will be here at the head of a great Roman army. He will burn down the house of this impostor and reclaim his office. But don't worry. I will beg the king to pardon you on that day because you have saved my life and been a friend to me."

Bahraum-e Siavoshan, who had had doubts about the rebellion from the start and was unhappy about the way the rebel commander had forced the issue of his kingship, listened to his captive with interest. "We all saw how this man declared himself king. I was opposed to his rebellion from the beginning. Will you swear on the holy scriptures to stand by me when the king comes?"

"I do solemnly swear to the scriptures and pledge my life and good name that I will champion your cause before the king."

Assured by this oath, Bahraum-e Siavoshan released Benduy of his chains and unlocked the door of his jail but kept him there to preserve the appearances. He was planning to assassinate his friend during an upcoming polo game. On the appointed day, he wore armor under his shirt. His wife noticed this strange act and reported it to Bahraum-e Chubineh, who decided to stand at the entrance of the arena, and pat every participant on the shoulder. Upon discovering the hidden chainmail on the would-be assassin, he said: "Who wears armor under a polo shirt, you venomous snake?" He then disemboweled the culprit on the spot and sent for Benduy to see if he was behind the conspiracy. The soldiers came back and informed him that the prisoner had been allowed to escape. Now it was obvious that Benduy had suborned Bahraum-e Saivoshan. He regretted that he had not killed Benduy when he had the chance. If he had done that, his hand would not have been tainted with his friend's blood.

He who scorns a friend and befriends a hostile
Might as well lay down on the razor's edge
Or jump in the Nile and swim with a crocodile.

Benduy fled Ctesiphon and did not stop until he reached the wilderness camp of the Armenian commander Mushil. There he rested near the temple of Azar-goshasp with his host, hoping that the king would soon come back to take back his throne.

THE REFUGEE KING IN ROME

Khosrow-Parviz and his men continued to traverse the wastelands in search of the Roman border until they reached the city of Bauhele. Having brought no provisions from the monastery, they were close to starvation. They had barely dismounted when the lord mayor of the city came with a letter that he had just received from Bahraum, commanding him to imprison all Iranian stragglers as he was in pursuit of escaped criminals.

Clearly, that city could not afford to protect the rival king of Iran without endangering its safety. So the weary group rode away, hoping to find something to eat at a thicket that stretched along the River Euphrates. Gostahm was an expert hunter, but he failed to find any game. However, as their hopes of survival dimmed, a caravan appeared on the horizon. Its leader was a young man named Qais bin-Hareth, an Arab with some Iranian ancestors returning from Egypt to his home by the Euphrates. He slaughtered and roasted a three-year-old female camel for Khosrow's men. They devoured the meal and fell asleep around a glowing bonfire. In the morning, they woke up restored and in great spirits.

Khosrow-Parviz declared that when he regained his throne, he would richly reward all who had helped him in his hour of need and forgive those who had been disloyal to him. Then he asked Qais how far away the Roman border was. He said it was seventy leagues away and volunteered to act as the group's scout. As luck would have it, the group was treated to another lavish feast from a caravan headed by an Iranian named Mehran-shataud. After the banquet, wine was served, which put the king in a good mood. He asked his host where he was from. He said that he hailed from the village of Karzy near Khorreh-ye Ardeshir in Iran. This was written down so the king could later reward the generous merchant.

After a few days, Khosrow-Parviz and his companions entered the Roman territory and camped at the walls of the city of Kaurstan. But the Christian residents of the city feared the armed Iranian band and kept their gates closed. Three days later, menacing clouds appeared in the sky. In the ensuing storm, one-third of the city's fortifications crumbled. City elders interpreted the calamity as divine punishment for denying hospitality to the destitute Iranians outside their walls. Thus, they sent three priests to apologize for their neglect and offer them residence at a luxurious palace inside their city. The group ate and rested in the palace, and Khosrow penned his first letter to the Caesar. He wrote that he had come to seek help against a usurper of the Iranian throne.

From Kaurstan, the group went to the city of Banuy, where they received another gracious welcome and invitation to sojourn there for three days.

The group's next destination was the city of Uorigh. But Khosrow-Parviz wished to first stop at a desert monastery to converse with a famed clairvoyant monk. The Christian divine knew who Khosrow-Parviz was as soon as they met. "I can see you were unhappy with your father's conduct as king. Now, you are escaping from a conceited subordinate."

"I am but a servant of the king taking a message to the Caesar," said Khosrow-Parviz. "Please tell me if this journey is auspicious."

"Lying is forbidden in your religion. I know you are a king and that you have had a difficult escape."

Khosrow-Parviz apologized for uttering a falsehood. The austere monk proceeded to speak. "It is your good fortune that has led you to this monastery. I prophesy that the Caesar will provide you with a well-equipped army and make you his son-in-law. The general who has rebelled against you will be defeated by you and killed by your agents."

"May your prophecies all come true," said the king. "How long will it take to regain my office?"

The monk continued, "It will take twelve months to wipe out your enemies and another fifteen days to formally assume your office as the king who illuminates the world."

"What of this company? Who among them is disloyal to me?"

"They are all loyal. But be on your guard against a man called 'Bastaum.' He will cause you much pain."

The king pointed to his uncle and asked: "Is that the man you were referring to? He is my maternal uncle who goes by Gostahm. But his birth name was Bastaum." The monk confirmed that he was the man he had in mind. Finally, Khosrow-Parviz asked about his fate after regaining his crown.

"Your rule will be long, uneventful, and prosperous," the monk replied. "You shall prevail against your enemies."

After leaving the monastery, Gostahm swore to all that was holy that he did not harbor ill will toward the king and begged him to disregard the dark prognostications of the Christian monk. Khosrow-Parviz responded that he trusted him insofar as his past conduct was concerned. But, he added, people change.

In the city of Uorigh, the king received a heartening response from the Caesar, promising to help him in his campaign against the rebellious general. Khosrow sent Gostahm, Bauluy, Andian, Khorrad-e Borzin, and Shaupur as his ambassadors to the Roman court, advising them to display their skills in chess and polo and be clever in conversation with the Caesar's philosophers.

The delegation of the five knights was received with due honors at the royal palace. The Caesar greeted the delegates warmly and invited them to recline on golden daises. All sat down but Khorrad-e Borzin, who said he was not permitted to sit before delivering his message. The Caesar gave him permission to read the king's letter:

> Praise God who created time, space, the revolving heavens as well as the wild and tame beasts. Kings Kayumart, Feraydun,

and Kay-Qobaud founded the Kay dynasty whose golden chain was never broken until a presumptuous mercenary usurped their throne. Will you help me rid myself of this vicious rebel?

The color drained from the Caesar's face, and tears rolled down his cheeks. After a pause, he told the ambassador, "It is no secret that I consider Khosrow my kin and love him more than anything. Take from my treasures, armaments, and soldiers as much as your king needs. I will not deny him anything."

He then called a scribe to commit his pledge to writing. The document was given to the ambassadors, who then took their leave and returned to the Iranian camp.

Once the envoys left, the Caesar called his council of four wise philosophers to consultation. They advised that it would be rash to pledge unconditional support for Iran. After all, Rome had never been free of Iranian harassment since the days of Alexander. Iranians were constantly laying waste to their land, occupying their cities, and demanding heavy tributes. What was the guarantee that Khosrow-Parviz would not continue that pattern if he regained his power? It is prudent for us to keep our distance from succession wars in Iran.

This conversation impelled the Caesar to write another letter to Khosrow, mentioning the past conflicts between the two nations and prevaricating on his unconditional support for Iran.

The change of the Caesar's tone in his second letter was appalling to Khosrow-Parviz. He sent an impromptu, oral message to him by his trusted knight Nakhar. "Give the Caesar my best and tell him that true sovereigns don't vacillate. Nor do they go back on their word. Regarding the past, let the Caesar investigate the historical record. Who initiated the hostilities between our nations? My ancestors were God-fearing, generous, and humble. They did not invade Rome without cause. But let us not dredge up the past. I will turn my face east for help as soon as my ambassador returns."

Upon hearing the message, the Caesar realized the grave danger he faced if Khosrow allied himself with the khagan of China. He called upon his prognosticators to cast the fortunes of the war. They poured over their charts and astrolabes, and finally declared that Khosrow-Parviz would win a decisive victory and rule for thirty-eight years. Based on their assurance, the Caesar wrote an ingratiating third letter to Khosrow-Parviz:

> I am not conceding that your side was right in their attacks against Rome. You raided our towns, enslaved our women and children, and laid waste to our land as recently as the time of Hormazd and Qobaud. So, it should not come as a surprise if the Romans entertain doubts about Iran's intentions. But our religion commands us to forgive those who trespass against us. We ought to forget the past and forgive one another. We must stop bringing up such divisive myths as the story of the martyrdom of Iraj.
>
> You should pledge not to demand tribute from Rome. To solidify our kinship, I will give you my daughter Myriam as a wife in accordance with the solemn rites of our religion. Maybe this way, the future generation will forget the legends of fratricide between our nations.
>
> Regarding your current conflict with your insubordinate general, my firm decision is to help you win this war. I shall open the treasure houses of Constantinople and call upon all provinces to send in their military divisions.
>
> Read this letter yourself and write a reply in your own hand. I do not wish scribes to learn of the contents of this exchange. You will have all that I have promised upon receipt of your response. God loves a magnanimous king.

The Caesar put his stamp on the letter and sealed it. As soon as the ink was dry, the letter was dispatched. Khosrow-Parviz readily accepted the Caesar's terms and wrote back that he would be honored to wed the princess of Rome. Iranians would be glad to bury old grudges and mark the royal union as an auspicious turning point in the history of the two nations. The two nations would henceforth respect each other's borders.

Khorrad-e Borzin, who was chosen to carry the historic letter, jumped on his bay horse and disappeared in the dust raised by the steed. This diplomatic mission promised a fresh start in the fraught relationships between Iran and Rome.

The Iranian delegation, consisting of Gostahm, Shaupur, Bauluy, and Khorrad, was graciously received in the Roman capital Constantinople. The Caesar himself saw to their luxurious lodging and amenities.

As Iran and Rome were finally at peace, the Caesar thought that friendly competition and intellectual challenges should replace violence and bloodshed. Thus, he decided to amuse himself at the expense of the Iranians, using an ingenious contraption fabricated by Roman artisans: an automaton of a crying maiden that leaked liquid from her eye and wiped it away with her right hand. The artifice was meant to represent a mourner for the passion of Christ. The Caesar sent Gostahm to where the beguiling machine was set up, telling him that it was his daughter grieving her dead husband and asked him to comfort the sad princess in her chamber.

Poor Gostahm tried his best to reason with the machine. He told it about the transitoriness of life and the inexorability of death that awaits us all. But his words fell on the automaton's deaf ears. So, he returned and confessed that he had failed. Shaupur and Bauluy were also sent in and came back crestfallen. They said that the pitiful damsel was inconsolable. Finally, Khorrad was sent into the chamber.

The entire show appeared suspicious to him. The movements of the seated lady were repetitive, and her statuesque attendants stood there without trying to console her. It didn't take him long to figure out the nature of the elaborate prank. Khorrad went back with a smile and praised the Roman artisans for their ingenious craft. He added that this was a clever trick, and he could not wait to entertain Khosrow-Parviz with its story.

Excited by Khorrad's intelligence, the Caesar showed him another wonder of his craftsmen, a life-size equestrian statue suspended in the air. The ambassador nodded and said that he knew the secret of the gravity-defying object as well. He had seen a similar hovering idol in a Hindu temple, which worked with magnets.

The Caesar admitted that his statue was also kept floating by magnetic forces. He then asked Khorrad about the creed of the Hindus. The ambassador spoke of their veneration of the cow and the custom of a widow entering her husband's funeral pyre believing that she would thus burn off her sins in an invisible fire called Ether. Khorrad closed his discourse with a critique of Christian beliefs, posing a rhetorical question: How could Christians square their love of opulence with the ascetic life of Jesus Christ? And why would they call a humble but mortal man the Son of God when God does not have a human family? Greatly impressed by the depth and width of the wisdom of the ambassador, the Caesar gave him worthy prizes that included a diadem.

When the preparations for sending Myriam, the royal bride, were complete, an army of one hundred thousand well-equipped soldiers accompanied the litter. The celebrant cavalcade set off on the auspicious twentieth day of the month that was associated with the planet Mars. Gostahm was chosen to act as the princess's personal assistant during the journey. Four Roman philosophers, three hundred golden-belted slaves, and forty dazzling female servants accompanied the long trail of camels carrying the trousseau of Princess Myriam. It was estimated that the value of the trousseau exceeded three hundred million dinars. The Caesar went three milestones to see his daughter off. Then, he kissed her goodbye and advised her to remain behind the curtains of the litter during the trip. He then entrusted Myriam and the Roman army to his son, Niatus. They said a tearful farewell and parted ways.

When the Romans reached the Iranian camp, Khosrow-Parviz embraced Niatus and kissed the beautiful Myriam's hand before leading her to their wedding chamber. After three days, the king emerged from his pavilion to meet with Niatus, and his top commanders Serges and Kut. Seventy junior officers of the Roman army were also in attendance.

He gave both the Iranian and Roman warriors four more days of rest, and regaled the Roman commanders with praise and promised them lavish gifts upon victory. The next day he brought both armies to the plain of Duk in the province of Azarbaijan, where he put Niatus in charge and rode up the slopes of the sacred mountain leading up to the Chichast lake and the fire temple of Azar-goshasp.

These ramps happened to be where Mushil and Benduy were waiting for the arrival of their king. As Khosrow-Parviz's standard came into view, they galloped toward the Iranian army to greet their king.

Khosrow saw the approaching horsemen and asked who they were. "Without a doubt, the one on the piebald horse is my brother Benduy," Gostahm said. Khosrow-Parviz was incredulous! There was no way his uncle could have survived the siege of the Christian monastery after his ruse was discovered. But as they came closer, everybody could see that Gostahm was right. The king embraced his long-lost companion and asked him to relate all his exciting adventures—from the monastery to his imprisonment at Bahraum-e Chubineh's camp. Mushil also received accolades for the help he had provided to the king's uncle.

THE SECOND BATTLE AGAINST THE REBEL ARMY

When the news that Rome had joined Khosrow-Parviz's army reached Ctesiphon, Bahraum dispatched a letter to Gostahm, Benduy, Shaupur, and Andian, urging them to defect. The knights of Iran had to stand together against the treacherous king, who was beholden to the Roman enemy:

> Nothing but duplicity and deceit has come from the Sassanian dynasty. Didn't the disloyal Ardeshir betray his benefactor Ardavan? Didn't Qobaud kill Sufrai, who had avenged his father and saved his kingdom? This king, too, bought his crown at the price of blinding and then killing his father. It is easier to pluck rubies from the red willow or extract ivory from blackwood than to find honor in the progeny of Sassan. Join forces with me, for we are all from the same stock. Let us crush these Roman mercenaries and cleanse our land of their abomination.

He gave this letter to an envoy named Dauna-panauh, who went to the Iranian camp disguised as a merchant leading a caravan of precious merchandise. But instead of delivering the letter to the Iranian commanders, the opportunistic messenger gave it to the king; figuring he would be rewarded for switching sides. Khosrow-Parviz read the letter and wrote a deceptive response on behalf of his knights to the effect that they would gladly defect once they were on the battlefield. Based on this false assurance, Bahraum defied his advisors who wanted to stay and fight a defensive war from the capital and left the fortifications of Ctesiphon to fight on the open plain of Duk in Azerbaijan.

On the day of the battle, the Romans asked Khosrow-Parviz to lead the fight, and he agreed. Niatus, Benduy, Gostahm, and the king ascended to a hilltop to view the battle. On the other side, Bahraum gave the heart of his army to Yalaun-sineh and led the vanguard himself.

When the armies collided, the plain of Duk turned into a sea of blood. The king was praying for victory when Kut, one of the Roman commanders, approached him and demanded: "Show me this insolent slave who bested you in war and forced you to come to us for help. I want to teach him some manners."

Khosrow was deeply offended by Kut's impertinence. "He is the one on the piebald horse," he said after a long pause. "He is sure to fight you if you challenge him to a duel, and I expect you will stand your ground and fight like a man. Don't dishonor yourself by running away."

Kut took his lance and galloped full tilt toward the enemy like a raging elephant. Khosrow-Parviz stood from his dais to better view the confrontation. Seeing the charge, Yalaun-sineh warned his commander. Bahraum drew his sword and urged his horse to a full gallop as well. But, seconds before contact, he slowed his horse to a halt, deflecting his opponent's heavy lance. Then he brought down his sword on Kut's helmet with all his might. The sound of this strike echoed across the battlefield. Bahraum's blade had pierced through Kut's helmet and slashed down to the middle of his chest. The king laughed with derision. Niatus took umbrage at this reaction.

"You consider this a laughing matter? Kut was a commander equal to a thousand warriors."

"I was not laughing at his demise," said the king, "but reflecting on the way the proud are brought low. Kut shamed me for fleeing from a mere slave. I dare say there is no shame in fleeing from a slave who fights like that!"

Bahraum had Kut's corpse tied to his horse and sent to the Roman lines to demonstrate the power of his sword hand. The Christian patriarch, who had accompanied the army, wept for their fallen hero and presided over his funeral. The king ordered the body to be taken to the Caesar with all the due honors. The stunning success of the rebel commander over the formidable Roman champion had vindicated Khosrow-Parviz, and he made sure the Caesar was appraised of how easily Kut had been dispatched.

To exact revenge, the Roman army launched a general assault. But they failed to break through the lines of Bahraum's army. So many were killed in the ensuing counterattack that their piled-up bodies resembled a range of macabre hills. Khosrow knew that another day like that would finish off the Roman army and end his hopes of crushing the rebellion. Thus, he advised Serges against bringing their forces to the battlefield in the next day's confrontation.

When the luminous flag of the dawn was hoisted over the eastern horizon, the Iranians went forth to the pounding of the tin drums and the blare of the trumpets. Having been deceived by the false letter of Khosrow-Parviz on behalf of his commanders, Bahraum expected the Iranian knights to come over to his side as soon as he appeared on the battlefield. But Gostahm, Andian, and Shaupur stood firmly as commanders of their flanks. Even Bahraum's own brother Gorduy was at his post.

With a sinking feeling, Bahraum suspected that treachery was involved. In great fury, he drove his white elephant to Khosrow's right flank, which was commanded by Shaupur.

"Answer me, you repugnant, double-crossing fiend," Bahraum screamed at the commander. "Didn't you and your friends respond to my letter, pledging to switch sides on the battlefield? Is this your idea of living by the knightly code of honor?"

Shaupur was bewildered by this address. "What letter? What promises? What on earth are you talking about?"

Khosrow-Parviz scornfully interjected from his position at the vanguard of the army, "There is an amusing story behind this letter, Shaupur. I will tell you about that when the time is right."

Hearing this, Bahraum's suspition was confirmed that his letter had been intercepted and the message he had received from the Iranian generals was nothing but a clever forgery. Now he had to win by the force of arms what he had wished to achieve by cunning. Thus, he turned his elephant back around toward the Iranian lines and charged. But the beast was stopped by a barrage of arrows that the Iranians had sent through its trunk.

Bahraum-e Chubineh jumped off his collapsing elephant, switched to a reserve horse and continued his advance until the horse was shot, whereupon he dismounted and advanced behind his shield. The soldiers shooting at him fled as he got closer. From that opening in the lines, he ravaged the heart of Khosrow's army and turned to demolish the right flank, which was commanded by his brother Gorduy. The brothers locked eyes and accused each other of treason.

"Only a bastard suits up to fight his own brother!" Bahraum said.

"Listen, you two-faced wolf! You are the one standing against God and the king. A stranger is better than a brother who betrays his homeland."

But they stopped short of an actual duel to avoid the sin of fratricide. Bahraum turned his horse around and went back to his army. Gorduy went to the king and received accolades for his loyalty.

As the battle continued, Khosrow-Parviz grew concerned that the Romans would take all the credit if they played a major part in crushing the rebellion. This would give them the right to brag that Iran owed its sovereignty to them. To prevent such a development, he proposed that they organize a duel between the elite Iranian warriors of each side. The victor of the limited combat would be declared the winner of the war. His commanders agreed to the plan. The king chose fourteen paladins, including his top commanders Gostahm, Benduy, and Gorduy, and went forward to signal his intention to Bahraum.

By the number of warriors coming at them, the rebel commander guessed that the king was proposing a decisive duel between the best warriors of the two armies. He welcomed this challenge, and turned to his commanders Yalaun-sineh and Izad-goshasp, saying:

"This pretender is approaching us for a duel with what he considers to be his top warriors. They appear to be no more than twenty in number. It would be beneath our dignity to bring more than four to this fight."

Khosrow-Parviz saw Bahraum-e Chubineh and his three prominent commanders galloping toward them and told his comrades: "I will fight Bahraum if you stop his companions." However, this plan fizzled before it could be implemented. All the Iranian warriors except Gorduy, Gostahm, and Benduy had already fled. From the vantage point of Niatus and other Roman generals who viewed the battle from a hilltop, the Iranians appeared like a flock of sheep running from a pack of wolves. Shaken, the king told Gostahm that he feared he might lose to Bahraum in hand-to-hand combat. And yet he was ashamed to show his back to the enemy. Gostahm assured the king that there was no shame in redeployment.

Taking this as his cue, Khosrow cut the barding to lighten up his black horse and galloped away, trailing behind his deserting men. Bahraum gave chase, taunting: "Your time of reckoning has finally come. There is no point in escaping. You threw your life away when you imagined you were a match to me in close combat."

At the end of the battlefield, there was a massive rock formation. The king abandoned his horse, hoping to find a hiding place there. But he was troubled to see the cove he had chosen offered little protection. He then tried to scale the mountain wall but ended up on a ledge surrounded by the vertical rock face on every side. Meanwhile, Bahraum had alighted from his horse and was running toward the rocks wielding his unsheathed sword.

In his despair, the king ardently prayed for divine intervention. In a moment that seemed to stretch time, an angel adorned in green robes and riding on a splendid horse appeared before him. "Who are you?" the awe-stricken Khosrow-Parviz asked the otherworldly figure. "I am the angel Sorush. Rejoice, for you shall be the king of Iran." Then, with a firm grip, the angel took the king's hand, and they soared over the towering boulders, effortlessly crossing to the other side of the mountain.

Bahraum, who had witnessed the miraculous event as he stood at the foot of the mountain, turned pale and mumbled to himself: "I never shrank from facing up to a man. But I have never had to contend with angels! Maybe I should not have raised the flag of rebellion against a king who commands such powers."

The Roman generals were also following these events from their vantage point. They had assumed the worst when they saw the king disappear into the boulders, followed by his sword-wielding nemesis. Princess Myriam, who had left her tent to watch the fateful duel, was weeping and clawing her face in a gesture of mourning. But then, just as everyone had given up on Khosrow-Parviz, he was seen walking back toward his people. To the amazement of the onlookers, he was approaching from the opposite side of the mountain. A cheer went up at the miraculous reappearance of the king.

Upon returning to the Roman side in triumph, the king explained the incredible events that had occurred. "You saw the way I was transported across the mountain. That had nothing to do with sorcery and black magic. It was a pure miracle. God sent the archangel Sorush to my rescue. Such kings as Feraydun, Tur, Salm, and Afrasiab also had divine visions. But what happened today was a direct intervention by the Almighty."

Overjoyed by the divine succor he had received, the king rallied his troops and mounted a general assault, ready to finally confront Bahraum head on. The rebel general shot an arrow that pierced the king's belt. But the silken doublet worn under his armor stopped the projectile. A soldier stepped forward and pulled out the arrow. Then Khosrow-Parviz charged Bahraum and slammed his sword into his helmet. The mighty blow ripped open the metal. Although the rebel commander was not injured and could escape, the sound of the blow reverberated in the arena, inspiring admiration for the king.

Heartened by the courage of their king, Khosrow's soldiers pushed back Bahraum and his forces. Once the withdrawal turned into a rout, Benduy advised the king that it was unseemly for Iranians to shed the blood of their compatriots. Khosrow declared an immediate amnesty. As the sun began to set and the two armies hunkered down to rest, Benduy sent criers between the two armies to announce the king's general amnesty: "You are all forgiven by the king," they said. "The more implicated you are in the rebellion and the more aggressive you have been on the battlefield, the more you shall be inundated by the royal clemency."

This led to such a massive defection that Bahraum, walking through his deserted camp at dawn said: "If there is a time to flee, that time is now." Then he ordered his treasures to be loaded on fast-trotting camels and escaped with his commanders under cover of darkness. He chose the desert path to avoid capture.

THE REBEL LEADERS ON THE RUN

In the morning, Khosrow sent an army of three thousand soldiers under Nastud's command to arrest the fleeing party. Bahraum and his companions didn't stop until the descent of the cloak of the night. They stopped at an old woman's hut and begged for food. She returned with a water-skin, a bowl of whey, and a few crusts of bread. Yalaun-sineh handed his commander a bundle of ritual Barsom to bless the meal. As they were famished, they commenced eating without finishing the Zoroastrian rite of humming the Bazh. Women of the nearby hamlet gathered to watch the commotion. The old woman offered her guests a quantity of wine in a gourd as well. Bahraum quaffed a little and addressed her:

"Tell me, old woman, what have you heard about what is happening in this world?"

"I have heard so much that my head is spinning," she told him. "The city folk say that the rebel Bahraum-e Chubineh was defeated by the king and that he took off running for his life."

"Be honest. Do you think it was wise or foolish of this Bahraum to pick a fight with King Khosrow-Parviz?

"I think some demon has blinded you, my dear sir," she replied. "Don't you find it laughable that this obscure soldier, the son of an even more obscure father, squared off against Khosrow-Parviz, the son of King Hormazd?"

Bahraum-e Chubineh smiled and airily opined:

"In so far as I can see, this fellow Bahraum deserves to drink wine out of the skin of an old gourd if he ever fancied that he could become a king!"

The next day as the rebels continued their trek; they came across a thicket where workers were harvesting bamboo. One among them whispered to Bahraum: "Why have you come this way? Don't you know an army is lying in ambush for you?"

Bahraum turned to his companions. "I knew that Khosrow would send one of his worthless commanders after us. It's time we brought their tedious journey to a dramatic end. Surround the thicket and set fire to it. Let's wait and see who we can smoke out."

As the fire raged, some of Nastud's troops perished, and the rest ran away. Nastud was captured, bound, and brought to Bahraum. He groveled on the ground and asked to be spared. "Please don't kill me. Forgive me, for I am the victim of bad luck. Spare me and I will serve you as a slave."

"I don't need a cowardly slave like you," spat Bahraum. "It is below my dignity even to kill you. Just go back and tell your master what occurred here."

Nastud kissed the ground and ran away. Bahraum continued his journey through his ancestral land of Rey, hoping to seek asylum from the khagan of China.

AN UNFORTUNATE QUARREL

Back at the battlefield, the king confiscated what remained of the rebel's abandoned camp. The rebellion that threatened his life and royal career had been crushed. In gratitude, he rode to a dry field overgrown with thorn bushes to offer prayers. He prostrated himself before the Almighty and thanked Him with all his heart.

Next, Khosrow sent a report of his victory to the Roman court. Upon hearing the good tidings, the Caesar descended his throne and humbly thanked God. He then sent his royal son-in-law a crown he had inherited from the past Caesars along with a torque, earrings, a gold-worked green gambeson, a bejeweled cross, and one hundred sixty royal garments. Four philosophers led the thirty camels that delivered Caesar's gifts to the royal pavilion at the Azar-goshasp temple.

Glad as the king was with the gifts of his royal father-in-law, he hesitated to wear the garments emblazoned with Christian symbols. Doing so could give the impression that he had converted to Christianity. But not wearing the garments would be considered an insult to the Roman court.

Royal advisors debated the matter and concluded that the king must wear the Roman robes. People of consequence would understand that accepting the gifts of the Caesar did not mean that the king had abandoned his ancestral faith. Khosrow agreed and on the appointed day, presided over the banquet in the lavish Roman garments.

The repast started with the customary Zoroastrian rites of holding the bundle of sacred herbs and humming the Bazh mantras. Niatus considered it an abomination to mix the rituals of a pagan religion with the sacred cross of Jesus that was embroidered on the garments of the king. He threw down his bread and angrily withdrew. Benduy slapped Niatus with the back of his hand for this breach of decorum. Khosrow was furious at this interaction, which could have grave consequences for both countries. The Roman commander left the feast only to come back in full military gear with his guards to demand that Benduy be surrendered for punishment. The king left without a response.

"What do these Romans expect?" he said, turning to Myriam. "That I drop the required rites of my religion just because I am wearing the garments sent by your father? Now Niatus is threatening me with his military—whose performance was far from inspiring on the battlefield."

"Let me manage this quarrel," Myriam said. "Deliver Benduy to me, and I promise no harm will come to him."

"I will give you Benduy. But remind your brother that I never pledged to convert to Christianity as a condition of this union. Tell him to embrace Benduy and make amends. This silly event has gone too far."

Myriam lived up to her promise. Benduy was released, and Niatus apologized for his drunken outburst.

"I am glad," Khosrow said. "I was not happy with what Benduy did. No love was lost between this man and me, considering the circumstances surrounding my father's death."

Two-thirds of the wealth recovered from Bahraum's camp was given to the Roman side, and a document was written whereby border cities annexed by the previous kings of Iran were returned to Rome.

The king went to the Azar-goshasp temple to pray and meditate before rewarding his loyal commanders. Gostahm received the northwestern province of Khorausan, and Andian was given the southwestern region of Kerman. Gorduy received a significant promotion at court, and Bauluy was appointed governor of the city of Chauch. Another prominent knight by the name of Raum-Borzin was entrusted with the central regions of Daurab-gerd and Estakhr.

I am sixty-five and I know it's uncouth
To think of wealth, as death beckons
Those who've squandered their youth.

I've lost my son who was my very soul
It was my turn to die, but he preempted me
Tis the kind of loss none can console.

At thirty-seven, he hated this world despite
His tender age and was impatient with me,
So, he went to the realm of the eternal light.

I picture him up there saving me a place
I see him awaiting my imminent arrival
As he basks in God's eternal grace.

I pray for the forgiveness of his sins.
He left me too soon. Destiny's dice
Are always loaded. In this game nobody wins.

Now it's time I stopped to meander
About and come back to the fate of Bahraum:
The defeated but unbroken rebel commander.

BAHRAUM AT THE COURT OF THE KHAGAN

When the rebel leaders crossed the Oxus, they were greeted by ten thousand troops sent by the khagan. Bahraum-e Chubineh was escorted to the royal pavilion by the khagan's son and brother. He kissed the ground and said: "You are aware of Khosrow-Parviz's greed and recklessness. No one is safe while he lives. Now I have come to seek your protection. I pledge to obey and serve you from the bottom of my heart. But if you do not wish my company, I beg your permission to cross this land and seek my fortunes in India."

The khagan graciously accepted the Iranian general as a respected ally, provided him with lavish lodgings, and invited him to participate in polo, hunting, and nightly feasts. He was also made a member of the royal entourage. One of his privileges was to attend the morning audience of the khagan. During these meetings, he noticed an uncouth commander named Maghatureh, who came often, touched his lips with two fingers as a sign of respect, and brazenly demanded one thousand golden dinars for his expenses.

Exasperated by this impertinent behavior, Bahraum went to the khagan and asked: "Why is this Turk given all this gold in addition to his regular salary?"

"According to our custom the khagan cannot refuse anything to his top commanders. I know he is abusing that custom. But I fear he might sow discord among the soldiers if I don't appease him."

"You have allowed this man to take advantage of your generosity," Bahraum said. "A subject should never gain such power over his king. If you are bound by the obligations of your office, say the word, and I will rid you of this pesky begger."

"You will have done me a great favor if you remove this nuisance," said the khagan.

"Then I shall do it. Don't speak to him when he returns. Don't smile at him. Don't even recognize him."

The next time Maghatureh went to the khagan, he noticed the change in his treatment and protested: "I will not be treated so shabbily, my Khagan. I know it is all due to the evil influence of this Iranian interloper. Beware that he will tempt you to the kind of injustice that will soil your reputation and spoil your army."

"Keep your voice down and know your place," Bahraum stepped in.

"Get it through your thick head that I will not allow you or anyone else to siphon money from the treasury of my benefactor. They say you can take on three hundred soldiers on the battlefield. Be that as it may, your military prowess does not entitle you to show up every other day and extort the king."

Maghatureh was flushed with anger and demanded satisfaction. As was the custom of the warriors of the east he reached into his quiver and handed Bahraum-e Chubineh an arrow. The gesture was reciprocated, and the duel was set for the morning.

When dawn broke through the eastern horizon, the contenders suited up for battle and came to an arid plane far from the city. The khagan and his retinue had also come to view the duel.

Maghatureh's brother had tied his feet together under the belly of his horse to keep him from being knocked out of his saddle in combat. He rode into the battlefield wearing a glittery gambeson over his armor:

"It is time Bahraum proved his mettle and matched action to words. Do you want to initiate, or should I?"

"You demanded satisfaction. You start."

Maghatureh nocked an arrow in his bow, pulled the string, and let the shaft fly. The missile bounced off his opponent's armored belt and fell to the ground. Bahraum did not move, making his opponent think he was dead on his saddle. As Maghatureh spun around to return, he roared: "It's too early to return to your tent. You spoke first. Wait for a reply."

Bahraum chose a deadly arrow from his quiver, pulled the string and shot it through Maghatureh's belly, forever quenching his thirst for unending sacks of gold. He expired on his saddle. The hero turned to the khagan and said: "I believe this man needs an undertaker." Upon ascertaining Maghatureh's death, the khagan returned to his pavilion, trying to hide his happiness. Then he enriched his new Iranian ally with a well-caparisoned horse, a complete set of arms, and a crown worthy of a king.

SLAYING THE LION-APE

A ferocious beast known as the Lion-Ape roamed the mountains of the Khagan's realm, preying on anyone who dared venture beyond the city limits. There was scarcely a family that was untouched by the marauding predator. The khagan and his wife, the khatun, had also lost their beautiful daughter to the Lion-Ape when she was on a hunting excursion. As she sat at the spread with her friends to drink wine the Lion-Ape had descended on them and killed the princess. The khatun could not get over her grief as long as the terrible man-eater was alive. But there was no one brave enough to slay the beast.

One day Bahraum-e Chubineh, who had gained a certain notoriety after killing Maghatureh, was strolling around the royal compound and he happened to attract the attention of the khatun. She asked her attendants who the impressive fellow was. They told her that he was the favorite companion of the khagan who had once been the king of Iran. The khatun decided to appeal to him to avenge her daughter. But such a request could not have been made without her husband's approval.

The khagan did not relish the idea of a foreigner avenging his daughter, but noting the distress of the khatun, he reluctantly consented. She then approached Bahraum at a feast and said: "Great hero, hear the appeal of a mother who asks for a boon.

"Speak, my queen, and your request shall be granted, whatever it might be."

"Not far from here there is a pleasant meadow that is a favorite of young people. It is adjacent to a forbidding, tall mountain where a man-eater known as the Lion-Ape lives. He regularly preys on our people, and my daughter was one of his victims. He is so fearsome that our men are afraid of confronting him. I ask that you kill this ogre and avenge my daughter."

"With the help of the Almighty I shall slay this beast tomorrow when dawn breaks over that meadow."

The next day at sunrise, Bahraum put on a gambeson over his armor and went up to the beast's favorite hunting grounds. With ten arrows in his quiver, he gingerly scaled the mountain using his lariat. The beast sensed the hunter's approach and immersed himself in a pond, as his pelt would act as armor when it was wet. But his natural shield proved ineffective against Bahraum's arrows. The Lion-Ape was felled with a few shafts, but Bahraum sent seven more to make sure it was dead. He then unsheathed his sword, cut off the beast's head, and put it in a pouch before rappelling back down the mountain.

Victorious, Bahraum returned to the royal compound to present the Lion-Ape's head to the queen, and he was welcomed by an enthusiastic crowd that cheered in his honor. He was showered with gold and silver coins as he marched to the khatun's pavilion. To show the extent of her gratitude, the khatun stepped off her dais and kissed the intrepid avenger's hand and rewarded him with many gifts. She also arranged to give her younger daughter to him in marriage. And thus Bahraum's fame reached its zenith in the court of the khagan. He was now a member of the royal family, and it was rumored that his treasures surpassed those of the king of Iran.

Khosrow-Parviz was rankled by the news of Bahraum-e Chubineh's rise in China, so he sent an envoy carrying a terse letter to the khagan:

> Praise be to God, the Creator of the sun, Saturn, and the moon. He punishes the wicked and helps those who seek wisdom. I hear that a treasonous soldier who rebelled against me has found favor at your court. He was a nonentity. My father pulled him out of obscurity and gave him an army. The ingrate has repaid these favors with insubordination and rebellion. He could not find refuge anywhere after escaping Iran. But you have opened your gates to him. This will not redound to your glory. Extradite this man if you don't wish to see my army at your borders.

The letter arrived at the khagan's camp a month later. After hearing of Khosrow's extradition request, Bahraum went to the khagan and said: "I have not seen this ambassador, but I have heard of him. I know what his message is. Khosrow continues his intrigue against me. Just command me, and I will conquer that land for you with a small, elite force of my choice. I will kill this malignant man and purge Iran of the Sassanian blight."

The prospect of an easy conquest of Iran was appealing. Agreeing to this plan, the khagan appointed two of his top warriors, Januy and Zanguy, as lieutenants of Bahraum and charged them to prepare an army on the banks of the Oxus River. While these preparations were going on, the khagan sent the following reply to Khosrow-Parviz:

> I have treated your envoy with respect, and I have read your letter with care. It does not behoove you to address the king of the Turks, the Chinese, and the Hephthalites as if you are chiding a slave. I have not violated our treaty of peace. Giving refuge to Bahraum was an act of kindness. Nor am I intimidated by your army. I only fear God. A final word of advice: Listen to the council of reason if you wish to increase your glory.

Khosrow-Parviz' advisors thought that the khagan's position was reasonable. One could not expect a sovereign to betray his son-in-law because of a threatening letter. The best course would be to send an ambassador to thoroughly explore various avenues for eliminating the danger posed by Bahraum-e Chubineh, even if it took a year. The king nodded in agreement and appointed Khorrad-e Borzin as his special envoy to the court of the khagan. He went to work immediately, preparing his journey to the eastern kingdom. Upon arrival he presented his credentials, praised God, and declared that he was sent by the king of Iran, who had fraternal ties to the east as he had descended on his mother's side from the great emperor of China. Khorrad-e Borzin then retired to his luxurious tent without asking for favors. He was hosted in great luxury thereafter, and his privileges included membership to the khagan's retinue in hunting and drinking. Confident that he had found favor at the court, he finally said to the Khagan: "Bahraum-e Chubineh is a lowborn and ungrateful slave. He mutinied against King Hormazd and his son, although he owed them everything. Such a man is bound to turn against you as well. Great would be the rewards if you were to extradite him to his master."

The khagan frowned. "Do not speak of this matter again if you want to be respected at my court. I am not the kind of man who breaks his promises and betrays his friends."

Knowing he had no chance of budging the khagan's loyalty to his Iranian friend, Khorrad turned his attention to the khatun. She, too, was beholden to Bahraum as he had avenged one of her daughters and married another. But the devious ambassador did not lose hope.

A MURDEROUS PLOT

As he cast about for a way to obviate the king's enemy, Khorrad-e Borzin came across a poor old man named Qalun, who was a marginal member of the clan of Maghatureh. He wore a tattered pelt and survived on millet porridge. Khorrad surmised that the man might resent Bahraum for killing Maghatureh, so he gave him money for a suit of clothes and victuals. Soon he put on some weight on a diet of fresh bread and roasted lamb, and started to fill his new garments.

To show his appreciation, Qalun informed his benefactor that the khatun was desperately seeking a healer for one of her daughters who suffered from a mysterious illness. As luck would have it, Khorrad had studied medicine and was able to cure the princess with a concoction of pomegranate juice and chicory flower extract. The khatun asked the Iranian ambassador to name his reward. He refused payment for his services and said it was enough to be considered a friend. This meant that the queen owed him a favor.

A plot to assassinate Bahraum by Qalun's hand was slowly taking shape in Khorrad's mind. He had decided that the old man could slip through security guards as he accorded to nobody's idea of an assassin. One day Khorrad broached the subject with him:

"I have a thrilling proposal for you. I want you to kill Bahraum for me. It's a perilous mission, though, at your age, death is not a great risk. Just think of the rewards if you get away with it. You will spend the rest of your life enjoying pleasures that you cannot even imagine. And if you are killed, you will leave a rich legacy for your children."

Qalun seemed persuaded by Khorrad's offer and after a pause nodded his approval to carry out the mission. Khorrad explained: "Bahraum considers the twentieth day of every month that is associated with the planet Mars as inauspicious. On that day he goes into seclusion in his tent. I will give you a letter with the khagan's seal, which will get you past the sentries. Enter his tent and tell him you have a secret message from his wife and need to whisper it in his ear. Then stab him and escape. There will be pandemonium in the camp, and no one will suspect an old man like you to be the assassin." Qalun was ready to carry out the grisly mission. All they needed was a letter sealed with the khagan's seal.

Khorrad went to the queen and asked for a favor. "Some of my relatives have been arrested and imprisoned on false charges. A letter with the khagan's signet would secure their release."

She said her husband was in a drunken stupor, but she could impress the sealing clay on his ring without waking him. Khorrad received the seal and kissed the ground.

The plot went forward with ease. Qalun was received in the camp and gained access to the general's pavilion on the strength of his humble appearance and the letter he was carrying.

As he entered the tent, he saw a slave offering Bahraum a plate of pomegranate seeds, a quince, and an apple. Seeing that an envoy had arrived with a letter embossed with the royal seal, he dismissed the slave and bid the messenger to approach and whisper his oral message in his ear. Qalun crept up to Bahraum's bed, slashed his victim's belly from side to side and turned around to run.

Bahraum managed to scream for his guards, and the killer was apprehended. An angry mob beat him severely, but despite his broken bones, Qalun refused to divulge who had sent him.

As Bahraum was bleeding to death, his sister entered the tent. "Who brought you so low, my heroic brother?" Gordieh said, scratching at her cheeks and pulling at her hair. "You bowed your head to neither king nor God. But look at you now! Didn't I warn you against raising the flag of rebellion against the house of Sassan? Didn't I tell you that people would sooner crown a girl than make you a king? Your soul is bound for the house of death, leaving your clan defenseless, as roaming sheep among a pack of wolves."

Bahraum gazed at his sister's tearful face. "You were right all along," he said, "and I should have listened to you. But my path was set by the stars. I wasn't the only one who lost his way. Many kings have also been led astray, including Jamshid and Kay-Kavous. I was deceived by a demon. But what is done cannot be undone. I hope you and Yalaun-sineh will take care of each other. Go to Khosrow-Parviz if he will have you. Bury me in Iran.

"I have made many sacrifices for the sake of this khagan, so I trusted his messenger. I didn't expect him to send a cutthroat after me. But again, the old assassin was most probably an agent of Khosrow-Parviz. He was never going to let me live."

Bahraum dictated a letter to the khagan, begging him to take care of his family after his death. Then he kissed Gordieh's neck and departed this world, his cold face dripping with his sister's tears.

Life is brief, so be steadfast
Don't get used to its delicious nectar
For such pleasures will never last.

Bahraum-e Chubineh's body was placed in a luxurious coffin and buried. When the khagan heard the news, he ordered Qalun's execution. He also had his two sons locked inside their house as it was set on fire. The khatun was subjected to insults and her wealth was taken away.

Having masterminded the assassination, Khorrad-e Borzin slipped out of the camp, jumped on his horse and galloped to the Oxus River. He was received at the Iranian court like a hero. The king enriched him with fabulous riches and announced a seven-day feast in his honor. Money was sent to various fire temples in thanksgiving, and alms were distributed among the poor.

THE HEROINE OF THE REBEL ARMY

The khagan dreaded the accusation that he had been negligent or complicit in Bahraum-e Chubineh's murder. Thus, he sent his brother Toborg to assure the Iranian camp that nothing had changed despite the assassination of their leader. In a separate letter, he praised Gordieh as a chaste and respectable woman and proposed to marry her. This was the ultimate sign of respect for Bahraum's followers. Toborg delivered this letter and added his personal guarantee that she would enjoy the highest honors at the khagan's seraglio. Gordieh sent this reply:

> The great khagan has acted as a kind and compassionate king. He has honored me with this marriage proposal. A good husband is a blessing for every woman. But it is far too early to speak of such matters. We can return to this matter after our four-month period of mourning.

Then she called her council of advisors for consultation, as the fate of the group was at stake. She started with an account of what had transpired between her and Toborg. "The great khagan has extended us an offer of friendship that includes a marriage proposal. He is a veritable king. But the union of Iranians and Turks has never ended well. Consider Siavosh's fate after he married Afrasiab's daughter. He was killed and long wars of revenge ensued. We are not welcome back in Iran, but we must somehow return to our homeland for this is an alien world, and I feel we will never be safe here. I have written to my brother Gorduy and begged him to present our case to the king. We were part of Bahraum's rebellion, but I am sanguine on the prospects of a royal pardon."

The council of leaders sang the praises of Gordieh and declared her their leader. "You are the bravest and the wisest among us. Where you stand your ground, a mountain cannot move you."

With this resolution, Gordieh chose a regiment of one thousand, one hundred sixty cavalrymen to spearhead the group's return to the borders of Iran. Each one of these warriors was equal to ten soldiers on the battlefield.

"I only need intrepid fighters in this force. Let cowards hang back," Gordieh said to her elite guard. We are on our way to our ancestral land. The khagan is sure to send an army to stop us. Banish fear of death from your hearts and fight with everything you've got."

The cheer of agreement was unanimous. Yalaun-sineh and Mehr, the son of Izad-goshasp, rode ahead of the guards chanting: "*Death with honor is better than living with the shame of defeat.*" Three thousand camels carried the group's provisions.

The khagan was infuriated when Toborg informed him that Gordieh had decamped and was going back to Iran. He charged his brother to stop them from crossing the Oxus River.

"Block them, but don't be harsh," he ordered. "Do not humiliate them. Persuade them with honeyed words. Maybe they are running out of fear. Reassure them that we don't intend to harm them. That said, you are authorized to enslave or kill them all if they persist in defecting."

It took four days, but Toborg caught up with Iranian troops and told them that he had a message from his brother, the khagan. Gordieh stopped the trail of camels, donned her brother's armor, and came forward to identify herself in front of her guard.

"Be advised, worthy lady," said Toborg, "that the khagan considers you a friend. You are the sister of his late son-in-law. He did not mean to force marriage upon you. That was just a gesture of friendship. You are free to marry him or live in this territory as you wish. Either way, you and your group are under our protection. But you are not permitted to cross the Oxus River. If you defy me, I have orders to carry you back as slaves."

"Let us continue this conversation in private," Gordieh replied. When they had moved away from their troops, the heroine removed her helmet and said: "Bahraum was like a father to me. You have seen his feats on the battlefield. Now try my mettle, and see if I am marriage material."

Then she spurred her horse on and struck Toborg with her lance, knocking him to the ground and killing him. Then she motioned to Izad-goshasp and Yalaun-sineh. They waded into the enemy lines, followed by their men. Many in Toborg's army were killed and the remainder ran away. Gordieh pursued them for two leagues before returning to her troops.

After another four days of rapid marching, what was formerly the army of rebellion stopped at the eastern bank of the Oxus. Gordieh sent a letter to her brother Gorduy, who had remained loyal to Khosrow-Parviz, and asked that he redouble his efforts to obtain a pardon from the king for the house of Bahraum-e Chubineh. Gorduy was trying his best, he replied, but Khosrow-Parviz was preoccupied with another affair.

AVENGING HORMAZD

After crushing the rebellion, Khosrow-Parviz became consumed with avenging his father.

"I have to gratify my desire for vengeance," he told his vizier. "How can I stay calm while my father's murderer walks around without a care in the world? How can I rule as a king while my mind is awash in impotent rage? How can I let the dastardly Benduy and Gostahm get away with murdering my father?"

At long last, the king had resolved to avenge his father on his uncles. For this purpose, he drank copious amounts of wine and drunkenly ordered the arrest of his uncle Benduy. He then commanded his henchman to cut off his hands and feet and let him bleed to death. Once this was done, he sent an envoy to Khorausan to summon his other uncle. Gostahm began to head toward the capital but stopped when the news of Benduy's gruesome execution reached him.

In retaliation, Gostahm sparked a rebellion in Amol, laid waste to a vast area in the north of Iran, recruited a large army from among its discontented peasants, and attacked a number of royal garrisons. The king sent several armies to crush the uprising, but they were all defeated. Gostahm's next move was to cross the Oxus, hoping to join forces with Gordieh and form a united rebellious front.

He had tears in his eyes when he met the heroine. "Worthy lady!" he mused. "Accept my condolences for the cowardly assassination of your brother. Our brothers had a similar fate. They both trusted this bloody king. He sent an assassin after your brother after he saved his kingdom from destruction. And, he paid Benduy back for his crucial support by brutally murdering him. How can you expect such a dastardly man to honor his word? When Khosrow-Parviz speaks softly, violence is never too far behind."

Gordieh's resolve to return to Iran faltered after this conversation.

Khosrow-Parviz's cruelty toward his close allies was disheartening. Gostahm wanted to strengthen his alliance with what remained of Bahraum's army by marrying Gordieh. In accordance with the custom of asking for a woman's hand, he chose Yalaun-sineh to carry his proposal to her. She accepted to marry Gostahm. The bridegroom was most cheerful as the wedding was solemnized, and treated his bride with utmost respect thereafter.

The king was alarmed by the news of this marriage as their union posed a serious threat to his eastern border. Thus, Khosrow-Parviz and his advisor Gorduy decided to tempt Gordieh to do away with her husband and come to their side. In return, she would receive an offer to marry the king and a general amnesty for her troops. Gorduy suggested that his wife act as a go-between, since Gordieh would be more likely to consent if the plan was conveyed by her own sister-in-law.

Khosrow-Parviz's letter was written on sumptuous paper and sealed with his signet. Gorduy wrote his own letter to his sister, indicating that their brother Bahraum had soiled their clan's name and that she would restore their honor by consenting to the plot. Gorduy's wife took both letters and set off for the eastern border.

Gordieh was delighted to see her sister-in-law after their long separation. They caught up in a private pavilion, where they shed tears over Bahraum's tragic fate. But the mood lifted when she read the letters that were placed on her lap, and a smile broke on her face. Her mind was made.

That night, Gostahm stumbled drunkenly into his tent after an evening of merrymaking and fell asleep. Gordieh, who was waiting for him, snuffed the candles around the tent and called upon five of her loyal maids to assist in the grisly act she had planned. They entered Gostahm's bed chamber and smothered him. The victim managed to scream for help a few times before succumbing.

The commotion woke up many in the camp. They were roaming around in confusion when Gordieh came out in her armor and addressed them. She explained what had happened and gave them the good tidings that they had an amnesty and soon would be returning to their homeland. A cheer went up from the crowd.

Gordieh then sent a message to the king that she had fulfilled her side of the bargain. Khosrow-Parviz sent a beautifully illuminated letter inviting her to come back to Ctesiphon along with her troops. Her face shone like a brilliant sun surrounded by the dark night of her hair as she rode ahead of the army into the capital. The king took his new bride's hand, and their marriage ceremony was solemnized by the Zoroastrian priests. Gordieh happily went to her chamber as one of the king's favorite wives.

After two weeks, Khosrow-Parviz arranged a feast for the women of his seraglio to celebrate his new marriage. When Gordieh arrived, the king asked her to regale the company with the story of the battle with Toborg. She had a better idea: she would reenact that battle. The king ordered all the necessary props to be brought to the arena, including caparisoned horses, weapons, armor, and helmets. With royal permission, she vaulted on her horse using the butt of her lance as a pole. She then galloped left and right, wielding her weapons and sounding her war cry. She explained the story as she reenacted her feats: "I went against Toborg like a mad wolf, and this is how I vanquished the enemies of the king."

One of Khosrow's favorite consorts objected that he was being imprudent: "Why would you arm your enemy to the teeth and let her come so close as you sit here in your soft, silken robes?"

"This woman is steadfast in her devotion to me," the king assured her.

At the end of the outstanding performance, the king made Gordieh the mistress of his twelve thousand imperial guards and put her in charge of the security of his palace.

Times were good, and nothing seemed to mar the king's pleasure. And then, at one of the banquets, he was handed a goblet embossed with Bahraum-e Chubineh's mark. The bitter memories of the past came rushing back, and the king declared that the city of the rebel general, Rey, should be demolished. He had a mind to have the city trampled under the feet of his war elephants. But the royal advisors convinced him that it was not the kind of thing a king would do to one of his own cities. Khosrow-Parviz stayed his hand, but he was intent on destroying Rey by other means.

"I will appoint a fool to serve as the lord mayor of Rey," he decided. "A bad mayor is sure to run the city into the ground. Find me a malformed, foul-mouthed, and dishonest man who is offensive in both aspect and character."

The courtiers kept searching, but they could not find anyone with the attributes the king had listed. Finally, someone came to the royal court to report that he had found the man matching the king's specifications. The assembly laughed out loud when they cast eyes on the ridiculous visage of the would-be lord mayor of Rey. Khosrow-Parviz interrogated him to make sure he was as wicked as he looked.

"What is the worst thing you've ever done? What are your bad habits?"

"You name it, Your Majesty, and I have it!" the man replied. "I never tell the truth when I can get away with a lie. I never keep my word and viciously attack anyone who finds my behavior wanting. I love dishonesty."

"You are indeed a repugnant man, born under an evil star. It is a sign of your misfortune that you are happy with your lot in life. In other words, we have found the right man to govern Rey." With this, the king issued a royal decree and sent him off.

In his new position as the lord mayor of Rey, the man issued two proclamations: the city's rain gutters and downspouts were to be filled with mud, and its cats were to be massacred. As a result of these ordinances, the city's roofs collapsed with the first rain, and the streets were infested with mice that thrived in the absence of cats. People moved away, and the prosperous city turned into a ghost town. Gordieh was dismayed by what had befallen her former home.

Back at Ctesiphon, spring had arrived, and Khosrow-Parviz was spending time with his wives at his pleasure garden. Gordieh put on a diverting show in celebration of the season. She had cats dressed up as children riding horses around the garden. They sported earrings, their claws were painted with nail polish, and their eyes were made up with mascara. The king laughed with abandon at the amusing spectacle and granted her one wish.

"Please, oh great king! Dismiss the malevolent fool who runs my hometown."

"Your wish is granted," he relented. "Sack the idiot and send a wise man to restore the city to its previous glory."

Learning of the new governor's arrival, people returned with their cats and rebuilt their roof gutters, downspouts, and eaves. Within a few months, Rey was thriving again. And it was not the only city that fared well during this period. The king chose forty-eight thousand brave warriors to secure the borders. They were divided into four divisions of twelve thousand and sent off in four directions. Some went to the Roman border in the west and some to the Alan tribes of the north. The other two divisions were stationed at Zabolestan in the southwest and Khorausan in the northwest. These standing armies were charged with protecting the country from foreign invasions.

COURTLY LIFE AND THE STORY OF BARBAD

At the peak of his power, when Iran was secure and thriving, Khosrow-Parviz divided his time between the country's administration, meeting with foreign ambassadors, merrymaking, edifying discourses with friends, prayer, consulting with astrologers, conversing with learned men, and romancing. Playing polo, backgammon, chess, and hunting expeditions were also allotted a period in the monthly calendar.

In the twenty-eighth year of his reign, a skilled musician by the name of Barbad set his heart on auditioning for the king. The virtuoso was not motivated by worldly gain as he had enough wealth. But he knew that he was on par with, if not better than, the king's best entertainers and deserved a royal hearing. Serges, the music master of the court, had heard that there was a young man with exceptional talent who could pose a threat to his position. Thus, he bribed the gatekeeper to refuse Barbad entry into the palace.

But Barbad was not deterred. He knew that the king was in the habit of going to a particular orchard on a given day of the month to enjoy music. On the appointed day, the ambitious young man took his lute to the garden in the morning and bribed the groundskeeper to let him in. He then climbed a lush old tree, comfortably nestled himself in its thick branches, and waited for the king's arrival.

When Khosrow-Parviz reclined in his chair and took the first goblet from his cupbearer, Barbad started to sing one of his melodious songs to the accompaniment of his lute. The entire group was entranced by the heavenly music that filled the garden. After the song, the king commanded his retainers to search the place and find the source. But they found no one. Some speculated that the sound had a supernatural origin, for none but the ethereal fairies could sing and play so well. Then, there was a repeat of the virtuoso performance. By the end of the third song, however, there was no doubt that their talented entertainer was a human. The king issued strict orders that the musician be found, for he intended to fill his mouth with precious jewels. With this promise, the trickster came down from his hiding place and kissed the ground before the king.

Delighted to see the musician, the king reprimanded Serges for keeping such a talented artist from coming to him earlier. Thereafter Barbad functioned as the highest musician of the court.

BIRTH OF THE CROWN PRINCE

Six years after the royal wedding between the King and the princess of Rome, they were blessed with a son who was given the public name of Shiruyeh. His secret name, Qobaud, was known only to a few courtiers.

According to royal customs, astrologers were summoned to cast the infant's horoscope. They returned with downcast eyes and reported that the newborn was destined for an evil future: "Disorder will pervade the land under Shiruyeh, and the army will despise him."

The king ordered the astrologers to keep the prophecy to themselves and withdrew into isolation. In his despondency, Khosrow-Parviz stopped amusing himself with hunting, games, and merrymaking. The courtiers sent a wise cleric to learn why the king's routine had changed. He placed the record of his son's prognosticators before the magus.

After a moment of reflection, the magus said, "We must seek refuge in the mercy of the omniscient God. He is sufficient for mankind. If a disaster befalls us due to what is written in the stars, we cannot avoid it by our worries. I would advise you to forget this prophecy and live your life as happily as possible. May the stars and God be with you."

The king dispelled all worries from his mind and dictated a letter to his royal father-in-law to give him the good tidings of the birth of his grandson.

The birth was lavishly celebrated in Rome. The Caesar's extravagant gifts were loaded onto fifty camels and one hundred hinnies. Among these gifts were two hundred bolts of Roman brocade, hundreds of thousands of gold dinars, and the statuette of a jewel-encrusted golden peacock. Four hundred philosophers were sent to accompany the cavalcade, headed by a commander named Khaunegi. At the border, the commander of the Iranian forces, Farrokh-zaud, received his counterpart and ushered the caravan of gifts to Ctesiphon.

Khorrad-e Borzin was given the task of reciting the letter sent by the Caesar. He had congratulated the king on the birth of his son and reminded him that the common progeny of Iranians and Romans going back to King Feraydun had been reinvigorated with a son born to a Roman princess and a Persian king. He requested that the True Cross of Jesus Christ, which had been carried away by the Iranians during a battle, be restored to Rome to mark the renewed friendship of the two nations.

The king honored Khaunegi and invited him to join his retinue in hunting, feasting, and drinking. After a month, Khosrow-Parviz gave the following letter to the Roman envoy to deliver to the Caesar:

> I thank you for your praise and generous gifts, which I have put aside for Shiruyeh. I am fortunate to have such a magnificent ally who rules over a vast territory connecting the earth to the constellation of Pisces in the heavens. Your realm extends from the land of the Slavs to the borders of China and India. You gave me refuge and treated me like a son when I was abandoned by my friends. Yours is a righteous religion with beautiful rites like fasting and contemplative prayers on Sunday. We, too, are proud of the ancestral religion given to us by King Hushang. We worship an exalted God who has no associates and does not sire earthly children.
>
> As for the True Cross, I will say this: A religion that assumes God has children and venerates a piece of wood is not guided by

> reason. It puzzles me that you believe God had a son who smiled on the gallows, died, and joined his father in the sky. But then you mourn his death and worship the timber on which he was hanged.
>
> Besides, were I to consent to your demand and send over this object, my subjects would suppose I have given up my ancestral religion and converted to Christianity. This will not bode well for my reign. I have nothing against my wife holding onto her Christianity, and she is perfectly free to perform the rites of her faith. I wish you God's blessing in doing the same.

Khaunegi and his philosophers, who had been enriched with precious gifts, carried the letter back ahead of a caravan of royal gifts. It was composed of three hundred redheaded camels, laden with such offerings as one hundred forty thousand bolts of Chinese silk, one hundred sixty rubies, each approaching a pomegranate in size. It also included one hundred sixty thousand pandavasi, the currency minted by Khosrow-Parviz that was equivalent to five gold dinars.

Thereafter Shiruyeh received elementary instructions in royal arts. At the age of sixteen he was taller than a fully grown man. But ominous portents about his future continued to weigh on the king. He had tried hard to provide the best moral education for his crown prince. But retaining learned magi and renowned tutors did not yield favorable results.

One day a tutor went to check if Shiruyeh was reviewing his Kelileh and Demneh assignment. But he was found waging a mock battle between the dried claw of a wolf and the skull of a buffalo. The tutor did not merely feel disappointed in his charge, who was too old for such games. He also took the mock battle as a bad omen and reported the whole affair to the king.

Khosrow-Parviz's old unease about his crown prince was revived. Reluctantly, he confined Shiruyeh and his fifteen brothers to a vast but enclosed compound. Thereafter they and their three thousand friends lived a luxurious if restricted life. They were given a complex of connected houses and facilities for hunting and polo. All their needs were served by a regiment of retainers, skilled cooks, and beautiful entertainers.

The ancient book of kings needed to be revived
So, I verified it in sixty thousand couplet lines:
If a longer poem was ever penned it hasn't survived.

These are all euphonious verses, well crafted,
Except maybe five hundred or so
That may be slightly wanting or ill-drafted.

Somehow the sultan hasn't read this book
I'm convinced my enemies have kept it hidden
From His Majesty by hook or by crook.

Once the king realizes what I've done
The sapling of my labor will bear fruit
And I'll be the richest of all poets bar none.

MARRYING AN OLD FLAME

As a young man, Khosrow-Parviz had a beautiful concubine named Shirin. He worshipped his beloved the way the heathen venerate an idol. But fighting the protracted uprising of Bahraum-e Chubineh banished love from the king's heart and he forgot his lover. Thus, the two remained apart for many years.

But the old flame was rekindled when the king came across his companion during an excursion in the royal hunting grounds. This meeting was not purely accidental. The king was riding in the company of his gamekeepers and attendants, hunting with cheetahs, dogs, and falcons. Shirin, who lived not too far off the area, wore a yellow garment woven in gold thread, donned a dazzling diadem, and stood in the king's path. When he came to pass, she recited a poem with tears in her eyes:

Once, you cried tears of blood if we were apart
Whatever happened to our intense love?
Why did you exile me from your heart?

The king wept at the sight of his beloved and ordered his servants to escort her to the royal seraglio. Upon completing the hunt, he called the magi to solemnize their union with the sacrament of marriage.

The courtiers were scandalized that the king had wedded a mere concubine of his youth and avoided the court for three days. Khosrow-Parviz summoned them and asked why they had absented themselves. The chamberlain spoke on the group's behalf: "We know that you have undergone difficulties during your reign," he said. "Of course, you are experienced and know better than anyone that nothing good can come from mixing blood. No king has ever married a woman of low birth and easy virtue."

Disappointed, Khosrow-Parviz motioned to him to adjourn the meeting. As the next day's dawn broke, the courtiers were called back. Still, most of them were riled by the marriage. Some were still firm on their critique of the king. Others were ready to take it back and repent. A third group maintained that they should await clarification in the upcoming meeting.

As they stood in the great hall before the throne, a servant came in and placed a basin of blood before them. The courtiers winced in disgust, as in their faith blood was considered a polluting and foul substance. The servant took the basin out, emptied its contents in the fields, washed, and dried it. Then he brought it back filled with wine mixed with musk and rose water. As the courtiers marveled, the king said:

"Note that the basin has not changed. It is the content that has changed. Shirin outside my palace is not the same as Shirin inside of it. She is cleansed by entering these halls. This woman has never known anyone but me. I alone was the cause of her suffering. Now, I have restored her to her innocence."

The courtiers admired the humanity of their king.

Shirin's position improved with time. Soon, she was placed above all women of the seraglio. Only Myriam, the princess of Rome, held a higher position. The king spent most of his time with his Roman queen. This made Shirin jealous. She had waited so many years to be reunited with her lover and could not bear to see him in the embrace of another.

Eventually, Myriam mysteriously died of poisoning. No one would ever know that Shirin was the culprit.

THE PLATFORM OF TAQ-DIS AND THE GREAT TAUQ-E KASRA

At the end of life's journey, we must fix
Our exit. There's a time for everyone
And mine is nigh at sixty-six.

This glorious poem I'm composing will glow
Like a beacon. The words I scatter are seeds
From which a lush Persian forest will grow.

Khosrow-Parviz's grand ambition was to build a unique palace that the world would envy. He wanted it to remain in pristine condition for at least two hundred years. The king sent heralds to China and Rome to search for the most skilled builders and adept masons. Three thousand candidates were identified for the position of the head architect. Of this group, one hundred were selected. The list was narrowed down to thirty, and then to three: two Romans and an Iranian. The man selected to build the king's vaunted monument was a world-famous Roman architect.

The master architect dug down thirty cubits to lay a foundation of stone and plaster on which the walls would be built. The arches would be placed on these walls, bending toward a focal point high in the sky. Before the arches met at the summit, the head architect called for silken measuring ropes to be hung from the top until they reached the ground. He marked the length of the ropes, and cut and placed them in a sealed box that was delivered to the king's treasurer for safekeeping. The king was impressed by the rapid progress, but he demanded an exact date for the completion of the structure. The architect responded that such matters could not be rushed. He said he needed at least forty days to gauge how the foundation was settling.

Khosrow-Parviz did not believe this claim and suspected the architect was angling for more rewards. Money was no object, so he ordered an additional thirty thousand dirhams to be disbursed and sent to the construction site. Realizing that the impatient king would never abide by the unpredictable process of building such a structure, the architect absconded in the dead of night. In his fury, Khosrow-Parviz imprisoned all the workers and tried in vain to find another architect to complete his palace. None dared to take on the risky project.

Finally, after four years, the fugitive architect turned himself in. The king demanded an explanation. He asked for the return of his package from the treasury and had the silken ropes dangled from the top of the foundation walls. Eleven cubits of rope remained on the ground, demonstrating that the foundations had settled by that much. Had the architect obeyed the king and completed the building, the whole edifice would have collapsed. The king acknowledged the wisdom of the architect, freed the imprisoned workers, and enriched them with bags of gold. The architect received wealth, property, and arable land with deeded water rights.

The construction of the palace continued, and after seven years it was completed as a wonder of the world and a delight to behold. Thereafter the king sat at the center of the hall of Tauq-e Kasra. The heavy crown of the kings of Kay was suspended by golden chains from where the arches of the dome met. At the spring festival of Nowruz, the king ascended the throne to present the courtiers and commanders with gifts. He also distributed alms to the needy, and announce an amnesty to the prisoners.

Khosrow-Parviz also restored the ancient platform throne of Tauqdis that had been designed and built at the time of the Serpent King Zahhak. King Feraydun, the founder of the Kay dynasty, had commissioned an artisan named Jahn, the son of Borzin, of Damauvand Mountain, to refurbish it. He was so happy with the result that he enriched the builder with thirty thousand dirhams and gave him the governorship of Saury and Amol. The magnificent throne was bequeathed to prince Iraj, and thereafter it was the seat of authority for the Kay dynasty from Manuchehr to Kay-Khosrow, and then to the line of Goshtausp and Lohrausp. Each of these sovereigns repaired the throne and added embellishments.

King Lohrausp's learned vizier Jamausp rediscovered the hidden properties of the throne that allowed it to be used as an observatory. He added signs for the twelve constellations, the seven planets, the sun, and the moon to the rounded roof of the Tauqdis platform. Thereafter the structure was used for astronomical measurements as well. It was plundered by the Touranians and later hacked to pieces by the minions of Alexander. What isolated fragments remained of the luxurious platform were passed down as heirlooms from generation to generation.

When Ardeshir-e Baubakan, the founder of the Sassanian dynasty, recovered some of these pieces, he ordered the reconstruction of a smaller replica of the old throne. But it was Khosrow-Parviz who decided to fully restore the enormous edifice using extant descriptions. For this purpose, he recruited eleven hundred sixty craftsmen from Rome, India, and China to work on the mammoth structure that was 512 cubits long, 165 cubits wide, and 622 cubits high.*

The throne was encased in jeweled sheets of gold and silver and adorned with one hundred forty thousand turquoise medallions. Pegs that kept the pieces of the structure together were made of silver. When the sun was in Aries at the outset of spring, the revolving Tauqdis throne turned, so the garden appeared in front of it. In June, it would turn toward the orchard to allow the aroma of ripening fruits to waft in. When the sun entered Leo in July, the platform turned on its axis opposite to where it had been in March. In winter, the open porticos would be boarded, and its walls were covered in luxurious beaver pelts to provide comfort for the people inside.

The seating within the throne was arranged as a pyramid composed of three platforms separated by four steps. Each platform was dedicated to a class of subjects. The rural nobility sat on the low ewe platform, so called because it was emblazoned with the head of an ewe. The warriors reclined on the middle, indigo platform. The highest turquoise platform was reserved for the courtiers, high clerics, and advisors to the king.

A tapestry stitched by a Chinese artisan hung behind the throne featuring the planets and the moon. The seven realms of the world and the crowns of their kings were also stitched on the tapestry. The king reclined on a golden dais at the peak of the pyramid of seats. From this position, he presided over the annual celebration of Nowruz, which falls on the vernal equinox.

* These measurements are obviously exaggerated. But, given the monumental astronomical devices in observatories of the region, the existence of this throne cannot be dismissed.

THE DEMISE OF THE KING

This king enjoyed such repute
That none had enjoyed before, and yet
He was killed by a knave, a vagabond, a brute.

For almost four decades, none dared malign
Khosrow-Parviz: Neither the Hephthalites khan
Nor the Empror of Rome, great Caesar of Byzantium.

He had such musicians as Sarges and Barbad
Twelve thousand women adorned his seraglio and
His twenty-two hundred war elephants were ironclad.

The lesson of the demise of such a king
Is that even the most fortunate among us may fall
And none escapes death's venomous sting.

Toward the end of his rule, King Khosrow-Parviz grew careless and unjust. He entrusted the welfare of his subjects to greedy administrators and refused to rein in wicked functionaries like Farrokh-zaud, an avaricious and overbearing officer who siphoned state funds and took bribes. He so impoverished the king's subjects that they cursed him, and many even migrated to foreign lands. Another courtier was the scheming and disloyal chamberlain Zaud-farrokh, who restricted access to the king and distorted his understanding of the nation's affairs.

The third member of the corrupt triumvirate was Gorauz, who was in charge of defending the Roman border. Instead of protecting the boundaries of Iran, he entered a treacherous alliance with the Caesar, inviting him to invade. The king learned of this plot and summoned Gorauz for an explanation, but he refused the invitation.

When the Romans started to move their troops toward Iran, Khosrow-Parviz devised a clever counterplot. He wrote a letter addressed to Gorauz but arranged for his messenger to let it fall into the hands of the Roman forces. Thus, his ostensibly secret letter made its way to the Caesar himself.

> Gorauz! Kudos to you for tricking the Caesar into launching an attack on us. We are waiting for the Romans to walk into our trap. The benighted Caesar thinks you will be fighting on his side. Wait for your cue on the battlefield before attacking him from behind. He is going to be crushed between us.

Shocked by the perceived treachery of his Iranian collaborator, the Caesar withdrew his troops. Gorauz was puzzled by the sudden redeployment and asked for an explanation. The Caesar replied that his treachery had been discovered and there would be no attack. Gorauz denied the charges, and begged the Caesar to reconsider. But his entreaties fell on deaf ears.

The king then sent another letter to Gorauz, reprimanding him for his insubordination and ordered him to send the disloyal elements of his army to the capital for punishment.

Gorauz brazenly ignored the king's direct command again and brought twelve thousand warriors to Khorreh-ye Ardeshir to await further developments. This time Khosrow-Parviz sent his chamberlain Zaud-farrokh to force the unruly officer to purge his army. Instead of carrying out the king's orders, however, the chamberlain advised the troops to stick together and goaded them to publicly defy the king.

"You are a brave and powerful army," Zaud-farrokh said. "Don't be afraid of this weak king. I represent him and I should know. Do not fear me either. I empathize with your cause. Even my own brother Rostam-e Farrokh-zaud has rebelled against this king. If you despise us, don't hold back. Express your feelings. Curse the king and me, for we have earned your disdain!"

Thus encouraged, the troops shouted imprecation against the king and his chamberlain. Zaud-farrokh returned to the king with the bad news that the entire army was in open rebellion and that they had publicly cursed the king. Khosrow-Parviz did not fully trust this report as he was leery of Zaud-farrokh. But he did not wish to push him too far lest he should switch sides and join his rebellious brother. Little did he know that Zaud-farrokh was the ringleader of the rebellion, colluding with his brother Rostam-e Farrokh-zaud, the able knight Nakhar, and the defiant general Gorauz. The task of crushing the contingent of soldiers guarding the crown prince's compound was entrusted to Nakhar.

The crown prince Shiruyeh was surprised when he encountered the knight who had broken into his well-protected compound. "What are you doing here? What have you done to my father?"

"Don't be obtuse. You will cooperate with us if you know what's good for you. There are fifteen more like you at this compound, and any of them would do for our purpose. Live as a king or die and be forgotten. The decision is yours."

The choices were stark and Shiruyeh had to decide. Thus, he acquiesced to the plans to overthrow his father.

Zaud-Farrokh, who was still acting as chamberlain, kept Khosrow-Parviz ignorant of the developments around the capital while inciting the street crowds to unrest and destruction.

By nightfall, everything was set for the final blow. To signal the success of the coup, the chamberlain changed the city guards' cry of "All Is Safe in the City" to "Long Live Qobaud." Hearing the strange announcement, Shirin awakened her husband. The king's complexion turned a shade of green. He realized that Zaud-farrokh was behind the plot as only he knew that Qobaud was Shiruyeh's secret name. Khosrow-Parviz had no choice but to escape to Baluchestan, lesser China, or even greater China for help. He needed to bring a foreign army, as he had at the outset of his rule, to regain his crown. But such a journey was impossible in the middle of the night and without preparations.

Thus, he simply donned his armor, picked up his weapons, and ran into the vast orchard surrounding the royal palace. This way, at least, he would avoid immediate capture by the rebels. He hid in an isolated alcove, hung his golden shield from a branch, and sat on his armor on the ground near a patch of saffron and narcissus flowers.

By this time, rampaging crowds had broken into the royal compound. Not finding the king, they ransacked the palace and plundered its riches.

At noon the next day, Khosrow felt the pangs of hunger. He ripped a gem off his belt, gave it to a gardener, and sent him to buy some bread. The man went to the bakery and tried to pay for the bread with the gem he was given. The baker, who did not know the gem's value, went to the jeweler for an appraisal. The man recognized the stone and suspected that they had stolen it. The matter was reported to Zaud-farrokh, who, upon interrogating the three men, discovered the king's hiding place. A contingent of six thousand guards was sent to arrest the king, but they dared not draw their swords on their sovereign.

Zaud-Farrokh went up to the king and advised him to surrender, saying that resistance was futile. Even if he could fight off the guards, there was no way he could fight the entire nation that no longer wanted him.

Khosrow-Parviz despaired. An oracle had once told him that his end would come between two mountains of gold and silver, above the iron ground and under a golden sky. The two mountains, he surmised, were symbols for the two coffers of gold and silver that he had hidden on the two sides of the orchard. The golden sky was his shield, and the iron ground was the armor on which he sat.

Shiruyeh had his father confined in a mansion under the watchful forces of general Golinush. Confused and uncertain of his position, the young crown prince ascended the royal throne wearing the Sassanian crown. But his reign would not be a long or prosperous one.

Such are the ways of this wicked world
Do not expect fairness, justice, or integrity
In this vale of tears where we've been hurled.

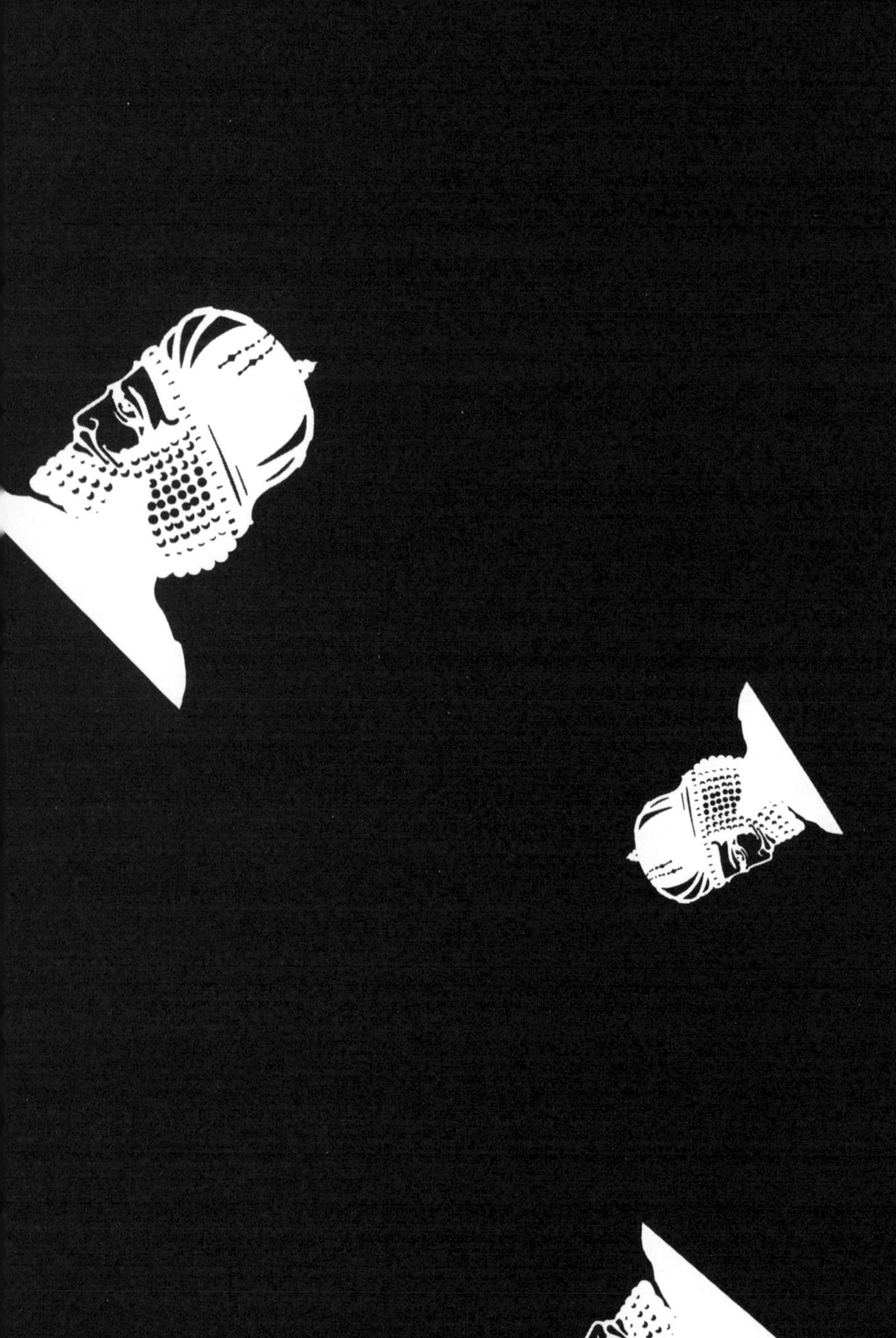

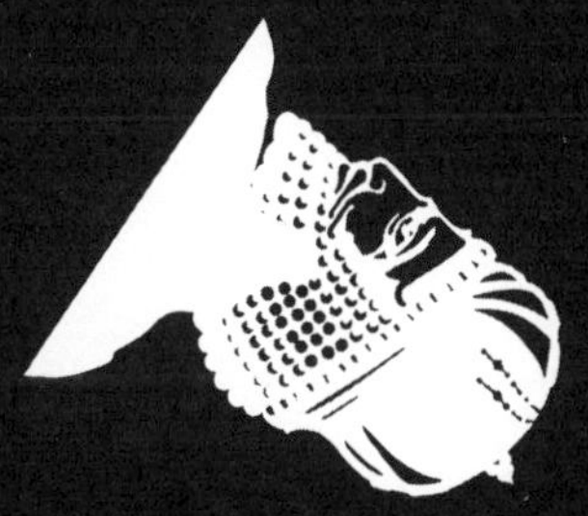

CHAPTER 26

The Beginning of the End: Shiruyeh to Farrokh-zaud

When Shiruyeh was crowned as a king of Kay
He invited eloquent courtiers to sing his praises.
They also prayed for his progeny to hold sway.

The new king reclined on his father's throne to receive the courtiers. "I will keep the land safe and eschew evil deeds," he declared. "I shall send a messenger to tell my father that his wretched end and the bad name he leaves behind are the direct results of his misdeeds. I hope he atones for his sins and returns to the path of righteousness."

Two old and respected knights, Khorrad-e Borzin and Ashtaud-goshasp, were chosen by Shiruyeh for the unpleasant mission of purveying these accusations. They were surprised to find the mansion chosen to confine the king was surrounded by General Golinush's guard in full armor. The ambassadors questioned the need for such extreme measures when the transition had already occurred, and all was calm. The general responded that his orders were to keep Khosrow-Parviz in complete isolation. No one was allowed in without a sealed letter from the crown.

Upon reading the young king's letter, the general went to Khosrow-Parviz with hands crossed over his chest. "Will His Majesty permit Khorrad-e Borzin and Ashtaud-goshasp to enter and deliver a message from the king?"

Khosrow-Parviz was reclining on a dais covered in brocade embroidered in gold, holding a fragrant quince. He laughed. "You make no sense, my good general. Why do you address me with that title if someone else is king? And if I am the king, what am I doing in this prison? Isn't it obvious that I am in no position to admit or reject visitors?"

Golinush had no answer to these rhetorical questions. He led the envoys in to deliver their message. Upon their entrance, Khosrow-Parviz sat up and placed the quince on a stand. But it rolled off the edge, onto the pillows, and over the edge of the bed onto the ground. Ashtaud-goshasp quickly picked up the fruit, wiped it clean, and put it back on the stand. Khosrow-Parviz took it as a bad omen, looked skyward with a woebegone expression and entreated, "Who can put back what the Almighty God has knocked over? When good fortune forsakes a clan, who can bring it back? The fall of the quince revealed the fate of this dynasty just as the portents about my evil child have come to pass. Iran will be conquered and plundered. Friends will turn into enemies. The exalted will be humbled, and the humble, exalted." He turned to face the emissaries. "Carry on your duty. Read me what that ungrateful son and his wicked advisors have written."

Ashtaud-goshasp recited the letter:

> Don't blame your son, these messengers, or the Iranian people. God is chastising you for your wickedness. You shed your father's blood, stuffed your coffers with gold at the expense of the people, imprisoned the innocent, and sent troops to the ends of the world, separating them from their families.
>
> Finally, you made an enemy of your father-in-law, the Caesar of Rome, over a trifling. What harm was there in returning that worthless piece of wood that they venerate as the True Cross of their Lord? And I won't even mention the long imprisonment of your sixteen sons.
>
> You have sown the wind and reaped the whirlwind. Your son was destined to be the instrument of your punishment. Atone for your sins. Apologize so the Iranians may forgive what you have wrought.

When they finished, the deposed king heaved a cold sigh. "Go tell your master that these are not your words, and he who put them in your mouth was an imbecile. My accounts are clear with God, and I have nothing to confess to mere humans. But I will answer your charges because future generations deserve to know the truth.

"Regarding your accusation that I killed my father and stole his crown, note that he was the one who wanted to kill me! He was deceived by Bahraum-e Chubineh's trick of minting coins in my name. Fearing I was about to dethrone him, Hormazd sent an assassin after me. I barely escaped with my life. Later, while I was away, he was overthrown by his own courtiers. I fought several battles against the rebel general. It took a long time, but when I put down the rebellion, I executed my uncles, Benduy and Gostahm, for their regicide.

"You charge me with imprisoning my children. First, it was hardly a prison. You lived an easy life within your compound, enjoying hunting, polo, and beautiful entertainers. Your confinement was due to the astrologers' warnings who foresaw your betrayal of me. The portent was again confirmed two years ago by a messenger who came from India riding a white elephant. The emissary had brought me many gifts, including a letter from Rauy, the king of India, addressed to you. It predicted that you would become king two years hence, specifying even the day of your coronation. I knew that your happiness would come at my expense. And yet I did not act on that letter. I only sealed it and gave it to Shirin for safekeeping. Obtain that letter and read it if you don't believe me.

"Your complaint that I imprisoned innocent people is frivolous at best. A king must rule with a firm hand. I did not detain the innocent but the criminals who must be in jail if good people are to live in safety. Incidentally, I hear you have released some criminals I had jailed. Let me give you a piece of advice. Don't be greedy for the bribes that come from the ill-gotten wealth of the prisoners.

"And then you speak of the fullness of my treasury as if it is a sin. I have exacted fitting taxes and extracted legal tributes from our neighbors. A state runs on funds, and the treasury must be full. How do you think I managed to suppress a rebellion and fight many wars?

"Sending troops to the borders was neither cruel nor arbitrary. I had to secure our borders. When you let the walls of your orchard fall into disrepair, don't be surprised when intruders break the branches of your apple, pomegranate, and quince trees and trample on your narcissus and basil plants.

"As finances of the country surpassed ten million dinars, I minted a larger denomination called the pandavasi to facilitate financial transactions. Such matters are beyond your ken. But I must set the record straight.

"I did not hoard money. Nor was I stingy with the army and the officials of the state. They got their portion of the wealth in cash and such provisions as armaments, horses, slaves, musk, camphor, and luxuriant pelts. The Green Treasure and the Bride's Treasure are full because they are our reserves for national emergencies.

"I am under no illusion that my treasures are safe from thievery. They will be squandered to the four winds because you have surrounded yourself with scoundrels and promoted ungrateful and greedy underlings. A bankrupt king cannot maintain an army, and a nation without an army will be enslaved. Remember the advice of King Nushin-ravaun: 'He who arms his enemies has signed his own death warrant.'

"You accuse me of intransigence because I refused to restore the True Cross to Rome. Once more, you are out of your depth. And as usual, you play judge and jury right after you bring your charges. Do not listen to Zaud-farrokh's account of things. The Romans did come to our aid. But they were well compensated for their trouble. Regarding that old piece of timber that they venerate as the instrument of their savior's death, I will say that a nation that prides itself on wisdom and philosophy should not call a man God or worship a chunk of decomposing wood. If this timber was somehow divine, why didn't it fly back to its devotees of its own accord?

"Shiruyeh dares to call me to atone for my sins! Go tell him that God crowned me king. After thirty-eight years of successful reign, I will not ask a mortal for forgiveness. Only God the Almighty can forgive sins. Nor do I have anything to confess to a child who does not know right from wrong."

Khosrow-Parviz took a breath and paused for a while. Then he resumed his speech. "Now, go my honorable emissaries, and convey my message to your master. And add these final words: 'Son of man is born to die. I will die as did the olden kings from Hushang to Goshtausp and such glorious heroes as Arash the bow master, Rostam, and Esfandiar. My reign was not the longest or the most successful among my forefathers, but I had my accomplishments. I vanquished rebels and enemies alike. Iran thrived under me, and my treasuries were full. I shall soon leave this world to walk across the Chinvat bridge into paradise. My son will not linger long after me in this world."

Khorrad-e Borzin and Ashtaud-goshasp were wiping their tears with their sleeves as they left the king's chambers. Shiruyeh, too, wept when he heard his father's message. He called his advisors to an audience and presided over a meeting in a pensive mood. They simply reminded the new king that having two leaders in one nation was politically unsound. Shiruyeh ordered that his father be kept in luxurious isolation for another month. His victuals were to be delivered from the royal kitchen.

The deposed king did not allow anyone to serve his meals but his queen, Shirin.

Barbad, the musician, was disconsolate when he heard that his king had been deposed and imprisoned. He rushed from Jahrom to Ctesiphon to visit with him for the last time. Upon seeing the king in dire straits, he wept so hard that even the guards were affected by his sincere sentiments. They, too, shed tears as the master musician sang a dirge for the lost splendor of his king:

Tell me, my generous benefactor, and bold
King. What came of your throne and crown
And your black horse caparisoned in gold?

What did you do to end up so lonely?
How did your noble son fail you?
Or was he a son in name only?

The Sassanians will be toppled once you're gone
In the absence of the shepherd, the meadow
Will crawl with the wolves' savage spawn.

Barbad swore to never entertain another man while he lived. To demonstrate his resolve, the despondent master amputated the four fingers of his right hand and burned his musical instruments.

The generals who had overthrown Khosrow-Parviz kept up the pressure and pushed Shiruyeh to issue orders for his father's execution. The young king was not a resolute man; and at any rate, he was no more than a figurehead who ruled at the pleasure of his generals. Thus, he signed off on the plan to eliminate the deposed king. Ordinary executioners did not dare commit regicide, so a vagrant was found to perform the deed in exchange for a square meal. Zaud-Farrokh tipped him with a few additional gold pieces.

Khosrow guessed the purpose of the loutish man when he entered his cell. "State your name."

"My name is Mehr-Hormazd," said the man. "I am a stranger in this city."

"Then I am to be killed by a drifter, a knave."

Khosrow-Parviz called on his attendant to bring a basin of water, musk, ambergris, a bundle of holy Barsom twigs, and a clean garment. He held the Barsom and started to hum the Bazh mantras while repenting his sins. To avoid the face of his murderer, he draped himself in a blanket. The killer stepped up, pulled out his dagger, and slashed open the left side of his victim. Khosrow-Parviz bled to death.

The world is erratic and most fickle
Muzzle your greed for fortunes won't last
We live in the shadow of the grim reaper's sickle.

When news of Khosrow-Parviz's death spread in Ctesiphon, the generals sent a band of ruffians to the royal palace complex to murder his remaining fifteen sons. Shiruyeh had no say in the matter, so he shed impotent tears. His only act of nobility was to save the compound's women and children.

AN IMPERTINENT PROPOSAL

Fifty-three days after the death of Khosrow-Parviz, the erratic Shiruyeh sent a harsh message to the former queen Shirin:

> You are a sorceress from hell! Witchery has been your only trade, and there is none more culpable in the corruption of my father than you. Your days of luxuriating in the king's seraglio are over. Do not provoke my wrath. Come to me as soon as you receive this writ.

Outraged by Shiruyeh's insults, she snarled: "What else should one expect of a man who sheds his father's blood? I will not cast eyes on this monster even from a great distance. I refuse to see him either in feast or in funeral."

Despite this outburst, Shirin knew that defying the king was not an option. Thus, she prepared for the fateful encounter by having her properties listed and recorded by a scribe. She placed a lethal amount of poison in a small flask sewn into her garments. Only then did she send her reply.

> You ought to be ashamed of inventing such lies. How dare you accuse your father of consorting with witches? I greeted the late king every morning as he wanted to start his day by beholding my face. I was not his witch but his amulet of good fortune. Don't let such falsehoods slip from your lips ever again.

Shiruyeh sent back his envoy with the message that she had no choice but to appear before him. She responded that she would not come to a private meeting, for as the dowager queen she was entitled to certain privileges. She had to guard her modesty and good name. Thus, Shiruyeh summoned a group of fifty old courtiers and sent word to Shirin that he was ready to receive her in a public meeting.

She wore a combination of black and indigo garments and sat behind a veil in the flower garden of Shaudegan, where the meeting was convened.

"In a few days, two months will have passed since my father's demise," the new king told her. "It is time I brought you into my own seraglio where you will be accorded more respect than you enjoyed under the late king."

"I will be yours, body and soul, if you meet my three conditions," she replied.

"And what might they be?"

Shirin demanded to be given a chance to publicly defend herself against the calumny of sorcery. Shiruyeh protested that it was unnecessary as he had not meant to literally accuse her of witchcraft. It was merely a figure of speech. Surely the young are entitled to their impetuosities! She ignored this interjection and continued with her oration.

"I was the wife of the king for thirty years. Has anyone in this gathering seen anything but righteousness in my conduct?" she asked. "Has anyone seen anything but modesty from me? Women are praised for three things: property and propriety, giving birth to worthy sons, and a combination of beauty and modesty. I came from nobility and wealth, gave birth to four princes of the blood, and shone as a paragon of decency and discretion. As to my beauty, you be the judge. Behold my face, a sight that no man other than the late king has ever seen."

With these words, Shirin took off her vail. Her beauty caused the audience to gasp. But none was more smitten than Shiruyeh.

"You are the only companion I seek," he said, "and I shall not settle for a lesser woman."

Having secured the public recognition of her virtue, Shirin demanded the fulfillment of her second wish: the king had to issue a writ that her property would never be confiscated. When this wish was granted, she asked for a brief leave. She rushed to her quarters, freed her slaves, and distributed her wealth among her loyal servants, family members, fire temples, and such public causes as the repair and refurbishment of hostels for travelers. Then she addressed her companions.

"I will pose a question that I hope you will answer truthfully," she said. "Have you ever witnessed any sinful behavior on my part since I wedded the late king?"

They rose and collectively affirmed her modesty as the royal consort. Relieved, Shirin said:

"But this villainous patricide has maligned me as a faithless witch. I fear these accusations will blacken my name forever. You must come with me to the court and bear witness to my innocence."

The servants accompanied their mistress to the Shaudegan garden and praised her as their blameless queen. Shiruyeh, who was in a hurry to wed her, asked her to declare her third condition. She said that she wished to say farewell to her late husband. Shiruyeh ordered the royal vault opened for the bereaved queen.

Shirin entered the enclosure tears, streaming on her cheeks. She put her face on the cold face of the late king and softly spoke of their love and the good times they had shared. Then she whispered farewell and ingested the poison she had brought along. As the toxin took effect she leaned against the wall and let death carry her to the other side.

The young king was stricken with grief when he was told what had happened. He retired to his quarters and refused to appear in public. Shirin was entombed in Khosrow-Parviz's vault. Shortly thereafter, Shiruyeh was poisoned by those who had put him on the throne. He had ruled for seven months.

His horoscope made the oracles wince
Shiruyeh would kill his father and die young
How could a darker fate befall a prince?

THE GRIM INTERIM

Shiruyeh was succeeded by his son, Ardeshir, who pledged to follow the way of his forefathers, elevate the meek, and smite the proud. He appointed a man named Piruz as the head of the royal army. Shortly thereafter, Piruz received a secret letter from Gorauz, the commander of the Iranian forces at the Roman border, who considered Shiruyeh's short reign as a sign of Ardeshir's vulnerability.

> I advise you to form an alliance with me. We must get rid of this callow youth who has inherited the crown. Wait for me to arrive with my armies, and we will take care of this situation.

But Piruz did not wait. That night he cornered Ardeshir, in a drunken state, and strangled him to death. When Gorauz arrived to occupy Ctesiphon, he learned that the king had already been killed. Strangely enough, no one seemed agitated about the regicide.

Gorauz changed his name to Fara'in and declared himself king. His maxim was simple enough: better be king for a day than a commoner for sixty years! He fantasized about crowning his elder son when he was ready to retire. Was it so unthinkable that he could be the founder of the next dynasty? His younger son thought that it was. "We don't have a drop of royal blood in our veins," he said. "Amass as much wealth as possible before this crown is taken off your head."

But Fara'in's older son shared his father's ambition. "You are a veritable king indeed! Keep your treasure houses full and run the government. Don't worry about not having royal blood. Abtin, the father of the founder of the Kay dynasty, didn't have royal blood either."

The foolish general squandered the entire treasury in two weeks. He gave it away, hoping to buy friendship and popularity. He was extravagant in his habits as well. Eight ambergris candles burned before and after him when he stepped out to the garden at night. He ate and drank excessively, used foul language, and shed much innocent blood. Thus, instead of buying the love of the courtiers, he became the object of their loathing. The commanders unanimously agreed that the boorish pretender had to be eliminated. Thus, one of them went to the arena and shot Fara'in in the back with such force that the arrow went through his body and came out of his abdomen. In the ensuing chaos, many from different factions were killed.

The noblemen were scandalized by the senseless bloodshed and wished to return the crown to the Sassanians, but the massacre of Khosrow-Parviz's sons had left no male progeny to ascend the throne. Thus, the courtiers acclaimed a Sassanian princess named Puran-Dokht as the queen of Iran.

She wore the crown and declared she would rule like a true king. Her first act was to avenge Ardeshir. She had Piruz tied to the back of an untamed colt that slammed his rider to the ground and dragged him around until he died a painful death. Unfortunately, the queen was suddenly struck by an illness and died within a week. Her entire reign lasted for about six months.

Then, a second woman wore the robes and crown of royalty. Her name was Azarm-Dokht. She declared that she wished to be a righteous queen as well. But she, too, was carried away by illness after four months.

Finally, the courtiers brought a distant relative of the Sassanian family named Farrokh-zaud out of the city of Jahrom and acclaimed him king. His was the shortest tenure of all, as he reigned for just one month before succumbing to a mysterious illness.

The world being so uncertain, it might be best
To be merry while you live. Eat, drink;
Be cheerful and give away the rest.

CHAPTER 27

The Last King: Yazdegerd III

When Yazdegerd ascended the throne, the common belief
Was that the troubles were over. But soon a pitiless enemy
Appeared on the borders, and the nation drowned in grief.

Ponder the fate of this king, although you aren't one
You, too, can be caught in destiny's insidious web
Which cannot be torn asunder or undone.

After a series of inept kings of questionable pedigree, Iran was ruled by Yazdegerd III, who wore the crown of his ancestors. People were glad that once more, a true scion of the Sassanian dynasty was installed as their legitimate king.

"As a descendant of Nushin-ravaun, I hold the midday sun in my grasp, as I do the Pleiades and Pisces constellations of the night sky," he declared at the occasion of his coronation. "Rest assured that I will spread justice and purge the world of wickedness."

The king had ruled for a blissfully uneventful period of sixteen years when an Arab potentate named Omar sent an army to Qadesi at Iran's southwestern border. The purpose of this army, which was led by Sa'd-e Vaqas, was unclear, and their demands were vague. But it was obvious that they followed a new religion and were spoiling for a fight. Yazdegerd appointed his distinguished general Rostam-e Farrokh-zaud, the son of Hormazd, to confront the enemy. The wise and pious warrior brought his well-organized divisions in pomp and ceremony to the border to meet the strange foe.

Rostam, who was in the habit of consulting his astrolabe on important occasions, cast the horoscope of the war when he arrived at Qadesi. He was dismayed when he observed that all signs pointed to a crushing defeat. The sun presided over the disaster from its fourth sphere. Mars and Venus were at the worst possible locations, and Saturn was in conjunction with Mercury in the constellation of Gemini. This was not merely an ominous portent for the coming war. The stars had doomed Rostam as well as Iran to utter destruction. In his hour of despair, the commander wrote a letter to his brother to share his dire prognosis.

Good and evil come from God. Woe is me, a sinner beset by darkness from every side. The stars have foreordained our bitter end. The sun, Mars, Venus, Saturn, and Jupiter have lined up against us, and Mercury is in Gemini.

I must keep my peace even though I have seen the gathering stormclouds. I weep for Iran and Iranians and for the children of Sassan. All this glory will be lost in time, and our name will be washed from the annals of history. Nor will we have recovered from this calamity after four hundred years.

I have spoken to the Arab envoy. He says that their aims are limited to a stretch of land and some trading rights. They even propose to pay taxes. They lie. None of my commanders believes a word of what they say. Negotiating with them is futile. Whatever we manage to preserve of Iran will have to be won by the edge of our swords and the pounding of our maces.

Of course, I will do my utmost. But it will come to naught. As for you, take whatever you have of treasures, servants, horses, and garments and go to the temple of Azar-goshasp in Azerbaijan. Recruit anyone you can into the army. Wait for the time when the stars offer us another chance to regain our lost glory.

Share this letter with our mother, for I shall not see her again. Tell her not to weep for me. Death is written for the son of man. Gather our clan and pray to God. Be generous, and don't fear what tomorrow will bring. Above all, protect our king with your life, for he is the last of his line. Iran will be lost without his leadership.

These invaders will replace the throne with the pulpit and use it for sermons about Abu-Bakr and Omar. They will rule without a crown, a throne, golden boots, or a flag.

By then, morality will have vanished. Pedigrees will be lost, social distinctions will be blurred, and castes will mix. We will turn into a nation of mongrels, a travesty of our former selves.

Hypocrisy will dominate the land, and dishonesty will be ingrained in every transaction. Common peasants will become soldiers, and braggarts will be elevated to knighthood. Chaos and thievery will prevail. Father and son will draw on each other over a crust of bread or some worthless rags. Spring and winter will be indistinguishable. People will not partake in wine when they are happy. Nobility will be forgotten and shedding blood over worldly possessions will not raise an eyebrow.

It fell to my lot to be the knight protector of Iran at the time of its demise. I will fight hard, with a sword that will not cut and a mace that will fail to pound the enemy into submission. Knowledge is a curse, and ignorance is bliss. Lucky are those of my commanders who think they have a chance of defeating this enemy.

Let me close. I wish you the best. Qadesi is my graveyard, and my armor will be my shroud. May you have the good fortune of helping our king in these dark days.

The mighty knight sealed his letter and gave it to a herald. Then he penned another letter on white silk and addressed it to commander Sa'd-e Vaqas.

This is from Rostam, the son of Hormazd, to warlike Sa'd, the son of Vaqas. In the name of God, the just and compassionate king of the universe and the ultimate source of authority on earth.

Tell me who your king is and what possessed you to bring forth this poorly clad army that is bereft of both arms and armor. Instead of coveting the throne of your benefactor, you should thank your lucky stars we let you live under our protection. How can a bunch of shameless vagabonds compete with a king who is more resplendent than the full moon on a dark sky? Yazdegerd can ransom your entire nation without a noticeable diminution in his treasuries. His twelve thousand hunting dogs and cheetahs, all festooned in golden chimes and chains, eat more meat in one day than your entire nation consumes in a year! How can someone without learning, virtue, or a drop of royal blood nurse ambitions of royalty?

Now, let us be reasonable. Listen to me if you don't wish to become an object of ridicule among nations. Send me one of your elders. Tell me what you want. I promise to dispatch a herald to His Majesty and appraise him of your requests. Being the issue of the magnificent Nushin-ravaun, he is bound to be just and generous to you.

Rostam pressed his signet at the bottom of the letter and gave it to Shaupur-e Piruz, whose armor was engraved in gold and silver and whose honor guard shone in their golden kamarbands and splendid shields. When this grand delegation arrived at the enemy's camp, Sa'd came out of his tent to offer them hospitality.

At his humble camp, the Arab commander spread a cloth on the sand for the Iranian ambassador and said: "Manliness is not measured by the quality of one's brocaded seat, his exquisite silverware, or sumptuous meals."

Shaupur-e Piruz delivered his letter. Sa'd acknowledged receiving it and promised a speedy reply.

Once the Iranian delegation departed, Sa'd wrote his response to the Iranian king in Arabic.

He referred to the races of Jinn and man and the Hashemite prophet who was sent to them by the one and only Creator. He spoke of the prophet's message to humanity enjoining them to worship the one and only, eternal, and omnipotent God. The letter was replete with Quranic promises of paradise where rivers of fresh water, wine, milk, and honey flowed under lush trees, and the air was redolent with the aroma of ground camphor. All the pleasures of this world could not compete with the beauty of a single heavenly virgin. Hellfire and molten pitch awaited those who refused the new faith. Finally, the writ guaranteed that the prophet would personally intercede on behalf of the Iranian king at the divine tribunal if he accepted the true religion of Islam. He would then enjoy pleasures of this world and the world to come. Otherwise, torments of hell would await him. He closed the letter by offering salutations to the prophet Muhammad.

Sa'd had intentionally chosen a wise but undistinguished envoy to carry his letter to Rostam. Moghayrah, the son of Sho'beh, was old, weak, blind in one eye, and without a steed. His only weapon was a thin sword hanging by a rope around his neck. His garment was threadbare and slashed on one side.

To impress the Arab envoy, Rostam had decked out his pavilion in brocade curtains. A plush purple carpet was laid out to connect the entrance to the center of the lavish pavilion. A luxurious dais was placed at the end of the rug, and sixty knights in their golden torques and earrings stood in attention on each side.

But Moghayrah refused to act as expected. He skirted the carpet and limped forward on the sand floor using his sword as a cane. Instead of reclining on the dais, he chose a patch of dirt for his seat. Rostam greeted him in ornate phrases: "Welcome to our pavilion. May your body and soul be exalted."

The messenger's response was curt: "Peace be upon you, too, if you accept the faith." Rostam frowned and motioned Moghayrah to hand over his letter to the scribe. The letter was translated and read aloud for Rostam. He was not pleased.

"Go tell your master that he is neither a king nor a contender," Rostam raged. "You are a nonentity dreaming impossible dreams. Keep this new creed to yourself. We don't need it, for ours is the ancient faith bequeathed to us by our royal ancestors. That is all I will say for the time being. Our main negotiation will take place on the battlefield. I consider death in combat superior to life in humility."

Crushing this ragtag army would be easy if the stars were not against us, Rostam thought to himself. *Alas, this faithless hunchback, this eternal dome of heaven, has turned its back on us.*

THE DUEL THAT SEALED THE FATE OF IRAN

The buglers sounded their horns, and the Iranian army stirred like a swelling sea. In the black dust plumes risen by the soldiers, their lance tips sparkled. The battle was joined, but it was inconclusive. The armies fought each other to a stalemate. After three days, a shortage of fresh water started to have a tangible effect on the Iranian side. Rostam led his soldiers with a dry throat and cracked lips. His men and horses were so parched that they tried to squeeze water out of the wet mud. It did not help that, unlike the Arabs, they had to fight in heavy armor that burned their skin under the scorching desert sun.

Finally, the two commanders decided to fight a duel whose victor would emerge as the winner of the war. They chose a secluded corner of the battlefield and commenced hand-to-hand combat. As they approached, the Iranian general struck a deadly blow on his opponent's steed, causing it to collapse headfirst. Sa'd nimbly jumped off and parried Rostam's sword as it swung for his neck. Then, under the cover of dust, he shifted his position to hide from his opponent. In a state of confusion, Rostam gave up his advantage and dismounted to see his foe. He tied his horse's tether to his belt to prevent it from wandering away. Sa'd, who could make out the outline of his adversary, landed a blow on his helmet. The wound was superficial, but it caused blood to stream into Rostam's eyes, obstructing what remained of his vision. Exploiting this handicap, Sa'd slashed his neck. The limp body of the great commander tumbled to the ground.

When the Iranian troops found their field marshal's corpse, they broke and ran. Those who had not died of thirst were killed as they fled from the battlefield.

Top commanders died on their saddles of thirst
The great royal army of Iran was routed
And the fortunes of Yazdegerd were reversed.

What remained of the Iranian army took refuge in Baghdad, where the king had chosen to reside. Rostam's brother, Farrokh-zaud, crossed the Arvand River and engaged the Arabs at the Karkheh River to avenge the death of his brother at Qadesi. Despite some initial success, however, his army was defeated and routed. He rushed back to Baghdad and importuned the king to leave.

"Western Iran is lost," Farrokh-zaud reported. "You are the last of your line, and this nation will be doomed without you. Take refuge in the rainforests of the north. There, you can start anew, as did the exalted King Feraydun. People of Amol and Saury are your devotees. You can raise a formidable army and return to fight the Arab horde."

The knights and commanders endorsed this plan, but Yazdegerd had lingering doubts about going to the mountainous north. He thought it best to go to Merv in the western state of Khorausan. For one thing, that region bordered the Turkish khaganates as well as lesser and greater China from where he hoped to seek help. For another, the governor of Merv, a man by the name of Mahuy, was one of his acolytes.

"It is true that Mahuy was a lowly shepherd at the beginning," said the king. "But he was ambitious. I championed his cause and promoted him through the ranks until he became a governor. He owes me everything. The magi have said that one must associate with those he has benefited and avoid those he has harmed."

Farrokh-zaud thought the opposite was true. "Do not trust wicked men, especially those beholden to you. They are bound to be greedy and unreliable. Mean nature does not improve with kindness."

Yazdegerd disagreed. He believed it was worth a try and issued orders for his retinue to move the royal camp across the Iranian plateau. Despite everything that had happened, the Iranians were hopeful because as long as their king was safe, it was still possible to expel the enemy and restore order to the land.

Denizens of the city of Nishaupur came out to welcome Yazdegerd with teary eyes. The king was moved by this display of emotion and wept with them. A delegation of those related to the khagan renewed their compact with the king and immediately went to ask their leader to support

Iran against the Arab invaders. The commander of the army, Farrokhzaud, followed the king through the cities of Rey and Gorgan and joined the royal camp after one week.

The king wrote a letter to his vassal in Merv appraising him of the calamity that had befallen the country. His commander had been killed by a lowborn Arab called Sa'd, his army was routed, and his capital Ctesiphon was lost. Mahuy's orders were to prepare an army and await his arrival from Nishaupur within a week. The king intended to stop in Merv and send for help from the Turkic khaganate and the emperor of greater China.

The king also sent letters to the regional chiefs of Khorausan in preparation for his arrival:

> In the name of the Almighty God of victory and the protector of royalty. He is the one who rules the mosquito and the eagle, the elephants of the land, and the crocodiles of the sea. This is an epistle from King Yazdegerd to the guardians of Iran's eastern borders. Your loyalty never faltered during the mutiny of the accursed Bahraum-e Chubineh. You left your cities and took refuge in the mountains rather than bear the yoke of the rebellious one.
>
> You have undoubtedly heard that terrible times are upon us. We are attacked by a wicked race of savages. They are bereft of knowledge and shame. Nor was this unexpected. King Nushin-ravaun had seen this all in a dream: A hundred thousand Arabs would cross the river Arvand to invade Iran like musth camels. Eternal fire in the temples would be snuffed, and the holidays of Nowruz and Sadeh would be forgotten. The parapet of royal castles would crumble, and the crops of Iran and Babylon would burn, sending up a thick smoke to the constellation of Aries.
>
> All that has come to pass. We face an abysmal future if we are slow to move. The high will descend, and the low will ascend. Evil will suffuse the world, and the good shall be supplanted with the wicked. A petty tyrant will rise everywhere, and ugly spirits will haunt the world.

I have come to Khorausan to see if we can stop this nightmare. Farrokh-zaud is mobilizing from Altunieh, and his son Kashmgan is resupplying the impregnable castles of the land. But we do not intend to hide in these castles. We will mobilize an army and take the battle to the enemy. To this purpose, my court needs provisions and victuals. What we have is hardly sufficient to feed our cheetahs and their keepers. We ask that you provide the following items. Of course, you will be reimbursed in the future. Make two ledgers of what you give. Send one to the treasury and keep the other in a safe place. Here are the provisions that we need:

Forty thousand oxen loaded with wheat,
Twelve thousand donkey loads of rice,
Ten thousand camel loads of millet,
Ten thousand camel loads of pistachio,
Ten thousand camel loads of pomegranate seeds,
One thousand oxen loaded with salt,
One thousand oxen loaded with sugar,
One thousand oxen loaded with dates,
Twelve thousand loads of gum and nectar,
Twelve thousand loads of dried and salted meat,
One thousand skins of ghee,
Three hundred skins of naphtha.

All these provisions must arrive within the next two months. I have issued orders that you receive five courtly garments and gold-embroidered diadems as tokens of my appreciation. Also, each of you will receive forty gold dirhams freshly minted for this occasion. My image is embossed on the reverse side of this coin, and on its obverse side, you will find the holy name of the Almighty God.

THE KING AT MERV

Mahuy came with a great host to the region of Tous to welcome the king. He dismounted and kissed the ground. Farrokh-zaud embraced Mahuy and said, "I have come this far to personally entrust the last of the Sassanian kings to your care. Gird your loins and serve him, for I must return to Rey to fight. I am not sure if I will ever see the king again. Much worthier commanders have perished in this war, not the least of whom was my brother Rostam."

"This king is dearer to me than my eyes," said Mahuy. "I appreciate your trust and hope that you solemnly assume the responsibility of serving this king."

Mahuy promised to protect the king with his life. But his warm sentiments evaporated soon after Farrokh-zaud's departure. The ambitious son of a shepherd was nursing dreams of royal grandeur and devising plans to depose the exiled king and replace him. He malingered for a while to justify his absence from the king's court, while he was secretly enticing the prince of Samarkand to invade Tus. The name of this prince was Bijan, and he was descended from the Tarkhan noblemen of Touran. Mahuy had promised to collaborate with his invading forces and pledged that it would be a relatively easy victory whose prize was nothing less than the entire homeland of Iran.

Bijan was tempted, but he also had reservations. If he went against Yazdegerd and lost, the khagan would laugh at his incompetence. But if he refused Mahuy's bold proposal, the khagan would call him a coward. His vizier advised him to hedge his bets and send his commander Barsaum on this mission. It sounded like a good compromise. Thus, a well-organized army of ten thousand warriors was organized to wage war on the exiled king of Iran.

When the invaders arrived, Mahuy rushed to the king and breathlessly reported that a horde of hostile Turks had appeared on the horizon. Furious at the impertinence of a local prince to challenge him, Yazdegerd wore his armor and led his men into battle. There was no decisive win for either side on the first two days of the battle. On the third day, the king broke the enemy's lines and penetrated the heart of the enemy's army. But as he was slashing away, he got a sinking feeling that he was alone. The deceitful Mahuy had called back his men, leaving him to the enemy's mercy.

There was no option but to escape. Yazdegerd found his retreat through a thicket that led to the shore of the Zarq River. Having evaded the enemy, he came across a water mill, released his horse, and hid inside until his pursuers were gone. There, he collapsed on a bundle of dry hay in complete exhaustion.

Such are the visions of this funhouse of delusions
Nectar turns into poison and palaces into old mills
Beware of life's flimsy props and cheap illusions.

The king lingered at the mill until the sun rose. He was famished as he had had nothing to eat all day and all night. In the morning, the miller opened the door and found a melancholy young man wearing opulent garments and a diadem.

"What does a man shining with the halo of divine sanction want in my ramshackle mill?" asked the miller.

"I am an Iranian and a fugitive of the Touranian war."

"And I am a poor miller, who has nothing to offer you but whey smeared on a crust of bread and some watercress."

"Bring me what you have," begged the king. "But I need the Barsom bundle for my eating rites as well.

The miller went to the headman of Zarq as he had no idea what Barsom was and where he could obtain it. The headman sensed the importance of the report and sent the miller to the governor's office. Realizing the identity of the man at the mill Mahuy barked:

"Go and cut off that man's head right away. That's a direct order. I will kill you and your entire family if you disobey me."

The magi and noblemen present at Merv's court were scandalized by this wanton plot to kill the king. They tried to dissuade him from the sinful act and told him that even such powerful people as Tur, Afrasiab, Garsivaz, Benduy, and Gostahm had not gotten away with regicide. But the dim-witted governor was so blinded by greed that he dismissed the meeting, preferring to consult with his son and his army commanders. They, too, said that he should not have embarked on the perilous path of deposing a king. But having done so, it was too late to change course.

"Once you hurt an enemy, you must kill him," said his son. "If you let Yazdegerd get away, he will raise an army from greater and lesser China and come back to destroy us."

Needing little persuasion, Mahuy forced the miller to assassinate the king. He sent along some soldiers instructing them to remove the king's garments, regalia, and signet so they wouldn't be soiled with his blood. Then they were told to throw the king's naked corpse in the Zarq River.

The miller was reluctant to carry out the dastardly plot, but he didn't have the courage or the character to stand up to the governor. He went to his mill, greeted the king, and came close as if he wished to whisper something in his ear. He then unsheathed his dagger and slashed Yazdegerd's side. The king let out a muffled sigh, and his head fell into the wooden tray still containing the whey-smeared bread. Thus ended the life of the last king of the Sassanian dynasty.

Heaven is unjust. It cannot be denied
That it would be better to be unborn than witness
Worthless scoundrels getting away with regicide.

The soldiers of Mahuy relieved the corpse of its regalia, torque, golden slippers, and the royal seal. Then they waited for darkness before throwing the corpse into the waters of the Zarq. They detested this bloody chore and cursed the lowly governor for making them accessories to his crime.

In the morning, two Christian monks pulled the body from the river that flowed by their monastery. The abbot and his hermits recognized that the body belonged to their noble king and carried it to their cloister in a solemn procession. They stopped the gash with resin and tar before washing and perfuming the cadaver with camphor and musk. Finally, the body was shrouded in white linen, clad in yellow silk, and placed in its vault. The hermits approached the body one by one and offered their eulogies. The abbot said the final benediction: "May this crypt be a garden for your soul. May this shroud envelop you in eternal bliss."

Yazdegerd fell into everlasting sleep
No sage has unraveled the mystery of death
What can we do at its approach but weep?

Ferdowsi's life was wrecked by this recent hail
That ruined his wheat, lambs, and even firewood
Pour the wine, for justice in this world is an old wives' tale.

THE END OF MAHUY

The cruel governor was furious to learn that the monks had found and respectfully interred the king's body. "Since when do these agents of Rome care about what happens to an Iranian king?" he screamed. Then, he ordered his henchmen to loot the cloister and slay those who had participated in the king's burial.

Only after Yazdegerd's assassination did Mahuy pause to think about what he had done. Nobody considered him a person of consequence, let alone a king. He had no pedigree, no learning, no accomplishments, and no charisma. He only had the king's personal effects, which his henchmen had salvaged from the regal body. *I wish I had been less rash in making these decisions*, he thought.

One of the governor's advisors suggested that he come up with a story about how he had come into possession of the king's personal effects. So, he told the elders of Merv that Yazdegerd had given him the symbols of royalty and appointed him king before his battle with Bijan. Having only one daughter and no sons, he was afraid of perishing and leaving Iran without a king! Telling this tale had seemed like a good idea at the time, but no one believed it. The local nobility and generals laughed at the governor's obvious lies.

But Mahuy was too obsessed with his maniacal plan to notice the incredulous reception of his peers. So, he proceeded as if he was the acclaimed king of Iran, appointing his son to govern Balkh and Herat and sending his cronies to rule various principalities of Khorausan. To stay in character as the king of Iran, he embarked on the conquest of Samarkand and Chauch, declaring war on his erstwhile ally, Prince Bijan. His cause of the war was seeking revenge for the blood of his martyred king Yazdegerd.

Bijan was thoroughly confused by this claim. He asked Barsaum to explain the actions of the unhinged governor. The general related the story of Mahuy's betrayal of Yazdegerd during the battle and his subsequent assassination at the mill. Now he had declared himself king of Iran and the avenger of the king he had killed!

Bijan asked if there was anyone left they could appoint as king of Iran once he had exterminated the mad pretender, as he had resolved to do. "Alas, there is no one left from the line of Sassan to carry on the dynasty," Barsaum responded. "And at any rate, Arabs have taken over most of western Iran, so there is little hope of restoring the dynasty or saving the country."

In great fury, Bijan brought his well organized army to the eastern shore of the Oxus to receive the minions of the mad governor. But he waited for the enemy to cross the river first. Once Mahuy reached the other side, he lost his nerve, beholding the size and the organization of the army he had come to fight. There was row after row of gold-embossed shields held by the heavily armored warriors, backed by endless rows of lance and mace holders. Further back stood divisions of bow masters holding their composite bows at the ready. Many camels stood with arrows and armaments to resupply the troops during the battle.

As soon as Bijan urged his troops to attack, Mahuy turned to escape the battlefield. But the Touranian prince, who was keeping a close eye on the wily governor, commanded Barsaum to give chase and capture him before he could cross the Oxus. He grabbed Mahuy's belt just as he tried to ford the Farb tributary, lifted him off the saddle, and slammed him to the ground. Then he dismounted and tied his hands. The soldiers urged their general to behead the worthless regicide with his hatchet. But his orders were to capture Mahuy alive.

Prince Bijan ordered a canopy to be set up on the soft sands of the Oxus and had the treacherous Mahuy dragged there. The governor nearly perished in fright when he saw Bijan's angry face. "Why did you kill your noble king, the grandson of Nushin-ravaun and the last scion of the Sassanian kings?"

"I confess that it was a despicable act, the punishment for which is death by beheading," Mahuy replied. "No one would fault you for executing justice. Cut off my head and throw it in the middle of this assembly, for that is what I deserve."

Bijan was wise to Mahuy's tricks, and could see that he was seeking an easy death.

"Of course, I will kill you. But I will do it in my own way. A dastardly slave like you does not deserve a painless death."

The prince ordered Mahuy's hands and feet cut off, and then his body was flayed and put on hot sands until he was near death. Then the prince ordered his executioners to cut off his head and carry it around to demonstrate the fate awaiting traitors. Mahuy's sons, who were exalted leaders of the army, were burned alive on the pyre of their father's corpse. And thus, the world was cleansed of the vile Mahuy and his progeny.

Now, we have arrived at the end of our story. With the defeat of Iran, the religion of Omar prevailed, and the pulpit replaced the throne.

I versified the chronicle of the kings to amaze
The learned men. I also needed bread to eat
But people kept plying me with empty praise.

I am thankful to God that three men gave me a hand
Ali-Deylam and Budalaf, who copied and collated
This long poem into tomes, well-bounded and tanned.

And I pray for Hoaya-e Qotayb, the lord of Tous
Who forgave my taxes and sustained me with victuals,
Garments, and even soft comforters to use.

At seventy-one years of age, I still hope
To receive the bounty the sultan has promised,
For I don't believe magnanimity is beyond his scope.

My hard work is done though it was never a drudge
*On March tenth, four hundred years after the Hijrah**
In the name of our Lord, our Omnipresent Judge.

* March 8, 1010 CE.

ACKNOWLEDGMENTS

We would like to thank the Shafipour and Amin families, who have been the flag bearers of this project from the very beginning, Rostam Zafari, who embodies the essence of the new generation of Iranians committed to promoting the culture of Iran, Hamid Eshghi, at the Mowafaghian Foundation, who championed this translation, and the late Jim Mairs, who published the first edition of *Shahnameh: The Epic of the Persian Kings* and gave us the freedom to open up this masterpiece to a new generation of readers.

We would like to express our gratitude to the incredible community who have heartened us with their support, to the folks at Liveright who encouraged us to complete the translation for this edition, to the tireless Dr. Ahmad Sadri, whose commitment to the spirit of Ferdowsi is felt throughout the text, and to our daughter, Sufi, who inspired us to embark on this decades-long adventure of keeping these epic stories alive.

—Hamid Rahmanian and Melissa Hibbard
Brooklyn, NY

I thank my lucky stars and all the planets that lined up just right to afford me the honor of abridging and translating the magnum opus of the sage of Tus, Abu al-Qasem Ferdowsi. This a bittersweet moment, so I chime in with the poet: "My hard work is done though it was never a drudge."

This work would not have been possible without Hamid Rahmanian's vision, commitment, and immense efforts to monitor the minute details of its artistic and literal creation.

Finally, I wish to thank my wife, Panthea Golzadeh, for her unstinting support during the intense work on this translation that absorbed every minute of my free time for many years. My cats Aladdin, Bilqis, and Altan were not much help unless you consider sitting on the keyboard help. But their love soothed me as I labored on this volume, so they have also earned their honorable mention.

Ahmad Sadri,
Summer of 2024

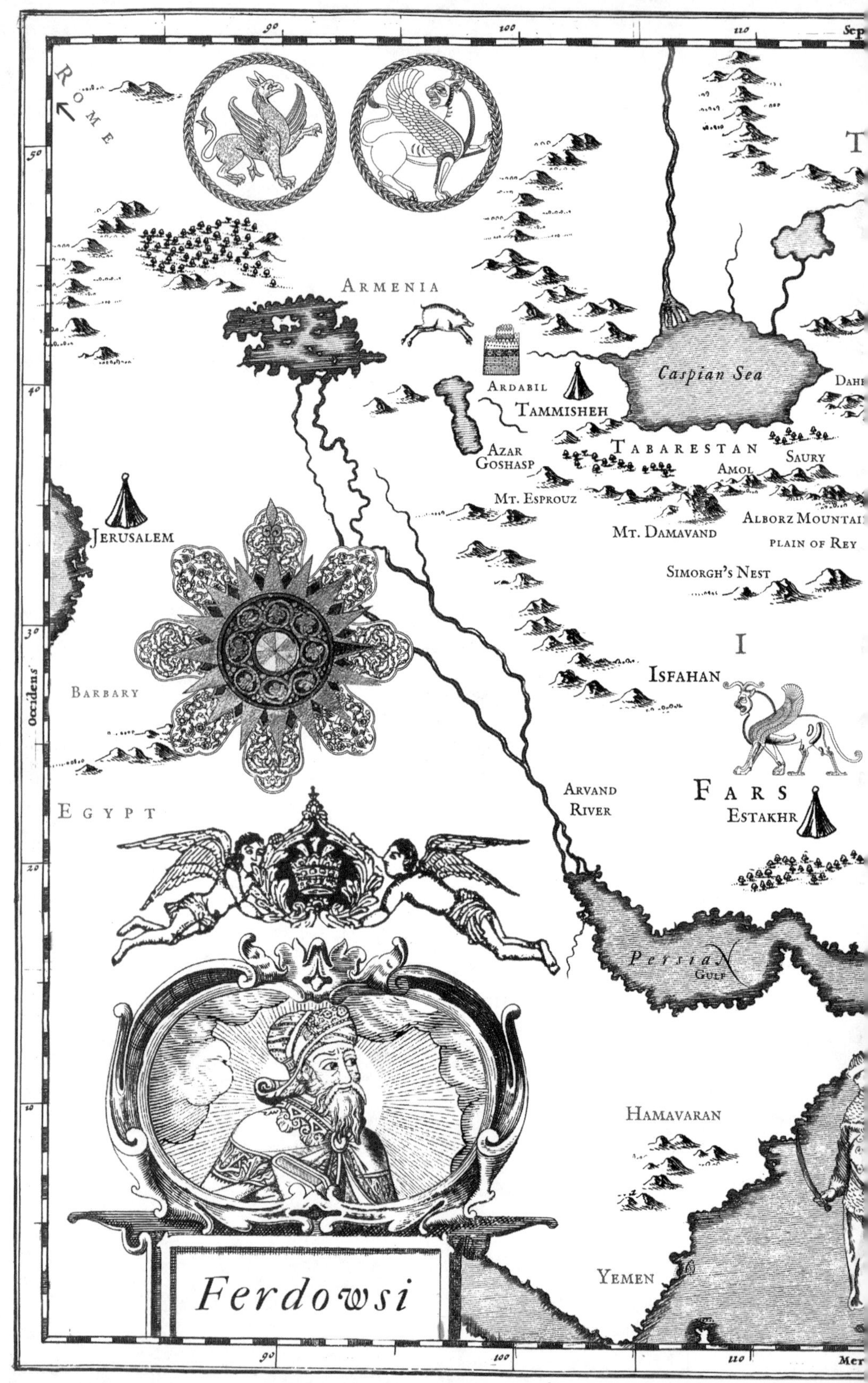
ROME
ARMENIA
Caspian Sea
ARDABIL
TAMMISHEH
AZAR GOSHASP
TABARESTAN
AMOL
SAURY
MT. ESPROUZ
MT. DAMAVAND
ALBORZ MOUNTAI
PLAIN OF REY
SIMORGH'S NEST
JERUSALEM
BARBARY
ISFAHAN
I
FARS
ESTAKHR
ARVAND RIVER
EGYPT
Persian Gulf
HAMAVARAN
YEMEN
Ferdowsi
Occidens
90
100
110

A fictional
Geography of
Shahnameh
U R A N
Invincible Castle
Kang
Oxus River
Siavoshgerd
Bactria
Gorgsaran
Mt. Hamauvan
Mt. Gonabad
Pashan
Zibad River
White Fortress
Samangan
Koushan
Khorasan
Kalat Fortress
Balkh
Daghuy
Haftelites
Khotan
Plain of Hamoun
Alanan Fortress
Kabol
R A N
Zabol
Kandahar
Mazandaran
China
Oriens
Gourabad
Bost
Hirmand River
Kashmir
Chichast Sea
Nimrouz
Ocean
India
Sea of China
Some locations on this map vaguely correspond to real places on the geographical plane of Iran and its bordering lands. Others are fictional loci of the mythological and epic traditions that found expression in Ferdowsi's poems.

Genealogy of the Main Characters in Part I

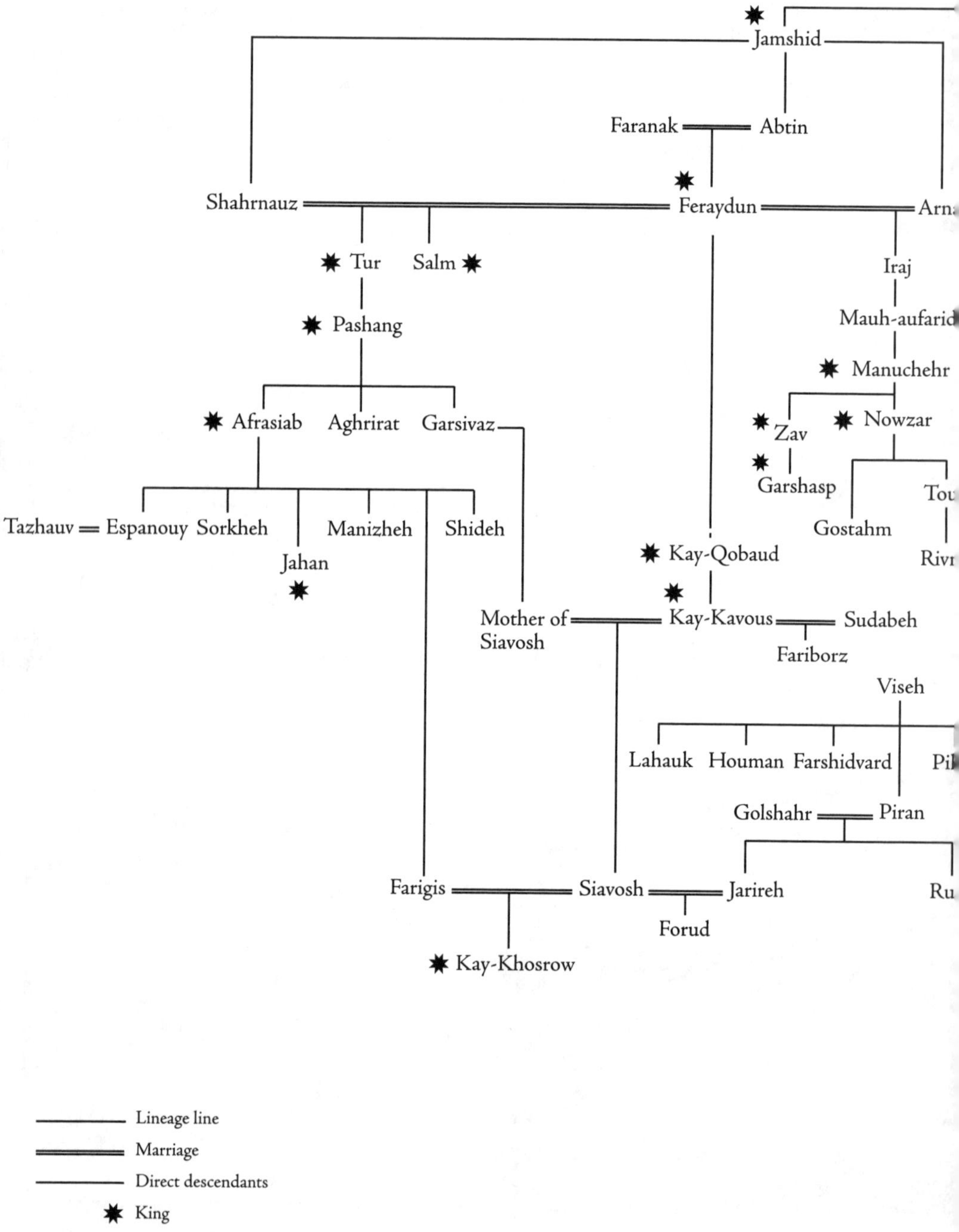

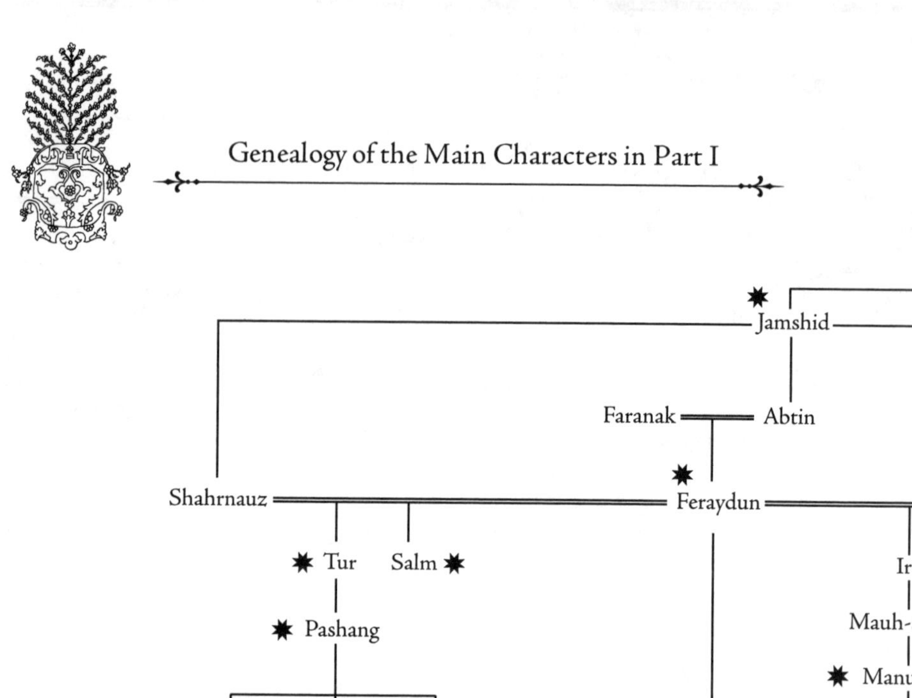

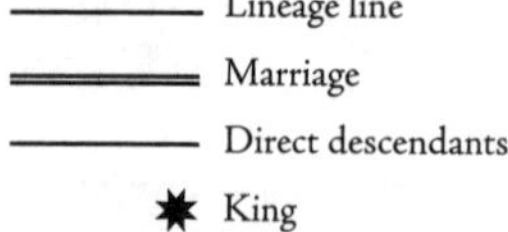

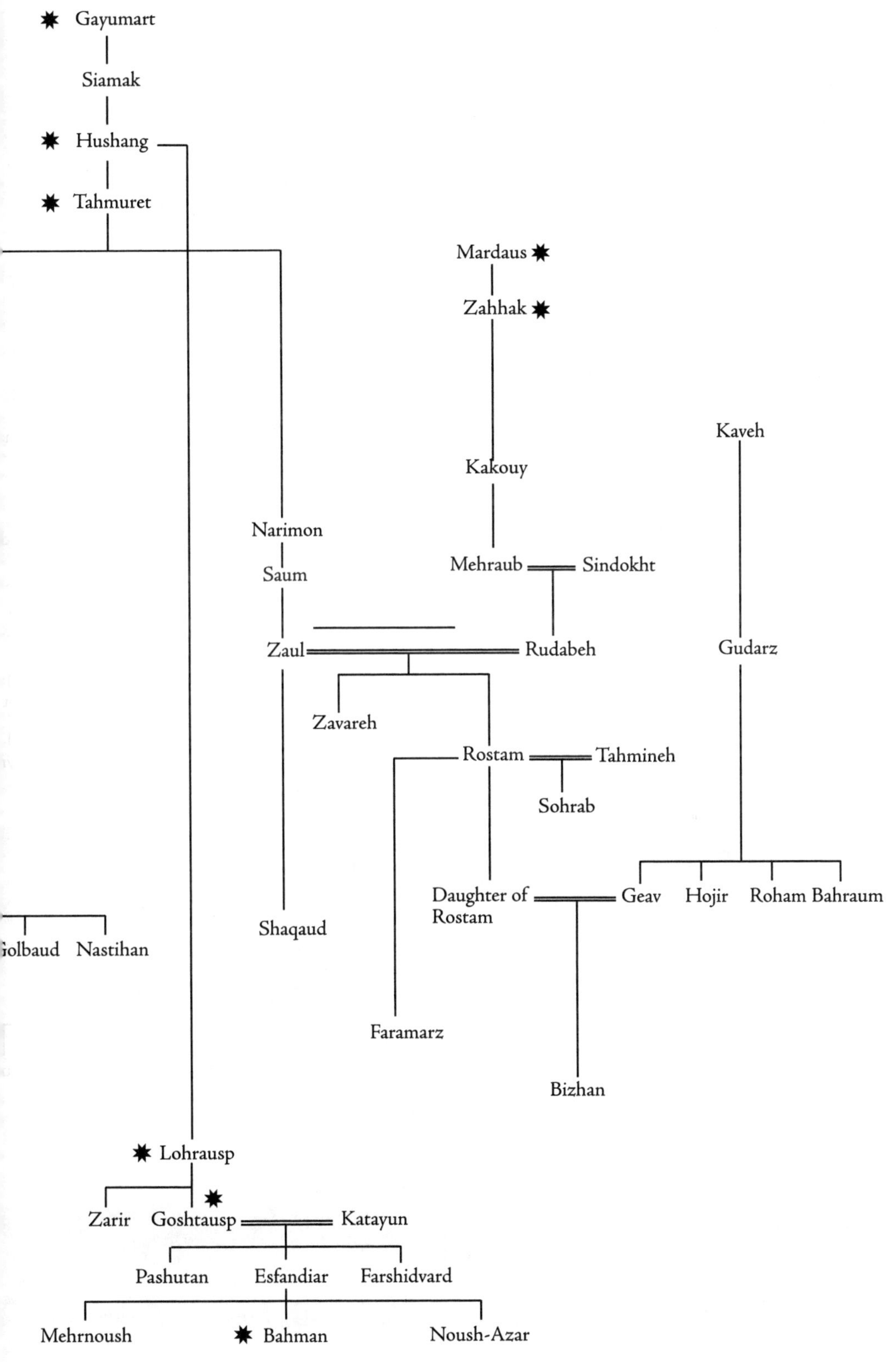
Gayumart
Siamak
Hushang
Tahmuret
Mardaus
Zahhak
Kaveh
Kakouy
Narimon
Saum
Mehraub
Sindokht
Zaul
Rudabeh
Gudarz
Zavareh
Rostam
Tahmineh
Sohrab
Daughter of Rostam
Geav
Hojir
Roham
Bahraum
Golbaud
Nastihan
Shaqaud
Faramarz
Bizhan
Lohrausp
Zarir
Goshtausp
Katayun
Pashutan
Esfandiar
Farshidvard
Mehrnoush
Bahman
Noush-Azar

ABOUT THE AUTHORS

An Iranian sociologist and translator, AHMAD SADRI is a professor of Islamic world studies, sociology, and anthropology at Wake Forest College, and lives in Illinois. HAMID RAHMANIAN is a John Guggenheim fellow and multidisciplinary artist based in New York. MELISSA HIBBARD is a writer/producer and cofounder of Kingorama's Shahnameh Project, also based in New York. LLOYD LLEWELLYN-JONES is chair of the Ancient History department at Cardiff University and director of the Ancient Iran Program for the British Institute of Persian Studies.

DISCOVER MORE ABOUT THE SHAHNAMEH PROJECT AT:

Kingorama.com

شاهنامه
فردوسی